Night Studies

Night Studies

a novel

Cyrus Colter

TRIQUARTERLY BOOKS
NORTHWESTERN UNIVERSITY PRESS

Evanston, Illinois

TriQuarterly Books
Northwestern University Press
Evanston, Illinois 60208-4210

First published 1979 by The Swallow Press, Inc., Chicago. Copyright © 1979
by Cyrus Colter. Northwestern University Press/TriQuarterly Books edition
published 1997 by arrangement with Cyrus Colter. All rights reserved.

Printed in the United States of America

ISBN 0-8101-5065-4

Library of Congress Cataloging-in-Publication Data

Colter, Cyrus.
   Night Studies : a novel / Cyrus Colter.
      p. cm.
   ISBN 0-8101-5065-4 (alk. paper)
   I. Title.
   PS3553.0477N54 1997
   813'.54—dc21   97-16024
                                                        CIP

The paper used in this publication meets the minimum requirements of
the American National Standard for Information Sciences—Permanence
of Paper for Printed Library Materials, ANSI Z39.48-1984.

To Imogene

. . . The dialectical process is thus like the dialogue of a continuous drama, and just as drama is the Greek word meaning conflict, so dialectical is the adjective corresponding to dialogue—the dialogue of action and reaction between conflicting social forces. It should be added that in society, action and reaction do not occur with the mechanical simplicity which we imagine when we think of an experiment in physics; and it is noteworthy that Marx and Engel's favorite example of the dialectical process was the germinating and growth of a plant from its seed—again the biological analogy—in which the germ is destroyed by its opposite, the plant; but is still in a sense part of it, in the same way that the new seed which the plant produces replaces its parent while continuing its form.

—Jacques Barzun, *Darwin, Marx, Wagner*

Masks! Masks!
Black mask, red mask, you white-and-black masks,
Masks of the four points from which the Spirit blows.
In silence I salute you!

—Leopold Senghor, *Prayer to Masks*

Book I

Convergence

Chapter 1

End and beginning. The Ray Charles concert was over though it had been—and still was to be—a strange, bizarre evening. It was the girl—Griselda. For the last two hours, throughout most of the music, Marvin had sat so utterly distracted over her he hardly knew where he was. It was her face, her strange, her holy face—so tinted, odd, and ravishing, yet delicately pale one moment, so softly darker the next. Never had he seen such beauty hallowing, purifying, a face—there it was, upturned toward the stage, her eyes first riveted, then glazed, soul entranced, hair cascading down the belted corduroy jacket of her mod attire. She was watching the artist and devouring the music. The blind black singer, first assailing the piano, then cajoling the organ, his tinseled orange shirt darkened with sweat, dead eyes behind amber shades, wailed out of a soul in ecstasy, frenzy, so it looked, to cast his sorcery specifically over her. And in her trance she seemed receiving the exclusive and powerful message as if it carried some relevance to her own personal history.

But before Marvin had noticed her—little Marvin the runt, the champion typist, the secretarial school headmaster—he had sat slightly to the left in the row behind her and the older woman with her, uttering little grunts of involvement with the singer's music and digging his fingernails into his moist palms, as meanwhile the perfervid music came down onto the audience like the spirit of the Holy Ghost at Pentecost. At last, if only briefly, her head turned to the left and he saw her profiled face. He stared, transfixed, and continued staring, soon even at the back of her head. To him now, in his quickly transposing imagination, she had become some enraptured though pure force of nature—say, an artless gazelle.

In a moment he saw her hand wander to that face, to coax aside a filament of hair, and it was then he glimpsed those strong, stub-nailed—typist's!—fingers that instantly sent a charge of mad

excitement through him. It was the dual discovery he had made—
first her dark porcelain beauty, and now these unmistakably decisive clues, these nail-clipped, ringless fingers, that so aroused,
thrilled him. His intuitive powers at work, he was convinced he
could not be wrong, for he had trained too many girls at his
clerical school for that. There was the same steely, manic strength
in these fingers he had once seen in the concert pianist Rene
Gasparo's—who when finally insane had each day to be forcibly
pulled away from the piano where he insisted on playing scales
ten hours at a stretch. Marvin, glimpsing her fingers, sensed the
paranoia. At one time or another in her life, if only as a child, he
thought, she had bitten those nails to the quick. He thought it, if
not ironic, fitting, this evidence, and felt the kinship. For he, as
much as anyone, anywhere, knew the signs.

After the concert everyone, the throng, excited, elated, spent, had
pushed and crowded through the foyer and out into the rainy night.
Marvin, furtively elbowing his way, following, in the crush even
sometimes ahead of, his gazelle, was particularly struck by her now
more fully revealed appearance. And when, on the street, he found
himself walking almost beside her, he became frightened and fell back
a few paces. He was awed, overpowered, by her green eyeshadow,
the Philip-of-Spain huge brass necklace, the configurated flare-leg
trousers, her wafted gait. But he did not like the looks of the woman
with her. Severely bronzed and weatherbeaten, she still appeared
not over fifty. She wore brogues, a Breton surcoat with grain-
leather — Napoleonic — collar, and swaggered noticeably as she
walked down the street. She seemed harshly unmindful of the quiet,
deeply-absorbed girl at her side and was sometimes a half-step
ahead of her. Ocean mists and California fog lay across the Bay
tonight, creating a ghostly indistinctness out of everything and all
but fading out the pointillism of a million city lights. And as a
backdrop to the north there loomed, gaunt and forbidding, Golden
Gate Bridge, Griselda's unknowing prophecy.

Marvin, nevertheless, doggedly stalked the two women. He was
a distasteful, almost pitiable, man to watch—five feet one inch tall,
or short, large heavy head, his squat, little body soft, swollen,
potato-shaped. Yet he was a near-genius—a typist wonder: when
younger, in a national competition in Baltimore, he had won by

typing 168 words per minute. Typing, the teaching of it, and perhaps his piano, were the insubstantial fillers in the otherwise hollow existence of this strange Nob Hill scion, this patrician dilettante. Soon now he had followed the women two blocks and finally into a new colonial-style coffee shop on the boulevard. But once inside, the surcoated woman turned on him like a she-puma. Furiously crinkling her eyes, at the same time somehow forcing a grimaced smile, she challenged him: "Sir, I noticed you in the concert, and later in the foyer, watching us—and again only a block from here." Her voice was a deep, hard *mezzo*. "I believe you're following us. Am I right? Tell me, *what gives?*" She plunged her hands in the Breton surcoat.

At once Marvin quailed. Yet in a moment he rallied, and smiled, humbly, contritely, doffing his soft, expensive little hat. "Oh, damn it, yes—you're right," he said in mock disgust, his voice its true very high tremolo, and lilting. "Everyone sees *me!* . . . Oh, how I wish I could go around like other people sometimes—unnoticed. Yes . . . yes, frankly, I was following you." He nodded toward his gazelle—"I was so intrigued by her hands."

The woman glanced once at the girl. "Her hands! . . . Oh, come now—what is this?" The three of them stood just inside the coffee shop, which had tables in the center and booths around the walls. A busy young waitress was pointing out a booth to them already. All the while, though, the weather-beaten woman was noting Marvin's expensive clothes, his elegant English shoes, the hat. Yet she frowned. "What about her hands?" she said. But the girl with her had started toward the booth and now she followed the girl.

Marvin pursued them breathlessly to explain. "She has the strong, purposeful fingers of an artist," he said. "Could she . . . could she by any chance be a typist?"

"Oh, my God," the woman said as she and the girl sat down.

"Great typists are artists too, you know!" insisted Marvin the typist brightly, smiling self-indulgently, almost simpering, and somehow now more sure of himself. And next, before the women realized it, he had eased his round, lewd little body into the booth-seat beside the girl. Aghast, the elder woman half stood up. But the girl seemed frozen. "Now, now, don't be so upset!" Marvin laughed coaxingly— "I'm not Jack the Ripper! I'm a man of

3

standing . . . of some reputation." Already, from inside his suit coat, he was bringing out his wallet.

"The nerve! . . ." the woman said.

". . . Although I guess I'm only a teacher, at that," he went on obliviously—"A humble typing instructor, ha, yes! Oh, well . . ." Uneasily, the woman finally sat down again as he fingered in the wallet. "Here, take one of my cards," he said to her, at the same time smiling beatifically at the girl. "See? . . ." The woman took the card as the young waitress came now and they ordered sandwiches and coffee—Marvin, Sanka.

The woman first looked at him, then studied the card. It read: *"Career Commercial College.* Marvin T. Freuhlinghausen, Founder and President." And after the address and telephone number, and in fine print: "Superior instruction in typing, shorthand, IBM key punch, comptometry, and the various clerical and secretarial skills. Day and evening classes." She glanced at him again, inconclusively, peevishly, and finally her tanned, lined, hardened face seemed to set in a kind of vague stubbornness. "What do you want of my daughter?" she said.

Marvin started. Finally he turned and gazed at the girl. "Oh, of course, of course . . . your daughter. Yes, yes—I should have known. How tender, how beautiful, she is. Look . . . look—that mournful alabaster face . . . ah!" He was thoughtful now, slightly puckering his lips. "I'll be honest with you," he said—"I don't know what I want of her." Then he brought himself up abruptly. "But tell me, isn't she a typist? . . . I'm almost sure of it!"

"She is—yes," the mother said. "You weren't able to tell that, though, by just looking at her hands." Her tone was accusatory as she turned now to the girl. "Griselda, have you seen this man before?"

The girl looked at Marvin and shrank as if she had been jerked forward and pressed to identify a tumid corpse. "Heavens no!" she shuddered.

Though not unaccustomed to such reactions, Marvin was momentarily in despair. He wrung his puffy little hands, sighed, and clucked his tongue. "But how else would I know she's a typist, madam?" he said to the woman. "Did you call her 'Griselda?'— what an unprepossessing, in fact, ill-suited, name for so lovely a

4

girl. Why on earth did you name her *that?*" But before the shocked mother could protest, Marvin went on: "I knew, though, she's a typist. It's her hands. Now, you mustn't make the mistake of judging me, and the things I can do, by ordinary standards." He laughed—"No, not at all! . . . It's weird, but I have a very high, a very sensitive, personal antenna . . . it's a fact! I can almost gather things—sensations, impressions—out of the air! I sensed Griselda's vocation practically on sight—for it's also my own. The only other possibility could have been that she was a pianist, but you can tell she lacks that horrible ego, the smug vanity, of the musical artist. Oh, I'm sure you're aware of that! . . ."

The mother sat up straight and laid her palm grandiloquently across her breast, saying: "It is *I* who knows about musical art . . . but I won't go into that." Her deep voice, however, had been somehow wistful, before she began watching Marvin again with her clear, hard, curiously-piercing eyes. "What's so special about *you?*" she finally said.

He smiled elatedly. "It's really beyond defining! . . . I swear it! You know, I could have been a great musician—just as well as a great typist . . . I'm sure of it! As it is, on my piano I play parts of *The Well Tempered Clavier* of Bach's not too badly—certainly with emotion, with real inner passion . . . which is important, you know." At this he cocked his large, heavy, neckless head proudly. Then suddenly some idea jarred him. For a moment he spoke only with his lips, no sound, as if first consulting himself. Then he blurted the words. "How would you like to come to my *apartment!* Tonight! . . . yet tonight! I'll play for you! . . . Oh, wouldn't you like to hear me play? Do you like Brahms? His piano music is simply beautiful! . . . and, oh, divinely rhapsodic! Oh, come on!" His smile was so ingratiating, so exigent, it became almost a manic leer.

"Heavens no!" Griselda breathed again, fearfully—though in his ardor Marvin did not hear.

The young waitress brought their sandwiches and coffee now, and for some inexplicable reason, perhaps the interruption, Marvin sighed. Then he shook four packets of sugar into his black Sanka. But the echoes of his plea still rang out in the booth. Griselda was visibly distressed, but her hard, hawk-eyed mother,

5

at the same time both purposeful and indecisive, watched Marvin —again taking note of his expensive suit, the rich, subdued colors of his elegant cravat of a tie, the platinum cuff links. Suddenly, peremptorily, then, she put out her open hand. "Let me see your driver's license," she said to him.

He laughed. "Oh, why, of course!" And quickly got out his wallet again and showed her his license. Once she had seen his name and photograph, she pushed the wallet away. "Do you trust me now?" he beamed. "Oh, I'm the solidest of citizens, believe me! Ha-ha! My family before me, too. Now will you come? . . . Oh, you *must*!"

"Yes, we'll come," the woman said almost offhandedly.

Griselda gave a muted little cry. "Oh, Mother! . . . *Hell*!"

"Eat your sandwich, Griselda." Her mother spoke grimly. "The trouble with you is you lack sense." She turned to Marvin. "Last spring Griselda lost her husband—in Viet Nam. I try to tell her the world didn't come to an end. But she insists on acting as if it has—although I don't doubt the genuineness of her feelings."

Marvin's jaw slackened. "Griselda . . . married? . . ."

"She *was*. Look at her."

Griselda's eyes were glazed with tears.

"I'm sorry," Marvin said, very humbly, emotion in his voice. "Oh yes, death, young death, is a plague-spot, a sort of obscene visitation, as I heard my father once say. Oh, I'm sorry, Griselda."

But both women had resumed eating.

Marvin wolfed down his own sandwich now, then taking up his cup in two swollen little hands, sipped the syrupy Sanka. "Griselda . . . married . . ." he mused sorrowfully. "I can't believe it. . . ."

"I'd have thought all those special mental powers of yours would have told you that," the woman said. "I guess you thought she was some kind of nymphet—which tells a lot about you . . . although I wouldn't quite class you as the typical 'dirty old man'."

Marvin's eyes flew open in surprised dismay. "Old man! . . . why, madam, I'm only forty-four! I'm not dirty, either . . . if you're talking slang—oh, what *are* you saying?"

While the woman did not exactly smile, she came nearer to it than at any time they had been together. "You reveal much about

6

yourself, you lecher," she said. "Why else would you follow us?" Her eyes twinkled.

Marvin grinned sheepishly now. "Yes . . . it's true. It was Griselda. Her hands at first perhaps. But then her. Oh, it's so!—I confess it. But I confess nothing wrong!" He had become suddenly agitated. "I'm no lecher! . . . I'm no dirty old man, either! You are insulting, ma'am! . . . the least bit, anyway." His eyes were thin slits, but soon he turned away and gazed at Griselda.

She put down her sandwich at once and a tear came out of each of her green-shadowed eyes. She dabbed at them with her paper napkin, then suddenly, her small breasts heaving, she looked daggers at her mother.

The mother was oblivious. "Well, I certainly didn't mean to insult you, Mr. Freuhlinghausen, but the object of your curious, actually funny, behavior was plain from the start. Of course, you're not the first to admire Griselda. Are you married?"

Now Marvin emitted the heaviest of sighs. "No . . . Oh, damn it, no . . . I'm not. I've never been married." He slitted his eyes in defiance again, yet had spoken guiltily.

For a moment the mother was reflective. "I must say, though, Griselda was married to an awfully nice boy—Alan. A colored boy."

Griselda dabbed at her eyes frantically now.

Marvin looked very confused at them both. ". . . A—" He paused. ". . . A colored boy? Is that really so?" He gazed at Griselda in wonder. "I see, I see. . . ."

There was another, a long, pause. Her sandwich finished, the mother occasionally, idly, moved her large freckled hands back and forth across the tablecloth. Then studying her hands, she said to Marvin: "Are you wealthy?"

"O, gosh!" He gave a startled, uneasy laugh. "I wouldn't say that. My parents are deceased. No, I'm not wealthy, actually— maybe my father could have been called that, and his father . . . perhaps my mother too. But I only live comfortably. Ha, you frighten me. . . ."

". . . Comfortably . . ." the woman mused aloud. "Comfort to some, you know, can be wealth to others," she said. "You like women, don't you?" Her spiny eyes went into him.

7

At once Marvin was offended again. "Oh, why would you ask that! . . . of course I like women! Do you like *men*? . . . ha, answer me that! Tell me a few things about yourself, ma'am! . . . You haven't as much as mentioned your name. You've surely asked me plenty, though. Gosh!—have you!"

"Who followed whom here, Mr. Freuhlinghausen?" the woman said. "You're entitled to very little, I'd think. I hope I'll keep my name to myself. Besides, my name's irrelevant—*I'm* irrelevant. But Griselda is not. Let me ask you again, do you really like women?"

Marvin gave a hollow laugh this time, then seemed fidgety, uneasy, ready for them all to go. "Yes, I do," he said soberly. "But I confess women don't much like me." He sighed. "I must say it hasn't been a bit pleasant, either. . . . I wasn't blessed with great physical beauty, you know."

The mother nodded solemn agreement.

Marvin now beckoned for the waitress to bring the check. "My car's still over at the College—just a few blocks from here," he said. "We'll catch a taxi and go get it, then drive to my place." Getting up, he laughed. "Okay, ladies!—here we go!" He put down a tip, paid the check at the cashier's stand, and they left. Outside now a fine drizzle was falling into the fog and the whole atmosphere gave off a kind of dense, translucent haze extremely unsettling, confusing, to the senses, as he led them up the boulevard in search of a taxi. Suddenly, almost breathlessly, the woman said to him—"My name is Nancy Hanks. . . ."

"What? . . ." Marvin turned to her and laughed again. "You're a little young, aren't you, to be Lincoln's mother?" Then suddenly sighting the taxi that was upon them before they knew it, he hailed it and herded the women inside. The elder woman, still breathless, intense, could hardly let him give the driver their destination before leaning toward him, saying—

"Nancy Hanks, the singer. . . ."

He looked at her. ". . . Should that mean something to me?" he said. "I'm sorry—the name doesn't ring a bell. . ."

"Oh, Mother," Griselda said in exasperation, "he's never heard of you. He probably doesn't like opera, anyway."

"He claims to be such a music lover—and he says he's forty-four . . . why shouldn't he have heard of me?" Nancy Hanks spoke bitterly.

"Oh, I'm sorry, I'm sorry!" cried Marvin. "Forgive me, will you, Mrs. Hanks?" Yet he tittered: "Well—opera, eh?"

Nancy Hanks glared out the taxi window.

When a few minutes later they alighted at the address Marvin had given and were walking through the haze to his car in the rear, he pointed out the sturdy, neat, three-story building on their right that housed Career Commercial College. "We've been here seven years now!" he said cheerily, proudly, his enthusiasm brimming—"We outgrew our other place. Oh, I've got loads, simply loads, of expensive teaching aids . . . instruction gadgetry, in that darn place there—Gosh, yes! We have four hundred and thirty-some students this time, you know!"

The two women gazed at the handsome building as he took them around to its rear, which abutted on a lighted alley. There he unlocked and opened a small side door and immediately they saw parked at a loading dock his shiny black Bentley. "Here we are!" he exulted.

Nancy Hanks was very formal, magisterial, as he opened the car doors for them. "You sit up front, Griselda," she directed, and climbed in the back herself. Soon they had driven out into the ghostly mists before the large automatic door closed down. As Marvin turned left now and, this time, passed in front of the building, Nancy Hanks got a better view of its wide frontage and imposing exterior. "Griselda," she said, "how is it you didn't come here for your courses?"

"A good question!" laughed Marvin as he stopped the car at a red traffic light. "A terrific question!—why didn't you, Griselda?"

"Mother wasn't giving me much money in those days," Griselda said, sullen scorn in her voice. "I was more or less fending for myself." Now her voice rose mockingly—"Remember, Mother?" There was heavy silence. "Besides, I've never heard of his school," she lied.

"She's being difficult . . . nasty," Nancy Hanks said over Marvin's shoulder, and, sighing, changed the subject. ". . . She types beautifully, though—beautifully and very fast . . ."

"I know it, of course!" beamed Marvin.

"She types all kinds of manuscripts—literary and scientific manuscripts . . . for graduate students and faculty people out at State College. Her work is very much admired."

"Oh, thank you, Mother," Griselda said cuttingly.

Thus the prickly, ill-willed conversation went. Marvin, at first amused, was soon intrigued. And later, as the Bentley climbed a wide, hilly avenue in the spectral mists, a feeling of portent, irresolution, came over him as though some life-changing event impended. They were in an area of large, opulent houses, many with faintly gleaming post-lanterns on lawns stretching back into a vaporous infinitude, and the drizzle had wet the pavement so that it shone impotently wherever the car passed a tall street light. When they had reached the top of the hill, he turned right, into an avenue lined with majestic trees.

"Where do you live?" Nancy Hanks asked, but, peering hard out the window, she was already impressed.

"Oh, never you mind!" laughed Marvin—"But not far! . . . in fact, only about three blocks." He turned to Griselda beside him. She was silent, dour. "You know, I have a sneaky suspicion Griselda doesn't much like me," he said with mock seriousness. "Yet I like to think it's only because she's presently grieving—yes, a sorrowing widow. But that won't last forever."

Griselda gave him an angry look. "You freak," she said under her breath, then glanced up in the rear view mirror at her mother —" . . . You too," she whispered, "both of you."

But Marvin sensed her displeasure, yet was somehow strangely pleased by it. "Oh, what temperament Griselda has!" he said. "Her hellish little traits, the gloominess, spite, are all appealing, enthralling, beyond words! Oh, it's true! And her beauty, her bizarre looks—the tangerine complexion, and especially her green eyeshadow! . . . well, it's just all beyond describing! . . ."

"Mr. Freuhlinghausen," Nancy Hanks said, "you mystify me more and more—in your attitude toward my daughter. What on earth's going on?—are you bent on satisfying some curious lust, or are you sincerely thinking of marriage? . . . Clear that up for us, will you?"

"Oh, my! . . ." Startled, Marvin gripped the steering wheel hard as he turned the corner into a narrower street. Soon, though, he was pensive. "I guess it could be either or both, you know," he said at last. "It's atrociously hard to say. Tell me, with how many men have you tried to place her?"

"*Place* her . . . !—My God! . . ."

"It's true!" cried Griselda. "She's always wanted to be rid of me! . . ."

"Jaded Christ!" breathed Nancy Hanks.

"Ha!—you didn't answer my question, Mrs. Hanks," said Marvin, now almost gleefully. "You *are* trying to 'place' her, now aren't you? Ha, ha!"

Harried Nancy Hanks finally sighed. "I want her, this time, to take up with a man of some substance—preferably, of course, as his wife. Griselda is in so many ways an unusual, a really rare, human being. You seem to need that kind of woman to match all those high-flown aesthetics of yours, your art, and all; all those strange whims you harbor . . . maybe even certain droll sexual longings, for all I know. An alliance with an extraordinary person like Griselda might be well worth your trying."

"For me, yes . . . *maybe*," Marvin said, reflectively. "But for Griselda, I'm not at all sure." He paused and took a deep breath. "What do you say to that, Griselda?"

Marvin had been driving slowly, carefully, in the fog—almost creeping. But Griselda, nearly oblivious, stared straight ahead through the wet windshield. "Your longings—ha!" she said. "Both of you make me laugh. You're so funny, so ridiculous—so alike, really. It's *you two* who ought to be together! But, yes, Mother, I'll do whatever you say—although he wouldn't think of marrying me. So you're really talking about a shack-up job, right?"

"Oh, Griselda!" Marvin tittered again— " . . . That awful, that vulgar, expression! There are surely more euphemistic ways of putting it than that—Gosh!"

"Name one," Griselda said. "One."

"You know," Marvin said to Nancy Hanks, "I'm beginning to see something of your problem. You have in this young lady quite a cross to bear, all right. What I can't understand, though, is your solicitude, your anxiety, for her welfare."

"My welfare!" Griselda laughed. "She's practically throwing me out. I cramp her style."

Marvin turned to the girl. "*Would* you come live with me, then, Griselda? . . . and be my mistress?"

At this Griselda's face grew long, sad. "I only know . . . I only know I would never, *never*, marry you."

"Why, you little minx, you!" Nancy Hanks said. "It just goes against your grain, doesn't it, to do anything respectable—and in your own interest! First you run off and marry a hapless, godforsaken black, then when he gets killed in war you refuse, so far, at least, even to process the necessary army widow's benefits papers. Now you tell a man who may have the means and station to lift you up some in life that you would never marry him. Yet you imply you'd live with him!"

Griselda spoke wearily now. "I haven't *said* it yet, though, have I?" Then she gave her smile of scorn—"I first want to see his apartment."

This remark somehow sent Marvin into a bizarre, hysterical, laughing spell. *"Ha-ha-ha-ha!* . . . Oh, you fantastic child! . . . Oh, Griselda! You're absolutely mad, but adorable!—no matter what I've said before!"

Nancy Hanks looked alarmed.

"Monsters," breathed Griselda.

But soon they pulled up in front of a four-story apartment building—sleek, rather new, of white stone facade. "Here we are, Griselda!" Marvin cried. They got out and he led them in out of the weather, but going up to the top floor in the shining automatic elevator, he became noticeably subdued, and spoke quietly, soberly, almost confidentially, to them: "Please, let's have a spell of peace, can't we? . . . what do you say? Whew, my heart's fluttering so. Let's just have an unforgettable evening together—no more fights . . . okay?" He smiled wistfully, weirdly. But as they got off the elevator, Griselda gave a low, contemptuous laugh.

In its elegance Marvin's eight-room apartment was everything Nancy Hanks had secretly hoped for, yet expected. Except for the beautiful chaos of the wallpaper, the large parlor was light and airy in a pink and yellow color scheme of the most daring mood. The chaise lounge was fuchsia, but after that every chair in the room, and both sofas, were covered in whole or part in Peppermint Pink, creating a dazzling, luminous frame for the ebullient Mimosa and Lemon Peel rug which had been especially designed to highlight the room. Yet the bright colors were all subtly held in check by the Black Pearl of the slate floor. Hugely monopolizing one corner sat an immense Knabe orchestral grand piano. Nancy Hanks was awe-struck, and stood at the edge of the lemon rug gaping.

But Griselda, in great bladder discomfort, looked plaintively at Marvin. "Can I go to the bathroom?" she said.

Marvin started. ". . . Oh, why, of course you can! Here—this way, my sweet." He led her down the ornate central gallery to a powder room off an alcove. When they were out of the line of sight of the parlor, at once he rushed her, wrestling her as best he could into his arms and kissing her ravenously. "Oh, God! . . . Oh, you sweet thing! Griselda, Griselda!—come live with me! . . . Oh, please, please! . . ." She laughed at him again as she fought him off, and, wriggling free, slipped into the powder room and locked the door.

Marvin, trembling with excitement, desire, finally returned up to the parlor.

When Griselda came out of the powder room, she decided suddenly to take a quick, unguided tour of the apartment. She went back to the farthest room, the gleaming copper kitchen, then glanced in each room returning. The extravagant luxury throughout, including Marvin's sauna bath, impressed her, though ambivalently. The last room she entered was his book-lined den, containing an elaborate four-channel stereo sound system, with turntable, tape deck, and headphones as well as loudspeakers. Also there on his desk sat a silver-framed photograph apparently of his deceased mother, and on the wall over it hung his Stanford diploma. Against the opposite wall sat a brass-legged trophy case displaying all his medals, cups, statuettes, and other memorabilia and insignia—prizes won by the young typing champion.

When Griselda returned up front to the parlor, Marvin had made them all drinks—rye whiskey and soda. "Ah, there you are, Griselda!" he said. Handing her her dark drink, he could see she had applied fresh green eyeshadow and his blood jumped. Nancy Hanks, drink in hand, seated in one of the downy-plush sofas, was staring around at the marvelous landscape paintings on the wall, but soon she saw the two stacks of music scores on the piano and got up to go look through them.

"Sing something, Mother," Griselda said derisively, already well into her highball.

Nancy Hanks drew up her shoulders in a virile primness, then

13

—"Haw"—gave a short flinty laugh.

At once Marvin ran over to her. "Oh, by all means! . . . by all means, Mrs. Hanks! Sing something!—Oh, look at all this wonderful music I've got here! Find something!"

But Nancy Hanks seemed uneasy, indecisive.

Griselda, a sudden wild look in her eyes, brashly raised her highball and took another drink. "Sing about the love child, Mother," she said, bitter sarcasm in her voice.

Nancy Hanks shot her an outraged look.

Griselda turned to Marvin. "Ask her to sing about the love child—really, it's Monteverdi's music." She smiled—"Yes, the love child . . ." Already her face was flushing scarlet from the whiskey.

"Spare us a maudlin drunk tonight, will you, Griselda," Nancy Hanks said.

"*I'm* the love child, Marvin!" Griselda said. "Do you see? . . . I'm a love child!" She turned to Nancy Hanks. "Mother, you slept with a man without benefit of clergy—didn't it, ha, technically, at least, make you a mistress? . . . Then, why can't I be one if I want to?"

"Jaded Christ! . . ." breathed Nancy Hanks.

"Now ladies!—now ladies!" Marvin sang out. "We agreed not to fight any more . . . remember? Griselda, cut it out! Why, hell, we're all love children—children of *lust*. Now, stop harassing your mother—stop trying to embarrass her."

They were all strangely silent for a moment. Nancy Hanks, still standing beside the piano, hung her head in self-contemplation. "Ah . . ." she sighed incomprehensibly. Griselda, taking her drink along, went over to the far sofa and sank moodily into it. At last Marvin sat down at the piano and began to play—softly, dreamily, closed eyes toward the ceiling. The music was Brahms—an *intermezzo*. Soon a peaceful lull had settled over the room and for the moment Griselda's glowing face was in repose. "Mother, sing something for Marvin," she said seriously, her tone free of sarcasm now. "Go on—sing Brahm's *Sapphic Ode* . . . or *May Night*."

"Oh, my God," said Marvin, dramatically, in a whisper of excitement—"Does she know *May Night?*"

"Ah, *Die Mainacht* . . ." Nancy Hanks mused aloud. "No, it's been too long . . . too long. There are too many memories. . . ."

14

Marvin now stood confronting the unhappy woman. "You must, you must!" he whispered again, feverishly. "I have the music right here somewhere!" He began rummaging, pawing madly, through the music scores. "I'll accompany you! . . . Oh, yes—come on!" When he finally found the song, he began humming it in his high tremolo even as he placed it up before him on the rack. "What a beautiful *lied* Brahms came up with here!" he said, again excitedly. "He's brooding over the beauty, you see . . . the poignant sadness . . . of a tranquil, a lovely, spring evening in May. Ah, yes . . . !"

"Hogwash," Nancy Hanks said. "Who knows what was in his mind? Forget all that and try to play it with a certain detachment, will you, Mr. Freuhlinghausen—musically, of course, but spare the pedal."

Marvin was crushed. But he soon sat down again and, after a silent, grandiose, pause, began the introduction—a quiet, languorous, flowing melody—as Nancy Hanks, with gravest dignity, stood waiting in the bend of the piano. Then she began to sing, in a velvet-rich *mezzo*—her German diction flawless. In a moment she had clasped both hands in front of her, singing with the closed eyes and rapt concentration of a concert singer before a tense, packed house. After the first minute Marvin was crying, blubbering; big, salty tears ran off his cheeks onto his expensive suit, as he played sentimentally, mushily, contrary to all Nancy Hanks' instructions, and finally ended with a huge, gauche, empty chord. She looked displeased, yet said nothing. But they could get her to sing nothing more.

Marvin, however, was ecstatic over what he had heard. He embraced the singer fervently, at the same time trying with his handkerchief to dry his eyes. "Oh, I'm such a big crybaby!" he said. "But you sang so beautifully! . . . I couldn't help it. Listen! . . . listen, Mrs. Hanks—if Griselda does come to live with me, *will you come too?*"

Nancy Hanks' mouth opened. She stared incredulously.

"Oh, I've got plenty of room here!" Marvin said. "We could live like one happy family. . . . You could have the Jupiter room. Ha, that's what some of my friends call the room back there an English chap occupied for a year . . . a very brilliant boy, Basil Thorne, who was teaching drama at State College. Basil had a portable phonograph in that room he played *all* the time! . . . and played nothing, absolutely nothing, it seemed, but Mozart's Jupiter symphony!—just incessantly. He said Mozart was God. Well, it caused some of my wacky friends to name the room Jupiter! . . . Oh, what a character, that Basil!—with his tweeds, and boots, and long, dramatic blond hair! . . . a sweet lad, actually."

"I'll *bet*," Griselda said.

Marvin looked at her, and took a deep, injured breath, but beyond that ignored the remark.

"May I have another drink?" she smiled now, holding out her glass.

Still pouting, he made the drink quickly, brusquely, and, having thrust it in her hand, turned to speak to Nancy Hanks again. "It would be no problem! . . . you could live right here, Mrs. Hanks—in the Jupiter room. Now, now, don't be so quick to say no! . . ."

Nancy Hanks was thoughtful, grave, suddenly imbued with a strange understanding, if not compassion, for Marvin; also with a sense of their mutual need, which in some conceivable setting they might both share—a desperate affinity of necessity. But she shook her head. "No, I cannot come," she said. "I really hope Griselda will, though, now—if it will make you happy. But you should be warned. She is vain and selfish, and often mean . . . really, a little crazy—look at her marriage. As time goes on you'll learn all this—I hope not to your sorrow."

From the second highball Griselda's face was cherry red. "I've told you she doesn't want me, Marvin!" she said, sipping the drink erratically. "You see now! It's best she and I do part. If *you* want me, I'll come. . . . I'll come live with you and be your faithful mistress. If you'll take me home now to get my few clothes, I'll come back here gladly!" With an effort she at last stood up from the Peppermint Pink sofa, the wild look still in her eyes, and summarily turned her back on them both.

Nancy Hanks gave a long, bitter sigh.

Marvin hung his head in earnest, questioning, thought, then gazed for a moment at Griselda's back. ". . . Yes, my sweet," he said meekly. Soon they had left the apartment and driven off into the dark, swirling fog.

*   *   *   *   *

Griselda moved in and the liaison began auspiciously. At once, almost unwittingly, she made Marvin's household over into a kind of psychological museum that held for him the most engrossing secrets as well as discoveries. At close hand now, he saw her revealed in all her various and captious moods—her childish curiosity, the wary observing, a capacity for awe over trivial things, her surprising talent for cooking and sex, yet her frequent boredom, her petulance, sometimes her cruelty. Bizarrely, the last trait soon all but obsessed, engulfed, him and removed a block in his mind; freed him to revel in a weakness he had managed, until meeting Griselda, to quell: the craving, the utter necessity, to be dominated—to be harshly, cruelly, ruled.

But his method was at first careful, indirect—he was determined to ingratiate himself. In only the second week he took her down to I. Magnin's and bought her five thousand dollars worth of new clothes. Although she was impassive in the store, when they left and were walking down the street, for the briefest moment she caught his hand and held it—until he warily pulled it free. And at home that night she let him have all his fanciful sexual ways with her that so excited, enkindled, his soul. Yet, obscurely, it also depressed him. She had been too pliant! he told himself with concern. But other times he was all but consumed with the pure pleasure of her, and so became an optimist and bought her her own new Porsche to drive.

Matters went on this way for nearly three months. Then the raw, damp winter seemed at last to affect her adversely. She became morose, gloomy, uncommunicative, often contemptuous. Marvin of course took special note, and watching her with bated breath, missing nothing, experienced a subliminal elation bordering on the ejaculative. Whenever she sulked, or gave him a withering glare, he would smother her with fawning, abject kindness, scurrying about the apartment in a ridiculous dither, nervously—ecstatically—finding her favorite television programs, making her hot chocolate or mulled wine, washing her stockings in the bathroom face bowl, or even reading to her from *Robinson Crusoe*. It seemed only to increase her contempt.

17

At last a rarely-felt ambivalence brought him to phone Nancy Hanks for advice. As expected, she was blunt, unkind, and negative. "What shall I *do*, then?" he whimpered. "You can do nothing, absolutely nothing!" she said—"Someday I may be able to be of help to you, but certainly not now. The only thing you can do is *wait*." For days he wondered what she had meant.

Then one night Griselda had a nightmare. Ordinarily she slept silently, seeming hardly to breathe at all, although sometimes, Marvin had noticed, she lay curled on her side sleeping with clenched fists. But tonight she cried out in her sleep for her dead husband. "*Alan!* . . . *Oh, Alan!* . . . *You come back, now!*" Lying beside her, Marvin sat bolt upright in the bed. Finally he shook her awake. At once she began to moan and cry and he could not comfort her. He tried to take her in his arms, but she fought him off savagely, cursing him through hot-breathed teeth. It was then for the first time he realized he had fallen in love.

The following evening he coaxed her into dining out—at the St. Francis Hotel. In their bedroom as they were dressing to go, she— in only panties and a slip—was sitting in a chair putting on stockings, when suddenly, impetuously, he threw himself at her, on her, and, as best his five-foot one inch potato-shaped body could manage it, tried to take her in his arms. The frenetic suddenness of it frightened her, at first, then she rudely pushed him away, whereupon he knelt, almost fell, down before her, clasped both her hands in his, and, quaking, shivering, looked up pleadingly into her face. "Oh, you unhappy little bird of paradise!" he cried—"How you fill my heart with sadness and at the same time the wildest ecstasy of joy, of craving, of longing! . . . ah, just as in *Tristan and Isolde*, my sweet! . . ."

"Oh, for Christ's sake, Marvin!—get up off your knees!" she said. "I loathe you kneeling there like that! . . . Get up!"

But he kept writhing and threshing about, then threw his mammoth head in her lap, causing her quickly to close her legs. "I won't get up! . . . I won't, I won't!" he cried, still shivering, and slavering now, as she tried to push his great head away. "I won't get up!—I won't, I tell you! Oh, don't make me get up, Griselda! . . . I worship you when you're like this! . . . I *do*! I could die for you! . . ." Finally he raised his head from her lap and gazed up dreamily into her glaring eyes.

"Oh, Marvin, come on!—*get up!*" Now with all her strength she shoved him back hard by both shoulders, then, eluding him, quickly got up and left the room. Alone now, he sobbed bitterly, and cursed himself with stammering lips. But soon, feeling much relieved, strangely sated, he went into the den and made himself a very dry martini.

They arrived at the St. Francis in Griselda's Porsche at seven-thirty. It was late January, a raw, damp night, yet she wore a mini-coat and mini-dress. The dress was a daring I. Magnin creation reaching halfway up her slender thighs—a jet black hugger-snug-ger garment, tiny and smouldery, with its high hem set deep in jet rosettes and ruby-red sparklers that cast off a shower of fire. With this she wore scarlet crepe boots flamed with embroidery and her hair, parted simply in the middle, fell below her shoulder blades. Marvin, walking behind her as the *maître d'hotel* led them to their table, was beside himself with excitement gazing after her.

The elegant room, almost completely dark, was like a gloaming, such light as there was coming from low romantic lamps on the tables, and over the quiet talk of the fashionable patrons a violin played *Begin the Beguine*. When the waiter came, Marvin ordered a vodka gimlet for Griselda and another very dry martini for himself.

They were quiet, subdued, reflective, until the drinks came. Then suddenly, impulsively, he grasped her wrist across the table—startling her. "Oh, God, you're so beautiful, so exciting, tonight!" he whispered. "Griselda! . . . Griselda, marry me! Marry me and put me out of my misery . . . will you? . . . oh, my sweet! . . ." His lip quivered and in a distraught gesture he dropped, almost flung back, her hand.

She only looked sadly into her cocktail, and said nothing.

"I can *somehow* make you happy!" he said, much too loudly.

"*Shhhh!*" She put her finger to her lips. "Don't make a scene, Marvin—please!"

"I *know* I can make you happy! I know it! You yourself are certainly not happy now, that I know. You're still living too close to your past. Do you realize what you said last night? . . . in your sleep? . . . Do you remember?"

She stiffened, looking frightened, but at last shook her head.

Marvin leaned forward breathlessly, melodramatically. "You sort of cried out, 'Alan, you come back, now!—*you come back!*' It was like you were commanding him, or something. It was eerie . . . God!"

"That's what I said to him at the airport." She spoke in resignation and gazed off in space. "It was the day he left—a year ago last Sunday. I felt so terrible at the time, so helpless, alone now in the world, that I guess I thought maybe I could *will* him back. It was all pretty silly, though—useless." She looked impassively around the room now as the romantic violin played gaily in the soft, low lights.

Marvin watched her distressfully; soon he was twisting in torment. "He had such a morbid hold on you, Griselda! . . . my God! . . ."

"There was nothing morbid about it. It was the most normal . . . natural—the healthiest thing that ever happened to me."

"Oh, I'm so envious," he whined now. "I'm really jealous! I've thought a lot about it, too . . . and I've wondered . . . I've wondered how he *ever* got such a hold on you!" He leaned across and whispered: "Tell me, Griselda, was it sex?"

She looked at him in astonishment, then exasperation. "Heavens *no!* In fact, Alan was inept about sex. I had to lead him. He was a shy, sweet boy. . . ." Pensive now, she said no more.

"Why have you always refused to talk about him, Griselda? . . . even about how you met him, or anything."

She took up her vodka gimlet, idly poising it before her green-shadowed eyes. But instead of sipping it, she said with a desperate shudder: "I don't want to go into it . . . ever." Then angrily—"Spare me, will you! . . ."

"Okay, I *will!*" He went into a savage pout.

"Alan repaired shoes," she said at last. "I met him in a shoe repair place, not far from where I was living at the time—where I'd go sometimes to get my heels fixed."

"You can't mean it. . . ."

"It's true of course." For a moment both were silent. "In the shoe place he would smile at me," she said, ". . . and smile again, and try to talk to me—I guess he thought he was flirting. It was really funny. I was indifferent to him at first. . . . And when he asked me to go with him to a Ray Charles concert, I only went to make him happy. That's how it started."

"But even overlooking the fact that he was black, what could you two have *possibly* had in common? . . . Oh, it's so weird! . . ."

"Nothing—so I thought. But then he never referred to race, never brought it up, so I soon forgot he was black—he was just another boy I knew . . . at first. He was so happy whenever I'd go out with him, though, that it finally started making me happy—at a very unhappy time in my life . . . when I'd just found out my mother didn't want me any more. I soon realized he was a cast-off too, like myself—most blacks are, you know—so we sort of grew together, I guess. We never discussed it, though—never. He didn't like to talk about serious things. I knew why, of course—life for him hadn't been any joke."

"Ah, but what did Mama have to say about all this?"

Griselda made a face. "She couldn't have cared less. Anything to get rid of me—she didn't want me around with a front-seat view on her activities."

Marvin had lapsed into deep, incredulous thought now. "He made you happy . . . happy . . ." he kept saying, almost inaudibly.

"Yes, yes! . . . I've told you—he made me happy because I made him happy. Oh, if I do say it myself, I made him very, *very*, happy! . . . So don't you see how happy that made *me*?"

Marvin looked away and gave another of his long, heavy sighs. ". . . It's . . . it's almost holy, isn't it? . . ." he breathed.

"That's true, that's true," she said.

Finally he motioned for the waiter to bring the menus.

* * * * *

But something else these days in addition, something very significant—though it was a mystery—had happened to Griselda. It was a kind of strange inner happening, an ambition, a new aspiration, that now imbued her—singular enough almost to defy explanation. It had to do with a sharp change in outlook, or even a brand new outlook, for until recently she could be said to have had none at all. But now she had begun to see a potential, a promise, that her life, her whole existence—which she had seen as drifting, aimless, having no future—might take on at last some focus, meaning; yet—did she realize it?—in the strangest, and ostensibly least motivated way.

In short, for a month now, and certainly without Marvin's knowledge, she had embarked on a clandestine adventure which not only gave her respite from the tedium of her ordinary day when he was at the office but much sober reflection in other ways—obscure, baffling ways. In late December, for reasons she herself could not have understood, unless it had been her time with Alan, she had gotten the bizarre notion, soon to become a burning ambition, of allying herself with a group called the Black Peoples Congress. This militant black organization, national in its scope and activities, was presently headquartered in the city but it was rumored because of its fast-growing membership across the country that the national office would soon be moved from the west coast to a city more centrally located.

Her first awareness of the Congress had come from reading a Sunday newspaper supplement article on its fiery leader, one John Calvin Knight. This ascetic young man's angry preachings, even though rigidly exclusionist—i.e., "Black"—had intrigued her not only by their bitterness but also their inflamed moral tone. Knight then had also figured prominently in a local TV newscast—in an incident of racial protest, with its accompanying threats of picketing and possible violence. It had all had a strange—in time, mesmeric —effect on her. She now began to read everything about the organization—and especially its leader—that she could find anywhere, sometimes only after great effort. She wanted, moreover, to talk with someone, anyone, at all familiar with the Congress, its activities and aims—though eventually in this she failed. But it was Knight himself, the inflammatory leader—some said moral leader—who most interested, fascinated, her. She went on studying everything about him she could lay hands on—it became a passion, fixation. The great mystery, however, she knew, remained in the question of her motivation. What really was it?—why had she embarked on this outlandish venture? She herself soon became intrigued by her new state of mind though fully aware also of her inability to unravel any part of the riddle. Yet daily, symbolically, she felt the compulsion to reach out to this explosive black organization and whatever it was that, under its tireless, feverish leader, it sought to achieve, especially what she saw as its great moral goals.

Finally, impulsively, she had gone to the organization's office to volunteer her free services—as a part-time typist if nothing else. There, however, she was coldly received. The people in the office were all but rude. She had difficulty, even on her third visit, merely seeing Knight's secretary, a wiry little black woman, about thirty-five, named Mamie Campbell, who curtly told her they presently had no need for volunteers. Griselda of course knew this was untrue and realized why she had been rebuffed. Her reaction was one of anger, then stubbornness. She now resolved to see Knight himself.

But her questions and doubts always returned as she asked herself again and again why it was she persisted in forcing herself on these people and their closed, for-blacks-only, organization. For the $n th$ time then she told herself it was because of Alan, the memories of him she cherished, that motivated her. Yet she sensed this was far from all. Throughout all this crucial time she would sit alone at home during the day, in Marvin's opulent apartment, pondering the mystery, her dilemma. Also she had brought home much of the literature she had seen strewn about the waiting room in the headquarters. She studied it painstakingly, exhaustively, now. One bright yellow brochure, its title—"John Calvin Knight Speaks!"—emblazoned across the cover over a grim, gesticulating likeness of Knight, in part read: "Power, Pride, and Struggle are our watchwords! They will bring us to a fuller awareness of the true virtues of BLACKNESS!" It was cited as an excerpt from a speech Knight had made the past summer in New York. The quotation went on: "We shall throw off our bitter persecution one day—when we learn to love ourselves for what we are instead of hating ourselves for what the white man says we are! It is a question of knowing ourselves, of where we have been, of our neglect, our brutalization, the fact that no one cared about us, and of the common experience which will forever bind us together—our 'long night of suffering!' " A surge of emotion went through her as she read it, making her eyes smart. Still she did not know why. Was it, she wondered, that Knight's words had somehow a strange relevance to her own personal history, especially its sadder aspects—the sense of loneliness, the "neglect," the fact that "no one cared?"

Though during this time her moods changed from day to day, the fire, the glow, of her identification with what Knight preached remained unswerving. Finally she sat down and wrote Mamie Campbell a letter—unwittingly, in a rather quarrelsome tone: "I frankly don't know why it is I've felt so strongly, really angry, about the way I was treated in your headquarters the other day, the callous brush-off I got. Think of it, someone comes in your office and volunteers her services—I told you of my skills—but because she's not the right color, that is, black, you're barely civil, not even that. Maybe I should have told you that I'm the widow of a black man, which is the truth, and that I revere his memory, but I doubt it would have made any difference with you—your mind was made up the moment you saw me. Yet your organization continues to blast discrimination, though only the kind *you've* suffered from. I can't believe, though, Mr. Knight would have turned me away like that—I refuse to believe it. I've read his articles and speeches and, whether he knows it or not, beneath the blackness that he preaches there's a universal moral tone that's possible of the widest application. Can't you see?—it's an added reason why what he's saying and doing is important; he's capable of speaking for *us all*. That's why I'm going to try to see him." Sealing the letter, Griselda now realized that merely writing it had, almost as if by magic, cleared up many of the mysteries that had so long plagued her about her motives, her reasons. It brought temporary relief.

A few days later then, no less stubborn, insistent, she returned to the headquarters and asked to be given an appointment to see Knight. When she was vaguely told he was out of town and it was not known when he would return, she sighed and asked again to see Mamie Campbell. As she sat waiting in the large, unsightly office with the others, all needy blacks bringing a variety of problems, she thought of her situation and became discouraged, even briefly questioning her own sanity. The woman sitting next to her, with whom she had tried to strike up a conversation, held a baby in her lap and related how an even younger one at home badly needed a doctor. The woman was confident, though, she would get the help she sought and heaped her praises on Knight: "He'll help me get my baby in the hospital, you watch—I know he's on the road a lot but he'll help me, or these people here in the office sure will. Oh, what a great man Mr. Knight is—he's doin' everything he can think of to help black people, here and all over the country; oh, Lord, yes. I heard him speak at the big rally they had for him here last fall. He set everybody on fire, I'll tell you. He lifts you up, gives you hope."

Griselda at first said nothing—a feeling of great futility had come over her. Hope for whom? she thought, now bitterly, her anger again rising. Suddenly she turned on the woman—"Why doesn't he give hope to *everyone*?" she said, "not just a few. You say he's a great man—then how can he speak of hope for some and not for others?"

At once the woman was offended. She turned and frowned at Griselda. "What're you talking about?" she said. "You people got the President of the United States, and everybody else, for that matter, to speak up for you. We ain't got nobody—at least we didn't have till Malcolm X and Martin Luther King come along. You people don't need anybody to preach hope to you—you've got it, have always had it, but that ain't kept you from kickin' other people around. We never had hope, though, till Malcolm and Martin come on the scene. Ah, but just think of it . . . both now are dead—heroes, heroes, they was. But John Calvin Knight is movin' heaven and earth trying to fill their big shoes, and a whole lot of black folks are sure hoping that in time he'll make it!"

Griselda sighed, and said no more.

Five minutes later then wiry little Mamie Campbell came out and confronted her. "I got your nasty letter," she said. "Now you want to see me—I'd like to know what for."

Griselda stood up. "I didn't necessarily mean for it to be nasty," she said, now almost timorously.

"Whether you did or not, *it was*. You expect us to fall all over ourselves when you walk in the office. Well, it's not like that any more; those days are gone—even if you did have a black husband. We're busy here—trying to do a job for our people, *black poor people*. We haven't got time to coddle anybody—especially the ones that have caused our troubles. You say you can help us—well, that remains to be seen. But busy as I am, and despite your rude letter, I'm going to give you a hearing. Come on in my office and let me hear just what it is you can do for us that's so great—other than just claiming you were married to a black man. Let me be the judge. Come on!" But Griselda was crying. Undaunted, Mamie Campbell led her back into her office.

Yet this was how it came about that on the following Monday Griselda began volunteer work, three to four hours a day, in the headquarters of the Black Peoples Congress.

*   *   *   *   *

Marvin had never quite recovered from the night they dined out at the St. Francis Hotel—it had been Griselda's revelations. He felt he had learned more about her that evening than during all the other time he had known her. Much of the time in the weeks that followed he was silent, glum, or would sit playing his great piano, often sadly humming and mumbling to himself for hours. And one Saturday when Griselda was out—he did not know she was on her "job" at the Black Peoples Congress—his intuitive powers, seeming to sense things were even worse than he knew, produced an hour of maudlin despair. He dissolved in tears and yammered like a calf. He had come to wonder if from here on this was to be his life. All of a sudden he was grimly determined it was not. That evening after dinner, having consumed a bottle of red wine with the beef *Delmonico* Griselda had come home and prepared for him, he provoked a fight with her. She seemed more startled than angry or afraid when he slapped her hard twice and sent her sprawling across the bed. Curiously feeling her cheek for a moment, she gave him a slow, contemptuous smile. "You freak, you miserable midget," she said—"I didn't know it was in you." Then she jumped up and stood squarely, defiantly, before him, her eyes blazing crazily. "But hit me with your fist, Marvin!" she said—"Come on, I dare you! You haven't got the guts!—Oh, you wouldn't hurt a flea! . . . Come on! . . . belt me one!" Her laugh was mad, shrill.

He dropped on the bed and, crinkling up his face, was about to cry.

"Marvin!—honest to God, if you start crying again, I'm going to whip *you*! Get up!"

Shivering with hidden delight, he would not move—"Oh, Griselda, you're so cruel to me! Why are you like that? . . . why do you hate me so? . . ."

"Oh, come now, you love it."

". . . Oh, God, I wish I were dead. Why won't you have pity on me? . . . and marry me?" The tears came at last.

She stood over him. "Get up, Marvin, and go wash your face. Then we'll go to a movie—it'll do us both good. Come on, now." She tugged him up. "I don't hate you—I don't even dislike you. I really feel sorry for you sometimes . . . when I'm not feeling sorry for myself. Come on, I know where there's an Italian film."

But in the following weeks they seldom went out. Griselda preferred it that way—she had found new interests, pursuits which

26

were already overwhelming her. Almost daily now she was in the Congress' office by noon and stayed until four. It was little less than a miracle—she had proved herself to most of them in the office within a fortnight and was presently on the way to becoming indispensable. The other aspect, of course—it had come inevitably —involved John Calvin Knight himself. Whatever it was that had happened to her—her emotions could not encompass it all—had transformed her life. At once she had fallen under his unwitting spell and to her now these were days of dreams—perfect, incredible dreams.

Then came April and the news that brought the shock of her life. The office was closing down. Knight was moving the national headquarters—as well as himself—to Chicago. The bottom had suddenly fallen out of her world. At first she was unbelieving, in agony, then she began to mope, and when two weeks later the office actually closed and moved, she was inconsolable. Home all day now, she sat alone. In the evenings Marvin, ever watchful, knew something was wrong but could not know what. Moreover, he was hesitant about inquiring, for he feared her in so many ways. As a consequence he was more miserable and mystified than before as matters went on unchanged for a month.

Then one Tuesday morning—it was early May—she was up early and made his usual breakfast of one poached egg on a slice of dry toast, a teaspoon of strawberry preserves, and two cups of black Sanka viscously sugared. But when later he went out the door on his way to his office, she turned sadly aside from his customary parting kiss. It worried him, and at Career Commercial College all day he was restless, depressed, then angry—all of which he took out on poor old Eleanor Duffy, a veteran shorthand instructor, whom he called in and complained to harshly, pettily, about what he charged as her "pedagogic failings." Then about three o'clock as he sat staring out his office window, unmindful of the beautiful spring day, his head began to ache. It was the old migraine, he knew. He longed to rush home now to Griselda, though never knowing whether she would show him sympathy or cold unconcern. Soon he began to feel sorry for himself, and locked his office door as if to make a private phone call and put his elbows on his desk and cried a little. By four-thirty he could stand the separation no longer and left, went down and got in his Bentley, and drove hurriedly home.

27

When he entered the apartment it seemed like a tomb. At once he went to the rear and, seeing no Griselda, called out to her anxiously. "Hey! . . . Hey, Griselda! . . . where are you, my sweet? . . ." No response—a ringing silence. He made himself conclude she was still out shopping—although he had just seen the Porsche parked outside. His head was splitting now and he went in the bathroom and took two Anacins. Suddenly he panicked. He began running through all the rooms, looking, crying out for her— "Griselda! . . . Oh, my sweet! . . . where *are* you! *Griselda!*" There was terror in his voice. Yet no response.

Then two minutes later, in their bedroom, he found the scribbled note. She had left it on the nightstand under the corner of a crystal ash tray. "I've gone, Marvin," it said simply. "I won't be back. I'm going to travel some—I've got to try to pull myself together, find myself. Wherever it is I'll look around and get a job of some kind —I'll have to. But I'd reached a dead end here—feeling lousy, lonely, so much. A couple of times I'd thought of doing something drastic, but I don't think I have that kind of nerve—the thought frightened me, actually; made me afraid of myself. What I've got to do is go away somewhere and try to help myself—as if I'm worth all the effort. But maybe it will sort of pry me loose from my past, I don't know. Thanks, anyway, for being nice to me— at least part of the time. I wish you well." That was all.

He swallowed as he eased down on the bed, still holding the note in his hand as if he did not know where he was. Soon he was shaking. Yet he was rational enough to know he ought not be that surprised, really—though he sat there, his face pale, heart pounding. At last he got up and, in a futile gesture, began opening the clothes closets in the room. All the expensive shoes, coats, and dresses he had bought her were there and he wondered what he would do with them. And on the dresser he found her keys to the Porsche. Next he went in the bathroom again, looking—for what? he asked himself hopelessly. But there he saw the few remaining miscellaneous trinkets, her articles of beautification—little ghosts. Also, on the wall hung the still-damp pink wash cloth, and in the niche above the tub a perfumed bar of soap yet moist. But it was not until, in the medicine cabinet, he saw her small vial of green eyeshadow that he lost hold on himself, sat on the closed toilet, and wept uncontrollably. The migraine too was racking now. Finally he stumbled from the bathroom and went up in the parlor.

There it seemed even more like a tomb than before. He looked around the elegant room—remembering so well her first night there —as if any minute she would reappear. He felt the reckless urge to cry out for her again, but understood it was futile and restrained himself. At last he wandered over to the grand piano and sat down, yet could not bring himself even to touch the keys. He only sat there, his despair total.

He did not leave the apartment for two days and three nights. When his office called he said he was ill, and in a sense he was, for he was helpless. The second night, in his book-lined den, he had only an excess of Scotch whiskey and the incessant migraine to keep him company. There, the lights low, he put a Ray Charles record on the stereo turntable and let the singer's desperate black art flood his soul. "Oh, *Griselda*! . . . my sweet! . . ." he cried out, but it was driveled. Suddenly his sotted rage exploded: "*You little bitch, you!*—I'll . . . I'll follow you to the ends of the earth! You came here to be mine!—you have no right to live apart from me . . . ah, you haven't, Griselda! You are *mine*! . . . my souvenir of something unspeakably blissful in my dreams!—even if it does frighten, appall, me. . . ."

He was quivering drunk now. Yet he kept trying to clear his mind in order still to think—to rue the night he had first seen her. Why had she gone to hear Ray Charles anyway? he asked himself, but now so nostalgically. She herself probably wouldn't have known the answer, he thought. He felt, however, she had virtually dragged her mother there, and, though obscurely indistinct to Griselda, perhaps for a purpose—maybe to Griselda Ray Charles was to sing a belated requiem that night, a *Grande Messe des Morts*, for all mute, fallen blacks in Viet Nam . . . including her own. Soon Marvin poured himself another Scotch, weaved back to the stereo, and started the record over again.

He stayed up most of the night drinking, and on finally staggering to bed was too stuporous in his earlier sleep to dream. Yet later, as if relentless, inescapable, the old dreams returned—rambling, erratic, half-remembered fragments, sometimes nightmares. He seemed in the longest, most significant, of them as much wrought up over Griselda's leaving as he was in his waking hours—in a furor of anger, frustration, and sorrowing confusion. For he seemed in the dream to have been expecting great things of her, preparing her in the crucible of their dissonant temperaments, their clashes,

29

for something not, at certain moments at least, entirely clear in his own mind. Moreover, he was not always eager to define it. But the plans, however misty, evanescent, had been going so beautifully, he assured himself in the dream, his purposes moving toward that brink of his truest desires in a way that bedazzled, excited, him, made him as he slept want actually to hop, skip, and jump. Then she escaped. She saved herself from her fate—without the slightest notion of what had eventually impended. Now he would have to go out into the world and find her. Track her down, if necessary— yes, to the very ends of the earth.

Three days later he returned to his duties at Career Commercial College, but his agitation and desperation accompanied him. Moreover, he was thinking constantly now of Nancy Hanks, though against his will, for she somehow made him feel unpleasant, insecure, more troubled. But he needed help—he knew he must talk to someone or go mad. A far-seeing person, she had long ago offered her services—he had not understood at the time, but much had happened in the interim. He needed her now. Yet he repulsed the urge to call this strange, difficult, haunted creature. Two more days passed. But at home on the evening of the second day he could stand the trial no longer. He capitulated and called her. His feelings were beyond anything but the vaguest description—exhilaration, foreboding, hope, guilt, uncertainty. And, always, in the chaos of his will he saw his life.

So at last. "Mrs. Hanks? . . ." he said hoarsely into his phone.

"*Well*—I've expected this," the voice of strength came back to him at once. "I've been waiting."

"You know she's gone, then? . . ."

"Yes—I *felt* it."

"Oh, what shall I *do*, Mrs. Hanks? . . . What shall I . . ." His voice broke.

"Go find her and bring her back."

"Find her! . . . She disappeared in thin air—I wouldn't know where to begin looking for her! . . ."

"We'll have to talk. I may have a clue. I'm busy for the next few days—call me again next week."

"Yes, yes—I'll come see you!"

There was a pause. "No," she said—"I'll come there."

One evening the following week, by prearrangement, she came

to his apartment for dinner. He saw her alight from the taxi, dressed femininely today—green pumps, yellow-spangled spring coat, tasteful jewelry. Her hair, however, was short and severely coiffed—her mien dignified, grave.

"How well you look!" he said, admitting her.

"I survive—somehow." Replying, she viewed his flamboyant sport shirt.

"It's nice of you to come—I'll drive you home. You can imagine I've been pretty desperate." He took her coat and with apologies led her back to the kitchen where he meant to broil two lobster tails. But, making drinks, he was frantic to get to the subject of their meeting, even before dinner, yet saw the wisdom of observing at least the barest amenities. "Tell me about yourself," he said. "What have you been doing?" This was a mistake.

She was seated at the kitchen table with a Scotch before her. "I have my problems," she said, toying with the drink, though her gaunt, leathery face had assumed a resolute cast. "My dear friend and young colleague Lily Heller, who shares my apartment, has opened a small music store. Considering the modest capital we were able to put into it, she managed to stock it well enough—she has voluminous sheet music and music scores of every kind, plus a fairly adequate stock of both popular and classical records and cassettes. And business has been good, but she hasn't been able to generate all the cash she needs to re-stock the inventory she's sold. In other words, Mr. Freuhlinghausen, she needs a banker—a business loan. I immediately thought of you, of course; that with your business contacts you might be able to direct us to a banker . . . or"—she looked away—"to some other source of funds. The business needs temporary stimulation—a blood transfusion, so to speak."

"Ah, yes . . ." said Marvin, taken completely by surprise. "I may be able to do something. . . . I know a man I think she might go see—at Harper Trust. I'll give him a call and try to set up an appointment for her. You mustn't let me forget—I've been so upset about Griselda."

"I won't let you forget," Nancy Hanks said, a slightly malicious twinkle in her eye. She got up from the table—"Now, I'll help you with dinner. Did Griselda leave an apron?"

Marvin turned to her, offended—"Griselda took nothing, absolutely nothing. You should see all the clothes in there—and I've put her Porsche in storage. Gosh, Mrs. Hanks! . . ."

31

"The girl is not bright," Nancy Hanks, shaking her head, claimed. "I've always said it."

Later, in the dining room, they talked as they ate dinner.

"What about Griselda—what happened?" Nancy Hanks finally said.

Marvin's face at once showed his distress. "I don't *know!*" he said in an anguished voice. "I just came home that evening and found her note, that's all." He quickly got out his wallet, handed her the worn scrap of paper, and she read Griselda's farewell note. "We were on pretty good terms, I thought," he said— ". . . for us. She was even up early that morning and got my breakfast, as she nearly always did. Then this! Oh, it's been a terrible blow, Mrs. Hanks!"

Nancy Hanks, returning the note, continued looking at him. She thoroughly masticated the food in her mouth before she spoke. "Did you know that she had been working?" she said—"That she had a sort of job?"

". . . When?"

"For some weeks—or months—before she left."

"No, no—that's not so! She couldn't have had!—she was home almost all the time."

Nancy Hanks set her jaw. "She spent part of nearly every day working in the office of a black militant organization located in the heart of the ghetto—on Fulton Street."

"Oh, this is incredible, Mrs. Hanks! I don't believe it! . . . Where did you hear that?"

"How could you have known where she was?—weren't you at your business all day? A boy who went to high school with her used to see her going in this office regularly. His father—a slum-lord type, probably—owns the building. I had a suitable person—a black woman acquaintance of mine—check on the story, and it's true. Griselda was going there doing volunteer work for this organization. Actually, she has some kind of hang-up about blacks— she's always been attracted to them, even as a child."

"Oh, are you kidding about this job . . . or what, Mrs. Hanks? It's so weird. Griselda's always been a puzzler, though. Maybe I shouldn't put it past her." He sighed—"Yes, I know she's got this strange identification with blacks. . . . She was very emotionally involved with her husband. She looks at herself from a peculiar perspective—probably the same as a mistreated black might view his life. I've thought a lot about this attitude of hers—to me it's aberrant, maybe a little eccentric."

"Not at all." Nancy Hanks spoke slowly, deliberately, as if in deep concentration. "It's *not* so strange, maybe. She may, although unconsciously, have reason to feel as she does. She herself has black blood."

Marvin's jaw slackened. He rested his wine glass on the table with great care, for he had almost dropped it.

"Oh, perhaps not a lot of black blood," Nancy Hanks said—"but enough."

Marvin, his eyes staring, leaned far forward toward her—"What do you mean, Mrs. Hanks? . . ."

"It's very simple. Her father was part black."

Marvin lowered his gaze and seemed inert, past shock.

"I met him in Buenos Aires," she said—"at the Opera there, the Teatro Colón . . . when we both sang in Verdi's *A Masked Ball.* He was a baritone, and, while maybe only a serviceable one, he was a very handsome man—olive dark, with a great stubborn mass of brown-black hair, and an imposing stage presence. He was said to be Portuguese. The fact is, though, he was part Portuguese and part black—from a tiny island off Antigua. He told it himself— that he had had an African grandmother who as a girl was a slave in the Caribbean."

Marvin was tense now. His throat, despite the Chablis, seemed dry. But soon he tried carelessly waving a hand about—"Hell, of what consequence is it?" he said. "I don't have much of a color complex, myself—it doesn't bother me . . . I seldom think of it."

"Ha, not much," Nancy Hanks said.

He ignored her taunt and said: "What you say, though, is interesting—especially as it sheds light on some of Griselda's psychological problems, which are pretty complex, maybe manic, and, I might say, at times vexing. In sum, good or bad, she's a rare human being, right?" Now he recalled the taunt. "And if I may say so— with all deference, to be sure; with no offense meant—you yourself had quite a part in making her what she is . . . mysterious, I mean, frustrated, lonely. Did you really care about her, Mrs. Hanks? . . . as the average mother would've?—I've never understood if—"

"—I'm not interested in going into that," Nancy Hanks interrupted. "I was talking about her father—though that itself, actually, could explain some of the things you asked . . . in terms, that is, of what it did to *me*. Despite his indifferent voice, Christian Hattam could have been a great success—he *was* with the ladies—but as a singer he was inclined to be lazy, I later came to learn. Yet he had become a fairly well-known artist—at the time I was much younger than he and really just getting started. Maybe that's why I admired him so—I was star-struck. He wasn't at all vain, either, or cheap— he was a generous man, in fact—not hard to get along with. I was considered quite attractive, if not pretty, in those days, as well as talented—and he was estranged from his wife, a terrible woman, a Croatian dancer, who would not give him a divorce. So we were two very devoted friends together—I was sort of a factotum to him, if you wish to call it that—for almost eight years, and we traveled to many parts of the world. Griselda was born in Sydney, Australia." Nancy Hanks had spoken with great seriousness, almost solemnity.

"Yes," Marvin said, "she told me once—in passing—she was born there. She never mentioned her father, though—never."

"She didn't know him—she was too young to remember him. But his career eventually hit a plateau—ironically, mine overtook his. When this happened I had to follow my own opportunities as I began to get better roles to sing. We were now often in different, far-distant, places—sometimes we didn't see each other for months. Finally we separated for good—though without any rancor or recriminations. In fact, for the first of the four times I sang at the Met—for me the most significant happening of my life—he came all the way from London to be present. The role was 'Ulrica,' in *A Masked Ball*, that I had sung with him in Buenos Aires the first year we met. But I was shocked now by his appearance—he had aged so . . . and was terribly emaciated, and deathly sallow white. After the performance, I remember, we went with friends to supper. He seemed as talkative, cheerful, as ever, and complimented me repeatedly on my performance—though next day the reviews were mixed. But looking at him, remembering how handsome, how striking, he had once been, I could hardly restrain my tears in his presence. He wanted to see Griselda, who was then only four—he insisted I take him. So we went to a friend's place in Queens where I had left her and he stood over her bed for a few moments as she slept. I've always wondered whether I should have awakened her. Watching her, he smiled, remarked how beautiful she was, and otherwise tried his best to seem unmoved. I knew better, of course. I could not then let him leave New York without inquiring—discreetly—about his health. At once he was furtive, defensive. He said he'd had a peptic ulcerous condition brought on by intense overwork—this I doubted, as I'd never known him guilty of overwork—but that the condition had now improved spectacularly, to the point that he meant next month to sing 'Gérard' in *Andrea Chénier* at Covent Garden. He returned to London the following evening and within three months, after horrible suffering, was dead of stomach cancer."

"My God! . . ." breathed Marvin.

Nancy Hanks gave a heavy sigh and stared off at nothing. "That night at the Met," she said, "was the high point of my career—but after that for me too it was mostly downhill. Christian and I—in those early years—would certainly have married had he been free. Maybe Griselda wouldn't hate me so today. I've never professed complete innocence—though she, I think, is a quite paranoiac person. You see, then, my life at times has been a great burden to me —as well as to others. Yet one's life takes many strange, unforeseen turns—it's the nature of it. And no less so in Griselda's case. So there are some who would say she is black. She of course does not know she is."

"Poor, poor Griselda," Marvin said. "I adore her now more than ever."

"Yes, 'poor Griselda,' " said Nancy Hanks harshly. "But no one ever thinks of me, of what I've been through for her—of what as a result life has done to me. It's something, though, I've learned to live with. . . . Ah . . ." She gave another of her long, dread sighs, then fell silent.

". . . Poor Griselda," Marvin, oblivious, repeated in a whisper. "I wonder where she is tonight."

When they had finished dinner, Nancy Hanks, dour still, helped him clear the table, after which at her request he prepared to take her home. But in the foyer as they left she said to him: "Should I call to remind you about the bank appointment for my friend?"

"You needn't—no," he said. "I won't forget, if"—he looked at her—"you do everything possible to help me find Griselda." He added, almost reprovingly: "You said last week you might have a clue."

She seemed surprised, irritated—"I *gave* you the clue. It's that black organization she worked for. I'll wager that whatever she's doing, wherever she is, has still got some connection with those people. That's the clue." Then she paused as if debating something with herself. "Maybe sometime soon," she said, "I can ask my friend again, my black friend, to make inquiries in the community about any new developments. Shall we go now?" They left and he drove her home.

Coming back, he of course thought only of Griselda. But now it somehow brought him a strange exhilaration he had not known since she left. He felt pouring on him the bright light of his highest hopes—and his love for her had never soared higher. He went to bed at last, tired but heartened. Then in the middle of the night the bad dreams returned. Soon he awakened paralyzed with fear and drenched in sweat. Though not a religious man, he now prayed for deliverance from himself in his dreams.

Chapter 2

This would be the crucial day and no exaggeration, although Mary Dee's daemon, her whirling dervish spirit, voluble and self-assertive, and who seemed now always at her side, was given to bombastic, and often excited, talk. "Life's tricky, dear girl!" he insisted on warning her. "Take heed, then, be more cautious, less headstrong—life can really hurt you, you know. Yet one can hardly afford to live all one's days in inactivity but in tension. So, yes, try to have a good time, travel if you like, be open to romance and adventure, wear your pretty clothes, *haute* fashion; and men—move only in the company of *outstanding* men; others are beneath you. Yet, as you may soon see, this rarefied domain, of lordly men, is the real danger zone—as it were, full of land mines. *Achtung*, then! If you sense danger, flee, my pet—flee for your life!" Mary Dee, however, was oblivious of it all—even of her wily daemon's very presence; sober, reflective, yes, but oblivious. Later she did indeed sense a kind of gnawing uneasiness, yet was strangely unaware of its character; she rather thought what she sensed was her own nettling curiosity. She hadn't, though, long to wait.

It was Friday noon. A warm autumn drizzle fell in the streets as she suddenly appeared—emerging from the iron-girded courtyard of the École des Beaux-Arts where she was a graduate art student—and, flaming, captious, intense, also puzzlingly self-conscious, looked quickly down the rue Bonaparte toward the Seine. She was marvelous to watch—eyes alert, hands thrust in pockets, her pretty chin so defiantly high and exposed. But the belted raincoat she wore, the calf-length lizard boots, the green cloche hat, all conveyed the quaint, arty, image she loved so much to affect as she came out of the École through its ancient portal. Now slightly frowning, lips pursed, beautiful head cocked to the right, she peered hard up the street in the opposite direction. ("Be wary, my angel," whispered the daemon.) Damn it, Raoul was late, she thought.

The drizzle was a nuisance. How different from the week before

—the last week in September. Then it had been ideal—with a profusion of sun and vast blue sky, and with red and yellow horse chestnut leaves on all the trees along the boulevards and quays. But now this week had brought rain—heavy, then warm, tranquil rain for days. The leaves, splayed, black, and wet, adhered to the pavements, the mansard roofs, and newspaper kiosks, and the leaden skies hovered low. But here in the crooked, crowded streets of St. Germain-des-Prés people were oblivious. They went about their chores—menial, academic, or business—with the Parisian's usual aplomb, ironic exuberance, and nonchalance. Yes, Raoul was late, she reflected, insisted, tightening the belt of the raincoat; yet, even if only for the moment, she was not overly disconcerted, as if more were required than his tardiness and the grey, sodden day to daunt her *café au lait* beauty, her dazzling though sometimes petulant looks, her colorful, utterly feminine charm.

Oh, no . . . there he was! He was coming up from the river—from the Quai Malaquais. She saw him hurrying, jostling, bouncing, peering out merrily at her from between a tall, bearded student and a prim gendarme. Good, brave, little Raoul. She smiled quickly, lovingly, as he came up.

"Mary Dee! . . . Mary Dee!" he said—"Hallo, hallo!" His words came barely before his mirthless, metallic laugh—"Ha-ha-ha-ha!" At thirty now he was elfin, nervously energetic, and precocious—the precocity, when he had begun teaching, had made him the butt of frequent jokes by his waggish art students at Beaux-Arts, who had dubbed him "the genius." He wore thick glasses, a black trench coat, and no hat—his dark forelock of hair falling to his glasses—as he stood smiling at her. "I was not late—no!" He laughed again and waved a tattling forefinger. "Am I ever late?—no, no." His too-precise Gallic English, learned entirely in French preparatory schools and universities, was somehow at once sibilant and throaty. He smiled mockingly at her now—"I would not be late for *you*, *bébé*," he said. She gave him another adoring look. It was for his selflessness, his gamy outlook on life, his character—she considered his character as pure as any human being's she knew, not excepting even that of her father, an admired surgeon back home in Chicago, whom she idolized. Toward Raoul, though, it was gratitude she felt; she was grateful for his confidence in her—in her promise, her talent with charcoal pencil, brush, and paints. And throughout these last months, the period of her confusion and anguish, he had been a spotless mentor-friend.

"You're really such a nice man, Raoul," she teased him now. "You *are*—haven't I always said that?" She was twenty-three and tall, her color a wild peach on crested Negroid cheekbones, her body lithe and willowy. But then with a sudden grave twinkle—she was more uncannily prophetic than she knew—she asked: "What have you got up your sleeve today?"

"Come!—come with me," he said in his bookish English, catching her elbow and turning her around. "We shall eat something good, very good, eh? *As-tu faim?*" They were already walking.

"Oh, why would you ever ask that?—you know I'm always hungry."

"I shall tell you what." He feigned deep study. "We shall go up to Le Canary. It is just off St. Germain—down that little passageway of a street, rue du Dragon, remember? They have even hamburgers *et gruyère* there, yes. You remember it. Also a good enough wine *ordinaire*. The place is not *trop* expensive, either. Ha, ha, *d'accord*?"

"*D'accord*—I remember it." She smiled at him and nodded assent as they walked. She was a head taller than he, yet thrust her arm through his as they marched along with a comic little swagger —going up the slender, constricted rue Bonaparte toward the Boulevard St. Germain. But soon because of the scant ribbon of sidewalk on which they walked, Raoul had to drop behind and for a time they went in single file. From the opposite direction the one-way small car traffic rushed headlong at them, and, fearful, Mary Dee crowded the buildings at her elbow as she squinted into the puny rain; yet there was a kind of mystic humming in her head, not of despond, or elation, not of stuffiness or ennui either; it persisted, though, this lightness of sensation, as if some slight opacity of feeling bordering on the curious, the oracular, had slowly invaded her senses; then the rain brought her back to her consciousness, for she finally gave a little cry of irritation: "Oh, Raoul!—The Canary is five or six blocks! I *would* come off without my umbrella!"

"Maybe only four blocks, *chérie*—though, ha, blocks mean nothing in Paris." But he seemed preoccupied, thinking doggedly of something else. Soon, on the right, they were approaching the little sidewalk cafe Le Bonaparte, and, across the street on the left, the ancient church of St. Germain-des-Près, its thirteenth century stone and mortar scaling and decaying, the Romanesque tower a dunce cap in the drizzle. Mary Dee looked longingly at the cafe Le Bonaparte; its red, white, and blue awning gave protection to its patrons having their aperitifs and lunch, or reading newspapers, on the *terrasse*. She made another grimace: "Raoul, why can't we stop here and eat? . . . this drizzle's so messy!"

"No, no, *chérie*—let us go on."

Her daemon seemed suddenly scurrying ahead of them now; he had not left them. Entirely enveloped in the mists, he laughed and capered, indulged, diverted, himself. "Turn back, turn back, dear girl!" he cackled—like the he-witch he was; soon he came scampering back to them. Scarecrow arms flailing, he tried to confront her, impede her footsteps, head her off. "Read the cards, my beaut!" he cried, breathing his hot breath in her face—". . . now that you're out, stay out of the tall blond man's bed!" He ran on ahead again, as quickly, soon hidden, enshrouded, in the damp heavy haze; disappearing, as it were, into his own very disappearance. Mary Dee was oblivious, unaware—though ever hearing the mystic humming.

When they reached the Boulevard St. Germain, and before crossing, Raoul looked up the Boulevard to his right, past the cafes Deux Magots and de Flore, and blinked guilefully into the rain. "It is not far now," he said—"and that is good; otherwise in this little wetness, despite your raincoat and snug hat, you might dissolve; ha, it is secure to say we would not want that." In his tone there was delicate irony.

She smiled at him—"Have it your way—and stop insulting me." Yet she glanced at him with quizzical eyes, sensing in him some vague but stubborn purpose about The Canary. The humor left her; her curiosity quickened; soon vibrating suspicions were at work in her, sending her mind back . . . inquiring, stumbling, searching; nothing came . . . until at last the glimmerings of a possibility; it was in the blurred, amorphous outlines of a face. Philip's face. Philip, their friend—only a magnificent vagueness to her now, formed by bad visions from so many yesterdays. Could it possibly have something to do with Philip? she thought—hopefully not, pray God; but almost at once she began to feel the slight malaise as of old, and soon again the catching, the tearful swelling, in the throat. No, no!—it could not be Philip! she pleaded with herself;

he, the sole source of her four months' lovesick wretchedness. Yet she confronted herself—it was mandatory; it was her *feeling*, the feeling that it could be no other. The thought sent a knife into her heart. She was certain now Raoul's phone call last night, asking her to lunch today, had in some way something to do with Philip. It was a presentiment.

They had crossed to the other side of St. Germain and gone right, past the drug store and the Brasserie Lipp; almost at once then they turned left into the narrow little rue du Dragon. The Canary was not far, and when they reached it, Raoul's hair and glasses were wet; yet he was smiling—deceptively so, Mary Dee thought. They entered the little restaurant to find it already nearly full, and the headwaiter asked if they would wait a few minutes at the bar. Instead, Raoul's eyes quickly swept the place and she knew he was looking for someone. Then they both saw Philip at once. He was seated over at a table against the wall—tall, poised, saturnine, his ash blond hair worn longer than she had seen it before. He saw them now and a surprised, then defensive, look seemed caught on his patrician face. At last he vaguely waved to them, then appeared confused, flustered, displeased. Again Mary Dee felt the thickness, swelling, the tears in the throat; soon her eyes began to sting.

"We will join our friend," Raoul said to the headwaiter in French; then touching Mary Dee's elbow, he steered her deftly, gently, forward to what she knew would be an hour of the old misery. It was not new to her; she had borne it for a year now and understood its demands, its wanton foolishness, the hurt, even if these were sometimes eclipsed by memories of good times, the bliss. But during the past four months, the time she and Philip had been estranged, apart, it had become a cup of anguish, a cross of stoical heartache to bear. She tried to steel herself now by holding in her breath.

It was a rare and bizarre history involving two willful people. One, Mary Dee Adkins, brown, talented, beautiful, impetuous, woman to the core, preening in her fierce ego, yet torn and confused. The other, Philip Morgan Wilcox, twenty-six, also studying at the École des Beaux-Arts but in the school of architecture, himself satanically handsome, vainglorious, morose, alternately lovelorn and stubborn, a Philadelphia scion, generations-rich and overindulged. Both of them single and in love with each other, yet in

41

their pained and muddled frustration at last seeing, and agreeing, it was all hopeless, inept; besides, both families, had they known, would have ruthlessly condemned. At last Philip, in a towering dudgeon, had walked out of his classes at Beaux-Arts and gone off on a wild holiday in Nice. At once Mary Dee deserted her own studies, flew home to Chicago, and spent ten fretful days with her unsuspecting family—sister and brother Jocelyn and Ronald, teenage younger siblings, and parents Dr. and Mrs. Horace M. Adkins. Although eventually the lovers returned to their classes, accepting the departmental disciplinings and warnings, they had not once, until today, seen each other since the angry, tearful breach.

When Raoul and Mary Dee reached Philip's table, he stood up, but, barely smiling, still showed his confused discomfort; he ignored Raoul and gazed at her. "Hello, Dee," he said, emotion already in his voice.

She had held her breath so long she could hardly speak— ". . . Hello, Philip," she said; then realizing she must show no fear, added boldly, too boldly: "What a surprise!"

Raoul exploded in his mirthless laugh: *"Ha-ha-ha-ha!* Yes—for *both* of you!" Beaming, he helped her out of her raincoat before she removed her wet cloche hat. Philip watched her. Her dark hair was loose, curly, and fine, although she wore it short and very chic; she also wore a persimmon-colored wool knit dress and much costume jewelry including many rings. As Philip sat down again Raoul quickly got out of his own trench coat, then wiped the rain from his face with his handkerchief. "Sit here, *bébé*," he said, pointing Mary Dee to the tiny space beside Philip on the wall seat, a red art-deco banquette. When she sat down beside him, Philip would not look at her. Raoul, oblivious, smiling in triumph, settled himself in the chair opposite them. "You see," he said excitedly, "I had this storm of the brain! *Ha-ha!* I thought how good, how excellent, it would be for us to have lunch together again—as in the old days. *C'est ça.* It was near this time last year—very early October, yes—when we three first made our great, our grand, acquaintance, although of course I already knew Dee. *D'accord?"*

"Yes, Raoul." Mary Dee's reminiscent gaze hovered far away.

Philip had been having an aperitif; he looked around now for the waiter to order two more. *"Amer Picon, deux,"* he said when the waiter came, not consulting them.

"Bien!" cried Raoul on hearing the order—"Ah, Philip has not forgotten. Yes, yes, as in the old days, when we would have an *Amer Picon* before lunch or dinner. *Trés bien!"* But suddenly he lapsed into the briefest wistfulness: "Sometimes it is good to remember . . . really. *D'accord?* I think so, yes. . . ."

Philip turned and moodily devoured Mary Dee with his eyes. "How've you been?" he said at last.

She looked at him; she started to speak; but her voice failed. Raoul laughed: *"Mon Dieu,* Philip, you can see for yourself! Was ever a woman so beauteous? . . . what do you say?—gorgeous? *Oui,* gorgeous. Ah, *bébé."* He patted Mary Dee's hand. She smiled at him; then she looked at Philip and sank into a reverie. When the waiter returned with the two aperitifs, Raoul, still exulting, at once proposed a toast: "To just one day—today! . . . *Aujourd'hui!"* They drank.

But Mary Dee's mind had slowly taken flight. Again was it the daemon? . . . had he returned already?—for it was true her brain had gone into a spin. Strange—she wasn't thinking of herself, her own feelings; never that, there wasn't time; she was thinking of her situation, the plight of it, how to deal with it. "Be careful, dear girl!" enjoined the blithe daemon now—"Merely enjoy the day. Don't ask too much of it. Be reasonable, not insatiable. Be cool, clear-headed—smile some, occasionally laugh. But keep the mind *alert!* And, by all means, keep the mind away—*away,* do you hear? —from the past; the dead, dead past! Rather, be involved with the future—your future. He already has one—do *you?"* Yet her mind continued its slow, ranging, sad flight; there seemed no stopping it: it went soaring back, back, over the weeks, the months, over, as it were, the causeway of time linking incident to unforgettable incident, examining the actors' frailties, the missed opportunities and fatuous hedonism of it all, yet so much, so very much, of it sheer rapture. Suddenly up went the daemon's warning finger—"Ah-ah-ah-ah! . . . you're forgetting already what I told you—you dear, sweet, disobedient girl! . . . *Eschew* the past!" Would that she could have heard him, for it was not possible for her to forget the felicities of the past; yes, Raoul had mentioned the beginning, she thought; the first meeting—earliest October, a whole year ago; on that now seeming far-off day, after an agreed-upon meeting and a talkative lunch, he and she had gone to examine Italian Renaissance pigments in the Louvre; they fascinated Raoul; afterwards they experienced the brilliant late afternoon from a sidewalk cafe table at Fouquet's, on the Champs Elysées; it was dreamy, quixotic Paris, the onset of gentle evening, the streets in movement, cars and taxis swarming, the great neon signs flashing Cinzano, Moet, and Pan Am in red, green, yellow, and aquamarine; and across the boulevard the office personnel leaving Air Afrique and the Assurance Generales. All the while the two of them sat luxuriating in, trying to possess and hold, it all, as they sipped their *fine à l'eaus*. The air was unseasonably mild, and it was so thrilling to sit outside and watch the day recede into a salmon-colored glow. "Oh, this is lovely!" she had said; yet, then in Paris only two months, she was still tentative, groping, though inwardly eager and in a perpetual state of exhilaration; also she was flattered by the platonic attention of an instructor who thought her gifted; as for Raoul, he was diverted, amused, at first; then slowly he felt himself developing a strange involvement he could not understand, and did not wish to probe; he suppressed it; but at that time she was still in awe of him, of his precocious and encyclopedic knowledge of art and art history, and felt fortunate to be his student.

It was all yet so very vivid to her—how that same evening the big party had arrived and were seated only two tables away; there were six or seven of them—young men, young women, smart, fashionable, insouciant people, all a little reckless yet well enough behaved, and led by a tall, blond, godlike youth the others called "Philip." She even remembered what she had worn—a kingfisher-blue pants suit, almost the same costume jewelry as today, with a cerise scarf at her throat. Soon, her quivering sensibilities at work, she became conscious of "Philip's" awareness of her. Then she caught him watching her. Immediately she kept her eyes away, talking straight at Raoul. Soon just once she dared look again. He was gazing at her and her eyes flew away. Raoul had seen—and laughed: "You are being admired. I have seen him somewhere— perhaps at Beaux-Arts. . . . It may be so, yes." Then about ten minutes later, to their amazement, "Philip" rose and came over to them; he spoke to Raoul in uneasy French: "Good evening, Monsieur. Excuse me, my name is Philip Wilcox—I'm a graduate student in the school of architecture at the École des Beaux-Arts. . . . I think I met you about three weeks ago at the Brunes—at the reception for foreign faculty. I recall you were introduced as a member of the faculty in the art school, but your name doesn't return to me now." He smiled uneasily, though he appeared intent on being ingratiating. Raoul at first only listened; then with some dignity said: "My name is Peyret, Monsieur Wilcox—Raoul Peyret. Yes, I remember you now—you were with the Stuttgart couple, the young German architect." "That's right," said Philip, "and also, I think, with one of your students—Georges Le Bec." "Ah, yes, of course," Raoul smiled—"Le Bec, one of my brightest." Though this led to more and easier conversation between them, Mary Dee, tense, sensing something she could not decipher, kept her eyes away. At last Raoul, looking uncertainly at her and hesitating for an instant, said to Philip: "This is Miss Mary Dee Adkins, another of my students." Philip made what seemed the slightest gesture of a bow—"Good evening," he said, his smile coming like an afterthought. But for the first time now Mary Dee experienced the faint malaise, a kind of tremulous indisposition, that she would know again; soon then came a portentous tingling of the nerves. That was how it had all begun. Shortly, at Philip's insistence, she and Raoul had joined the larger party for introductions all around and more pre-dinner drinks. Later they all dined at Lasserre on the Avenue Franklin D. Roosevelt.

*   *   *   *   *

"One more toast!" now said Raoul—looking around again for the Canary waiter. "Just for luck—for I want to propose the *Future!* The future, you know, is imminent!" He gave his short, sharp, cacophonous laugh. "It is upon us, my friends! *Parce que j'ai faim!* . . . oh, I could eat a horse!" He seemed trying to be festive, joyous, ridiculous, his purpose apparently to break the awkward tension. Finally, waving, he got the waiter's nod.

Philip watched Mary Dee with glowing eyes. Soon he repeated his question: "How've you been?"

"I sold a picture the other day." She tried to smile as she said it, and her voice was low, submissive, at last; she laughed: "I got a grand total of a hundred and thirty new francs for it. I won't be rich, will I?"

The waiter came and Raoul ordered another round of aperitifs and asked for a menu. "She is painting well, Philip," he said. "It is true she got a very small sum—it was her first sale—but, ha, so did Gauguin!" Then laughing, a little wistfully again, he sat appraising Mary Dee. "She is talented, yes. Why else would I give her so much of my time, my pedagogy?"

"I've wondered," Philip said, slightly raising an eyebrow.

"*Bébé!* . . . do I hear right? Is he *jealous?*"

"She *is* your protégé, isn't she? You've sort of taken her under your wing since—"

"*Mon Dieu!* The man is unhinged! He is frantic, desperate, lashing out in every direction—even at poor me! *Of course* she is my protégé, Philip! *Of course* I have taken her under my wing! And all before you ever knew her—before you ever inveigled out of me an introduction to her! Also, under my pedagogy, and that of my admired friend, the painter Jean Vitry, she will become a painter!" Just then the waiter brought the new drinks and the menu, but now Raoul in his agitation had forgotten all about his intended toast to the Future. He looked at the drinks curiously.

The moment, however, the waiter left, Philip turned on him savagely: "Why did you bring us here!" he said, quivering. *"Why?* Your trickery! . . . your damned—"

"Wait, Philip," Raoul said. "Please do not speak to me in that voice. Remember that you are a student, while I am faculty. Besides, we are good friends." Philip glowered despairingly into his drink and said nothing. But soon Raoul was cheerful again, and when the waiter returned they ordered lunch, wine, and a bottle of Vichy water.

"Show Philip the photos," Mary Dee, mollifier, said to Raoul now —"The snapshots of Nadine." Raoul was a widower. His wife Pauline had died in a Paris auto traffic accident, and Nadine was his seven-year-old daughter who lived presently with his mother in Arles in the south of France. His face darkened and for a moment grew sad; and Mary Dee regretted her suggestion, for she knew he worshipped little Nadine, and that his necessary long absences from her were a source of great unhappiness to him. She felt maybe this was why he sometimes seemed so strange and lonely, and why he tried to hide his feelings behind his harsh, mechanical, sometimes hysterical laughter. Was it this void somehow that made him want to see her and Philip reunited, as in the old, happier, days and nights when the three of them were so much together? She was not sure. Raoul was a complex person, she knew; more complex even than Philip and mystified her most of the time. She gazed at him now as he took the two snapshots from his wallet and handed them to Philip. "Isn't she growing?" she said eagerly, leaning forward to see.

"Yes, a lovely child," Philip said. They were waiting for the food to come and the conversation had lagged. Raoul tried to revive, stimulate, it; knowing Mary Dee's adulation of her father, and Dr. Adkins' recent illness—a coronary—he asked of him. She answered almost too quickly: that he had completely recovered. She spoke with a tense, compulsive confidence, as if by the mere saying she could make it so, could by some means ease, reassure, herself of his good health. Raoul turned and inquired of Philip's family then. Philip said he heard regularly from his four brothers and sisters in Philadelphia, that he doubted his parents were coming to Europe this year after all, and, casually, that his father had recently become a member of the Harvard Board of Overseers. By the time the food came the talk was freer, more relaxed, sometimes animated, and soon Raoul was beaming again.

The luncheon had gone through to dessert, when suddenly Raoul looked up front toward the big window fronting on the street. "Look!" he said, pointing. "The sun! . . . the sun is out!—it is a miracle! Oh, how glad we should be to see the sun again! *D'accord?*"

"Oh, yes—yes!"—Mary Dee had turned to see. "It's wonderful! . . . Oh, look!—and after all the dark, depressing rain!"

"Now, I have a significant idea!" Raoul said—"This time no storm of the brain! My friends, let us cross the Seine and go up to Fouquet's again—for coffee! As in the old days . . . and sit outside and have a cognac or a Triple Sec. Is it not *our* cafe?—where you two first met? Ah, what do you say? Look how the sky is clearing! The sun!—the sun! *Merveilleux!*" Soon he had the waiter and was paying the *l'addition.*

They left The Canary and returned to the Boulevard St. Germain where Philip had parked his humpbacked, mustard-colored Citröen. Raoul put Mary Dee in the front seat with Philip and himself climbed in the back. He could detect her excitement; she was by turns radiant, pensive, restless, uneasy, yet despite everything thrillingly happy again. As he drove, saying nothing, Philip's eyes seemed afire. The streets were wet but it had never been cold, and now that the sun was out the day had suddenly turned glorious.

They took the Pont Royal across the river, driving fast to stay in the swift, catapulting traffic, as the sun seemed trying to dry the pavements. The water below the bridge lay quiet again after the two, old, blue-grey *bateaux mouches* had passed under and gone on. At last over on the Right Bank, they proceeded up the Quai des Tuileries past the Gardens, spacious and formal, past the Orangerie, and, turning right, on into the sweeping vista and frantic traffic of the Place de la Concorde.

Raoul was rapturous. "It seems we have done all this *before!*" he cried. "Or was it in one of those worthless cosmological dreams of mine?"

"We *have* done it before, Raoul!" Mary Dee spun around to him. "Many, many, times before! But a thousand years ago!"

Finally emerging from the riot of traffic in the Place de la Concorde, they found themselves already moving up the Champs Elysées. The great avenue was alive with humanity, commerce, and the inevitable darting roustabouts and other species of the combustion engine: Dauphines, Simcas, Peugeots, Fords, Citröens, Fiats—all rushing, rushing, past the signs, shops, and signaling gendarmes in a sea of motion and myriad color. The trees lining either side of the stately boulevard, though now almost bare, yet gave a majesty to the view all the way up to the Rond Point, from which still farther into the distance, grand, cool, dappled in sunlight, rose the Arc de Triomphe.

*   *   *   *   *

Fouquet's was a smart, popular restaurant and sidewalk cafe and occupied a prominent corner site on the Champs Elysées at the Avenue George V, with a clear view up to the Arch of Triumph. Its great awning was blood-red with a straight golden trim, the chairs honey-yellow wicker, the tables circular and tiny. Correct black-coated waiters with their long, white aprons moved about outside among the patrons, bringing them food and drink of a wide variety. As the front terrace was almost full, Raoul, Mary Dee, and Philip were given a table on the Avenue Georges V side, well back from the sidewalk yet where they got a shaft of the sunlight as well as a breath of the breeze. When the waiter came, Raoul and Philip ordered Triple Secs and small coffees; Mary Dee, a Crème de Violette.

At the second table over sat, silently, a couple in their sixties, presumably husband and wife, and French. The woman had been writing a letter, as her husband casually observed other patrons. Soon he was looking at Mary Dee. At last he leaned forward to his wife, whispering: *"Regarde la belle Negresse."* The wife turned and looked at Mary Dee but showed no reaction, then returned to her letter. Mary Dee had not noticed.

After the liqueurs and coffees had been brought, Philip let his eyes travel over the place, remembering so much. "Yes, this is okay," he said, almost to himself—it was as if he were musing, but Raoul had heard. "I've always liked this place," Philip went on. Mary Dee's heart turned over watching him.

"Yes, this place is good," agreed Raoul—"It is Paris . . . it is also *us.*"

By chance now Mary Dee glanced to her right. Across some four or five tables sat a black man. He was staring at her—a truculent, hostile stare. Thirty-two or three, ebony-hued and thin, almost tall (about five feet-ten), he wore his hair in a fierce Afro but was conventionally, neatly, dressed. Mary Dee quickly averted her gaze when she saw his stare. Who was he? she wondered, a shadow crossing her heart. Was he American?—somehow she was certain he was. How could he show such hostility to a perfect stranger? Soon it angered her. The nerve! she thought—he was a fool, an arrogant fool . . . a boor! Coldly, defiantly, she turned around to him again, determined to stare him down. But he moved his eyes away in disdain and gazed moodily at passers-by on the sidewalk.

Raoul was slouched happily in his chair. "Ah, this is nice, nice, nice," he said and sipped his Triple Sec. "Like last year, *d'accord?"* But Philip was watching Mary Dee now who seemed strangely distant, frozen—Philip had not seen the man. "In fact," said Raoul, "it is so nice, so reminiscent, that it has brought me another storm of the brain! Ha-ha-ha-ha! Listen—Dee, are you listening?—do you recall Adrienne? . . . Adrienne Delavigne? She was here with us once or twice—she went to the opera with us, too, I think; to *Tosca.* Ha, occasionally I have been her escort—do you remember?"

"Of course," Philip said.

Raoul glanced at Mary Dee. Though her face was still cold and drawn, she finally agreed: "Yes, Adrienne was fun. I liked her— she was good for you, Raoul."

Raoul laughed again and shook his head sadly, bravely: "What are you saying, Dee? . . . is anyone good for me, after all I've been through? I married the woman I loved—Pauline. Adrienne is a friend; we were never really serious—although she is now divorced —for she knew my bad moods too well; she and Pauline were good friends, you know. Oh, what got me on this?—let us order again." He threw up his hand to the waiter—*"Garçon, s'il vous plait."*

Mary Dee, straining to keep her mind from the oppressive presence across the tables, finally smiled: "Go on, Raoul—you didn't finish telling us about your new storm of the brain."

"Oh, no I did not! . . . well, it is simply this, *chérie:* Why should I not go now and telephone Adrienne—at her office. If she is free tonight, then I want us all first to go to dinner, then afterwards to some quaint, *very* interesting, little night club, maybe—as we used to do; ha, to some dive over in Montparnasse—some veritable den of iniquity! What do you say, my prudish friends? *Ha-ha-ha!"* His shrill jerky laugh distended the veins in his neck.

Mary Dee laughed at last: "Oh, you wouldn't know a den of iniquity if you stumbled into one!—not you!"

"Oh, yes, I would! . . . I know one already—over on the rue Brea, off the Boulevard Raspail. If Adrienne can come, that is where I shall take you tonight. It is called the 'Caveau d'Alsace'— a wonderful little basement place . . . very indigenous. What marvelous entertainment they have! But truthfully, the place is not really very naughty—I was joking you; it is only very frantic, very loud. Let me go call Adrienne, *d'accord?*—now." He got up from the table and hurried inside to buy a *jeton* for the telephone.

Already Mary Dee was trying to control her excitement—"It *will* be wonderful if Adrienne can come," she said to Philip, whose eyes would not leave her face. She was fully aware of his attention and her mercurial mind swam in a kind of unsteady, buoyed-up ecstasy;

she was experiencing now a strange new need for people, especially for Philip and Raoul; it was the hostile oppressiveness—she felt it still; it seemed much, much nearer even than the few tables away and made her imagine herself some solitary creature, unprotected and vulnerable, who somehow wished always to be surrounded by people, never to be left alone. A distracted, wild look came in her eyes. Unconsciously, it may have been the daemon's presence, for her head went into a spin. She turned eagerly to Philip again— "I'd *love* to go tonight!" she said, her breath coming fast. Unwittingly then, she looked away and her eyes collided with the black man's baleful stare. For a moment panic rose in her throat as if it would make her cry out; she was shaken, distraught, then soon angry again before eventually the frozen look returned on her face. "Ah," said her daemon at last, "you're confronted with something very unusual here, something pretty extraordinary. Eh?—do I misrepresent things?—no, not in the least. The question *you've* got to face is not, after all, a very hard one. It's simply this: Why does he frighten you so? Why? Have you thought about it? . . . you should, you know—you're going to have to, sooner or later; probably sooner. *Why* does he send chills through you?—aside from the uneasiness and dread you feel, and also the touch of mortification? What have you done to *him*? . . . and those he would represent? For a moment you turned and looked him straight in the eye, didn't you? But when he turned away in disgust, your terrible fear returned and perched right on your shoulder, as it were, as if it would caw: 'Nevermore!' Why, why, are you so afraid, dear girl? Is it his stare of hate? Why should he hate *you*? . . . and at first sight. It's something to think about, isn't it? Yes, yes, it is for sure . . . and for one's sense of what's real and unreal, it's gotta be faced up to, lamb!"

Philip had at last noticed the man and his exchange of stares with Mary Dee. "Do you know him?" he asked her.

"Of course not," she said, her voice hollow.

"Why in hell is he staring at you?"

She tried to laugh. "How would I know?—ignore him, Philip."

But Philip turned and glared at the man, only to find him contemptuously turning away to stare into the street again.

Soon Raoul came back in triumph. "Adrienne will come!" he announced joyfully. "It is all set, yes! Now that is good—oh, boy!

After awhile we shall leave here and go home and maybe change our apparel. Then later we shall pick up Adrienne at her apartment and go to dinner. Where would you like to dine, my long-lost friends? Think it over!—choose with care; let us be fastidious, for it is the beginning of an exciting evening. After dinner then, yes, to the Caveau d'Alsace. And—listen!—when the floor show is over, *we shall dance!* . . . yes, right there, *dance!* Maybe, later on, then a light supper somewhere. . . . ah, *merveilleux!* What do you say? My arrangements, Philip—how do you like them? They are as we used to do them—very sudden, very swift . . . impromptu, eh? Do you like them?—*do you?*" Exhausted from his efforts, he plopped down in his chair, smiling blissfully.

"Right," Philip said, "I like them."

"Yes. . . . Oh, yes!" cried Mary Dee, giving Raoul a nervous smile—"I can hardly wait to descend into your awful den of iniquity!"

The black man was sitting too far away to hear what was being said but he was a sullen, watchful observer. Finally in seeming disgust he paid his waiter and left the cafe. A cold shudder went through Mary Dee seeing him walk down the Champs Elysées. His loathing disapproval of her was naked, undisguised, and she thought now she knew why. "Ah, ha!" cried the daemon—"And what of your father, dear girl, your ill, doting father? Would his reaction be any different?—you see, another easy question for you." Though her mind was spinning, it had traveled the great expanse of ocean before, and that very afternoon. She had lied to Raoul and Philip about her father. He was still convalescent from his heart attack. He would be curious, puzzled, concerned—to say the least—were he to see her now, and conceding this to herself she felt empty, helpless; but what if he knew *all?*—the thought made her wince; he would be shocked, beside himself with grief and anger. Yet—a wise man—would he? Dear, dear Papa!—she sighed and stared off in space. Now she was aware Philip again was watching her. On impulse she grasped his hand and desperately held it—as Raoul pretended not to see. Even the daemon was pensive, disturbed; but suddenly, as if ashamed of his lapse into a banal sentimentality, he turned evil, gleeful: "Have a great evening, dearie! . . . a *grand*, an *exciting* evening—ah, while there is yet time."

*   *   *   *   *

By common consent—with Adrienne now with them—they dined
at Chez Regent, off the Avenue Matignon not far from Elysée Pal-
ace. Three of them had poached eggs, sweetbreads, and a seafood
terrine; Raoul, roast woodcock; the wines were first a Sancerre,
then a claret of great character. Raoul and Adrienne were the life of
a dinner that went on for an hour and a half; throughout the two
talked volubly of French politics, until finally at a few minutes past
ten they all left the restaurant and headed circuitously for Montparnasse. The autumn night was lovely, the slightest chill in the
breeze, the moon a smoky orange and swollen, and the Seine at
rest under shimmering lights. At last they crossed over at Pont de
l'Alma and turned left into the Quai d'Orsay, as Raoul and Adrienne, in the back seat of Philip's car—they were laughing now and
still talking with great animation—left Philip and Mary Dee in the
front seat to their own awkward devices.

Adrienne, already a promising scientist at twenty-nine, was petite, pretty, enterprising, and covertly opinionated: she had gained
a Physics Ph.D. at twenty-five. Tonight she wore a suit and broadtail jacket, with her thick, coppery hair piled high in an outlandish
belle époque coiffure. Though at times cynical, she could also be
understanding, especially with Raoul; with him, sometimes tender.
She was in a happy, quipping mood tonight: "No matter, no matter,
Raoul!" she laughed—they were speaking French—"Admit it, in
Monsieur Pompidou we have our own Nixon!"

"Oh, Adrienne!—*nonsense!*" cried Raoul, intensely Francophile
and excited from the wine. "*Le President* is French to the bone—
as Nixon is American. Can you imagine Nixon, as President, living
in a house once the home of a courtesan—Madame de Pompadour?
Ha-ha-ha-ha! Americans would never stand for it! French politics
has always been romantic, emotional, theatrical! Thank God for it!
France wept even as it executed its king. It has manned revolutionary barricades that brought tyrants to power. Adrienne, I will not
allow you to render us so prosaic!"

Philip and Mary Dee were silent, oblivious, restive, thinking only
of themselves, caught up in the emotions of the moment, of the surprise and difficulties of being together again. Occasionally in the

53

low dashboard light he glanced at her; he thought her breathtaking tonight: she was bareheaded and now wore hoop earrings, *à l'Africaine*, and a fashionable bright red officer's-style coat with double-breasted brass buttons down past the waist of its wide-flung Cossack skirt, with her lizard boots. He reached and took her hand and gripped it as the car moved over the cobblestones. They were back on the Left Bank now, had passed the rue St. Dominique and were entering the Boulevard Raspail. The moon was behind them at last, still hovering over the river and the Chamber of Deputies; but Mary Dee kept turning around, looking over her shoulder, as if she would never see it again; now she gazed at Philip driving and became very quiet, for he seemed consumed with some fiery silent passion. The lights were bright along the Boulevard Raspail and cars and people thronged the street, which always caused Mary Dee to wonder if Parisians ever stayed at home at night or slept; but soon again her thoughts were on the swollen moon behind her; then she imagined she heard Philip in an agitated sigh and hoped she had not heard amiss. Suddenly Raoul leaned forward, laughing: "Say, say, you two up there!—where is the funeral? Come, my dear friends, let us make a joyful noise, and so forth—eh? We do not do this often!"

Mary Dee smiled and turned around to Adrienne, saying: "Have you been to the Caveau d'Alsace before?"

Adrienne laughed: "Never!—Do you really think there is such a place? Or is it another of Raoul's storms of the brain?"

"Ha!—you will see!" said Raoul—"It is more of Paris!"

When they arrived and had finally found a place to park, they still had over a block to walk—down the narrow rue Brea. Philip and Mary Dee did not mind. Lagging behind Raoul and Adrienne, they could not keep their eyes off each other. At the entrance of the Caveau d'Alsace there was a low iron fence on either side of the narrow stone steps leading down into the place. But they first encountered the seedy-looking doorman—an ungainly, tall, toothless, red-faced man; in his greasy formal tails and battered top hat, he resembled a circus clown. "Come in, come in, *mes amis*!" he greeted them effusively in excited French—"The second show has only just this minute begun! Oh, you are in fine time! This way! . . . *Par ici, s'il vous plait*!" Already they could hear the raucous music pouring out from below as he passed them along to an unkempt matronly woman wearing a buttoned sweater and standing at the bottom of the narrow stone steps. When they had descended she led them inside. The place was half dark, in a fog of cigarette smoke, and jammed with noisy people, as the motley little band blared. The sweatered woman peered around for a vacant table but, seeing none, took them to the rear where she found one wedged between two large, boisterous parties. There was a candle and two ash trays on the table, and, as they sat down, the woman reached across with a lighted match and lit the candle for them. The cigarette smoke was at first oppressive, hanging in a purple haze over the expanse of guttering candles. In the murk the patrons' faces seemed ghastly, a macabre bluish-white. The six-piece band—piano, trumpet, drums, flute, electric guitar, and accordion—played from seats on a dais against the far wall. The dais was at the edge of the tiny dance floor which was presently in use for the floor show.

At their table Raoul yelled something to Philip but could not make himself heard over the din of the music accompanying the first act of the show. At last he gave up, clapping both hands to his ears in a riotous laugh: "*Mon Dieu*! . . . What a frightful hubbub!" he cried. When a harried waiter finally came, Raoul had to shout the drink orders—for Adrienne, Philip, and himself, *kirs*; for Mary Dee, a *crème de menthe* frappé. At the moment unable to talk, they sat back and watched the show. The band was playing a loud rock ditty while two roly-poly women in tights and a little shrimp of a man with a waxed mustache went through a wild tumbling act. The little man seemed out of condition, for he was plainly winded from being thrown about by his two great Amazon colléagues—all as the little band crashed out the shrill, blatant rock.

Mary Dee, fascinated, watched with unbelieving delight. Excited, her hoop earrings flying, she would suddenly whirl and over the noise of the music try to say something to Philip, or to Raoul or Adrienne. Philip would smile wanly and Raoul and Adrienne would laugh or make faces. Then, as suddenly, she would lapse into silent wonderment again, or from a reverie turn to Adrienne and break into a great, disarming smile. Adrienne adored her ingenuousness but well recognized her complexity also—as Philip sat stealing enraptured glances at the earrings.

The second act of the floor show was a mezzo-soprano singing popular love songs. Tall, gaunt, fortyish, cheeks heavily rouged, she was introduced to the patrons by the Master of Ceremonies as

"Denise, une chanteuse fabuleuse!" The muscular little M.C., wearing a turtle-neck sweater and rough leather boots, and holding a wet cigar butt in the scissors of two fingers, was apparently the proprietor of the place, as he bawled out an incredible chronology of Denise's successes last year in "the States." Then tall, haggard Denise took the floor and, stepping scrupulously around her mike cord, sang three songs, sang them well, and was ecstatically applauded. The last song Mary Dee loved. She had heard it before, on Paris television: *"L'effet qu'tu m'fais"*—"Your Effect on Me." It went: "Some know how to express their feelings. I can't. I don't know how to put into words the effect you have on me. The only solution is for you to take me in your arms. My life-line can be read in *your* palm, not mine. If I could only tell you the effect you have on me!" Caught in the spell of the song, Mary Dee did not once take her eyes from the singer's gaunt, rouged face. Her songs finally over, Denise retired amid stormy applause, as Philip, feeling the old pain and frustration, savagely gulped his drink and was silent.

A comic came on next. He was at least sixty, with white, bushy sideburns down his face, and costumed as an English butler. But his jokes were delivered in such a rapid, nasal, French dialect that only Raoul and Adrienne could catch the nuances, flavor, the risqué innuendoes, of his routine. They laughed uproariously, while Mary Dee and Philip could only smile their lack of comprehension. The patrons loved the butler and howled with delight.

The fourth and final act brought on the chorus. Six flesh-powdered, big-thighed, near-naked chorines rushed on. They danced in two rows of three, for the tiny floor would not have accommodated them abreast. Meantime, the flute player had got out his piccolo, and although the little band now let loose with all its might, the piccolo could be heard shrilling over the blaring noise of drums, trumpet, electric guitar, and other instruments. The chorus girls were stamping, whirling, squealing, and kicking their heels and big thighs high as the scent of their damp powder and sweetish perfume wafted out into the darkened crowd. When at last they went off, Mary Dee was completely bedazzled and applauded to the very end, as Philip sat motionless. Finally the three prior acts returned on stage, followed again by the chorus, all to take more bows— their "curtain calls"—and share in the deafening applause. It seemed Raoul's and Adrienne's wild clapping would never stop. Philip in stealth seized Mary Dee's hand and crushed it to him, as they sat futilely staring at each other. Her daemon, possibly back somewhere in a murky corner by now, is likely to have preened forward on tiptoes to glimpse the lovers again; and was soon clucking, shaking his head: "You're hopeless, really, dear girl! . . . what a pity!—after being warned, too . . . warned against your own insatiability; it's bad—especially after all my admonitions . . . to *stay out* of his bed—where, alas, you spent some months already. Do not—please do not!—repeat. And—ah—think of your father, your poor father . . . tsk, tsk, tsk! It's still not too late maybe to turn back—or *is it*? I somehow seem to see you, though, as being swept away—before my very eyes . . . somehow . . . somehow. But listen to me, you sweet, luscious peach, you beauty with the throbbing heart—listen to me, before it's . . . before it's—"

Everyone was getting up! . . . The show at last over, everyone was getting up and surging onto the little floor to dance. The band, led by the accordion player, a lanky, bearded Basque wearing a black poncho, began playing with even greater fervor and abandon than before. Raoul and Adrienne were already on the floor when Philip led Mary Dee through the tables to the front to dance. The floor was jam-packed and the other dancers were curious, friendly, watching the handsome pair, who were unmindful of all their surroundings until Raoul and Adrienne, smiling knowingly, mockingly, danced by. "Ah-*ha*!" cried Raoul·

"That Raoul!" Philip spluttered angrily, dancing away from them —"His damned maneuvers! The great reunion, eh? He's due no thanks from *us*."

"He's wonderful," said Mary Dee, suddenly defiant.

"Certainly—he brought us together again! . . . great! A *favor*!"

"Then don't abuse him, Philip!" She could hardly breathe, he was holding her so close to him. For a moment she disliked him. She always thought of her father at such times—when subconsciously seeking protection—but at once the image frightened, saddened, her. She adored her father almost to the exclusion of other members of the family and always felt a strange panic whenever, as now, she was brought to think of his reaction to her life if he knew it all. His pride in her was deep, intense, and he took few pains to conceal it. The family accepted it as a matter of reality, a fact of life, they could do nothing about. Had she no obligation to him? she thought now—no love, respect? What of the money he lavished on her? . . . on her education, her clothes?—despite the recent heavy expense of his illness and absence from his practice. He did not have *that* much money. What if he ever learned the truth and abandoned her? How would she live without his support? —she had never worked a day in her life. Could Philip be depended upon? Quickly, with deep embarrassment, she put this question out of her mind. It tormented her and she did not want to have to examine it too closely. She only thought of her father now, and felt flawed.

"What's the matter with you?" Philip said, dancing her almost to the floor's edge.

Before she thought, she glared at him. "I was thinking of my father!" she said. Strangely at that moment a chill passed over her heart. "My father," she repeated bitterly.

"Oh, you're so selfish, Dee!—things must be your way or not at all. Life's not always like that, though!—you'll see!"

She seemed not to hear him. Her eyes were curiously, fanatically, alight. "I was thinking of my father," she said once more, though this time almost inaudibly—it was as if she were reliving some sad, sweet memory.

"Do you hear me?" Philip said, his voice rising. "You think only of yourself!—you love to deal out punishment. But I'd be careful if I were you!—if I can't have you, I'll . . . I'll harm you! *Dee*!" But the music blared out now.

Mary Dee sighed as though bored. She waited for the music to subside. "Oh, you've belabored all that before," she finally said, coldly turning her face away. "You had your chance to 'have me,' as you call it."

He was silent at the accusation.

Suddenly she melted. "Oh, Philip!"

"Dee, why do you stand in our way?"

She drew back and gaped. "Why do *I*! This is incredible. . . . You really seem serious. But you know better, Philip. You've never quite made up your mind about me, despite what you say—or maybe you *have*. Yes—negatively. Only you just haven't come out and said so. And all along I've postured about it. Oh, you know it all too well—my pride, and all that. I'm so ashamed about everything.

If my father knew, he'd drive me from the house. But it's you—
you! . . . deep inside you, you fear our relationship. You fear *me*—
what I represent to your family. Oh, how you fear your family,
Philip! Yes, yes—it's true! . . . admit it!" She was writhing and
twisting in his hold on her. "Oh, *please* admit it!"

For a moment, flustered, Philip said nothing—then: "No, I *won't*
admit it. I wrote and told my brother, Randy, about you. . . . I
even sent him your picture—the clipping from *France-Soir* when
you modeled for the students' ball. I haven't heard of your telling
anyone in your family about *me!*—have I, have I?"

"Oh, Philip, you're quarreling!" But she loved, reveled in, his
protestations. She felt temporary relief, a transitory victory. Then,
however, the sense of indefiniteness, insecurity, which she always
felt when she was with him returned and soon she was miserable
again.

Suddenly Philip was impetuous. "Dee, come to my place tonight!"

She seemed unsurprised, almost lethargic. "No, why start all that
over again?" she said—"I'm not all of a sudden turning virtuous on
you but there's no future for us in that . . . only more troubles, more
headaches . . . more heartaches." She shook her head. "We've been
through it all before."

"Will you come if I invite Raoul and Adrienne—for a late supper? Then I'll deliver all of you home. *Dee!* . . ."

She was silent. She took a deep breath. But already her resistance
had crumbled, dissolved. "Yes," she said at last—"I'll come. . . .
Oh, how weak I am." Soon the music stopped and, saying no more
to each other, they left the dance floor with the others.

Soon Raoul and Adrienne came alongside. Again Raoul was
laughing—"Come back to earth, you two!" he said.

Philip smiled glumly, saying: "When we leave here, why not
come to my place—for a potluck supper?"

"A *grand* idea!" cried Raoul—"Oh, by then I'll be hungry again,
do not be afraid!"

Later Philip danced with Adrienne, Raoul with Mary Dee. But
Mary Dee could not dispel her depression. On the other side of the
floor as he danced, Philip's face was a mask.

*   *   *   *   *

Philip maintained two residences in Paris. One an apartment in the *Quartier*, on the rue St. Jacques, in a noble old building of yellow, unattractive exterior but with six extremely elegant apartments inside. He also kept a suite of three rooms in a small but very refined hotel over on the Right Bank, in the 8th *Arrondissement*—the Hotel Vilar, at No. 7 rue Chateaubriand. Sometimes on weekends, with the best of intentions, he would take a briefcaseful of homework over to the Vilar, but then, because of the intrusion of friends, or chess matches, or gala cocktail or dinner parties, he might on Monday morning bring the briefcase back to the Quarter unopened. Yet at other times, at either residence, he could study long, grueling hours, ambitious one day to please his father, a tyrannical investment banker, by becoming an eminent architect.

Mary Dee, who had been in Paris exactly half Philip's time, also lived in the Quarter, in a third-floor apartment on the rue des Écoles which she shared with two other girls, one French, from Amiens, the other Roman, both students at the Sorbonne. She and Philip, during the eight months before they quarreled, had seen each other almost every day. In the process, their experiences—escapades— were various, legion; more than a few thrilling. Mary Dee had never known such perfect happiness—nor really had Philip. Together, occasionally with Raoul, they had explored nearly the whole of Paris and environs—eaten in a variety of restaurants and cafes, gone to theatre, opera, and ballet, sightseeing to Versailles and Fountainbleau, to the races at St. Cloud, soccer matches at Colombes Stadium, and even driven three hundred kilometers west to the Normandy D-Day beaches. The prior May they had spent a three-day weekend in the chateau country—just the two of them—where they shared a small gilt *Louis Quinze* suite in the Hotel Bievre in Chaumont. Back in Paris, they had gone to Vespers in Notre Dame, considering, in their dizzying involvement, their love to be a really holy affiliation. All this, while both carried full academic loads at Beaux-Arts.

It had been a blazing affair from the start—from that first mauve evening at Fouquet's where Raoul had introduced them to each other. All the correct, the necessary, ingredients were there for what would follow. Mary Dee, from earliest years told by her father how intelligent, talented, beautiful, she was, how desirable, how special, had developed a preening vanity that soon became fastidiousness. Until Philip, she had yet to meet the man she felt really worthy of her, of her hand *or* body, though at home there had been the two or three adventitious boys—she had not arrived in Paris a virgin. But at Fouquet's, after the first ten minutes in his presence, her instincts told her Philip was something highly unique. Though poised, clearly vain, with perhaps even a streak of cruelty, he could also be easy-going when he wished, relaxed, and was as comely as a prince. She calculated his family to be not only blue-bloods, but Croesus-rich, and her later information would bear this out with room to spare. She was wise, however—a realist. No absurd optical illusion of marriage entered her head—that is, at first. It was the prospect of chic foreign adventure, of hobnobbing with smart wealth, the thrilling vogue, an interesting, bold mind, the careless opulence and hauteur—these were the considerations which at first attracted her. She was determined, nonetheless, to protect herself, guard her self-interest, her name. She was confident. She would merely see more of this beautiful, rich Teuton of a man, this brazen Apollo, and set him on his ear. That was all.

Philip's original enticement had been different only in the mirror of his experience—which reflected prurience. At Fouquet's his eyes had literally feasted on Mary Dee's gorgeousness. He rather took her to be a fashion model, very *haute*, or a starlet in Paris shooting a film, or some extremely high-toned black in the theatre . . . beautiful, aloof, even haughty, and, he was sure, sexually-tornadic—appealing beyond any woman he had recently seen in Paris. Then he noticed, and vaguely remembered, Raoul with her. He had met him somewhere. Now he was puzzled . . . this odd little joker, this fusty academician, could hardly be out with someone not of his own prosy world. But he soon forgot all that in gorging his senses. He took action. Leaving his own ebullient party and approaching them—her—the thought of love, aching, involved love, would have seemed to him farcical. So both of them, alike, had been blind to the possibilities—the probabilities. And in this fact lay very irksome difficulties—at once they fell ridiculously in love.

61

*   *   *   *   *

Philip, Mary Dee, Raoul, and Adrienne arrived at Philip's apartment in the *Quartier* thirty minutes past midnight. As they ascended in the mahogany-paneled old lift, Raoul and Adrienne were in hilarious spirits and entered Philip's living room still laughing at the English butler's risqué jokes at the Caveau d'Alsace. But Mary Dee, despite her smiles, was subdued, fearful, preoccupied—remembering this apartment and her unworthy times in it. Philip was quiet, courteous—too nonchalant.

The apartment was handsome, striking—with expensive furnishings. It was not really large, yet plainly a man's place. The walls were a cool military gray; and the floors, bare except for a small oriental rug, were stained dark oak and burnished; much of the furniture was leather. But most of the rest was pictures. They hung everywhere—two even leant against the wall. Many were brashly modern, and most in vivid, clashing colors. One such—the artist, Mary Dee—was a great black cubistic goose strutting across the background of a red mosaic floor, and hung low over the left stereo speaker. Now Philip took Mary Dee's Cossack coat.

"Oh!" uttered Adrienne, looking around at the walls—"Many of these pictures are new, aren't they, Philip? Most I haven't seen. You love pictures so!—why don't you paint?"

"Ha!—not a very bright question," said Raoul, going over again to study Mary Dee's gamboling goose. He had never liked it.

"It's simple," Philip smiled, taking Adrienne's broadtail jacket— "I have no talent. I didn't care much about pictures at all until Dee showed me some things she liked. Then we started going around to the shows—that's how I got interested, especially in the new things." He nodded then toward the stereo—"Raoul, how about you and Adrienne putting on a couple of records and making some drinks, while Dee and I go back in the kitchen and forage for food?" Soon then he and Mary Dee, trying to be casual, went back through the dining room to the kitchen. But before putting on the kitchen light, Philip suddenly seized her. In the dark he kissed her hungrily, vengefully, then whispered: "*God damn it!*—what happened to us? . . . Why did you put me down, Dee?"

She struggled with him. "*I* did nothing! . . . we both *agreed*,

62

Philip!" But he fought to hold her, grasping her head in his hands and forcing open her mouth in another groaning kiss. "Oh, Philip! . . . don't! . . . *Philip!*" she whispered. Mauled, disheveled, she finally managed to push him away.

"I'm *telling* you!" he said hoarsely—"You're staying tonight! We'll drive them home, then come back here! Do you hear me?— I'm crazy for you! . . . I'm crazy *about* you!" He reached for her again.

But she clumsily eluded him and put on the kitchen light. Her eyelashes were wet with tears. "That's just it!" she said—"You're only crazy *for* me! Oh, Philip! . . ." But in a moment, now willingly, she moved toward him, then into his arms again, and they kissed with passion, she kissing him back, until they heard Raoul's laugh and approaching footsteps in the dining room as he came for ice cubes. Quickly, they stepped apart, but not before, as if in a daze now, she breathed to him—"Yes . . . yes, I'll come back with you!"

Philip went to the refrigerator and took out a roast capon, as Mary Dee, her eyes kept away from impish Raoul's, went into the dining room to put plates and silverware on the table. In a few minutes when they all gathered to eat, Philip poured a chilled white Bordeaux. Raoul had put on a Honegger record up front which played rather too loudly as they ate. In addition, he talked incessantly on a variety of subjects, all the while watching the lovers, sensing, understanding, their stormy travail. His feelings were mixed, complex, an amalgam of curiosity, wistfulness, amusement, loneliness, envy, always envy, though now somehow also pity for them.

When later they had finished eating, they all returned to the living room. Adrienne went over and found Berlioz' song cycle *Nuits d'été* among the records and put it on. "Ah, Berlioz!" Raoul said the moment the music began. "Another glory of France—Berlioz. Am I right, Adrienne?"

"Yes. But, sad to say, Raoul, *mon cher*, Berlioz is our only *truly great* composer. The only possible addition could be Debussy— maybe Ravel. It is our painters, our fabulous impressionists, whom we must look to for our true grandeur. But I don't have to tell *you* that."

"The same is true of the Italians," said Raoul ruefully. "After

63

Verdi, whom do they have? Donizetti, possibly—Bellini. But then they have Leonardo, and Buonarroti, and Raffaello—ah. Also the mighty Dante. Different categories, true, but—"

"Don't forget Rossini," Adrienne laughed—"and Puccini. You hum their music—I hear you."

Raoul set his jaw grudgingly. "Yes, but it is the Germans—it is the Germans and their cousins, the Austrians—who have the giants in music. When they took Paris in 1940, they used *our l'Opera* to stage their victorious music dramas, especially *Götterdämmerung*. Bah! What they did not know, though, was that their own 'Twilight' was later to come."

Adrienne laughed again. "Raoul, will you *never* forget that? It happened before you were born!"

"What Frenchman can forget it?" he said. But soon he brightened —"Do not overlook literature, though. That is the domain of the English! Yes, you must admit it, hands down. Ha, they need only Shakespeare, Milton, and Keats!" He seemed relieved at the thought.

But Adrienne, smiling sweetly, indulgently, said: "Only we weren't at first talking of literature, *mon cher* Raoul."

Raoul fell silent, glum.

An hour later, after many Edith Piaf records and more talk, Raoul yawned and looked at his wristwatch, saying: "*Mes amis*, it is a good thing that tomorrow is Saturday, when we can sleep late. And—ha!—Philip, I will not be devious and say that I will call a taxi. Instead, and quite forthrightly, I will ask your unfailing kindness in driving us home—in your splendid car. Besides, we all live on this side of the river—ha, not far. *D'accord?*"

Philip, nervous, edgy, eager quickly to be rid of Raoul and Adrienne, smiled. "Of course," he said—"I had planned to take you home." He went and got the women's wraps.

Going down in the lift, Raoul watched Mary Dee's drawn, pre-occupied, though smiling face. It made him wonder; again his envious curiosity began to stir; at last his suspicions too. Soon he was feeling protective of her; yet he remained cool, casual—watchful.

Philip's Citröen was out front, facing south on the rue St. Jacques —in the opposite direction from Mary Dee's flat. When they were all in the car, he started off straight ahead south in the direction of the Boulevard de Port Royal, where, first, he meant to take Adrienne home, then come back northwest to the rue de Rennes, where Raoul lived. But Raoul, in the back seat with Adrienne, at once leaned forward—"Dee lives closest, Philip," he said, smiling, ". . . quite close, in fact. Why do you not drop her off first? Dee, you can be in bed one half-hour in advance. *D'accord?*"

Words of reply froze in Mary Dee's throat.

Raoul knew then. All suspicions were confirmed. "Please take her home first, Philip," he said, still smiling but with slight firmness in his voice now.

Adrienne turned on him with an irritated laugh: "*Mon cher* Raoul!—suppose he is not ready to take her home? Is it any business of ours? Ha, ha!—Oh, you kill-joy!"

Raoul was unmoved. "Yes, Philip—who we all know is a bred gentleman—will take her home first. For she is closest. I have some responsibility in this. It was my storm of the brain, you know, that produced our long—our twelve-hour—convocation, yes." He laughed, but quickly grew serious again—"We have had *beaucoup* fun today and tonight. Ah, how nice, how capital . . . how reminiscent . . . like old times, *d'accord?* Let us complete it that way, eh? Let us remember this day, this night! It was beautiful . . . *oui*, as formerly. For a time our minds were free of the shadows, the dark vapors, of life . . . ha, the setbacks—and the vagaries, yes—and so forth, and so forth . . . ah, my friends . . ." His voice expiring, he sighed.

Adrienne, smiling now, gazed at him fondly—"Aren't you wonderful," she said.

Philip's face was crimson with anger and frustration. Mary Dee shuddered beside him. But suddenly he swerved the car right, into a side street, went over to the Boulevard St. Michel, and headed back north—toward the rue des Écoles and Mary Dee's flat.

When they arrived at her building, he stopped, leapt out, and, after she had said good-bye to Raoul and Adrienne, saw her to her door. He followed her into the entrance and, out of sight of them, said to her breathlessly: "I'll be back! . . . right back! *Do you hear?* . . . Sit by your window—and come down!"

She was silent entering the stairwell, and did not once turn around, though her eyes gave off a strange, manic glitter. But at last, a little hysterically, over her shoulder, she said: "*Yes!* . . . I'll be at the window. Hurry! . . . it will seem so long!" Then she hurried up the stairs.

When she let herself into the apartment, the two girls with whom she shared it were long asleep. She went back into her own room and turned on the light. She saw the azure envelope lying in the middle of the bed. It was a cablegram. But she would always remember, as she tore it open, her terrible impatience to get to the window. The cablegram read simply: "Friday. Your father died today. Telephone when you get this and arrange to come home at once. (Signed) Mother."

Slowly, trembling, she sat down on the bed, staring around her as if she had suddenly been put down in some very strange place. She brought the cable up again, feebly, but high, before her eyes, read it this time in one swift glance of fright, then was somehow quiet before she screamed.

*   *   *   *   *

It was a bright, cold day—a week before Christmas. Raoul and Mary Dee met for a final lunch at The Canary. She had gone home in October for her father's funeral and returned only to finish the Beaux-Arts term, her full graduate work to remain uncompleted. Tomorrow she would be off again, going home for good—her Paris days over. Sitting there near the front of the little restaurant—it was as usual almost full today—the two of them were at first uncommunicative. Both seemed thinking of things far, far away. Mary Dee had just addressed three farewell post cards to Paris friends and returned her pen to her purse, as Raoul fingered an *Amer Picon* and gazed out the window up toward busy Boulevard St. Germain. Finally he got the attention of their waiter and they ordered food and half bottles of Evian water and claret. They did not see their nemesis. It was not the daemon this time. It was the black man. He was sitting far behind them, in a remote corner of the place, sipping his dessert coffee and smoking a cigarette. They had not seen him when they entered, and now their backs were to him— he had been there for almost an hour, as if, by some strange, rare divination, awaiting them. He gazed at them now—coolly, calmly.

Raoul at last looked at Mary Dee and smiled: "What are your thoughts, *chérie*? Come, come—they must be very serious . . . I

66

sense it. Your mind—it seems always engaged, never at rest. How I admire your searchlight imagination—it is so fertile, yes. So creative. That is why you must resolve, wherever you are, to continue your studies, your training. You must, you must, *chérie*. Your future, your life, what will happen to you, is involved—ah, yes, yes, your future. What will it be like? . . ."

Mary Dee gazed out the front window. "My future—" she said. "I feel my life's over already. I *do*. How could I feel otherwise?—how could I, possibly?"

"You should not feel so. Ah . . . Philip, too, is quite broken-up, you know."

"Oh, Raoul!" There was bitter anguish in her voice. "How can you say that! Then why did he fly off home for Christmas before *I* left? He could at least have stayed to see me off—to say good-bye. He knew I wouldn't be back. But he had to rush home—to the protection of his family. Raoul, didn't you see? . . . didn't you see how uncomfortable he had become?—especially since my father's death. Oh, everything has changed. Yet maybe he was the same all along and I just wouldn't see it—I was so blind! . . . I was blind because I wanted to be, I guess. Yes, he was uncomfortable before—it's true!"

Raoul gazed toward the street again. "How can you be sure, *chérie*?" he said at last, though unconvincingly. "Maybe . . . maybe you should not be too hasty—these have been bad times for you and you have been upset."

"Raoul, be realistic. It's the end . . . the *end*! . . ." She bit her lip.

Though still looking away, Raoul tried to speak soothingly: "And for you . . . for you, *chérie*, maybe it is the chance for a beginning."

She stared at him.

"But, in any event, you must come back to Paris," he said— "You must complete your studies." He seemed furtive, uneasy, now, though. At this precise point her daemon, as if coming out of the woodwork, could control himself no longer: "Brace yourself, dear girl!" he says—"The little man, your most valued, beloved instructor, is about to toss a bomb your way. You never expected *this*—oh, no!—and on the same day, the same occasion, that the black sits skulking in the corner there behind you! . . . menacing you. Look at him, pulling on his cigarette, eyeing your plight! . . . what foul deeds lurk in his malevolent heart? Be *alert*, daughter!

. . . ah, but you have ignored all my other warnings—why heed me now? . . . eh? . . . what? . . . I'm not reading you clearly, my poor melancholy peach! . . . the pity of it—tsk, tsk—we specters operate under such cruel handicaps. I've wanted *so* to protect you! But now, for weal or for woe, the black will always be with you—alas, as both your *conscience* and your *cross*! You shall not be alone— ever! . . . Now hear your weird little professor—" All the while, Raoul was trying to bring himself to face her, to make his eyes stay put on her face, to somehow camouflage his furtiveness—"Yes," he finally said, "the chance for a new beginning, *chérie*. . . . There are others, you know, who care for you. You must already know this, yes—ha, *d'accord*?"

For a moment she leaned forward. At last she sat back again— "Oh, Raoul . . .!" Tears glistened in her eyes.

"It is true, *chérie*," he said—"I have thought of Pauline, my wife, in her grave. Now I think of you." As if just realizing what he had said, he seemed embarrassed, then diffident. He tried to drain his already-empty aperitif glass.

By the time the waiter brought their food, both of them had fallen silent again. Mary Dee sat shocked at the revelation, then confused, agonized. "I go home tomorrow, Raoul," she said—"I won't be back. I *can't* come back. For one thing, my mother can't afford it any more." She sighed: ". . . There are other reasons, of course. But I will miss you—terribly. You have been so wonderful, so sweet to me. I will cherish it—always."

"*Chérie*, forget *me*. Think of your future—your talent. Who can teach you what I have—what I can? Tell me. And my painter friend Jean Vitry—he is equally dedicated to you. But certainly— go home. See how it goes. Meantime, you will have grown up much. Even now you are a more mature person than you were, say, in August or September. You may want to try your own wings now, and in time may come to appreciate those who see, and wish to serve your talent . . . ha, I almost said 'genius,' but that is just an expression, a compliment, *chérie*. So, yes, go home—it is the right thing to do for now. But soon you may get the desire to reassess your life. It is possible, you know—yes?"

Suddenly, impulsively, she grasped both his hands in hers. The black man watched. "No, no, Raoul!" she said—"I can't bear to look at my life! . . . I can't, I can't! You don't understand me at all.

You think I'm a nicer person than I am. You're wrong. I'm selfish, I'm heartless—I was heartless to my father—I'm cruel . . . Oh, Raoul, I can be a real witch! I've been a very, very bad woman . . . always—even as a girl! . . . Oh!—"

Raoul only smiled. "Do not flagellate yourself so. It is not merited. We shall rather wait and see. Forget all that I have said to you. Go back and try Chicago. . . . It will be a test. But you will think of Paris."

Mary Dee's face showed her distress. "Oh, I will, I will!—I know it. But for me can Paris *ever* be the same? . . . You know it can't."

"Of course it cannot, *chérie*. It will be quite different. So will you—you will be wiser . . . perhaps not as happy, yet not so miserable, either. You will have begun to understand the way life is. It is—what do you say?—a mixed bag. Eh?—ha! So for the present let us ride with the tide—yes? These recent events should not be treated as anything so earth-shaking—so . . . so cataclysmic? . . . yes. *D'accord?* Ah, now, let us again this afternoon hail a taxi, cross the river, and go to the Louvre—to the Jeu de Paume. We shall see the beautiful Cezannes, Degas's, and Sisleys once more—like old times. What do you say? Then tomorrow I shall come for you and take you to Orly airport. There we shall say good-bye." He smiled. "But then—who knows?—maybe also hello. Yes, ha, good-bye-hello. It is possible, *bébé*, yes? Ha, ha, ha."

Mary Dee was crying. Suddenly she bent far forward and kissed him clumsily on the nose. The black man, a scarf of cigarette smoke curling lazily from his nostrils, watched them. "Yes, Raoul . . . yes, yes!" she said. But her mind was filled with a thousand doubts.

Raoul, though, laughed again and seemed somehow confident. He ordered another half bottle of claret.

The black man had finished his lunch now. He paid and tipped his waiter, rose, and with studied deliberateness put on his rather dapper overcoat. He started out. But as he passed Raoul and Mary Dee—almost brushing their table—he stared straight ahead.

Mary Dee, suddenly seeing him, froze. She could not move, until at last her hand vaguely searched for her face.

Raoul saw her. Then he looked at the man going out the door. "Who was he?" he said.

At first she was too shaken to speak. "It was the man who watched us that day . . . at Fouquet's," she finally said, though barely audibly. ". . . the last time we were there, with Philip—the day my father died . . . *oh!*—" Her hand went to her face again—it was the fear.

Raoul, frowning, seemed not to comprehend.

"Maybe you didn't see him," she said. "Philip and I did. He was sitting a few tables from us—glaring holy hate at me."

"No, I did not see him. Who is he?"

"Oh, Raoul, how would I know? . . . I haven't the slightest idea! —I've wondered so many times." Now she tried to smile—"Maybe he's just an apparition. . . . Ha, I've certainly hoped so, though you can clearly see he's not." Soon her laugh was forced, almost hysterical—"Maybe he's my *conscience!*" Her daemon—an egotist—smiled broadly at this. "*At last,* beautiful dove, you've listened, eh?" he surmised—"Sweet of you, you know. I fear, though, it's late . . . too late. Yet—there's so much ahead for you—you may well beat the rap. If so, fine—who would predict doom so early? . . . who needs tragedy? There's far too much of it already—tragedy's a drag. Here then, dear, sweet girl, is all possible best luck to you! . . . Whee-e-e-e! . . . *Adieu!* . . ." But her fear, foreboding, would not leave her. Imploringly, she studied Raoul's impassive face. Something mysterious had happened to her and she felt now that tomorrow at Orly it would be good-bye, sadly not hello . . . goodbye to Raoul forever? It was the specter—he'd just walked past their table. She still wanted to insist to herself this sudden second encounter could not possibly be reality. True, this time there had not been the melting glare of his hate—it was almost as if he, the "apparition," with his cold, enigmatic, straight-ahead stare, his seeming imperturbability, had passed their table in order to view, study, her as the chosen object of some perfectly innocuous salutation. Would he rather, she wondered, defer, patiently wait, and make his appearance later?—at some other critical juncture in her life? This vaguest of premonitions persisted. But almost at once she summoned the will to dismiss it. She smiled again. And when their lunch was over, she still sat smiling—fondly, at Raoul. "Be sure to think of me," she said, patting his hand. "Always think of me."

Raoul looked at her quizzically; then he too smiled; yet somehow even he appeared to share the strange experience; he seemed able to sense something he could not quite fathom. "Yes, *chérie,*" he said, "I shall. . . . I shall *always* remember." But he was vague, then reminiscent again—soon thoughtful.

Outside, the sun was high over the narrow little rue du Dragon. The sky was flecked white against the bright blue, the day crisp, invigorating. Mary Dee turned to him once more, yet could not face him. Both of them seemed oddly inept, hesitant to look at each other. ". . . Think of me," she whispered a final time.

Raoul still could not bring his eyes to rest on her lovely, unhappy face. At last he pushed back his chair and looked around for the waiter and the *l'addition*. "Yes," he said to her, a kind of breathless stoicism in his voice, "now we shall go to the Jeu de Paume. There we shall see for the last time—for awhile—your two favorite pictures. Ah, the Cezanne *'Pommes et Oranges'* and Sisley's *'Le Canal St. Martin.'* Your love for these pictures, *chérie*, tells so much about you—your sensitivity, the capacity, yes, that you have for emotion. Artists must be capable of emotion—oh, it is true. So we shall see them again, yes, and a few others besides. Then after a taxi ride up the Champs Elysées, we shall get out and walk, just walk—ha, an arm-in-arm stroll—by Fouquet's. Not to stop—no, not to go inside . . . nothing so heavenly as that. Instead, we shall be brave—we shall just glance at it, in passing. But you *must* see it once more, so that you will always remember it. Eh, *chérie?* Is it not something to remember? . . . if only as a token, maybe a symbol . . . of our three persons, our three lives, here in Paris . . . of our happiness—ha, our foolishness . . . and so forth, and so forth—" He turned at last and gave her his radiant smile.

Yet for a moment longer they sat, silently, with their thoughts, uncertainties, their private longings and confusions, perhaps hopes —a briefest time of communion.

Chapter 3

It had been a smooth ride, and not at all dull, in this blackest of nights; there was much to talk about and the going had been peaceful all the way—coming on east from Denver. There had been much giving in to fantasy—the mind ranging, searching, pondering, as the bus moved over the perilously wet concrete. And, fantasizing still more, she had noticed, in the obscurest and remotest recesses of her mind and memory—*true* remembrances—that the skin of his jaws and neck was becoming darker and rougher all the time, a perpetual black shadow, with large patches of stubborn ingrown hairs around and under the chin. She knew it came from his busy, hectic, way of life; he was preoccupied, in a hurry, all the time; it caused him to ignore or forget himself, especially during the two years now he and his wife had become irrevocably estranged; an example was the way, from all the evidence, he must have shaved— hurriedly, much too fast, and apparently with a dull blade in the razor. It had been the same with Alan, though his lifestyle was of course very different from Knight's. But she had surprised Alan with the gift of an electric shaver, which, perhaps because of the gesture, had pleased him very much; yet he seldom used it, preferring his rusty old Gillette. Nonetheless the experience had made her want to tell his successor-in-her-affections that, being the public figure, the idol, he was, he should take better care of his face. This had occurred to her one day back in the San Francisco office as she returned a batch of typing to Knight; she thought his once-handsome face now almost a disaster. Standing before his desk, however, she had trembled in fear. Who would dare broach so personal a matter to the leader? It was unthinkable.

Earlier tonight the dark rain for a time had been a spring freshet; now it had nearly stopped. The sleek Greyhound bus, its headlights glaring, made its way down the drenched expressway—eastbound toward Kansas City, a junction for innumerable points beyond. At the moment she was silent; she sat in a kind of sad, fanciful state of reverie; even in the bus's darkness she could see his face as clearly as if it were in sharpest daylight; as if he were there riding beside her, instead of the old black woman with whom she had been talking for so many long miles since Denver. The old woman, who for a moment had been dozing, stirred now and resumed her religious admonitions. "The Apostle Paul was a great preacher," she said—"Oh, Lord, yes! It was him that told us in the first epistle to the Corinthians: 'For Christ sent me not to baptize, but to preach the gospel. Not with the wisdom of words, lest the cross of Christ should be made of none effect. For the preaching of the cross is to them that tolerate foolishness; but unto us which are saved it is the power of God.' That's what Paul said! . . . It's something we can all think about, I wanta tell you. Ain't that right?"

Seated on the aisle beside her, Griselda was still thinking of that face—his face. "Yes," she finally said to the old woman—"I guess so. I don't know much about the Bible, though."—in the dark her face loomed pale, uncomely, haunted, her lank, long hair down the middle of her back. She smiled to the old woman—"How can you recite so much of it by heart?"

"It's God's written word, ain't it?" came the reply—"What'n the world can you put ahead of it? I read some Bible every day, rain or shine." She patted the worn bible she held in her lap—"Paul said this too: 'Know ye not, brethren, how that the law hath dominion over a man as long as he liveth? For the woman which hath an husband is bound by the law to her husband so long as he liveth; but if the husband is dead, she is loosed from the law of her husband.' That's from Paul's epistle to the Romans. I tell you, you might be running away, but you're still bound as long as your husband's alive—the Apostle Paul said it and I didn't misquote him. Running away ain't going to do you no good—Paul says you're still bound."

Griselda turned away slightly and gazed up toward the front of the bus. The driver, coatless, bareheaded, seemed relaxed at the wheel as the giant wipers kept the windshield clear of the glistening raindrops. She laughed. "We weren't really married," she said to the old woman—"I didn't tell you! He would have married me, though, but I didn't want that." She wondered why she had unburdened to this old busybody—a perfect stranger. It was comical, she thought—bizarre. Yet what harm would it do?—they would never see each other again. It was good maybe to get it off the chest. She smiled—she hadn't told the old woman about Alan, though. Only about Marvin. She knew she wouldn't have understood—and certainly not about all that had happened to her most recently.

"You didn't want marriage," said the old woman with a snort meant to be a laugh, "but look at you now—you're on the run, ain't you? Let me tell you something, there's nothing like a good husband. I had one for thirty-eight years—ah, Henry's in Glory now, praise God. Young people today are doing more common-lawing than they did when I come along—ain't that right?"

Griselda still saw the face. She saw it in its many and various moods, her imagination moving, twisting, scanning, fiercely tossing about, making her wonder what this troubled visage looked like when he was delivering one of his famous speeches—she had heard only snatches of one or two of them on a tape recorder someone had played in the office; she remembered thinking that his voice was at times too high, excited—strident. "Well, times have changed, I guess," she said to the old woman, and smiled—"Maybe marriage doesn't do the job for some people." Then she gave a sudden, strange, laugh.

"It's the people's fault, then, if it don't," said the old woman. "What'd your father think about you living with a man you wasn't married to?"

"I don't have a father."

"Oh, Lord—poor thing. You got a mother, ain't you?"

"Yes, I've got a mother. . . ." Griselda's voice faded.

Soon the old woman was dozing again—until the bus driver spoke into the intercom: "We're due in Kansas City at 10:20, folks. That's about an hour and five minutes from now." He gave a number of connecting schedules. Farther up front a baby was crying, and in the aisle seat directly across from Griselda a tall black youth sat slouched, listening to Aretha Franklin on his little transistor radio. Griselda listened to the music now too, wanting above all things to avoid hearing further mention of her mother. And Aretha was singing so sweetly:

> I say a little prayer for you
> The moment I wake up,
> Before I put on my make-up,

I say a little prayer for you.
While I'm combing my hair now
And wondering what to press to wear now,
I say a little prayer for you;
Forever, and forever, to say in my heart
That I will love you forever,
Forever, forever, and forever . . .

The music filled Griselda with a kind of wild, stoic sadness. She
had burned her bridges and felt utterly alone. Yet her decision had
been deliberate, and, ironically, had brought her a sense of freedom
she had never known before—though there was always the terrifying, lonely fear. She had been gone ten days now. How was Marvin
taking it? she wondered. The entire past week, during which she
had stopped over in Denver, had been spent in struggle. She had
tried with all her will to summon the resolve to stay put there for
awhile, or if she did move on, to go anywhere but to Chicago. So
far, however, her will had failed her—she was still traveling eastward; a powerful magnet was pulling her; she seemed powerless
against it—San Francisco was no more than a mirage now, with
great, misty chasms of time intervening; it was the future, more
immediate than ever, that held her in its grip. Yet, leaving Denver,
she had bought a ticket only to Kansas City, hoping even here to
make a last stand in behalf of rationality. Aretha's high, plaintive
voice of song came out of the little radio across the aisle straight
at her now. On impulse she turned to the lounging youth. "I like
music," she said to him, and smiled—"Especially Ray Charles and
Stevie Wonder." The youth, scooting even lower in his seat, glanced
at her, and she thought he smiled back but in the darkness she
could not be sure. Yet she could see him well enough to make out
his gaudy jacket, bell bottoms, high-heel clogs, and his Afro. She
could even see he too needed a shave. She was sure now he had
smiled at her; she imagined it to be perhaps a bravado grin. And
when he put the radio up on his aisle armrest and held it there to
let her hear better, she was pleased. "Thanks," she said. Again he
glanced uncertainly at her and clearly smiled this time; yet he made
no reply. "Do you live in Kansas City?" she said to him at last.

He laughed and vigorously shook his head now. "It's my auntie
that lives there" was all he would say, his voice a rasping, gravelly
bass.

75

Negroes, or black people, or whatever, she thought, were real enigmas—unpredictable, puzzling. Yet they had intrigued her from her earliest memories. She recalled as a child the strange, very religious woman who had worked for her mother, as a sort of maid--of-all-work, whose name was Sima. She was slight and brown, with large, staring eyes. She it was, not Nancy Hanks, who had put Griselda to bed every night and quietly read her to sleep; she, who bathed and dressed her, took her for walks, who lived-in with her when her mother was on an opera or concert trip, and who had first told her about "sweet Jesus." It too was Sima who clearly, beyond any doubt, loved her; Sima from whom alone, until Alan, she had received all her love. She was nine when her mother dismissed Sima, who had, quite innocently, accidentally, stumbled upon telling evidence of Nancy Hanks' preferred lifestyle. Sima's sudden leaving was Griselda's first calamitous, traumatic, experience. It was as if she had lost the closest, dearest protector and friend she would ever have, the only person or object in life that had meaning for her. After crying for days and nights she finally went into screaming tantrums, rages, against her mother. The years with Sima, however, had had their ineradicable effect, for the little girl, growing up, came to equate all love with Negroes. She was convinced they had worlds more capacity for love than other people and were by far preferable to be with.

In high school her favorite teacher had been Mr. Newsome, who taught history. Mr. Newsome had smooth, cocoa-colored skin and neat stubborn hair; he wore sparkling, steel-rimmed glasses and each morning smelled deliciously of after-shaving lotion; he also used words like "perspicacious" (of Metternich), "nefarious" (of Nero), and "impedimenta" (with much of which Hannibal crossed the Alps). She liked him because he always smiled at her and gave her high grades, made her feel good—cheerful, vain—and singled her out with special little gestures of attention, fondness, sometimes calling her "dear child." She extravagantly admired him too— though easily forty-one or two, he was said by the boys in class to be a "whale of a" tennis player. One day after class when, alone, she had lagged behind to bask in his smiles and compliments, he told her she was so sweet and tender, so "nubile," as he put it— she was fifteen—that he feared she might have problems in her future. Then he laughed and put his arm around her shoulders. She could sense his powerful, though deeply secret, desire for her, but she did not mind at all; she was neither resentful nor afraid; she liked him and when he hugged her around the shoulders ever so slightly, she went limp with this strange, dulcet, insistent feeling she had never known before. She felt he alone appreciated her, really liked her, might even secretly love her; nor was this in the least made inconsistent to her by the existence of his wife and four children. Negroes with their mountainous capacity for it had enough love to go around, she was sure, more than enough for everybody. It had been her experience in life that love was a very, very precious, scarce, dear, commodity—and dealt in mostly by Negroes. She could not understand why this was so, why they were more capable of love than other people; she was only convinced beyond any doubt that it was true.

The youth's radio across the aisle was playing music not familiar to her now. But soon Dionne Warwick's voice came on, singing "It Had To Be You," and she sat back, trying hard to relax, and listened. The old woman, clutching her worn bible, now with a thick rubber band around it, still dozed. Griselda, again seeing that face—*his*, the leader's, face—wondered what made it seem so tense all the time, so absorbed, though sometimes mean and malevolent too, mistrustful, suspicious. Knight, she had noticed, seldom ever smiled, unless possibly when someone happened to bring children into the office. There were many, many reasons for this, she knew, and she sometimes felt sorry for him—when she was not feeling sorry for herself. His only child, a boy, had died at age four, and she'd heard it had nearly destroyed Knight. Moreover, he was doubtless still harried by, taxed with, the shrew his wife had turned out to be—an angry, grieving, jealous, unstable woman, whom, it was said, he had vowed never to return to. There were also all his elusive, tormented dreams of black liberation, black self-awareness, black final triumph. She thought of Knight and sighed. At last she turned to the youth across the aisle again. "Do you live in Denver?" she said.

He laughed his gravelly laugh once more; it was strangely loud, hilarious, this time. "I don't live no place!" he said. "I travel! Travel with a circus!"

She stared at him. ". . . With a circus? . . ."

77

He stared back, in the darkness his eyes fairly glowing. "Sure," he said—"Why not? I dig it. Get to see a lot of places, too."

"What do you *do* in a circus? . . . you're kidding."

"Naw! I walk a tight wire—with an umbrella over my head."

"Oh, my!" Her hand flew up. "I'd be scared to death."

"I work the trapeze too—me and my auntie."

"Your aunt . . .?"

"Yeah—but she's younger than me. She's terrific. Got a lot of nerve, too, up there in the top of that big old tent. Whew!—Aunt Della is somethin' else." He unwrapped a stick of chewing gum now and put it in his mouth, then withdrawing the radio onto his lap, slouched low in his seat again. The music, a rock band, was suddenly wild, savage, and he turned the volume down.

"Who's that?" Griselda said.

"I don't know—some crazy acid-head outfit. You gotta get used to those cats—that kind of music. We got a bunch of kooks like that in the circus—they play all kind of instruments, though; good musicians; real weird—they wouldn't take a bath for their mother; stink all the time—women worse'n the men. They wanted me to join up with them—I can play a flugelhorn a little—and said it'd save my life; ha, from falling outa the top of the big tent some day. I wanted no part of them, though—in my work you got to live clean and regular; no carousing around. Aunt Della is with me all the time of course when the circus season's on, and she's sure a clean-liver. You got to keep in good shape to do what we do; it's dangerous. And besides working with her on stunts, the trapeze, *I* walk the tight wire—yeah, holding a crazy umbrella over my head!" Though not so loud, he gave his rough, grating laugh again.

Griselda was fascinated. "What *ever* got you into it?" she said.

"Aunt Della was in it first—she was only eighteen. And had one pretty bad fall trying to walk the tight wire. She gave that up. But she started showing me how then. Said she'd lost her nerve, but I don't believe it—shoot, the trapeze takes as much, or even more, nerve than a tight wire. She says, though, it's better when you can work with another person—especially somebody like me she's trained herself. Besides, of course, I'm kin to her—I'm her oldest sister's child. That helps, she says—to have your own kin up there with you. Whew, is she strict!—is she tough! Ha, ha, ha!—now

78

she's living in Kansas City with her third husband. She's twenty-two, I'm twenty-four, and her husband, old Cleet, is older than God!"

"So you're coming to visit them—I get it."

"Yeah—the big season will soon be here. Crazy old Cleet wants her to stop, though. But she won't—the circus is our life. I'm coming to have a talk with them, for she's fixing to leave him like she has the others if somebody don't do something. Yeah, she likes circus work, and ain't about to quit—she'll quit *him* first. We're a drawing card—people like to see us, and always give us a big hand in our final act when I catch her from my trapeze after she flies all the way through the air to me from hers. It's something!—gives you a feeling there ain't no way to describe."

"Sounds like the work of the devil t'me," the old woman beside Griselda said—she had clearly been awake and listening. "You'all are tempting the Almighty himself." She stuffed her bible in her handbag now and folded her hands in her lap.

Displeased at the sudden intrusion, Griselda ignored her and turned to the youth again. "But the danger," she said—"don't you worry about the danger, about falling?"

"Sure—all the time." For a moment he seemed reflective; then laughed—"But when you get way up there in the big top, you gotta think so hard, you ain't got time to be scared. You *better* concentrate!—you can't afford to be scared; you'll kill your fool self."

". . . Why on earth do you do it?" Griselda appeared troubled by all the questions in her mind. "But I guess when you've learned how to perform so well, it's not all that dangerous any more."

"Naw, naw!—then it's *more* dangerous. If you ever get to thinking you got it down pat, look out! That's bad. Aunt Della always says to try to think you're still a beginner—even if it means being shaky and afraid all the time. Take one of those hot days last summer. We had a close call—a near-miss. It was ninety-five in the shade, and you can imagine what it was in that big tent—well, I almost didn't get a good hold on her wrists when she come sailing in the air toward me from her trapeze. It was the sweat, y'see. Yeah, it was a close call and both of us knew it. That evening, when we were havin' a coke in the motel, I asked her why she was in this kinda thing, anyhow—putting her life on the line half a dozen times a week, and so forth. She said it cleared up a lot of things for her. I asked her what things—I didn't know what she was talking about. But she got all mixed up then—trying to explain it to me. I don't hardly think she knew herself."

"It didn't clear up *God* for her, I'll tell you that," the old woman put in again. "That child sure needs Him."

"Why do *you* do it?" Griselda said to him.

"I don't know—just for the hell of it, I guess. You always got somebody with you, though—that helps. It makes a big difference when you ain't by yourself—lonesome."

Pondering his answer, Griselda was still unsatisfied. She wanted to pursue the subject and all the elusive questions it raised; yet did not know how. Suddenly she began twisting and turning in a strange confused anguish, thinking of herself as one who, except for the few months with Alan, had always been alone. She said no more.

The bus pulled into the Kansas City terminal out of a drizzle. She had two bags and, although neither was heavy, the youth, with his own val-pak, insisted on carrying the larger of them for her into the busy terminal waiting room. She wanted to find some inexpensive motel in the vicinity where she could rest and think for a day or two—where she could try once more to make up her mind about where she should go, what she should do. Had she followed her secret but almost overwhelming desire—even if it had meant sitting up all night in the terminal—she would have waited and boarded the next bus for Chicago. But now she could only endure her chronic state of misery, foreboding, loneliness, and indecision; her mind was blocked, the confusion total.

"Where you staying?" the youth said. They were in the passenger concourse now, after saying good-bye to the old woman, and for the first time got a chance to see how each other really looked. She wore jeans and a long dark green coat, and, despite her natural beauty, was pale, wan, her hair loose and hanging, her eyes puffy from the need for sleep. The youth was as tall and skinny as he had appeared on the bus to be, with rough, dark skin the color of gingerbread. One thing she hadn't clearly seen before: his teeth were large and prominent, protruding in an unsightly way whenever he laughed. He asked his question another way: "You know where you going, young lady?"

"I'm going to try to find a motel around here, if I can," she said, tossing her hair back and knitting her brow. Then she realized the necessity to seem confident, self-sufficient, in need of help from no one. "There's one, I'm sure, not far."

"Do you know anything about this big old bad town?" Furtively, he scratched his right eyebrow with his little finger. "You gotta watch your step, you know," he grinned, yet appeared somehow giving her only half his attention.

"I haven't been here before, no—but that's no problem, is it?"

He shook his head in disagreement. "I been here *twice* already. I *still* ain't figured out this dadbloom town." But as he spoke, he would not look directly at her. "Be careful," he said—"It's crazy." He stopped, put the bags down, and, inexplicably, took a pair of dark purple sunglasses out of his pocket. When he had put them on they changed his appearance completely, giving it an odd, partly sinister, cast that his former manner had done nothing to create. "If you don't know nobody here, you better ask somebody that does," he said, but still as if in some quandary, or debating something with himself. At last, now staring at her, he picked up the bags and continued through the busy terminal.

By the time they neared the main entrance, she was trying to keep up with him. "I'll only be here a day or two," she said— "Then I'm going on east."

"That don't make no difference," he said, but rather vaguely. "I better take you to the Travelers' Aid—then you can locate a place right around here, maybe. . . ."

"Oh, don't bother—I'll find out from the cab driver."

"What you talking about?" he grinned. "No indeed—a damn cab driver might start getting ideas." He glanced away from her again —"Want to go with me out to my Aunt Della's? We can get something to eat there . . . then we can phone around and get you a place somewhere—no problem."

She was somehow not surprised at the invitation; it seemed natural to her—almost as if what he had said had been pre-ordained. A strange feeling came over her. She did not want to go with him. The idea in fact terrified her. Yet her feelings were more complex than that. Again she felt so desperate and alone. That was why she had talked, perhaps imprudently, to the old woman on the bus; and why she had struck up the conversation with the youth; actually most of the time she had been frightened—just as, although she did not appear so, she was frightened now; frightened not only of this odd, loose-jointed-looking circus performer, but also at coming into a strange city at night, all alone, knowing no one; frightened too of herself, of her own weaknesses, impulsiveness, of the fatalism she seemed to have been born with. Yet she was determined not to go with him. Almost at once then she asked herself why she was afraid of *him*—if in fact she really was; she could think of no specific reason she should be; then she knew she must acknowledge fear of a kind at least; to refuse to acknowledge it would be foolish. What then was the nature of it?—if it was not of him, of what was it? She had an intimation it was not physical—not a fear of molestation. It was something more elusive, strange, morbid, perhaps nasty—she felt like telling him *yes* she would go! Instead, smiling, she said: "No, thanks—I'll make out all right; don't worry about me. Ha, I know my way around."

Suddenly giving a kind of high-floating hollow laugh, he dropped the bags and grabbed her arm. "I know you do," he said—"I *ain't* worried about you, because you ain't going nowhere but with *me*!" He seemed, though, essentially flippant, playful, in his way—not threatening. Yet she quickly pulled her arm away as though she feared his very touching her. "What's the matter?" he said, surprised—"You afraid of me?" His arms were at his sides.

"Of course not," she said, careful to smile—"but I'm going to go grab a cab now. So long—it was nice talking to you and listening to your radio." She was about to reach down for her bag he had carried, when he grabbed her arm again. Eyes wide, she tried to wrench free of him. "Okay, now . . . no rough stuff," she said— "I'm not going with you."

"You sure'n hell *are*," he laughed, showing his huge, protruding teeth. "I ain't leaving you by yourself in this ratty town. Where you think one of these cab drivers would take you?" He was pulling her away from her bag now. "Come on—you're going with me out to Aunt Della's. Then when she calls and gets you a place to stay, I can take you there in her car—see? *Come on*!" With all his strength he pulled her to him.

An elderly couple, apparently man and wife, seated on a front bench, had been watching them. Now the blanched, furious old woman got up and hurried to the entrance of the terminal, where a young policeman stood laughing with two bus drivers. The policeman came at once—his walkie-talkie radio strung across the front of his tunic—staring at Griselda as he approached. The youth saw him and at once let go Griselda's arm—but still stood smiling sideways at her. "You coming?" he said to her, before glancing again at the policeman.

The policeman, ignoring him, still stared at Griselda, and asked her: "Do you know him?"

"We were talking . . . on the bus from Denver," she laughed nervously. "There's no problem. Thanks, Officer." She reached down for her second bag.

The youth grabbed it from her—"*No!*" he almost shouted, ". . . I'll help you!" The policeman observed his strange, excited behavior.

"No, I don't want you to," she said. "I can manage. . . . Give me my bag, now."

He only stood smiling at her, though still trembling from his excitement.

The young policeman was cool, deliberate, malevolent—he wrenched Griselda's bag from the youth and handed it to her. "You'd better get going, now, girlie," he said to her. In possession of both her bags now, she looked at him, then at the youth. She backed away—yet seemed somehow reluctant. The policeman turned to the youth. "Get lost—*you*," he said.

The youth stood studying him for a moment. "Okay, my man," he said with a bitter smile. "You win. But she don't need you to protect her—I was lookin' out for her all right."

"She don't want your protection."

"How d'you know that? She didn't say so, did she?"

"I said get lost!"

Instead the youth turned to follow Griselda.

The policeman, his face white with anger, grabbed him and shoved him violently back against the end of a bench. "Get out of this terminal," he said—"before I call and have you hauled down and locked up. Can't you see you're making a nuisance of yourself?"

"Don't put your hands on me no more, Officer, that's all," the youth said, still curiously smiling. "*You're* the nuisance." In the scuffle his dark purple sunglasses had become partly dislodged; he adjusted them on his face now and, making an odd movement as if squaring his shoulders, reached down for his val-pak. By then

Griselda was fifty or more feet away and had looked back only once. "Young lady!" the youth called out after her—"Just wait a minute, will you?" His voice was full of exasperation. Suddenly he started after her—in a sort of wild, oblique, clumsy trot. At once the policeman, now spluttering saliva, ran and caught him and threw him sprawling to the floor. Strangely, the youth offered little resistance as he was virtually sat upon and frisked for weapons. Soon the policeman had handcuffs on him and was holding his head down hard on the pavement floor. A cluster of people had gathered; then a second policeman appeared. Griselda was nowhere in sight. The first policeman pulled the youth to his feet and started with him to the door, as the second followed with the val-pak. Outside, their squad car was parked at the curb a few feet beyond the line of waiting taxis. They had emerged from the terminal at the moment Griselda was climbing into the lead cab. In a loud, quavering voice, as if in great distress, the youth called out to her again —"Don't leave! . . . Where you *going*? . . . don't leave me—you know they'll beat me up! . . . I told you about this town!"

Griselda, halfway in the cab, looked at him and hesitated. At last, sighing, shaking her head, she stepped back out and asked the provoked driver for her bags again. A third policeman sat at the wheel of the squad car as the other two put the handcuffed youth in the back seat. Griselda came toward them with her bags now, a guilty, distressed, confused, expression on her face. "He didn't do anything to me," she said to the second policeman who had the youth's val-pak. "He was just playing when he grabbed my bag— we'd been talking on the bus and listening to his radio!" She was becoming more distressed, almost hysterical—"He didn't do anything to be *arrested* for! . . ."

The second policeman, a pale, weary-looking man of at least forty-five, smiled. "He was disorderly, young lady," he said.

"Oh, what's the matter with you! . . . Let him *go*!" She spoke directly into his face. "He came here to visit his relatives—don't spoil his trip over something as petty as this! . . . Oh, Officer! . . ."

The policeman, looking more weary, bored, than ever, stood observing her for a moment. Finally he turned to his two partners in the squad car with the youth and grinned. "The prosecutrix is having second thoughts," he said, adding with an inflection of contempt—"Now she probably wants to go home with him."

Griselda's eyes blazed. "What if I do!" she cried—". . . Oh, hell! You're all being ridiculous—mean!—now. . . . Come on, let him go!" Another cluster of onlookers had gathered.

The first policeman at last turned to the youth in the back seat beside him and took off the handcuffs. "Okay, get out of here," he said; then almost yelled: "And get out of my sight—both of you!"

The youth clambered out at once, took his val-pak from the grinning second policeman, and began trotting down the street alone, as Griselda, her two bags flapping against her legs, hurried to follow him.

After two blocks they sighted a roving taxi and the youth flagged it down and gave the driver the address of his Aunt Della's house. He seemed to have forgotten all about the incident with the policemen and never once acknowledged Griselda's help, mentioning only at last, and then almost in a whisper, "those dadbloom smart-alecky cops." A slow rain was falling and Griselda thought the drab, narrow streets they were entering now were uncommonly dark despite the yellowish lights. Ten minutes later the youth was peering hard out the cab window. "Lord, I hope Aunt Della ain't moved," he said, staring at the rundown buildings. Suddenly he pointed to a short, monotonous row of frame houses. "It's along in here somewhere," he said to the driver, then turned to Griselda again: "Lord, what if Aunt Della has moved?" Shivering from the damp, discomfort, and real fear now, she did not answer him. "That looks like the dadbloom house *there*," he said, once more pointing, with apparently some special prescience, and got out money to pay the driver. "Aunt Della don't know I'm coming," he grinned to Griselda—"I sure hope she still lives here." He looked at her queerly. When the driver let them out it seemed to her the street was darker than ever; the only object she could see was the small motley grey frame house they approached up a shattered cement walk. The youth chuckled—"Wait till you meet Aunt Della. She's somethin' else. Ain't but the one. Won't she be surprised! Tries to be so tough. But don't let her scare you—that little gal's got a heart inside her big as a dadbloom basketball. Don't pay her no mind, hear?"

Griselda said nothing. His inane talk strangely heightened her fear. Yet somehow, at least for the moment, she no longer felt lonely—though she knew this to be a deceptive feeling that could both come and go. Then again, as always, she berated herself for her foolish, erratic, impulsive ways. Why had she done this? . . . why had she come with him? . . . it was all so absurd—and dangerous. She didn't even know his name. She thought too he acted at times as if he weren't very bright . . . and performed in a *circus*! So he had said. "Aunt Della"—did such a woman exist? It would soon be determined. At any rate it was good to know—if such was the case—that there at least would be another female in the house, for whatever security that represented; her thoughts were tumbling, her brain in a whirl. At the end of the crumbled cement walk they climbed three wooden steps to a small, dilapidated porch or stoop. She was all too aware of her stiffening fear now. Strangely, she thought of Knight. But he seemed so far, far away. Yet she wished he were there with her, to advise her, if not to protect her. Suddenly the eviscerating feeling of loneliness returned in a great rush of emotion. She had never felt so utterly solitary in her life.

Groping their way onto the porch, they set the bags down and the youth tried in the dark to find the doorbell. When after a moment he failed, he knocked on the door—hard. "Come on outa there, Aunt Little Bit," he half-soliloquized in his low, raucous voice, laughing and rubbing his hands together. It was almost eleven-thirty. "Oh, Lord, she's *gotta* be here!" he said, crinkling up his face in distress. They could see the vague reflection of a light inside, somewhere in the rear; then suddenly a brighter light came on nearer them, in the living room. "*Somebody's* in there," the youth said.

Now they heard an old man's querulous voice through the door —". . . Who *is* it . . .?"

"Lonnie!" the youth cried at once, triumphantly—"Open up, Uncle Cleet! . . . It's Lonnie!" Then in another barely audible aside —"Open this dadbloom door, you old limber-dick galoot, you." There was a pause. Griselda, though frightened, somehow wanted to laugh.

They heard another voice now—an irritated woman's: "It's Lonnie, Cleet! . . . Open the door!—here, I'll open it."

Suddenly the door came open as the light burst out. There, in their pajamas, stood two of the most fantastic people ever witnessed by Griselda. The extremely tall old man was at least seventy, but the girl was tiny and could almost have passed for a teen-ager. The old man was very black and stooped and wore long, grizzled sideburns extending down the entire length of his emaciated jaws—like an ancient, unctuous, plantation butler. The girl's color was a kind of light, sorrelish tan but she wore her hair meticulously plaited down flat on her head in a severe, African-style, "corn-row-tight" hairdo. Apparently in her rush she had been trying to get into a white bathrobe and now at last wrestled it on as she let out a little cry of ecstasy and rushed to embrace the youth—"*Lonnie!*" Then she became suddenly aware of Griselda, and almost recoiled, her eyes moving back to Lonnie—in reproach.

Lonnie made haste to explain. Even before presuming to cross the threshold, he stood there awkwardly saying: "This young lady came in on the same bus with me, Aunt Della. . . . We talked some. She ain't got a place to stay yet, no hotel . . . she's a stranger here. She'll just be here a day or two—d'you know a place where she oughta go? . . ."

The petite girl studied Griselda for a moment. "Come in, you'all," she finally said to them, ignoring Griselda's presence now as well as Lonnie's question. They entered what in another house would have been the living room, but here, though not at all high-ceilinged, the room resembled a small gymnasium. There was no furniture in it anywhere; the polished floor was completely bare. An intricate series of wires, ropes, pulleys, and cables, including a short trapeze ladder, all fixed into the troublesomely-low ceiling, hung a third of the way to the floor. Lonnie gaped around at the room. "Lord, have mercy," he soliloquized aloud—"What's Auntie got here? . . . what'd she *do* to this room?" He turned and grinned at Griselda. Della's husband, old Cleet, stood piously looking on in his pajamas.

"Cleet, go put on your robe!" little Della said hotly. "You'all put those bags down and take off your wet things," she said to Lonnie and Griselda—"then come on back in the den."

Lonnie was still looking around at all the contraptions hanging from the ceiling. He laughed—"Ah, little old Auntie's been hard at it, looks like! You been getting ready for me, ain't you?"

"I've been practicing some, sure," little Della said—"I bet you ain't, though. You'all had anything to eat?"

"We sure ain't," said Lonnie. He put the bags against the wall and the coats on top of them before they went in the den. The den was clean but drably furnished, though in the corner it had for an ornament an old-fashioned, highly polished, brass spittoon. "We're just two poor starvin' children!"— Lonnie added, giving his gravelly laugh.

Humble old Cleet, now in a robe, greeted them in the den, coming forward with a docile smile like a grizzled old dog wagging his tail. He extended his hand to Griselda—"What might be your name, darlin'?" he said.

Griselda smiled though his hand in hers felt like a lukewarm steak. "Griselda," she said, but unflinchingly now, almost boldly.

"Hey, *that's* your name, huh?" spoke up Lonnie—"How you say it again?"

"Grr-zeld-aaa." There was somehow icy irritation in her voice.

"Have a seat," little Della said to them. "Just traveling, eh?" she added, suspiciously, to Griselda.

Griselda blurted it before she thought—"I'm going to Chicago to join John Calvin Knight and the Black Peoples Congress." Then she was appalled. She realized what she had said. Why had she done it? she thought; then knew something had made up her mind for her without her volition. But had there really been any doubt? She thought not. The decision had long been irrevocable—to Chicago. But by saying it just now, acknowledging it, her life seemed to have been made simpler. Except for the loneliness. Would she ever rid herself of it? she wondered. Why else was she here in this bizarre house, with these strange, almost grotesque people? She searched her mind in fear, but when no other answer came, the fear mounted and she looked helplessly about her. Lonnie, as if sensing something he could not understand, smiled at her and, touching her arm, insisted she sit on the sofa. Then he sat down beside her.

But Della, still standing, her fingers absently, minutely, examining the corn-row-tight coiffure, studied Griselda. "You're going with Knight's people, eh?" she said. "I'da swore you was white. You sure had me fooled. We'll get you fixed up in a motel okay after you've had something to eat." Griselda, caught off guard, confused, could think of nothing to say. She was silent. "Cleet," Della said, "go turn on the oven so we can fix them some food."

Old Cleet, his posture stooped as if arthritic, gave her his wide, knowing smile, then slowly made his way into the kitchen. But almost at once his voice came wafting back—"You want me to reheat the chitterlings, darlin'?"

"Of course not! . . . Christ!" Della shouted. "Fix them some ham and eggs—and hot rolls!" She turned to Lonnie, lowering her voice —"Honest to God, I don't know how much longer I can take it. He gets on my nerves so damn bad—more and more every day. I knew I was making a mistake but didn't know it was this big!" She shook her head in a strange, violent, little motion. "He won't let me outa his sight."

"Yeah," laughed Lonnie, "but you wanted them good old pension checks coming in every month, didn't you? Well, you got 'em."

Della gave a tiny, petulant squeal of a laugh—"He wants to go on the road with us this summer! I'm not lying, Lonnie!" She was whispering now. "Says he wants to protect me! . . . Christ, I'd fall and break my neck the first night!"

"Ho!" Lonnie slapped the sofa arm in glee. "Lord, have mercy —marriage! . . . ain't this one pannin' out, either? Looks like little Auntie gets herself a new bridegroom every year, just like it was a new car. By the time you're thirty you'll be world champion!"

"Champion trapeze artist, I hope," Della said with a rueful smile—"If I live."

"You'll live, all right," said Lonnie. "Long as you're working with me you'll be a *live* champion."

At that moment old Cleet returned to the room—unsmiling now, for the first time grave. He turned to Lonnie. "I've been getting all kinda vibrations from Frimbo today," he said—"all day long. Maybe it was because you was coming and we didn't know it—Frimbo was trying to tell me *something*, I know that."

"Ho!" cried Lonnie. "You don't mean it!" He went into riotous laughter. "Not my man Frimbo again!—you ain't starting in lecturing us half the night on Frimbo, are you, Uncle Cleet? Ha-ha-ha-ha!—Oh, Lord!"

Griselda gave them all uncomprehending stares.

"Frimbo is real," old Cleet said, still grave but more assertive now. "We got to reckon with him."

Lonnie turned to Della. "Still the great philosopher, is he?" he said, nodding at Cleet—"Things, them big thoughts, still coming to him right outa the blue, are they? He shoulda been a preacher—ha! Still got Frimbo on the brain, huh?—Lord, have mercy!"

"Frimbo is real," old Cleet repeated. "Only you'all ain't got the nerve to face up to what he's telling you."

"*Who* ain't got the nerve?" exploded Della again—"You come talking to *me and Lonnie* about nerve! There ain't no such person as Frimbo, anyhow—he don't live, exist. It's *Cleet* that's Frimbo—don't deny it." Della laughed now, her voice shrill, full of derision. She turned to the others. "Cleet dreamed up Frimbo—years ago. No fooling—I believe it. All this time he's had Frimbo saying all those deep, crazy, things about life that're over everybody else's head, and himself going around—yeah, just like a preacher—talking all that gloom and doom, when it's *Cleet* that's the culprit. He's the one that dreams up all that depressing doubletalk that's enough to scare the living daylights outa you—it's *him*!"

"Hosea Frimbo is a prophet," said Cleet stubbornly.

"Frimbo's a bonehead!" Lonnie said. "What's he come up with now? Still talking about how it pays to suffer? Huh? Yeah, put your head down, grit your teeth, and suffer, man! Right, Uncle Cleet?—how God's put us blacks down for keeps; how we do what we do because we can't help it; because we got bad problems; that somethin's feedin' on us, on our minds, and all that jazz, right?"

"I've been telling you'all ever since I knowed you," Cleet said, "that Frimbo tells us *why* we do the things we do. Why do you'all spend your time up in the top of some big circus tent, on all them dangerous ropes and wires, flying through the air and making a fool of yourself, when you could be down safe on the ground with a job like other people with some sense've got? Why is it, huh?—ever think of that?"

"Who *ain't* thought of it?" said Della spitefully.

"Frimbo teaches it's because somethin's eating you." Cleet, concentrating, his mind deeply involved, went over to the spittoon, peered down into it, but did not spit. Now he raised his eyes to the ceiling for a moment, as if mesmerized, under a spell. "The very devil's at you, that's why," he said—"driving you crazy-like. What person in his right mind would go up on one of them rope apparatuses every day, teeth chatterin', shakin' like a leaf, flirtin' with a horrible death, if it wasn't because they're after something they can't half-understand themselves. You'all spit in death's face every day up there, don't you? Ah, but you don't know why, do you? Yet you try to act like you know everything. But you don't, quite—ha! The world is so bad, so evil, so awful, it makes *most* people wanta puke. But not you'all—instead you go up on them high wires *wishin' for death,* hopin' for it, courtin' it, prayin' for it, because you can't *stand* your life, you two; can't bear the thought of it—because you want to be together all the time and *can't!*" Lonnie's mouth fell open; he half stood up. "Sit down!" Cleet said—"I ain't no fool. Your life like it is now makes you'all wanta do something desperate —it turns your stomach and makes you fit for the insane asylum. So what do you do?—you go up in the top of some big circus tent and fly back and forth catching each other by the heels. But you won't listen to Frimbo—who could tell you why, and maybe save you all them headaches you go through up there. You'all act like you know everything, yeah—but you know you don't; that's what makes you so afraid all the time—you *feel* the awful fear! . . . Ah, Lord, you feel it. . . ."

"Cleet's senile," Della said, but as if with the fear Cleet spoke of in her voice, then sighed and looked around at the others—"Don't pay him no mind."

But Lonnie's angry nostrils were open.

"Frimbo's got answers," Cleet said, still standing over them. "I heard you'all talking a minute ago, all right—about John Calvin Knight. Why, he's one of the biggest liars and fakes that's come along since Marcus Garvey. You'll get no answers from *him.*"

Griselda sat up at once. "Who's Frimbo, sir?" she said in a stinging tone of challenge. "I never heard of him!"

Old Cleet gave her his beatific smile again now. "I know you ain't, darlin'. You know why?—it's because Frimbo ain't no so-called 'leader,' no 'savior.' That right there's worth a whole lot. The first thing we gotta do is get rid of all these 'leaders.' Frimbo's a follower. His *people* are the leaders. There ain't many of them, either. They don't need many—because all they gotta do anyhow is act as examples. They don't need no big offices, no thousands of followers across the country, no big mass meetings, no messiah for a leader—*none* of that stuff does Frimbo's people need. There ain't but about eight or nine of 'em maybe—why, not even as many as Jesus' disciples. They tell Frimbo what to do and what to say, knowin' all the time, though, he's smarter than they are—in *some* things, that is. . . . Get it?"

"See what I mean?" Della, shaking her head, said to Griselda— "Cleet's senile." Meanwhile Lonnie, sullen, resentful, sat glowering at Cleet.

91

"Let him explain!" Griselda said irritably.

"They don't wanta hear it, darlin'," Cleet said to her. "Frimbo's smarter than they are because he's a follower. He's willin' to humble himself—he *wants* to humble himself. He lets them do whatever they want to him. He suffers their mistakes, and all their shenanigans and bellyaching, with a cheerful, even a thankful heart. As a black human being, y'see, he knows he's alone in the world and *expects* to be mistreated and imposed on. So he's their leading example—they're smart enough to see it, too; understand it. But they're nowhere near the example *he* sets—they know this. They hope, though, to get better at it as time goes on—hoping, always hoping, to improve themselves as examples to others; examples of misery-lovers that don't fight life. But they're still the leaders, even if they do call themselves his group—his band—and they'd tackle a mountain lion for him. Ah, I wanta tell you, darlin', they got answers; answers not only for black people though, but for everybody; people that are by themselves in the world—and that's all of us— and people that have been kicked around a lot and ain't got the know-how to make it in this jungle-land. Believe me, they got answers for us." Old Cleet smiled at Griselda again now—"You ain't heard of Frimbo, eh? . . . ain't heard of Frimbo's band. Well, that's your hard luck, darlin'."

"Go back and fix the food, Cleet," Della said disgustedly.

But Cleet's eyes had not left Griselda's face. Suddenly he was trembling with emotion. "Go tell your John Calvin Knight to stop misleadin' the people," he said to her. "Tell him to start usin' the heart instead of the head so much—*his* heart. Then he'll be a real leader—but he'll be leadin' the people in a mighty different direction from where he's trying to take 'em now; that's a sure thing; for he's *mis*leading 'em now!" Griselda gaped at him but could somehow not speak. "Tell him," Cleet said, "to find out about Frimbo's little band of men and women, of all colors and creeds, that have found answers—that are goin' to change this old world, darlin'. Ah, but Knight won't wanta hear this—no, no! There's nothin' in Frimbo's teachings about big leaders and little followers. Frimbo tells us that in this horrible world we must learn to bend our vanities to our sorrows; that people cursed with Nothingness— and that's everybody, darlin'—must overcome it by long suffering and smiles." Cleet looked around at Della and Lonnie now. "These two young folks here—especially *her*—don't understand that; they're headed for an awful disaster, I tell you. I wait and shudder for the day when they'll bring her back, bring my pretty little wife in here from Buffalo, or Richmond, or Indianapolis, or some place, every bone in her body broken, and drop her cheap casket on my doorstep for me to weep over—just like *I'd* killed her!" His voice rang, then trembled. "Expectin' this, I keep in close touch with Frimbo's band, preparin' myself for this awful judgment—because maybe *I* have sinned somewhere along the line too. But my little wife here and her nephew won't listen; they suffer, though—knowin' what's going to come. . . . Oh, how they suffer—only they don't know *why*!" Cleet had grown cruel, triumphant, now.

Suddenly Della was crying. "I don't *want* to die," she sniveled. Then her face darkened with anger. "God damn it, Cleet!—why do you talk like that!" she shouted. Lonnie glared.

"It's Frimbo talkin', dear—not me. You know that." Cleet's tone now was both unctuous and scornful. "He's tellin' it just like it is— he's always told us we're only here to be victims, and the sooner we find it out the better; we won't be so shocked then when the blow falls, he says—as it sure will, all right. You see if Frimbo ain't right, dear. He's put us on notice—forewarned us like. We know, of course, it's all because we're so by ourselves in the world—nobody to look out for us but ourselves. It's kinda a shock, ain't it, all of a sudden to realize you're alone. I ain't got used to it *yet*. It makes you do crazy things—Frimbo's people laugh and tell about some of the strange things people do to hide this from themselves. The only way you can deal with it, Frimbo says, is to get outa the rat race, especially when you can see plain as day it don't bring you nothing but grief. Start livin' by the heart, as I said, instead of so much by the head." Cleet's eyes lit up with a diabolic light—"*Get it?*"

Griselda had leaned far forward on the sofa. Though understanding nothing of what he was saying, she yet felt somehow deeply, fatefully, involved.

"Why don't you come clean, Cleet?" Della said, blowing her nose into a Kleenex. "Confess up—that there ain't no damn Frimbo; that it's *you*!—that all these long-winded spiels you go into, all this gibberish crap you spout, come from nobody but you. Confess it, Cleet!"

93

"No, I won't neither, dear," said Cleet. "I won't confess nothin' I don't know for sure. These things come to me from somewhere but they ain't *all* in my imagination—no matter if I do get all kinda vibrations day and night. Sometimes I can *see* Frimbo—and I can see his few people around him, tellin' him what to do, and what not to do; and sometimes scolding him. He just sets there and smiles at 'em—but all the time he's listenin' mighty careful. I *hear* him, though, clearest of all, especially when he speaks what I call his 'great truths.' I know they're truths because I can *feel* 'em. I never did doubt a one of 'em for a minute. If I was an educated man I'd try to write 'em down—maybe write a book on 'em. I don't feel short-changed none, though, because I didn't get an education; no indeed. The things we're talkin' about don't come from great thinkers anyhow; they come from great *feelers*! . . . get it? These things come right outa the blue—not from the brain but from the blood and heart. Like I said, you can feel 'em. So how can I deny Frimbo? . . . He's the one that puts all these big thoughts and ideas, these 'great truths,' in my heart, vibrating out to me in the name of the prophet Hosea—yeah, Hosea Frimbo and his band. These ideas of the heart are truer than any gospel you'll ever read in the Good Book, I'll tell you that—comin' like they do right from Frimbo's little band. What a grand group that is—only eight or nine of 'em, yeah; so I know most of 'em by name. Yeah, a great group—a little band of *saints*!"

Della's face was long again. She had been deeply reflective as Cleet spoke. "Why do you keep talking on and on like that?" she said to him now. "I don't know what you're talking about—I don't think you do, either. Don't say things like that, Cleet! I think maybe Frimbo's told you something about *me*—put a *curse* on me or something! *I* don't wanta die! . . . I don't! You oughta know how it makes me feel—you would if you had all that *feeling* you've been talking about! . . . instead of telling us all those horrible things about the dangerous circus, and about caskets, and my broken bones, and all that morbid stuff, on and on! You're terrible! . . . it's awful! Why do you do it? . . . *why*? . . .!" She was on the verge of hysterical tears again.

Old Cleet's face was stony. "Take my advice, my lamb," he said. "Heed Frimbo. Do what he says—have faith in him and quit that circus."

Lonnie's jaw was set. He stared angrily at the floor. Finally he raised his eyes and said to Della: "D'you wanta give up the circus, Aunt Little Bit? If you do, it's okay with me, I guess. I can find another partner, maybe." But his lip quivered. Then he stared violence at Cleet.

"No, no!" cried Della. "Oh no!—I won't! . . . I *can't* give up the circus!"

"I can't, neither," said Lonnie mournfully.

Cleet turned to Griselda again. "You see, darlin'?" he said, "—how they suffer? . . . Lord, you don't know how much. And I can tell you've got heavy burdens yourself. I can *feel* 'em, y'see. Don't ask me how. You probably think your troubles are heavier than anybody else's, but they ain't necessarily. You sure don't face certain death young, before your life's hardly got started—like these two here. They've enlisted in a war—a battle of will power; it's a nasty business, because they flirt with death every day. But I'll admit they don't complain; they got guts; they're hurting, though, even if they do try to act like they ain't, like they enjoy what they're doing. Yeah, I admire 'em in a way, for they're scared to death all the time—don't my little wife here wake up in the middle of the night screaming? . . . I know what I'm talkin' about. Ah, they're sufferin' because they know sooner or later they got to pay the supreme penalty. But, sad to say, they don't know why. When they do finally pay the price, though, nobody'll be able to say any longer they're afflicted with Nothingness. Nobody—because they'll be examples for all of us. It's the only bright spot in the picture." Then bitter derision came in his voice: "But it'll be a sad time, I'll tell you—ah, yes. It'll be a sad time for my little wife here and her nephew, who—you see, I know—are a whole lot more to each other than *that!*" Cleet quivered as he said it.

Suddenly Lonnie, who had first reached down to his right ankle, was standing.

Della screamed—"*Lonnie!*"

Lonnie stood directly in front of old Cleet now with a switchblade knife, drawn from his sock, in his hand. The blade flew open. "You old motherfucker! . . . You'll die before *we do!*" he said, and, grunting, drove the knife to the hilt in Cleet's breast.

"*Lonnie!*" Della screamed again—". . . Oh, *Lonnie!* . . ."

Cleet gasped, then groaned once, and went to his knees, arms flailing limp. He tottered on his knees for a second, then fell over, landing on his side; and finally settled partway onto his back, the knife still in his heart.

Suddenly Della had stopped screaming. She was cringing, quavering, in fear. Lonnie came over now, took her tenderly, passionately, in his arms and tried to comfort, reassure, her. Griselda had run into the front room and grabbed up her coat and two bags. Now she ran to the front door and out into the night and a pitch-black driving rain.

* * * * *

"The man you referred us to at the bank was very nice—very understanding. You are a person of considerable influence, Mr. Freuhlinghausen." As she spoke, Nancy Hanks gave Marvin her weary, jaded, weatherbeaten smile. She had just arrived on this fine spring Saturday afternoon and they were in his parlor. But as yet Marvin had been too nervous, agitated, to sit down.

"It went all right, did it?—well, I'm glad," he said absently.

She was seated deep in one of the downy peppermint pink sofas. "The loan they were willing to make to my friend and me was generous . . . certainly generous enough," Nancy Hanks said—"though perhaps the interest rate was not quite equally so. But, all in all, it was a great—and necessary—convenience to us. So my friend at home is very happy—she and I both thank you."

"Fine, fine," said Marvin hurriedly, but again with his mind far elsewhere. At last he sat down. "But nothing at all has happened in Chicago, Mrs. Hanks! . . . Almost two weeks and she hasn't shown up there *yet!*" He was in great distress and, pausing almost tearfully, bit his lip. "Investigators are making frequent checks of Knight's office there but she hasn't been there at·all so far; no sign of her whatever; it makes you want to tear your hair!" He wrung his hands, but then suddenly directed at her a look of the greatest displeasure—as if she were to blame.

Nancy Hanks found it difficult to hide her irritation at this. He spoke, she thought, almost as though she had failed on her part of some bargain, some solemn pact; when there had merely been the tacit understanding between them that he was to try to help the woman she lived with, Lily Heller, get a bank loan for a music and record shop while she was to try to get any information obtainable —through a black woman friend, among others—on Griselda's present whereabouts. But, she thought, the fact that the loan had materialized and to date Griselda had not was no fault of hers and he was unreasonable to imply it. Yet, though she managed to smile one more time, she was still unable to suppress the urge to pester, afflict, him further. "Why are you so frantic, Mr. Freuhlinghausen?" she said, eyeing him suspiciously. "Why is this such a life-and-death matter to you? Can this possibly be *all* love?"

Marvin seemed subdued, crushed, by her probing—and soon uneasy. "Oh, how would I know that!" he said, almost pleadingly. "I only know I must have her—have her back. I must!"

Nancy Hanks gazed at her large freckled hands in her lap. "I warned you about Griselda," she said. "She can be a real harridan sometimes, yet can have a strange satanic power over some people. I think of poor Alan, her husband, for example. Now she's got you in that power. What *is* there about her? . . ." She sighed, and for a moment desisted. "Yet," she went on, "there's that seeming innocence about her, too. She's a very complex person, Mr. Freuhlinghausen—very. She always was, even as a child; she's never fit into any mold and never will. This makes it hard, very hard, though, on anyone who has to deal with her—I've told you before, Griselda's kind of crazy."

"I only know we must find her." Marvin seemed determined now —grim. "We *must*. I've retained an investigative firm that has the widest possible connections, in Chicago as well as out here, and they'll tell me the minute she shows up there. And she will, Mrs. Hanks—she's bound to end up there. You were right—I've had it verified by professionals—she was very much involved with those people. Black people, as you've said all along, somehow have this strange fascination for her—it's almost as if it were some very strong, unconscious, attraction of the blood, her own black genes running silent and deep. It's hard for us—for you and me, Mrs. Hanks—to fully understand this, but I believe it's true; it's a factor. . . ."

Nancy Hanks, throwing up both hands, almost snorted—"*Well*, you talk like she's a rank stranger to me. Remember, *I* told *you* all these things."

97

"I know, I know—forgive me!" Marvin said. "Yes, I can see the whole pattern now. Griselda is really one of the most extraordinary human beings either of us will ever know. She's your daughter, but I doubt if even you know how true this is. You say she's kind of crazy—well, she's searching for something, trying to find herself. Oh, well, maybe she is a little 'off,' but if she is it's because of her legion moral instincts; she wants so much to be able to solve all the mysteries involved with happiness and unhappiness, with the real purpose of life, and the nasty human soul—"

"Oh, rubbish! There you go, moralizing again. I tell you, she's a little crazy—she's not really interested in *any* of that." Thoroughly exasperated, Nancy Hanks turned her head away.

Marvin gave a long sigh. "What a pity," he said. "Tsk, tsk, tsk—I can see, Mrs. Hanks, why things are as they are between you two; you've never appreciated her for her true worth. She is really a very noble, courageous, though utterly feminine person, but you've never seen that—and in your own daughter. It's sad—very sad. Griselda no doubt would be a very different person if you had taken the time to really try to understand her. Now she feels the world's abandoned her—it's changed the whole course of her life. Don't you see that?"

"Of course I don't see it!—you're naive to the point of—"

"—She has this secret, gnawing yearning, you see—yes, to find herself! Maybe in so heedlessly helping everybody else she feels she'll help, even save, herself. Oh, Mrs. Hanks—"

"—You're the world's greatest, mushiest, romanticist!" Nancy Hanks' laugh was coarse, hard—"Ha, just as you play the piano! . . . Oh, my God!"

Marvin was crushed again. "That's not a very nice thing for you to say to me, Mrs. Hanks, is it? Certainly, I know Griselda's very mixed-up—who isn't who feels the way she does? But, oh, how appealing it makes her! You can't imagine how much—especially to someone like me, whom life and everybody have completely abandoned, written off, and shat upon. *I* know the meaning of being lost, too—of being, if you will, a 'solitary,' of living, or trying to live, a life that has absolutely no moorings. Yet—an irony—I say Griselda's mixed-up, when who's more mixed-up than me? I have a galling nerve, don't I?—though, ha, not a bit more so than you; ah, it's something to think about, Mrs. Hanks—you've had your ups and downs, too, you know. But in some other, very different, better world, Griselda might be called a saint—she's moral, I think, in the most convincing way. It's her compassion. Her living with me—ha, in 'sin'—and her other shortcomings, are of no importance whatever; for, yes, she's as moral as a saint—I believe it!" In his excitement Marvin had jumped up, still staring anxiously at Nancy Hanks, but, seeing her stony face, soon regained control of himself and sat down again.

"Oh, don't get so carried away with yourself, Mr. Freuhlinghausen," Nancy Hanks said. "She can be a veritable little bitch, too, don't forget. You talk of her compassion. She had little for you, certainly—she walked out on you."

"Oh, why, of course she did—who knows better than I? But that's so insignificant when you see her whole, as an entire human being—as you've apparently never been able to do, Mrs. Hanks— for then you sense the pure good that lives in that terrifying complexity of hers, the strange ambivalence, and, above all, in that holy innocence! Oh, it's so powerful a feeling I get when I think of it, I dare not keep her on my mind!—you can't imagine, Mrs. Hanks!"

Nancy Hanks gave him a look of perfect disdain. "Claptrap," she said—"Horrible sentimental mush!"

Suddenly Marvin scooted forward on the edge of his chair. "I've only known one other person," he said breathlessly, "who even approaches Griselda in this almost bizarre holiness. It was Basil Thorne. He's the darling English lad, the drama instructor, who lived here with me for a year. Basil, too, had many strange, yet saintly traits. Though, of course, not to the extent that Griselda does. But he was truly unusual, in his way—so good, so generous, and, yes, mixed-up. Oh, what a pair they would have made, had they ever met!—both, yes, are a little crazy. What a pity they shall never meet!—he's back in Britain now. . . . Oh, what a pity. . . ." Marvin sighed reminiscently and gazed out the window at the bright spring sunshine.

But Nancy Hanks persisted in her irreverence. "You pine so for Griselda," she said, "—I *guess* it's she you're sighing about—but what happens when you, or your operatives, locate her? What then?"

Marvin looked astonished, incredulous. "Why, I'll go bring her back—at once."

"Suppose she doesn't want that?—suppose she won't come?"

"Why, of course she'll come—why shouldn't she? She's mine,

isn't she?" He jumped up again, very agitated, his face red with passion and excitement. "Why, Mrs. Hanks, *I need her!*" He was almost in tears now. "I need her! . . ."

Nancy Hanks was silent at this—not knowing what to say, or do. She only gazed down at her hands again. Finally she looked at him. "There are strong indications, you know," she said, "that she has other interests. Have your professionals turned up that possibility, Mr. Freuhlinghausen?"

Marvin turned and stared at her. At last, disconsolately, in resignation, he dropped his eyes and she knew that he knew. "Don't worry about that," he finally said—"don't worry at all. He shan't have her, though—I shall see to that." But he spoke without confidence.

"You say you need her," Nancy Hanks said, staring back at him now. "This seems rather incredible to me; it doesn't seem possible, really; after all the trouble she's caused you. Who needs trouble, Mr. Freuhlinghausen?"

Marvin shook his great head—"But I'm in far, far more trouble without her! . . . don't you see?" His face was more distraught than ever. "It was the same with Basil—he gave me a bad time too, before he up and left! Yet I needed him so—just like I need Griselda now! It's my fate, don't you see? . . . I *need* beautiful, spirited, gifted—even if cruel—people around me! Can't you see why? . . . can't you, Mrs. Hanks? It's because of *me*, the kind of person I am—a despicable, burdensome, little creature, who ought to be stamped out like a bug, like a cockroach, on the sidewalk! Oh, yes, of course I'm despicable, and loathsome—a bug—an ugly, evil, depraved little beast! Nothing, absolutely nothing, is so morally low as I! . . . I'm cursed, you see—I was cursed before birth, in my mother's womb; I was! Neither she nor my father ever loved me; they couldn't bear the sight of me; the only thing they ever did for me was to bequeath me money; it was meant, I guess, to compensate for all their coldness, cruelty, and neglect! They loathed me!— do you hear? . . . yes, how they loathed me! All my life I've suffered from it—few people in the world have suffered as I have, Mrs. Hanks. Life, the whole hellish mess, has been a trial for me— and now *this*! I need something to heal me, you see! . . . yes, that's it!—or as I've said before, something to heal, truss up, my malignant soul. Of course Griselda, like Basil, was unthinking, callous, mean to me sometimes. Yet they were sorry for me, too—for they knew how I suffered; they felt compassion for me—Griselda told me one time she felt sorry for me; she told me so! Yes, it was because she saw the extent of my suffering—yes, yes, it's true! Oh, how I need something, something somewhere, to heal me! . . . to heal me before I go under, suffocate in my own misery. Something! . . . oh, something to heal me—to suture up my execrable soul, yes! . . . Can't you see it, Mrs. Hanks? . . . oh, can't . . ." Dissolved in tears and sobbing now, he flung himself in a chair and covered his face with his hands.

Nancy Hanks looked on helplessly. She found the scene unpleasant, almost repugnant, and longed to leave now, nearly as soon as she had come. Yet she too somehow felt sorry for him, though she could think of nothing at the moment to say to him. Finally he recovered his composure, and soon got up and left the room. Left alone now in his dazzling parlor, she too began to think of her daughter. She had never really wished for a reconciliation with Griselda, although she did wonder about her new life; and its risks, its dangers. What had made Griselda so rebellious?—from the very beginning, even as a child. Nancy Hanks did not know. She had only wanted, in her own way, she felt, to love her daughter and provide for her life. What had caused her to fail? She hated Griselda in some situations, especially when she charged her, Nancy Hanks, with neglect and then laid it to her alleged wayward lifestyle. It infuriated her and she thought her daughter ingenuous, totally lacking in understanding, and bigoted about the way her mother chose to live. Griselda could be both spiteful and dishonest, she thought. As a mother, she had supported her throughout her spasmodic schooling, and paid for most of her secretarial training after Griselda, a junior with excellent grades, inexplicably dropped out of the local community college and refused to return. She felt Griselda had always resented her help, even though she had accepted it. Then she had met the black boy, Alan, and the relationship between mother and daughter, never a happy one, came to a bleak impasse, and end. Nancy Hanks thus sat in profound communion with herself. The sun's rays out of the west came in through the windows and emblazoned their luster over Marvin's Mimosa and Lemon Peel rug. She uttered a heavy sigh before her face became a stony mask—she would never accept the whole blame for the collapse of affairs, never! She thought Griselda too often mean and unreasonable; and, yes, a little crazy. She, Nancy Hanks, could not be properly held accountable for this, certainly. Nevertheless she worried about Griselda. Not the least of her concerns was Marvin's violent, neurotic, attitude toward Griselda's leaving him. He seemed sometimes virtually paranoiac, unhinged, and, she thought, might at such moments be capable of the most irresponsible, in fact dangerous, acts. She wondered now if it had been right to give him those few clues about Griselda's whereabouts. What if he took matters into his own hands? In such case she, the girl's mother, could not escape grave moral responsibility. Marvin well recognized his own terrible shortcomings, she knew, and had this tragic, psychotic, loathing for himself. What then *wasn't* he capable of? She felt the future obscured, precarious indeed. It worried her.

*　　*　　*　　*　　*

Little Ferdinand Bailey, seated at his cumbersome second-hand desk, tossed aside an auditor's report he had been trying to study and stared absently at the blank wall of his office. He was puzzled, confounded. Strange, unlikely, suspicious-looking people had been occasionally turning up in the office—the new Chicago office of the Black Peoples Congress—for at least the past fortnight and he did not know what to make of it. He decided to talk to Mamie Campbell, Knight's secretary, about it again. Though they had already discussed the matter at least three times, neither had been able to come up with a plausible explanation. They had merely agreed to be vigilant, watchful.

Dwarfish Ferdinand's office was spartan plain—clean and unfussy, yet somehow drab, in the ghetto office building which itself was ancient and drab. But the floor layout and partitions of the space the Congress leased were brand new and freshly carpentered, providing a greater number of smaller offices where before there had apparently been only two or three. As Knight's second in command, the hunchback Ferdinand occupied the second largest of the new offices, where he daily performed prodigious feats of organizational work and arranged besides for all of Knight's complicated, strenuous, speaking tours. Little Ferdinand, however, was glad to be back in Chicago—had in fact been influential with Knight in its selection as the national office's new home site—for it was the city of his adolescence and where his very few friends still lived. He had thoroughly disliked San Francisco. In the embattled sixties he had been an undergrad at the University of Wisconsin for almost three years but had left to follow Knight after hearing, in Madison, one of the young firebrand's speeches, his fanatical appeal for Blackness. It had literally transfigured Ferdinand, enkindled both his heart and mind. Now nearly four years later, following a period in which he had advanced in the Congress to a position of near indispensability to Knight, he had assumed a proprietary, almost authoritarian, attitude toward the organization that in its intensity and persistence all but outstripped Knight's itself. Yet at other times he could be understanding, generous, even noble—especially where Knight, whom he idolized, was concerned.

He pushed back from his desk now, struggled out of the chair—which contained three cushions to afford him greater height as he sat—and left to go across the banistered aisle to Mamie Campbell's little office. Knight, as now, was away most of the time, traveling about the country speaking and organizing, addressing great gatherings of black folk who searched for hope and a better way of life. Ferdinand, now gritting his teeth for no apparent reason at all, as was his habit, meant to tell Mamie he was almost convinced the strange office interlopers they had been lately speculating about were probably government agents—snoopers. He thought it the only plausible explanation for what they had recently seen. Mamie's door was open. "We're being infiltrated, that's what," he said to her as he entered—"Also probably every phone in the place is tapped."

"Oh, Lord, I hope not!" Mamie, seated at her desk, was a chain smoker, and having just mashed out one cigarette, she now lit another. "You may be right, though," she said. "Ferdie, sometimes I'm scared."

"They may be only police spies but it's still surveillance," Ferdinand said. "If I had to bet, though, I'd bet it's the federal government. Don't put anything past that Nixon gang in Washington. That man in the White House will stop at nothing. He's got an iron-fisted control over the C.I.A. and F.B.I., hasn't he, and will use undercover agents in a minute—especially against people like us who're trying to shake up the country and change things."

Both now fell silent, envisioning the dread minions of the federal government becoming privy not only to the long and short range goals of the Black Peoples Congress, and its whole organizational structure, but even to its most petty, routine, activities as well. Soon Mamie got out some files containing personnel rosters and volunteer lists and they discussed every office and organization situation they could think of capable of any possible outside exploitation. They even exchanged and assessed various bits of gossip and rumor. Except, however, for one or two minor incidents, they once more found they had reached a dead end. "The girls in the office tell me, though," Mamie finally said, reluctant to give up, "that there's a character who pops in here every few days—he was here yesterday —apparently just to look the office over. They don't like his looks, even if he is black."

"What's his pretext?—what's he want?" Ferdinand said.

"He's always got a suitcaseful of ladies' toilet articles he says he's selling. Sometimes, though, he just comes in and sits down with the others there waiting—until somebody finally asks him what he wants. Then he brings out all his lipsticks, face powders, and bottles of cologne. But all that time he's been looking us over real good, seeing who's coming and going—who's here. Oh, I realize, Ferdie, it could just be our imagination—this office is always so full of people—yet it's a sign, I think, that here in Chicago we're going to be in for more *action* than we ever had in San Francisco. It's in the cards—I feel it. You watch—it's going to be different. I see all the signs of it—almost every day among our visitors we get some new type, some real character. Just this morning there was a young dude in here who claims he's a poet. He was leading a delegation that wants us to set up another big mass meeting for John Calvin sometime soon—like the one he came here to address last year that turned out so terrific. The poet was passing out a lot of printed stuff to everybody in the office—his poetry on John Calvin, he said —and proclaiming that Chicago's now on the road to a new day, a great day. He was real weird—wild-acting. They called him Gideon, of all names!"

Again Ferdinand innocuously ground his teeth. "Yeah," he said, "I saw that bunch milling around out in the front office—a tough-looking delegation. Yet that's the kind of people we really need; am I right? We need blacks that are out on the streets—they're mad as hell. We'll wake this town up with people like that."

"That's what that crazy poet said this morning—he and his sonnets dedicated to John Calvin. Well, we shall see." Mamie blew a plume of smoke in Ferdinand's direction and mashed out another cigarette butt. "There're plenty things, though, we're going to see before this is all over—mark my words. I'm not talking about snoopers, either. But, yes, I do think we're being watched—and there's no telling, really, by whom. That baffles me."

Ferdinand somehow laughed at this. "It can affect your mind— I dream about suspects. The other night I even dreamed Griselda, back in San Francisco, had been a government agent of some kind —right in our very midst."

"Oh, Ferdie, how could you?—she was so wonderful, so faithful, after we got to know her. Hardly a day goes by that I don't wish she was here with us right now—she can turn out the work of two or three people, you know."

Ferdinand nodded—"I know how you admired her." Then he gave a wily smile and lowered his voice. "John Calvin admired her too," he said. "It was getting out of hand—it might have become a problem."

At once Mamie seemed embarrassed, displeased, at the innuendo. "It might have but I doubt it," she said—"though Griselda *was* extremely attractive. But you're not underrating John Calvin, are you?—his strength, his purpose, where the organization's concerned?"

"Oh, not at all!" said Ferdinand, flustered, contrite, now. "He could have handled it all right—no question."

Mamie sighed. "Well anyway, thank God, it's over and done with."

"Yes," said Ferdinand—"thank God indeed." He yawned wearily, then went to Mamie's window and gazed down on the congested street of pawnshops, "soul" restaurants, jazz record shops, undertaker parlors, and taverns, and shook his head. "We've got so much to do," he said half-aloud. He was tired. His deformity, moreover, the mountainous hump on his back, put added strain on his twisted little body and spidery legs. Pain and fatigue consequently came to him more quickly than to others. He knew he needed rest now, sleep. But Knight would return from out of town tomorrow and the matters in the office to be attended to would double. Whenever, though, he thought of his own burdens he was also made to think of Knight's, which he knew were heavier by far. He became less sorry for himself then, even if there still were times when he grew morose, depressed—he could not help it. He even occasionally felt unappreciated, despite his single, stubborn, dedication to Knight and the organization, but would then quickly purge his mind of such thoughts. He knew Knight never complained, though he had known grief—the leader's only child, his little boy, Ferdinand also knew, had died and the marriage now was finished. But he was well acquainted with Knight's habitual remedy. When the pressure of events got the better of him, he would merely take off somewhere, to some distant place, "for thought and study," as Ferdinand had heard him put it. This meant travel abroad. One time he had stayed well over a month, with his luggage full of books—almost always biographies of great leaders—and kept in touch with the office only by air mail or sporadic phone calls. Last autumn it had been Paris.

"You look beat, Ferdie," Mamie said at last.

Slowly Ferdinand had gone to her door to leave. Yet he stood for a moment almost with his back to her. "I was anxious to come to Chicago—to leave San Francisco," he said. "But I wonder sometimes now what will happen to us all here. Now that we've made the move, I can't seem to see into the future anymore. I somehow have the feeling, though, things will get more complex."

"Complex?" said Mamie. "Is that good or bad, Ferdie?"

He left without answering.

*   *   *   *   *

In flight. Though on bus wheels, she had been running, still running. Never before had she witnessed murder. It had brought her terror, the sense of fugitive panic, and fatigue almost to the point of numbness. But, as suddenly then, she had seemed no longer to care; she was as cold as ice, and totally unrepentant. Now she was only conscious of her writhing belly, her hunger. Yet earlier she had known the feeling of a criminal in flight, though she had committcd no crime—unless failure to inform police of a killing, or her present unavailability as a witness, were lawbreaking. But she had panicked and fled, up here into Iowa—Des Moines.

Yet Cleet was so troubling. He grieved her. She had known him thirty minutes; she still saw him as he was—surprised, fumbling, old, though finally shocked at his impending death; giving a gasp, then a sigh, as he went to his knees, the knife still with him. She remembered her flood of pity for him as she—yes, running—took her leave. Now she could not oust his leaden image from her mind, her conscience, nor from the domain of her sense of obligation—hadn't he unveiled Frimbo? Incredibly, throughout her escape from Kansas City and her bus ride here, Frimbo and his band of saints had traveled with her—in her awareness and in her heart; in back of her consciousness the prophet Hosea had hovered, ever the perfect agent of both confusion and hope—yes, not a thinker, he, it was said, but a feeler . . .? The image, the awareness, ticked in her mind like a time bomb; yet there was always the failure of comprehension, the utter distraction and bewilderment. And she was still running . . . running.

Soon now the first light of dawn would be coming through the draperies of this cheap motel room where she had just taken a hot shower and gone to bed hungry. There had been the all-night ride and the accompanying nightmare of old Cleet's death—his fated end. He had died without remonstrance or protest; only surprise. He had been almost supine, actually permitting, *suffering*, death . . . as if it were Frimbo's very tenets at work, the old man just one more exemplar; perhaps he was now a member of the band itself—in a kind of canonization, or creation of sainthood with great suddenness; also, maybe he might love this conferring of sainthood. Yet two maniacs had killed him—the girl as well as the other grotesque; what a weird incestuous pair!

A tangent thought hit her now. She remembered that two men had been loitering in the motel lobby at the ungodly hour of her registration; and, looking her over with lewd approval, they had smiled at each other. She had not forgotten them. She got out of bed, went to the door of her room, and tried the double lock again. It was secure. Nonetheless she could feel the old lonely fear. She looked around at the walls for other doors and was relieved to see none. Her room was on the second floor of this drab, two-story structure and back at the very end of the hall, with the kitchen apparently directly beneath, for she could hear the clatter of breakfast pots and pans and the boisterous talk and banter between the chef and his help. Unable to sleep, she sat on the side of the bed trying to marshal her memory, make some system out of her unruly and exhausting thoughts.

Inevitably she thought of Knight, regarding him as the only focus her life could be said to have—until Frimbo. What else had been drawing her so inexorably to Chicago but Knight's image, his spirit? At times the realization angered her, for sometimes she disliked him—for his coldness, self-possession, and, most of all, for what she considered his utterly simplistic view of life; she not only thought him at times naive, but that too frequently he let Ferdinand Bailey influence him to his detriment. She thought Ferdinand, even if sincere, a grudging man, to whom her race, her color, was, in the circumstances, an offensive, even hostile, matter. Hadn't he stubbornly opposed her continuing to work in the office, even as a volunteer, until Mamie Campbell had shown them all how beneficial, vital, her services were? It was a paradox that it had been Ferdinand, not Knight, who was the last to relent. She could not forget this. Knight had merely ignored her, acted in the office as if she didn't exist. But she had always felt that Ferdinand was watching her.

It was true that Knight's first recognition of her had been subtly forced on him—and by Mamie Campbell, who, in her own right, was not without power in the office. "This is Griselda," Mamie had said to him one day as he passed Griselda, who was typing outside Mamie's office, and then, as if he had never heard it, she added: "She's a volunteer who's come in to help us." Mamie, Griselda well knew, in getting at least Knight's tacit approval of her addition to the staff, must have given him this information more than once before. Before responding, however, he had looked at her with what seemed deliberately vacant eyes. "Good," he said, and for a moment seemed not intending to stop. Then he paused at her typewriter. It was their first encounter, her first opportunity to really see him, observe him close up. He looked older than his now thirty-four years, she thought, and was slender and medium tall in his dapper tan checked suit, sharply pressed and semi-mod. The features of his face had great symmetry, and, nobly black, seemed chiseled, acutely etched, although the skin was rough and seemed uncared-for. His hair was worn in a modest-sized yet somehow fierce Afro, and his gaze could be penetrating, his manner intense. She thought him handsome, though frightening. She had then bungled his first and only question: "What made you want to come work with us?" he said. Her mind went blank; she could think of nothing to say. ". . . I don't know," she had finally said, as Mamie Campbell almost laughed. He gave a dry, deigning smile. "You ought to find out," he said—it seemed not so much advice as a command. Then he went into his office. She had tried to resume typing but could no longer keep her mind on it—she realized he had asked her the central question: why had she wanted to come work with them? She didn't know the answer—then or now. She only knew that her condition, predicament, was her sense of being so alone. Had Frimbo affirmed it, calling it Nothingness? Was this what he had meant? She could not know for sure—his sayings were so confusing. Yet she felt she would someday understand them better; meanwhile, she sensed some efficacy in their mystery.

The racket in the kitchen below went on unabated. Besides making it impossible to sleep, it reminded her again of her hunger— she hadn't eaten since at the bus stop-off in Salina, Kansas the afternoon before. She decided now to stay up until she could order breakfast sent to her room. She went to the window and parted the cut-rate draperies enough to peer out at the city in the earliest light. It was so far a grey morning and the streets were not yet as active as she knew they would be soon. What was Des Moines like? she wondered. She had never been here before. In her panic, she had caught the first bus leaving Kansas City—for anywhere—just, fortunately, missing by five minutes a departure heading back west, eventually to Tucson. No matter—in her confusion and fugitive's fright she would have taken it. Yet she well understood she would eventually have returned east, and that what she had told Della, Lonnie, and old Cleet was all too true—she was going to Chicago to join Knight. Why was this motive so compelling, overpowering? She could not say. She only knew it was complex—partly Knight, partly something else she could not fathom.

But what of Knight?—slowly, imperceptibly, grudgingly, he had changed. She was convinced of it—she *felt* it. Her first three weeks in the office had seen only his curtness, actually his boorishness, yet also the beginnings of his self-doubt, his perturbation of spirit.

She knew—again she sensed—that he was all too aware of her presence now. She also sensed Ferdinand Bailey—ever watching. Knight's change had begun when Mamie Campbell asked her to type the draft of a speech he had poorly, hurriedly, dictated to Mamie—who that afternoon had to be out of the office as Knight's stand-in at a funeral. The task occupied Griselda for a full afternoon of concentrated work. Midway in the typing she was obliged to go in his office to ask two questions involving his careless syntax, which she thought at best dubious usage. He barely glanced at her, saying, "The people who listen to my speeches are less interested in grammar than in what makes sense." But he approved her recommendations—which she had been careful to couch in tactful questions—and went on clearing his desk for a hurried departure to Detroit where he was to make the speech the next evening. Secretly, however, his approval of her suggestions gave her much pleasure, and late in the afternoon she returned to give him the triple-spaced, immaculately-typed final draft.

He seemed to have been waiting—"Thank you," he said noncommitally, and at once began reading it, paying her no further attention. At last she withdrew and returned to her desk to await any reaction from him, but after waiting ten minutes, and seeing the lateness of the hour—4:30—she prepared to leave, pressed by the necessity to get home before unsuspecting Marvin's arrival. But when she had gone over to the coat rack along the far wall to get her coat, he emerged from his office, looking around for her when he realized she was not at her typewriter. He saw her then. He seemed jittery, ill at ease—she wondered if it was because Ferdinand was watching from his open office door—and when he came over to her, he spoke too loudly, boldly, and with a false offhandedness. "Will you come back in my office again for a moment?" he said. His face was grave, tense, and at once she was filled with fear.

When they were in his office, he stood studying her for a moment, as if not knowing how to begin. Neither of them sat. "You read the speech, of course," he said. "—Typing it, you had to. You couldn't miss some of the things I said about white people." He gave her his steady gaze.

Startled, she could only return his look. She could not collect her thoughts; she remembered somehow feeling disheveled, that she had been too hurried when he interrupted her as she was getting into her coat; also her hair was in disarray, and she thought she held her bag, in her left hand, terribly awkwardly. But yes, she had thought at last, she recalled everything he had said in the speech. She had not been surprised—though she did not entirely agree, she expected him to say such things about whites and had not reacted one way or another. She had been too busy thinking of other things involving Knight—for instance, how she both liked and disliked this man. Finally now, unable to think of how to respond to his statement, she said nothing.

"Why did you want to come work with us?" he said.

She swallowed; then smiled weakly: "You asked that before."

"I know I did. Why did you?"

"Oh, I don't know." She gazed away.

"You know what we're trying to do—you know our stand on the big issue of black oppression and on how it will be stopped; and how we feel about white people. We obviously don't think you're here for any ulterior reason—we wouldn't go for that. Do you believe in our work?"

But she was thinking about how the two of them had been thrown together in his office earlier that afternoon—alone, in close, serious contact—as they discussed her suggested language changes for the speech. She disliked having to admit to herself it had somehow been a thrilling experience for her. The thought made her irritable as she answered his question—"I don't know."

He frowned and shook his head. "That's hard for me to believe," he said.

"I don't! I'm not sure at all I know what you stand for." Then she said it before she thought: "I'm not even sure *you* know!" Strangely, she was angry, and also confused. She really wanted to scream at him. He stood there, staring at her. "I only know," she said at last, "that whatever it is you stand for doesn't cover enough people. You preach hope but you leave a lot of people out of it— that's what I didn't like about the speech." Even until the present she remembered so well what she had said to him, and how she had said it, that day. Now at the crack of dawn in a drab motel room in Des Moines, Iowa she thought again of what Cleet had said about Frimbo's band—that they had answers for everybody. And Frimbo was black.

He grimaced. "You're as typical as whites come," he said.

"I don't think I'm typical at all. If I were, would I be here?" She frightened herself.

He was very grave again. "I won't argue with you," he said—"I'd sound like an ingrate. The organization appreciates it that you've come in like this to help us." His voice hoarsened slightly. "And I thank you personally. . . ."

Standing there, her coat feeling only half on her, her hair disheveled, face shiny, both angry and moved, she felt hot tears glaze her eyes. She left quickly.

Three days later, when Knight had returned from Detroit, she stepped to his office door, very unobtrusively, apprehensively, and asked him how the speech had gone. He raised his eyes from the stack of accumulated mail he was reading and, seeming to comprehend nothing, stared at her. No sign of recognition came to his face. She fled at once, feeling foolish, inane, humiliated. Yet the next afternoon, returning from lunch, he came to where she sat at her typewriter and told her her Porsche, parked down the street—and almost entirely in a no-parking zone—had had a parking violation ticket on it. He produced the ticket from his pocket then, held it up, and told her he would pay it. But she rose immediately and, refusing, tried to take it from him, only to have him turn and stuff it in his pocket again. Then, for almost the first time, she saw him smile; it was nearly a laugh, and she was astounded. After that, on entering the office, it was not unusual for him to pause as he passed her and speak to her, or say something funny, or half rude and flippant; he could also be serious or show the briefest trace of wistfulness. This was how it had all begun, and soon at night she was dreaming of him. Then, in a matter of only weeks, came the shocking, dreadful, news that the office was closing, moving away. She felt that the bottom had dropped out of her world.

Now the grey morning had somehow vanished—changed into a miraculous flood of golden light. The sun was up—shining through the motel's skimpy draperies—as she lay there in bed indulging her sleepless memories, reveries. But by eight o'clock, despite the kitchen noises below, she had partially dozed off to sleep. Then hunger pangs would awaken her—these heightened by savory food smells coming up from the kitchen, it seemed to her, through the floor. Soon, however, fitfully, she slept again. She dreamed. The two sleazy men she had seen loitering in the lobby downstairs turned up in the dream—knocking on the door of her room. When she answered through the door, then refused to open, they had laughed and made the expected indecent proposals. Then in the dream, Knight, somehow hearing, rushed down the hall from his room. He cursed and threatened the men, and chased them away. Yet when she had called out to him, to ask him in, he had already mysteriously disappeared. The shock of her disappointment awakened her again. Her compulsion to go on to Chicago became an obsession, and she knew the sooner she left, the better. After food and sleep, she would take the first bus leaving. She could not rid her mind of the dream or its after-effects; where was she now?— in actual reality; what would have happened in the dream had he remained and accepted her invitation to enter her room? Her mind fled from the possibilities. Lying there in the bed, it soon became difficult for her to distinguish between what was real and the stuff of her dream. She only knew something significant, decisive, had happened the day he brought in the no-parking ticket off her car and they had faced each other in the office. She would never forget it and wished so passionately now the moment could be relived. What would it be like in Chicago? Her heart sank with fear, for she knew she could not possibly envision what the future held. Would her fantasies of all the bright possibilities be dispelled at once? Would the whole Congress office force be different?—and Knight inaccessible? How would she be received?—if she was received at all. She knew besides that her services to the Congress could no longer be donated, for her money was dangerously low (two hundred twenty-five dollars in travelers' checks) and she must support herself. Under these much changed circumstances, how would Knight and the others in the Chicago office react to her now? It was something at the moment she did not care to explore—it brought back all the fear and loneliness.

Food aromas still wafted up into the room—the smells of bacon frying as if rising through the floor. She could smell hot coffee too, and realized she was unendurably ravenous. She went to the telephone at last, called the coffee shop, and ordered bacon, eggs, toast, and a pot of Sanka. But the order was a long time coming—thirty minutes—and when finally the timid knock came at the door, she hurried to open it. In her absentmindedness, somehow expecting to see a female, she wore only pajamas; then opened the door to a

113

tall, lanky boy of sixteen with hair almost to his shoulders. He seemed for some reason unhappy and spoke in a kind of harried murmur—"Breakfast order, ma'm. . . ." Entering, he held the tray of food straight out in front of him, hazardously, awkwardly, as if this were his very first day as a room service waiter. And he wore a sweater, no uniform. She thought him gawky and unsure of himself but almost pretty, though she wondered why he seemed so downcast, put-upon, defeated. At once she felt sorry for him; she did not know why, denying it could be his melancholy beauty. The very presence of this strange boy, however, only made her more than ever aware of her own wretchedness, the sense of desperation she felt. She had opened the door widely, eagerly, to let him in. A flood of emotion she could not have explained, part bold, animal wantonness, part unaccountable demonism, part sorrow, came over her as she stared at him. She wanted to console, pamper, even pet him, and ask him about his young life and the source of his dejection.

". . . Where do you want it, ma'm?" he asked, lowering the tray.

She smiled queerly, her eyes aglitter. "Put it over there." She pointed to the decrepit chest of drawers, then closed the door.

The boy, his light brown hair flowing, went over and put the tray down. When he turned around to give her the check, he found that she had followed him. She lifted the metal cover off the plate of bacon and eggs and inspected them, then stared at him again, her eyes afire. He proffered the check, which she ignored. "Two-forty," he said to her, in almost a whine, or pout—"Two dollars and forty cents. . . ." He watched her, though, as if some kind of tension were building inside him.

"What's the matter?" said Griselda. Her voice, soft, cajoling, was pleading, sympathetic, almost to the point of hysteria. "What's made you so unhappy so early in the morning?" Then she gave a strange little laugh and took a step even nearer him. "Tell me."

He hesitated. Then, without saying a word, he proffered the check again. When, once more, she ignored it, he opened his mouth, speaking haltingly, dejectedly: ". . . My dad—it's my dad." He seemed embarrassed, and gave her a hangdog smile—"He makes me get up every morning at five-thirty. I have to come to work here before I go to school—he owns the motel."

"Oh, that's it, is it?" She laughed. "That's a very serious matter

114

—and I thought *I* had problems!" Her laugh was wild and full of irony. "My problems are *nothing* compared with yours, are they?"

The boy still held the breakfast check as if not knowing what to do with it. He viewed her out of the corner of his eye. Whereupon, she went and got the ten-dollar bill she had earlier put on the nightstand and gave it to him. "I'll have to come back," he said, apologetically, "—I haven't got change for a ten." His eyes were big, sad.

"That's okay," she smiled, almost lovingly now. "When you come back, you can keep me company while I eat—talk to me a little. Hurry."

The boy smiled, though also giving her a look of disapproval, doubt. "I've got to go to school," he said, "—I'm late now. . . . My father will—"

"Oh, to hell with your father!" She laughed in derision. "You ought to want to get even with him for making you get up at five-thirty in the morning and come work for him—don't be a patsy. What's your name?"

"Clifford," said the boy gloomily.

"Clifford, go down and get my change and then come back and talk to me—keep me company. You and your piddling little troubles!—you don't know what it's like to be by yourself almost all your life, do you?" But the boy too looked lost. "You don't know what I'm talking about, do you? Clifford, look at me!" Then her voice fell almost to a whisper. "Have you ever been to bed with a girl? . . . made love to her?"

Clifford's jaw dropped. At last he eyed her strangely, and grinned.

"*Have* you?" she said.

"Are you one of—" He stopped and began again. ". . . Are you a bad woman?" he said. "My father'll put you out, if you are—he doesn't allow them . . . he won't let them stay here."

"I say to hell with your father, Clifford!—answer my question. Have you ever been on top of a girl! . . .?"

Clifford grinned again. "Sure," he said. He suddenly looked pleased.

Griselda gave a plaintive sigh. "Hurry," she said, "—go down and get my change and come back. Bring your coat with you—tell your father you're going to school. Hurry!—if you don't come back, I'll call down and tell your father you kept my change. Do you hear, Clifford?" Her eyes shone.

"Sure," he said again. "Don't call *him*, though—Jeez. I'll come back." Hair flowing, he loped out.

Her hands were trembling as she pulled a chair to the bed, put the tray of food on it, and, sitting on the bed, began to eat. She had felt starved, but now she ate obliviously; yet, in her deep absorption, she was soon gulping the food down. Her thoughts troubled her—a dreary guilt enveloped her. She was about to seduce a child. It filled her with a vague moral dread—and with a tenderness, a scalding pity, for herself as well as for the boy. Yet would he return? Would he, if so, accede to her tender, desperate desires? She wanted so to hold him in her arms, to let the warmth of this inept young spirit flow into her own body and, if only for a few minutes, somehow give it peace. She ate the food slowly now, savoring every bit and taking her time. Yet she was aware of her excitement, her sense of curiosity, anticipation, a strange concupiscence born of loneliness and desperation. She had hardly eaten the food, when she heard his knock at the door. She went and let him in. He seemed breathless, excited, and really looked different to her—wearing now a heavy suburban coat, too short for his height, and a brown leather cap sitting high on his head. She thought him comical and very dear. He also held her change, a fistful of coins and one-dollar bills, tightly, and at once pressed it in her hand. "I haven't got much time," he said, still grinning. She could see how nervous he was, almost as nervous as herself. He tried to speak again, but his voice was a hoarse whisper and she could not hear him. He could only grin nervously, and finally repeated—"My father'll ask you to leave. . . ."

She had put the money on the nightstand, and now reached up and took off his cap. "Will he really, now, Clifford?" she said, unsmiling, her voice mocking. She began unbuttoning his coat.

He shuddered from the excitation. "You *are* one of those bad women, aren't you?" he said, then unbuckled his belt himself, as she unbuttoned his shirt. Soon she had him naked and sitting on the side of the bed before her as she went to her knees, her long hair cascading down over her gluttonous, frenzied face, and gave him fellatio. Then she took off her pajamas and got in bed with him. Soon they were locked in churning, hot-breathed embraces as she tried distractedly to tutor, guide, him into giving her that maximum pleasure, violence, release, she was so mad for. Afterwards, in tears, she admitted to him that she was a bad, a very bad, woman indeed. Clifford, though, was dressing. Briefly, clumsily, he tried to comfort her, but seemed in a hurry to go.

"Don't go—don't go and leave me like this," she said, wiping her tears with the back of her hand.

He was buttoning his shirt. "I gotta go!" he whispered fearfully —"Honest!"

She sighed. "I know," she said, and seemed at last resigned. Seated naked on the side of the bed, she did not even rise as he slipped hurriedly out the door and left.

*   *   *   *   *

She had thought of Frimbo's ambiguous but powerful message all the way—coming on the bus from Des Moines into Chicago. It had somehow given her strength, as if it were returning afresh, or in a rescue role, and steeped in some grand, beclouded revelation. As a result, having just arrived in the afternoon, she walked almost in a trance. Carrying her two bags, she left the big bus terminal on Randolph Street and crossed over to the Civic Center complex, the seat of city government, where she soon emerged into the great expanse of municipal plaza dominated by Picasso's huge and famous rusty steel sculpture. The Picasso was controversial. During the few years it had been in place and on view it had been an issue, not only aesthetic, but political as well—though meant to be non-representational, it vaguely resembled a young, lean, sober-eyed, squatting baboon. Griselda had never seen it before—this was her first time in Chicago since babyhood—and now in her trancelike state she stood looking, smiling, at this great, grotesque configuration. She was almost totally oblivious of her other surroundings, innocent even of the time of day, and knew only that the skies were partly overcast though the sun came through on occasion to give this bemused, demure-looking simian primate its dappled, almost elegant aspect. Again she smiled at the sculpture; then made a strange sort of little genuflection toward it, giving it at the same time a mild wave of the hand, a very beautiful, very feminine salute. She was clearly pleased with it—in awe of it, too. Hadn't

117

Frimbo just been saying to her on the bus that man was, in greater part, animal? But that this was no great cause for alarm?—might in fact be good, for in its lack of deceit, dishonesty, and guile, the animal gave man much to emulate? Frimbo had imparted it, she felt, with the same authority he must have employed to so impress old Cleet. She felt edified—until all the horror of the murder came back on her like a frightful dream; now she found herself staring at the sculpture with a kind of hideous fascination, yet almost in dread; it carried a strange portent. She stood there between her two bags that rested on the plaza pavement and continued gaping up at this huge, ferrous-rusty, linear baboon—until she became aware of another presence.

A man, another onlooker, was suddenly standing beside her. Staring up at the sculpture, he made a grimace. "Uugggh!" he groaned—"What an ugly thing!"

She looked at him, surprised. "Oh, I don't think so at all," she said—"It may someday lead us."

The man looked at her strangely, curiously. At last he grinned. "Are you kidding?" he said, and walked away.

Still oblivious of most of her surroundings, she felt a great sense of euphoria—as if she herself were now, by some magic, a member of Frimbo's little band of men and women, "saints, of all colors and creeds," who truly understood the profoundest meanings of life. She went over to the sculpture and gazed at the rusty steel girder-plate of its base, that might well have been considered, in a more naturalistic creation, to be the baboon's two feet, and paused, reflectively. She stood there for two minutes, then stooped low, humbling herself, and kissed the "feet," the bare rusty steel, her hair falling as it had over the boy, Clifford. Now she rose, retrieved her bags, and headed out of the great plaza—at Washington Street. Turning left toward State Street, the congested main thoroughfare of the Loop, she was wandering almost aimlessly—asking herself why it was that Frimbo made her feel so holy. On the way, she passed many shops, notion stores, office buildings, and a food market. Soon she paused in front of the display window of a wig shop. There she saw a wide variety of wigs, of all shapes, sizes, textures, styles, and colors—both Caucasian and Afro. She suddenly entered the store and asked to see a black Afro wig similar to the one she pointed out in the window to the puzzled salesgirl. When the girl brought it out to her, she carefully examined it, feeling its tight, kinky, harsh texture, appraising its bold size and militant air, as the girl curiously looked on. Next she went to the mirror and tried to put it on, but found she did not know how. The girl then showed her how to gather her hair up so that the wig, once on, would fit and look normal. With the wig soon in place, she observed herself in the mirror again. Her sallow olive skin, nonetheless beautiful and satin smooth, was not at all inappropriate for this strange, new guise. She stood studying herself. She thought of Knight and smiled.

The salesgirl smiled too now. "Going to a costume party?" she said.

Griselda thought for a moment, and turned and looked at the girl. "Do you think it would work?" she said, smiling prankishly and primping the wig with both hands.

The girl hesitated. "You could put on some very dark tan powder, maybe," she finally said. "That might help—your skin is already a bit swarthy."

"You probably think, though, I should try something else?" Griselda's eyes swept around at the other wigs.

"Why do you want to be . . . why do you want to go as a black?" the girl said.

"*I'm* black," laughed Griselda, as if on an escapade, and stared at her.

"You *are*?" The girl gaped.

"Oh, of course not—I'm only putting you on." Griselda became reflective, however, and did not laugh again. It was as if she were puzzled by her own remark, and, unsmiling now, still stared at the salesgirl. "I'll take this wig," she said at last.

But the girl had already reached for a blond wig—one with long, flowing tresses. "Why don't you try this one?" she said, in a tone almost imploring.

"*Blond?*" said Griselda, startled.

"It would be even more dramatic, don't you think?—with your dark skin color."

"Oh, yes?—then I could use a blond *Afro* wig, couldn't I?" Griselda, very serious, turned around to the other wigs again.

The salesgirl looked deflated. "Oh, I don't know about that," she sighed, dubiously. "Why must you be *black?*"

Griselda stopped and studied her, as if the question had never occurred to her before. She could not think of an answer. But finally she smiled—"Oh, I don't think it's a compulsion, quite. But I'll take the black Afro wig." It was only then she seemed to remember she was wearing it. She quickly pulled it off and gave it to the girl to wrap. Then she paid for it, put it in one of her bags, and left.

By five o'clock, after eating a hamburger and wandering the streets for an hour and a half, she had checked into the Stacy Arms Hotel—a modest but clean little hostelry located on Michigan Avenue at the southern end of the Loop. Her room was a cheerful one that faced Grant Park and beyond that the lake where the sun's red rays at her back cast their fiery reflections out over the water. As she unpacked, she turned on the television—to Walter Cronkite. After national coverage came local news, the weather, then more local news, the attractive young woman newscaster reading the brief item almost whimsically:

> Extra police details that were assigned Wednesday to two trouble areas of the predominantly Negro near-Southside— following the shooting Tuesday of black activist leader John Calvin Knight—have been withdrawn as tensions somewhat lessen and order is restored. Knight, at Mercy Hospital, has been taken off the critical list though doctors describe his condition as guarded.

Griselda, heading to the bathroom to launder panty hose, had frozen in her tracks. Now she wheeled and faced the television— only to hear the pretty newscaster, in her whimsical way, go on to other items of local interest.

Chapter 4

The third day of March had arrived in a blinding snowstorm. From out over Lake Michigan the snow seemed driven, hurled, catapulted in great cyclonic chunks inland, bringing traffic to a crawl in the twelve-inch accumulation on the city's streets. The condition, arctic, perilous, frightening, rare, had persisted since earliest dawn, three hours before, with no sign of let-up save the possibility that plunging temperatures might eventually slow, perhaps stop, the onslaught. Meanwhile the cars kept trying to plow through.

The two black children, hand grasped in hand, frosty breaths wraithlike, waited at a traffic light for the desperate chance to cross. The sky grew wilder still and soon the wind set up a fearful howl. Ernestine gripped little Vernon's hand harder now, but for a moment let it go, the better to gather her thin, squalid coat about her. Vernon, in his outgrown mackinaw, stood at the curb shivering, his teeth chattering. How hateful, old school! Ernestine thought; especially when you had to go out in a blizzard after being yanked from bed and sent off with only a bowl of cornflakes in your stomach—and with Vernon already with a hacking cough from the cold he'd had two days. Why had their mother done it, when they had begged and cried to stay home? She couldn't understand it, unless maybe Momma had a new boyfriend coming by—since Clarence, her steady, was out of work and away a lot. As Ernestine looked at her brother Vernon, eight years old and in the third grade, standing there, cold, shaking, his hands gloveless and aching, she was by turns angry, sad, then, from experience, resigned. It was their life.

Vernon was standing on one foot now. "M'*toes*'re cold!" he cried, grimacing. He put one foot down, then lifted the other, as the raw snow blew in their faces. Yet Vernon seldom complained. If matters he could not understand became unpleasant, even painful, he would look at eleven-year-old Ernestine, his only sibling and his deputy mother, whom he knew loved him above all things in this world, and would pucker up his mouth and cry briefly. But Ernestine could stop these half-hearted emotional moments by giving him her un-divided attention for a minute or two—by wiping his nose, say, rudely pulling his cap down over his eyes, or punching him in the ribs to make him laugh.

The traffic light went green and Ernestine reached for Vernon's hand again. "Only two more blocks," she said—"Come on." The wind nearly blew them down as they stepped off the curb into snow almost to their knees. Vernon gripped her hand fearfully as she half-dragged him through and across to the other side. When a block west of 60th and Cottage Grove they had reached A. O. Sexton grade school, they found it closed and locked. It was later known their mother had drunk half a jug of muscatel wine the night before and gone to bed without the usual TV stint to tell her that because of the blizzard schools would be closed next day. Ernestine tried the school's stubborn front door again, in vain. Vernon, watch-ing, began to cry—"M'*feet*'re cold! . . . *Owwwww!* . . . Open the door, Ernestine!"

Ernestine shook the door handle hard, angrily. "Damn school's closed today," she said. "Momma didn't tell us. Hell, now we gotta go all the way back." She looked at Vernon's thin, snow-caked shoes, then at her own. "Hell!" she said again. Once more she took Vernon's hand and started off back in the direction from which they had come. "Owwwww!" bawled Vernon. "M'toes hurt! . . . Ernestine! . . ."

"Shut up!" Ernestine said. She muttered to herself: "Momma's evil, yes she is. Hell!" Leaning into the blizzard, they had returned only a block, when Vernon, gasping for breath, stumbled and went down in the snow on one knee. He stayed down, unable to move. "What's the matter with you?" Ernestine said. But her eyes were wide with fear. "Get up . . . get up, Vernon!" Breathing wildly as if his lungs would burst, Vernon could only look up at her. She tried not to panic. "Vernon!" She bent down to him. "Vernon, what's the matter?—you tired?"

"I can't breathe! . . ." he said, choking—then whimpered: "M'leg won't move. . . . It's froze. I can't breathe, neither."

She tried with all her strength to pull him up, but she could not. Suddenly frantic, she ran out in the street and began flagging traffic, which was barely creeping in the drifting snow. A Commonwealth Edison line-repair truck, marked "Chicago Central Division," stopped and the two men in the cab peered down at her. "My brother! . . . he can't walk no more!" she cried up at them. "He's give out! . . . he can't walk!" The men sat and looked as if wondering what they were expected to do about it, until the halted cars behind them began sounding their horns, at which they plowed over to the side, let traffic pass, then the driver got down and came over. Vernon was on his hands and knees in the snow now.

The fourth or fifth car in the line of traffic behind the truck was a flashy—new—little red Datsun 1200. It also paused when its driver, a lone young woman, saw the commotion and the children. Curious, she put her window down and stared out. Although in the maelstrom of snow her face seemed alien, indistinct, remote—it was also partially obscured by the fierce hood of the great fur parka she wore—it could readily be recognized by almost anyone who had ever seen it before as that of Mary Dee Adkins. The horns were blowing again now. As the Edison driver had done, she pulled off to the side as best she could and stopped, still peering out at the children through the flying snow. At last she got out—wearing heavy suede boots, a thick wool pants suit, and the shaggy fur parka—and joined the Edison man standing over Vernon. The man had pulled Vernon to his feet, but when he relaxed his hold, Vernon, still whimpering, sank back to his knees again. "He's give out!" protested Ernestine. "We went to school but there ain't no school today! . . . We was coming back and Vernon he give out!"

"Where do you live, little girl?" Mary Dee said.

"Round on St. Lawrence."—but Ernestine was busy bending down to Vernon again.

Mary Dee turned to the Edison man. "If you'll help me get him in my car," she said, "I'll take them home."

The man picked Vernon up under the arm pits and, dragging him along as Vernon moaned, stowed him in the back seat of Mary Dee's car—at once prompting Ernestine to climb in beside him. The truck drove off as Mary Dee started her motor. "Where on St. Lawrence?" she said to Ernestine.

"Near 64th, lady." Ernestine then sighed, theatrically: "There ain't nothing to eat at home, though. My Momma's check ain't come yet, and I'm hungry. Vernon's hungry too." She gave Vernon a crafty, threatening look, cuing him in to corroborate. But Vernon, frightened from his experience, painfully winded, cold, seemed for the moment content in the heated little car and did not react, said nothing. Moreover he was already wondrously impressed with Mary Dee and kept his great eyes on the back of her head encased in the ferocious cowl of her fur parka.

"No food!" Mary Dee almost turned around to them. "Don't you have a father?"

"No'm." They answered together. "But Momma's got a boy-friend," explained Ernestine. "Clarence ain't working right now, though, and's gone most of the time. Momma says we ain't got any food because her check's late this month. She made us leave in the cold this morning, too—when there wasn't any school. Oh, Lordy." This time she gave Vernon a vigorous nudge—"Vernon, you hungry?" Vernon still did not answer. His eyes were riveted on Mary Dee.

Some mother! thought Mary Dee, incensed—a clear case of child neglect, almost abandonment. She watched what little she could see of them in the rear view mirror. Ernestine had a rough-hewn, stubborn, intelligent face, and seemed already shrewd, worldly-wise, tough. Vernon, though conspicuously her blood brother, was more naive and trusting. He was pixyish, winsome also, and gave the impression of wandering or rambling in his thoughts, or spending much of his time in daydreaming. Mary Dee did not know that, despite his dogmatic reliance on Ernestine, he had also come to feel now he had chanced upon a great new friend, a protector, indeed a beautiful guardian angel, in herself. Hadn't she saved him from the awful snow and cold? . . . Wasn't he riding in her warm, newfangled little car? . . . Also hadn't she been enough interested in them to ask if they had a father? He was in-clined to think his fortunes had immeasurably improved. But now his limbs had begun to thaw and he was feeling genuinely starved. "I'm hungry!" he said, and looked imploringly up at Mary Dee.

"You sure are—I can tell," Ernestine quickly confirmed. "So'm I." Her eyes too went up to Mary Dee—"You got any food at your house, lady?"

"I don't live around here," Mary Dee said. "I'm on my to my job."

"Oh, Lordy," Ernestine sighed. But then suddenly she turned and frowned hard at Vernon.

Vernon, enough intimidated at last, twisted up his face in a fit of mock crying: "I'm hungry! . . . I *am!* We ain't had nothing to eat but some old cornflakes!"

"Too bad, too bad, Vernon," clucked Ernestine, at the same time glancing hopefully up at Mary Dee again. "This lady's on her way to work—she ain't got no time to be feeding *us*. When we get home we'll have to just drink some water."

Mary Dee smiled to herself at this ploy. Yet, and quite suddenly, she made the decision. She would take them to a restaurant— if she could find one near—and get them food. With all the weather, an hour's delay would mean no problem at the office. She turned the car around at the first opportunity and headed back toward Cottage Grove. Ernestine, ever watchful, alert, immediately sensed some change in the course of events, perhaps too in their fortunes, though she knew better than to inquire. She wanted actually to clap her hands in joy, but realized life at the moment was far too serious, precarious, for any such presumption. Besides, Vernon now was coughing—a deep, croupy cough. "Vernon needs some cough medicine for that old cold of his," she said, rather too loudly. "It sure ain't getting no better." Quickly Vernon gave another hacking— substantiating—cough. ". . . *Gee!*" said Ernestine in seeming great wonder, alarm, glancing at Mary Dee—who pretended not to hear.

The snow seemed slackening some as they reached Cottage Grove and turned toward 63rd. Besides the crawling car traffic there were many pedestrians on the street, people picking their way around snowdrifts to get to the "el" trains taking them to work. Mary Dee, peering forward over the Datsun's windshield wipers, kept looking for a place to get the children fed. She turned at 63rd and proceeded west, where not more than a block and a half on the left she saw the lighted sign: "Andy's Trocadero—Restaurant and Lounge." Fearing 63rd Street's deep snowdrifts, she parked off the street in the alley behind the restaurant. When they had left the car and were passing the Trocadero's kitchen on the way around to the front, they caught the smells of frying food. "Ooooooh!" Ernestine said—"I smell bacon, or ham, or something!"

"Me too!" whispered Vernon incredulously.

But the moment they entered the place Mary Dee realized her mistake. By her standards it was sleazy and dirty—deplorable. What had looked presentable enough from the outside turned out now to be a crummy and unsightly ghetto honky-tonk in an advanced state of deterioration. The furnishings were the worse for wear and tacky, the light fixtures murky, and the walls grimy—sooty over the door leading from the kitchen, where she could envision cockroaches scurrying about and a greasy chef wearing cut-up shoes at the range. The customers, many engaged in horseplay and boisterous talk, were eating, not drinking—the bar and lounge were closed, or not yet open. But they were all here, some *still* here, or had gathered or just trailed in, singly or in pairs, fugitives from the blizzard—all denizens of this all-night hangout, a few of them even young prostitutes, dope pushers, and pimps. The bar and lounge dark, the patrons were all in the restaurant part, seated as they capered and ate at the U-shaped counter or at tables around the walls. The men, young and predominantly Superfly hipster types—known as "cats" or "farmers"—preened and loitered as they talked, or "rapped," and played the records in the jukebox. The women were mostly young too, and garrulous, in their tight skirts and vehement Afros, and seemed chattering and laughing only to attract attention to themselves.

Mary Dee, furious at herself for her blunder, felt a sickening disgust. She considered it only further evidence of the luckless fortunes of her life now, the curse of this forced return to the city of her birth, and of her brash, naive, ill-omened nature. She had the sudden impulse to turn and leave, then remembered the hungry children at her side, and, at last resigned, led them to the nearest unoccupied table.

One of the Superfly youths put another coin in the jukebox and the place exploded in an uprising of instrumental and vocal music with a hard, riotous, gutbucket beat. Many of the customers began singing now, or shouting across the tables at each other, or just sitting and snapping their fingers in time with the chant—though one couple, squealing in glee, the girl still in her overcoat, went into an unrestrainable hip-slinging dance in the middle of the floor. It was an amazing, novel, experience for Mary Dee—unprecedented. In all her sheltered life she had never been in a place even faintly resembling this and it filled her with shame and anger, convinced her this was the crude, vulgar behavior one expected of the true "nigger" types she had so often heard her mother castigate. Ernestine and Vernon at first sat staring around at everything in wonderment, but soon they were smiling knowingly at each other, then in perfect delight.

"You wanta dance, Vernon?" Ernestine said seriously.

126

Vernon hesitated. He glanced at Mary Dee.

Mary Dee was staring violence at them. "Don't you *dare* leave your seats!" she said.

The other patrons were oblivious, seeming under a spell, as if to every one of them the Trocadero had become a welcome haven in the storm, and that no one ever intended leaving it or going out into the cold, disagreeable world again. A waitress, heavy, mulatto, not yet in uniform, brought over three glasses of water and placed them down at Mary Dee's table. By her attitude of hostile apathy she seemed to have sensed the children were not Mary Dee's and, ignoring her, talked directly to Ernestine, who responded without batting an eye: "I want sausage and eggs, and fried potatoes, and biscuits—milk too, and butter, and some jelly. Vernon he wants the same as me, but he just likes grits instead of fried potatoes." She had not once looked at Vernon or Mary Dee. The waitress laboriously wrote it all down, then deigned turn to Mary Dee.

"Nothing for me," Mary Dee said, frowning and turning away.

"Y'want some coffee then—or something?" the waitress, persistent, said.

"No—nothing!"

The waitress clumped off.

Vernon was gazing dreamily at Mary Dee now. In a petulant gesture she had just thrown back the cowl of her parka and for the first time he saw her entire face in its grave, tense beauty: the vaguely aquiline nose, the cheekbones rising gaunt and smooth-crested, the liquid brilliance of the eyes, her peach skin, the inevitable air of impatience and hauteur. "You pretty," Vernon said.

"Shut up, Vernon," Ernestine laughed. But she too looked at Mary Dee—"You sure are, though, lady. You married?"

". . . No," Mary Dee, momentarily flustered, said. Then with impatience she looked at her watch.

"We like *you*," said Ernestine, her tone important, honor-conferring. "Don't we, Vernon?"

But Vernon's attention had been distracted. A Trocadero habitué, a brash, disheveled, Afro-ed youth, had approached the table. Ernestine and Mary Dee looked and saw him now. He was slight, though tall enough, with a pimply face the color of copper and pale gray eyes that popped. He wore a maxi-length GI overcoat, purchasable at any Army surplus store, thrown over his shoulders and held in his hand a sheaf of pamphlets with which he appeared to have been canvassing the place in behalf of some fervent cause or other. In a great sense of urgency he thrust out a pamphlet at Mary Dee. "Here, beautiful sister," he smiled, though somehow bitterly— "Take a look at a couple of my poems. Eighteen of 'em for only a dollar—revolutionary poems that I wrote." His voice rose slightly —"They're something else, sister! Black revolutionary poems!"

Mary Dee, taken by surprise, for a moment could not react. "No, thanks," she finally said, shaking her head.

The poet was tenacious. "Sister, this ain't just some more of that grass or jive poetry . . . about puppy love, and castles, and golden hair, and beautiful blue skies, and all that jazz!" He spoke still with an acrid smile, his goat's eyes jumping out at her. "These are poems about what's coming! . . . about the new day! . . . about liberation, *Black liberation,* and how to cope with 'The Experience!'—with our pain . . . the pain of being black in a rat-trap, racist society! They're dedicated to how you go upside whitey's head with a machete—and about letting a little blood run and so forth! These poems come to me sometimes even in the middle of the night, sister!"

Mary Dee had stonily turned her face away from his torrent of words.

"Here," he said, "let me read you one—just one!" He opened a pamphlet and began reading in a feverishly exalted voice.

At once Vernon broke into a fit of raucous coughing.

The poet, eyeing him, stopped and waited.

"Drink some water, Vernon!" Ernestine, in awe of the visitor, whispered. Vernon obeyed.

"Pardon me," Mary Dee, half frightened, trying to be conciliatory now, said to the poet, "but we don't wish to buy any of your poetry today—now will you excuse us?"

Instead, the poet took a clumsy step forward and sat down directly opposite her in the empty fourth chair at the table. She was speechless. "Sister," he said, "let me fill you in on what this is all about—not only liberation, not only whitey, and not that white traitor, God the Heavenly Father, ha . . . not only all that! I'm writing about *the Black soul too!*" He began trembling with excitement at the words, half rising from his chair. "It's the only soul on earth that's *pure!* . . . purified by slavery, by all the horror and brutal treatment, by the lynching and burning! . . . all the suffering and so forth! And now, yes, hate! Hear me out, beautiful sister!—listen, listen! *Yes, hate! . . .* purified by hate!"

Mary Dee was shocked and blazing angry at his intrusion. She opened her mouth to speak but he would not be interrupted.

"Yet," he said, "we shall redeem ourselves—redeem ourselves in *blood!*" The words were constantly punctuated by his forefinger stabbing the air.

Suddenly he was joined by one of his two friends whom he had left sitting at the counter—the three had come in together—for the purpose of taking him back. "Cool it, Gideon," the friend said, putting a hand on the poet's shoulder—"Come on and eat your breakfast, man. . . . It's already cold."

The poet was irritated. "Go away, Hugo, go away—I'm talking to the sister here."

Hugo, a thick-set, flat-nosed youth, also drew a frown from Ernestine. "Will you gentlemens leave us be," she said, "so we can eat *our* breakfast when it comes?—Lordy!"

But the poet, his zealot's eyes ever on Mary Dee, would not be diverted: "I go around everywhere, beautiful sister, telling our people about what's coming. I tell them in my poems! . . . Here, I'll *give* you a set of 'em, free of charge!" He quickly put a soiled pamphlet on the table before her. "Take these home and read certain ones to the children here, sister—the youngsters must be taught too, from the cradle! . . . oh, yes!"

"Gideon," said Hugo, "we're gettin' ready to go, man—we've finished our breakfast and ain't hanging around here no longer. I'm sleepy." He turned and started back to the counter where the third youth still sat. Promptly, without another word, Gideon got up and followed him as if sleepwalking from his marijuana, though when seated at the counter he could not help glancing worriedly over at Mary Dee as if wondering whether he had convinced her or not.

The children's food came at last. The heavy waitress, in uniform now, came through the door from the kitchen bearing high her loaded tray. As she approached the table the children's eyes shone —"O-o-o-o-h!" uttered Vernon. Detached, businesslike, the waitress began placing down the various dishes on the table. Ernestine, leaning forward, carefully noting each item, checking for accuracy, said to her: "We might want some more milk tereckly—these glasses ain't so big."

"Hokay," the waitress grunted and, shaking her head, left.

Vernon, though fidgeting with eagerness, still waited. "You ain't said the blessing yet," he said to Ernestine.

Without ceremony, Ernestine bowed her head and closed her eyes. "Jesus bless this food for our bodies," she said, almost in one breath—"and keep us from harm and the devil till the day's over and we get home to pray again tonight. Amen." She reached across at once then and began buttering Vernon's biscuits.

Mary Dee sat watching them eat. They were ravenous. Yet she had no thought for them and wished they might hurry and finish. She would take them home then and get on to her office—the advertising firm where she had temporarily taken her first job, as a commercial artist. Although it meant some income—no negligible item with her now—it also took her out of the house each day and filled her mind with sundry office projects. She felt less deserted while working, more successful at keeping Paris banished from her mind. The year just past was a mental affliction, a sorrow, weighing on her like some nocturnal and massive force irrevocable in purpose, consuming in design; a symbol of her abandonment to oblivion. Here in this wretched dive these thoughts brought the pain rising as a lump in the throat and she caught her breath. Where was Philip at this hour? she wondered. Nine in the morning here—even in this place of revulsion—was three in the afternoon in Paris. Blessed Paris. Suppose he were to see her at this moment? . . . he would refuse to believe his eyes. Pride and anger sent up her blood—even more so than the jukebox. She tried to quiet herself. What was Philip doing today? she asked herself. He was still in one of his classes perhaps . . . or a participant in some Beaux-Arts seminar where certain tenets of architecture were under learned, tedious discussion. Where would he dine tonight?—and with *whom?* Which girl in his eager seraglio would receive the nod—the thrilling phone call in Philip's halting French? Then to the *Mediterranae,* say, a favorite fish restaurant, for turbot after the hot bouillabaisse. Or to the more quaint, plebeian, *Le Pot D'étain,* for black bean soup, lamb shanks, and the robust red Rhone wine the waiters brought out in carafes. Where to afterwards? . . . to hear *The Italians in Algiers* at *l'Opera?* Or perhaps merely to a cinema on the Champs Elysées. Later? . . . to his little suite in the Vilar? Ah, or to the apartment in the *Quartier.* Soon her eyes were swimming in tears. Why didn't

130

he write? She lived these days only for mail, a hunger constituting her chief means of salvaging sanity—though when, as was most times the case, no mail came, she lapsed into her old refuge of self-castigation and doubt. Driving home each evening was a drawn-out exercise in dread as she assessed the chances of mail and hope. Raoul wrote not infrequently, but Philip had written only twice . . . twice in over two months!—and then probably only at Raoul's subtle prompting.

Ernestine, wolfing her food, glanced at her. "You feel bad, lady?" she said.

Mary Dee looked away and said nothing.

Suddenly a tall black man, youngish though slightly stooped, entered the place. The poet Gideon, eating at the counter, jumped up. "Torres!" he cried, laughing sycophantly—"Where'n the hell you been, man? . . . Come over here!" Gideon's two friends, though keeping their seats, smiled both in deference and caution. An impassive grin on his face, Torres Coleman came over and sat down with them at the counter. He wore gloves, a snappy gray hat, and an undertaker-like black overcoat. Gideon went into a gravelly laugh, fawning and servile—"Ha-ha-ha! . . . Out tom-catting, eh?—where you been, Torres?"

Torres replied ruefully—"Yeah, out all night, like a fool." He took off his gloves and stuffed them in a pocket of his undertaker's overcoat, then vigorously rubbed his hands together to warm them. "I been up on the Northside—went to hear Art Blakey at the Jazz Showcase. Got hung up with a crazy-ass chick and lost my sleep. Spent some bread too." He yawned.

"Hey, now!" Gideon began snapping his fingers in rhythm. "Art Blakey and the Messengers! They're cool, man!—but still got that hard bop sound, I bet!"

Gideon's friend Hugo grinned—"The Jazz Showcase jumps."

The slender, bewigged counter waitress came and Torres ordered breakfast. "Blakey's got a new hornman with him," he told them. "He's good. Ha, oughta be, with that name—'Oh Lu Dara.' A young stud, yeah. Art Farmer ain't along this trip, but you don't miss him none. This cat Oh Lu Dara stretched out Monk's 'Round Midnight' like it was his own. They got a new tenorman too—Carter Jefferson. He took 'I Can't Get Started' and kept building and

131

building spirals on the melody like Sonny Rollins. Mean man. Heavy. But so's this new hornman."

"But don't tell us the cat's good as Sonny Rollins, Torres," laughed Gideon's second friend, Felix, a handsome ebony youth, wearing glasses and a thickly-matted beard.

"Damn near—no foolin'," Torres said. "He can blow in *any* front line."

"Wow!" said Felix.

"Hey, now!" Gideon repeated.

Torres frowned: "But in spite of all that damn weather you see out there, you couldn't hardly get in the place for honkies." His voice was cutting, contemptuous. "They thin : they dig the stuff like we do—like it's *their* music."

"Man, don't I know it?" Gideon also curled his lip in scorn.

"The motherfuckers," Torres said.

Someone with a coin provided more music now. Out of the juke-box came James Brown's frenzied, squealing voice taking the song high up over his band's fervid beat. Appearing out of nowhere, the same dancing couple as before, the girl this time rid of her overcoat, resumed their act. Both crouching low, doing a mad wriggle while rising, letting out little shrieks of ecstasy in company with the singer's cry, they threw back their heads and flailed their elbows about over gyrating hips. Torres, waiting for his food, finally turned around and in boredom watched them. "Looka there," he said, shaking his head—"Niggers in their element. All they wanta do is cut the fool—*there's* your 'liberation.'"

Gideon's eyes opened wide as he giggled accusingly—"Where'd you say you've been all night, Torres?"

"Yeah, that's right—cuttin' the fool just like them," Torres said. "It's our weakness, man—all of us. Pleasure before business any time." He stared hostilely at the dancers.

"It ain't so much cutting the fool, Torres," Gideon said, "as it is the poet in us. See what I mean?—it's just that we're all *poets* at heart, man."

"Shit," Torres said, and turned his head.

Gideon was unmindful. "It's a damn good thing we are, too," he said. "Sure, we suffer for it, but it's our heritage. We have feeling—*soul*—for each other, man. We want to *be* with each other!—see what I mean? The black soul is the purest thing on earth—I say so in my poetry!" The music had stopped and he picked up one of his pamphlets of poems off the counter. "Here, you'all, listen to this!"

"Oh, no—no!" In defense Torres threw up both hands. "I ain't up to it—don't start readin' me any of that shit this mornin'!"

But Gideon, his voice strident, unfaltering, was already reading:

> Black heads high,
> Eyes aloft in that trance,
> Our song, not others' deaths,
> Is the soul—black and pristine pure,
> Eternally. First, gifts of hate,
> Then words of love, though - - -

The front door burst open. Two men, one with a blue, snub-nosed revolver in his right hand, entered and came directly toward Torres at the counter. Torres, mouth open, sat petrified.

"Oh, God! . . . it's *Quaker!*" Gideon breathed, and tried to duck down behind his friends Hugo and Felix.

"Okay, you ready for Hell, Coleman? . . ." the man with the gun said to Torres. He was almost as tall as Torres, and near his age—youngish—but not quite as black, and instead of a hat and overcoat wore a black beret and a weird maroon cape.

Torres, though shaking, finally found his voice. ". . . No, I ain't ready, Quaker. . . . Say, man, what is this? . . . I ain't done nothing to you—put that heat away! . . ."

Ernestine, staring, had dropped her fork to the table. "He's got a gun!" she whispered—" . . . See it? Oh, Lordy! . . ."

"I can see it! . . ." said Vernon, his eyes big.

Mary Dee, furious with herself, sat frozen with fear for their lives now. She could not move.

The man "Quaker" answered Torres scornfully. "Yeah, put the heat away, huh?" he said. "You mean it, don't you? . . . I'm gonna put it away, all right—after I put a slug in your eye! You won't muss up no more of our people with your brass knucks. You go for bad, but you got the guts of a chicken, man—phony as a three-dollar bill! . . . *Stand up!*'

The place was quiet as death, everyone gaping and frozen in their tracks. Torres still sat, but gave him a wild, worried stare.

"You hear me?" Quaker yelled, glaring. "Okay, stand him up, Jimmie," he said to his squat, burly partner.

The partner reached and grabbed Torres by both upper arms. Torres stood up then, and Quaker with his left hand quickly frisked him for weapons. The slender, bewigged counter waitress, alert, eyes big, heart pounding, had been awaiting her chance. Now she ducked into the kitchen for help.

The poet Gideon was trembling. ". . . Quaker!—why . . . why you want to hurt somebody?' he stammered, pleading. "This ain't no time for us to be fighting, man—we oughta be having a meeting or something! . . ."

"Your friend here don't want no meeting," Quaker said, nodding toward Torres. "He'd rather beat up on our organization people— that is, whenever he can catch one of us alone!" He lunged and swung the pistol at Torres's head. But Torres ducked and was missed, the blow glancing off Hugo's shoulder, as Hugo dove for the floor.

At that moment a big black policeman rushed out from the kitchen, wild-eyed and looking belligerently around him. He was bareheaded, had a paper napkin tucked in his tunic, and was still masticating a free breakfast. "Hey, what's wrong, fellas?" he said, at once coming over to them—"Oh, we have firearms, do we? Let's see that blue pistol, man," he said to Quaker. Quaker hesitated. *"Give it here!"* he shouted, confronting both Quaker and Jimmie and putting out his palm—"Then I won't have to get out *mine!*"

Quaker, breathing hard, eyed him. At last he handed over the pistol and the policeman slipped it in his tunic pocket before frisking them both. Suddenly the policeman squinted at Quaker. "Hey . . . ain't you Quaker Ferguson? . . . You damn right you are— there's been a bench warrant out for you for two weeks. Where you been hiding, man?—we been looking all over for you." Quaker stared at the floor. "What you guys altercating about?' the policeman said, turning around to the others—"Good thing I was back there, or somebody mighta got hurt. What's happening, people?"

Gideon, greatly relieved, at once tittered—"Oh, it's a long story, Talley. . . ."

Quaker now spoke up in righteous anger. "Torres is outa his head or somethin'—tryin' to be such a *bad* dude. . . . He upped and got out of our organization but still won't leave us alone. He's tryin' to get together an organization of his own—everyone of 'em thugs—but still won't lay offa us. Keeps followin' our folks around —threatenin' 'em, tryin' to make 'em come in with his group. Night before last him and one of his goons sapped up one of our men, Haley Scruggs, with some knucks—yeah, marked him up bad. We ain't taken' that, Talley. Jimmie and I seen him come in here and I was fixin' to pistol-whip his fuckin' brains out if you hadn't stopped me. But why's he tryin' to break up *our* organization?—he don't have——"

"——Wait a minute," Talley, the policeman, said, turning toward the kitchen—"Mabel, baby," he said to the bewigged waitress, "bring the rest of my breakfast out here, will you?" He then led Quaker and the others over to the nearest empty table—only one table from Mary Dee's and within easy earshot—and sat down. "Pull up enough chairs," he said to Gideon and the rest—"We're gonna have this thing out. We got too much violence in this community. People're suffering from it—*black people*. It don't make no kinda sense." Soon all seven of them—Quaker, his friend Jimmie, Gideon, Hugo, Felix, Torres, and policeman Talley—sat bunched around the table, and when the waitress brought Talley's plate, he ordered coffee for the others. Shocked and frightened Mary Dee could hear with no difficulty everything being said. Talley took out his notebook and pen and placed them on the table. "Okay, now," he said—"I know about your organization, Quaker. It's okay—you're doing some good things in the community. But to hear you guys, you'd think it was a couple of street gangs involved, instead of people in uplift work—I mean the violence. It's stupid. It's gotta stop. I was at that big meeting myself, Quaker—the mass meeting, when you'all brought John Calvin Knight here to speak. It was a *great* meeting, man—great! I read somewhere Knight's moving the national headquarters here maybe."

"You read it right, Talley!" Gideon's eyes lit up. "He's coming, man—we'll be the center of everything, right here!"

Quaker spoke up—"It'll be a great thing for the blacks in this town."

Gideon, in great excitement, turned to the others at the table—"Hey, Talley was at the mass meeting, huh?" he said. "Dig *that!*—he heard The Man! Ah, we all were there too, Talley—everyone of us—to receive his inspiring message. It was something, wasn't it?"

"No question," said Talley.

"He took us up on the mountain top!" Gideon said. "He's the only leader *I* recognize! . . . He'll turn this town wrong side out,

135

you watch! I must have written over a dozen poems about him and that meeting!—yeah, poems to Brother John Calvin Knight! The title of one is 'Knight, the knight'—hey! Here, let me read it to you right quick. . . ." He was opening one of his pamphlets already— "Oh, what a man! . . . he——"

"——Hold it, Junior! . . ." Talley had put up his hand.

Gideon was unheeding—"It's my best John Calvin poem, I think! . . . about his mighty vision!—his iron will, his wrath, man! . . ." Wetting his thumb, he went hurriedly through the pages.

"Oh, God," groaned Torres.

"Now, wait a minute!" decreed Talley, staring at Gideon—"*I* called this meeting and I ain't got time to listen to any damn poems! . . . I don't care if they are about Knight!—I'm doin' *police work!*"

Gideon did not look hurt, and closed the pamphlet.

Talley now turned to Torres. "Why did you leave the organization?" he said—"Huh? . . . It's a great enough organization, ain't it? I'm a member myself, y'know—so's my wife and kids."

Torres had worked up a slow fury. "God damn it!" he spat. "The organization's turned chicken, that's what! It's outa step with the people—with the black man and woman in the street!" His face clouding with outrage, he could hardly keep his seat—"We don't need no church people, we don't need no school teachers, we don't need no doctors and lawyers! What we need is people we can depend on—I'm talkin' about *street niggers!* They don't fuck around, man! . . . They see things like they are! The only way we can get these honkies off our backs is to '*waste*' some of 'em! We gotta *come down* on 'em, man!"

"*Thass* whut I'm talkin' 'bout," his man Jimmie said.

"*I* ain't no leader, and know it," Torres went on. "I'm just tryin' to get some people together that think like I do on this thing— maybe then we'll turn up somebody that can lead us. We got to, Talley!—black kids are starvin'!"

Mary Dee realized the truth of the latter statement. Her eyes flew from Ernestine and Vernon and did not soon return.

Talley was chewing a piece of ham but shook his head vigorously in protest: "Oh, don't hand me all that!—I know there're black kids that ain't getting enough to eat, but you're more interested in whipping somebody's head, or shooting out of a window at whitey, than you are in getting black kids fed or starting any new organization. Violence and bloodshed are *out,* man—I'm *telling* you! Okay, now, let me hear about this *new* organization of yours—I know already I ain't goin' to like it."

"We oughta have a good *local* leader," Torres said at once—"None of this shit of Knight's about runnin' things from two or three thousand miles away . . . from San Francisco, or New York, or London, or Paris, or wherever he happens to be. . . . What the hell's Knight know about what's happenin' here in Chicago—huh? He ain't been here but once since he spoke at the big meeting last fall. It's dumb, man—plain-ass dumb! . . . *Knight!*—hell! . . ."

"He's *moving* here, Torres!" Gideon spoke up witheringly. "The national office of the Black Peoples Congress will be right here in Chicago—and on the Southside. You'll see some action then!—you better believe it. John Calvin's not only our spiritual leader—he's our intellectual leader too. It's from him we get our *ideology!*"

"Shit," Torres said again.

"Never mind," said Gideon, "he's already had some effect without even being here—we have his writings, don't we? . . . and his speeches. He writes articles about his travels too, don't he?—where he's gone to study the poor peoples' condition in other places around the world, like in Asia, and Africa . . . ah, Mother Africa . . . and in Europe and a lot of other places. What you need, Torres, is to read more—ha, instead of jivin' with the chicks all night up at the Jazz Showcase! *Read* Knight, man—study him! He's got answers!"

"It's the *violence* I'm interested in!" said Talley loudly. He bit off half a biscuit and chewed for a moment. "It's bad, damn bad, for our people—this violence. We gotta get rid of it—yeah, and that goes for the two of you, Torres and Quaker. We can talk, and argue, and make speeches, and call each other all kinda grannydodgers we want, but when it comes to takin' up violence about it, that's where *I* come in! I'm goin' to be promoted to sergeant before long, y'know, and I'll still be right here in this district—you can bet on it. That's where I wanta be. And I'm goin' to be doing something about this violence, hear?—you hear me, Torres and Quaker? I got kids myself." He noisily sipped his coffee. "And after we get through here this mornin', Quaker, I gotta deliver you to the station on that bench warrant—for some of your other shenanigans. Keep on—you'll learn one of these days. As for the other things you'all—*all* of you'all—been doing, I'm giving you a pass. *For the time bein'.* I'm gonna be watching you, though—you see if I ain't." There was silence around the table.

At long last Ernestine and Vernon had finished eating. Mary Dee, in a terrible state of agitation to go, her purse in her lap, kept looking around the room for the waitress and the check. Ernestine sat stuffed, her manner now languid, eyes dull. Vernon in a parting action sopped his plate well with his last biscuit. Ernestine then turned to Mary Dee and whispered—"You know where the bathroom is, lady?"

"Of course not!" Mary Dee turned on her—"I'm taking you home! Can't you wait until you get home?"

"I'll try." Now Ernestine looked at Vernon. "You gotta go to the bathroom, Vernon?"

Vernon grinned proudly. *"No!"* he laughed.

As they sat waiting for the waitress, Mary Dee seemed getting more and more frantic. She placed her purse up on the table, finally returned it to her lap, then, frowning, grimacing, looked at her watch again. But Ernestine, too busy before, had now begun taking interest in the men's conversation nearby, and soon turned around and was watching them steadily, especially Gideon again and policeman Talley. At last, pointing to the sheaf of poems in front of Gideon she said to him—"Can I have one of them too?"

A look of incredulity came on Mary Dee's face.

Gideon, extremely pleased, laughed. "Why not? . . . Of course you can, Kidada! Ha!—do you know what Kidada means? I'll bet you don't! . . ."

Ernestine solemnly shook her head.

"Kidada is Swahili—our mother tongue. It means 'little sister.' You *are* my little sister, you know. Now, here." He reached and handed her a booklet of poems. "You be sure and read them, now—you can understand them all right. If you can't, it's my fault. I write poems for the people—black people—and if they don't understand them, then I ain't writing them right. Take them to school with you too—ask your teacher to read them in class. And be *sure* to tell her to read the poems in there about our great leader— John Calvin Knight. Don't forget that! What's your name, Kidada?"

"Ernestine."

Suddenly Gideon was standing over their table again. "I can tell this young man here is your brother," he said, pointing to Vernon. Ernestine nodded, smiling. Gideon then merely glanced in Mary Dee's direction—"And the lady, Ernestine? . . ." Mary Dee coldly turned her face away.

Ernestine looked at her, hesitating. "She . . . she's with us."—was all she could think of to say.

"I know she's with you." Gideon laughed—"I could see that when I was at this table before! . . ."

Mary Dee's anger was on the point of exploding, when at that moment the waitress came with the check. Mary Dee quickly turned to the children—"Hurry! Get your coats!" She paid the waitress, gave her a token tip, and got up at once.

Though Gideon had returned to his friends, he sat watching as Mary Dee pushed the children ahead of her toward the front door. Ernestine clutched her poems in her hand. It was only then he noticed Mary Dee's poems left on her table. He jumped up, as the men at his table frowned—"Sister! . . . Sister!" he called. Mary Dee half-turned around. "You left your poems—the poems I gave you! . . . shame on you!" he laughed. He retrieved the poems and caught up with her. She took them glumly, without a word, and stuck them in a pocket of her parka, then herded the children outside into the snow.

"Whew-w-w-w, it's cold!" Vernon said on the sidewalk. The snowing had almost stopped.

As they went up the alley to the car, Ernestine somehow maneuvered Mary Dee between herself and Vernon so that each of them could hold her hand as they walked. The familiarity made Mary Dee uncomfortable.

"What's your name, lady?' Ernestine smiled.

". . . Names are not important," Mary Dee finally said—"Vernon, pull up your coat collar. You've already got a cold—we'll stop somewhere and get something for it." Vernon tugged futilely at his mackinaw collar.

"Why don't you want to tell us your name, lady?" Ernestine said.

"My name is Mary Adkins," Mary Dee sighed, and wanted to withdraw her hands from theirs—though hers were gloved and theirs were not—but she lacked the will.

"You got any children?" Ernestine said.

". . . You certainly are an inquisitive little girl!—no, I don't have any children. I've already told you I'm not married."

Ernestine smiled. "You can have children without bein' married, lady."

Mary Dee, remembering so much, was silent at this.

Ernestine looked up at her now and laughed. "You sure are good to us," she said, swinging Mary Dee's hand to and fro. "We ain't hungry no more—are we, Vernon?"

Vernon pondered the question—it was important. "No," he conceded, then, preoccupied, said—"Hope m'toes don't start hurtin' again; it's cold."

They had reached the car now. As Mary Dee opened the door to put them in the back seat again, Ernestine said—"Can I ride up front with you, Mary?"

"All right—hurry up."

Vernon was upset—"I don't *wanta* be back here by m'self. . . . Ernestine! . . ."

"Oh, God," Mary Dee breathed—"Okay, we'll all sit up front. Come on, Vernon." Soon she started the motor and, the tires heavily crunching the snow, drove out onto 63rd Street with Vernon sitting up front between them. He smelled unpleasant to her, like the rancid odors of the Trocadero, until she realized she herself must by now also smell almost the same. Again she was furious with herself.

"Do you like children, Mary?" Ernestine inquired.

"Oh, I guess so, sometimes, but maybe not the ones who ask so many questions."

"Are you gonna have kids sometime?"

"How would I know *that?*"

Ernestine laughed. "If you like kids, then you must like us—me and Vernon!" It was not a question but a statement of conviction. But then Ernestine seemed suddenly jarred back into reality. An almost stricken look on her face, she turned to Vernon. "Momma's gonna be mad," she said—" . . . us coming home like this, before noontime."

"What kind of mother have you *got?*" broke out Mary Dee before she thought.

Ernestine was resigned. "Oh, she's all right. She's got lotsa troubles, she says—ain't got a man. You got a man, Mary?"

Mary Dee dropped the subject.

Vernon was coughing again now. "Oh, Lordy," said Ernestine. Soon he seemed about to hack up his insides—spraying the dashboard with tiny particles of saliva.

"Vernon, put your hand over your mouth when you cough!" Mary Dee said—"That's not polite—you'll give other people your cold." She reached for her purse and handed it to Ernestine—"Give him some Kleenex out of there."

Ernestine, complying, said again—"Vernon needs some medicine for this old cold of his."

"I know, I know," Mary Dee said, and headed for 63rd and King Drive where she remembered there was a drug store.

Twenty minutes later they pulled up in front of the rundown apartment building where the children said they lived on the third floor. But Ernestine, the medicine in the bag in her hand, had grown serious, thoughtful, apprehensive, again—she had said very little and now made no move to get out; nor did Vernon. "You going up with us, Mary?" she said—"so Momma'll know why we come home?"

"I don't have time," Mary Dee said. "And I'll get stuck if I try to park!"

Vernon's eyes were wide. "Momma might throw me out the window," he said.

Ernestine laughed. "Oh, Vernon—hell, she didn't mean that; she was just tryin' to scare you."

"Said she was gonna throw me out the window," Vernon said, reflectively, then with a long face glanced at Mary Dee.

Mary Dee, shaking her head, surrendered. She pulled out of the middle of the street into the deeper snow on the side and got out. "Come on, come on," she said to them—"Get out."

Ernestine and Vernon, subdued, uneasy, clambered out and soon the three of them were in the vestibule of the building. Though the decrepit stairwell door appeared to have been ajar for months, Ernestine pushed the bell and they climbed to the third floor, where she barely knocked. There was a wait. She knocked again.

"Who is it?" the woman inside shouted.

". . . Us, Momma," Ernestine said. "School's closed today. . . . We come back."

The door flew open and they confronted a short, stoutish, slovenly woman, about thirty, in a nightgown with a sweater worn over it. Her face at first showed surprise, then truculent suspicion on seeing Mary Dee.

"This here is Mary, Momma," Ernestine said. "She brought us home in her car—Vernon give out and fell down in the snow."

"She took us and got us some breakfast," Vernon said.

The woman studied Mary Dee.

"She bought Vernon some medicine for his cold too," Ernestine said, showing the paper bag.

"Well, thank her and come on in here!" the mother, ignoring Mary Dee, said.

"Thank you," Ernestine said dutifully to Mary Dee. Vernon's echo was whispered. Both then passed by their mother, went in, but stopped.

The mother finally turned to Mary Dee. "Okay, much obliged," she said. "These kids're a mess—you can't keep up with 'em, no way!"

"Sometime you coming to see us, Mary?" Ernestine said, peering from behind her mother.

"Hummmph," the woman grinned—"for whut?"

Mary Dee spoke on impulse. "Sure, I'll come." And gave the woman a caustic glance.

"When?" Vernon whispered, before going into a fit of coughing.

Mary Dee waited. "Oh, sometime," she said—"maybe real soon."

The mother, offended, insulted, looked at Mary Dee's chic pants suit, her fancy boots, and fur parka. "You must be kiddin'," she said, and closed the door.

Mary Dee returned down the filthy stairs. "You slut," she breathed. Then she was sorry.

*　　*　　*　　*　　*

That evening by five-thirty it was already nearly dark, though Chicago's modestly affluent Hyde Park-Kenwood area had gotten the snow plows only at dusk. Fragile, light-skinned Irene Adkins, nervous, restless, pacing the front part of her ornate house, at last left the parlor and went back to the kitchen, where Mrs. Grier, the housekeeper, was getting dinner. Irene went to the window and peered out, keeping her vigil for Mary Dee. "I worry about Suky coming home after dark," she said to Mrs. Grier—"and with all this snow it's even worse."

Laconic Mrs. Grier, a big-boned black woman, put a chicken casserole in the oven. "Mary Dee drives good," she said.

Irene Adkins still looked out onto the snow-banked driveway that passed the big house and went back to the two-car garage in the rear, where darkness had sent on the tall, automatic floodlight. The blizzard was over, the sky had cleared, and even stars would soon be visible. Yet the temperature had fallen and, according to weather reports, would go down tonight to almost zero. "She may be late," Irene Adkins said—"Should you have put the casserole in already?"

"Sure," Mrs. Grier said, thinking herself of getting home in the weather—"By the time it's ready, she'll be here." She broke out a package of rolls.

But Irene Adkins' mind seemed already elsewhere as she smiled —"Could I please have a cup of tea? . . . maybe it will settle my nerves some." She then grew pensive, self-indulgent, almost maudlin. "I'm not very well today," she said.

"Okay." Mrs. Grier slid the teakettle onto the burner. "If you'll just stick to the tea, though," she said—"You know how Mary Dee fusses when she catches you putting that brandy in it."

"Suky fusses at everything these days," Irene Adkins said, sighing, as she looked out on the lighted driveway again. "She gets upset so easily—at any little thing. But we should be tolerant with her, I guess—she's going through a trying period. She'll never get over her father—never."

Mrs Grier, however, nodding, had wondered recently whether there were not other things on Mary Dee's mind as well, though she did not know what. When the water was hot, she took down a cup, saucer, and tea bag, and made the tea. She knew from experience Irene Adkins would take it with thankful, trembling hands and disappear somewhere up in the front of the house. But soon she would be back with the cup empty and an incipiently mad gleam in her eye—though her hand would be steadier. Then she would ask, sometimes plead, for "just one more cup, please." She had been faltering in spirit even before her husband's death. Now she was fading in that delicate, near-white beauty which until lately even her fifty years had done little to impair. Yet there had been those small earlier signs—like the secret taking of sherry and brandy; in her utter privacy she had felt this necessary in order to maintain her former dash and verve, the social élan, and synthetic high spirits. For Horace Adkins, in his unwitting enamorment of his eldest daughter, had all but forgotten her. Mary Dee, in her self-centeredness insensitive to so many things, had no really true inkling of her mother's state. Otherwise she may not now have shown such impatience, exasperation, when of an afternoon her mother might lace her tea with half a fifth of Three Star Hennessey.

Shortly after six o'clock the little red Datsun, its headlights stabbing the darkness, plowed down the driveway toward the rear. Irene Adkins ran to the kitchen window—her thin blood tingling, eyes crazily alight, from the brandy she had slipped into two cups of tea—and stared out again. *"There's* Suky!" she cried. (The sobriquet, given Mary Dee by her laughing, doting father, originated in her childish pronunciation of "Suzuki," the character in *Madame Butterfly,* her first witnessed opera.) Irene Adkins now scrambled for the light switch to the back stoop.

Mrs. Grier, invariably so-called by the family she had worked for since the three children were small, opened a package of frozen vegetables, then put the rolls in the oven. She was tacit, imperturbable, and responsible, and for years had been in unquestioned charge of the house. As Mary Dee, after stomping snow from her boots, entered through the kitchen door, Mrs. Grier glanced once at her, said "Hi, girl," and went on cooking the broccoli. Irene Adkins, eyes more aglitter than ever, face a cherry pink, gave Mary Dee a great, beatific, mothering smile—"Ah, Suky," she said. Mary Dee greeted them in passing, only to keep on through to the front of the house in desperate quest of mail. She approached the bombe chest in the foyer, heart thobbing, throat tight, dry, for it was here her mother placed each day's delivered mail. Suddenly she hesitated, thinking of, fearful for, herself now—it was also here each day she went through all the lonely stages of a fresh martyrdom. Would it be different today?—she all but knew it would not; yet hope fired both her head and heart. She picked up the seven letters off the silver tray, most of them business mail, and went through them swiftly. The same old story—nothing. She wondered if she would ever get used to this—this purgatory, this seeming self-vivisection, and the shame of it. Yet, repeatedly, for some time now, she had regarded it as an immutable way of life, some apt retribution, and went and stowed her boots and parka in the closet under the stairs and, putting on loafers, went to wash her hands.

Irene Adkins had remained in the kitchen—feebly, hilariously, gay. Mrs. Grier at such times took little notice of her, but Mary Dee could seldom hide her displeasure and would often sulk. Yet when Irene Adkins came into the dining room and seated herself at the table—this a persistent perpetuation of family ritual—she always seemed somehow to have regained much of her poise, her thoughtful earnestness. Mrs. Grier served them dinner and they began the meal in silence, each absorbed in her own thoughts. Mary Dee, home less than three months, still fighting off Paris memories, sought to hold, confine, her mind to the most mundane of things —the dining table, for instance, at which they both now sat. She knew at dinner in the old, the better, happier days, the table never held fewer than two, frequently three, leaves in it. Now Mrs. Grier had removed them all, which, Mary Dee felt, left the table sadly reduced, humiliated, in spirit abandoned. Yet with Jocelyn and Ronnie away at school, she knew Mrs. Grier had been right to do it. Before, there had been an interminable parade of company for dinner—an assortment of friends and relatives, boys seeing Mary Dee and Jocelyn, and Ronnie's pals, with Horace Adkins' white hospital colleagues and their wives, as well as all the black society figures and community leaders—but now only mother and daughter were left. Realizing the futility of dwelling on those nostalgic days, Mary Dee glanced across the table at her mother with somehow new compassion and understanding; with contrition also.

When Mrs. Grier had finished serving them dinner, her nephew came in his car and took her home. At once her absence seemed to affect Irene Adkins' spirits adversely as she ate. Her giddy cheer in the kitchen, the inanity of her "tea" talk, even later her earnest concentration, entirely disappeared. She became strange, distant, morbid. She only picked at her food and soon sat in a vacant-faced pout. Mary Dee saw the change but chose to ignore it. One moment her mother would not look at her, or talk to her, but then suddenly, a now frightened gleam in her eye, she would turn and study Mary Dee with riveted attention. At last, almost hysterically, she said— "Suky, I want to sell this big old house!" Mary Dee looked at her at first as if she had not understood. "It's nothing but a great worry for me!" Irene Adkins said. "Its so expensive! I never realized until now the load your father carried all these years—it makes me feel guilty. This house is a burden!—we must get rid of it!"

"Mama, you can't be serious. . . ."

"I *am* serious! How could I be otherwise? The expense of this place is out of all reason. Ask Mrs. Grier."

"Oh, Mrs. Grier!" Mary Dee threw down her napkin. "I won't ask her anything!"

"You children don't have any idea about money—expense! . . . you've never had to. Certainly it's hard for me to face the fact we can't afford this house any longer. But it's true—the taxes and up-keep on this place are terrible, and going up every day. Thank heavens the mortgage was paid. You must remember our income is nothing like it was in your father's best days, although he left some fairly good stocks and a sizeable life insurance program. These are adequate—we certainly won't starve—but I must think about our day-to-day living. There's also the rest of Jocelyn's and Ronnie's college education to be provided for. I worry about these things! Then . . ." Irene Adkins faltered, sighing. ". . . Then there's your own life—your father would be very disappointed to know you've had to give up your art studies and take a job. He was so keen on your finishing your work in Paris—although, like every-thing else, it was an awful strain on him at the last. You're aware he had to turn most of his surgery over to others in the final year."

Mary Dee threw up her hand—"Oh, Mama, do we have to talk about it?"

"We need a smaller place, Suky. An apartment—a condo-minium, maybe. One day before long you'll all be married—all be gone. If we don't need all this space now, *I* certainly won't need it then. Mrs. Grier agrees with me."

"Mrs. Grier! . . . Oh, hell, Mama!"

Irene Adkins frowned—"Is that the language you learned in Paris? You're unfair to Mrs. Grier. In those last months I don't know what I'd have done without her—especially when you re-turned to Paris after the funeral. Everyone left me—everyone—except Mrs. Grier. She even stayed with me some nights—I was so lost. She's been more than a servant or a housekeeper—she's been my friend." Irene Adkins quickly rose now, went in the parlor, and stood staring out at the piled-up snow the snow plows had left under the street lights. She seemed lost still.

*　　*　　*　　*　　*

Next day Mary Dee had a cold. She was sure she knew why and put the blame squarely on Vernon—his coughing in the car. It served her right, she told herself, for her stupid Samaritanism. Vernon and his wily sister, she thought, had caused her an experience, introduced her to a world of abomination, squalor, violence, vulgarity, and filth the like of which she expected never to have witnessed in life, and hoped never to see again. The nightmare of the Trocadero had last night invaded her dreams and even today disastrously moved in and out of her consciousness. Nor on the other hand could she entirely free her mind of the two hapless children involved, their lives and dismal prospects. Try not as she might, they excited her pity, and she regretted now having promised to come see them, for of course she now had no such intention. She nonetheless felt remorse and knew she would not soon forget them, if for nothing more than the unpleasant thoughts they provoked about the way some people lived—or had to live. But the afterthought came tardily.

Her coughing and sneezing were particularly embarrassing to her at lunch with two of the girls at her office—the office of Aico & Aleshire, advertisers, whose modest but lively establishment was located out near the University of Chicago. Nevertheless, despite her cold, the luncheon turned out to be a boost for her morale in that one of the girls, Katherine Reinecke, had recently divorced her husband and throughout their sandwiches delivered herself of a series of comic tirades against men in general. There was much to laugh at, which, notwithstanding the child involved, was apparently Katherine's intention. And when they returned to the office, Mary Dee, though sneezing into Kleenexes, was in better spirits than she had been for weeks. She could not understand it—could it augur something? she wondered. No matter, things could be worse, she thought, and most of all she herself vowed never to become entangled with the ne'er-do-well, womanizing type Katherine Reinecke had married and so vividly described. Mary Dee somehow by this resolve felt superior, her natural bent in any case, and this state of mind coupled with her recent friendly reception at Aico & Aleshire's gave her reason to feel not altogether unpleased with things—this at any rate was what she told herself. It was a necessity. Moreover, there was Mr. Aleshire himself, the senior partner and along in years, to whom she reported, who much admired her work as illustrator for his selling conceits. Her colorful drawings depicting his imaginative ideas for touting soups, soaps, candle sticks, and tape recorders pleased him greatly—though she had no intention of making it a career, for Raoul's admonitions still rang in her ears.

Yet she felt she must summon the practical good sense to rise up somehow out of this slough of melancholia in which she had so helplessly threshed about for months. She must retrieve herself at last. Driving home that evening she even tried forgetting the daily problem of mail—though it was in vain, she tried. Again the attitude was a necessity. Much of the snow had been cleared from the middle of the streets now, and at first she operated the Datsun in a kind of half brooding, half light-hearted, daze in which she hoped, at least for a time, to be out of touch with reality. But soon she was sober, reflective, again. She thought what the Reinecke girl had said so hilariously nonetheless had much substance, made sense. It had been an experience to hear it—women *were* often used, she told herself. She had always abhorred Women's Lib and regarded, condescendingly, those carping females who always seemed, because of their unattractiveness, unable to cope in the free market of pure appeal—which, she thought, was how one got men, wasn't it? Here too she had always felt superior—that is, until meeting Philip. The very passing thought of him now was a fresh danger. She fought to keep her mind free.

It was near dark as she passed her dear Lab Schools—the University of Chicago Laboratory Schools—where she, and later Jocelyn, then Ronnie, had received a very private grade and high school education. Sweet memories flooded back to her. It was here she had first known, say, Homer, Pliny the elder, Wagner, Toussaint L'Ouverture, Phidias, John Dewey. . . . Here too that she had once dreamed of becoming a famous cellist. Then with other students one day she had been taken to see the great canvases in Chicago's famed art museum, the Art Institute of Chicago. There ever since first encountering Gauguin's pictures, their ravishing deep-pastel coloration so evocative of the South Seas verdure, she had been a perfect thrall to painting. Her father, himself a weekend and vacation

148

painter, was beside himself with joy when he suddenly realized her promise, saw the talent burgeoning so indisputably. At once he encouraged her, pressed her, lavished on her all manner of art supplies—easels, brushes, fixatives, tubes of exotic paints, and more. Later, before Paris, he would send her for her formal training to the classes of the Art Institute, where four years later she graduated—then on to Beaux-Arts. Accompanying all this however came, inevitably, his own advice—impractical, romantic. Counsel came also from others—family friends and kinfolk—when they saw her fierce beginning works. But her grandmother—Horace Adkins' mother, of the distinguished frizzy snow-white hair and pince-nez, the family matriarch and emeritus professor of Latin and Hebrew at Fisk University—saw danger. Danger not only from the ferocity of the canvas colors, or the brash, hedonistic romanticism revealed, but the personality of the artist herself, the signs of spoiled, doted-upon precocity, incipient arrogance, airs. She counseled time therefore, forbearance, hands-off policies to her son. And to her granddaughter: *Do,* yes, was her admonition in a letter from her home in Atlanta. Make your mark. But treasue patience and humility. Who can clear up muddy water?—asks the proverb. But if left to remain still, it will clear itself. A violent wind seldom outlasts the morning, nor a rain squall the day. This is nature, all-powerful, as in art— for art is untampered-with nature. How then can mere man long sustain the efforts of a natural force? But, yes, in all things look to beauty—even passion. Yet recognition of beauty implies perception of ugliness, as recognition of good implies the idea of evil. The artist does not forget that nature is anything but benevolent. With ruthless indifference it makes all things, certainly art, serve its purposes—like in olden times straw dogs were used at sacrifices. You, the young artist, my dear, must dare, even at this early time— indeed, the earlier the better—to look deeply into *yourself.* This is pre-Socratic—he who knows others is clever, but he who knows himself is enlightened. He who vanquishes others is strong, yet he who overcomes himself is mightier still. But, alas, those who know these things seldom speak, while those who speak do not know them. Be wary of life, my child; and above all in your ambitions as an artist, do not look to Western values to solve all problems—as I sometimes think your father may do—for while attaining much, these values have also failed in much; their formulators bear the inborn curse of rapacity and cruelty of which my own generation has been made so aware; so pick the best of them and abjure the worst; be self-reliant and discerning; and, again, be wary of life; it can be dangerous, especially for the proud and gifted; for the beautiful female with these qualities, almost impossible. Humility therefore has many virtues, practicality being not the least of them. Take these words and put them under your pillow.

How she does go on! Mary Dee remembered thinking then—at that far, far-off time. Grandma's mind wanders so.

On arriving home that evening, her mother and Mrs. Grier were in the kitchen as usual, Irene Adkins' eyes wild, mirthful, inane, her face inflamed, as Mary Dee spoke cheerfully to them and, today avoiding the front of the house, used the backstairs up to her room. As in the car coming home, she felt an uncommon malaise, though it was not perhaps so distressing after all, for she had at last resisted the monster—that veritable griffin!—of *mail*. Once more she felt the ruse to be a necessity—why, though, was everything so necessitous? Her reactions were vague, puzzling, to her, until suddenly it occurred to her that her weird, erratic, state of mind today was temporary, that its origin was the menstrual flow. Women were different—she felt it altogether possible—more imaginative, intuitive, if often testy, during menses. Perhaps then it was not too improbable a paradox at all that she had felt better all day—and despite the cold Vernon had given her. She made no pretense of understanding any of it—basically. She was a mystery to herself, though she believed this true of all unusual—by which she meant gifted—women. So be it, she thought.

That night just before she went to bed her mother, of course steadier now, her recuperative powers uncanny, came in her room and stood bewilderedly. "Suky, you know," she said, "there was no mail today. . . ." She paused then and, looking at Mary Dee, thought for a moment, as if it was a matter mysterious indeed, beyond all fathoming. "Isn't that strange?" she continued. "No mail at all. Not even a bill or a magazine. . . . I don't understand it." To Mary Dee the intelligence was like a slow, delayed electric shock. She saw the utter irony of it. Unable to inhibit herself, she quietly laughed— which startled her mother into greater nervous confusion. Of all the days, thought Mary Dee, to resist going up in the foyer for mail was the day there was no mail at all—for anyone. She could hardly suppress more laughter.

Next morning at eight, while her mother still slept, she was down in the kitchen getting herself breakfast before going to Aico & Aleshire—when the front doorbell rang. She went up to find neighborly little Dr. Maceo Buckley, who lived three doors up the street, standing on the steps holding a handful of mail. "More Post Office efficiency!" he laughed when she opened the door—he also, furtively, eyed the form-fitting red sweater she wore. "Probably a new man, or a floater, on the route yesterday," he said—"He left this with us. It's all Adkins mail." The old inveterate dread returned—and her heart, after a moment of erratic behavior, seemed almost to stop. At last, with a kind of preoccupied profuseness, she thanked him, took the two magazines, junk mail, and the three letters, then clumsily turned her back. Closing the door, she allowed herself to glimpse just one of the gaudy, tri-colored tissue envelopes bearing the French legend *Par Avion* and a menstrual cramp hit her. Her knees went slack. Yet she returned to the kitchen, sat down, her grapefruit vainly waiting, and looked at the envelopes with trembling hands. There was a letter from Raoul . . . but *two* from Philip! She felt a trace of vertigo now and tried to sit very still to let it pass. The irony was complete. Soon tears came in her eyes. She was also cramping terribly now, yet fifteen minutes later, when she had read and reread the letters, though the discomfort had subsided, her heart was in blissful chaos; she was numb and hardly knew where she was. She only knew she would not go to work today. She wanted to be very private, very alone, and, finishing her grapefruit and toast, took the letters and a mug of black coffee with her upstairs to her room and closed the door.

The skies had fallen in. . . . Philip was coming! Coming from Paris to see her! At least that is what he asked her permission to do. It was incredible! . . . after all these months! She was so distraught she wanted to cry out. Could it be true?—had she read the letters right? . . . Yes, yes, it was true! Ah, but Raoul—was Raoul's letter some kind of veiled caution? Philip in a way seemed changed, "vaguely different," as Raoul put it, though he said little more on the specific point. What did he mean?—*how* was Philip different? But dear, dear Raoul!—how she adored this sweet little man. She sank on the bed and began reading the letters all over again, reading Philip's first letter, postmarked two days before his second, first. He was in a black, yet somehow contrite, almost distracted mood, it seemed to her. Knowing Philip, she could tell, as of old, there had been much wine. His tone was so ardent, impetuous, at times truculent. Where had he been? . . . to *Prunier* for dinner, or *Drouant,* or having the sweetbreads Sarah Bernhardt, with the heady red Bordeaux, at *Chez Regent?* Ah, the *Regent*—where he, she, Raoul, and Adrienne had dined that beautiful, that glorious, night . . . with the moon over the shimmering Seine as they drove across, headed for Montparnasse and the Caveau d'Alsace. Mary Dee began to cry at eight-forty in the morning. Once again she read from the first letter: "This is a hellish town without you—I have found that out." (What tardy sentiments, Philip, she thought.) "Paris is such a miserably bleak scene since you left—it's in the very air, and I——"

A violent cramp hit her, making her catch her breath. It was while pausing, waiting, resting the letter on her knee, that she entered momentarily upon a strange, improbable, vision. She saw Katherine Reinecke's sharp ruddy face again and heard her sardonic laugh at yesterday's luncheon. The laugh seemed to mock Mary Dee and she was awed by it, wondered at it. Following her brash, cynical laugh, the Reinecke girl seemed saying: "Men, men, men! . . ." The words were spoken in bitterest derision. When the cramping had eased, Mary Dee raised the letter again. "When I think of a year ago," Philip was saying hotly, "I realize now I'm only existing, not living. Then we lived!—you know it's true, Dee. I've deliberately tried not writing you, thinking the problem, my unhappiness, might eventually go away, but it hasn't. I know you've thought terrible things about me—hated me, actually—and you're justified if you have." Mary Dee rested from reading again—the emotions the letter generated were too intense. She thought of Philip's strange Paris coolness—his virtual neglect—following her return there after her father's funeral. The recollection saddened, mystified, her. She picked up Raoul's letter now. "You know, Philip has become an enigma to me, *chérie,*" it said in part—"He seems somehow vaguely different. Yet, *is* he? I keep asking myself—is he really? We recently had lunch. He said he is getting 'fed up' with Paris and may make a quick trip home to Philadelphia soon—his favorite uncle is quite ill, he says, and he might come home to see him. Is this believable, *chérie*?—I do not know, frankly. I do think Paris has palled a bit for him, though—it is not like when you were here. Ah, he and I *both* feel that. So he wants to come to Philadelphia for a few days—ha, to see his sick uncle. I do not have to tell you that our friend Philip can, on occasion, be somewhat willful, and selfish. Or should I state it more politely—self-indulgent. This sudden anxiety over his uncle does not strike me quite right. There may be other reasons, *chérie*. He has been very restless lately, and is often rude to all those so-called friends and hangers-on around him so constantly. When we are together he talks only about the old days, our good times of last year together, et cetera, et cetera. I verily believe it is because of you—because he misses you so. Philip is willful, yes, and he likes to have his playthings around him when *he* wants them—although I am sure you are no plaything to him and never were. Yet do not be surprised if you suddenly hear from him—maybe telling you he may come home for a short time soon. I know how he feels, though, *chérie*—we both miss you, yes, so very, very much." There was more—mostly gossip and news—yet nothing lessening the subtle warning of the letter.

Mary Dee reached for Philip's second letter—written with no trace of stimulants. "My Uncle Ambrose, my mother's brother," it said on the last page, "has prostate cancer. We haven't given up on him yet, but he is back in the hospital. I plan to come to Philadelphia for a few days at the end of the month, and, if I may, I'd like to phone you before I leave there to come back and maybe fly out to Chicago overnight and have dinner with you somewhere. To see you again would mean very much to me, Dee—I've never missed anyone so much in my life. Whether you believe this or not, it's true." She could bear to read no more, and carefully folded the letter and returned it to the envelope. Her happiness was a great tidal wave, inundating her, lifting, sweeping, her and everything before it. The whole world had changed within an hour.

* * * * *

The next ten days were doggedly preparatory, though with a kind of fatalistic impotence—she moved and acted as if most of the time in a trance, or as if static, like some inert, ferrous metal, unmalleable, quiescent, dead. She was not herself, and even, on a most unlikely occasion, found it helpful to drink—one day getting tipsy while shopping for the right dress to wear if Philip came. That day, a Saturday afternoon, her ankles tired from walking, she entered an insignificant-looking little restaurant up on North Michigan Avenue near Saks and ordered a sandwich—also a Manhattan on the rocks while she waited; for her a most rare resort, as she cared nothing for alcohol. Surprisingly, though, the first cocktail called for a second and when the sandwich came her head was in a whirl. She gave the waitress a dazed, glowing smile and asked for coffee. But she was happy, deliriously happy, for the first time in months. On masticating the food, however, she found she had no sensation of chewing at all; her jaws seemed soundproof; moreover, she could taste little of the sandwich itself; and her ears rang. From two drinks! she thought. Yet at it all she smiled, a wonderfully stupefied smile to everyone around her.

Suddenly she wanted to write Philip a love note on her paper napkin. She laughed at the thought. But the letters, his two letters, the hope, the balm they supplied, their dissipation of her heartache, filled her with feelings both of thankfulness and guilt—guilt the result of her decision not to answer them. But to do so, she felt, would be tactically unwise. Philip could not be played with; he was serious business. And though, like ice cream in a torrid sun, her heart had melted completely, she knew she must hold the line, avoid over-eagerness, project self-esteem and independence, or risk ruin again. Why, though, had he changed?—if he had changed. She had read the letters so often she knew them by heart, yet this she still could not decide. He said he missed her, terribly. Why then hadn't he felt so before? He said he had resisted writing her—was this meant as a palliative for her, his excuse? It was so bewildering, especially now to her spinning head. But would he really come?—or would he change his mind? She knew though she was in no state to deal with these complexities now—they would have to wait.

Yet, unavoidably, there was Raoul's strange reaction to be considered—his veiled admonition. Did he know more than he told? Or could it be that he harbored in his heart, though very covertly, the tiniest spark of jealousy? She dismissed this at once—Raoul was too noble for such a thing, and too proud. He merely wanted her to be cautious—to be wise. Dear, dear Raoul. Still she wondered if he, any more than she, knew Philip's real intentions. Philip, yes, had said he missed her. Wasn't then the next step to missing someone, *wanting* them? she asked herself—wanting them beside you always? This was the rub. She grew sad. Had Philip at last made up his mind about this? It was crucial. If he had, it was for him a clean break with the past—this she knew. He could have so conveniently cleared the air by suggesting, for instance, that she meet him in Philadelphia—and be taken to meet his family. At once the thought plunged her into doubt and gloom. It was something she knew she dared not think of now. It was too anguished and difficult.

She finished her sandwich, then glanced at her watch. It was three o'clock. She looked out the window onto the sidewalk, at the trooping pedestrians, more apparel shops opposite, and cars and taxis on the boulevard in the chill mid-March sunshine. It was her inner self that she somehow now felt—delineating a fanciful earlier life. Even as a child she had often sat musing, in deep studied reverie, about herself—sometimes before a mirror—searching her mind for clues to the kind of being she really was or would become. She was curiously awed by the possibilities and was at times, in secret, afraid. At other times she was confident, fully so, for her father had always told her how unique she was and what extraordinary things lay ahead for her. She of course believed him, her occasional fears at once vanishing. During the past year, however, she had met colossal doubt. To her, Philip, and what he represented, symbolized the great vistas of which life, at its very best, its most fruitful, was capable of realizing for special people—among whom she counted herself. Was it then unreasonable to envision some such grand life for herself with Philip? She thought not. And it was ironical that her father might, after all, have agreed. At one time, especially in Paris, she had been in mortal fear of his wrath and sorrow had he known about Philip, but on reflection since his death she was less sure. How would he have reacted had she sat down and told him the whole story with background? He may, yes, have agreed with her—who knows? It was not inconceivable to her now, though it had certainly been then. But why not?—hadn't he told her to prepare for great things? She regretted now not having summoned the courage to confide in him about Philip—to warn him, prepare him.

155

How would he have *really* reacted? She would never know, of course. Would he, for instance, have said: "It's too risky, Suky, honey. You might get hurt—psychically—and bear the scars for the rest of your life. I love you too much not to say it." Or would— as she believed—her *real* father speak?: "Go ahead. Who is more suited than you?—or more worthy? All your life you've been reared, prepared, for such a moment. You deserve the best and you are equal to the best. Don't run from life. Don't be afraid to live it. Whatever happens, you may in the end have fewer regrets."

She found new strength in his memory. Before the stores closed that day, she found a lovely dress—rainbow chiffon—at Bonwit's, bought it, and took it home to brood, dream, over.

*   *   *   *   *

It is night and she cannot sleep. In bed she has read until her eyes are sore, yet only fatigue and a blind passion of worry and fretfulness beset her. Exacerbating matters, her mother has been pressing her about Lloyd Stark, the young widower and insurance executive—"tycoon," as he is referred to by admirers in the black community—who has called her three times. But now, late Sunday night, the start of the crucial final week of the month, she longs only for sleep. She has work to do at the office within hours and needs rest. Yet she is denied it. Lloyd Stark!—her mother makes reference, subtle or direct, to this man each day God sends, until Mary Dee could wail, scream, like the banshee in Irish folklore. God!— and at this fateful time in her life! She gets up and walks the floor, then realizing the phony theatricality of it, sits down on the bed and stares across at herself in her dressing table mirror. He should see her now—Philip—she thinks. And she was said to be good to look at. Regard the distraught eyes, at the moment weak and bleary, her hair, not so loose and curly now, the beige pallor of her facial skin, the naked, humorless lips. A frowsy woman—no beauty visible, she thinks. If she could only hear something! What was happening? Was he back?—was he home? If so, how could he call her without her telephone number? Long distance directory assistance —using her address which he possessed? Perhaps. But she should

156

have acknowledged the letters and included the phone number. So now—what to do? He might wire her. An iffy service at best. She could only wait. This, though, was what was killing her.

Waiting, yes. It was not her first time—there had been other waits. Philip too had waited—that night, for instance, when she got the cable about her father's death. Her scream had awakened both of her roommates and as they worked over her, Philip, gnashing his teeth downstairs in the car, had *waited*. Finally after twenty minutes, thinking he had been tricked, he rang the bell and, in an angry quandary, came up. He witnessed disaster. On learning everything, he seemed so inept, ineffective—lost. In the small sitting room of the apartment he had sat staring helplessly at her as Yvette and Carla, in their wrappers, stood over her trying to assuage her, staunch her tears. Then he did what she later thought a bizarre, clumsy thing—he had gone to the phone and called Raoul. Dear Raoul, though, was there as quickly as a taxi could bring him. He took charge. Next day they had both, Philip still helpless, taken her to the airport. Philip was a very strange young man.

Monday passed now, Tuesday passed, Wednesday passed. But by Wednesday night she was sleeping better—knowing now Philip would not come. She was almost relieved, grateful. Life was so much easier without the clawing tensions—who needed them? Then Thursday at the office—she had just returned from lunch with Katherine Reinecke and the others—there was this message for her to call Operator 62 in Philadelphia. This was it! Life was treacherous but fulfilling. Now the eruption of developments. She could not cope with them in all their variety and complexity. At first confusion was uppermost, excitement so handicapping. That evening her mother sensed something afoot—the noontime phone call from Philadelphia had been diverted to Aico & Aleshire by Mrs. Grier. "It was a fellow I knew in Paris, Mama," was the offhand explanation—sincere and cunning. "At Beaux-Arts. He's passing through here tomorrow on his way back and I'm going to meet him downtown for dinner." That was all. Irene Adkins, pointedly sober tonight, pondered it. Why downtown?—why wasn't he invited home for dinner? She said no more, however—even today spared mention of Lloyd Stark, for which Mary Dee was desperately grateful. First there was the issue of dress; it *yet* was not solved—no matter the new rainbow chiffon from Bonwit's. It was a question—a prob-

lem—of role, she thought. What part—role—must she play? . . .
should she play? The dress seemed now unsuitable. It was too sheer
and lovely, too feminine, helpless, overly alluring. Too obvious. It
cast her in the incorrect mood. It did no justice to her honesty and
seriousness in the matter. Besides, he could not be influenced by
such things—frilly baubles. It was unnecessary anyway. He knew
her. She would wear then the simplest dress she owned. And her
hands. They were a problem or not a problem. He had seen her
hands the worse for wear before—paint-smeared, smelling of fixa-
tive and turpentine, unsightly. She was, after all, a painter. She
would brush-scrub them good and let it go at that. Her hair was
okay—she would shampoo it tonight. It was her heart causing the
trouble. He had gotten her phone number before leaving Paris (ah,
at the word she felt already, sensed again, the presence of the
daemon—the daemon flouting his confinement to Paris, his writ
of *ne exeat*) and said on the phone Raoul had supplied it. Of course
—who else? Raoul the soul, the dogmatist, of responsibility. The
arrival tomorrow—O'Hare at two. In the hotel—the Plaza Royale
—by three. Yes, she would meet him in that gaudy little peacock
lobby at four. Things were thus ordained. She could not have described her feeling.

*   *   *   *   *

It was strange next day, indeed annoying to her, the way, at first
sight, he affected her. Crossing the royal carpet of the Plaza Royale's elegant little lobby toward him, she had seldom if ever felt less
sure of herself. Philip looked so fine—superfine. She had never
seen him more imposing, commanding, romantic—his plenitude
of ash blond hair more *distingué;* and dressed in a suit of fine British tweed, with a Sulka blue madras shirt, and his tan leather boots.
It was the way a famous young symphony conductor, poised, German, chivalric, should look, she thought. The situation was anything
but easy for her. He seemed too, for him, in excellent spirits, smiling
a lot, though of course never losing the unobtrusive dignity and
hauteur—he was Philip Morgan Wilcox, no less, son of William
Vincent Phineas Wilcox. "Dee! . . . thank you for coming!" was his

almost whispered first greeting, smiling and for a moment holding her hand in the middle of the lobby. There were stares, but if not overtly hostile, they differed markedly from Parisians' casual unconcern. He led her aside to a red velour sofa. "You look great," he said—"Gosh." They sat down.

She hoped he meant it, for under her open coat, casual camel hair, she wore a plain wool dress—sienna brown—that he had seen before. "So do you," she said at last, unsteadily, then remembered to smile—finally to laugh. Yet she felt herself fighting tears. Philip saw it and grew tender, asking about her family, her mother, something he had not often done before. She declined, however, to reciprocate and asked about Raoul instead.

"Raoul's busy—you know Raoul," he said. "He's also spending a lot of time in Arles—seeing his daughter. Nadine's eight now, I think. If he'd thought I might see you on this trip, he'd surely have sent his best."

"Wonderful Raoul," she said. "When do you return, Philip?"

"I'm on an eight o'clock Paris flight tomorrow evening."

Paris—she heard it. That word, that *world*, again. . . . with the consequence that here *he* was, the daemon—as if in overseas transit perched on Philip's shoulder in TWA first class ease. Philip—the carrier of pestilence. "I presume to advise you no longer, my triste madcap of a spoiled girl!" said he, her Gallic daemon-praetor, though as if showing the effects of a great tedium. "The point of no return you've passed long since, dear girl. I'm now a mere observer. Yet I take no glee in what's probably to come. I'm only tired, footsore, disillusioned—under the encumbrance of jet fatigue, too. Your case affords no joy to people of healthy mind—so let nature, impersonal and clownish though it is, take its course. . . . ah, dear girl. . . ."

Talk began—though smaller than small. Philip at first did most, but at last drew her in. It was exhilarating to neither of them. He told about Adrienne, now married to an "English chap." She told about Mr. Aleshire, for whom she drew pictures of toasters, lamp shades, and outboard motors, who worked in his office wearing bedroom slippers. Both then talked of Raoul still, bringing overdue levity and laughs. She felt good at last to be able to laugh with Philip again. It led to other sundry matters and soon she had told him she was glad, *very* glad, he had come—to which, oddly, he seemed unable to frame a ready reply.

"Philip, tell me, why did you come?"

"Where?—here to Chicago? . . . To see you, of course—didn't you read my letters?" He laughed.

"Why did you want to see me?"

He faltered. "How do I express *that*?" he said. "It's not easy—there're so many things involved. One is, I think about you all the time."

She watched him.

"Every day, every night—constantly—I think about the wonderful times we had," he said. "And that they are gone. I've been very unhappy. It's hard for me to say it right—I feel it, though. It's been sheer hell."

A slow fire came in her eyes. She could bear to listen to no more for awhile. It was painful and lovely. "Let's go for a drive," she said, suddenly.

He seemed surprised. "Okay—yes, I'd like to." He looked at his watch. "What about dinner?—where would you like to go? Maybe I should make a reservation somewhere, for later. I've heard about the Pump Room. . . ."

"Oh, we can eat anywhere—I don't feel fancy tonight. Skip the reservations. My car's down the street—we'll take a ride. I'll show you some of the South Side—Hyde Park-Kenwood, where I live. Would you like to?" She got up.

"Absolutely—whatever you say." He rose and they left the hotel amidst more stares—curious, bemused, some grudgingly admiring. It was not Paris. Outside, March, true enough, was going out like a lamb. The snow of three weeks ago was gone completely, the air was mild, the streets dry.

She took him south on Lake Shore Drive to 5100, then west on Hyde Park Boulevard. The sky was clear and dusk, a tranquil pink, was enveloping the city before the street lights came on. She laughed. "I'll take you by our house—but not in." The moment she said it, though, she was sorry.

"Yes? . . ." he said.

She would really have preferred some sort of protestation from him—polite insistence that he be taken in to meet her mother. She drove on, however, soon turning right, into Woodlawn Avenue, where a block and a half farther, on the left, the big Adkins house, a few lights on, sat back from the street swaddled in trees and a sizeable lawn—premises fairly typical of this prosperously integrated community. "That's our house," she said, pointing—"there. Gee, to think of it!—I was ten when we moved over here."

Philip leaned against her and peered out her side of the car. "Handsome," he said. ". . . A good neighborhood." Nothing about meeting her mother.

She was disappointed—slightly miffed—and for a moment had the impulse to turn the Datsun around, go back, and take him in. It would make their few hours together seem more respectable, less clandestine, equivocal, if he were to meet her mother. She soon abandoned the idea, however, and went on. After a short further tour of the area she headed back north toward the Loop. As they neared Soldier Field on the Outer Drive, Philip, looking to his right, saw a small plane, lights blinking, coming in from over the lake for a landing at Meigs Airport. He inquired and she explained that Meigs was a small facility accommodating only smaller craft carrying business men who thus could land nearer the Loop hotels and avoid the twenty-mile ride in from O'Hare. The thought hit her then —Meigs parking lot. She wanted *so* to talk to him—away from everybody. She was in torment. "Let's go watch the planes for a minute," she said, already turning off the Drive. She realized then how inane, obvious, this was—what was so remarkable about a Twin Beechcraft taking off in the dark?

"I'm with *you*," Philip laughed, though. It was reassuring. "I'm happy to be along for the ride—as long as it's with you!" He put his arm around her shoulder—lightly, unobtrusively. Yet it sent shivers up her spine. She felt already like putty to his touch. She drove into the lighted lot and parked in the first row of cars in clear view of the runway. The moment she turned off the motor he, as if prescient, took her chin in his hand, turned her face to him, and kissed her hungrily. She almost swooned from the old sinking feeling she had not had since her last time in his apartment. Now he moved his hand down over her left breast and held it there, his fingers gentle, caressing. She saw fire and her head fell back helplessly as he kissed her again, deeply. "Philip! . . ." she whispered, whimpered. His lips were soon past her face, in her hair, against her ear now, saying—"Oh, Dee! . . . it seems like I've lived years for this moment! . . . It's been so damned long!" She began crying but quickly checked herself, determined she would not, must not, lose control.

The daemon, as if in the back seat, exclaimed—"How right you are, dear girl, my erstwhile pet! . . . Hold on!—don't let go! Save those tears for some more auspicious, more worthy, occasion! See first what his proposition is, his mission—ha, if, that is, in his blind confusion and innocent racist egomania, he has one. Lose your head now and you'll lose more of what you've lost already—which is pretty grim, no? It may be a painful moment for him too—excruciating—who knows? He's got his problems. He's hurting. Yes, like us all, he has his handicaps—think of his world, his background, teachings, forebears, and that older Tom Buchanan of a father he's got. The son never knew excitement and passion until you—you beautiful, luscious-brown, pulsating peach of a girl, you! —until you swam into his ken. Passion is a bad word where he hails from, dearie—you don't clip coupons *passionately*. Now, do you? In his milieu, passion equates with weakness, decadent spleen, hateful non-Nordicism. He understands none of all this he faces now. How then can he understand the way he feels?—or what makes him tick, what makes *you* tick, or makes the heart burst the iron bonds of his Mayflower traditions? . . . How can he cope with it all? To him it's incomprehensible, confusing—damned frustrating, my friend. Yes, he's hurting. He's used to having what he wants, when he wants it, the way he wants it, in circumstances *he* controls. Think of this, my sweet! . . . Then you'll think only of yourself. It's *your* test now more than his. Don't *you* give—until he gives! If you would overcome, don't meet vacillation with more vacillation. Meet it with your simple strength—inherited from *your* great forebears. You are entirely capable—or are you? Oh, if I were a praying being, my prayers would go up (or down) for you, dear girl! . . . I'm your nether-world partisan—your inconstant shield! . . ."

Bravely, obliviously, she drew back from Philip and smiled through her wet lashes. Then she laughed—but it was a quiet laugh, with some shyness, then some sadness. She felt better, though—almost good. In the car everything, the kissing, had stopped between them—and by her own force of will. About this she also felt good. Again laughing—"I think I want to go home and put on a different dress," she said. "I'll dine with you then—in the Pump Room. How about it?"

He smiled in her eyes—"Whatever you say," and kept his arm around her shoulder.

"You can talk with Mother while I change," she said.

A hesitation—" . . . Okay." He said no more.

Laughing as if suddenly overtaken by a strange, subdued hysteria, she started the car and was soon headed south again on the Drive. She talked freely, while he sat mostly silent, occasionally smiling or laughing—it was like they were in Paris again. She was happy and wanted her mother to share her joy by meeting this man of her emotions' most extravagant dreams. In her state of mind, consequences, reactions, implications, were all but forgotten. When they arrived home, the front of the house was dark, which she knew meant in her absence her mother had had dinner in the breakfast nook instead of the dining room, insisting Mrs. Grier go home early. She got out her key and let them both in. Philip seemed tense again—she could sense it. She hung his coat in the closet under the stairs and took him in the parlor. "Let me go get Mother," she said—"And I won't be long changing. I'll call the Pump Room, too." She gave him the evening paper.

At first Philip was grave, then he seemed trying to be jaunty to dispel any impression of uneasiness, as he sat down in the great wing chair. "Take your time," he smiled. He gazed around him at the fireplace, the heavy damask draperies, the fragile chest of ancient chinoiserie, the rugs, the enveloping elegance of the house, and took a deep, protracted breath.

Mary Dee, after bounding up the stairs, found her mother's bedroom door closed. She could hear the television inside however and knocked once, then turned the knob to enter. The door was locked. She knocked again, calling through the door softly—"Mama! . . . why've you got the door locked? Let me in! . . ."

"Just a minute . . . Suky?—is that you already? . . ." came Irene Adkins' quavering, hollow voice. "I'm coming . . . I'm coming, Suky!"

Mary Dee's heart sank. She knew the problem now. And tonight of all nights! After a moment, and some groping fumbling, her mother unlocked and opened the door. The worst fears were confirmed—Irene Adkins was staggering and weaving from the brandy she had drunk, and had been asleep. Mary Dee entered quickly and closed the door. "Oh, Mama! . . . what have you done to yourself?" she whispered. Irene Adkins' dress was disarranged at the collar and left shoulder and had sustained a rent along the side seam as if she had fallen. The eyes were wild and frightened in her

163

withered octoroon face and her breath reeked of alcohol. Mary Dee was distraught—"Mama, you've done it again! . . . Oh, God!—but why lock the door? . . ."

"I'm sorry! . . . Oh, I'm sorry, Suky! . . ." came the long, wailing cry—"I'm *afraid* in this big house by myself!—You went off and left me! . . . Mrs. Grier left me too! I'm afraid, Suky! You're not going out again, are you? . . . Oh, I know you won't leave me—I'm so glad you're back already! . . . Suky! . . ." Her lament had become a low cry as she extended her arms imploringly toward Mary Dee—who was paralyzed with fear that the voice might carry downstairs. She glanced then at the bed behind Irene Adkins. There were five or six framed family photographs lying face up on the bedspread, pictures of the family in former, happier, times—a younger Horace Adkins in golf togs, the whole family on vacation in Montreal, a large backyard cook-out for a Nigerian diplomat, the three children at various ages, and Mary Dee, age fourteen, at the easel. It was clear Irene Adkins in her brandy had been brooding, grieving, over her lost family, and instantly Mary Dee's compassion and love burst all bounds. "Oh, Mama! . . ." She turned the television off and led her mother back to bed, where she removed the photographs to a chair, and tried to get her to undress and get in bed.

"Yes, yes—I will, Suky! . . . I'll do whatever you say!" Irene Adkins dropped helplessly to the bed. "You come in now, Suky, and we'll look at television together—don't leave me again! . . ." Her beauty gone, the muscles of her face lax, drained, and tired, she gave Mary Dee a dazed smile.

"Mama, I've got to go back out again," Mary Dee said. "I changed my mind and came home to put on a different dress—my new dress. The young man, Philip Wilcox, is downstairs!—he's sitting down in the parlor! . . ."

"Oh, I might have known! . . ." moaned Irene Adkins—"You're going to leave me again! . . ." She began crying, wailing, again—"Oh, Suky! . . ."

"Mama!—*Shhhhh!* . . ." Mary Dee got the nightgown out of the closet and began undressing her, and soon put her, feebly protesting, whimpering, to bed and turned out the light. Soon Irene Adkins had sunk into a stuporous sleep. Mary Dee now hurried to her own room and changed into the rainbow chiffon dress—certain though that Philip had heard the commotion. How would she explain her mother's absence?—it terrified her. Quickly, she examined herself in the mirror, unable to avoid seeing her harried, jittery, put-upon look. She tried to compose herself by sitting down for a moment in a chair in her room. Finally—it was an antidote—she remembered to call for Pump Room reservations. When she returned downstairs, Philip, hands behind him, stood before the parlor window, gazing out toward the lighted street. He turned to her—expectantly—smiling. "Mother's indisposed, Philip," she said. "I didn't insist she come down. Maybe another time. Shall we go?—I called the Pump Room."

". . . I'm sorry," he said. "Of course, shall we?" She got him his coat and soon they left.

But driving north, she felt the awkwardness and was convinced he had heard her mother's travail. "My mother's going through a difficult period," she said. "She had never imagined life without my father—now it's bad, very bad, for her. She's drinking. You heard her. She was in no condition to come meet you—I regret it. I feel so sorry for her—I feel I have somehow let her down. She didn't want me to leave her. Oh, well. . . ." She sighed.

Philip wrinkled his brow, seeming ill at ease again, as if searching for the right thing to say and do. ". . . I know it's been a bad time for you," he said. A long pause. "I've come to ask you something, Dee. . . ." His voice quit on him then. She gripped the steering wheel to keep control of herself and the car. He seemed unable to say more and she fought off the urge to prompt him to go on, to say something, anything, that might furnish a clue to his thoughts. They rode in silence as her frustration screamed inside.

The sky, though cloudless, was black with but few stars, the night calm. They by-passed the Loop and stayed on the Drive until Oak Street, then west and north to the Ambassador East Hotel and its Pump Room, where one of the red-coated doormen took the little Datsun. Once inside, they heard the orchestra's gay dinner music even before Philip gave his name to the tuxedoed *maître d'hotel* and they were ushered in. The atmosphere was subtly various, distinctive—both blasé and secure; there were no stares, curious or otherwise; by other patrons they seemed unnoticed; and to the personnel it was clear this extraordinary couple were somebody and inured to the best—entitled to the establishment's serious attention and a good booth. The ceilings were high, the colors light and airy, the waiters sedate, experienced, the prevailing motif elegance itself, as Philip, already in easier spirits now in this his metier, gazed at her across the table and told her her dress was well worth going the distance home for. Despite what she had just been through, she too felt she looked good and accepted his appreciation with a nervous smile. She did not really want a drink, knowing there would be wine, but she let him order her a Campari over ice anyhow as he ordered himself a Scotch. She loved the music and knew later the little floor would fill up with dancers, though she herself did not wish to dance. Suddenly on impulse she turned to him—"You said you had come to ask me something," she said, and tried to laugh. "But you didn't say what it was."

Philip glanced at her quickly, then away; he tried to smile. "I guess I lost my nerve," he said. "I was probably afraid of a 'no' answer."

It made her whole body ache with anguish and anxiety. And she was afraid to push him, nor could she, in her confusion, possibly think of a comment of her own that would not betray her ordeal or would not be gauche. At this moment the waiter came, with the great menus for consultation, followed almost at once by the sommelier, his stately chain of office dangling on his breast. These details took most of ten minutes.

"How was your family, Philip?" It was a last resort—the only way she could think of resuming the conversation.

"They were fine," he said. "Of course, I told you about my uncle. He won't make it, I found out. He knows it, though, and is stoical—a very courageous guy." He sipped his plain Scotch with no ice. Then unheralded—"Your mother's very dependent on you, isn't she?" he said. "Psychologically, I mean."

She looked at him for a moment, not sure of the answer. "She probably is," she said—"though I hadn't thought of it that way. My sister and brother are still away. She also relies heavily—too much so, I think—on the woman who's been with us a long time, the housekeeper. It's only natural, though—through this period, at least—that in many ways she should look to me."

"What about your work—your painting? Have you given it up altogether? . . . Raoul's very unhappy about this."

"I haven't given it up. I'm not going to. This is just a difficult time—I'm trying to adjust as best I can to the changes my father's death has brought about. It's necessary that I have a job. Already Mother's talking about selling our house and moving into an apartment—the upkeep on the house is so great, she says. So these are all problems that must be dealt with." She laughed. "I do paint—like mad!—on weekends. Though I doubt Raoul, or his painter friend Vitry, would approve of much of it." There was another awkward silence. "Is that what you came to ask me?—about my painting?" she smiled.

Troubled, he studied the tablecloth. "What I've asked about your mother and your painting is at least germane," he said. Then the waiter brought the oysters Rockefeller and he said no more.

She waited and waited. Suddenly she was nettled—"Germane to what, Philip?"

He cast the tiny fork aside. "Oh, hell, Dee—I don't know! . . . I'm up a tree! It's—it's just that I can't get it out. You should be pursuing your career—your life's work. . . ."

"Of course I should!" she said impatiently. "Oh, but how you talk in riddles! . . . you've never spoken freely with me!"

"But that's what I've wanted to do—now. That's why I came. But it's not all that easy, I tell you! . . . Don't be so tough."

She was offended, but held her tongue. She knew she was in less than an advantaged position—at least that of subtle pursuer. And that he felt it. Also that he abhorred being even nudged, no matter how gently. She denied however being "tough" He should not have used the word, she thought. Now she pouted.

The waiter came and poured a great chilled Puligny-Montrachet the sommelier had brought. Mary Dee would not look at Philip. "Tell me," he finally said, "do you believe me when I say that for me Paris isn't fit to live in with you gone?"

"Maybe I believe you feel that way at certain times—when you think about us this time last year, say, or our holiday together in the Chateau country—but I doubt if I'm justified in going beyond that." She tried her best to smile. "That is, if I'm an intelligent person—which often, where you're concerned, I'm not. But even suppose you do feel that way, all the time, it's 'germane'—to use your word—to *what?*" Pursuit again, she realized, but did not care.

"It means I'm unhappy when you're away from me," he said.

Though still trying to smile, she leaned forward and spoke almost into his face. *"Philip, which is 'germane' to what?"*

He looked at her but no words came.

"You speak of *your* unhappiness," she said. "Do you see what I mean? . . . the significance of it? So you came all the way to Chicago to tell me *you're* unhappy when I'm away from you. Don't you see we're right back where we were when I left Paris? And I don't know what we can do about it. Do you?" Pursuit again, she realized. *"Do you, Philip?"*

"You can come back with me and continue your schooling!" he blurted. And looked shocked.

She sat staring at him. Helplessly they stared at each other. What did he mean by that? she thought. She took up her drink for a moment, not knowing what to say, how to react. But by his manner it was evident to her he regarded what he had said as some kind of impulsive, accidental revelation. "I don't understand you, Philip," she said at last.

His eyes left her face. He did not reply.

She was afraid to continue but did not know otherwise what to do. If he meant merely what he had said, her reaction was of course certain and negative, she knew. Such a proposal she thought indecent, insulting. Yet she was not prepared to decide on the spur of the moment whether it had eventual—or potential—possibilities. Did it represent the utter, absolute, limits of his thinking? Or was it capable—in skillful hands—of further development, being made something of? She did not know and therefore did not want to act precipitantly. "I've got my mother to think about, Philip," she finally said. "You know, though, how much I'd love to be in Paris now if she were okay—I don't have to tell you that." She waited.

He frowned at her and seemed in torment. "What are you saying?" he said—"that you won't come?"

She somehow felt sorry for him. Then felt more sorry for herself. "Oh, Philip, don't put it that way!—it's unfair. You know my mind as well as I do myself—you know my preferences, my *longings*. So please don't put words in my mouth I don't want there. As you say, don't be so 'tough.' "

He thought about what she had said for a moment. "I don't want to be," he said with great soberness, and stared futilely across the room. The waiter came now with the roast rack of lamb for two and poured the sommelier's burgundy, a soft ruby red *Côte de Beaune*. They ate in virtual silence, until Philip said—"Are you angry with me?"

"Not necessarily for anything you've done today." She spoke reluctantly—"But you must be aware you didn't treat me well when I returned to Paris after my father's death—a time when I so needed you. I'd be untruthful if I pretended I'd forgotten. Why did you do it, Philip?—what was in your mind? . . ."

"I worried about us all the time! . . . about our relationship." He wrinkled his brow again. "It was hell—you were a terrific burden on my mind. I was trying to put some distance between us, I guess, but didn't know how. I bungled it. I didn't know that without you it would only be worse."

She knew at the moment it was profitless to pursue the obvious point: That he had not been able to bring himself to consider the one true solution. She might, she thought, be able to suggest this a little later, and get his reaction, but not now. "Oh, well," she sighed, "let's talk about something more pleasant." They ate, talked about mutual friends and the instructors at the École des Beaux-Arts, and listened to the violins of the orchestra. Eventually, later, the wine changed her mind about dancing and they danced—to a few indecipherable stares. Though on the dance floor Philip was proper, not demonstrably ardent, she sensed his wrought-up feelings—especially when, though holding her ever so correctly, he whispered to her fragments of love talk and pleas that she try to understand him and his problem. The latter was at last elucidating; her misgivings were confirmed; she could no longer avoid the plain, hard fact that his Paris proposal was incapable of expansion. She was not surprised by the realization, actually. She had in her inner intuitive feelings suspected, anticipated, it. She was filled now with a kind of weary insensibility, callousness, a resigned fatalism, and knew that when soon he asked her to have a night-cap at his hotel she would not demur. Hadn't she foreseen this and ingested The Pill? But in the process she would pursue her "obvious point," nail it down, remove all dubiety, and have it out with him once and for all.

Two hours and fifteen minutes after they had come in, Philip asked the waiter for the check and for the sommelier to be summoned for his stipend. Later as they waited outside for the Datsun to be fetched, she felt a strange ennui, a tiresomeness of it all, yet knew the feeling to be false. It was not fatigue, it was dread. And her usually chattering daemon had not a word to say.

*   *   *   *   *

Philip laughed and called them the "Magic Mirrors." This, he told her, was how the Hispanic bellboy had described them when the latter had brought up his luggage to the suite (1020) and placed it in the bedroom. She stepped inside his bedroom and, wide-eyed, looked around her. It was like a fantastic, bizarre, expensive, carnival. The walls and ceiling were grotesquely-refracting shafts and panes of mirrors—both clear and cloudily opaque, some convex, some concave, others on a plane—and all vaguely illuminated by a garish, revolving three-way light, intricate and multi-colored, securely fixed in a far corner into the floor and at the moment trained generally ceilingward. The unnatural lighting transformed the bedroom into a kind of psychedelic Dante's inferno. No color in the spectrum seemed missing. Philip laughed again and used the same fixture both to reduce the light's glare—the wattage—and slow the rate of rotation. "Ha! Pleasant setting, isn't it?" he said. "A real passion pit!" The room at first frightened, then brought her to laugh, wryly, too—she thought it ridiculous. "The bellboy says this is the most expensive suite in the Plaza Royale," Philip laughed— "You can see why!" He had not yet even taken her coat. He did so now and, after she had let him kiss her again, they returned to the parlor of the elaborate suite. "Let's have a drink," he said. "I've some stuff in the kitchen—and there's ice."

"No thanks," she said—"I'm still reeling from the wine." She was not interested in this ploy. Philip went and got himself a Scotch and soda and came back and turned on the low, velvety music of the FM radio. She laughed, again ironically—"What is this, Philip? —the old build-up? You're slipping."

"It's no build-up," he grinned. It was a boyish grin and she had always thought it attractive; loved it, in fact, though it was rarely in evidence. She was suddenly sad—how she adored, worshipped, this vain, selfish young god of a man who had mistreated her so and broken her heart. It was distasteful to have to carry this affliction, yet she viewed it as a condition of her life. They sat across the room from each other as he grinned at her still—"No, I'm not stupid enough to think I could ever fool you, trick you, into doing

170

something you didn't want to do," he said. Again she felt helpless; putty in his hands.

"Intentionally or not, you've tricked me plenty," she smiled ruefully. "No, you're not stupid," she sighed. "Only me."

He came over and got her and took her back to his sofa—then kissed her again. She was supine to the point of inertness—the reemergence of her fatalism. "What's the matter with you?" he said. "You're cold as ice."

"Should I be hot?" she said, a half-smiling, crazy glitter in her eyes. "Yes, I guess I should. That's the way you like me—*hot!*" She gave her ironical little laugh again; then, momentarily spiteful, resentful, said—"I'm a *hot* piece, aren't I, Philip? . . . right?"

"That's insulting," he said at once, no longer grinning. "It's insulting to you too!" He took a swallow of his drink. "You can be bitchy sometimes, Dee—and a little crazy too. You imply I have less than respect for you as a person. You may deny it but that's what you really mean, for——"

"——Wait. I *don't* deny it." Her voice fell then, despairingly. She spoke in great distress. "You've used me, Philip! . . . Or maybe I've let myself be used. I don't know which is worse. Either is bad enough."

He grew very serious. "Its nonsense for us to keep up these endless recriminations, Dee—Oh, Dee! . . ." He took her in his arms again and they kissed passionately. Then, as of old, he began undressing her. Though her face was sad, she did not resist. She was not being swept away, but was in full charge of her faculties. When she saw him, his hand trembling with hot passion and expectancy, toss the rainbow chiffon dress across the chair, she was conscious only of her briefest shudder of mortification—that was all. She remembered with perfect clarity the moment in the car in Meigs Airport parking lot when she had made the decision, felt the compulsion, to go home and change. She had sensed what it meant—discarding a garment of dignity and strength for one frilly, weak, and self-destructive. She realized at that moment the die was cast. But once more it was her thought, persistent and recurrent, that it was a condition of life. She made no resistance now as he carried her naked into the garish circus of bedroom mirrors. Again she was suddenly overcome with a great sense of fatalism and put her arms around his neck as he carried her in and rolled her onto the bed.

171

Then he threw off his own clothes amidst the green-violet-orange-white-purple-yellow-red-celadon-vermilion miscellany of gyrating lights and joined her on the bed in a paroxysm of wild caresses. She would always remember the mad gleam in his eyes as he took, penetrated, her, uttering his sighing, desperate moans of long-denied fulfillment. Her upturned face to the now-muted revolving lights, evil, kaleidoscopic, dizzying, their continually changing, symmetrical forms full in her vision, had on her both a horrifying and lascivious effect. She realized the present peril of going equally mad from terror and bliss. She felt them, two God-abandoned human beings, locked together now in a kind of ceaseless, imperishable ecstasy—the lurid self-reflections above and around them spurring them on. From every imaginable angle she could see his back and buttocks in writhing, grinding motion—at first pale blue flesh, then lemon-banana skin, then red and bottle green garnishing the nape of the neck and the ears, now the whole body a screaming orange-black-silver, then his hair sable, now white, but quickly violet. Her own shoulders, arms, and legs wildly flailing, had assumed a macabre new beauty—heavenly, shapely, balletomanic, in a coloration of changing Harlequin hues—as Philip, throat, mouth, groaning on her neck, deeply possessed her. Soon, beyond all restraint, able to bear it no longer, she cried out in a frenzy of rapture—*"Oh, Philip! . . ."* His vocal cords were paralyzed and incapable of response. Then the slow, sweet spasm took him, driving his voice up and out of him, high and incoherent, and drowning out her shattered cries. *"God damn you! . . . Oh, Dee, I love you, my angel! . . ."* Then they were borne up, up, up, on the pinions of the explosion, to be returned only after long incomprehension of where they were at last. It was an experience of sweetest gluttony and together, as one, they were conscious of only their own mad presences against each other. Soon, panting, spent, but still one moist dual-body, they could hardly move and, now feeling a deep lassitude, lay whispering love devotions to each other, as the bizarre, low, multi-colored lights and images came and went in slow, sad revolution. At last they separated, turned, and lay on their backs and gazed silently, thoughtfully, around them into the magic mirrors.

Minutes still later Philip finally stirred. "How do you feel?" he said, and kissed her damp brow.

"Don't move," she pleaded. "Don't start the world up again.

Will it stay this way if we try not let it change? . . . Philip!—will it? . . ." She saw her face then in the changing mirror-light—the eyes grotesque, the nostrils pinched as in a skull, the mouth hideous, before the image quickly vanished. "Do you wish it would stay this way, Philip?" she asked, and turned her face from him.

"With all my heart," he said.

"Wish it, then—it will stay. You have the power."

He was silent, and shifted his leg slightly on the bed.

She was patient. She gave him time. "Do you want me, Philip?" she finally said.

"Yes . . . yes, more than anything in the world." But his words seemed somehow inhibited. He shifted the other leg.

She wanted to press him—to ask him: "More than *anything*, Philip?" But she did not. Yet she felt he should not have said it, carelessly or not, for she knew both were well aware it was not true. For one thing, he wanted family approbation more. She was incensed. "If you want me more than anything in the world," she did say, "then why don't you take me? You've just seen how available I am, ha!"

"Dee!"

"Why, certainly. All you have to do is reach up and pluck me off the tree—like you have tonight—it's that simple. Ah, but I forgot —it's *not* really that simple, is it, Philip?" Her anguish and frustration were soon turning to anger, but she was determined not to cry again. "The problem seems to be marriage—am I right? As if that just occurred to us." She spoke calmly, trying to contain herself. "Quite a stumbling block, eh, Philip?" She waited. "*Marriage*, Philip—I've spoken the dastardly word, you see." She did not yet turn her head toward him, and only heard his struggling discomfort when he cleared his throat. She said: "I know you've thought a lot about it—in my petty, sinister little way I've forced you to— but, Philip, what have you thought?"

He bristled. "I've thought plenty," he said.

"No, no—*what?*"

"Dee, I don't want to talk about it."

"What's the difficulty, Philip?" She tried to say it innocently yet could not keep the bitter scorn from her voice.

He flounced over on his side, away from her, but soon, half muttering to himself, spun onto his back again. Still she waited. "I talked to my father about it yesterday," he said. "He hit the ceiling."

She turned to him at last and raised up in the bed on her elbow, her voice a deadly purr. "He *didddd?*" she said, mock wide-eyed.

"Yes. It makes it a problem. . . . People of the past generation sometimes don't see things the way we do—they have different notions about things . . . about—"

"—About race, yes. I know, Philip. Your father would prefer you married a white girl—right?"

"God!—'*prefer!*' He almost climbed the wall. My mother in the next room wondered what on earth was happening. When he told her, she broke out crying. They were both upset as hell. They've never known people like your family, and when I try to tell them it only makes it worse. I was glad to get out of Philadelphia."

"Yes, Philip, I can tell you're still frightened. You speak of your parents' notions, but what are your *own?* That's what I'm interested in."

"How can you ask that?—Dee! You know what *I* think—I've proved it."

"Proved what?"

"That my feeling for you is for *yourself*—I'm not interested in anything else. . . . I couldn't care less. I admire you for so many things—not only your good-looks . . . your intelligence, your character, talent, personality, and all the rest. Color doesn't enter into it a damned bit. I want *you.*"

"Did you tell your parents that?"

He swallowed. ". . . Yes, I did."

"They were unmoved?"

"Yes, Dee."

"And you say you want me—I understand now. You asked me to go back to Paris with you, but you meant as your mistress, didn't you?"

"Oh, don't put it that way, Dee!—you make it sound so . . . so demeaning! . . . when, these days, it's not at all!"

"Philip, you've got many good traits—many. Otherwise I don't think I'd have fallen in love with you as I did. But courage isn't one of them. Maybe I'm a masochist, but please have the courage just this once to tell me that you won't marry me. Just tell me."

"It's not that I won't, Dee. *I can't.* . . . My family . . ."

"Sure, I understand—it's the same thing. That will do for an answer, Philip. You rose to the occasion beautifully." She scooted off the bed, went in the parlor, and began gathering up her clothes.

He ran naked after her. He grappled with her in the parlor and began pleading with her. "Dee, you've got to listen to me—you slander me. I've got no less courage than you've got. Where is *your* courage? . . . answer me that. I want you to come back to Paris with me and right away you start referring to yourself as my 'mistress,' as if you were calling yourself my whore. Such bourgeois mentality! Yes, I want you to come live with me—in my apartment in the Quarter. I need time to try to work things out the way you want them—it's not as easy as you seem to think. Living together!—hell, some of the most prominent men and women in the world, respectable people, share a place without being married. Don't you know that?" He pulled her down to him on the sofa. "This is a new day!—what's wrong with two people in love with each other living together? I don't demean you when I ask you to return to Paris. This sort of thing is entirely acceptable nowadays. It's our happiness isn't it? You've got to consider my side as well as yours. Look, I have all the money to spend I want—my father, until this week at least, has had a hundred percent confidence in me, and in my judgment. No father's been more generous with a son than he's been with me. I'm sure you know all the money I have—all of it—comes from him. And at his pleasure. But he can discontinue it as quickly as he gives it. Tell me this: Would you like me as much as you do if I were flat broke?—with no money at all coming from Philadelphia? Have you ever thought of that? Yet you say I'm gutless. It's not that damned simple, Dee."

"Philip, the more you talk, the worse you make it," she said. "Of course I'd like you as much. I'd like you *more*! What I don't like is your willingness to let your family, your father, run your life—run *our* lives. You're twenty-seven now—you're no kid. Most men have families of their own at your age!" He was silent and turned her loose, whereupon she quickly got up, took her clothes into the bathroom, and began dressing.

Behind the closed door now she tried to calm her anger, her hurt. She should not be surprised, she told herself in the mirror—she had seen all this coming, really. She had asked for a clear answer, too, and had got it. Now she knew where she stood—he had told her. Yet he defended himself. For that matter, on reflection, she felt neither of them was being completely honest. Yes, what *if* he were a poor architecture student living in a dingy Paris walk-up, unable to squire her around among his well-heeled young French friends, or to take her to expensive restaurants, cafes, the

175

theatre, and the opera? What if his family were of lowly, blue-collar origin, his father a plant foreman instead of a Harvard over-seer? Would Philip really excite her as he did now? Would she be so exercised about his hesitancy in marrying her? She knew she would not, and that she had been untruthful in telling him she would like him even more. But she had never considered such a contingency—Philip poor? Impossible. Her image of him would admit of no such version. It would not be *her* Philip. Perhaps he had this idea of himself also, she thought, and was determined not to give it up—wealth, breeding, and position were not so easily come by. Sensing now his determination in the matter, she con-sidered the possibility she may have accused him wrongly of lack-ing courage. Maybe in fact this was what he *had* in his refusal to precipitate a family crisis. But how did she know he was telling the truth? she thought. Had he really tested his family in the way he had said? She was confused, yet somehow she believed he was truthful in this—or was he? She knew, however, she would *never* live with him as his mistress. No matter his euphemisms, it was unthinkable. This was so even had she been free to leave her mother —which she was not, she knew. Maybe he was right—many "re-spectable" people did live together unmarried. The idea in the ab-stract did not much bother her. If she were white, with no hinder-ing ties, such as her mother, she would not be averse to coming to Paris as his mistress. But she was not white. She might not even be averse were he black. But as it actually was between them, with all the historical implications adverse to her, the idea was ren-dered so far out of the question as to be ludicrous. So this was finally the end, she reflected. It still seemed incredible. Yet some-how she felt wiser—perhaps, though embittered, calmer too.

Dressed now, she returned to the parlor to leave. She found Philip also fully dressed and ready to see her home. "May I ride out with you?" he said—"Maybe you'll be willing to brew me a cup of coffee as we sit a brief moment in your kitchen. Then I'll have you call me a taxi to return. I won't keep you up." She looked at him, sighed, and nodded. Soon they had left.

In the car they were silent most of the way. But when they had turned off the Outer Drive and were almost home, he turned to her. "I guess your answer is no," he said.

She hesitated and looked at him—having forgotten the ques-tion. "What? . . ." she said.

"I asked you to come back to Paris."

"Oh, Philip, of course not! I wouldn't think of it. And please don't bring up the subject again—it's distasteful to me."

"I had to be told, though," he said. "It's better to have things clear."

Her frustration and anger returned. "Yes—I agree," she said. "Things are clear between us now. You won't marry me and I won't become your mistress. Things couldn't be clearer." Tears welled in her throat and she could hardly speak.

He gazed ahead through the windshield. "Well, we've got a lot to remember," he said. "We'll be rich in memories, at least." He heaved a heavy sigh.

She was silent.

"May I write you occasionally?" he said.

"No—I wish you wouldn't, Philip. It will be easier this way. No more letters—no more waiting for letters."

As they reached the house, he said something barely audible— "I hope you're happier than I am. . . ."

Her daemon then, as if veritably from the glove compartment, delivered the eulogy. "The end? Well, maybe—though I'm not sure, for one never knows about you two, does one? What gluttons for punishment you are, though—like two handsome punching bags. Why didn't your all-wise and ever-loving God, way, way, up there in that terrific celestial splendor—ha, so far from my own native habitat in the fires below—make all people raceless? Ah, think of the heartache it would have spared. You would by now have had the expensive nuptials, with much champagne and throwing of rice, and now be just returning from a global honeymoon. But look at you—you miserable pair. You're not a very pretty sight—especially you, my dear, sweet, peach-brown beauty of a girl! How sad and crushed your comeliness tonight after all those horrific magic mirrors. So it's the end—or is it? It is the end for me, I feel—I am old and bitter at seeing young beauty despoiled —by, ironically, the innocent despoiler. It offends one's sense of poetic equity and invites the goddess Nemesis. Yet through the world of the spirits there had been manifold warnings—unheeded, of course. So let's say, whether it's true or not, this is the end— and be damned thankful therefor. I do not rejoice—I deplore and commiserate . . . for it is man's stupidity! And soon the Western death knell. Alas, alas . . . but now *au revoir*."

177

Philip, climbing out of the car, in almost a whisper said it once again—"I hope you're happier than I am. . . ."

*　　*　　*　　*　　*

Weeks passed. At first, the turn of events seemed only to have blunted, dulled, Mary Dee's senses. She walked around in a kind of nascent bewilderment—dazed. Yet she had in no way been shocked by Philip's performance, by what she now considered his gall, the revelation of his true character; nor even surprised. She somehow accepted it, and its meaning, in an attitude of fatalism. In the very beginning—after he returned to Paris—she did not even dislike him. She merely did everything possible to keep from thinking about him, and performed her duties at Aico & Aleshire and pursued her painting at home with a new, an intense, concentration. The painting seemed for awhile a form of therapy during the interim her faculties were so numbed and leaden. She cleared out and had decorated the upstairs of the Adkins capacious garage in the rear, a former coach house loft, and made it into an artist's studio. Here she brought all her painting equipment and supplies from the basement of the house and set up her easel. This period of false calm, however, was not to last. Soon spells of blackest depression came over her and gave her no rest, followed by days and nights of frantic anger and outrage as the time-anesthesia of the weeks wore off like novocaine after a painful tooth extraction. In her refurbished studio she was painting furiously now, using harsh, lurid, abrasive colors and great awkward forms. Moreover, in her confusion and state of malaise, she had sought to join a group of militant black writers, photographers, and painters whose vow was to depict, if not glorify, the trauma of black ghetto life and to foster all forms and concepts of exclusively black aesthetics.

Irene Adkins was shocked and dismayed at the latter development, and mystified by the great change that had come over her daughter. She tried to sort things out by long talks with her housekeeper, Mrs. Grier. "What will Suky be up to next?" she said to Mrs. Grier one beautiful Saturday afternoon in May. They were in the kitchen and had just watched a young black couple saunter down the driveway on their way back to Mary Dee's studio over

178

the garage. The young woman looked all of seven months pregnant and wore sloppy denim pants and a colorful green and red African headdress. The young man, big, muscular, wore a dashiki and sparse, scraggly beard, and carried a good-sized painting. "You know very well they wouldn't be going back there if she hadn't invited them," Irene Adkins said. "Oh, I want to sell this house so badly!—it's becoming more and more of a trial for me. I don't seem to be able to keep up with what's going on here any more—I can't control . . . oh, well." She threw up her hands. "You saw for yourself what she did to that garage loft," she went on. "Certainly, it needed cleaning up, but not what she did to it—one whole wall a big, ghastly, monstrosity of a painting about black children! It's a horror—a nightmare! I thought at first *she* had done it and that she was finally deranged, but then she told me the fellow did it—the big fellow who just went back there with his *enceinte* wife. So *he* must be deranged. Oh, what do you make of it all, Mrs. Grier? . . ."

Inscrutable Mrs. Grier, her bulk perched on a high chair at the kitchen counter as she polished the Adkins' silver, thought for a moment. "I don't know," she said. "Mary Dee's got her own mind about things—she don't talk much, seems like."

"I know she doesn't. She's very upset about something—that I'm sure of. Why else, all of a sudden, would she take up with people like those who just went back there? That fellow and his wife—I *guess* they're married—may not only come here, you know; Suky may go to their place too, for all I know. Goodness knows what that must be like." Distressed, Irene Adkins turned away from the window and, almost pleadingly, asked Mrs. Grier if she would make her a cup of tea. "It's true," she added, in deep, troubled, reflection, "Suky's joined those people."

This was not entirely the case. Rather, Mary Dee had *tried* to join them. But except for the couple just arrived—the Hungerfords —she had been treated coolly by this group, icily by some. They knew who she was and knew about her family, were aware of what over the years she and her family had stood for—or what they had failed to stand for—and treated her accordingly. Mary Dee, sensitive, insecure, defensive, felt the cut of their disapproval and was unhappy, also confused by it, and always uncomfortable around them. Yet her determination was firm not to give up; she meant to prevail. Also, she had suddenly come to share many of their beliefs—especially their hatred of whites—and loved to listen to their conversations, their diatribes, for this was the talk, the ideas, that gave her the vengeful pleasure she, a short year ago, would have thought impossible, incredible. She had formed a bitter, implacable, hatred for Philip's parents and all their kind, and only wished she could talk about it with her new acquaintances as freely as they gave vent to their opinions, feelings, and frustrations. But this she knew would be laughable—they would only berate her and tell her she'd got what she deserved. She had finally begun to hate Philip now also, considering him equally racist, and a weakling besides. She was therefore inevitably attracted to this group of angry militants and in so many inept ways persisted in seeking them out. Yet only Rosabelle and Ornette Hungerford had been in the least receptive to her—even if warily so at first. Ornette, himself an amateur painter, though ambitious to paint well, had seen three or four of Mary Dee's paintings at an art fair almost three years before and knew of her spreading and promising reputation. He was much impressed. Yet it was her ability, her talent, that impressed him—not the subjects she painted, which he considered ridiculously "Western" in light of the current realities as he saw them. He and his wife Rosabelle were convinced Mary Dee badly needed instruction—a crash-course orientation toward Blackness.

Mary Dee now welcomed them into her light, airy studio again. Ornette was a hulking, ebony-black young man, with huge arms and hands, all making him appear to have the strength of a Goliath. Rosabelle, light-sand brown and big-eyed, herself no small woman, moved about awkwardly in her late pregnancy; and although clean, and otherwise capable of real attractiveness, she seemed careless of dress and used no cosmetics. Both she and Ornette wore large, aggressive Afros. "What have you got there?" Mary Dee laughed to Ornette as they entered and she glanced at the wrapped painting he carried, "—a Rembrandt?"

Though attempting smiles, Rosabelle and Ornette showed they hardly thought this funny. "What would we want with a Rembrandt?" Rosabelle said in mild reproof. "The Dutch were the cruelest conquerors and slavers of them all—real bastards."

"Oh, I was only joking," said Mary Dee contritely—"Of course they were." Humble, nervous, she took the painting from Ornette and, unwrapping it, asked them to sit down. Neither, however, at the moment complied.

But Rosabelle, pointing at the picture, smiled now. "Ornette's latest," she said. "Tell him, will you, Mary Dee, whether it's any good or not."

Ornette, ignoring them both, had gone across the room to inspect, admire again, his stretch of mural on the large newly-white plaster wall. He had completed it ten days ago, and though he had done it in only three nights, he loved it, thought it great. Mary Dee's secret estimate of it was mixed. She thought it strong, imposing, though terribly violent, but also crude and simplistic, demonstrating what Ornette readily, almost proudly, admitted, that he had had absolutely no formal training. The mural, in vivid, warring colors, was a kind of panoramic depiction of thirty or more black children. Many of them were marching and shouting, or singing, with clenched fists raised high in defiance. Four others were pitiably crumpled, crushed, lifeless figures sprawled in the rubble of a bombed Birmingham church. Two more, a boy and a girl not over fourteen, were shown, sleeves pushed above the elbow, shooting dope. A third, comatose, eyelids half closed, lay ill or dying of a drug overdose on a mangy pallet in the corner of some ghetto room. Others, ragged, some shoeless, all seeming crazed and lost, were milling about and crying. One little girl, blue-black, stark naked, her short hair a fright, had, in some earth-shuddering race violence, lost an eyeball, which yet hung, a grisly pendant, suspended two inches down her cheek. She was screaming. The whole mural was surreal, a nightmarish vision of hell. Upon finishing it, Ornette had then lettered in, at very top-center, the mural's legend, its title: CHILDREN OF OUR LANDSCAPE. Now he stood studying his handiwork, his face stern, smoldering, proud —determined.

Mary Dee had now unwrapped the new painting Ornette had brought. It was an oil on an unframed canvas, about thirty-six inches square, and portrayed, in rather artless, broad brush strokes, still another black child—a sad-eyed boy with huge ears and drooling mouth. She held the painting out and studied it, thinking it not very good, but that she must not say so.

Rosabelle, watching her, laughed—"Mary Dee, you never did

181

say whether Ornette could paint or not. Come on—what do you think?"

Mary Dee hesitated, feigning further study of the picture. "My, how he loves to do children," she finally said—"Almost everything I've seen of his is about children."

"Well, he's got four of his own and a fifth one on the way," Rosabelle laughed, then grew serious—"Can he really paint children? . . . or is he just fooling around?"

Ornette interrupted them. "Well, I ain't fooling around—*I* can tell you that," he said contentiously. "I paint children—black children—because I'm concerned about them, concerned about what's gonna happen to them in this society, this racist society. What's more important than our children?—name me something, will you? You can't. We got to do something about our kids—got to try to make things better for them—or else we ain't no damn good ourselves. It's simple as that." Ornette loved to affect ungrammatical street talk, but he was a city commuter college graduate and sold insurance for a black-owned company for a living. Rosabelle was a check-out counter cashier in a food supermart. "But never mind about the children," he said—"What about the picture? . . . What d'you think of it?" He grinned at Mary Dee.

She still hedged. ". . . I don't know if I understand it," she said. "The child is strange—although that doesn't necessarily mean it's not well rendered." She held off the picture again. "I guess I'll have to get used to it—the boy is so sad."

"He's sad because he's hungry," Ornette said—"No mystery about that. You never saw a hungry child, did you?" His short little laugh was derisive. "Not *you.*"

Mary Dee, thinking of Ernestine and Vernon, was nettled but tried not to show it. Yet she did not know what to say, and was defensive again.

"Kids get hungry, y'know," Ornette went on. "If folks ain't got no food for them, they get hungry. Then they look sad—because they *feel* sad."

Inwardly Mary Dee sighed, wondering why she had taken up with these two domineering, perhaps actually resentful, people. Yet, she asked herself, why had they chosen to associate with her? There were reasons on both sides, she knew. It had begun in early April, when, in her desperation following Philip's visit, that tragic

182

fiasco, she had gone to a showing of paintings which was billed as a "Festival of the Committed Black Artists," then afterwards to a fund-raising cocktail party held in a rented union hall. Almost two hundred people were there. She had gone alone, as she did almost everywhere now, and throughout the afternoon and evening she felt lost—although many of the men, until they learned who she was, were flippantly friendly. People who were aware of her identity mostly avoided her. The exceptions had of course been Rosabelle and Ornette, though even they had at first seemed stiff, reserved. On sight Ornette knew who she was. Also, he had seen, and well and favorably remembered, several of her paintings from the days when she was regarded as a local prodigy before she left to study in Paris. But it was Rosabelle who broke the ice—"You should join our movement," she had finally said to Mary Dee after some small talk, "and help give pride and hope to our people, especially the black poor whose lives are so awful that they've lost hope. We need people like you — you can do a lot." Ornette, though less ready to be friendly, agreed —"Think it over," he said at last, "but there ain't no glamour in it. It ain't 'society.' " Yet, despite the barb, but perhaps because they were the only ones to show her attention, Mary Dee had somehow liked them, almost from the start, even if by now, after some six weeks of acquaintanceship, the relationship had had its ups and downs; for now she sometimes thought they still resented her and felt she took neither them nor their movement really seriously. Though this was not true, their situation at times produced its touchy moments—for example, the present.

"Oh, Ornette," chided Rosabelle, defending Mary Dee, "she knows there're a lot of black kids hungry—what do you take her for?"

Ornette gave his testy laugh again—"I said, did she ever *see* a hungry child."

"Of course I have," Mary Dee said. "Who hasn't? I've fed hungry black children."

Ornette smiled at this. "Well, I'm glad to hear it," he said, his sarcasm only half playful.

Really irritated now, Mary Dee ended the subject. "Please sit down," she said to them again, but remembered to smile, "—if you can find something to sit *on*." She looked around the studio—

"I've got to get some more furniture if I'm going to ask people in."

"Oh, I think your place is okay," said Rosabelle, surveying the clean, bare floors and freshly-painted white walls. "You wouldn't want to clutter it up with a lot of furniture. Anyway, it's too big to furnish. It's clean and that's enough. I like it."

"Ornette's mural is what makes the difference," Mary Dee said, wishing to flatter. They all turned now and viewed the mural wall.

"Do you really think Ornette's any good?—that he can paint?" said Rosabelle. "You've had a lot of training and the best teachers."

"Wait a minute, baby," Ornette said, grinning. "Don't put her on the spot like that—don't make her lie."

"I don't have to lie," Mary Dee said. "You're certainly a *gutsy* painter—your work has a lot of boldness and force." Then she hesitated, as if wondering whether to risk a negative comment. "It's pretty polemical, though," she said.

Ornette's reaction could have been expected. "You damn right it's polemical. You didn't mean it as a compliment but I'm taking it as one. I ain't one of your 'art-for-art's-sake' black painters. In my book, art should teach. Yeah, it should *preach*."

"Don't get loud, now, Ornette," Rosabelle said. She finally backed up and sat on a straight chair, her great belly, it seemed, in her lap.

Ornette gave her an impatient frown. "Don't you see, baby?— that's where Mary Dee comes in," he said. "She's got to be changed, turned around—we gotta show her the way, the *new* way." He looked at Mary Dee now: "You gotta get active with us, girl. You gotta get to know the *people*—yeah, some street niggers. It'll do you good. If these problems are ever gonna be solved, they're the ones who'll do it, don't forget that. But they need help. They need us. We need *you*, too. We need your painting, we need your money, we need your influence—we need your *know-how*, girl." He paused and studied Mary Dee for a moment. "And you know what?— something tells me you need *us* too. I don't know what it is—I just feel it. . . . Something's come over you, something's happened to you, to make you change like this, to come down off your high horse. Wow, what a change—I don't get it. When we saw you that day, saw you standing around looking lost at that raunchy Black Arts Festival, my mouth fell open and I couldn't get it closed. I couldn't believe my eyes—neither could Rosabelle—although we read somewhere, after your father's death, that you'd come home from Paris to be with your mother, and later that you lived here again now." Ornette laughed—"Yeah, girl, when I saw you I said to myself, 'Well, what brings Miss Society out to mingle with us common niggers?' " His laugh was edgy, cynical.

"Ornette!" scolded Rosabelle.

"But something's happened, baby," he went on, to his wife now —"I don't know what it is, but it drove her into us, into the movement. She sure didn't learn to love niggers in Paris, I'll tell you that. I've watched her for over a month now, listened to little things she says every once in awhile, little things she unconsciously lets out. And you know what?—why, she hates whitey worse'n anybody. It's a fact."

Mary Dee had stoically turned her back and gone to the window. She stared down onto the Adkins backyard and still-well-cared-for lawns. It was mid-May. The flower beds, in a riot of color, were already in bloom, the sun, though descending, was still golden bright, and the expanse of lawn grass a luxuriant, deep-sea green. She made no reply to Ornette.

"Ornette, why go into all that?" Rosabelle said—"What right have you got to get all in her private business like that? Mary Dee, tell him to go to hell."

Ornette grinned at Mary Dee. "Ain't I right?" he said to her. "You *hate* paddies, don't you?"

Nervously, Mary Dee looked away from him. ". . .It's not that simple," she said.

"Oh, ain't it, now." He stepped around her, confronting her. "I think it's very simple. It finally happens to *every* black, don't it?— no matter how stand-offish he's been or how long he's stood aloof from the fight. The time finally comes, don't it, sooner or later, when whitey gets to *him* too—puts him down, gives him the shaft, real hard. He reacts *then*, all right—and how. But what he apparently didn't know all along—I say *apparently*—is that whitey messes with rank-and-file niggers every day in the week, three hundred and sixty-five days a year. Ordinary niggers catch hell the year around. So think of them once in awhile, will you?—especially their *children*. Lord, just think of their kids and pitch in and help. Bring some hope into these families—for instance, like John Calvin Knight is doing. He's moved his national headquarters here to Chicago now, you know."

185

"She don't know anything about Knight, Ornette," Rosabelle said.

". . . I've heard of him," Mary Dee said weakly, her mind going back to that blizzardy morning and the poet's blatherings in the Trocadero.

Ornette laughed to Rosabelle. "See what I mean, baby?—she's heard *of* him. But at least that's a start. Mary Dee, my friend, you're gonna hear a lot more *of* him before long. Big things are brewing for this town now since he's come—*big* things. What a terrific nigger—that Knight! . . . *God damn*! . . . this town's gonna jump! You better come on in with us . . . get into it—be a part of it. Look what a person like you can do—and you'll get the damnedest sense of fulfillment you ever got out of anything in your life. I guarantee it. There's nobody in this movement, y'know—from Knight on down—that got into it just by accident or chance. Everybody has his reason, his own reason—you ain't by yourself, girl. Come on in here with us and let's *help* Knight."

"Yes, yes, Mary Dee," Rosabelle said—"Ornette's right, honey."

"You see, John Calvin Knight *knows* black folks," Ornette went on. "He's an expert—he knows what's in their minds and hearts, knows what makes them tick. And that, he says, is their *children* —their hungry, suffering kids. They'll tear up the world for their kids."

"Ornette," Rosabelle said, "Mary Dee don't want to hear no more of your preaching—let's get on something else." But Ornette kept talking.

Mary Dee, though facing them again now, stood motionless. She heard everything Ornette was saying, but her mind was deeply involved with herself. It was a paradox—she somehow felt good, very good, realizing these two people wanted, had even said they needed, her. Though they apparently did not know it, she in fact already considered herself a part of them and their movement. Despite Ornette's biting bluster, she was almost sure the three of them would be friends now. But what of *their* friends?—the people in the movement who had thus far been so cold to her? She vowed, in time, to win them too. Yes, she told herself, she had joined them, and all that that meant—which was much. She would even, if need be, become a devoted disciple of their great John Calvin Knight. She thought Ornette entirely right; now she knew what it was like to hate, to want to even old scores with people like Philip's parents, and all others like them. She felt so right about it all, that it was such a perfectly natural thing to do, and that in the end it would give her very existence a new meaning. Her attitude now shone in her eyes. "Can I get you something?" she said to them, almost cheerfully. "Would you like a drink?—though I'm afraid I only have some Chianti."

"No, thanks," said Rosabelle, placing her hand on her swollen stomach and laughing—"Not for two more months, anyhow."

"How about you, Ornette?"

Absently, Ornette looked at Mary Dee as if he had not heard her. "We got a big, busy summer ahead of us," he said. "It'll take money, though—organizing takes lots of money. But we gotta help Knight raise it—it's our duty."

Both women agreed—Mary Dee eagerly now.

Soon they asked to see some of the paintings she was at work on, and she brought out three. "Wow, girl," said Ornette, looking at a garish green, blue, and yellow hexagonal figure monopolizing the first canvas. "What *is* it?"

"Whatever you like," smiled Mary Dee, unwilling to try to explain.

"Lord, I'd give anything to paint like you," he said, studying the other two pictures now. "I could do so much with it. I wouldn't be painting no big rocks, though, or deserts, or railroad tracks—no indeed. I'd be painting the *black struggle*. We gotta change *you*, girl—your head's messed up." All laughed, Mary Dee nervously, and soon they were seated and making big plans.

First, there would be a party in Mary Dee's studio, at which a committee would be formed to raise money for the Black Peoples Congress. Also, all the artists must be contacted and readied to pitch in and paint the hundreds of signs and placards Knight would need for the big day launching his summer effort—a giant downtown march and rally in June. But equally important, said Ornette, was Mary Dee's "situation"—by which he meant her indoctrination. He and Rosabelle, after the baby came, would take her on what he termed "field trips," into the bowels of the inner city, the ghetto, in order to let her see, first-hand, conditions about which she had only read or heard. There, said Ornette, she would see the rat-infested buildings, the children dirty and hungry, the rip-offs and crime, the filth, disease, and squalor, the plight of human be-

187

ings wretched, half-crazed, and bereft of hope. And yes, he said, from now on her paintings must reflect the conditions she saw—it was an obligation. Ornette's graphic, dramatic, descriptions of what she would see made her recoil inside. Yet, she told herself, she had chosen her course and must not waver, that in opting for her new way of life she had covenanted with herself to be artificial, squeamish, bourgeois, no longer. Again she thought Ornette right—she had obligations now.

The three of them talked for almost two hours, yet Mary Dee wondered where the time had gone, for when Rosabelle and Ornette finally left, the sun was down. But she experienced a strange satisfaction now and felt something crucial to her life had been achieved today. She closed and locked the studio and went up to the house. Her mother was nowhere in sight and Mrs. Grier had gone home. Though Mary Dee was thankful for the solitude, she knew her mother, dinner over, was up sleeping off her "tea." She warmed her own dinner now and sat down in the kitchen to eat. The big house she so dearly loved was silent as a tomb. She recalled other, happier, days and was sad—and soon grim. Life had played tricks on her, she told herself. It could have been so different. Now her very existence, *her essential self*, had been despoiled, she thought in a silent fury. She had not only been insulted, but dishonored, symbolically spat upon, by those racist wretches in Philadelphia. Who were *they*? . . . what license had they to adjudge *her* unworthy?—what credentials, what *right*? Had they considered *her* family?—*her* background? . . . her scholarly, patrician grandmother, for instance, her successful and extravagantly respected father, her refined and beautiful mother, her precocious sister and brother, her own talent and intelligence, some said her rare beauty, her schooling, her culture, her character—her *superiority*? Had they considered any of these? They had not, of course! They had only considered the sheerest accident of the color of her skin. She would never take it lying down—it was so incredibly obscene! How she hated, hated, hated, them!—and irresolute, fainthearted Philip as well. She would get even with them all—*them all*—she would! . . . *she would*! From today it would be her task of devotion! Mary Dee was almost hysterical now, but fought to control herself and hold back the tears. Too distraught, though, to finish her dinner, she dumped the food in the garbage pail and went upstairs and secluded herself in her room. She turned on her FM radio. It was playing Bessie Smith singing the blues, and, for the first time in her life, she listened.

*   *   *   *   *

One morning—four days later—before leaving for work, Mary Dee took in the newspaper off the front porch. Pausing in the foyer, she saw the glaring headline—and below it the man's face. She could only stare—as if paralyzed. It was that face! . . . that troubled, handsome, black face—that never-to-be-forgotten, outraged, Paris, face—that she had so often since seen in her dreams, her nightmares. The shock of recognition weakened her limbs. Eyes almost popping now, she stared long at the page and somehow wanted to cry out—"*No! No! No!* . . ." Said the headline: JOHN CALVIN KNIGHT SHOT!

Her daemon, though now strangely, inexplicably, aged, and hypochondriacal besides, had not yet expired—he spoke to her unhearing ears as if from the parlor, the otherwise silent fireplace. "The prophecy has been fulfilled, my beautiful lamb—and so be it . . . Amen. Now, now, dear, dark-fair one—at last the wheel has come full circle. What did I tell you, my sweet, on that beautiful, mild October afternoon on the *terrasse* at Fouquet's?—the day my message was so lost on both Philip and Raoul. . . . Ah, but not on you. *You*, with your delicate, your fastidious, sensibilities, at once grasped the portent and were shaken by it—not without cause, to be sure. So now it has come to pass—for he may not die, my dear . . . he may *not* die! . . . Pray, then, *pray*—my ravishingly beautiful, wayward, tormented, sweet girl—pray for the extinction of his life and for the preservation of your own! And, alas—think of it!— you have, unwittingly, been eager to enlist in his cause. But now, I exhort you, contemplate it. Your new-found friends do not know this history—that for you Knight is *night*. Yet maybe I, the supreme melodramatist, overdo things. If so, thank me and be glad. But I have now done my deed; as it were, shot my bolt. In the words, however, of lonely Hamlet's spectral father, 'Adieu, adieu, adieu!—remember me. . . .' Yes, dear girl, remember me. . . ."

189

Book II

Chronicle

Chapter 1

Knight, like some reminiscing, palsied dotard, thought back on his life. The tears, tasting like what seemed bitter brine, then came overrunning his trembling mouth, his chest, his gown, as he lay in the hospital bed between cool white sheets, the horrid tubes up his nose, and gave way to a tragic, suffering spirit. The pain, though, came and went; yet in his prostration his emotions had become near unmanageable. The sedation, its effect intermittent though at times assuaging, had, or at least seemed to have, undermined him, creased his brain, raised plaguing questions involving his very existentiality. He was meant—by persons unknown—to have been dead. What had happened? What had he done?—or what had he *not* done? And why was he like he was? Who was he, really? How did he come to be—as a man? What was behind him?—in all the centuries of years? . . . what was his history, the inherited composition of his mind, the fanaticism (psychosis?), the harrowing self-doubts? What was he made of? . . . ha! he thought—what made him think and act? What had brought him where he was here? Yes, yes, *who was he*?—and the millions of others like him. . . .

The sedation again, the euphoria, soon transported him back, deeply, profoundly, into his genealogical—his racial—past. Through the mists of time-space he saw now Tenkamenin, he descended into the Wangara gold mines, he hailed the grand Mansa Musa. It was, despite all, a kind of cherished reverie—this Afric history. Yet at times it would torment him. Though, he thought whenever lucid, it was only because he so often wished to be able to lie on his side in this bed, instead of always on his back, and face the impersonal wall, rather than eternally to have his hot, wet eyes fixed on the ceiling, where at night, the lights gone low into a kind of gloaming, he saw the hordes, the "people," the forebears (his and the ancestors of those for whom today he suffered), the venerable ancients panting from their exertions, faces bearing tribal scars or grotesque masks, bodies ceremonially painted, moving to the psalmody of the village medicine men and musicians whose drums and reed flutes prepared them all for the communal ancestral feasts of the earth goddess Ani, source of all fertility. Then his salt tears, his psalter, would run again and become rivulets on wasted cheeks and infantile, quivering mouth. What was behind him? . . . Who was he? . . . *Why* was he? What was the history, political, racial, psychological, out of which he had come—that had produced him as he was today and yesterday?

During these transports, half-sedated and wild, which the hospital gave rise to, the torment yet would sometimes cease; during these intervals, feebly gasping, parting his teeth, smiling, he would see somewhat more contemporary legends in the redd foxx, moms, dick, slappy, dusty, simple, and other grim but sly-faced jesters who taught brothers and sisters the techniques of the dodge, the laughing escape, then the grim "get-even." But soon trauma, a shivering desperation, would return; would, as it were, come perch on his breast like an Awikam vulture, plucking deep at his heart before suddenly vanishing into what might have been the swift rushing air of some dry Upper Volta harmattan. Yet it was those other, dubious, vexatious, those inevitable, moments he most hated, when of necessity a sort of acquired punctilio made him go Western. His mind, already frustrated and torn, would spin, traverse the one hundred eighty degrees to, say, Camus: "If one believes Homer, Sisyphus was the wisest and most prudent of mortals, but, according to another tradition, he was disposed to practice the profession of highwayman." Knight himself, throughout his consecrated, turbulent career, had also been thus dually accused, and saw, conceded, some truth in the "slander." Yet, yet, what had gone wrong? Why had they so wanted his death? But this was only a token—of something deeply fundamental. Would resort to the roots of history, to chronicles of another time and place, of brooding darker lands and peoples, of sin, rapacity, and greed, of blood, and bleeding—would such resort, to the root and rock of this history, inform? . . . reveal what he was? . . . what he truly was?—and why?

Then later, the hospital bed now slightly elevated, there might come a quite sober, almost deliberate, return to his blackest roots of tradition, to moments of exhilaration, radiance, of euphoria, when, though still flat on his back, he luxuriated in the imagined, fantastic chronicle set in the African bush, the savanna, or in the dark, dense rain forests, though all in due time under an equatorial sun. They were annals that he knew had made him whatever it was he had finally become as a fleshed-out human in this somehow still-new, still-strange, land and hemisphere Columbus had stumbled upon. Here generic, lineal Knights had sojourned now since the far, far earlier times of black diaspora. Ancestors, yes. From the Ivory Coast, from Cape Three Points, the Gold Coast, from Elmina, and old Cape Coast Castle, had come the proud, fierce Fanti and Ashanti, a strange, driven prodigy of a people, who on his now murky hospital ceiling loomed immense, solemn, brooding, marching before, above, him, a people of whom, in the early seventeenth century, an English slaver captain sailing the Spanish Main had said: "They despise punishment but never Death itself, it having often happened that on their being in any ways harshly dealt with, twenty or more have Hang'd themselves at a time—a haughty, ferocious, & Stubborn people, call'd in the Americas, Coromantees, and, more often than not, leaders of the most barbarous, troublous Slave Mutinies, thirty-three of them, newly imported, having murdered no less than nineteen Whites in the space of an hour. Yet, not unlike ourselves, an exceeding brainy people, but unmitigated in their mean, fractious, and piteous ways, terrible in their visions, and spurning all our endeavors to Christianize them—to show them the true way."

Knight indeed lay tormented. It was the effrontery of this testament, its irony and naivete, the insulting presumption, from a captain of a slaving vessel hauling souls to their perdition and ruin, that so dismayed, disgusted, him. Yet the core of the torment inhered in one pressing question: If the Coromantees were brainy, if they were bloodthirsty, moreover suicidal, why then were they slaves? This was his heavy burden and he carried it with him eternally. His vulture, that beast-bird, pertinacious, cruel, though ever hilarious and gloating—tormenting—picked deep at his heart and gave him no rest. What had happened? he grilled himself. On a vaster panorama of events what fate had impended, intruded, triumphed, to produce this grand, this grisly, tragedy? . . . the three and a half centuries of Atlantic slave trade, in the process at home and abroad perhaps forty million dying; brutality, torture, terror, and extinction on a scale so colossal, so near continent-depopulating, as to be unmatched in human history. He pondered these

195

things. Though a .38-caliber slug had coursed through his right lower lung and his liver from the swiftly vanishing car's ambush, he did not want to die before somehow trying, straining, to understand the grand complexities, riddles, the larger whys, of a racial past so steeped, baptized, in disaster and sorrow, in ancestors' blood. Though now, the surgery over, the pain for a time eased, respited, with drugs, he wished for a tiny drink of water, then, his bed once more level, to lie with his face to the wall. Instead, still on his back, he soon slipped dreamily, stuporously, into the fantasies of some imagined long, long-ago; for it was this past that had created him, brought him to this point in an uncertain reality. Fantasies, yes . . . tokens, deeds, vestiges, of ancient Africa, of forebears, black kings, and ghosts, of the Middle Passage, diaspora, death. . . .

*   *   *   *   *

Mozart was to die late that year in Vienna and be borne to an unmarked grave, while, in the New World, George Washington served his first term as president of the new slave-importing nation of freedom zealots. But in Africa . . .

There were four of them on the hot, interminable, July trek—children. There were of course also the many others—the adults and their captors. The three boys were brave but perplexed. Osei, thirteen and the oldest, had injured his right foot in the so-far seventeen days' march from the interior, though even now they were little more than halfway to the seacoast, their intermediate destination. Serious, grave, almost grim, Osei walked behind the girl, Nene, and the other two boys. Bondzie, his half brother, was emaciated and sickly, but Rufai, ten, the youngest of the four and no relation, with a face both impassive and resolute, seemed incapable of tiring. Nene, her gait slow and shuffling, eyes glazed by fatigue, was merely pensive and resigned. It was not her first experience with the bloody havoc and dislocation of tribal wars and now she held the conviction that it was her family's lot to bear this curse of the evil spirits in resignation, though she no longer knew to what parts her family was scattered—a year ago her father and two of her brothers had been taken in battle with the Kodwo tribe, leaving Nene, her mother, and baby brother, behind to be fed and sheltered by neighbors, merciful villagers; and now had come the Odoewu attack and final disaster. As a consequence, Nene, at least for the moment, had far less faith in the priests and medicine men than her father had had; he who thought them effectual, indeed all-powerful; and, even if at times renunciative, fatalistic, she also knew moments of starkest fear, for a future blackly foreboding and unknown.

There were forty-five or more of them in all—men, women, the four children, and the ten or so Odoewu guards or drivers—in the coffle, the captives all taken from the same village before it was sacked and burned and seven of the defenders killed, the calabash drums beating for holidays and baptisms forever stilled. The Odoewu, a fierce, if agrarian, people, who had in no wise abandoned faith in the war-spirits of their dead elders, had then, as was the custom, taken all survivors slaves. Nene's mother and remaining brother had been put in another coffle, contingent, starting out for the seacoast two days ahead, so that now her only friends in this protracted ordeal were Osei, sickly Bondzie, and dauntless little Rufai.

The coffle had been traveling through dense forests, but now its trail widened as it came into miles, days, of mute bush and grasslands. The children unmanacled, walked beside the adults, who in double file were chained to each other by the neck, as the drivers with their heavy muskets walked up and down the column, exchanging crude banter among themselves in a melange of tribal tongues more often than not unintelligible to their prisoners.

"What are they saying?" Nene asked Osei.

Limping on his sore foot, Osei first glanced furtively around at the drivers. "They speak of their king," he said—"that much I understand. They say he is brave and good, and a mighty king, who has twenty-six wives and uncountable cattle and slaves; that if he was not a generous king, we who have been taken would all be dead; that instead we are going on a long, long journey . . . to a new and happy land."

"Are they first taking us to him?" spoke up intrepid little Rufai. "I will ask the king that he let us return to live again in our village—they say he is good."

"No," Osei said gravely, "I do not think they are taking us to

197

him, for by now we have left him far behind. They say we are
going to the big water; that we have never seen it before—to the
great sky of water."

"Oh! . . ." uttered Nene, fearfully, her eyes large. "No, I have
not seen *that*—never."

"Nor have I," Bondzie, weary in his illness, said. "And what
then? . . ."

"The journey, I guess," said Osei, "the long journey across the
sky—across the sky of water."

At this they all bowed their heads and trudged on in silence,
absorbed in their vagaries, uncertainties, their dire misgivings. It
was well into the afternoon and the trail, if wider, had also become more difficult, rough, then dusty—to the extent that later,
as the sun was near to setting, the dust took on a fiery red glow
terrible in its beauty and a smarting irritant to the eyes and throats
of the children. Nene, choking, almost longed to be back in the forests again, though there in the awesome night at the end of a long
day's march she had been fearful of being carried off by some marauding lioness or ingested by a python hanging from a tree. Now,
as the sun went down, the drivers halted the coffle, ordered camp
to be made for the night, and the evening meal of yams and goat
soup to be prepared. Within an hour of their eating, the children
were asleep, curled up and huddled together in the tall grass to
be warm as best they could in the quick-chilling air. As darkness
descended, the drivers, after they too had messed, sat off to themselves around a log fire and tippled palm wine from a gourd, passing it from one to another as, slyly, covertly, they joked in envy of
the delectable wives of their aged and impotent king.

There were also the mosquitoes—it was much later, in the dead
of night, when Nene awoke to the singing in her ear of a huge
mosquito. As she lay scratching the welter of bites on her body,
she could no longer sleep. Scantily clad in her raiment of the tribe,
with only waist beads, her *jigida,* entwined about her for ornament,
she was cold and shivering to the point of hoping for tomorrow,
when, she knew, however, the sun would be high in the heavens before her flesh had expelled all its chill. She thought long of her
strange, calamitous, predicament, unable to fathom it; her future,
a great void, made her fear to let her thoughts go—despite what
Osei had heard the drivers say about the journey to a "new and

happy land." Wherever it was, she did not wish to go there and coveted only a reunion with her kin, a family, however, she felt the spirits, the tribal deities, had not smiled upon. Soon she began to suspect she may have sinned in some way that she was unaware of, that perhaps now she must prepare to appease the powerful spirits who held her fate so precariously in their hands. She saw the big moon rising above the dark jungle horizon and, though her faith had long since been shaken, she wished she might somehow consult the Oracle of her clan for succor, guidance, as was her family's practise when the moon was full over her father's compound and the dancing, raffia-skirted medicine men sent up their fearful chants. But knowing such consultation, with all its required intricate ritual, here impossible, she only lay shivering in the dew-wet grass and hugged her knees for warmth, for strength, and for the ingenuity to invoke the spirits of the past.

Next day on the sweltering march amidst the swarms of tsetse flies and shortly before the coffle stopped for the midday meal, the young driver Yao, his musket slung awkwardly across his shoulder, came alongside her and, smiling brazenly, gave her a rough jostle with his elbow. She sought to elude him, yet, fearful, hastened to smile back at him. Yao, short, squat, bowlegged, and hardly twenty, was nevertheless muscular and strong, his face now drenched with sweat from the broiling sun. But somehow, of all the drivers convoying them, she disliked him least—it was his callow play, the rude sportiveness, which he then at once tried to hide by a fit of wild talk and bluster, that made the difference to her. He grinned at her again now as he spoke: "Hey, how do you do today, little one of the long legs?"

Her response, naive and instant, was to show him her bare arms covered with mosquito welts, then her long legs bearing the same. "The nights are not good, Master," she said urgently, appealingly, to him, "—nor, for that matter, are the days; and always I am tired." Then the thought hit her. "If, Master Yao, I am to finish this dreadful journey, I must gather to me the strength of my ancestors' spirits—I must consult our Oracle. Even my father— ah, if he were here!—would tell you this is so. It is also the same with the others—the young ones here." She gazed around at the three boys walking behind her. "We must be allowed to call upon the spirits of our past—they are still alive. Already Bondzie is sick,

199

and Osei is lame. Only little Rufai is strong among us. We need to pacify, to placate, the spirits—maybe by chanting, praying, by dancing in the moonlight as our witch doctors would do if they were here; all will be in homage to our Oracle, who will then cast these evil spirits out. It must be arranged—you must help us, Master." She watched him with burning, innocent eyes.

Yao seemed surprised, then very uneasy; at last shocked. "You speak dangerous words," he warned. "There can be no rites, nothing . . . nothing, of that kind—it is not permitted. You would be killed for a witch. So would I—for treason in wartime against my clan."

"Help us, help us!" Nene cried. "We are far from our village and people—we have no medicine men."

"Shhh! Quiet—stop it! . . ." said Yao in a fierce whisper. He had turned around to see another of the drivers—brutal, suspicious Mogho—overtaking them. Farther back, Mogho's distant relative, the squinting albino Karfa, head driver in charge of the coffle, followed the column. "It is Mogho coming! . . . lieutenant to Karfa!" said fearful Yao.

Nene in her fright dared not look. When the giant Mogho, his eyes bloodshot and treacherous, reached them, he stared directly at Nene. "What were you saying?" he demanded—"Why do you cry out? What do you want?" Her heart raced as she gazed at the ground and was silent. Mogho, frowning, now turned to Yao. "What is her complaint?"

Yao laughed nervously. "It is soon time to eat," he said—"She is hungry."

"You do not speak the truth!" shouted Mogho. "I also saw her show her arms to you—then her legs. What was she saying? Boy, do not joke with me."

Yao, afraid, relented. "Each night the mosquitoes come to her—they bite her. She wants to perform rites—petition her Oracle. I told her this was not permitted."

"Oracle! What have mosquitoes to do with an Oracle?" Mogho spun around again to Nene. "Do you think us frogs and fools? Say truthfully what you want of your Oracle."

Nene only looked at the ground.

"One consults his Oracle on matters of life and death!" shouted Mogho, "—not on such trifles as food and mosquitoes. Is it that you wish us, now your masters, dead? You wish, I think, to invoke your evil spirits against us—then, when in the bush we lie dead, to escape. Is that so?"

"No, no!" said Nene, but alarmed and indecisive, then at once lapsing into silence again.

Mogho turned on Yao. "Why did you not report this, you young dog?" He wheeled and looked back toward the rear of the coffle where his kinsman, Karfa, marched. "Instead, you try to protect her—while she would bring the evil spirits of our enemies down on our heads and destroy us." At once he started to the rear to report to the albino.

Osei, Bondzie, and Rufai, all of whom had seen and heard it all, marched on in silence, though Rufai, rebellion suffusing his childish face, turned and glowered after Mogho; a few of the coffle's adults, all manacled, did the same. Yao looked worried. At last he brought his musket off his shoulder and, glancing back warily, carried it, ready, in his right hand. Nene, still rigid with fear, regretted ever talking to him.

But, for the moment, nothing happened—though Mogho in the rear could be seen waving his left arm and stamping his musket butt on the ground as he exhorted Karfa to do something. Karfa, however, who bore only a sheathed machete, and looked perennially dour and downcast, seemed impassive, unmoved. Mogho at last returned up the column and, in sullen silence, marched with Yao alongside the children. Nene was even more fearful now that no words passed among any of them and that some seemingly mortal, bodeful, suspense weighted the air. Why, she asked herself, had her mention of the Oracle caused such a to-do? She had not wished —despite Mogho's charge—anyone's death, though, she knew, escape might well entail, indeed necessitate it; there could be no question, she thought—it was deliverance she wanted and she still believed only her Oracle could bring it about. It made her think of the past, her family, memories now sweet. Ahmadu, her father, had been a prosperous and respected herdsman in their village, holding two titles from the clan, as he tapped and drank his palm wine, farmed a modest but rich piece of land, and, with his five slaves, tended a herd each of goats and cattle. His compound, comprising his own dwelling, called his *obi,* and a hut for each of his three wives and their children, was kept orderly and in good repair.

His slaves, except for customarily living a short distance apart from himself, were treated as members of the family, and when ill were brought to live in his own *obi* until Ahmadu's strong herb concoctions had restored them to health.

Nene's mother, Abena, at this time still young-looking though in age and length of marriage the middle of the three wives, was of Dahoman stock, of Ewe-speaking people, and known for her stately height, poise, and beauty—Nene, even if then only eleven, had often been told she could pass for her mother's youngest sister. Even now it made her proud to think of this. One evening her father, smiling as he observed mother and daughter together, said the gift to him of Abena had been greater than the gift to man of fire. Ahmadu then, as was too often his habit, began telling one of his long, tedious tales, this time a tribal myth handed down through generations, of "How Man Stole Fire From the Lion," as Nene and Abena, though inwardly smiling, listened attentively, respectfully. Nene remembered these times. Happiness had been taken for granted—for example, the beautiful, starlit nights, the moon rising above the dark, solid rim of trees, when the three wives, their children around them, would sit outside her father's *obi* listening to the billion insect night noises coming out of the forest, with never a thought of soon-approaching disaster. She could never forget; now she yearned for the spirits embodied in the all-wise Oracle of her clan, or some effective substitute, to reverse her fortunes, as well as those of her tribespeople in the coffle with her.

Later as the column was about to stop for the midday meal, she, unthinkingly, reached inside her tunic, above her budding breasts, and fingered a small wood carving, a charm, hanging from a leather thong around her neck. It was a black tortoise, small and hard, its red eyes bulging, tiny cracks carved in its shell, and the protruding head painted a muddy gold. It was her father's, Ahmadu's, personal god, his *chi,* and known to intercede for him with the Supreme Being itself—with Chukwu, the all-wise. Ahmadu, just before being taken away, had given it to her, he said, for her protection—though with a pointed admonition—as he was being hustled off after the tribe had lost the war with the Kodwo clan. Though she had worn it ever since, she had scarcely thought of the grim, ugly little object till now. Could it in any way be significant, of help? She was full of doubts. Yet she grew stealthy now as she fondled it, turned it over in her fingers again and again, pressed it against her breast, and squeezed it in desperate hope. Then suddenly she remembered—Ahmadu's admonition.

"It is like the masks of our clan," he had told her as he gave her the charm. She had been puzzled at first. "Like our masks, it is not for the women," he insisted, warned. "Have your brother when he is older, or some other male of the tribe, use it in your behalf. Only then will it serve, will it protect you. You are a woman, and, as such, must eschew it as you would the *egwugwu's* masks."

She knew what this meant. She remembered those scary objects. The great grotesque tribal masks of the village were used by the elders in ceremonies requiring they impersonate their ancestors' spirits. The masks' powers were so great that women must at all costs be protected from them. They were powers reserved for the males' use against evil spirits to prevent further individual or tribal mishap. Nene's thoughts came fast; she knew what she must do.

The sun was high in the sky now. The coffle, still in the bush, at last stopped for the midday meal. The four children sat eating together. Nene knew she must rid herself of the tortoise by turning it over to one of the boys to use as Ahmadu had said. She pondered which boy it should be. Osei? . . . he was oldest, and, though temporarily lame, the most experienced. Bondzie? . . . No. True, Bondzie was shrewd, intelligent, but carping, caviling, and weak from his sickness. And brave little Rufai? . . . he was too young, really only a child. Yet she remembered Rufai's uncle with whom the boy had lived. He was Okolo, the medicine man—who, despite his occult powers, had been captured and sent off in the first contingent by the conquering Odoewu along with the others. With Okolo, Rufai had lived in the very midst of witchcraft, surrounded by all the paraphernalia of magic, the wildly-colored tribal masks, made of ivory as well as wood and bark, with raffia or bast strips for ornamentation and fish bones for the horrid teeth, amidst all manner of sorcery and legerdemain, of charms, talismans, amulets, and fetishes. Moreover, thought Nene, Rufai—even if but in his tender years—knew no fear. Her decision was thus unqualified. Rufai would receive the tortoise, their fearful sign of salvation, for he would know what to do.

Now, as they ate, she stealthily took the charm from her neck and gave it to Rufai. Though his face was a great question mark, he said nothing as she pressed the tortoise in his hand. "Wear this, Rufai," she said. "It is my father's *chi*. You are young but you are a male of the tribe who has learned from your uncle, Okolo, much about our rites. Use this talisman to bring ruination to our enemies who hold us slaves. Speak through this *chi* to Chukwu himself!" Little Rufai, serious of mien, at once put the thong around his neck, letting the tortoise dangle, hidden, inside his garment to his navel. Osei and Bondzie looked on in awe. But from somewhat afar, both resting against the trunk of a tree, cruel Mogho and the albino Karfa did the same—watched. Within thirty minutes, however, the coffle was on the move again.

By evening the charm seemed to have had a strange, mesmeric, effect on Rufai. Merely touching it as he walked made him bold and talkative. And as they made camp that night, he spoke repeatedly of his uncle who he said was by now doubtless an ancestral spirit and entitled to their most reverent respect. He described Okolo in minutest terms, though they all remembered him well—even the adults in the coffle, overhearing his fervent, childish recitations, nodded in agreement. This further emboldened him—and raised Nene's fears. When she tried to cool, quiet, him, he told her the black-white art of necromancy, the conjuring up of the spirits of the elders, was upon him and that he would not be stilled. His eyes were alight as he took the tortoise talisman from his bosom, bit it—tentatively, as if testing with his teeth the genuineness of a coin—and reminded her of her charge to him. "Okolo will not leave us to thirst and die in the chains of our enemies," he said, gripping the charm. Then all at once he stopped, as if a chill wind had blown against them. Darkness had come now and suddenly, for the first time—it was so unlike his true nature—he sat cringing as though under some hovering, umbrageous premonition. Through the light of the campfires he had seen Mogho and Karfa—still watching. Later, in the middle of the night, he was jerked from where he slept, dragged struggling into the bush, and butchered with a machete, his decapitated body left for the jackals and vultures.

*   *   *   *   *

The early yet smoldering African sun, as it rose out of the sea showering filaments of crimson gold over the water, lifted finally above a laceband of fleece, of clouds, and was free at last upon its own horizon. The day would be hot. Serious on finishing business early, the human traffic—a few white men and the natives— was already astir. The slave pens in the stockade, the barracoon, were still allowed their quiet. But, as always, the stink was rife —despite his score of years in the trade, John Mace, the factor here, yet could not abide it; to him it was the most peculiar, abominable, of stenches. Indeed, in general, no white man, certainly no American, in all the eclipsed dark continent stayed more constantly miserable from the filth and squalor—as well as from most other things —than Factor Mace. He felt his life, especially his health, entirely ruined. His emaciated body seemed to prove it. Originally from one of Rhode Island's respectable-enough families, he had invested inheritances in various slaving ventures until losses suffered while he dandied at home forced him to sea as a factor, a broker, bartering souls himself. Finally, after tours of duty in several slave-trading ports along the West African coast, the Gulf of Guinea, the last at Elmina, his fortunes progressively worsening, he had, unceasing in his El Doradoan quests, moved on now, somewhat up-shore—here to old Cape Coast Castle. He was of course older now too, fifty-one, with his thin, hawkish face, like the blade of an ax, splotched and red from drink and his former lank straw hair, never attractive, turned an ugly, mousy grey. Life had been baffling to him, burdensome, sad.

People were up and about early this morning, and native women, some with filled baskets and other impedimenta easily balanced on their heads, moved along the ancient, rock-and-sand-strewn roadway leading up from the sea to the old fortress. The fortress dominated the surrounding ignoble thatched buildings and huts where the factor maintained his shack of an office at one end of the stockade-barracoon. The office was called the "factory." As the factor was about to enter his office hutment, he paused to look out into the gulf, far beyond the shallows, where the slaver *Charleston Caper* lay at anchor awaiting, as it had now for over a month, its full com-

205

plement of black cargo—slaves. Matters were slow. Was the interior drying up? he wondered, though he knew of course it was
not. Then just as he was about to turn again to go in the door, he
saw, up beyond the stark barracoons, the bedraggled coffle slowly
approaching, its forward members emerging from a stand of man-
grove trees athwart the sandy knoll not more than a hundred yards
from where he stood. Some members of the coffle seemed to hesitate, then, frightened, to balk, at the sight of the water. At once
Mace's stare was eager, intense, his hatchet face flushed and expectant. How many were there?—it was his only thought—how
many? He knew the *Caper's* captain required at least a hundred
and twenty more chattels purchased before he would load and sail.
Now, as more of the coffle appeared, he began counting, but soon
stopped when the column was fully in view and he saw how few
there were—hardly forty, including many guards.

They had apparently marched all night—as if Karfa feared any
ship in port might sail before his arrival—for it was obvious the
drivers, as well as their captives, were footsore and exhausted,
though had they only known, they could, en route, have taken another fortnight. But suddenly the slaves had shown a strange im-
mobilizing terror. Some had stopped in their tracks, and only
Mogho's threats could move their splayed, aching feet again. It was
the sea. They were aghast, and quailed at the sight of it. None had
ever seen the sea before, nor even thought or heard of its possibility prior to the march; now they were petrified before the immense spectacle and the great, distant sounds of the surf and the
churning waves; they thought it was the roaring of some great beast
which possessed the power of their destruction; and the further
thought that they were soon to embark on a journey across the
frightful phenomenon rendered them terror-stricken. Also, there
was what remained of the hapless children—constantly harrassed
by Mogho. Bondzie, no longer able to walk, lay pitifully curled on
a litter carried by members of the coffle, while, despite Mogho,
Nene and Osei lagged wearily near the column's rear. Nene, after
days and nights of hysterical, remorseful, wailing over Rufai's fate,
was at last merely numb, inert, stuporous from fatigue and the experiences of the journey—though now she stared in fearful awe at
the sea. Rufai's murder for the attempt at fetishism against his

Odoewu captors had precipitated a sudden frenzied, though hopeless, uprising among the manacled slaves, resulting in death, by shooting, for three of them. Yao, the young driver, was also shot—executed by the albino Karfa for dereliction of duty and disloyalty. Karfa, egged on by Mogho, had put down the rebellion with a bloody hand.

The factor did not enter his hutment; he was too otherwise taken now—magnetized. And he wondered what people, what tribe, it was the captors represented—what victorious clan. Would he, from all the numerous and proliferating dialects extant, be able to understand their tribal tongue, to say nothing of making himself understood, in the coming parleys? He was not certain of this as he scanned the coffle formation for sight, or semblance, of its leader. Mogho, suddenly coming to the front, seemed, now on arriving at their destination and despite a bone-weary fatigue, to have regained some show of his former brute force and marched audaciously, head high, nostrils flaring, musket shouldered, as he sensed important events, negotiations, impending. The factor saw him and, all indecision behind now, nominated him leader.

Factor John Mace somehow harbored a grudging veneration for leadership, no matter the identity of the leader flaunting it, for his own life, long drifting and rudderless, had become a trial for him which in periods of depression he ministered to with prodigious quantities of brandy and rum, almost always followed then by consortium with some native woman. His morbid disability was in a way derived from his vocation, if mysteriously, tenuously, so—in the early days, slaving had, at least on occasion, nudged, if not disturbed, in him some vague moral quickenings which had been, originally, instilled by a pious Quaker mother. Those days, however, were of short duration. By thirty he had lost a wife—in a final, shrewish revulsion for his profession she had fled and taken his children with her—and had also lost some thousands of dollars, both, one as directly as the other, due to the "peculiar institution," the "trade," the curse. Now he had degenerated into a mere factor—and besides for some random absentee entrepreneur fattening in New York or Richmond or London or Amsterdam—buying hapless, bewildered, herded blacks and holding them in a "factory," a barracoon, until some Portuguese, British, Dutch, or

American slaver hove into port and bought and sailed off with their cargoes to a distant, chained and brutal bondage in Hispaniola, or Brazil, or South Carolina.

But at once now Mace left and went out to meet, to intercept, the straggling coffle. Mogho saw him coming and hesitated, then turned to signal Karfa in the rear. Karfa fiercely motioned him on. At this the factor paused, then waited. He saw he had been wrong—the morose albino, wearing a murderous, though sheathed, machete and guarding the coffle's tail, was leader. In all the years of his African sojourn, Mace had seen only one other albino—once, a Bantu child. Yet now as the coffle got nearer he marveled at Karfa's freckled, stark, pink-white skin; also the flattened nose, the thick lips, the blond kinky grapes of hair, and, upon exposure to sunlight, the squint of pained, vulnerable, pink eyes. Now Karfa hurried up to join Mogho at the head of the coffle, and at once those two were in earnest conference. The factor patiently—indeed, in an outward sense, respectfully—waited; and when they had fully approached him, he took particular note of Karfa's strong voice of authority in halting the column. Manacled, dusty, weary, frightened, confused, the men and women of the coffle stood still, many trembling as they kept their eyes away from the churning, noisy sea. The factor smiled broadly now, showing broken, decayed teeth, and greeted Karfa in Ewe: "In the earliness of this fine morning I hail, address, you, friend and doubtless minister to your king." Then, seeming to implement the words, he let an arm swing wide and low to do for a momentary bow.

Karfa, involuntarily frowning, shielded his eyes from the sun. He spoke no Ewe but, guessing he heard some ludicrous, and guileful, form of salutation, glanced forlornly at Mogho—who had not understood either.

Mace tried three other dialects he fairly well knew—Djerma, Hausa, and Twi—and Mogho, this time, caught at least the reference to the king and translated as much for Karfa. It only left Karfa noncommittal; instead, still shielding his eyes, he peered far out into the bay at the *Charleston Caper* riding at anchor and knew he had arrived in time.

"Your leader—what is he called?" the factor, nodding toward Karfa, said to Mogho. "His name?"

Mogho understood nothing now, but, resourcefully enough, looked down the column for an interpreter, a "linguister." He summoned perhaps the most emaciated prisoner of them all—a small, balding man, his manner half-mournful, half-defiant—but one with whom he had apparently had dealings on the march before. "You, you, of little hair!" cried Mogho—"Come here! Tell us what is said." The summoned one finally stepped forward, but too slowly, too glumly, for the blinking Karfa, who suddenly came out of nowhere and, not a large man himself, struck the captive hard across the mouth with the back of his hand, then put the hand menacingly on the hilt of his sheathed machete. The shriveled little man, now terrified, began translating at once. "He wishes to know your name," he said to Karfa. ". . . Shall I give it?" Karfa gave him a malevolent nod.

The factor now became voluble, and, through the prisoner, said to Karfa: "I have a storehouse full of many valuable objects and things that will please your king no end. I have bolts of the most favored and beauteous cloth of many colors, hogsheads of the finest and most pleasure-giving distilled spirits; also pipes, tobacco, cutlasses, gunpowder, ball and flint for muskets, plus bags upon bags of cowries. I warrant you will be treated well by me and those I represent." Mace then let his covetous eyes pass back over the coffle. "How many do you have here?" he said.

"Thirty-one." Karfa spoke bluntly through the linguister and turned his eyes from the sun.

"Some are children," smiled the factor.

"Only three," Karfa retorted.

"How many women?"

"Five."

"Along the way, did you see other parties coming?" inquired Mace. "Will there be others soon?"

"I saw no parties. So I cannot say." Karfa seemed impatient, displeased, at the factor's procedures. He also seemed fatigued enough to fall. "We want to eat and sleep now," he said. "We will palaver later regarding what my king requires." Turning his back on Mace, he contemplated the wide barracoon area, sandy, pebblestrewn, down before him.

"Very well," smiled Mace—"Bring them on and follow me." He

soon led the coffle down to the storehouses, barracoon, and slave pens, where armed guards, recruited natives of the environs, already awaited them. This rough constabulary separated—cruelly pried apart—Nene from Osei and Bondzie and sent her, with the coffle's five adult women, into a stinking pen harboring some thirty other women and girls. Nene fell on the ground and began wailing again.

*   *   *   *   *

By four o'clock that afternoon, Karfa and Mogho, now well enough slept and fed in the shack provided by the factor, were drunk on his cheapest brandy. The same was the case with the seven other drivers, though they had instead been plied with an even cheaper rum. Karfa, however, was not so drunk as to accede to the factor's cunning invitation to parley yet that day. He knew the perils, for it was not his first experience with a trader armed with a keg of brandy. Karfa had brought people out to the coast many times before—some of them not taken in war either, but snatched from the bush or from the outskirts of some village, singly, or in pairs or threes—though he had brought none yet here to Cape Coast Castle.

But it was never a pleasant experience for him, for he hated dealing with white men. The feeling was not the result of any squeamish moral compunctions over their being in his homeland, or the base reasons for their presence, but solely because of the way they looked, the execrable color of their skin—its whiteness; he considered white skin one of the world's marvels, and an evil, abominable, one at that, which neither he nor anyone he knew had ever been able to fathom. His own whiteness was the salient fact of his life, and the mystifying phenomenon for which he hated himself; mystifying because his mother, he knew, living all her life deep in the jungle interior, had never so much as even seen a white man. He could only attribute his misfortune, this personal calamity, to the malediction of some evil priest, witch doctor, or medicine man who, he suspected, had been in league at one time or another with some powerful spirits, enemies of his family. Accordingly, in his own behalf, he had caused numerous purification, exorcism, rites to be performed, invoking the fullest panoply of witchcraft and magic his tribal elders practised—all to no avail; everything failed, and he had finally come to realize he must carry this hated incongruous color, this social debility and curse, with him to the grave.

It—the whiteness—had rendered him in every way possible so radically different from his fellow-tribesmen that he well knew it was this that had set him apart as the object of their stares, smiles, the butts of their grisly jokes; the result, he was convinced, had been to make him cunning, murderous, and evil, when he had never wished to be. And in no way to be underestimated was yet another cruel effect he was sure his skin disorder had produced: he had no wives, not even one; this despite his reputation as a tribes-man of intelligence, of many skills, industry, of bravery both as a hunter and warrior, and a capacity to lead that was familiar to all his clan; yet no respectable girl's family would consent for her to become his wife. It was a sad, shameful, situation—especially, he reflected, when everyone knew that, unlike many men of the clan, he could easily have afforded three or four wives.

He felt his condition at last had brought him rejection on every hand, embittered his life, and caused him, more than once, to kill. And now, surpassing everything, he had come to be known, and feared, as the most ruthless of slave catchers. There was justifica-tion for the reputation, he knew; he had brought many a coffle from deep in the interior out to the white man on the coast, some of the experiences of brutal and infamous notoriety, captives sometimes attempting suicide by eating a noxious clay, only to be severely beaten for it when induced vomiting had brought failure of their plan; another time the coffle had been attacked by a gigantic swarm of bees and a woman captive so badly stung she had been aban-doned to die or while yet alive to be eaten by roving lions; often too a coffle, its members carrying heavy loads of corn or ivory, had to ford a river teeming with crocodiles, or wade through swamps in-fested with deadly, venomous snakes or surrounded by areas in-habited by many other species of marauding beasts. Karfa had lived through it all, had done whatever most profited himself and his king. In exchange for his captives he had accepted kegs of rum, bulging bags of cowrie shells (the native coins), or, for his king, hundreds of new, cheaply-made muskets; slowly now, though, at intermittent periods, he was coming to realize his moral predicament; that his ancestral spirits were sorely displeased with him and that he had hit bottom. At times it almost frightened him, briefly made him want to repent.

Yet at other times it seemed only to make him worse. That evening in the shack the factor had provided, drunken, stumbling about, having just vomited up brandy and food in a corner of the crude room, he experienced a kind of mad craving for the physical release that only a woman could give. In his rage and frustration he yelled at Mogho to leave, get out, before he killed him. Mogho, his long face displaying both an air of persecution and fear, got his goatskin bag and left. Karfa began walking the floor then still in a murderous mood; from his desire for a woman his groin ached; yet he knew his chances of satisfaction were slight—even the women in the slave pens were heavily guarded. But there were other women in this place! he muttered to himself in his fury—was this not the notorious Cape Coast Castle? But he knew it made little difference—wherever women saw him they were afraid, desperately afraid, of him, and not only because they knew he was capable of killing; there was another reason—his color, his whiteness; he had become prey to a body of folklore, had been proscribed and anathematized by a whole galaxy of evil spirits; it was believed that any child sired by him, at its very birth, brought on its mother a mysterious flux, a putrefaction of the womb, that she would carry to the end of time, even into the spirit world. In extreme situations rape had therefore not been unknown to him. He had resorted to it. Yet this was extremely dangerous, he knew—once caught, or even plausibly accused, one could suffer, at the hands of the victim's kinsmen, a swift and bloody death. That evening in the factor's shack then he had to put the matter of copulation out of his brandy-stuporous mind. He merely drank more and more and brooded over his affliction—his whiteness.

Early next day the critical parleying, the haggling, with the factor over what price each captive should bring began in earnest. First all the men and the two remaining boys of the coffle, Bondzie still on the litter, were brought out of the pens into full daylight and the sight and sound of the sea, all for Mace's purposes, his examinations. The physical inspection of slaves up for sale, plus the sharp bargaining that followed, could be a prolonged and meticulous procedure—so much so that the factor, from somewhere overnight, now produced his own native interpreter, linguister, a grizzled, toothless Yoruban of much gravity, fastidiousness, who wore a "grand baboo," a long, flowing, yellow tunic, and, as he shook hands first with Mogho, then with disdainful Karfa, volunteered his name to be Obiajulu. The factor, noting Karfa's grimaces of contempt, informed him, through Obiajulu, that the step, this change, had been more than necessary, for to have the coffle member they had made use of yesterday involved today in the negotiation of his own sale was, to say the least, unfeasible, unwise; perhaps dangerous.

The factor this morning in other things as well seemed to have adopted a firmer line with Karfa than formerly; this Karfa observed and disliked, though Mace quietly persisted. The factor had had his share of unsatisfactory experiences as a trader-broker and was determined in these parleys to be on guard; he moreover was fully aware of Karfa's extraordinarily keen intelligence and did not trust him to be truthful about the health of his captives; as the price of blacks went up yearly, their physical condition, the hardihood to withstand the horrible rigors of the voyage to the New World, became more and more important, crucial; yet native slave catchers and sellers had become so wily they could not always be depended upon to deal in slaves able to pass a careful inspection; a slave, though made in any number of ingenious ways by his seller to appear sound, might actually be in such poor condition as to drop dead a few hours after the sale. Mace therefore was serious, firm, and meant to be painstaking.

Karfa had already sensed this attitude and taken offense. This deplorable, ugly white man, he thought, impugned his honor; from weeks of close, constant observation he, Karfa, knew, that his captives, except for Bondzie on the litter, were strong and sound, even if presently debilitated from their long journey; he would stand up to this scurvy wretch of a broker whose fetid brandy breath this morning he knew to be more than a match for his own or Mogho's.

The factor, his linguister Obiajulu following, now went over and, to begin the inspection, bent down to Bondzie lying on the litter in the bright sunlight. Bondzie, his eyes large and frightened, lay trembling from his illness—a bleeding flux which had worsened.

Karfa did not move; he recognized the factor's stratagem; he, Karfa, would not consent to palaver about his one sick slave first, he angrily told himself; he would instead at the beginning discuss only the strong ones; if the factor did not like this, did not cooperate, he would break off negotiations with him, wait, and, eliminating this sordid middleman, treat directly with the captain of the waiting vessel. Speaking softly, with a great show of solicitude, interest, the factor now, through Obiajulu, said something to Bondzie which Karfa, though he could understand Obiajulu's dialect, could not make out. Bondzie was listening carefully, though, his eyes going back and forth between the factor and his interpreter. At last the factor, as indeed Karfa had anticipated, had the child, who was groaning in pain now, roll over on his stomach. There they saw on the seat of his loin cloth fresh blood and excrement. The factor turned, smiled, and looked at Karfa. Karfa charged over at once and began yelling, not at Mace but at Obiajulu. "I will not palaver with you! You see that he will die, yet you seek to imply his taint is on the coffle—so that it will go cheap! I am no fool—you insult me and my king! The boy's death has nothing to do with the coffle—you know this!" Bondzie began to whimper, then cry.

"He is not for sale, then?" smiled the factor. "I do not understand your displeasure."

But Karfa was still yelling at Obiajulu. "You cur! . . . I will not palaver with you!" Then, shielding his eyes from the sunlight, he tried to look at Mace, but the sight of the dissolute factor was so distasteful to him that he turned instead and squinted out to sea. Finally, waving an arm in the direction of the slaves, he shouted at Mogho now: "Take them away!—take them back to the pens! I will not palaver!" He turned on his heel and stalked off in the direction of his shack—as the factor, patient, understanding, wily, gave him an indulgent smile and concealed his loathing contempt. Mogho did as he was ordered.

Karfa sulked in his shack most of the day and drank the remainder of the cheap, throat-searing brandy Mace the day before had sent him. There had not been enough of it to make him as drunk as he had formerly been, but enough that Mogho stayed clear of him. In the evening, as canny Karfa had again anticipated, Obiajulu, his yellow tunic ceremoniously flowing, came to him with the factor's invitation to dine. Karfa was hungry and, if gruffly, accepted without the slightest hesitation. But before accompanying the linguister to the factor's hut, he went to his bag hanging on a nail and took out the charm—the little tortoise on the leather thong that he had taken off the child Rufai's body after, his machete dripping blood, he had hacked him to death. He studiously put the charm around his neck, for he had adopted the grim object as his own little god, his *chi,* now, and, as he had done daily, prayed to it that his color might somehow be changed from its present ghastly white to black. He was fully aware that his color—or what he sometimes, though always under great stress and anguish, thought of as his absence of color—had not come directly from his parents or either of them. He knew nothing of genetics, of laws dictating that separate characters were inherited independently of one another, each reproductive cell receiving only one of the pair of alternative factors existing in other body cells, some factors being dominant over others; nothing to the effect that albinism is inherited as a Mendelian recessive character; nothing about throwbacks, nothing . . . yet much about the torturing of the human soul.

The factor, who himself had been drinking all day, greeted him warmly, his mousy lank hair falling over one eye, his face, sharp, hawkish, now a cherry red. Karfa in response grumbled something which Obiajulu could not catch. The factor, though, jaunty, smiling, unsteady, seemed oblivious. Weaving slightly, he led them into one of two coarse rooms in the hut; the room was a small, rectangular, almost hall-like, chamber, its rough wooden walls unadorned save for two lizards staring at them before skittering up higher, up to a ceiling so low it made the room confining. On the table in the middle of the floor stood a jug of rum, pewter cups, and food— spicy soup, a boiled hen, yams, millet cooked in a dark, viscous sauce, and cassava. The factor had invited them to draw up stools and sit at the table, when the preparer of the food, his native concubine, a heavyset, wild-eyed, ebony-hued woman, came in the door through which Karfa and Obiajulu themselves had just entered the room from the outside. Mace and Obiajulu ignored her, but Karfa, lust at once dilating his nostrils, stared at her with wistful covetousness. Suddenly seeing him for the first time, the woman froze—a horrified look on her face. At this, indignant, Karfa turned his back on her. Obiajulu finally said to her: "What is the state of things in the pens, Elizabeth?"

She could hardly take her terrified eyes off Karfa as she answered. "Things are the same—quiet. But the boy is dead and his body thrown in the sea to the sharks. The dogs have eaten his excrement."

"Ah," said the factor, through Obiajulu, to Karfa—"Your sick boy is dead and disposed of. You have no worries now. The others of your coffle looked fit enough—although we shall see tomorrow, if your consent is forthcoming."

But Karfa had reached inside his cloth—the garment which passed under his right armpit and was tied above his left shoulder— and grasped the tortoise charm which hung around his neck. He rubbed it vigorously, then fondled it, as if in sudden great fear. "May the shades of the boy's elders rest his spirit," he whispered to himself—" . . . as I trust someday mine will mine." He turned to the factor. "Out of respect for the young departed's elders," he said, "I will not palaver with you tomorrow."

Mace listened as Obiajulu translated. Then, guilefully, he glanced at his woman, Elizabeth—he had insisted she give up "Anasi" and take this name—and went into a deep study. "Very well, if you wish it," he said to Karfa, then smiled to them all—"Now let us drink. It somewhat eases life." He took up the jug and poured four rums.

Karfa was quiet, subdued, and, at the news of Bondzie's death, had for the moment lost interest in Elizabeth, who now nervously gulped her rum and, setting the pewter cup down, kept her wild eyes far from him. The factor, as he drank becoming more sinister, watched his woman with a strange relish, a bemusement; then, smiling, looked again at Karfa. He clearly had something in mind, though his guest Karfa was pensive now, inscrutable. Yet there was a strange tension in the air. Obiajulu drank almost nothing and with his eyes monitored Karfa constantly, watching him even as they sat down at the table to eat. But Karfa and the factor went on drinking, Karfa silently, Mace with a kind of vicious, manic glee. Karfa's rum, however, soon took his thoughts from Bondzie back to Elizabeth, his gaze covering her and turning into a lewd, wanton stare. She was still plainly frightened, miserable, her flighty eyes darting about the room as if in a frantic appeal to someone for help. Each time she looked the factor's way, Mace ignored her, yet seeming, as he did so, to smile to himself.

Shortly after they had begun eating, the factor said to Karfa:

"We should palaver tomorrow, you know—the boy is dead and already eaten by the sharks; but you and I have much to do." He smiled. "You are not averse to a little dash, are you?"—"dash" being the word in the trade for a bribe and Obiajulu had no need to translate it, for Karfa knew it well.

He looked at the factor. "What *is* your dash?" he asked with a deadly directness.

Mace glanced once at the woman, then back at Karfa. "Well," he said, procrastinating, dallying, tantalizing, "I have much brass wire in the storehouse adjacent, that for neck ornaments would be of great delight to the wives of your king. Also I have bedsheets, for his own royal bamboo bed—ha, but which will elate his wives as well. Ah, but you, what about you, trusted Karfa?—what do we have in our possession that meets *your* fancy?" The factor then glanced again at Elizabeth, who looked as if she had had a sudden seizure.

But, waiting, Karfa had held his eyes on Obiajulu, who seemed slow, reluctant, to translate—as if he thought he furthered an enterprise fraught with great danger. When, though, hesitantly, he translated what the factor had said, Karfa looked away, embarrassed.

"Speak up, Karfa," the factor smiled—"I invite you." He glanced again at his flighty, frightened native woman.

Karfa said nothing; he seemed only to scowl at the pair of lizards coming heedlessly, playfully, toward him down the wall, but almost as if they had felt his glare—which had not been actually directed at them—they spun around and skittered back up to the low ceiling. "The woman does not want me," Karfa finally, simply, said—in sadness.

"He would bring injury to my body!" suddenly blurted Elizabeth, in great excitement, to the factor. "He is white!"

The factor, ignorant of the ominous folklore, was intrigued by this remark. He leaned forward toward his concubine, expecting more. ". . . White?" he finally said. "I myself am white."

Elizabeth seemed stumped by this. She sighed, moved her eyes away from him, and was silent.

"But they are somehow different, factor—the two cases," offered Obiajulu, leaving for the moment his role of linguister. With great care now he brushed a bit of cassava off his flowing yellow tunic. "In one, there is no wish to be white—it entails many complexities. There is a taint."

"It is true!" Elizabeth said.

"Although you are a part of it," said Obiajulu to Mace, "you cannot understand it. The taint is inborn, therefore you yourself do not see it readily. Only those to whom it is unnatural can experience its horror."

The factor's face was slack, uncomprehending.

Karfa rose in a towering dudgeon. "Enough!" he said. "I will go!"

"Oh, no, no," cajoled Mace now. "Do not leave us—it would be unceremonious of you. You are our guest, for whom we have prepared this feast. Afterwards we must talk, perhaps—eh?—far into the night."

Karfa heaved a heavy, troubled sigh, but made no further move to carry out his threat, which Elizabeth appeared agonizingly to regret. When they had finished eating, they withdrew their stools from the table over to the other side of the rectangular room. Elizabeth and Obiajulu refused more rum, but the factor and Karfa continued to drink. The factor was drunk, but Karfa, who had imbibed as much rum as his host, seemed now sad again, in a strange, secretive, melancholy mood of reflection. "The boy Bondzie is dead," he mused aloud. "He will not reach the land beyond the seas that is better, happier—for he is dead."

The factor, his rum cup in his hand, eyed Karfa unsteadily, yet started to reply, then at last said nothing. Instead he drained off the rum, shivered, and for a moment directed a maudlin stare at the blank wall, seeming completely unaware of the others in the room. Then, without warning, he began to cry. The tears coursed down his cheeks onto his stock and shirt as he stared into space. All were surprised. They sat looking on. Finally Elizabeth spoke. "Why do you cry, factor?"

"Yes, why this sorrowful outburst?" said Obiajulu.

The factor now only dove his face in his hands and sobbed.

Karfa, never having seen a grown man cry before, hastily got out his *chi*, the tortoise, and rubbed it vigorously, his eyes wide with apprehension, astonishment.

Soon the factor was beside himself, as if having a fit. "I cry for myself!" he shouted in a drunken, sorrowing rage. "Myself! . . .

and for the family and home I left! I cry for them! . . . I cry for my mother for whom I was such a trial, and who, full of tears, died so many years past! I cry for her! Yes, I cry for my wife, and for my children, all lost to me! I cry for the fortune I once had and which I also lost! I cry for my diseased and disgusting life, that ere long will send me flying into the everlasting fires of the Bottomless Pit where I shall suffer my just reward! *I cry for my soul!*— my dastardly soul!" He stood up, trembling in terror, as if now he actually beheld in the distance the gaping, fiery jaws awaiting his coming. Then he drew back and with all his might hurled his pewter cup at some macabre, grisly vision he seemed to see, the cup clanging up the wall and bringing the pair of lizards catapulting to the floor where they fled into the next room. Meanwhile, Obiajulu, though greatly agitated, yet translating as best he could, stood up and nervously, fastidiously, shook out his tunic.

Karfa, despite the dizzy swirling in his head from the rum, sat stunned, awed.

"Ha! 'Happier land'—eh, Karfa?" cried the factor. "How deluded you are! Rather, the boy Bondzie you mourn is lucky in his death—because he will never reach what you call that 'happier land.' You have been told lies! . . . lies! And you believed them or did not care—your countrymen whom you've brought here with chains around their necks will be taken far, far away, and, if they withstand the horrors of the sea voyage, will be sold again, into a living hell! . . . In this 'happier land' they will die slowly, worked, starved, and flogged to death! Do you hear me?" Mace shouted— "Do you understand what I say?" He wilted then and dropped down on his stool again, his head in his hands.

Karfa, his heart pounding, had almost held his breath as Obiajulu had translated Mace's wild, deranged remarks. He studied the factor intently. "Why do you say these things to me?" he responded at last, still staring, though now uneasily, at the factor. ". . . They are not true."

"They *are* true and you suspect it—I indict you along with myself! . . . We are dogs!—wretches!" Mace, already trembling drunk, took Elizabeth's cup and went and poured himself more rum. "Karfa," he said, "you too will pay for your villainy! You—*you!*— will not escape, either! . . ."

Karfa was visibly upset. "I do not believe your tale," he said weakly—". . . Nor does my king. He would not sell people into the condition you relate." He paused, reflecting. "Who are these people across the waters you speak of?" he asked—"people like yourself?"

Though Obiajulu repeated the question twice, Mace ignored it.

"Your slavery, then, is different from ours," said Karfa, with more confidence now. "We protect our slaves; we do not mistreat them; they live in our compounds and are a part of us. We do not work them to death and seldom beat them. I ask again who are these cruel people across the seas? People like yourself?"

"Yes!" said Mace, and turned his face away.

At once Karfa reached in and took out his *chi* again. He rubbed the little red-eyed tortoise fervently and, once again, prayed to it that his color might be changed. Instead terrible thoughts of his murder of Rufai entered his supplications and he became muddled, desperate, though not penitent; he had killed many and considered it a necessity of life; yet in a moment now he changed and felt this was not true—that killing was not always a necessity; rather, that he was depraved, cursed with evil; that it was because of the color of his skin.

Mace was looking at him now. "What troubles you so, Karfa?" he said—"that you resort to your talisman. I saw you. What do you fear?—or what is it that you yearn so deeply for? Again I fear you deceive yourself. It—the little crocodile, or whatever it is you carry—will not help you. I know—for these many years since abandoning home and a good life I have had a similar problem. I used the Bible, our holy book, as you now use that *chi*, but nothing happened. Nothing has happened, and nothing will happen. What is it you want, though?—what is the object of your yearning?"

Karfa spoke impetuously. "Color—my color! . . . I want it to be like others'. With it as it is now I have only troubles, bad troubles." He became excited then and began beating his breast— "What is it that makes me like I am?" he shouted, causing Elizabeth to quail as he stood up. "It is this whiteness! . . . this damnable whiteness!" As he said it, he savagely pinched and twisted the pink skin of his cheekbone as if he would wrench and tear the flesh away.

The factor shook his head sadly—"No, no, that will not do,"

he said. "Your color—you will have it always. Nor will your talisman help you any more than mine, my Bible, has helped me. We cannot change things, Karfa—I found after awhile I was not like Lazarus. He is one of the most hopeful figures in my holy book—but, unlike him, I learned I could not be restored. I could not be raised from the dead! . . . there was no miracle for me. I am only now as I was then—a poor, miserable, filthy wretch . . . abandoned by God. Ah, no miracles, Karfa—no miracles. . . ." Mace paused and drunkenly tried to think for a moment. "Why is it," he said, "that you do not like your color? Many great men, and conquerors, have, so to speak, 'worn' it. It is my color."

"On me it is a curse!" said Karfa heatedly. Again he reached for his *chi*, but, remembering what Mace had said of its powerlessness, he desisted. "Among my people I am an outcast," he muttered finally with bitterness.

The words seemed somehow to have a strange, sobering, effect on Mace. He appeared to lose some of his floundering unsteadiness as he tried to ponder Karfa's remark. At last he stared fixedly at him. "An outcast?" he said. "We're all outcasts—you are not alone in this. Look at me—I'm cast out of the ranks of men forever. Yet, as I say, I at one time thought that, like Lazarus in olden times, I could be restored. He was, yes, raised from the very dead! . . . ah, imagine it! What a miracle! My holy book tells of it—it is great, so inspiring, just to read of it. Lazarus was the brother of Mary and Martha, good women both, who were friends and followers of our Christian savior, Jesus—you have all, in coming out of the inland to the coast, heard reference made to Him, if only by a few of our hapless, futile missionaries. The Bible tells that Jesus was then on this earth, going about preaching good to the people, exhorting them to live righteously—we are taught that he was the son of God, in heaven, Himself. When Jesus and His immediate followers, who were called disciples, came to this little town near Jerusalem where the two women and their brother, Lazarus, had lived, He was met by Martha in mourning clothes with the news that Lazarus was dead, and with the sad rebuke that had Jesus been there at the time, her brother would not have died. Jesus said to her: 'Thy brother shall rise again.' When they had been joined by Mary and many others, on-lookers, Jesus asked about Lazarus: 'Where have you laid him?' They took him to the grave, which was a cave, its mouth closed by them with a stone. Jesus ordered the stone removed, but Martha, fearful, said Lazarus had been dead four days and that by now his body surely stank. But Jesus insisted and the stone was removed. Whereupon He said in a loud voice: 'Lazarus, come forth!' At once Lazarus, still swathed in his grave clothes, rose and came forth to them, to their great astonishment and joy. And Lazarus later dined with them at a feast for Jesus.

"I would read and reread about this great, this wonderful, miracle about Lazarus," Mace, eyes gleaming, inspired, unsteadily continued, "then pray with all my mind, heart, and soul to be myself so delivered. But it did not happen. I lacked the faith, you see! My sins had been so enormous that, deep down, I could not bring myself to believe they could be expiated—cleansed and purged away. But this faith, you see, was so necessary—absolutely necessary! Without it, nothing could possibly be accomplished. Yet I could not, and cannot, summon it. So my 'raising' will not come about—it cannot! Oh, this is so clear to me! . . . so now I only wait for death. It almost came last year, and because I was suffering such physical pain, I welcomed it—then the much-worse mental pain overcame me and I really longed for death. But it did not come just then. I was meant to be spared—to suffer even more— as, daily, hourly, I do now! So at last life is a burden—a terrible burden! But I shall soon die, and it will be over. It is all because of my sins—the human flesh I have dealt in, the suffering and death I have caused and witnessed. You too, Karfa—you are victim of the same disease; though, confused and fumbling about, you have not yet been brought to see the terrible truth of it. You think it is color, but color is an accident. It is rather the terrifying sins on your record, not your color, that afflict you like a maggoty pox and will at last bring you down! You have no confidence—no faith —in that miserable *chi* of yours, no matter where it came from, your elders or others; like me, try as you will, you cannot muster the faith; it will not come, for your sins are too great. Ah, Karfa, it is too late for us . . . too late." The factor, considering his agitated condition, had spoken at times with some calmness, dignity, at last resignation.

Karfa sat inert. As he learned from Obiajulu what Mace was saying, he seemed crushed, defeated. Obiajulu, however, seemed mentally to have extricated himself from any further involvement with the unpleasant issues discussed and interpreted with the cold efficiency of a robot. But Elizabeth appeared full of compassion for the factor, her anxious eyes seldom leaving his face. Suddenly there came a loud knock on the door. The factor staggered up from his stool at once, frightened out of his wits, and stared wildly around the room. At last he went and took a long, heavy pistol off a shelf and went and opened the door. There he confronted the giant Mogho, who had come for his superior, Karfa. Obiajulu too now stood up. "Yes, he is here," he said in answer to Mogho's inquiry.

Karfa docilely got his goatskin bag and prepared to leave. But as he did so, he observed the factor with a composed, almost stolid, face. "We shall palaver tomorrow," he said—"early. I want to leave this place—your Cape Coast Castle. It is an awful place —I shall never return to it." With that he spat on the floor.

But the factor seemed again to have lost contact with his surroundings—as if in a trance or daze. Saliva formed on his lips as he mumbled incoherently to himself, his eyes off in a maniacal stare, and the pistol hanging limp and pointed to the floor. Obiajulu went and took the pistol from him and returned it to the shelf, as Mace stood writhing now as if beset by demons. Soon tears came to his eyes and his voice grew louder, audible—"Lazarus, come forth!" he cried. *"Lazarus, come forth!"* Then he began sobbing again.

Karfa stalked out, followed by towering Mogho. When they were out into the night, Mogho said: "I found somebody—I found you a woman."

Karfa stopped and glowered. "Woman! Who told you I wanted a woman? I did not. You have a gall. Send her away—where is she?"

"In your shack."

This brought silence. Karfa, nostrils quivering, though extravagantly interested, was determined not to show it. He said nothing. The night was black, yet speckled with stars, as they walked up the gentle incline from the factor's hut—underfoot the soil was the soft loam of the seacoast where there was little foliage; the heavy, dank smell of the Atlantic ocean was in their noses now and its peaceful swell could still be heard some distance inland. Karfa stopped again, this time to urinate, and as he did so gazed up at the star-filled night and yawned, his breath reeking of rum; though he no longer felt so drunk. Such nights as this had always impressed him, filled him with wonder; there seemed some mysterious affinity between them, between himself and this awesome milieu, that permitted him to feel for a moment a fleeting happiness watching these blinking stars that did not make him squint as did the sun. In his rude reverie he started to reach for his tortoise, his *chi*, but again remembered the factor, who had spoken so incomprehensibly of their lack of faith. Karfa understood little of it . . . faith? . . . faith? He turned up his face to the stars; his pink flesh, even the tender, bloodless, kalsomine skin of his nose, absorbed their rays; he felt himself in perfect unison with this blackness of the night, with these cool breezes of the dark, brooding sea at his back. A rare moment came; for an instant he was at perfect peace.

"What put 'woman' in your tough elephant head?" he suddenly scowled at Mogho now—though the idea had never left him.

"When you are unhappy, and mean," complained Mogho, "I know the reason—no woman. You have been mean since you have come to this place. But it is always so—I know."

"Why did you bring her to my shack?"

"Where else, Karfa, was I to stow her while I went for you?"

They walked on, as Karfa's expectations rose. Finally his curiosity overcame him—"Who is she?"

Mogho grinned. "She is female."

"Hummph—and as old as the River Niger."

"She is not old."

Karfa realized Mogho was having fun at his expense and resented the familiarity, vowing to ask him nothing more. They went the rest of the way to his shack in silence, Karfa's eager heart beating faster every moment. What if she had fled? he thought. It would get Mogho a beating, it would. Then, for some strange reason—the female momentarily forgotten—he reached inside his cloth for his tortoise. He did not know why, when suddenly it came to him that he now invoked, entreated, his *chi* to grant him faith, the faith he did not understand, the state of mind the factor had said was so crucial. He rubbed the charm hard, imploringly, as he entered his door, put down the goatskin bag, and groped to

224

light a candle. Then he remembered where he was, and why. Faith was now forgotten.

In the pitch darkness he heard a slumberous, startled movement in the corner. But, still groping, he could not find the candle. Then Mogho, breathing heavily as he stood behind Karfa, found the candle and lit it. There, cowering in the corner, they saw the girl—no, a child!—with long legs and now sleepy eyes. Karfa gasped. It was Nene.

He wheeled on Mogho. "You dog! . . . you lout!—what is this? It is a child! And the witch who, on the march here, tried to call down all the evil spirits of her tribe on us!" Meanwhile, Mogho had stepped back out of range of Karfa's fist. "What do you mean? . . ." cried Karfa—"bringing her here? You big crocodile!"

"I knew, Karfa, you needed a woman."

"Brute! . . . She is a child! *Get out!*" He advanced on Mogho, who again, with a surprised, hurt look, retreated to the door and finally left.

Nene still cowered in the corner. "Master, do not rape me—do not kill me," she pleaded. "Spare me, master."

"Get up!" Karfa said, going to her, standing over her, candle in hand. "How did Mogho get you out of the barracoon to bring you here?"

"He 'dashed' the guards, master—he gave them cowries. I did not want to come. Don't kill me as you did Rufai." Nene then realized what she had said and involuntarily her hand flew to her mouth. She had not moved from the corner.

Strangely, Karfa did not react. He still stood over her, saying nothing. He watched her. At last he went and stuck the lighted candle in its tin holder. The miserable shack now took on a steady, blurred, lurid light, and still stank of his dried vomit. "I am not going to kill you!" he said gruffly—"I am not going to harm you in any way. Stop your pleading."

"Thank you, master—thank you." Yet Nene trembled.

"Get up," Karfa repeated—"Sit on that stool." Nene obeyed. He then took out the *chi* again. At first, in the strangely low, suffused light, Nene did not see it. He took it off his neck now and dangled it before her. Her eyes went large. Then, too afraid to speak, thinking fearfully of little Rufai's fate, she turned and

225

looked away. "I saw you give it to him—to the boy Rufai," said Karfa.

"Do not kill me, master, as you did him!" Nene implored again.

"I have already said I am not going to harm you." Karfa had lowered his voice. It expressed disappointment, dejection. "The *chi* is mine now," he said, "but it is no good. It will do nothing for me—nothing."

"Remember, it is a tortoise, master. It is slow, but very certain, like our people."

Karfa, studying her, seemed puzzled by the statement. He stepped back and sat on the other stool, staring at her. "Do you know how to make it listen to you?" he said—"to respond? It was yours."

"Oh no, master—I do not know. It was my father's. He gave it to me just before his captors, the Kodwo tribe, took him away."

"It was . . . ah, it was your father's . . ." breathed Karfa in wonder. "Did he tell you about it?—about how it was to be entreated? He must have told you." He stared at her in great urgency. "Think, think!—what did he say?"

Nene pondered the question, hard. "He said it could intercede directly with the Supreme Being—with Chukwu himself."

"Ah, *Chukwu*! . . . the All-Wise, the Omnipotent." Karfa almost stood up. "Is it possible? Then it is a very great *chi*."

"It is—yes, master. But not for me, a woman. It is like our ceremonial masks—only for men. My father told me to avoid its use as I would the *egwugwu's* mask. It is for men—as you."

Karfa seemed greatly impressed, encouraged. "Yes, yes!" he said, putting the thong holding the red-eyed little tortoise around his neck again. "You must teach me how to make the best use of it in the way your father admonished you—in time then we shall find how it can be made to hear our pleas, how it can be brought to talk to Chukwu!" His excitement grew. "Together the two of us will solve this tangled riddle. It is a necessity for me." He leaned forward, his rum breath hot, intense. "Do you see?—it is a necessity!"

"I fear, master, I do not know what makes it work—my father said it requires a man."

"*I* am a man!" Not realizing it, Karfa raised his fist on high. "You will help me, do you see?—it was the *chi* of your family, your father. Together we shall pierce the veil of knowledge lead-

226

ing through your *chi* to Chukwu himself. It is beyond all doubt necessary that we do this."

Nene sighed nervously. "You know best, master," she said. Though she had lost but little of her fear, she now quietly folded her hands in her lap as she listened to him.

"Yes, we shall take the matter to Chukwu," he said, now confidently, as if affirming it to himself.

Suddenly Nene asked: "Will I have to go far, far away—across the great, awful water? I shall die."

Karfa paused. He pondered what she had asked, as if he had not before considered it, for her, a possibility. He spoke firmly, resoundingly—"*No.* You shall not go on the great water. You shall stay—I will not sell you. You will help me solve the riddle—you will help me achieve the 'faith.' It is faith, I am told, I should have. Do you know faith?"

"I do not know faith, master—my father did not speak of it."

"Your father—it may be that he can help us, yes. Where is he?"

"I do not know. As I said, he was taken when we were last year overrun by the Kodwo tribe. I fear now he is dead."

"The Kodwo!—Ummph!" Karfa spoke with utter scorn. "A tribe of beastly cowards!—who attack only in numbers five-fold their enemies. We shall go to them and take your father, if he remains."

"It would be idle, master. It has been a year—if not dead, he may have been taken across the great water; taken to a happier land."

" 'Happier land!' That is a lie, child. It is not happier. It is a land of the hardest slavery and death. I have been told this—I believe it is true."

"I do not wish to go there," said Nene—"nor on the great water that makes such a stormy noise."

"You won't. I will hide you until the others are sold; then we shall leave this foul place. You will go live in my tribe with the other children there. The king will not refuse me this."

"Oh, master, will you save Osei, my friend, too? Bondzie is dead and, I hear, thrown into the great water. But I beg you to save Osei and take him with us—please, master!"

Karfa shook his head coldly. "I cannot do it," he said—"I cannot save the boy; he must be sold with the others; it is for the king. But you—you shall stay hidden until we depart."

227

Next day, after six hours of physical inspections and heated palavers, Karfa, except for Nene, sold the coffle to factor Mace, loaded Mogho and the other drivers down with the cowries and various other goods and baubles received from the sale, then began the long trek home. Nene cried the first night out, still thinking of Osei, Bondzie, and brave little Rufai, but for the rest of the journey she seemed absorbed in other things. In time she became composed, inured, not at all unhappy. She began to think of Karfa; how, through his *chi*, she might help him gain access to the great Chukwu. Karfa was in deep trouble over something, she told herself. He was desperate. Was it the evil spirits pursuing him about his deeds, about Rufai and Bondzie? Did he wish to escape the spirits, or did he yearn to atone? Somehow, though, she must try to help him, she thought—hadn't he rescued her? For a time now this became her mission, thoughts of which occupied all her waking hours and, day and night, filled her irresponsible, childish fantasies—before, inevitably, ennui set in.

As for Karfa, he lived with a new, a fanatical, determination to devote his life—and Nene's—to gaining contact with Chukwu in order to throw off the terrible yoke of his color. Safely back in his tribal compound among the Odoewu, where he lived alone, he would sit for hours gazing at himself in a piece of broken mirror, imagining even now that he saw, though vaguely, imperceptibly, changes in the color of his skin. Yes, yes, the white would in time turn black, he told himself—assured, promised, himself. *It would!* Chukwu would grant this, for it was just. Days, weeks, passed. Now he spent most of his time sitting alone in his grass-walled hut. On days when the sun was out strong, he would lean in his doorway and, though it was excruciating to his weak eyes, squint into the shard of mirror reflecting the sun. Yet, though he importuned his *chi* constantly, he could detect no change. Nene, he thought, had not been as useful in strengthening his faith as he had hoped —this strange, crucial faith!—although he felt she had sincerely tried. Otherwise he feared he might have killed her.

Then would come days of despair. He would not eat or leave his hut. The villagers were convinced he was sinking into lunacy and attributed it to the sad curse of color. Yet sometimes on these days he would send for Nene, who came to him now only when sent for. But she was still impotent to help him, he knew, still powerless to redeem the bright promise of the red-eyed tortoise. Children were strange, he thought, but recalled he had never before really known any; four children had started out in the coffle, yet only one, the boy Osei, would sail on the great water. Should he have saved him as Nene had asked? But to what purpose?—everyone was in time expendable, including himself; that was that. During such times Karfa would only gaze into the piece of mirror and leer bitterly at his ghastly pink face. If Nene was present she would sit watching him; the scene charmed her and stirred her childish fantasies of grotesque tribal masks and raffia-skirted medicine men, though she somehow felt not the slightest empathy with Karfa now. He was experiencing his fate, she thought. Day by day, he seemed losing ground, his periods of silent and deep depression ever increasing. Yes, it was his fate, she was sure; though she did not know exactly what it was; she only felt it must soon overtake him. Which it did. One night, his hand grasping the tortoise talisman, he died in his tortured sleep—on his bamboo bed on a white sheet he had brought back in trade from Cape Coast Castle.

Nene now took back her *chi*. Though she felt she would keep it always, she no longer had faith in its efficacy—for woman or man. Yet hadn't she herself been saved?—saved to remain in the homeland? For this, what or who was responsible? Karfa certainly—yet perhaps Karfa was moved to the act by the powerful hand of Chukwu. Nene raised the little black red-eyed fetish over her head and let its thong fall around her neck. She felt secure and at peace with herself, though the earth and her existence on it still baffled her. She would start afresh and maybe learn the great mysteries, she thought, kissing the tortoise. . . . Yes, the great mysteries. . . .

*　　*　　*　　*　　*

Knight rested now. It was five in the morning and the hospital was quiet. Many days and nights had passed and at last he was able to lie on his side, his prescience for the time being freed of the dark chronicles of Africa, his subconscious racial memories for the moment not plaguing him but at rest. Present conscious speculations, practical, mundane, had only to do with stitches—whether or not they would be removed today. The pain, however, at times severe, still came and went; yet he knew now he would live. He would have preferred to rejoice at this prospect of life renewed but lacked the resolve; it was not in him. Now must come the trying period of visitors, who until now had been limited to two—his secretary, Mamie Campbell, and Ferdinand Bailey, the ever-watchful shadow whose total devotion was currently involved with helping the police apprehend the would-be assassins. Busybody little Ferdinand also loved to sit in the hospital, in Knight's well-appointed private room, count the letters, telegrams, and get-well cards, and assure Knight how fantastically more widespread would be the organization's efforts the moment the leader was again ambulatory.

One matter persisted, however, which neither Ferdinand nor Mamie Campbell had yet mustered the courage to broach to Knight. Griselda Graves. She was in town—of all things! Ferdinand and Mamie had exclaimed it to each other. Griselda had "followed the Congress to Chicago," was the way Ferdinand had put it, then insisted he was not at all surprised. Not only was she in town, they had agreed—Mamie conceding—but badgering the office daily to permit her to return to work, at the same time pressing them for reports on the progress of Knight's recovery. He *must* get well, Griselda, appearing harried, distressed, had insisted; she seemed to have acquired a new, an almost frenzied zeal for the work of the organization, and, strangely, professed the aid and preached the precepts of some unheard-of group called Frimbo's band. It was all very confusing to Ferdinand and Mamie, and posed a problem—one they had deferred dealing with until Knight could be safely consulted. They thought, moreover, she seemed to have considerably changed, and not necessarily for the better; she looked strange—"wild," Ferdinand put it—and of all things wore an Afro wig! But Mamie defended her and said it was because she worried about Knight, for whom, as everybody knew, she had unbounded respect, if not outright idolatry. With this latter, certainly, Ferdinand agreed, barely able to suppress his acrid smile. But Mamie then refused to discuss the subject further.

This was during the time Ferdinand was having daily talks with the police officials and investigators. They were a group who intrigued him greatly—it was their methods; they—especially a captain of detectives, one Holabird—seemed far less interested in physical clues, hard data, facts, than in matters as nebulous as Knight's personality, "his approach to life," as one day it was referred to. This was amazing, thought Ferdinand; was this professionalism? "What's he like?" was the utterance Holabird always returned to—"What kind of a guy is he? What are his pastimes? . . . We gather he's something of a zealot, right? . . . although there's nothing wrong with that, given right principles." It would finally gall Ferdinand, though he became adroit at concealing it. Then in the process something else occurred to him, something he had not really considered before: He himself even had never thought deeply about Knight. It surprised him at first to realize it. Had he been too close to Knight to really "see" him? he wondered. Had he taken everything—virtues and vices alike—for granted? He pondered it and was not sure. He only knew he had thought constantly about it at the height of the crisis of these last dramatic, critical, days.

Knight lay in great perturbation of spirit. He saw the sky lighten in the east—the dawn of another day, but bringing to him the same tedium. He had lost much weight, his face was thin, yet though his hands shook, his steady eyes glowed like live coals. He wanted, and needed, more sleep, he knew—perhaps if he tried, if he really relented, he might get as much as three hours before his breakfast came. He would try to lie perfectly still, on his side, clear his mind of everything, and relax—surrender. Sleep might come. It was at least his modest hope. But then almost at once, for the hundredth time, he asked himself: What had happened? What actually had happened? He found himself as much interested in the solution of the shooting for its motives as for the identity and punishment of the perpetrators. That fateful afternoon, at about two-fifteen, he had just parked his car on the street near the new headquarters of the Congress and had gotten out to put a coin in the meter, when the other car, a rather new-looking, dark green Mercury, had driven up behind him and delivered the three handgun shots at close range— one, however, missing—and sped away. Despite the remembered horror of it, the blood, the unspeakable pain, the pitiable surprise, he still found it puzzling. They were blacks, three men, not necessarily youngish, he recalled, but everything else was a blur; it had happened so fast he doubted now if he could identify any of them even should they be brought into the hospital and made to stand beside his bed. It was all baffling like nothing he had ever dreamed of, as well as a profound, almost embarrassing, shock. And of course most baffling of all, yes, the motive. He had enemies, he knew it—he had attacked people in a variety of quarters, at many levels, high and low, black and white, but knew of only a few threatening reactions, and those, he thought, of crackpots. Yet now this. He was plunged into deepest depression again. When he did recover, could he now continue his work? he wondered. Or had this finished him, killed his courage, withered his resolve? He sighed again, realizing these thoughts, these doubts, for days and nights endlessly repetitive, could only prevent sleep. But somehow in due time he did sleep.

That afternoon, Mamie Campbell, after consulting two staff doctors, complimented him on their prognosis—optimistic enough, she said, to be really happy about. He was going to get well and return to the work of the organization, she vowed, beaming, showing a gold-capped tooth. Knight, lying propped in the bed, was only thoughtful, silent. At last, Mamie opened the long-delayed subject. "Guess what," she said, and laughed—"Griselda Graves is in town."

Knight glanced at her sharply, but with what seemed frightened eyes.

"She got in town just a day or two after it happened," Mamie said—"walked in the office that Thursday and said she'd heard it on TV, right after she checked in the hotel. Naturally, she was very upset. Lord, were we all flabbergasted when she showed up! She wanted to come to the hospital right away, but Ferdinand put his foot down. She wants to work in our office again, although she says she's on her own now and will need some kind of salary. Yet she comes in two or three times a week as it is and helps us out, for nothing—she doesn't know anybody in Chicago except us. But we thought we'd better wait till we could talk to you about it."

Knight watched her with his haunted, piercing eyes, then feebly moved a hand on the coverlet and looked away. "Can she still help us?" he finally said.

Mamie felt the burden shift back to herself, but spoke readily. "Sure, she can help us—her work's fantastic. Ferdinand might think differently, though—maybe you ought to check with him. And on salary, he'd know better than I what we could pay her now."

"Tell her she's welcome back," said Knight weakly. "Now, I

232

haven't the strength to talk any more." He looked away again, but soon brought his eyes back to Mamie. "I'm tired," he said. "Does she look well?"

"She looks okay—maybe a little different, though, sort of weird-like. And she's wearing an Afro wig!" Mamie laughed again. "You should see her!"

His eyes stayed on her with what seemed the faintest trace of a smile. "I'm very tired," he said again, but Mamie sensed he was for a moment happy and wanted to be alone. She was glad Ferdinand had not been present—the matter might not have gone so smoothly or turned out so well. What would it all produce? she wondered, though with somehow a sense of misgiving. She dared not give her mind its freedom to speculate.

That night—or was it the next night, or the next, or still the next?—Knight once again found respite, sanctuary, sorrow, in the dark brooding centuries of the past, in the annals of the homeland continent and the seas, in the tragic metaphor of black chronicle. . . .

Chapter 2

"Lay to it, there!" cried Cockle, the first mate, grinning elatedly and sweating last night's rum. "And tomorrow or so it'll be up anchor, won't it? . . . the old heave-ho and away we go!—what, lads?" The four ordinary seamen addressed, also sweating, sunburned, impassive except for one of them who likewise grinned, tugged at the oars of the longboat as the captain sat silent, musing, in the stern sheets and the mate went on exulting. "It's the very tidings we been awaiting to hear!" his rum babbled on, now to the captain—"For sure, Captain, it is! We'll weigh the old graplin with a shout the minute you give us the word and be glad. . . . Home!— no more salt beef for awhile, no more mouldy sea biscuit! I'll see my youngins again, and maybe the wife that was feeling so poorly with the milk sickness when we sailed—God grant she still lives. This is a great day, Captain! Tomorrow we'll beckon the canoes of the Krumen and fill the *Caper's* hold with the black cargo we come so far to fetch! . . . What a cargo!—nearly four hundred negars! I had long despaired we'd ever get the full complement for a ship our size—all two hundred tons of her. I raise my hat to ye, Captain, haggling there with that wily factor, Mace—at your best, you was!"

Captain Timon Stokes of the *Charleston Caper,* clad in knee breeches, silver-buckled shoes, and wearing a periwig topped by a tri-cornered hat, smiled faintly though he was not pleased—he had first smelled the rum on Cockle's breath as they had left the *Caper* to go ashore at sunrise; now, returning at high noon, he marveled at the spirits' obstinacy. At last, impatiently, he threw up a hand and silenced the mate—with the responsibilities of master of a vessel weighing upon him, he personally felt they could ill afford such glee. "Stay, stay, there a minute, Cockle," he said—"We're not home yet. We may well see the banner of the Jolly Roger, or some other fated calamity, before that."

"Ah, you're correct, Captain—I yield. But I'll take the pirate any time, I will, against laying at anchor these many sorry months in this heat-hell of a cape and risking the scurvy."

"Have it your way, Cockle." Stokes finally gave the horizon an imperious glance, then seemed impatient, as if feeling he talked to one with no conception of the demands, the rigors, of command. Yet he too was glad to be ferried back to his ship, with the impending prospect of sailing agitating, exciting, his mind; the complement had indeed been filled at last; there would be by this time tomorrow three hundred ninety-eight blacks—men, women, a few children—in the hold of the *Caper* and the departure for Virginia imminent; it was cause for true gratification.

The sea was calm, greenish-blue, with great gentle swells—the sun blazing. The grizzled sailors pulled steadily at the oars as Timon Stokes now sat again in deep contemplation. It was the beginning for him of another profoundly serious undertaking, an ordeal; it was his fifth slaving voyage in three years, and involved another cargo culled, hopefully, for its physical stamina to withstand, survive, the terrible experience of a slave ship's Atlantic crossing—called, by European-based slavers, the Middle Passage; it was "cargo"—as Stokes always referred to slaves—out of the African Guinea coastal stations to be eventually landed for sale again in the young, burgeoning United States of America. The ordeal, he knew from experience, consisted of a variety of challenges. The cargo was a precious one, its value highly monetary, yet no individual member of it would be spared in face of any peril to the enterprise, the voyage; instant ruthlessness was the watchword. There were also the outside perils. The captain of a slaver was by force of peculiar and hard circumstance required to be something more than a mere master of a merchantman; he was a sea fighter, an armed defender of his ship and cargo, as well; often arrayed against him were both pirates and privateers; in consequence, slavers sailed heavily armed for their runs. Captain Stokes' last voyage save one had been a hazardous winter crossing; moreover, the *Caper,* her hold jammed with blacks, had been attacked and ordered to surrender by a marauding British privateer armed with ten 6-pound guns. Stokes, his own ship armed but inadequately manned, yet refused to strike his colors. The Britishers, determined to seize a valuable slave cargo, attempted now to board the *Caper.* Stokes, his crew outnumbered, had no recourse—though riven with fear—but to bring up and arm with cutlasses the blacks (the Gold Coasters, the Coromantees), who gave an extraordinarily fierce account of themselves. As a consequence the British were repulsed in a bloody fight in which seven men from the two ships—three blacks from the *Caper*—were killed. Then the Atlantic's winter storms hit. The passage to Georgia took seventy-five days.

Nor did this exhaust the list of perils in the trade. There was always the danger of mutiny—by crew or slaves. There was also the constant prospect of the outbreak of epidemic, known in some cases to carry off half the ship's company and "cargo." Stokes now once more pondered the gravity of his imminent undertaking and was irritated by the first mate's raillery; it was the captain's natural mordancy revealing itself; he had never been a high-spirited man, nor really in any other way extraordinary; there was much of the deterministic automaton about him; throughout his life his reactions in almost any situation had been primarily innate, pragmatic; although he would have denied it, purely moral concerns were of little moment to him. Born in backwoods Virginia of poorest stock, he had mostly educated himself while apprenticed to a wheelwright, had then become dissatisfied and gone to sea at nineteen. Now forty-one, he had captained merchant vessels for eight years, the last three on the slaver *Caper*. Blacks to him were only a different, if more difficult, cargo. He took their transportation with the same earnest sobriety and practicality, the same grim conscientiousness, he before had taken with a consignment of cotton bales, Spanish sherry, or cast-iron cooking pots. He recognized few complexities, harbored few doubts, these traits simplifying his life and habits; the world, he believed, consisted of many races and peoples, some human, some subhuman, the former dwelling in western Europe and the new country of his birth, the latter in varying degrees spread in squalor and ignorance over the rest of the globe. Blacks, to him the most abysmal of all, were inert brutes and savages. Yet he took no particular pleasure in their enslavement, bore them no special malice; he only considered their abduction and sale quite a natural and logical circumstance; people who regarded the African a true member of the human species—for instance as did the missionaries —puzzled him, sometimes elicited his quiet mirth; he remembered, as a young seaman, watching an English slaver load its blacks at a coastal station in Sierra Leone; the captain of the vessel was hardly permitted to accomplish the task, in any case a difficult one, for the interference of an English bishop, by chance in the area, who insisted, before the ship sailed, on converting the slaves to Christianity; there then occurred a great convocation, including baptism, at the water's edge—all accompanied by the wholesale hilarity of the observing crews of other ships. To Stokes it had been one of the most ludicrous spectacles of his sea experience. He thought the English anyway a strange people; they lacked the method, hard sense, of Americans; it was probably why America was now a free nation. In other respects, however, he admired the English extravagantly—for their cool, easy, oblivious, sense of supremacy.

As soon as they were back aboard the *Caper,* Stokes took Cockle below for a final inspection of the ship's hold. In this process he carried, and frequently consulted, a large, rough sheet of paper, a chart of available hold space, the chart being more graphic for its use, drawn to scale, of tiny figures, replicas, of prostrate blacks for models; it reproduced the entire layout below, thus showing the most efficient ways of positioning, stowing, packing in, the slaves. The hold, the bottom-most compartment of the ship, afforded five feet of space between its floor and ceiling, the floor consisting of unplaned boards; this five-foot layer of horizontal space had been divided by a shelf extending six feet in toward the center from the sides of the vessel; the result: two layers of space, each two-and-one-half feet high; but on some slavers, of which Stokes had heard, if the original space was as much as six feet high, two shelves instead of one might be constructed, providing now only two feet or less of space between shelves for the stowing of the blacks packed uniformly together on their sides like rows of fetuses. Claustrophobia drove many of them mad.

Indeed the captains in the trade were divided into two schools of thought—called "loose-packers" and "tight packers." It was the theory of the former that giving the slaves slightly more space in which to lie reduced the number who went mad or died during the voyage and was therefore a practice more economically feasible. On the other hand, the latter group were convinced that despite a much higher death rate in transit, the net effect was still a larger cargo landed at the destination because more slaves had been packed into the hold in the first place. And even if, on landing, many of the

237

survivors were weakened, were skeletons, or near death, they could be treated by a surgeon or fattened up with food for a short period before being put on the block at the slave markets. Captain Stokes, however, took no notice of any division of opinion about how slaves should be stowed in the hold; he thought the dispute doctrinaire; conveniently or inconveniently, he merely purchased and brought aboard every black he could find any conceivable space for, sometimes even letting the children run loose and sleep on the upper decks. He felt himself far more humane, for instance, than the Portuguese captains who allotted a man slave a space only six feet long, sixteen inches wide, and two feet high; a woman, a space five feet ten inches long by sixteen inches by twenty; a boy, five feet by fourteen by twenty; a girl, four feet six by twelve by twenty. Stokes would not have countenanced this—it was inefficient.

"Never fear, Captain," said Cockle now. "Three hundred ninety-eight—but we can take 'em all. A little tight, maybe; some'll get ailments and distempers; but we got Whittier, ain't we?—when he's not settin' straddle-legged the rum keg—the best healing surgeon riding the seas. Ye don't doubt me, d'ye, Captain?" But Stokes was engrossed in other thoughts—telling himself that this time he would put the women slaves in the aft-hold, as far from the forecastle above, where the crew lived, as possible; for there was always the problem of crewmen forcing access into where the slave women lay, infecting them with the social diseases so many of the scruffy crew carried, and impairing the women's value come sale time. The men slaves, therefore, would be stowed forward in the hold, thought Stokes, the women aft, and, as usual, the few children given the tiny space between them.

"I've never seen ye in better fettle than today, Captain," Cockle insisted—"as I say, bargaining with that crafty factor, Mace. The merchant people in New Jersey and Virginia ye represent would be proud—Factor Mace met his match, he did. But he's poorly, ain't he? . . . a sick man—pale as death, and retching at both ends. Gads!"

"He's sick, yes." Stokes was matter-of-fact. "He's dissipated too long. Now it's fever and dysentery—probably delirium tremens too. It's the life he's led. He'll be dead in six months. Africa killed him."

Cockle marveled. "D'ye think so, Captain? . . . ah, the dark continent, eh? Many have died, it's true—why are we here?

But again Stokes was not listening. "Have the men ready the wrist and leg irons," he ordered—"There'll be much to do when the cargo comes aboard."

"That there will be, Captain. I saw them Gold Coasters, I did—a mean people. Though there are a hundred or more Whidaw negars, who don't give much trouble, there's another hundred of the Gold Coasters. A troublesome nation, I vow—bad, bad negars."

"Aye," said Stokes, "the Gold Coasters, especially the Coromantees among them, are a dangerous, villainous breed—handmaidens in one way or another in every black mutiny ever reaching my ears. Yet there's only a dozen or so of the Coromantees; we will handle them—but they mustn't be brought up from the hold, even for exercise or air; keep them below, and in both leg and hand irons constantly; chances mustn't be taken—I know captains who, in their careless leniency, seem to forget the havoc, the bloody slaughter, mutinous blacks, mostly Gold Coasters, have wrought in the trade; and the Coromantees despise the Whidaw and other tribes less turbulent, hate them with a more than ample avengement and bitterness—have not a few times forced them into mutiny against their will. Black mutinies have not, as some captains seem foolishly to think, altogether disappeared; this century itself, remember, has seen upwards of a hundred such; whoever in the civilized nations and cities think our trade a pleasant pastime, some sociality or other, voyages of romance, forget history—if they ever knew it. A black is dangerous when he knows the truth. Yet so often—I've never understood it—he insists on turning his face from the truth. A strange trait it is—I've watched it. On the other hand, a black that will force himself to look at truth becomes at once evil and dangerous—he'll have his way or die in a minute, taking many with him; but most times, almost as if abashed, he'll turn away from reality; otherwise these wretches could never be brought out of the bush and forest to be sold on shipboard and carried off like chained beasts into a harsh foreign bondage; they could not be handled; nor would their fellow-countrymen bring them into us as they now do if they knew what lay in store for them across the seas; instead many feel they send them into a better life—ha, like

239

we ourselves are taught that the mirage of heaven awaits us after our earthly deeds, and misdeeds. But blacks—in their almost moralistic fantasies—turn their eyes from the truth, from reality; think of the situation if they, too, had developed gunpowder; it would be different today, I tell you; the slave trade would not end for it would never have begun; but as it is, when they must finally confront the truth, it will be too late. It's want of the truth, Cockle— that's the black man's tragedy."

The first mate listened respectfully, though not wholly impressed. "Ye have real compassion for 'em, I think, Captain," he said, with a wry smile.

"I have no time for that," said Stokes—"for anybody." They ascended from the hold to the poop deck—which was being swabbed by three crewmen—where Stokes looked up at the hot, blue sky. "No matter if the weather augurs fair or heavy," he said, in almost a whispered prayer, "may this time our fortunes on the seas be favorable . . . though we carry a most fearsome cargo— cursed by God from within and without. I am sometimes called harsh, but it's God's harshness, not man's or mine."

"Ah, ye speak so bodefully, Captain," said Cockle, screwing up his face in half-spiteful vexation.

"What crossing, tell me, Cockle, have we so far achieved—with this black cargo—free of the most grievous troubles and privations? Last time it was the fever taking off nigh half the crew before we reached the Bahamas. Time before that attacked by the dastardly English privateer and almost boarded—save for the Gold Coasters that we, in our extremity, armed with cutlasses to help us. What warriors, yes, those Coromantees! Old Captain Brasheres, now long retired in Philadelphia, had a very similar experience some forty years ago on the Spanish Main off Dominica. Again the Gold Coasters it was who saved his ship from Dutch privateers in an all-day fight in which the Captain lost three fingers and much of his nose. He tells it that he would have been wholly dead except for the Coromantees. How he sings their praises!—'Not only the best and most faithful of our slaves,' says he, 'but all born heroes. There was never a rascal or coward in that nation. No man,' that old dotard raved on, 'deserves to own a Coromantee that will not treat him rather as friend than slave.' The Captain, to be sure, o'er speaks himself a bit there—they are also a cunning, villainous, bloodthirsty clan, given to a foolhardiness that makes mockery of our own cool but steady courage—yet no one can truthfully gainsay their fearlessness in battle. But don't forget too that voyage before the encounter with the English; it was the uprising of the crew itself—after that insubordinate dog, Jack Staggers, died of his flogging. That likewise was a bad crossing—that scurvy, mutinous crew would have loosed the blacks in the hold upon us if they hadn't feared being hacked to pieces themselves after the blacks had finished us off. And the voyage before that—you were not yet with me, Cockle, on my first slaver run—it was not only pirates on that luckless trip, but a score of suicidal blacks, both men and women, throwing themselves overboard to the sharks rather than become slaves. I tell you, it's the cargo we carry. It's tainted—blasphemed by God. Now, what will it be this time?"

Cockle flinched and seemed about to throw up a hand to ward off some phantom fist. "Oh, don't ye talk us up on something, now, Captain," he said—"Ah, don't tempt fate's blow."

But Stokes had stridden on ahead. "*I*, called harsh," he said, reflective now, half whispering again, repetitious. "Yet I have always opposed your infernal panyaring." Eyeing Cockle sternly, he was referring to a method of slave-stealing, slave-catching, by marauding whites unaided by native blacks—a practise accounting, during one period, for half the slaves taken off the African continent.

Cockle, grinning, placed a palm on his breast—"*My* panyaring, did you say, Captain? . . . You joke."

"It was you that told it—you were then mate, you said, for Captain Bledsoe on the *Serpentine*. Your whole crew would, on occasion, constitute a raiding party to go catch slaves and bring them back to the ship—if it lacks truth, you told it."

Cockle, thus reminded, relented, recalled. He suddenly laughed —"Aye, aye, and we had no idea at the time what a fearfully dangerous thing it was to do. Nothing—nothing, Captain—makes the black chiefs madder than panyaring. It gets their dander up— oh, how! It's because sometimes it's members of their own families that are caught; or, ha, other leading citizens, maybe. Then there's all hell to pay—look out! We stopped it—once a chief and some of his people caught two of our men and slowly tortured them to death. Aauggh! . . . a nasty business. It's one thing I like about your ship, Captain—no panyaring."

"A degrading practice," said Stokes—"degrading to us. Besides, why should we steal blacks?—rather let them be fetched out to us, so as not to offend the native chiefs. Then too, a panyared black is twice God-cursed and dangerous to have in our hold when encountering heavy seas—a superstition perhaps, but my belief. I will not, knowingly, take one abroad, Cockle. Let us buy our blacks honestly."

"Aye, Captain," laughed Cockle again—"even if with beads, calico, rum, and ornamental brass wire. Ha!—and maybe a few muskets too. Also a little gunpowder to go with 'em. Ah, but again I think not a little about what if they'd learned how to make gunpowder! As you say, it'd be a different story, wouldn't it? But it's too late now—too late."

*   *   *   *   *

Early next day, under heavy clouds and threatening August skies, the ferrying of the slaves out to the *Caper* began as early as seven o'clock. Guarded by armed natives and the *Caper's* crew —most of the natives carried great hippopotamus-hide bull whips besides—the slaves, three hundred ninety-eight in number, were taken from the barracoons and slave pens and herded down to the beach. There they were branded with red-hot irons by three busy crew members—males on the left buttock, females on the chest— and made to stand, painfully writhing and waiting, for the fleet of huge dug-out canoes that would ferry them out to the *Caper*.

Nearly a month in the slave pens had healed Osei's injured foot and he now walked erectly without a trace of his former limp. But, standing in line, his eyes large, watching everything, he was terrified at the coming branding. Also there was the big ship out there and the noisy, frightening sea—both this time closer up. Though they had all seen the sea, heard its roar, for weeks, some for months now, they quailed before it on actually having to confront it, knowing too it was the grand, mysterious, prodigious, watery marvel on

242

which they were soon to travel to the "happier land." A woman cried out as the branding iron, smoking of flesh, burned the legend of the firm of her absentee owner-dealer onto her chest. When Osei's turn came, he fainted dead away, only to be revived by the sharp, searing stamp of the iron on his buttock. Tears welled in his eyes but he did not cry out—though he was followed by a Coromantan boy, called Bymba, who took the brand disdainfully, smirking in contempt at Osei's horrified grimaces.

As the branding proceeded, a dozen or more of the great canoes suddenly appeared, propelled with unbelievable swiftness and dexterity by members of a tribe of fishermen called Krumen. These craft had been concealed behind the sand promontory of a neighboring cove and now, disciplined paddles of the Krumen flashing, darted through the surf and beached near the gathered slaves and their guards. The slaves had already sensed the ominous purpose of the big ship lying at anchor a distance out, but the sudden sight of this swarm of outsize canoes not only startled them but made clear the certainty of their own inpending departure. They could no longer harbor any doubt. They were leaving their homeland. Forgetting completely now what they had heard about going to a "happier land," some of them fell to the ground and began jabbering incoherently to themselves as they lay threshing about in the sand—until jerked to their feet again and threatened with the bull whips of the native guards.

The Coromantan boy, Bymba, about Osei's age of thirteen, stood in the midst of a group of other Gold Coast slaves. They were all muttering to each other as they hostilely eyed the canoes and their Krumen navigators. One of the group, Kano by name, a tall, sloe-eyed native in his thirties with a very slight beard lengthening the point of his chin, spoke with great attentiveness on the part of the others. "I doubt much of what we have been told," he said solemnly in a Fanti dialect—"though no one has returned from where we are to go, so we cannot be sure. But I dreamed in the night that in that far-off place, called *Jong sang doo* ('the land where the slaves are sold'), we shall be slaughtered and eaten by the white men there. I believe it. I have told many others—they all believe it too. Many had heard it even before my dream. Nor do I think it is a happier land—it is far worse." To much nodding of heads, this at once caused great consternation and murmuring among them again, Bymba included. But they were being observed by the guards now, who carried not only muskets and pistols, but, in the case of the men from the crew, cat-o'-nine-tails, and the native guards also their whips. Bymba saw them watching the group and immediately whispered warnings to his elders, who quickly sidled apart. Still the guards moved in, and, whips at the ready, stood glowering menacingly at them all. Yet the man Kano, who had spoken of his dream, turned again to his comrades. "We perhaps go to our deaths," he said, peevishly, impatiently, "and go so meekly—and I a Coromantee! For shame." The guards, luckily, did not understand his dialect.

"We have no choice, Kano, our respected one," said another Coromantee, a small frowning man and former herdsman as well as warrior, named Tippu—"What is there to do?"

"Die!" said Kano at once with flashing eyes—"or go to be eaten."

"Very well, then—we shall be eaten, and by the white man." Tippu, though of fierce aspect, seemed resigned now. "It is perhaps our destiny—but also his fate, which will bring misery to his stomach, manifold, for all time to come. He will regret his terrible, rapacious hunger when his belly aches from our foreign particles. Our ancestors' spirits approve of what I say."

Kano curled his lip in scorn. "I say no—it is unlikely they approve. What of our own kind, who have sold us into this condition? —or who, with arms, hippopotamus whips, and scowls now stand guard over us; or others yonder who will dip the paddles of their great swift canoes to carry us to our downfall and later devouring? What of their stomachs?"

"They have no stomachs—or heads," said Tippu, at last fiercely —"only ignorant and greedy palms with which to receive their worthless baubles, their bolts of cheap cloth, kegs of watered brandy, their bags of cowry shells. Yet history will not speak of them—though it ought."

Now a longboat was seen approaching from the *Charleston Caper*. It was Captain Timon Stokes being rowed by four seamen. He began giving orders the moment the boat touched sand. "Start ferrying those you've branded!" he cried to first mate Cockle who came running across the beach to meet him—"Why do you wait, Cockle?"

"I've already sent for the canoes, Captain—we're nigh ready." Cockle then wheeled and beckoned vigorously for the Krumen tribesman—whose canoes, some of them fifty feet long and requiring ten paddlers, were almost too large for the name. Each carried a captain-coxswain seated astern who gave his paddlers a loud-throated, cadenced beat, as he himself, wielding a deft paddle, steered the craft expertly, still precariously, through the dangerous breakers. Such a canoe and crew could in addition easily carry twenty-five slaves.

The skies were lowering and a wind was rising, hence Stokes' anxious impatience—taking slaves aboard ship in bright, calm weather could be troublesome enough, he knew, but when the seas were running high in a rain squall, it could be a hazardous operation indeed. Again it was the economics of the undertaking—the possible loss of just-paid-for slaves—that made it critical; for if in trying to run the tricky breakers, made more so by turbulent seas besides, the Krumen steersman allowed, even for an instant, the canoe to turn broadside to the surf, both crew and slaves at once were lost—drowned, or eaten by the sharks. Stokes' responsibilities were considerable and they worried, anguished, him.

Osei, his left buttock paining, burning, from the branding iron, stood in the midst of the throng of slaves on the beach and watched with awe the quickening pace of preparatory action. Now he saw Bymba, again in agitated talk with the adults of his tribe; he secretly admired, envied, him for his rash bravery, also for his inclusion in the discussions of his elders—something unheard of in his own upper Volta River tribe. He somehow wanted to get nearer Bymba, seek him out as a friend, for he sensed his innate strength. Soon now he found himself edging his way over to the Gold Coast group, arriving just in time to hear the man Kano, his eyes again flashing fire, say to his fellow tribesmen: "The spirits of our fathers and their fathers have deserted us! . . . Our time has come."

Already the guards, yelling threats and loudly cracking their whips, were segregating the branded from the unbranded. It was a scene of great disorder and confusion—except for Captain Stokes who, cool, grim, impervious, stood apart and watched. Now those in the first group of the branded were—according to their degree of resistance—being pushed, dragged, beaten, some even carried struggling, down to the canoes. Stokes still coldly watched. Three berserk women were running about and wailing, one falling to the ground on her stomach, arms outstretched, clutching great handfuls of sand in her terrified desperation at leaving Mother Africa. But the Gold Coasters moved out solemnly in a body—meekly, unobtrusively, followed by Osei—and on reaching the water's edge they tried as best they could to get in canoes carrying mainly their own tribe; those unsuccessful, however, were angered to the brink of violence and sat in the canoe they were obliged to take in a murderous sulk. Stokes looked on, icily bemused; though he studied the scene, he seemed no part of it; he felt no part of it; except possibly for the Gold Coasters, he felt only contempt for the blacks.

He thought eventually of his father, long since dead, whom in this regard he considered having been woefully misguided. Jubel Stokes was an impoverished Virginia farmer and preacher, fierce in his beliefs and intemperate in his sermons, especially in his revival jeremiads against slavery. His motives originally, however, were not unmixed; the true object of his wrath had been the landed gentry, the planters, who incidentally, because they could afford it, happened to own the bulk of Virginia's slaves. Jubel hated the aristocrats' wealth, elegant manners, their smug behavior—their loathing of the white poor. His attacks at first therefore were out of no compassion for blacks. Then in his older age, having now read numerous publications of the early abolitionists, and accomplished a lifetime of sedulous Bible reading, he changed—as though at long last he had begun to descry certain moral implications, complexities, in the ownership of human beings. Soon his sermons became philippics, almost exclusively anti-slavery, and violent as well, until he was threatened by the planters with arrest. Yet he continued haranguing his rural congregation as a prophet inspired. His son Timon, now grown and already a traveled apprenticed seaman, heard, on a visit home, one of his father's sermons. It surprised him. By now young Timon in his wide travels had seen and experienced much. He knew slavery first-hand and considered it logical. He had seen African blacks, chained, bewildered, sad, inert, herded onto ships headed for the dread Jamaican sugar plantations—an experience he had never imagined before going to sea—and, although he loved his father, he thought him now pitifully naive and uninformed; blacks were something apart, having little human potential, locked by God into their inferior state; the sight therefore Captain Stokes now saw—blacks in utter chaos about to be ferried out to his *Caper*—held his mind and tender memory all the more doggedly on the latter days of his father's evangelism; on, say, that long-ago hot Sunday afternoon, when the old man had preached to the few families of his flock in a grove of pine trees adjoining the sweltering little frame church of his ministry; he delivered himself of another of his warning, prophetic, tirades, his white shock of hair crowning an emaciated face dripping sweat, his frenzied upheld hands trembling, wild; he seemed furious, his son now remembered, that his hearers did not perceive what to him was rock-like conviction, truth. "There'll be an eye for an eye, says the Holy Book!" he shouted, "a tooth for a tooth! . . . the land will be torn asunder and run blood—slave agin free! Whole armies will be wiped out! For every black—naked, filthy, sick—hustled ashore in this land by your great and monied slavers, a white man will die in wars of the blood, fighting not agin England, not agin King George, but amongst themselves! For every example of white men treating other men as *things,* a white man will lay a'twistin' on his back in agony in some fly-fetid hospital tent, his wounds of war festering pus and stink! For every mulatto sold to strangers by his own white cousins, a white child will be orphaned! An eye for an eye, I say! . . . Oh, ye of no foresight and pity, take heed of what I say! God hath warned ye! . . . It is your children that will suffer for the eternal sins of these Godless planters that live like kings, buy and sell human flesh, and plunder the land! Awake! . . . Awake!"

Captain Stokes stood on the beach now pondering these ancient and gripping memories; how wrong his dear and zealous father had been, he thought; all because of an unreasoning hate for the true, the really qualified, leaders of the country, the very people who, like Washington, Jefferson, Madison, Henry, the Pinckneys, would engineer a nation's freedom and set its people on the high road of history—an attainment in which preordained and natural slavery had, and must, play a vital role. Stokes stood mute, detached, his conviction unshakable.

Soon, at last, the branding—which had left cries of women and children still echoing across the beach—was finished, though not before two or three canoes, heavy with their freight, had already departed for the *Caper*. Now the loading of the canoes began in earnest; and though the slaves had seen and heard, up close, the

247

tossing noisy ocean all morning, they were now required to confront it directly, embark upon it at first in a mere canoe; many were terrified out of their senses. Yet somehow the first three or four loadings went without major incident—the Captain watching. It was the canoe launched containing many of the Gold Coasters, including Kano, Tippu, Bymba, and also Osei, which produced trouble. There was a wide mixture aboard; in addition to some of the Gold Coasters and their Coromantees, there were people from the Baga and Susu tribes, who preponderated, as well as a few Ibo, Efik, and Ibibio, twenty-nine slaves in all besides the eleven Krumen paddlers and steersman. The Baga and Susu tribesmen and women, never having imagined, much less seen before their capture, anything resembling so stupendous, so overpowering, a sight as the great dark Atlantic waves threatening them, were now almost immobilized, petrified, with fear as they were flayed with the hippopotamus whips into the hapless canoe. The craft had barely pushed off when a rain squall hit, accompanied by thunder and lightning. Suddenly a Susu man screamed and leapt forward to jump overboard, before one of the angered Krumen swung his paddle at him, knocking him to his knees, as the steersman astern yelled out some untranslatable epithet in trying with his great paddle to right, to steady, the tossing, perilous canoe. Not only Osei, but Bymba and the other Coromantees, desperately clutched the sides of the canoe in despair of their lives as the steersman, eyes piercing, jaw set, his water-flecked and glistening body straining over the paddle, tried with all his might to keep the canoe from broadsiding the crest and capsizing. Moreover, there were some aboard who did not wish to live. Two such, two men, now sprang over the side of the canoe before they could be prevented, followed, in the midst of the distraction, by the very first attempter. None of the three now in the heavy-running seas made the slightest effort to stay afloat, each allowing himself at once to be swept under without a struggle. Osei sat trembling, awestruck. The Krumen, long paddles flying, redoubled, at the frenzied chant of the steersman, their utmost efforts to speed the canoe to the vessel yet three-quarters of a mile out before further casualties ensued.

Suddenly Kano, the gloomy, shaken Gold Coaster squatting near the stern of the canoe, his wisp of a chin beard slightly waving in the wind and rain, seized the steersman by the throat and tried to

248

twist, wrench, him about and throw him overboard. The nearest paddler, however, snatched up the musket lying at the steersman's feet and, aiming quickly, haphazardly, shot Kano in the left shoulder. But the ball, piercing flesh, cartilage, and bone, shattered the joint, where it stayed lodged. The paddler now wheeled and pointed the smoking musket at one or two others, as though it had just been reloaded; yet no one moved. Kano, knocked to the bottom of the canoe by the force of the ball, lay jerking in pain; then he ceased, shuddered once, dropped his head on his chest, and uttered a half-stifled moan. He was bleeding profusely. "Throw me over, my brothers," he said at last, weakly, to Tippu, the herdsman, and the others. "My time has come—I will not see your new land. . . . Nor yet will I now be eaten by the white man—for which I truly thank the spirits of my ancestors." The harried steersman, likewise knowing Kano would probably die from loss of blood, and bearing none of Stokes' commercial responsibilities, made no remonstrance as Tippu wrestled his friend Kano up off the bottom of the canoe and gently dropped, almost laid, him over the side. Kano, his face now in perfect repose, disappeared at once stiff-legged into an onrushing wave.

Strangely, in the furious wake of the beleaguered canoe, the slaves all looked back now and saw Africa moving away from them already in the distance, its remote treeline, dense, dark, impenetrable, looming up from behind the great expanse of sand, the barracoons and slave pens, and the old Cape Coast fort. Osei, still shaken, gazed in fear and wonder. So even did Tippu, the little herdsman as well as warrior, Kano's bereft friend, whose gaze was sober, plaintive, at last stoical. It all seemed to Tippu that an immense and brooding presence was receding, retreating, before him which had existed in eons of time—great epochs in which his and his ancestors' racial memories stretched back into an infinitude of mute history. A phenomenon, a hoary prodigy of a land, it was as old as time itself, while he, at say thirty, was as young as a mere twinkling instant in time. Viewing the silent, verdant tableau now slipping away from him, he felt as nothing—as the froth of the sea flying over the prow of the canoe.

Suddenly a great wave did break over the canoe, sending it, despite the steersman's frantic effort, scaling straight up a precipice of heavy, dark green water, then as quickly into a breathtaking dive back to the level of the rolling sea. Tippu's lips had parted. Osei had gasped. But soon now they could see that three more canoes behind them had left shore headed for the *Caper*. Osei was afraid to watch them for fear he would see someone jump overboard; instead he turned and kept his eyes on two of the canoes ahead of them that had almost reached the *Caper*. Tippu observed Osei's frightened look but felt no compassion for him. He preferred to look at Bymba, of his own clan, and took satisfaction in the boy's cool disdain of all the cruelty and hardship he had witnessed. Bymba, squatting amidst the others in the bow, was attentive, alert, his sharp eyes taking in everything, especially the *Caper* rocking at anchor yet a distance ahead of them.

Suddenly a huge, half-naked woman midway in the canoe let out a fearful shriek and dove headlong into the midst of the others around her, grappling with them as if they would save her. Now she began pointing wildly out to sea and screeching in an Ewe dialect, "What, what is this terrible beast?—this water! . . . I have never seen it before! It is a monster and will soon swallow us up! . . . Oh, it will devour us all! Where are our priests, our medicine men? . . . where are our witch doctors? Pray, pray!—that we may return to our villages. Oh, spirits of our elders, save us! . . . save us!" But soon her screams were drowned out by the noise of the sea as another great wave hit. Osei, clutching the side of the canoe, still gaped at her, but Bymba eyed her in disgust.

"*I* am a witch doctor," someone now said in a loud voice. They turned to see an older man, his teeth gone, wearing only a filthy loin cloth. His hand was raised to the sky. "But now," he said, "I fear I have lost my endowment, my power to communicate. It is because we have in these last few minutes left forever the land of our true knowledge. It is an evil day!"

"An evil day, yes. . . ." said young Osei, softly, before he thought—"It is true." But no one heard his muffled voice.

"They say, though," a frightened young woman cried out above the sea roar, "that we go to a better land. The land we leave was not always happy, we know—my niece, a baby of twelve moons, was sacrificed by the priests in the 'customs' just as they would kill a chicken!"

"What is unhappy about that?" called out the witch doctor—

"Our 'customs' rise out of our needs; out of our soil, the earth; they are our birthright, and appease the evil spirits!"

The young woman was silent at this.

"The land we go to is *not* better, not happier!" the witch doctor shouted. "We have been gulled—it is an evil day, I say!"

"Yes!" whispered Osei to himself. "It is true—I believe him."

The huge, near-naked woman, who after screaming had been moaning, now opened her mouth wide and let out another blood-curdling scream. Whereupon Bymba, able to control himself no longer, jumped up, leapt back toward the middle of the canoe, and struck her in the face with his fist, knocking her into the six inches of bilge in the bottom of the canoe. Now she lay moaning again— "We are consumed, my people!" she mumbled in a crazed, wallowing trance— ". . . We are swallowed up! Where did all our elders and medicine men go hide? . . . Why have they no means to protect us? . . ."

Bymba, glowering, moved threateningly again, until Tippu crawled forward and stayed his hand.

Most of the canoes ahead had reached the *Caper* by now and were already unloading their cargo. Osei strained to watch, knowing soon, if the canoe did not capsize, he too must board that huge strange-looking craft with its great heavy white cloths furled around towering spires cut from the forests. Now as he sat back, he saw Bymba, who was still grimacing; again he envied him his daring; yet why were Bymba, Tippu, and all the other bold and warlike Gold Coasters being taken away against their will just like himself? he wondered. Soon he saw the musket again, which this time rested between the steersman's knees. Although it had not yet been reloaded, it was not, he knew, the only firearm in the canoe; three of the paddlers, though hard at work, had muskets slung across their shoulders; the Krumen, Osei well understood, thus had the crucial power; yet against whom had they used it? he thought. He knew and it bewildered, saddened, him.

Cockle, the first mate, had left shore earlier and, on orders, was present aboard the *Caper* in time to oversee the arrival of most of the canoes. He exploded on learning the heavy casualties the ferrying had entailed—besides the four deaths in Osei's canoe, there had been other serious misadventures, some also involving deaths.

A man in one of the canoes, terrified by the heavy seas, went berserk, was clubbed with a Krumen musket butt into insensibility, and was dead on arrival at the *Caper*. In another canoe, a mentally-retarded boy of eighteen had seen a shark. Astonished, hypnotized, he began pointing and crying out—"Look at the fish!—the big white fish! . . . He shall not eat us—we shall eat him! Let us catch him!—come let us catch him!" And with that he dove overboard directly at the shark and, the mesmerized look still on his face, was snatched under with hurtling violence by the yawning teeth. In another incident, a woman and a girl, in suicide attempts before leaving the beach, had eaten, gorged themselves on, the ant-infested sand. En route they had collapsed in the canoe and were hoisted aboard the *Caper* unconscious and dying. Cockle was beside himself at the losses, knowing what Stokes' reaction would be. Yet he was not to blame, he reassured himself, though he knew such commercial misfortunes could cause the Captain to sulk in his vinegary meanness for a week. Cockle therefore made sure now the men slaves coming aboard were clapped in irons by the crew at once and hustled below into the hold.

These slaves, the men, most of them naked except for loincloths, were shackled two by two—the right wrist and ankle of one to the left wrist and ankle of the other—and bullied by the crew's cat-'o-nine-tails until herded below to lie in the suffocating coffin space of the platform shelves. The women were also crowded down into the hold, into their separate section, as were the children, with a separate shelf space for the boys and another for the girls. Occasionally, for short periods, the women and children were permitted up on the forecastle deck, for sun and air and to be fed, but the men, regarded always as mutinous and dangerous, were kept in chains in the hold except for brief ascents twice a day to the upper decks to be fed under heavy guard. The man to whom Tippu, the herdsman and warrior, was shackled was not a Coromantee, nor a Gold Coaster, a fact greatly displeasing to Tippu. At first he tried to ignore the man—Ezi by name and, by birth, of the distant Vai nation—but this was of course impossible. Ezi, moreover, was taller and larger than Tippu, which made their mismatched joinder in the shackles a gruesomely awkward and painful condition. Tippu next pretended not to understand Ezi's dialect, but when Ezi made the dexterous change to one of the more familiar Gold Coast tongues, Tippu could no longer pretend. They occasionally talked, though both were morose and inconsiderate. Tippu especially was inclined to be quarrelsome over the turn of events and had constantly to remind himself he must somehow be more agreeable; he was no longer a free, separate person, he realized, but, like a Siamese twin, doomed to go wherever his twin went; cooperation now was essential, especially at times when one or the other had to answer the call of his bodily functions and go to the stinking latrine tubs together. There was also general vomiting from seasickness.

By early afternoon of this first day the rain had almost stopped; the sun even occasionally shone through intermittent spaces in the clouds; once a beautiful if indistinct rainbow formed its great arc over the sky; then it would suddenly begin raining again, ever so briefly, so lightly, though in another part of the heavens the sun still shone brightly. The slaves' hold was humid and stifling; the men at first seemed bewildered by their shackles and tightly-packed, stinking ranks, as if this were merely some necessary initial exercise they must go through before being placed in more habitable quarters. They did not realize that, except for crawling out to visit the tubs, or twice daily to be fed on deck, they would not be permitted to sit upright during the entire voyage—which, depending on winds and weather, could take three months. Rather they were subdued now, expectant, curious, and most of them still frightened by their first encounter with the great sea. But by late afternoon, as the heat and suffocation increased, they sensed the ship was moving on some steady, rolling course, that it had at last set sail, and somehow a change came over them. While before they had been mostly silent, they now began to talk, loudly, volubly, even heatedly—in a dozen different dialects—crying out, arguing, speculating aloud on what might lay in store for them. Wearing only loin cloths, they lay packed together on their sides on the unplaned boards of their shelf, the curved shapes of their bodies fitting together like spoons in a silverware case. There were at least thirty other men slaves installed in Tippu's and Ezi's shelf, and about the same number in the shelf above it, all watched over by a sweating, red-faced seaman, armed with a cutlass and two pistols, who stood guard at the hatchway.

"Do you know where we go?" Ezi asked Tippu.

"I know nothing," snapped churlish Tippu, and would say no more.

Ezi, a former palm wine tapper and vintner, and about Tippu's age of thirty plus, was inclined to be pensive, thoughtful, careworn. He did not press Tippu. But soon he began talking to himself— aloud: "I think we will have our chance before long, before we reach our destination, to take over this house on the water and kill all the *Koomi,* the white cannibals, before they slaughter and eat us. Then we shall turn this house on the great river of salt around and go back to our villages. There again I shall tap the palm trees."

Tippu did not deign to comment; he now thought Ezi a fool. Besides, Tippu was so miserable and distressed in the stifling confinement of the tiers of sweating bodies in the hold that he could hardly think at all. Soon the men, who had not eaten since early morning, began to clamor for food and Tippu suddenly realized he too was hungry. He also began to twist and wrench his body about in the torment of his restricted space but the irons made it all but impossible for him to turn, or rise, or lie back down, without great discomfort, even pain, to himself and Ezi. Thus early in the voyage the sense of nightmare, insanity, from claustrophobia began to beset him; already he feared he might scream—an act heretofore unthinkable to a Coromantee. He tried now to lie perfectly still and not think of his entombment, to let his mind idle, rest. Soon something resembling a manic vision came to him—graphic, portentous, and in the sharpest outline; it somehow seemed to evolve out of the great body of oral recitation indigenous to his tribe. In the depths of the forest lived an elephant-king, Four-Tusk, by name. King Four-Tusk possessed a numerous retinue of other elephants and spent most of his time ruling them and protecting the herd. During one terrible period, however, there was a five-year drought; the rivers, lakes, ponds, and swamps all went dry. The herd appealed to Four-Tusk—"O King, our throats, and those of our little ones, are parched with this thirst; many of our babies are dead, and more are likely to die. We beg you to discover some way of eliminating this awful thirst; save us and our young." Four-Tusk, after much sympathetic palavering, conceded the thirst could of course be eliminated only by water, and sent forays of his elephants out in all directions in quest of running streams. The search party that went west at last found, after a long journey filled with hardships, a lake in the land inhabited by white men, a body of water called Loch Columbiana. It was a sight of great beauty and boasted all sorts of water creatures and fowls—fish, as well as ducks, osprey, heron,

254

swans, sheldrakes, cranes, and the like. The lake on three sides was bordered by lovely trees, embowered with flowering sprays of branches drooping under the weight of their fragrant blossoms; here brimming crystal water abounded amidst thickets of water lilies in full bloom. The elephant-explorers were delighted and even, in their great thirst, gave thanks for the wisdom of their king before wading in to drink. When they had drunk their fill and were ready to start the long journey back with the good news, they suddenly took notice of the fourth, the open, side of the lake. They were astonished to see a shy, handsome, young white man, in his early thirties, be-robed and wearing a gentle beard and dark brown hair to his shoulders, seated on a throne with a great vile-looking serpent in his lap. On being seen, the snake slithered down at once and disappeared into the beautiful water lilies, as the frightened elephants made off in haste. When after two hard days of travel they arrived back home and told of their experiences, good and bad, King Four-Tusk and the others, though expressing gratitude, were much in awe of, indeed unhappy about, what they had heard. The king slowly shook his head—"We cannot go there," he said sadly. "It is not the right place for us. It is ruled by a heathen—who himself is ruled by a snake." And the whole herd continued to go thirsty until the rains came. But Tippu did not understand his vision.

For the *Charleston Caper,* the first week of the voyage was one mostly of hot sun and becalmed seas, with, to Captain Stokes, only disappointing distances traversed. Moreover, at least a quarter of the crew ailed from one malady or another, predominantly virulent fevers contracted on the equatorial coasts. The condition constituted an additional trial for the captain and first mate, both of whom repeatedly urged Ship's Surgeon Isaiah Whittier to do his utmost to restore these men to health and duty. Whittier, in shirtsleeves and wearing an unsightly black peruke over his stubbled red hair, had smiled that morning at Captain Stokes and defended himself. "Aye, Captain, but I do my best, you know—all my profession affords. Much depends on the strength of the sailor himself; fever in this clime is a deadly augur, I don't have to tell you. Of the eight ill, two or three will surely die, Captain—and within a day or two."

This prediction seemed to anger Stokes more than it shocked or saddened him; death in the crew was not an uncommon difficulty for a sea captain, one he rather frequently had to face, but Stokes in this instance seemed unprepared, obdurate. Pretending to ignore what he had been told, he changed the subject to one calculated to put the surgeon on the defensive again. "Stay clear of the rum keg, Whittier," he warned—"We've got nobody to doctor *you*." Then adjusting his cocked hat, he left to mount to the quarter-deck.

But Whittier called after him. "We've got our fair share of the bloody flux, and the yaws, too, Captain—among the blacks. Did you know?"

Stokes turned and came back. This was a different, a more serious, matter. "What?" he said. "I did *not* know! Why so soon?"

"It's not soon, Captain—most of those that have disease had it when they came aboard. That infernal factor at Cape Coast was a wily fellow, even if he too was sick unto death; he was a rogue nonetheless. That's why I asked if I shouldn't go ashore with you for the examinations."

"I didn't want you ashore. You'd been at the rum keg most of the night before—as had Cockle."

"I was in shape enough to keep that man from swindling you, though, Captain," the surgeon grinned slyly. "He can hide disease. Take the yaws—he covers over the skin eruptions with a paste made of gunpowder and iron rust—the ruse works well enough, it does. And the bloody flux—he handles that too; he misused one poor black who before the sale was dripping blood from the arse by stopping the anus with a bung of oakum; the miserable wretch came aboard in greatest misery until the filthy plug was removed, much to his relief. Enough, it was, to make an abolitionist of ye, Captain."

"How many of the cargo are we apt to lose?"

"How can I say?—enough it'll be."

"Doctor them, doctor them, man! The underwriters do not insure against this."

"What am I doing now, Captain?—both day and night I doctor. But the hold needs sanitation, also more grates to let escape the terrible, noxious vapors; and cleaner, more spacious, platforms for the wretches to lie on. Now it's so crowded, so packed with sweating, stinking bodies, and the men shackled together, that many times they can't reach the tubs in time; they foul their nests, so to speak, and create the devil's own shitpit. And remember too, Captain, they must eat with their fingers."

"Nothing can be done about that!" said Stokes. "You must go down into that hold yourself and doctor them, and let me hear from you everyday, even oftener, about their condition—we've lost too many already." He started up for the quarter-deck again.

Once more the surgeon called out after him—"We've a pregnant woman too, Captain, who'll soon deliver. Ah, what a place to be born—Gads!" Whittier then turned and went to his berth for his first drink of rum of the day.

In a separate shelved section of the hold, Osei and Bymba had been stowed with the other boys, fifteen of them in all, while the women were directly opposite them, though behind a floor-to-ceiling impassable partition, with the few female children aboard crammed into a small shelf over the women and protected by the same partition. By an ironic coincidence, it was Bymba, the only Coromantee among the boys, who was the first to take compassionate notice of Mgboye, the pregnant woman Whittier had mentioned, whose delivery was each day imminent. The women on board, most of them barebreasted, and the boys and the girls, all three categories unshackled, were allowed more time out of the hold now, up on deck, during the day, after Whittier's repeated warnings to Stokes, than formerly. It was up on deck that Bymba had first seen Mgboye, heard her talk, witnessed her travail, and by her dialect discovered she was also Coromantee, though he had never seen her before. Sometimes, weakly, forlornly, she would sink down on the deck and talk in rambling soliloquies, as if in a daze, often wailing, crying out, for her other children, only one of whom had been brought out of the interior in her coffle but had then died in the Cape Coast slave pens. Watching her weakened daily laments, and now knowing she was Coromantee, Bymba at once felt close to, actually responsible for her; besides he saw that she was not only pregnant, but ill. She was near the age of his mother—whom he was not sure was alive since the sacking of their village—and somehow felt a compunction to protect her. On the sixth day out, while the ship was still mostly becalmed and the weather sultry, Mgboye, on deck, finally went into labor. Her groans and cries went out over the heat-shimmering water. Bymba, when he saw the other women on deck so wary of Mgboye and standing so uneasily apart, went over and bent down to her, yet could think of nothing to say. At that moment the sailor guarding the hatchway shouted to the linguister, an Ibo woman in the group, to tell Bymba to get back and stay away from the stricken woman. For a moment Bymba glared at the sailor, but finally complied, as some of the other women carried Mgboye below and a crewman went to notify the surgeon.

But it was not until an hour later that Whittier appeared in the women's section of the hold, strangely barefoot and half drunk. He would not deign to touch Mgboye, but presumed, as best he could through the linguister, to direct two of the women, one already a veteran midwife, in the art of child delivery. What more sober observation would have revealed to him was that Mgboye, who now lay prostrate on the unplaned boards of the hold floor, was not only in labor, but critically ill. Besides pregnancy, both a fiery fever and the bloody flux afflicted her. Even before entering labor she had been in such a weakened state she could hardly stand. She seemed now already delirious, and, her breathing sporadic, eyes wild, she cried out in her native dialect—"Take me to my village and my young'uns! . . . I thirst! . . . oh, I thirst!—and with water all around us! Where do you take us?"—she stared the question up at Whittier—"What far-off land will now claim us?—there, we hear, we shall be boiled alive and eaten by *Koomi,* the cannibal white man. Why do we go? . . . why are we taken?—and I about to put forth in the world of spirits another child, a man child, it is my feeling and hope, who shall be called Qwesi, the fearless and the good. I see the boy now!—*he* will not be eaten, but to his captors will take the bloody machete. Now, now, you midwives, my sisters, I shall spread my legs and let him come forth out of me and into this stinking house upon the sky of water where my pains come and go so hard. Prepare me, women!—help me! . . . give me a stick or a bar to pull on that I may bear down in my labor as was our way in our villages. Then I shall utter the boy. No, I shall not die—I suffer, but I shall not die! . . ."

Whittier, slightly weaving from his rum, still stood over Mgboye, and when the Ibo woman linguister told him what she had said, smiled, shook his head in mock exasperation, and directed Mgboye's skirtlike garment, covering her only from the waist to knees, be removed. By the time the ill woman lay naked on her back on the floor, the head of the fetus had already appeared in a welter of fecal-anal blood from her fluxes. Mgboye then desperately gripping both hands of the midwife's helper, strained and groaned until the birth was effected. The yammering child was a girl; yet it was not necessary the fact be made known to the mother, who already lay exhausted, stuporous, from her efforts, pain, and combined and worsening illnesses. In a moment however the cries of the baby seemed momentarily to arouse the mother, then almost at once Mgboye sank into a drowsy, apathetic lassitude. The surgeon, after squeamishly snipping the umbilical cord, shook his head again and, sucking his rum breath through his teeth, ordered Mgboye be got back in her scant garment and, with the baby, be carried up on deck for sun and air. Then he himself went above and found Stokes on the quarter-deck. "The woman has delivered, Captain," he said, "but she will not live."

"What have you done for her?" said Stokes, impatient, harried.

"Nothing—it's no use. It's their diet as well as the bad sanitation, Captain. I told you some time ago, we should have aboard more of their own, their native victuals—we have some, sure, but not near enough. Instead most of the time we have to give them salt beef, and sea biscuit, and even horse beans, while they're used to fowl, and goat soup . . . boiled rice, millet, cornmeal, yams, manioc or plantains—items of that nature. Most of all they hate horse beans, our cheap European beans, but they're fed them all the time now. You can hardly blame them, Captain—it's a frightful mess the ship's cook brews up for them from those horse beans. He boils the beans to a pulp, then covers all this over with an unholy mash made of palm oil, flour, water, and red pepper—the crew call it 'slabber sauce.' Many of the blacks, no matter how hungry they get, won't eat it—they throw it in each other's face. And the bad sanitation I've mentioned to you before, Captain—it likewise makes for a sick cargo. The hard shelf-platforms the wretches have to lie on ought to be swabbed down with scalding water and vinegar every day instead of every week—I know the crew well nigh mutinies at having to go down there and clean up the filth, blood, mucus, and excrement that's always to be found there, but it ought to be done; then maybe a surgeon could do you some good, Captain."

"I can't hear what you're saying, Whittier, for smelling your foul rum breath," said Stokes, in his classic diversionary way of dealing with the surgeon's suggestions that would cost the ship money.

"I only give you the facts, Captain—facts about your ship."

"Whittier, this is not a luxury packet cruising between London and Bremen with a complement of dukes and duchesses. It's not a hospital ship, either, evacuating the brave and wounded from some campaign. It is a profit venture—a slave ship."

"Well do I know it, Captain—I'm no tyro in the business, you're aware. What motivates the ship's owners and yourself motivates me alike—that, and that alone. But what if we arrive back home to the owners in Virginia with half the cargo dead and dispatched enroute—what then Captain?"

Stokes, breathing heavily, looked away. "It's my worry, not yours," he finally said, but thoughtfully now. Then he reddened— "It's yours to stay reasonably sober! . . . and go down in that hold and treat the ailing!" He stalked off. The surgeon then went to his berth again for the fortification that for him only rum could give.

In the hold two days later Mgboye died peacefully in a coma, the baby nestled beside her. Crewmen came and took both above, the dead and yet living, and threw them overboard to purposeful sharks trailing the ship.

Bymba, in the boys' partitioned-off section, knew nothing of what had happened to Mgboye, and in the days following attributed her absence on deck to her convalescence or possible forced reten- tion in the women's hold for some infraction. But in a few more days, amidst the great number of all the others aboard, he had forgotten her anyway. He had also learned to tolerate Osei now, who followed him wherever he went; Bymba talked constantly to the less venturesome boy of the possibility of trying to gain access to the men's section of the hold where they could visit Bymba's much admired fellow-Coromantee, Tippu. He was concerned for fierce, quarrelsome Tippu's safety, knowing he and the other shackled men were brought up only for the two daily quarter-hour periods—ten in the morning, four in the afternoon—required to feed them. Bymba had only seen Tippu on deck from a distance; no one was allowed near the men except their guards. Bymba was much impressed by the precautions the crew, outnumbered by blacks at least twelve to one, always took when the men slaves were brought on deck to eat; he could imagine the past bloody uprisings which had elsewhere taken place as explaining the precautions— every hatchway had its armed guard, and as the men ate, they were not only surrounded by armed crewmen but were the objects of cannon trained on them, the gunners standing ready with matches to be struck and lighted in an instant; moreover, on the quarterdeck an arms chest, plainly visible and open, was maintained brimming with small arms fully loaded and primed to be used on a moment's notice. This last enticement Bymba had noticed more than once; he reveled in the possibilities it presented if only Tippu and the others were not invariably shackled.

Time, inexorably, as the waters of the sea, moved on. Soon three weeks had passed, and, day on day, the ship seethed with more activity and ever more suffering. As to both slaves and crew it was as if the *Caper* carried a distressed multitude of pilgrims on their way to lands unknown; but mystery seemed hovering in the air as the sturdy hull rode the swells in the sprightly breezes. The sun was high and bright, the horizon limitless. Yet first-mate Cockle, a veteran in the trade, sensed something foreboding and thought it lay chiefly in the temper of the cargo. True, the *Caper's* slaves, during the long marches in coffles out to the coast, and while languishing in the seaside barracoons and slave pens, had, though miserable, in fear, resentful, nonetheless remained tractable. But now they seemed filled with a kind of low suffused desperation, rage, and bitterness. It showed, at least to Cockle, in so many little telltale signs. The more he thought of what appeared at first to be trivial indications, unsubstantial though they might now seem, the sooner he hoped the ship could complete its run—certainly, he almost prayed, in less than the three months it sometimes took when protracted doldrums, such as they were currently experiencing much of the time, stayed, slowed, the vessel's progress. One bad harbinger Cockle, in the last day or two, could not avoid having to deal with was the growing number of the "cargo" who refused to eat. Though a sporadic situation, it was getting no better, especially among the Gold Coasters—for whose spirit of defiance Cockle had a grudging respect—and he was now under strict orders from Stokes to ruthlessly stamp the practice out. Only that morning he had dealt summarily with such a case. The crew had brought word of two men slaves who, when on three straight occasions were brought on deck with the others, had refused their slabber sauce. Ingenious Cockle ordered up from the galley a shovel of glowing, hot coals, which he then held close enough to the mouths of the two offenders to scorch their lips; this was accompanied, through a linguister, by Cockle's threats that continued refusal to eat would get the coals poured down their throats. Only then did they eat. But the day before that, an extended flogging had been unavailing; the slave involved had merely been carried below unconscious. Use even in many instances of the "speculum oris" had shown indifferent results. This special iron device was a forcible mouth-opener, a jaw divider, with notched prongs or legs and a thumbscrew at the other, the blunt, end. To use it the iron legs were closed and forced between the subdued victim's teeth; when the thumbscrew was tightened, the legs of the instrument separated, gradually forcing open the mouth, into which the slabber sauce was then poured through a funnel. Yet even this sometimes brought unsatisfactory results, for immediate regurgitation often followed—necessitating resort to flogging again.

While the third week out had brought welcome trade winds to rescue the *Caper* from over two weeks of doldrums, the fourth week, thanks to Surgeon Whittier's ministrations, now saw a return to duty of a number of the crew who from the beginning had been stricken with fever. Captain Stokes throughout had been serious and taciturn, but now, though still never smiling, he seemed less preoccupied, more even-tempered. One reason of course was the favorable winds, improving prospects for making the run to Chesapeake Bay in shorter time. Because of this the crew too seemed more jaunty, spirited, and carried out Cockle's orders with less complaining. Then on some fine days, with the ship shooting through turquoise waters and its sails full and billowing before the friendly trades, the women and children permitted on deck were exhorted by the crew to sing and dance. Even the men slaves when brought up to eat had their stay lengthened if they could be cajoled, or threatened, into dancing, the purpose being—it was Stokes' theory—to flex stagnant muscles and possibly improve morale. But by now the leg irons, the wrist irons too, had taken their toll; the bleeding raw flesh soon made clear to Stokes that forcing the men to dance only increased the peril of further losses and he had the practice stopped.

Though the winds still accommodated, there now came long days of overcast skies. Then one night a full moon in all its opulence burst through the clouds over the ship, drenching the decks with a hard, eerie light. Mysteriously, then, the sea once more became calm—soon not a breeze stirred; it all had happened so suddenly; the ship seemed again to sit high on becalmed, almost motionless waters, its great gaunt silhouette of a hull, cavernous, specterlike, casting its profile across moon shimmers running to the sea's very horizon; the moon was like some heavenly lantern suspended aloft, betokening a spell, a respite, for man's reflection. It was midnight, and Stokes, alone in this apparitional light, stood on the poop deck placidly smoking his third pipe of Virginia tobacco. He gazed out across the glistening water, but he, a stony stoic, narrow in feelings, callous to all moral beauty, was in no way impressed by the sight; he only hoped, yet was confident, the winds would soon move again; the beauty entirely escaped him; this aspect of life did not exist for him; only facts, hard facts, immediate realities, affected him; this was why, despite his patriotism as an American, and contrary to his recent beliefs, he had now come to admire, was actually in awe of, his former British rulers; they, to him, because of what he took of late to be their vision and pragmatism, represented the powerful and civilizing influences in a world which so sorely needed this stewardship; the British had clear and discernible traditions, he thought; and they had produced, succeeded—the hard, tangible evidence was everywhere. Americans, Stokes, in a reversal of opinion, was now convinced, had attained their independence *because* they were hardy offspring of the British. He was therefore thankful for what he called his "fortunate heritage," one which prized ends, not means, which required concrete occurrences to enable him to react. Yet he was soon to encounter some such mighty happenings and to be impressed by them indeed.

The first of them came now as a mere sound. The strange, droning, discordant sound seemed as if it exuded from the very sides of the vessel below him, also to rise through both the lower and spar decks, to pervade the stillness of the entire ship's bosom. Then it ceased; not abruptly, but morbidly died away. Stokes, leaning against the taffrail, listened, straining to catch any hint of its resumption. There was none immediately; then shortly it was heard again . . . a soft wailing, a low moaning, gutteral and mournful— a sound of no hope. Then! . . . he knew now whence it came— from the hold of the ship. It rose slowly now as a great, swelling moan, then at last as a sigh. Ah, weren't blacks the strangest of creatures? he thought; they too could be sad, desperate, forlorn— even as himself at times; heretofore he had hardly thought them capable of it, had only known what he considered their savagery;

yet now they moaned so unhappily, wretchedly, that their sounds rent the gleaming night. He knew though he had not been alone in his former beliefs; other captains in the trade had claimed the same for what they were beyond doubt convinced was blacks' essential barbarism; they spoke for instance of the horrors of the blacks' torture of European sailors; first-hand accounts came especially from the captains engaged in panyaring, in the kidnapping of blacks, for they had lost many men to this, the blacks' retaliatory "savagery." Yet Stokes suspected these same captains had at one time or another heard the same doleful moanings coming out of the holds of their own slavers as he had heard now. What had been their reaction, reflections?—had it at all shaken their conviction, as he feared now it had his own, that blacks were nothing more than "pure savages," with no sensibilities evident?

He was not sure—for the panyarers told so many lurid tales of torture. Heavily armed, it was their practice to leave their ship, raid coastal villages, and carry off whole families—during this earlier period panyaring had, yes, accounted for at least half the blacks taken off the African continent. Sometimes as many as twenty or more seamen made up a raiding party; they were armed not only with muskets and pistols but frequently dragged small cannon up the beaches as they laid waste any tribal settlement encountered, killing the old and halt and taking off the able-bodied with them. The reaction of neighboring chieftains could of course have been foretold—it was outraged and violent. At once they held parleys, cracking many ceremonial kola nuts in the process, as they sat in a circle with the witch doctors in attendance standing behind them. Invariably, so Stokes was told, the chiefs first bemoaned their lack of enough gunpowder. Knowing this to be crucial, they would launch into long discussions of ways they could procure more gunpowder, and other arms as well.

At one meeting, however, a chief, a fiery Wolof, declared that if something was not soon done to stop the pillage, murder, and kidnapping, he would die by his own hand and take all his wives and children with him. It was the dishonor of the thing, he said. Then, turning to the witch doctors and uttering a terrible oath, he proposed his remedy. It was simply that they capture, at any cost whatever, at least one, if not more, of the marauders; then subject them to a slow, painful death by the most heinous tortures they could devise. At once the other chiefs threw up their hands in fervent agreement. Accordingly, the first raider captured was in fact staked prostrate and naked to the ground in the broiling sun and his body heaped with great ferocious ants which in one day and one night stripped him of most of his skin—though throughout the ordeal the man, screaming, sobbing, cried aloud to his captors for mercy, begging them to kill him. Instead, next day one of his hands was burned off by being held intermittently in a low fire. Later his testes were pincered into two gory polyps, and an eye removed. Yet, despite a further ingenious assortment of tortures, the captive lived for over four days. When at last he died, however, his devastated body was taken back out to the coast and thrown on the beach for his comrades to come view and learn from.

The panyaring captains thenceforth termed blacks "savages" but in that coastal area panyaring went into immediate eclipse. Now Captain Stokes stood pondering the phenomenon as he listened to the low, moaning sounds rising from the hold. In the quiet brilliance of the night the sea lapped gently at the bows of the *Caper* as if fearing to intrude upon those desperate tones from below. Stokes lit his pipe again and gazed at the moon. Though he felt no compassion whatever, his heart as cold as steel, the plaintive sounds yet gave him an uneasy feeling. Occasionally moreover in the midst of the wailing and moaning would come a piercing shriek as if from some man, woman, or child gone suddenly mad. Stokes was not a man readily to feel fear, yet now his uneasiness escalated to a gnawing concern for the well-being of the ship and its mission. Soon now he heard shuffling steps behind him. Turning, he saw Surgeon Whittier standing there. "What is it, Whittier?" he said.

"Do you hear it, Captain? . . . the yammering, the bellowing, from the hold?" The surgeon seemed now perfectly sober. "It woke me from my sleep."

"I'm surprised at that," said Stokes, his manner sarcastic, cold.

"It's the men among them that are crying, Captain. Already they pine for their Africa. It is aptly named 'Dark Continent,' don't ye think? Dark and mysterious—and deadly to boot; yes, deadly. I would not want it for a homeland, myself. Yet I was not born here, nor my father, nor his, eh?—it might be the difference. But with these creatures below—yes, they're the males, you see—howling like grieving wolves, it's another matter. They're human, Captain;

you can't get around it—just listen. . . . so sad, so mournful, what? It's chilling."

"I can see you're scared out of your wits," Stokes said cuttingly.

"Not at all, Captain. What's there to be scared of?—ain't every one of them in chains? There're other angles to it, though, that don't set so well, maybe. It's the way they feel—right now; tonight. You can tell it by listening to them—to their long, strung-out moans. There's a deep sorrow in them, Captain. It's almost like it came out of the bosom of the great Dark Continent itself. Listen to it! . . . ah, it's a tragic tone, it is."

"Bunk! It's their shackles hurting their legs—it's purely physical."

"Sure, their shackles hurt, Captain. But there's more to that weird moaning than shackles—it's something out of the soul, I tell you! . . . I feel I hear Africa moaning. . . . Listen, Captain—ah, listen. . . ."

Instead Stokes turned on his heel and went to his cabin.

Two days later the *Caper* encountered heavy rain squalls again. At first they were not alarming, but then winds rose hurriedly and by night a violent storm had struck, tossing the ship high on heavy seas. It was the roughest weather they had encountered and wreaked havoc on the blacks in the hold who suffered a multitude of abrasions and contusions in the violent lurchings of the ship; in the men's case it only added to the bleeding wounds made by the shackles. And because of the drenching storm, tarpaulins had been thrown over the few gratings in use below, causing the suffocating blacks—men, women, and children—to cry out hysterically: "Kickeraboo, kickeraboo, we are dying . . . we are dying!" The heat was so intense that steam came up through the gratings combined with a stench that sent the crew reeling. This continued until dawn, when Surgeon Whittier, sure there had been deaths, went again to Stokes. "Now that there's daylight, Captain," he said, "the blacks ought be brought up for air and their wounds and fluxes treated, or else more yet will die or go crazy. The shackles must be removed from the men for a time or we'll lose a heap of them—it's a fact, Captain. It'll give the crew time, too, to clean out the blood, vomit, and filth in the hold."

Stokes, his face grey and haggard from sleeplessness, pondered what the surgeon had said. Finally, ignoring Whittier, he called over to the first mate, who was directing crewmen up in the rigging contending with the storm, and issued his order: "Arm the crew, Cockle, and ready a deck cannon. Then when it's lighter bring the blacks up for medical inspection and take the shackles off the men until Whittier can treat those that are hurt or sick." Cockle's mouth opened. "I know the peril in it," said Stokes, "but do as I say!" He walked away.

Meantime in the hold Osei lay jammed against Bymba, both barely able to breathe. The night just ended had been the most horrible experience of their lives. Now they lay cramped, stinking, and exhausted, so weak they were hardly able to speak. Yet in the grey dawn the storm still raged, the ship pitching wildly as if in the throes of a great spasm. In his short spells of fitful, hallucinated sleep Bymba had raved like a madman, and now as he tried to utter a few words to Osei, his voice was hoarse, enfeebled. Osei lay helpless and inert, broken by what he had been through.

"I must get to Tippu," said Bymba, weakly, though excitedly— "I must talk with him! . . . and the others too. What can we lose? . . ."

"They will not let us come near him," breathed Osei—"It is better to die."

"Die like this? . . . like sickly chickens?" Bymba aroused himself and stared hostilely at Osei. "I will not die in this hold—neither will Tippu and the other friends from our region. Be sure of it, we shall die some other way. No matter what, today I will talk with Tippu."

"Tippu may be dead," said Osei.

The possibility, it seemed, had not occurred to Bymba. It jarred him now. "No, Tippu is not dead," he finally said. "He survived the night because he is strong, lasting, with a spirit of iron—they cannot kill him; he is of my nation."

The other boys, lying packed together on either side of them, were so weakened from the night's ordeal they were listless, stuporous, and only babbled incoherently, except for three or four of them who moaned quietly from their seasickness and bleeding fluxes. Then everything became silent as they all lay now in a nauseous stupor.

At last, his mind wandering, Osei stirred feebly and said: "Before the storm I dreamed of Nene." He stared wildly about him now.

"What?" said Bymba.

"Nene—the girl who came in my coffle. But after we arrived she

267

disappeared. I dreamed she was dead—as surely she must be. She longed so to see her mother and brother, who left in a different coffle. Now they are on this very house on the water—I saw them—but she is not here. She is dead—I dreamed it—because she lost her talisman, a little red-eyed tortoise."

Bymba looked at Osei again and frowned. "You have snakes in the head." he said. "Your mind has disappeared out over the water." He shook Osei by the shoulders.

Osei groaned. "Also Okolo is on this house," he said, obliviously, a blank stare on his face. "I saw him too. He was Rufai's uncle—a medicine man—who came as well in another coffle."

"Snakes," muttered Bymba.

"I dreamed," said Osei, "that if we die we shall return to our country, and our kinfolk and friends. I believe it. Is it not better then to die? Truly I wish for death. Others, many others, here believe this too—I have heard them say it."

"Ah, snakes," Bymba breathed again in resignation.

It was not until much later that morning, around ten o'clock—miraculously the sky had cleared—that the men slaves were brought up on deck. The air was tense and the crew armed to the teeth. After them came the boys. It was then revealed, as the surgeon had thought, that six men and two boys—one of the boys Nene's brother—had died during the night. When after the boys, however, the women and girls were brought up, it was found that, though many were ill, all had survived. Surgeon Whittier marveled at this as he watched them taking their turns at the slabber sauce. Then quickly, furtively, he disappeared—down into his berth to snatch a cup of rum before beginning the long ordeal of treating the ill; the decision for the time being, moreover, may have saved his life.

Osei had come on deck delirious; and staggering with every lurch of the ship, he was barely able to walk—his eyes staring aimlessly, apathetically, then wildly, about him as he babbled to himself: "Kickeraboo—I wish to die." Bymba, trailing him, frowned at this incoherent, weakened display, though Bymba himself was spent. Then, ahead over Osei's shoulder, he saw among the men two or three of the Gold Coasters he knew. At once his eyes searched for Tippu, but Tippu was nowhere in sight. Bymba, fearful, thought this strange, until, a minute or two later, Tippu, the only slave still in shackles, was roughly shoved on deck by two red-faced crewmen brandishing pistols and cat-'o-nine-tails. Tippu's back already bore bloody welts from the flogging he had just taken below. Bymba rushed over to him—only to receive a sudden lash across his face and shoulders from one of the same whips. "Get back, you black whelp!" said the crewman who had struck him—"One mutinous nigger on this ship's enough. . . . Get back, I say!" He struck retreating Bymba with the cat-'o-nine-tails again, then turned around to the other men slaves who looked on sullenly. But many, as they tried to eat, were so weak they could hardly stand.

Soon first-mate Cockle appeared among them, his long, heavy pistol stuck in his belt. But before he knew what was happening, one of the Coromantees—a great, tall, fierce man with a welter of filigreed tribal scars stamping his cheekbones, Wobogo-Woot his name, son of a minor chieftain—rushed him, seized the pistol, and turned it on him. Cockle blanched with astonishment, then mortal fear. But just as he gaped helplessly into the muzzle of his own pistol, his attacker, the giant Woot, weakened by the night's ordeal and the bleeding fluxes, fainted dead away—sprawling on his great back on deck as the pistol skittered across into the midst of the women. Cockle, shaken but at last recovered, bawled out the order that the cannon be brought and trained on the other men slaves until they were back in shackles and herded below. But already mutiny was in the air.

It was all action though at first it seldom appeared so—raw action, yet it seemed unreal. It was rebellion limned in lethargy, its start caught in slow-motion. The long debility of the blacks, especially the men, gave even the most frenzied, deadly, gesture the quality of stasis; there was a floating motion, together with a strange miasma, accompanying everything; it was illusionary. Tippu, making the first groping move, was of course manacled, his wrists in darbies; besides he had lived through the night—a feat— only to receive, for some random defiance, the bloody flogging within an inch of his life. Yet, though slothfully, as if under water, he moved first. It was the shackles motivating him; their mere thought incited him; they symbolized his hated plight, evoking now his shrillest exhortations in an Ashanti dialect that articulated the passions now aroused in all the black males on deck. "Come, come, brothers," he cried—"Death to the white cannibals! . . . We will fling them and their darbies into the sea and have our freedom!" He moved then. Wrists joined but elbows flailing, he hurled himself high at at petrified seaman whose belt held both a pistol and a dagger. Landing on the seaman's shoulders, he rode him to the deck, where with twin hands he jerked the dagger free. But alas then, his selective vengeance his undoing, he turned, not on the dagger's owner, but to stab the red-faced crewman who had flogged him. Yet just as he drove the knife deep in over the crewman's collarbone, the dagger-owner blasted him with his pistol at point-blank range. For turning his back on the better-armed, it was Tippu's end. Fatally pierced by the ball, he fell sideways, then toppled on his face. Bymba, gasping, had frozen into a rock. Now at Cockle's shouts the cannon had been moved into position, but first, having retrieved his pistol, Cockle, desperate, confused, fired willy-nilly into the ranks of the women, simultaneously with their anguished cries. This aroused the giant Wobogo-Woot. Though slowly, wanderingly, at first, he got up off the deck and, somehow now seeming charged with a miraculous sudden energy born of the pistol blast into the defenseless women, he led the beginning of the blacks' general assault. Thus was initiated on the grandest scale possible the mutiny itself, which soon became a widespread grisly convulsion.

But suddenly a crewman fired the cannon Cockle had ordered brought out, just as Captain Stokes rushed on deck. At the thunderous report the ranks of the slaves seemed to disintegrate; momentarily men fell back upon men and died an instant bloody death as screams from the women rent the air. Stokes stared crazily at a part of the bulwarks which had been shot away, then, appearing to come to himself, began shouting: "Reload! Reload!" Now he ran first to the two crewmen who manned the cannon and then, strangely, over into the ranks of the wounded blacks where the next cannon shot was very likely to be aimed. Yet despite their cries of anguish it was discernible an even further change had come over the raging blacks. Stokes saw it. "Cockle!—all hands on deck! . . . everybody! With muskets, pistols, and cutlasses! . . . Hurry! Hurry!" Stokes now had his own pistol out and was brandishing it in every direction including that of the women and children. Now six or seven crewmen came running on deck, panting, excited, in great fear, realizing, even though the blacks were unarmed, how far the crew were outnumbered. "Get the irons!" cried Stokes—"Get them back in the irons! . . . the darbies!"

But by the time Cockle and others had run to the chest of man-
acles against the splintered bulwarks, the black men, heeding Woot's
wily orders, had begun to disperse. There was much confusion and
disorder among them, yet they seemed somehow possessed of a
common purpose, a mission. It was then soon realized by Stokes
and Cockle that the dispersal was anything but a panicky rout.
Wobogo-Woot's giant heavy head and tiny, staring, beady eyes
seemed directing all this action, as if he had come at last to natural,
instant, leadership in the maw of war. Under his command the
blacks soon saw the folly of standing there in a solid manageable
phalanx to await further disaster. Suddenly now they were scattering all over the ship and crying out orders to each other in a
rash of variegated dialects.

"Watch, watch!" Stokes warned Cockle—"What are they saying? . . . what are they up to? Look!" Stokes was pointing.

One of the black men, a youth, was climbing the shrouds—
scurrying up toward the top of the mainmast as agilely as if it were
the trunk of a palm tree. The others too were scattering everywhere
—above and below the weather deck as well as aloft. Soon the boys
joined the men in spreading throughout the ship and also taking to
the shrouds, scaling the ratlines like veteran sailors. The young
black who had been first up the shrouds was now at the very top of
the mainmast, the pinnacle of the ship, a dizzying height, and holding sway over all the others below. He soon cried out in a great
wild shriek at the others scaling the shrouds—"They will never
catch us to put us in the chains again! No, no!—we are free,
brothers, if we resist! . . . Still more of us will die but there are
many, many of us—far more than the white cannibals—and we
can take them one by one! I can fire the white man's gun as many
others of you can, but those who can't can show the cannibals the
blade of a knife—that they can! Brothers, brothers, *we can take
this ship!*"

The few remaining crewmen were pouring on deck now. They
looked to Stokes beseechingly, as if pleading for leadership, for a
plan of action that would save them. But Stokes, and Cockle too,
seemed paralyzed; both gaped about them in total wonder, and fear.
The sun was bright, the ship rolling gently in a slight breeze, slipping through easy seas as if there had been no storm; and it would
soon be noon. Now the women and girls too, furtively, began to

271

wander apart from each other—until Stokes pointed his pistol at them and drove them back. Yet he still seemed powerless, inept, frozen by the suddenness, the unexpectedness, of these lethal events.

Suddenly now a black burst up from the galley with the cook held captive by a knife at his ribs. The cook was balding, potbellied, and pale as a sheet from fright; he stood shivering as if under sentence of death and looked at his captain, Stokes, with mournful, condemning eyes. "Free the cook!" at last yelled Stokes to the crewmen standing about as though they were petrified. Stokes futilely waved his big pistol now, but the cook was between him and the black. "Go around behind him!" he then shouted to a crewman with a musket—"Kill the black wretch!" The crewman shot quickly, his musket making a great roar, and the black fell forward on top of the crouching cook. The cook went to his knees but shook himself free, as the black, blood spurting from his neck, fell to the deck and gasped his last breaths. "The cannon!" now cried Stokes— "Kill them all! . . . kill every one of them you see!" Yet he himself stood as if glued to the deck, incapable of any action to restore the status quo. The blacks however for the moment also seemed experiencing some kind of indecision, powerlessness, indirection, doubtless due in part to their illnesses and bone-weary fatigue; their actions were no longer febrile; they seemed almost ready to lie down on the deck in a kind of frenzied death-sleep in which they would return to their native villages, their actions dreamlike, motions floating again, vague, almost lacking any purpose. This brooding, all-encompassing lethargy then seemed to rule the entire ship and every human on it. At last Stokes found breath. "Kill them all!" he repeated, though weakly—" . . . even if we arrive home in an empty ship! Show no quarter, men! . . ." But he seemed speaking to them from the depths of a well, his voice echoing faintly yet resoundingly to the crewmen around him, who seemed able to do nothing. Now he surveyed the weather deck stretching before him and assumed a very sober, contemplative mien. The deck was strewn, fouled, with blood.

The blacks throughout the ship had now begun a general, if confused and physically debilitated, assault on every crewman they could find. They hunted them down in every corner of the *Caper,* though many fell victims themselves to the muskets and pistols of the frantic crew. But there were always others to fill their places when inevitably the crewmen had to undertake the clumsy, laborious task of reloading. The blacks moreover had the cutlasses, knives, hatchets, and daggers they had taken and soon all quarters of the ship were a bloody, grisly sight. Some had even retrieved the expended, unloaded, muskets and pistols of dead crewmen and used them as clubs in the murderous melee.

"Fire when ready!" yelled Stokes to the two men manning the cannon. But suddenly there were no black men readily in sight for targets as the crewmen, outraged, panic-stricken, wild with fear, now eyed the milling women and girls, and glanced at Stokes. "Fire, I said!" he yelled again, apoplectic, his eyes blazing like a mad man's. The cannon's report was deafening, followed by a great, unison-like scream, then the piteous cries and moans, of the females, some of whom perished outright, while others, maimed, dismembered, bleeding, lay writhing on the deck. It was then the black men began the main, decimating, slaughter. Three or four of them, armed with knives or cutlasses, surrounded each crewman once he had fired his piece and hacked him to death. Blood ran across the decks and into the scuppers. Suddenly a black, who had witnessed the slaughter of the women and girls from up in the shrouds and who had now come down, observed Cockle firing his pistol in the fight. He confronted him before he could reload and, yelling something in a dialect ashen-faced Cockle could not understand, swung his cutlass at the first mate's head. Cockle, though ducking for his life, received a glancing blow over the eye that made the blood stream down the front of his shirt. Stokes then shot Cockle's assailant but not before he himself had received a superficial left shoulder wound from an anonymous galley knife. The crewmen were virtually surrounded now; there were wild shouts from all sides, the seamen still unharmed crying out great oaths against the blacks, yet resisting them ineffectively. The blacks were however also in disorder but realized their numbers meant the certainty of victory. Yet some, even those who so far had escaped wounds, seemed so weakened they could hardly fight—except for Woot, who, now that Tippu was dead, was unquestioned leader; everyone took this for granted. The boys, led by Bymba, seemed also somehow to have overcome their debility. They ran wild through the ship. Coming upon a sailor lying near death from multiple dagger stabs, Bymba

273

grabbed up a cutlass, and, wielding it with both hands, nearly de-capitated the crewman. "Death to the cannibals!" he shouted. "We shall return to our villages where we shall not be eaten and where our women will not be slaughtered! Death then to the white can-nibals!"

Just then a seaman was seen climbing, scurrying up, the shrouds as if in a frantic hurry to accomplish some vague mission while there was yet time. His lank hair was grimy and bedraggled and he wore a strange white garment resembling a long smock, a most unseaman-like apparel, and more like that of a portrait painter in his studio. As he frantically ascended the shrouds, nearing the top of the foremast now, he occasionally turned and, shouting some inco-herent message, stared back down at the devastation, at what was left of the ship's hapless company standing amidst the gore. Women and girls, killed or maimed by the cannon, were strewn about the deck and several of the men as well as sailors lay dead or sprawled with blood spurting from fatal wounds. Cockle, though still on his feet, was bleeding profusely from the cutlass wound on the head, while Stokes, waving his sound right arm like a fiery prophet, shouted futile orders to his routed and puny forces. The sailors however were too preoccupied with their own hurts, their fears for their lives, to pay him the slightest attention. It all seemed to stupefy and enrage Stokes, who was now raving again like a man entirely bereft of his reason. "You craven vermin, you!" he shouted to the remnants of his crew—"Will you malinger and be slaughtered by these black savages? . . . To arms, to arms! Think of your souls when you come to judgment for your cowardly misdeeds in the face of an ignorant and unworthy foe out of the jungle!" It was all like a fantasy. For a time the blacks around him, though they could not understand him, stopped their slow-motioned agitation as if they wished to wait and hear what more he had to say. They looked at each other as if in a quandary and one of them once made a vague motion as though shrugging his shoulders. Stokes seemed strangely exempt from their violence.

But now Bymba, his cutlass firmly in both hands, made a rush at the demented captain. At once the tall black warrior and now leader, Wobogo-Woot, stepped in front of the boy and prevented his reaching Stokes—who, though slightly wounded, stood ready with his own cutlass to defend himself. Woot said to Bymba: "No, no, little brother—he is the Captain and must not be touched. . . .

We shall need him to steer the ship, for we are untrained in such crafty skills. We will make the Captain, who is the leader of the white cannibals, return us to our villages. Then we shall disembowel him and throw his entrails to the hyenas—for this leader is unclean, having, cannibal that he is, devoured so many of our people!"

Bymba, appearing not to have considered these hard facts, at last desisted. He stared at the tall, almost naked, black giant. "Why, Master Woot, did not our leaders and medicine men teach us how to sail a ship?" he said vehemently—"Why did they not also arm us with pistols, muskets, and cannon with which to defend ourselves and our women? They have betrayed us!"

Just then, however, the sailor with the long, straggly hair and white smock aloft began yelling something down again at the weird gathering on deck as it went through its languid, surrealistic antics. His words could not at first be made out, yet he continued waving his arms and haranguing them all in a loud voice. Finally, getting no response from his spectators below, he stood on the ratlines in the shrouds and wrapped his smock about him in a most fastidious yet grandiose way, as if it were a Roman toga, but for another moment was silent. It was then seen he was bleeding freely from a cutlass thrust in the chest. Great blotches of blood showed through the front of the smock; he also appeared to be weakening, the volume of his voice falling. Holding onto the shrouds now with one hand, he placed the other across his bloody breast, as his long, tangled hair fell over an eye. He seemed trying to marshal all his remaining strength for one last, herculean effort to speak to the bizarre mob below. "We are finished!" he cried out, as if directly to Captain Stokes. "With all our guns, our compasses, spyglasses, cannon, with all our machinery, we are no match for them—for they are numerous and fight to return home! . . . They are at the edge of existence, where life is sweet, honor dear. We cannot withstand them!" Feebly swaying now, leaning, sinking, back into the shrouds, he seemed to weaken further as he drew the smock more tightly than ever about his quivering, wounded body—"Let me be content then to rest these last moments in the shrouds! . . . Our machinery has availed us nothing! . . . nothing! We are overcome by a more righteous breed who will soon know their strength. Our machinery, trappings, our science! . . . Bah!" He gave a bitter laugh, then seemed struggling to hold fast to the perilous ratlines.

At once Stokes began calling up to him from what felt to both of them as far, far below. "Hold fast, Buchanan!—hold fast! . . . We are not done!"

"We are finished, Captain . . . though you led us well," cried the sailor. "But they were on the edge!—do you see, Captain? . . ." With that he seemed to wilt, to give himself completely to the shrouds; yet, though he appeared dazed, he did not fall. "At the edge . . . Captain. . . ." he repeated weakly. Then quietly he began to whimper, cry, before he fell to his death.

The crowd below had summoned the energy to leap away from the spot where the sailor fell; his bleeding, broken body now lay on the deck in their very midst. The fall seemed to have stunned them, had a sudden, demoralizing effect on what remained of the crew. Stokes was also near tears; he addressed them now in funereal tones: "Buchanan was right. We are lost—and because of our grievous errors, it was. It cannot be righted now. But when we brought them up out of the hold we sealed our fate; only those of our civilization who show no quarter shall prevail; we were weak, misguided, and now we are vanquished. It will ever be thus." Stokes heaved a heavy sigh and gazed down at Buchanan's body; they all stood around him, even the blacks, everyone immobilized or in a vague bizarre slow-motion. Then a commotion at the hatchway aroused them from their torpor.

It was three blacks tugging the surgeon, Whittier, up through the hatchway and onto the deck. They rudely shoved him forward then at the feet of Wobogo-Woot. "It is their medicine man," one of them informed Woot. "We found him asleep on his pallet, drunk on spirits." Whittier stood sleepily blinking his eyes and weaving still; but suddenly he was rational, looking around at them all in wonder and bewilderment. Then he saw all the blood, the dead, and dying; finally he was aware of Stokes, who glowered at him; he knew why.

"You drunken dog!" exploded Stokes—"where have you been? . . . lying drunk, of course. It was you that brought this all on— it was you who said they must all be brought up, unshackled, and treated for their hurts. I was against it, as was Cockle, but, fool that I was, I gave in to you. Then you disappear to get drunk! . . . I should reload my pistol now and kill you! Ah, but your time is not long—these black savages will soon mete out proper justice to you, as they will to all of us who remain, before this is over. You won't escape next time, you rum-sotted miscreant! . . ."

Whittier was silent, penitent; he hung his head.

"Wobogo-Woot, he is their medicine man," repeated one of Whittier's captors. "He talked confused, crazy, talk when we took him—shall we kill him?" The three black captors moved closer to Whittier.

"Not yet, brothers," said Woot, though again weakly, yet raising himself to his full, magnificent height as if to remind them he was the son of a chief and their natural leader. "He has no firearms— we shall kill only those who have weapons and will not surrender them. Go and summon them all here, the white cannibals—bring them before me—and find a linguister. Go at once—hurry."

The three men left. But there were crowds of black men on deck now, completely surrounding, overpowering, the handful of crewmen who had survived the massacre. Whittier looked ruefully at Captain Stokes; finally he spoke: "Captain, why don't you parley with them?—we must bargain for our lives. They cannot sail the ship; they know it; and they know if they kill us, they too will die here in the middle of the Atlantic. We must somehow keep going; it's too late to turn back, as they doubtless want us to. We must beguile them, treat with them, Captain; stall for time and see what develops. Is there any other course—but certain death by butchery?"

"The great oracle!" sneered Stokes; he still seemed half crazed —neither Whittier nor Cockle had ever seen him so bereft of composure. "The fount of all wisdom! Whittier, you're going to die just like the rest of us—and, yes, most likely by butchery! I hope you're the first to go, I do—you deserve it! I want none of your advice—I will not parley with these brutes! I will die still superior to them—as a civilized human being, an Anglo-Saxon, an American, a Virginian!"

"Ah, Captain," said Whittier, "but suppose they torture you? . . . you hadn't thought of that, had you? The blacks are supreme at torture—and we are now at their mercy. It is better to make a formal gesture of surrendering all your weapons. This may somewhat appease them, play on their vanity. Then we could ask them to parley; tell them if they will spare us, we shall return them to their homeland—but instead take the straightest route to the Bermuda-Hamilton Islands off Hatteras. With the right winds, we might make, Captain."

"I will first suffer torture!" cried Stokes—prophetically. But his

277

chief mate Cockle also gave the captain an exceedingly displeased look; he had seen much logic in what Whittier had said and now shook his head doubtfully about Stokes' oracular vow.

"Others of us, though, Captain, may not wish to suffer torture," Whittier said. "In the face of nigh certain death, each of us has the right as best he sees it to provide for himself, to stay alive—you will concede that, Captain, what?"

Stokes was livid. "If we ever reach a civilized port, Whittier, you will hang higher than Haman for your mutinous insubordination! . . . I pledge it! . . . I will see it done!"

Meanwhile, the blacks—men, women, children—stood all around them, studying their faces as they talked. Wobogo-Woot and his people realized that matters of crucial importance were under discussion and were gratified to see there was passionate disagreement; more than ever it reassured them. Woot turned to one of the blacks—"Go, Kheti, and find someone among us to be linguister," he said, "for much is being discussed here." Kheti, a nervous, captious black, pitifully emaciated from the weeks of his ordeal since capture, looked irritated and surprised, then dismayed, at having been given so impossible an assignment.

Whittier interrupted. A veteran of the Guinea coast, he had understood what Woot had said and stepped forward now and spoke haltingly in the same Fanti dialect Woot had used: "King," he addressed Woot with unction, sychophance, "I myself, if I may be so bold, am somewhat a linguister. It is my wish, as well as that of many others of this crew, to assist you, to cooperate with you, to know your royal will. What would you know?"

Stokes, who had understood nothing, yet knew Whittier was collaborating. "Traitor!" he cried—"Have you no honor, no pride?"

But Whittier, in searching Woot's face, seemed not to hear Stokes. "King," he said to Woot, "until you have found a linguister to your liking, I shall be happy to serve you. I know, from many long African visitations, some of the most-used dialects. You are Coromantee—the Fanti language you use I do not know as well as some others, but much of it I still remember and understand. I will serve you, gladly."

Woot was nonplussed. Frowning, he studied Whittier. "What you say places you in the gravest danger, cannibal," he at last pronounced. "You are a menace. You hear and understand what both

I and your own leader say, and I know you are not with us. You are therefore a candidate for swift death—you imperil us with your many tongues, but we imperil you also. Take this man!" he shouted to his followers.

Two blacks leapt forward and seized the surgeon, who soon stood quavering in fear in their grasp. "Shall we dispatch him to his ancestors?" they asked of Woot.

". . . What?" cried Whittier, trembling—"when I can be of so much service to you? . . ." he pleaded. "Look . . . look at how many of your own lie there bearing almost certain mortal wounds!" He tried with his hand to make a sweeping gesture around the deck but was restrained. "King, I am a surgeon, a healer—a medicine man—with vast experience, who can yet save many of your people who groan here in agony—look!" Again he was restrained.

But a stricken expression came on the faces of many blacks at this. One of them with a gaping musket wound in his side feebly bestirred himself on the deck and spoke: "No, no—it is better that we die." He pointed a finger at Whittier—"He is *their* medicine man, not ours. He is no good for us—he cannot speak to our gods, but can only bring the evil spirits on us. It is he who should die."

Shrewd Woot, however, had had time to ponder the situation. "Let us wait awhile, my friends," he said to the blacks. "Trust me—let me find where our advantages are." He turned now to the few other crewmen assembled. "How many more of you will enlist in our cause," he said—"and save your lives? Come, is it not wiser? You will sail the ship back to our homeland and live," he lied. When Whittier had translated for the crewmen, Stokes cursed him. Cockle, though, held up a hand in fearful assent, but then, from mortification, was unable to speak. But eleven of the nineteen remaining able-bodied crewmen, hoping to survive somehow, vowed cooperation—to the accompaniment of Stokes' maniacal taunts; the other eight seemed too frightened to react at all. Whittier now gazed at his captain and was certain the stress of the day's cataclysm had driven him stark mad—Stokes' face was flushed, his periwig askew, his eyes wild; also blood from his slight shoulder wound showed through his shirt. Woot was still deliberative; he studied Stokes. "Your leader is an unwise man," he told the other crewmen. "He will lose your lives—if you too are unwise. Let us put this ship in order—deliver the dead to the sea and succor the hurt and ex-

hausted. With the consent of my people, I am leader here now."
There were ready expressions of assent from the blacks all around,
to which Woot reacted with a show of great dignity.

Two more crewmen, stragglers, were now brought on deck by a
roving band of blacks. "What?" said Woot—"are there still more?"

"These are the last," said one of the band—"the rest are dead."

"Why then do these two live?"

"It was my decision, Woot," said another of the party—"They
will do our bidding; they have said so. We shall maybe need them."

Woot was grave, reflective—contrite. "It is true," he said—"we
shall need them. Why is this? It is indeed something to ponder,
brothers. Why can we not kill all these cannibals?—as we would
surely like to do. . . ." He sighed now. "But these are deep considerations . . . of which I think I know little."

Whittier had heard and understood. "Yours are a great people,
King," he fawned, still trembling in fear. "In due time these mighty
matters will become clear to you . . . in, ha, your process of matura-
tion, let us say! Ah, but you will be no happier—look at us." He
turned and surveyed the mottled crewmen.

"I know you are not happy!" cried Woot angrily, but in anguish
—"You are cannibals, all of you! You prey on others like jackals.
Wherever you are there are misery and bloodshed. You must have
these plagues—it is your nature, your necessity! It saddens me that
we need you, but our gods have betrayed us—as yours have you.
Yet, as you have already today, you will pay in blood and sorrow!"

Whittier fought to conceal his contempt. "As if *you* haven't paid
in blood," he thought. "King," he said, however, with a bitter
though groveling smile, "one day you will be like us—ha, you deserve to be."

Though Captain Stokes understood nothing, he was sent into a
wild fit of raving when he saw Whittier's smile. "You capitulating
dog!" he shouted at the surgeon, then turned to the other crewmen
as well—"most of you! . . . you're unworthy of your heritage! I am
of Scotch and English stock—the purest—do you understand? I
cannot do what you do—death is preferable to me! I have become
a religious man too!"—Stoke's father's fire was in his eyes now.
"And I descend from the same stock as James VI of Scotland, who
was the James I of England—my religion, indeed my father's religion before me, comes down to me from him . . . James!"

"King, you see?—he is raving mad," said Whittier to Woot, in an aside. "Look at him—almost frothing at the mouth. . . . Ah, this is what you want, is it? These are all traits you too may have, if you wish—all your people too." Then again the bitter smile—"I'd almost swear you deserve them. . . ."

Stokes had taken a small black book from his pocket now. It was the size of a catechism or the New Testament, though it was neither. He stared around at them all and seemed near catatonic. He found the passage in his holy little book he desired and began to read in the loud voice of eloquence of his father: "Great and manifold were the blessings, most dread Sovereign, which Almighty God, the Father of all mercies, bestowed upon us, the people of England, when first he sent Your Majesty's Royal Person to rule and reign over us!" One of the few undefecting crewmen solemnly nodded his head and crossed himself. Stokes continued: "But among all our joys, there was no one that more filled our hearts, than the blessed continuance of the preaching of God's sacred Word among us!—which is that inestimable treasure, which excelleth all the riches of the earth! . . . because the fruit thereof extendeth itself, not only to the time spent in this transitory world, but directeth and disposeth men unto that eternal happiness which is above in heaven! . . ." Stokes paused to wet his lips with his tongue.

"Kill him!" a black woman suddenly shouted—"He will bring the evil white spirits down on us! . . ."

"Yes!" others agreed—"The raving cannibal is unclean and evil: he is now crazy besides; and has taken us away from our homeland, to devour us. Let us remove his head, brothers!"

But Wobogo-Woot raised a magisterial hand. "Be patient—that will come in due time," he said. "I wish to learn the meaning of what this despicable cannibal here is reading." He turned to Stokes —"Read on, while you still live!"

Stokes, understanding Woot's gestures, bent his head to the book again. But Surgeon Whittier intruded, smiling craftily to Woot— "What he reads, King, is from our 'Epistle Dedicatory.' It is not our Bible—it is trash, fustian." He too now was suddenly interrupted, as if by some divine decree, by a strange, almost ghostlike, noise from high above—the jarring, shuddering, ripping, motion of the huge white sails of the ship as they caught the full force of new winds moving the ship at a far faster speed than they had experienced before. Whittier did not resume speaking for a moment, as if reverential of, awed by, the obtrusive phenomenon. The others too gazed up at the open skies as if searching for the meaning of the events of the day in the bizarre, savage language of the sails and their ghostly whiteness. Again Whittier tried to speak, but once more desisted. At last, but still at times glowering at his erstwhile surgeon, Captain Stokes resumed his loud reading from the little book: "The eyes of Your people doth behold You with comfort, and they bless you in their hearts, as that sanctified Person who, under God, is the immediate Author of their true happiness!"

Whittier had translated for the others, when there came a piercing scream. It was from the black woman who, interrupting before, had called for Stokes' death. "Take him away, I say! . . ." she cried now—"He talks of his gods, who, in raising up a nation of white cannibals, must themselves be white! They are not for us!—they are our mortal enemies! . . . Look here at our dead around us! Must we stand here, Wobogo-Woot, and hear ourselves made victims of his vile white spirits? . . . Silence him, Woot!—cut out his tongue! . . ." There was widespread murmuring accord around her. Yet Stokes sneered his defiance at them all.

Woot shook his head. "I want to hear more," he said, with kingly finality.

Whittier, grinning, nodded to Stokes: "Proceed."

But Stokes seemed offended by any words addressed to him by Whittier. He set his jaw, returned his little book to his pocket, and stood in a towering dudgeon.

Woot looked at Whittier. "What is the matter?" he said—"Your man no longer reads. Has he spoken all the lies he wishes?—if so, what did they mean?"

Whittier shook his head in mock sadness. "King, he is fully demented," he said—"Can't you see? He is mad—completely out of contact with our own reality. What did he mean? you ask. Why, he meant nothing. What he said came out of his brain storm—it is all a confused lunacy; as I said, utter claptrap and fustian . . . though he would call it love for our civilization."

"I do not believe you," said Woot. "It has meaning—though I do not know what it is." He then looked out over the crowd assembled before him until he found the woman who had screamed. "Come forward," he said to her—"you, sister, who wishes their leader's death." The woman, tall, statuesque, brownish-black, a rag on her head, finally emerged from the crowd on deck, came across to where Woot stood, and faced him squarely. "What, to your mind, was the meaning of what their leader read?" Woot asked her. "Speak with care, seriousness, and truth, sister, for his life depends on it."

The woman spoke without hesitation. "We are not included in what he read, Wobogo-Woot—we are on the outside of it; it is not meant for us; we are only its victims." She paused and gazed up at the heavily shuddering white sails—Woot watching her with his beady eyes—as the sails rattled now even more menacingly. At last she seemed no longer able to speak; her jaw went slack.

"Go on, go on," said Woot impatiently.

I have finished," she finally said, and slowly, in defeat, turned and rejoined the crowd.

*   *   *   *   *

Ten days later the ship lay becalmed under a broiling sun; the heat was so intense that even the open decks were like a furnace. Woot, now solidly in command of the vessel, had spared all remaining lives when Whittier repeatedly assured him the ship had been turned about and was headed back to Africa's Guinea coast whence they had come. But Captain Stokes, at times now raving mad, was below in chains. Otherwise, under Woot's artful leadership, enhanced by the aid and counsel of a crafty deputy, Surgeon Whittier, an uneasy order had been restored aboard the *Caper*. But as Whittier and the remnants of the crew now under him had surreptitiously willed it, the ship, though temporarily becalmed, was still headed west, toward America, while Woot and the blacks harbored a blind faith they were returning east, to Africa. "How long now before we shall descry our homeland?" Woot continued asking Whittier, many times each day. The surgeon's reply invariably blamed the "infernal timid winds" but assured Woot of their steady progress, of their arrival after perhaps another moon. Yet Whittier on such occasions secretly trembled with apprehension, fear, whenever he caught Woot's absent, questioning, troubled, at times, bloodthirsty, stare on him. It made him quake. At once he would deftly lead the mistrustful leader onto some other subject, some other concern, such as that of the vital drinking water supply, the obedience of the remaining crew, or the convalescent rate of the sick and wounded—the dead had long since been dispatched overboard.

Again—one day near noon, the listless weather unchanged—little Bymba sought out his fellow-Coromantee, Wobogo-Woot. It was his third attempt to see his leader, in whom nevertheless he had developed an unbounded confidence, about a matter that sorely puzzled, troubled, him. Woot, Bymba however was certain, would eventually deliver them out of their captivity and lead them home. Yet twice Woot had refused him an audience, or at best had twice eluded him. Was it because, Bymba wondered, Woot felt his new position too august to bring him to parley with a thirteen-year-old boy? Today, however, Bymba had taken up a position outside Woot's cabin—that formerly occupied by Captain Stokes—and was determined to talk to Woot about this matter he did not understand but which had brought extremely plaguing questions to his mind. When now after an hour Woot finally arrived, Bymba approached him at once and exhorted him to parley. At first Woot was gruff, and stared at Bymba with his small, beady eyes. "Parley!" he said—"*You* wish to parley with *me,* eh, boy?"

"Yes," said Bymba—"in secret. I have questions."

"In secret! Children have no secrets, boy. But very well—come in and ask me your questions." Bymba followed him into the cabin and closed the door. But then he became confused, flustered, and could not find the right words. Woot was impatient—"Speak, boy! Do you wish to take all my time? . . ." He sat down and stared again at Bymba.

"Are we heading back toward our homeland, Master Woot?" said Bymba, his voice barely adequate at last.

"Yes—but not because of you." Woot seemed to relish the opportunity. "You wanted to kill all the white cannibals, remember? —you, running up and down the deck with a cutlass grasped by both your hands. But I stayed your stupid hands—else, where would we be now? Instead today we are making them, on pain of their very lives, return us to our homeland and our freedom."

Bymba pondered what he had heard; for a moment he was silent. "Very well then, Master," he finally said, backing away—"We are going home."

"Yes, boy—and may the watchful spirits of our ancestors grant it soon."

"I could not understand . . ." said Bymba—"I could not understand the setting sun. . . ."

"What?" Woot looked at him impatiently again.

"Before we subdued the white cannibals and took the ship," Bymba groped on, "the sun in the evening went down into the sea over the prow of the ship."

"Of course," said Woot.

"But, Master, it still goes down in the same place." There was silence—except for Woot's heavy breathing. "Have you observed?" said Bymba—"I have been puzzled, for I thought now it should go down over the stern."

Woot stared at Bymba. No words came from either of them. Then Woot slowly stood up. "This had not come to my mind," he said. "Say it again, boy."

"If the cannibals have turned the ship around," said Bymba, "why does the sun still go down over the prow as it did before?"

Suddenly Woot, his beady eyes now somehow dilated, staring, seized Bymba by the shoulders, steered him around to a stool, and pushed him down. Woot's breathing was very audible now. "You came to ask questions of me, boy," he said, "but I find I lack the knowledge to answer them. Ah, it is true—I have not the answers. . . ." Sweating profusely, he sat down again. Bymba watched him, feeling equally helpless. But soon Woot's face began to change, to take on a cunning, cruel mien, his little eyes darting back and forth, as he wiped sweat from his brow with his forearm. "There may be those, however," he said, "who *can* answer your questions—if they will; and with proper persuasion, I venture they will." Quickly he stood up again, towering over Bymba, and gave an ugly leer, then sucked air noisily through his teeth, his nostrils flaring. "Come, boy," he said—"you must go. I have things to do. No one must know of our parley, absolutely no one, you understand?—but return to me here once darkness has fallen. It is possible by evening I may have your answers already." He opened the cabin door and Bymba left.

Then the weather changed. It was all so sudden, freakish, as if fated. By four o'clock that afternoon the sun had disappeared completely; clouds obscured the sky; they began as gray, fleecy, scudding objects; then slowed, became viscous, obdurate; they soon darkened, were foreboding, just as the wind picked up and began lightly to flutter the sails and stir the shirt sleeves of the ship's surgeon standing at the taffrail anxiously surveying the precarious prospect. Whittier's years of sea duty rendered him fearful of sudden September gales; besides, the pitiful remnants of the crew had appeared at their posts clad to the teeth in their tarpaulin clothing. It was ominous. Within thirty minutes the ship was rolling in choppy seas that sent sheets of spray flying aft. Along the bulwarks on the starboard side the blacks stood in awed, silent lots, watching with fearful wonder, grave apprehension, the seas rise as fantastic, mountainous obstacles in the path of the faith they held in the return, homeward-bound, progress of the *Caper*. By five o'clock the ship was leaping on the waves like a steeplechaser. Most of the nervous blacks went below now, to what had formerly been the seaman's mess, where they were fed by the cowed crewmen and a contingent of auxiliary blacks assigned to the galley by Woot and his deadly serious lieutenants.

Suddenly the ship's bell rang. No one would ever quite know why —was it just coincidence? Yet the attention of everyone throughout the ship was arrested; there was a baleful silence. Then those on the weather deck were aware of a commotion at the hatchway. Four or five blacks were escorting, or manhandling, Captain Stokes onto the deck. He seemed composed, rational, however, and not unnecessarily perturbed, though he stooped a bit from his superficial shoulder wound; he was also extraordinarily well-groomed—as if he had had nothing else during his detention to do except wash and groom himself; he was almost foppish—resplendent in silk stockings, knee breeches, silver-buckled shoes, a flair-tailed, turquoise-blue coat, with his neck swathed in a high-reaching stock; his peruke, the hair brownish-red and tied up in a pigtail at the back with a black ribbon, seemed brand new beneath his tri-cornered hat. It was also apparent he was not at all downcast or depressed as he was led to the portside bulwarks and left by his escorts, or captors, to observe the rising imperious seas. Whittier left the taffrail at once and approached Stokes with an anxious expression on his face. Stokes took note of him impassively and Whittier became impulsive. "Oh, Captain," he said, twisting in anxiety, "I wish you were of some help to us! . . . we need you, we need your leadership—I fear the blacks have gotten suspicious . . . it's about the direction of the ship. That Woot—a sly, dangerous fellow—is asking queer questions. And he roams the ship constantly—from the bowsprit to the taffrail there, he does; he's restless, uneasy, as a cat. Something's bothering him, pestering his thick head, I tell you. And why is it he let you out of confinement, disburdened you of your chains; then—is it to be believed!—let you dress yourself up like an admiral of the fleet? It's strange, I vow."

Stokes, still impassive, occasionally glanced at Whittier, yet uttered not a word.

"What's going on, Captain? . . ." pressed the surgeon. "Has anybody said anything to you that should make us uneasy? Have any of the blacks approached you? . . . has Woot?"

Stokes' eyes lit up crazily; he smiled, almost sneered. "They know they're still headed away from their home," he said—"they know it. So what did they do?—though savages, they're no fools; there's a distinction—why, they enlisted my services, that's what they did. I'm in charge of this ship again. You'll all follow my orders now or I'll have you flogged within an inch of your lives. We may soon be returning to Africa!"

Whittier gaped at Stokes. Yet he could not believe him. He was certain now it was futile to talk to him in the hope he might have regained enough of his reason to be of service to the remaining crewmen; he was convinced it was all useless now; he would merely humor, indulge, him; provoke what was left of his imagination. "Is it your own wish that we return to Africa, Captain?"

"You say I have been disburdened of my chains; the choice then is mine, is it not? The blacks are fanatical in their desire to return home and have sought my services. Are they not sincere? They are indeed—as genuine as a force of nature itself; there is perhaps something to be gained by a study of their heated rectitude. It is Africa, you see; there lies buried, obscured, there an ingredient mysterious as it is brooding and profound; magnetic as it is enigmatic; so every black, no matter where—in whatever part of the widest world—he may be found, will ever in his fierce heart respond to that abstruse continent as to a lodestone. Is it possible, Whittier, there is some slight contagion here too for us? . . . is it seemly? I may not be averse then, let us say, to returning. But then again I may. I will study the matter further." Once more his eyes lit up crazily. "Yet, is it possible Africa could hold something precious for me? . . . oh, my mind is so confused—it is *not* possible . . . yet I think . . ."

Whittier became impish, shrewish, at last malevolent. "They have captured you, Captain, do you see?—captured your imagination, your sanity." He gave a cackle of a laugh. "They disburdened you of your chains, yes, but still hold you captive to their strange and fanatical love of homeland. But Africa is their lodestone—what is yours?"

At once Stokes flew into a rage. "How dare you question *me?* I answer to no one!" Yet his voice projected, trailed, into a pensive, hollow, echo—"I resumed command of this death ship today. I shall remain at the helm until the end. You will do as I say now. I have the power to enforce the will that propels us to whatever . . . to whatever—" His voice expired.

"Ah, but one little trifling, mundane matter, Captain." Whittier's choler had risen; he became excited. "Who in all this served as your linguister? . . . Who talked to that savage, Woot, for you?—there's no black aboard this ship who could ever talk or understand the English language. You're having dreams, fantasies! . . . you're deceiving yourself! What a pity it is your reason has fled."

Stokes sneered again. "Ha!—what presumptions. Are you the only one who speaks 'Africka?' Is it that none of this crew knows nothing at all of any of these hybrid dialects rife on this ship?—but you? Everybody aboard is a fool but you, eh, Whittier? You may see ere this is over that it may not be so. Now leave me, leave my sight—get below!"

Before he thought, Whittier, out of long habit, stepped with alacrity to do Stokes' bidding, finding himself already at the hatchway before coming to. He paused, then stopped, and looked back at Stokes. He had never been more mystified in his life as, docilely, he continued below. Now the ship was dipping, rolling; it was definitely no longer becalmed; and though what had earlier promised to be an awesome storm had not entirely materialized; the winds were high and strong, the canvas full, the destined *Caper* on the move—but where?

As soon as darkness fell, Bymba, as Woot had instructed him, presented himself at Woot's cabin door. Irresolutely he knocked. Soon there came a response in a language he did not understand;

realizing then it was no dialect of Africa's, he could not avoid the near certainty it was the voice of some crewman, speech out of the mouth of a white cannibal himself. His heart began pounding. Where was Woot?—why was his voice not heard? "Master Woot? . . ." he called through the door. The door opened then and he faced Captain Stokes. Both stared at each other. Stokes was still clad in his elegant attire, except, in relaxing, he had laid aside his periwig. Bymba's face clouded with anger, yet he could not conceal his surprise and bafflement at Woot's absence. He looked past Stokes into the cabin for a glimpse of Woot, but there was no one. "I've come to see Master Woot!" he suddenly cried—"Where is he?" Stokes, unable to understand the dialect, could only stare at him. Bymba's face now filled with rage. He pulled a dagger from his loin cloth and peremptorily repeated his question. "Where is Master Woot?" Stokes blanched and threw up both hands as if he were in fact about to receive the fatal dagger's blow. Then it vaguely occurred to him what Bymba might be asking and he began pointing a forefinger over, beyond, the boy's shoulder. Bymba, however, dagger still in hand, had not once taken his belligerent eyes off Stokes, who then finally stepped outside the cabin door and began an anxious beckoning for Bymba to follow him toward the bow of the ship. After many moments of this fervent summoning Bymba at last, grudgingly, came after him and they went forward, far forward, to the forecastle deck, passing on the way scores of blacks, men and women, lounging, murmuring, some, still exhausted and ill, asleep on the deck, others eyeing Stokes in his foppish finery suspiciously, hostilely.

Below deck in the forecastle itself, at last, they encountered an astounding sight. Twenty-five or more blacks, headed by Wobogo-Woot, were standing in a rough circle around six or seven crewmen, who like all their fellows aboard had long since been stripped of weapons. The blacks, however, were heavily armed, many even with pistols and muskets, as they stood huddled, crowded, listening intently to one of the crewmen acting, under dire orders, as linguister between Woot and another crewman who at the moment in the light of a lantern could not be clearly made out—yet it was evident he was manacled, hand and foot. Stokes, still leading Bymba, who in gawking around him had put his knife away, pushed his way to the inner circle where Woot saw them both but was so involved in what appeared a crucial life-and-death parley scarcely realized their actual presence. But now Bymba in the closer light looked again at the manacled crewman. It was Whittier!

Although Bymba appeared confused, uncomprehending, Stokes was unfazed at what they had come upon. He seemed to understand perfectly all that was going on and showed no surprise whatever. Whittier, disheveled hair down in his red face, shirt half torn off, an eye bloodied, stood trembling as if in mortal fear of his life. Woot was methodical, implacable, sinister; through the sailor-linguister, he questioned and grilled Whittier as though his guilt was a conclusion long foregone. Whittier was so spent and shaken by his ordeal he was almost in tears, as Woot now shouted at him and as the other crewmen looked on fearfully, aware of the revealed evidence of their own complicity. Bymba's thoughts now went back through old tribal memories; there was some vague, attenuated familiarity with the present experience—the endless parleying, probing, the denials and affirmations, the righteous, angry elders, the heat, the tension; they all somehow linked him with both past and present, and it was then he was suddenly aware he was witnessing a trial. Whittier was on trial for his life.

Nor had he ever seen Woot, now both prosecutor and judge, so bent on ruthless destruction. "Your fellow-cannibals," shouted Woot in the hapless surgeon's red face, "have said you were the leader in it all, so confess it! . . . though they willingly did your bidding, it was your plot. You filthy snake!—it was your determination never to return us to our homeland! Confess it! You were the leader of these other cannibals here, for you were their medicine man—you had power over them, though they should have resisted you, as they will well learn! But you persuaded them never to turn the ship around, as our people had ordered them to do, but to continue on course just as you had been before we subdued you. You were determined to deliver us into the hands of our enemies across this water where we would be devoured, or worse; where we would be stripped of our ways, our priests, our languages and dialects, our traditions, and made to become like you, villainous man-eaters who, for gold and shekels, or a miserable corner of your neighbor's land, would devour the hearts of your mothers—by the dozens!" With that Woot struck Whittier across the mouth with his open hand and the surgeon, trembling as if seized with an ague, went to his knees sobbing. "Ah, now you summon the tears, eh?" said Woot, curling his lip in scorn.

Stokes stepped forward now and, protected by the clever, loyal linguister, began to revile Whittier in even more bitter terms. "You are a despicable sight," he said. "Everything he says of you is true. Have you no principles?—you're a mean, low scullion of a wretch; a dishonor to us, a long-enlightened people. You first betrayed your own kind to save your putrid hide—betrayed *me,* your captain? You were unwilling to wait and trust me!—it was finally my design, after much study, to turn the ship around all right, yet still not head it for Africa. East, yes, but *north* and east. Ah, toward Europe—toward England? Yet you think me crazy? What a scurvy disgrace you are to the fellowship from which I hate to admit you come—you went over to these subhumans as soon as you saw their victory; but you have since betrayed them also and there's nothing in that apothecary's bag you carry about with you that will save you now, nothing!—prepare to die, Whittier." But the crewman linguister, translating, had taken pains to omit Stokes' grand strategy. The blacks remained oblivious, unaware.

Now Wobogo-Woot, with a strange detachment that went beyond the sinister, reached and shook Whittier by the shoulder, almost gently. "Which way is the ship heading, medicine man?" he said. Whittier only went on sobbing. The scene was eerie, almost ritualistic; the light from the lantern cast the shadows of the participants in the rite onto the walls of the gaunt, disordered compartment, as well as on each other; the blacks were intent, though they themselves seemed less sinister than serious, or partisan, or vindicated, as they craned forward into the circle the better to hear Woot's truculent interrogation; occasionally they mumbled comments, asides, assent, among themselves and were mutely absorbed in what the linguister said after each infrequent time Whittier spoke.

There were hardly enough crewmen left to navigate the ship in even the most favorable winds and seas; a bad storm equaled disaster; the sailors, subjugated and disarmed, little heartened by Stokes' plan, were by turns stoical, frightened, or downcast, and showed no signs of daring a further fight. But the reality was that the most malevolent and dangerous man aboard was Stokes—partially demented yet demonically brilliant. Yes, he thought now, viewing the grim scene before him, the whole crew, the ship's entire company, were totally helpless, defenseless, beaten—except, that is, for the potential of his and their minds. But to Stokes this difference was everything; he reveled in the conviction they would in the final test overcome; pondering it, foreseeing it all—even the end?—he could not help feeling fierce pride; they would overcome, yes, with the mind; he would never, he thought, while still alive, see himself and what remained of his crew in the end defeated; no, not alive, or, for that matter, dead. It was a zealot's vow he made to himself.

Whittier, depleted, consumed now, though standing again, hung his head on his chest like Christ on the cross. Woot, standing over him, repeated his question: "Oh, medicine man, you—which way is the ship heading?"

The surgeon at last partially raised his head and squinted at Woot through the eye, his right, which was not swollen shut; moments elapsed; it was not certain finally if he would speak at all. Then—"Toward heaven," he murmured. ". . . how I wish I had never left."

Woot and the blacks, uncomprehending, watched the sailor-linguister for a clue. "What? . . . where is that?" said Woot—" . . . Heaven?"

"The land of my birth." Sniveling Whittier tried to lift, square, his shoulders as he said it.

"Ah, yes," breathed Woot aloud—"The land of your birth. You wish to return there. I see. You wish to return there and take us with you—away from the land of *our* birth. It is clear to me now, yes." Woot nodded satisfaction at the linguister. Then he turned around to his followers. "You have heard," he said.

"He must die," said one of them to much murmuring agreement around him.

"I must parley with a chosen committee of you first," Woot said to the blacks. "Come with me to my cabin—the following among you: Popo, Loango, Tum, Gezo, and Tiy."

At once Bymba, frowning, pushed forward. "I must come also, Master Woot. We—you and I—were to meet, but you were not there."

Woot looked sharply at him, but relented. "Very well—you come too then, boy."

The caucus of the seven blacks in Stokes' former cabin was subdued, grave, grim, in the dim yellow light of the candle. "We have no ceremonial kola nut to crack with each other," said Woot to begin the meeting, "but we do so in spirit."

"It is true, Wobogo-Woot," the others, seated around on the floor, nodded gravely. Bymba sat up near Woot and missed not a detail.

"It is a deadly hour for us," Woot began, seated awkwardly on a stool. "We have the responsibility for the women and children also. What we decide here is everything. The white cannibals are at our mercy but we are also at theirs—else by now they would all be slaughtered and in the bellies of the sharks. But I think we cannot afford to kill any more of them—not even the hyena, their medicine man. For we cannot move the ship—and we do not know where we are. We only know we still leave our homeland and sail toward theirs. It is beyond thinking but it is true. Our question is what to do?"

There was silence. The men seemed embarrassed and glanced briefly at each other, then stared at the floor.

"Their captain," Woot continued, "said he could return us home and I released him from his confinement. But I think he is crazy, yet I would not trust him even if it turned out he was not. He is no friend."

"Is there no other course left us?" asked Tum, a decorous young Ebo—"Yet because he is crazy he may not lie to us, but turn the ship around and take us home. For us a crazy white cannibal is far better, I think, than one who is not."

"How do you know he is crazy?" said someone—it was little Popo, a favorite of Woot's, who with a cutlass in the battle had beheaded two crewmen. "He may be deceiving us," said Popo—"Maybe he is the sanest of them all. Shouldn't we kill him and put the medicine man back in charge?—he will do anything now that he thinks he is going to die."

"Master Woot," now spoke up Bymba eagerly, "why do we not ourselves sail the ship?"

There was total silence. Finally Woot, nettled, flustered, said: "This thing . . . this ship, is a contraption of evil, devised by evil men, by the white cannibals—it is not for us, boy."

"Yes, yes," said Bymba heatedly—"they are evil and they are our enemies! Then we should kill them all and return home ourselves."

Woot sighed now and shook his head. "We cannot sail the ship, boy. We do not know how—our elders, though they taught us many great things, did not teach us this. But you already know, in your deepest heart, that we cannot sail it—why do you try to make us believe you do not know?"

Bymba went into a slow pout. "I did not want to know it," he said. "I did not!"

Woot became firm, decisive, now as he said to them: "I think we should keep the captain in charge. Whenever the sun can be seen we shall know all right in what direction he is headed—we shall watch him. Also we will put the medicine man in chains. Does anyone have other thoughts?" Hearing none, Woot soon adjourned the meeting and sent them away. But as they left, he called Bymba back. "Boy, you must help me," he said. "You must go constantly throughout the ship, day and night, among everybody, and be my eyes and ears. You have the keenest powers of observation—you have proved that. You must now come to me often and tell me everything you find out. Much depends on it. We are trying to save ourselves."

Bymba was pensive. "How do we save ourselves, Master Woot?"

"That is an age-old question, boy. One must start early in order to save oneself—it must start with the elders, the wise men; they have the first responsibility, as had their elders. We were not told by them of this cruel outside world—they did not know of it; that it was ruled by these bloodthirsty white cannibals who know only pillage, ruin, and death. Nor were we told there would be some villains among our own who would sell us to these cannibals for rum, calico, or a brass necklace. We were left to learn these things for ourselves—ah, and under what dire circumstances! We must not ourselves be guilty of the same mistakes—we must warn those who come after us. If we live, boy, we must never let this experience be forgotten. It must be handed down to the young for ten thousand moons."

Bymba was in deep thought. "Shall we live?" he asked.

"I will not lie to you—the chances are small. I do not fear death; I only regret dying without having warned our people—that they must use the minds they have; that courage, a virtue we are widely known for, is not enough. What is vital is the mind. But if we die how shall we tell our people this?—we shall betray them as we have unwittingly been betrayed."

Bymba pondered this for a moment, and shook his head. "I do not wish to die, Master Woot," he said. "My friend, another boy here aboard named Osei, is ill, very ill—he lies on deck and speaks only of death; he wishes for it; but I do not; it will only betray us, yes—I would avoid it. Besides, Osei and I are too young to die. I then will help you in any way I can—I will be your eyes and ears. Now, good-night." Looking at Woot no more, he assumed an air of great dignity, an almost youthful pomposity, as he left to reconnoiter the ship.

Next day—it was heavily overcast and again threatening rain—Bymba stumbled onto Osei lying on deck on his side next to an aft-scuttle, his eyes half closed, fists clenched, his lips moving feverishly as if he languished in some dreamlike reverie. In addition to his grave physical illness, he had contracted a strange indisposition called in the slave trade "fixed melancholy." It was a deadly, stuporous malaise besetting slaves freshly brought on board and had the capacity to decimate a ship's slave population and bring on the owners commercial disaster; sea captains, callous, functional, did not understand it but dreaded it; slave men, women, and children, often died one after another for no apparent reason, harboring no desire to live. Captains and crews, alert to the danger, had learned from experience that if a black just brought aboard was not distracted and kept in motion, he often moped, squatted down with his chin on his knees, his arms clasped around his legs, and in the space of an hour died. Bymba reached down now and roughly poked Osei in the ribs—"How do you feel?" he said. "Would you like me to fetch you a cup of water?"

Osei seemed uncomprehending, though he opened his eyes; but then, gropingly, he tried to rise; yet, barely conscious, he sank back to the deck again and began murmuring: "Kickeraboo—I wish to die. . . . I wish to die so that I may return to my village. My mother is there—and my sisters and brothers also. Oh, Mother, I shall milk the two goats myself—you will remain inside the compound and make our soup. Do not forget our father—when the iron gong sounds, he will want his chicken hash and manioc brought to him at once. Later the venerable masked spirits of the clan will file in and look on as we all gather to do homage to the memories of our departed elders. Everyone will watch—as at a vigil for the dead. My father will watch me, however. Though I am not his first-born son,

I am his favorite—he says I am gentle and good and one day will be wise. He is partial to wisdom, he tells the masked spirits assembled—that only wisdom will bring greatness to our clan. Then, as once happened, a great red bird from the forest will come rest on my arm and give me a feeling of everlasting life and health. It is always thus."

Bymba was saddened by what he heard, for he knew now Osei approached death. Yet he himself was all the more filled with a fierce determination to live. "Be quiet," he said insistently, almost scolding, though his compassion knew no bounds—"Stop all that wild talk of yours and save your strength in order to live." But he knew Osei would not live. "You talk foolishness," he went on. "It never happened—the red bird of life never perched on your arm, or else you would not be here in this sorry state. No matter, *I* shall survive. I am a Coromantee—it is *my* arm to which the great red bird will return, for I have been chosen by the *egwugwu,* the spirit-elders, to represent them wherever it is my lot to go."

Osei did not answer. He was already dead.

That night, on Captain Stokes' orders, the course of the ship was all but reversed. They sailed now, according to Stokes' master plan, back east—but also north.

*   *   *   *   *

Next day Stokes' mind was a veritable maelstrom of plans, plots, and half-demented schemes of retribution. Wobogo-Woot watched him and understood he was driven by a demon, by some implacable force, a mission, that all but consumed him. The two men's relationship was bizarre in the extreme. They shared, first of all, the same, the captain's, cabin—Woot by threats insisted on it, though Stokes after the take-over had begged leave to move out. But vigilant Woot wanted him close to him. When refused, Stokes took to washing himself each day in sea water, then going into his sea chest for the finest, most resplendent coats, breeches, and shoes he could find. It was his way of dramatizing his notion of the distinction between them. Woot, however, understood it all, but had taken vows of patience, prudence, guile.

Then early one morning, two days later, chief mate Cockle came to Woot's and Stokes' cabin. When Woot, who had been asleep on Stokes' cot, heard the knock on the door, he started up, uttering a low, guttural growl, then motioned for Stokes, still in his underwear, to open the door. Stokes had been squatting on his pallet on the floor—where he was now made to sleep—energetically polishing a silver-buckled shoe. He stood up and, still stooping slightly from the superficial knife wound in his shoulder, went to the door. When he opened it and saw Cockle, his face at once took on a sinister, stealthy, yet somehow innocent expression. He did not ask Cockle in but stood staring blankly at him—Cockle's forehead bore the ugly, still-healing cutlass wound received in the fight for the ship. "Is it good for you to come here?" asked Stokes, but very matter-of-factly in order not to give away to Woot, who of course could not understand their speech, any semblance of their conversation. "You could have waited and talked to me on deck," Stokes added, his anger, despite his efforts, rising.

"It won't wait," said Cockle heatedly. "What's left of the crew wanted to turn this ship around again last night. It was all I could do to keep 'em from it. They don't believe you. They think we're returning to Africa—not going to England—and say they won't go back to their certain slaughter." Cockle showed little of his former respect for Stokes' leadership.

"They'll do what I say!" said Stokes, almost losing completely his false aplomb. "The blacks know, when the sun is out, as it is now, whether we're going east or west. They know I've turned the ship about—eastward—and are watching me like hawks. You tell that miserable crew if they don't want their throats slit by these savages, they'd better follow orders—my orders." His face was flushed with anger. Woot watched them both intently, his beady eyes darting from one face to the other, until he realized Stokes was giving some kind of order to Cockle. Then, cunningly, he lay back down again—as if he had no interest whatever in what was taking place. But he sensed, and knew, crucial matters were being discussed.

"Tell the crew again of my plan!" Stokes said to Cockle—"You have not sufficiently explained it to them!"

"Indeed I have," said Cockle. "But they're upset and desperate and will have none of it. You'd better talk to 'em yourself today—

or tonight they're goin' to turn this ship around toward home again. They keep sayin' if the blacks get us back to Africa, our lives ain't worth a penny—for the blacks won't need us then. This crew, I tell you, would rather die tryin' to get this ship back to Virginia than to keep sailin' in the direction we're goin'!"

Now came the sudden wild look in Stokes' eyes. "My plan may seem a rash one," he said, "but it is simply to make use of something we have that they do not have—knowledge. They are bewildered, confused, and as a result are very dangerous. They do not believe us, do not trust us; they do not think we are sincere in heading for Africa. Their leader, there, reclining on my cot, listening to my voice but understanding nothing, thinks we are eventually bent on our original course—home. It is true we are headed for Africa, though a little north too, but all this is only temporary; it's just to mislead, confound, them whenever they can see the sun. Our course, soon to be, is instead north-northwest . . . yes, toward England. It is much nearer—there we shall be saved and the blacks sold on board another vessel headed for Jamaica or some such place. This is my plan. Tell the crew again. Later I shall tell them also." Stokes now glanced in Woot's direction.

Woot lay on his back on the cot, his legs crossed high, gazing at the ceiling. Very audibly now he sucked air through his teeth—a sign always of his great inner agitation and concentration; a sign also that he was deadly dangerous.

Cockle looked at, studied, Stokes. "Time is running out for everybody aboard this ship," he said, forcefully, at last. "Food and water are already low, mighty low, for we no longer have discipline—the blacks have et and drank everything they could lay their hands on. It's parlous, Captain—we ain't got long to act. Your plan won't save us unless it gets us somewhere quick, I tell you!" Cockle was flushed and distressed.

Woot boldly raised up on an elbow now and, nostrils flaring, watched both men.

"When you go back," Stokes said to Cockle, "tell the crew that tonight, winds permitting, we change our course from generally east to north-northwest. The first time we get a cloudy day, tomorrow or whenever, the blacks, without the sun, will be thoroughly confused."

"But as you say, they'll be dangerous, too," added Cockle.

"It's a chance we must take—we can't go on forever floating

around in the middle of the Atlantic ocean. You say so yourself. Tell the crew what I say. Another thing—we've got to keep an eye on Whittier. He's a problem, a louse—gravely perilous to us. I can never feel safe in executing this plan with him alive—even if he is for the moment in chains. He is rotten to the heart—a disgrace to civilized man. Cockle, he must die. Otherwise, in the end, he will undo us; he will somehow betray our plan. Talk to the few crewmen left about it—the deed must be a joint decision." Stokes' bloodshot eyes bored hard into Cockle's.

Cockle equivocated. "There ain't many of us left, as it is," he said. "We may need everybody before it's over with—including Whittier." He scratched his head—" . . . I don't know."

Stokes leaned forward, confidentially, almost as if he had forgotten Woot's beady eyes upon them. "But do you remember?" he said—"Whittier knows many of the dialects spoken aboard this ship. Think of what he can do to us as linguister for His Eminence, here, presently lolling on his back on my cot—think of that. Whittier is only momentarily in disgrace with the blacks—it will no longer be so when he decides to offer them his services again. He must die, Cockle—and soon. By what means, you and the others, the crew, will decide—and by whom. But it must be done—possibly tonight." A strange, frenzied light then came in Stokes' face. "Ah, afterwards, then on to England," he said—"coveted England; even to King George. We are still his kinsmen, are we not? . . . upholding the ensign of a long-civilized race. Yes, I say coveted, blessed, England . . ." He turned, bent down, and took from beneath his pallet his little black volume which resembled a catechism, and in a moment, as if no others were present, began to read aloud, solemnly, from another of his favorite passages in it: "And now at last, by the mercy of God, and the continuance of our labours, these only texts being brought into such a conclusion, as that we have great hopes that the Church of England shall reap good fruit thereby; we hold it our duty to offer them to Your Majesty, not only as to our King and sovereign, but as to the principal Mover and Author of these works: humbly craving of Your most Sacred Majesty, that since things of this quality have ever been subject to the censures of illmeaning and discontented persons, these works may receive approbation and patronage from so learned and judicious a Prince as Your Highness is. . . ." Stokes paused.

Woot had sat up on the cot—rage beclouding his face—remembering having before heard a similar litany when Stokes had read from this hated book up on deck, with the black woman screaming her fearful execrations at him and calling for his death. It was a bad omen and, felt Woot, an overt, calculated insult to his person and people. He swung off the cot now and approached Stokes and Cockle. "What is it you now read?" he demanded angrily of Stokes in his swift Fanti dialect.

Stokes and Cockle, unable to understand, only gaped.

"As you did before!" shouted Woot at Stokes. ". . . calling down on our heads the wicked apparitions of all your kind—is it true?"

Stokes of course did not answer.

Woot then leapt outside the cabin door past them and yelled to a sickly, emaciated black youth leaning against the bulwarks— "You! Go find Tum or Loango! Tell them to fetch the cannibal linguister of the crew on deck at once!" Feebly, the black made off to do his leader's bidding, only to be called back. "And tell Tum," said Woot, "to also bring up that scurvy wretch of the red face, their medicine man who is under our sentence of death, in order that he may protect us, that he may inform us whether the first linguister tells us truly what is said. Hurry!"

As Woot's emissary left again, Stokes, his little book still in hand, turned to Cockle—both had followed Woot outside—"The savage is up to something," he said. "But we must show no perturbation. Go, as I say, and tell the crew things will be all right—tell them that tonight we shall act."

Cockle had started to leave, when Woot stepped in front of him and, scowling, shoved him back hard against the outside of the cabin wall, then glared at him. Several of the blacks loitering about the companionway leading down from the weather deck saw the incident and came congregating around Woot and his victims as if, contrary to fact, he needed help. At that moment Bymba appeared above on the steps of the companionway. He first stared at all the commotion, then called down to Woot in the Fanti dialect—"Master Woot, please come up here at once. The wind . . . it suddenly changed; now it has changed once more; and the sun comes out, then goes behind the clouds again. It is strange—the winds coming like this from all directions. I do not know in what direction the ship goes now—back to our homeland or elsewhere. I am confused —my head is whirling. Come up, Master Woot."

Woot, staring at Bymba, unhanded Cockle. Then he bounded toward the companionway from where Bymba led him up on deck. There, among light scudding clouds, they saw the sun rising higher off the horizon. The seas were choppy and the ship pitched a little as it put its bows into a small wave, sending spray flying back over the bulwarks. Two seamen stood looking intently into the binnacle at the compass. Soon then Stokes and Cockle arrived on deck, Stokes still only half-dressed. They too saw the crewmen at the compass as they looked around at the sea and up at the sky. Cockle licked, wetted, his forefinger and held it up to the wind. "The crew ain't waiting for tonight, Captain," he said to Stokes. "They're acting now—they've changed the ship's course."

Stokes was already looking up at the topsails where four crewmen labored. "Ah," he breathed, "but they're close-hauling her on the port tack." The ship had already come around, steadying on the port tack. "Though the wind is by no means fair, we're heading north—toward England! It's uncanny—they have read my mind, they have. Go to the wheel, Cockle, while I go below and consult the charts."

Woot and Bymba looked on bewilderedly. Then suddenly Woot spun around and yelled in rage for the linguister. Also the blacks had begun to gather on deck—as if sensing something of vast importance was imminent. Woot, confused, harried, breathing heavily, rushed over now to the two seamen who were still intently studying the compass. He began pointing at the binnacle and yelling incoherently at them. In fear of their lives, they stepped back from the instrument and stood behind Cockle at the wheel.

Soon then Stokes reappeared, now wearing pants and shirt. "I cannot understand it," he said to Cockle, "—how our minds were working together. It's like I had given them written orders. Minds, civilized minds, *are* capable of communicating; this is proof."

"I told you they wouldn't let you take the ship back to Africa— they were in a holy fit, desperate-like, last night; they almost done it then. All they need now is for you to rally 'em, Captain; give 'em a glint of hope."

"Our hope is England," said Stokes. "And its King George and all they both represent. We must not succumb to these savages, who, in their evil, benighted ignorance, call us cannibals—I've never understood why they, of all people on the face of the globe, so often refer to us as cannibals. It's baffling. Yet you see how our minds, the minds of civilized men, are in tune. Our men know, almost instinctively, what they must do. My necessary strategy, of taking the ship for these few hours back toward Africa, was to carry out my pact with these brutes. I kept it. We respect covenants. We can afford to do so; it's our minds, and our heritage—though these barbarous slaves call us cannibals; it's our genius to think directly, to know what to do next!" Stokes' eyes reflected a mad fire.

"Then what do we do next, now, Captain?" said Cockle, a little scornfully.

"Sail north toward England—as we're now doing."

An almost mawkish expression had come on Cockle's face, one of confusion and fright. "Have we a chance of reaching England? —with our stores goin' fast, with what's left of the crew sick and exhausted, and the blacks in command of the ship?"

"Who knows whether we shall reach it?" shot back Stokes. "But the blacks are not in command of the ship. We are; for we can navigate and they cannot. We know where we are—I have consulted the charts—but the blacks are confused and lost; they are at our mercy—if they kill us, they too die. We shall not change the ship's course again—never! I stand ready to die for it! I know our course and we shall stay on it."

"We are well past the Cape Verde Islands, I know," said Cockle.

"We are indeed—two hundred fifty miles past, west of, them. But we're heading nor'east by north now; in time we'll pass the Canary Islands, opposite the Spanish Sahara, then the Madeira Islands off Morocco. Finally we'll steer between the Azores and Portugal and straight up into the blessed port of Portsmouth!"

Meanwhile Woot was still stomping the deck and yelling for the crewman who during Whittier's arraignment had been translator, when at that moment both Tum and Loango came running and pointing up at the topsails where the four seamen were finishing their task. "He is up there, Woot," said Loango, "—the linguister is aloft. But they now descend."

"Then also go fetch their red-faced medicine man out of the hold!" cried Woot. "Through them we will parley with these cannibals to see whether or not they wish to live. We shall return to our homeland or we shall all surely die in the attempt. But they shall die first! Go!"

Stokes watched Woot. "Look at him," he said in a contemptuous aside to Cockle. "What's the savage up to?—what's he so excited about?"

"McCliff, the linguister, will be soon findin' out—he's the only one of us aboard, other than Whittier, that can understand any of these dialects."

"Don't mention that traitor Whittier! . . . ." Stokes' foot stamped the deck in anger, then, his eyes crazily alight again, whispered: "Do not forget—in him we have a snake in our bosom! Tonight he must be dispatched and thrown in the sea—before he seals our own fate. This is your mission, Cockle—talk to the men and see that it's carried out. I only hope it's not already too late."

Soon linguister McCliff and the other three crewmen were down out of the rigging. At once Woot, drawing his cutlass, went over to them. "Come!—I am going to parley with your captain," he said threateningly to McCliff. "It is a matter of most deadly importance—of life and death. . . . Come, tell him that!" He seized McCliff, a blond, though now darkly sun-burnt, man of thirty-five, by the arm and shoved him over toward Stokes. Stokes and Cockle stood dourly waiting, watching them come.

But suddenly Bymba ran up to Woot. "Master Woot, the ship is going another way!" he cried. "Where are we going now? . . . I feel the winds coming from so many different ways—and now the sun is hidden too. I am confused! . . . Ask them where we go!"

Woot stopped in his tracks and stared out to sea, both to port and starboard; then he glared at Stokes and Cockle. "We shall wait," he pronounced, "until the other linguister—their trembling medicine man—is brought up." Among the crewmen present only McCliff understood and, filled with fear, not thinking, he translated to Stokes and Cockle. Woot at once swung his cutlass at McCliff's head, the linguister falling to the deck just in time to avoid the blow. Woot then kicked him, but his bare foot was of no effect and McCliff crawled out of reach.

"Look, look, Master Woot!" cried Bymba, "—the sun is out! But look where it is! . . . where *is* it? Where do we go? . . . still toward, or away from, our homeland? Ask them, Master Woot!"

It was a paradox that Bymba's excitement seemed somewhat to calm Woot—to make him aware once more of his dread responsibilities, of the demands of leadership. He took on a cooler mien

303

now, at times a sinister coldness again, as they all stood waiting for Whittier to be brought on deck. "Do not panic, boy," he said to Bymba—"This is no time to show confusion. We must not be confounded by these evil cannibals. We will weigh carefully what they say before believing it—keep a clear head for the thoughts of our elder's spirits to enter into it readily. And yourself think great thoughts, noble thoughts, for we may soon be near death. Yet we shall never falter—death can sometimes be kind."

Cockle looked apprehensively at Stokes. "They smell something's wrong," he said to Stokes—"They're all mixed up and muddled, and that makes 'em dangerous as the devil's own hosts. They're probably spoilin' to ask you, Captain, if the ship's still on course to Africa. What will you tell 'em?"

"The truth," said Stokes, now almost quietly. "They may prefer to live, and go on north with us, than to kill us and themselves surely die. It's their test, their fate, as well as ours."

"Shouldn't you first take that up with the crew?—it's their lives too, y'know."

Stokes bristled. "Who turned this ship about and headed it north toward England?" he said. "Not I. They, the crew, did. True, I meant to order them to do that very thing, but they seized the initiative on their own—good men. It was possibly their lives then, and they knew it. No, I consult no one."

"But *tellin'* the blacks what's happened is another thing, ain't it, Captain? The crew oughta be talked to on this—the blacks could go berserk and slaughter us all."

Just then Tum and Loango dragged Whittier on deck. He was bleeding afresh from head lacerations taken in a beating just given him by Tum only minutes before. But immediately Woot summoned them all to gather around himself—he stood at the compass. This time scores of blacks—men, women, and children—began to congregate on deck, sensing crucial happenings. Woot, in the very center of the throng now, seized the two translators, putting bedraggled Whittier on his right, McCliff on his left, and confronted Stokes and Cockle directly. Bymba, still very excited, stood close behind Woot's right elbow. Woot began by looking hard into the binnacle—at the compass. He pointed his huge finger at it vigorously. "What is this?" he demanded of Stokes in Fanti. McCliff translated.

"The compass," replied Stokes, almost impassively.

Woot listened to McCliff's attempt at translation, then scowled at condemned Whittier for confirmation. When he had received it, he turned to Stokes again and asked: "What is the use made of this instrument?"

"It tells us the ship's direction," said Stokes, coolly, stubbornly.

"Does the ship, then, go towards our homeland?" Woot was both grave and sinister.

Stokes glanced at his men. "No," he said, "towards ours."

Linguister McCliff froze. Again he saw the deadly peril to his own life. His pausing however gave the appearance of inability to translate Stokes' answer. Woot stared at him, then spun around to limp and defeated Whittier. "How does he respond?" he yelled.

Whittier instead turned his swollen eyes on Stokes. "Ah-ha," he said, a vengeful grin, a sneer, on his face—"what do I say, Captain? I myself am under sentence of death, but you and the others have a chance to live if he hears the right answer—which for him is 'yes.' But you say 'no'—which means your certain end if it's truly translated. What would you have me say to him, Captain?" —Whittier, grinning, diabolical, evil, thus toyed with Stokes.

"You traitorous dog!" said Stokes, trembling with rage—"Your days are numbered! . . . stay out of this!" He turned on McCliff— "Find your tongue, rabbit! Tell this savage what I said!" McCliff, paralyzed with fear, still hesitated. The horde of blacks leaned in as best they could to see.

Whittier at last faced Woot. "You ask," he said in a crude Fanti, his voice ghostlike and raspy, "if we sail to your homeland. The answer is 'yes.' We all, the crew also, sail to our homeland, Woot! . . . Do you hear?—do you understand?"

Woot studied him. Bymba, eyes wide, body pressed by the throng against Woot's side, stood transfixed by happenings he could not fathom. Woot still pondered what he had heard though his bewildered expression showed he did not comprehend its meaning. Then—"Speak more clearly!" he yelled at Whittier. "You speak in riddles, you low hyena! . . . Tell us what you mean!"

Wasted, bleeding Whittier stood quivering with emotion. "We all sail homeward, Woot," he said, in a kind of manic awe. "Our home is death."

Woot seemed only let down by the explanation, impervious to the idea. "At some time we must all know death," he said scornfully —"that is no news. But do we sail to my homeland?"

Whittier seemed triumphant. "No!" he said.

Woot nodded, and appeared resigned. "Where, then, do we sail?" he said.

"Towards death," Whittier sighed now.

Bymba heard the wistful pronouncement. "I do not want to die, Master Woot," he said, but spoke boldly. "I want to live to pass your message to those who come after."

"Shut up, boy," said Woot absently, casting an eye over the throng of blacks—"Call the committee together, down in my cabin; I shall be down directly." At once Bymba disappeared into the crowd to find Popo, Loango, Tum, and the others.

Stokes, who had followed Woot's and Whittier's colloquy through McCliff, turned to them all and asked contemptuously: "Does Woot understand me?—that he will see Africa no more?—that it's England or death? . . . for us all? Make it clear to him and the others!"

McCliff, with Whittier listening, interpreted what Stokes had said. Woot seemed almost impassive. "I understand well," he replied. "But this place you speak of, where the ship now goes—what is it like?"

Stokes' eyes again took on their crazy light. "I have told you of it before," he said—"I have read to you of it from my little book. It is a great land, that from which my own homeland sprang. Although lately we were at odds, we are kinsmen nevertheless, and a great people. In going to them we, the crew, go to our homeland. If we are not meant to reach it, then we die."

"You speak truth," said Woot. "You shall surely die, and on this water—you shall pay for your damnable book!" He then left and hurriedly pushed his way through the crowd to go below to his cabin to parley with the committee.

But surgeon Whittier, reeling from his weakness, called out after him. "Woot, oh Woot! . . . you can still be saved. It is not too late. Do not accept death so eagerly—it makes fewer heroes than you think. I know well what is on your mind, but it is senseless. Trust me and you shall see your homeland again—you can still be saved. . . ." But by now Woot had disappeared below.

"You said we sailed towards death," said McCliff to Whittier

306

angrily, then glanced at Stokes, who glared hate at Whittier. "You can save no one, least of all yourself." McCliff spat and went over to the compass. "Our fate depends on the winds," he said to Stokes —"With foul, uncertain winds like today, we'll never make England; with fair winds we have only a chance."

"Foul winds or fair," spoke up Whittier, "you have no chance! Your fates are sealed. I am not alone. But I have sought to offer them hope—to ease the ordeal they face. But it's no good—Woot would not hear of it." Again Whittier sighed and Stokes still glared at him.

When Woot arrived below in the cabin, he found most of the committee already awaiting him, including the woman who had angrily screamed at Stokes for what she felt, by his reading from his little book, was his invocation of hostile spirits. Popo explained: "The decisions to be taken here are dread ones, Woot—we thought we should also have the wisdom of our women."

Woot nodded approval and sat down on the stool, as the others sat on the floor. "You were right," he said—"Our sister here, Buefi, was a well-advised choice. She has wisdom, hardness, and a love for our people." Bymba now entered with Loango and Tiy and the committee was complete. Woot, who had been perspiring freely during the parley up on deck, went now and got one of Stokes' towels and began mopping his face and eyes; he was clearly agitated and seemed loath to start the discussions. At last, standing now, he said: "Is it to be life or death for us?" Thus the meeting began.

"Our hope is not great," said Tum. "It lies perhaps, I think, such as it is, in their medicine man. He is a jackal, but he does not like their captain and, once we dispatched the rest of the cannibals, he might instruct us on how to sail the ship."

There was a lonely silence. "Will someone else speak?" asked Woot finally.

The woman, Buefi, spoke then. "How many days' food and water remain?"

"Food and water are low, considering the seas we have yet to cross," said Popo. "Wherever we are bound, we must get there soon."

A great pall came over the assembly. Bymba, though, was all eyes and ears. The woman Buefi, squatting in the midst of the men, seemed contrite for having asked the plaguing question. Yet they all, except for Popo, sat ineffectual, mute, as a heavy gloom fell over the cabin.

"What of their medicine man?" Tum said at last, returning to his prior suggestion—"I think he will help us if we dispatched the others forthwith and made him supreme. He dislikes their captain."

"But he hates us," spat Woot—"He is a slender reed." Again there was silence. "May I hear more discussion?"

"We can sail the ship," said Bymba. "Though our elders did not show us how, maybe the medicine man can show us, as Tum has said." His expression was perplexed, urgent.

"What if we do nothing?" put in Gezo, sickly, emaciated, tribal scars ornamenting his high, noble cheekbones. "Troubles sometimes solve themselves. The cannibals, though few in number, can still operate the ship. What does it matter where they take us?—we shall overcome in time."

Woot bristled. "In time!" he said—"but what happens before? . . . We have, even after our recent grievous losses, nearly fifteen score of our people surviving. What is to become of them if the cannibals prevail? This is our responsibility—how do we meet it? It is an aching question."

"We must first rid the ship of its evil spirits," said Buefi, her right hand belligerently in the air as if holding a cutlass. "As long as that cannibal with the book reads down on us these evil and pernicious spirits which raise all manner of perplexing and deadly questions for us, we shall suffer as we do now." Violent now, she stood up—"We must cleanse the ship! . . . the blood must flow again! The cannibals must be slaughtered! *Our* gods must be given sway of the ship—then we shall find out where we are and what we must do to save ourselves! . . . Brothers, we must have the yearning to destroy! Then we shall be saved—if not in body, surely in our fathers' spirits!"

"She speaks the truth," said Woot—"But after we destroy them, my sister Buefi, who will sail the ship back to our homeland? Without doubt you have thought of that—this is our awful question."

"The question does not bother me, Woot," said the fierce Buefi. "Once we free the ship of its evil spirits, brought down on us by that cannibal reading to us from his book, our fathers' spirits will return to us and help us guide the ship to our homeland. First, though, we must rid it of the spirits that now inhabit it because of that heinous cannibal's reading from his book of scapegrace evil and doom for us. As long as the cannibals inhabit the ship, so will the bodeful spirits that tie our hands against our homeward return. We must destroy them!—slaughter the cannibals as they have so many of our people aboard this ship with their guns and cannon! We must, I say, cleanse the ship!—then our elders' spirits will instruct us, guide us to our true destination. The cannibals' blood must run!"

Woot took a deep breath. "Who else speaks?" he said, looking around at the others.

"Perhaps we should do nothing," said Gezo again in a voice weak from his illness. "Let things come to a head more. And, as Tum and Bymba have said, maybe release their medicine man from his hard confinement and parley with him."

"There is little time to parley," Loango said—"little time to waste, with the food and water already so low."

Woot showed impatience. "Meantime," he said, "their hellion of a captain and the others are bent on taking us to an unknown land where we shall all be degraded and vanquished forever. Is there anything, my brothers and my sister, worse than this?"

"Nothing!" said Buefi.

"We must return to our homeland or die." Yet Woot said it without particular emphasis.

"But for that, Woot, we shall need their medicine man," said Tum. "We cannot hope to return unless we are instructed."

"He only administers to their sick," said Woot in disdain— "What would he know of sailing a ship?"

"Should we not parley with him first and find out?" urged Tum.

Woot, somber, reflective, did not answer directly. "You have all considered every alternative," he said, "except death. Why do you continue to avoid it? It is no disgrace if the cause is good. We have been seized and forced on this ship and are being taken by the cannibals to some evil place we know not of and from whence we shall never return to our homeland. Suppose we die now trying to return—there is no disgrace; and the spirits of our elders will smile in pride upon us. Is this not so?"

"It is so, Woot!" said Buefi—"It is so." Prayerfully, she placed both hands upon her breasts.

"But, if you think it wise, I am willing to parley with the medicine man—though, the wretch, he makes my stomach turn over." Woot then looked at Bymba—"Go, boy, and fetch their medicine man." Bymba left at once.

Woot resumed in a homily: "I learned it from my mother, who learned it from her father, a minor chieftain—as was my father— that the first human beings did not know death. It was greed that brought death. But at first when people grew old they merely turned into chickens, snakes, cows, or lions; or, if unlucky, into spirits called Gyi-nu, then later into still something else—the Gyi-nu were spirits with one arm, one leg, and green hair, and lived in trees and gave sickness. If you turned into a chicken or cow or something like that, you entered into another world where a secret language was spoken. Knowledge of this language was important. Ah, but alas then came along a man called Luemba. He wanted as much of the world as he could get—many wives, many children, much land and cattle, many slaves, and a great compound in which to live. He began plotting how he could get these things and in the span of five years had accomplished most of his aims. But then whenever he thought of the future, about how someday he must get old and change into a goat or crow, he was filled with misery and unhappiness. Yet his worldly goods continued to mount; and he had taken ten wives. Heavily the years accumulated. By the time he was almost eighty, and had eighteen wives and over a hundred offspring, he began to fail. He knew the time must soon come when he would undergo his inevitable transformation; his distress knew no bounds. Then one night a possible solution came to him in a dream. One of his many sons, Kamba by name, only now twenty-two years old, was in every way a model human being —strong, handsome, courageous, upright, intelligent—and he filled Luemba's breast with pride. It was hinted in the dream, as Luemba interpreted it, that, if he did certain things, he might send Kamba instead into an early metamorphosis and take Kamba's youth unto himself. Luemba was much aroused by this possibility. But in order to make the plan work, Kamba, after secretly being fed a slow-working, noxious potion, had thus to be brought to a state of feebleness and debility resembling exhaustion of the body just before its change into another form. Then, according to the dream, Luemba must lead Kamba into the remotest grotto in the forest, where he would hold his son, whom he claimed to love dearly, and whom he hoped would become an intrepid lion, in a deathless embrace for twelve hours—until Kamba's vitality was to have passed into his father's body and rejuvenated it as of old, and Kamba's metamorphosis into another form had been made complete. But when the experiment was tried, it was found Kamba had been denied by the angry gods knowledge of the indispensable secret language and was thus foredoomed to certain failure—they forbade Kamba's change and, in a weakened stupor, he died in his father's arms. So it was that he was the first human being to die. Next day Luemba also died—he was the second. Since then no human being has escaped death—it comes sooner or later to everyone no matter how we try to put it off. In the eyes of the ever-watchful spirits, it is *how* we die that matters. Had it not been for Luemba's greed for wealth and pomp, and, as a result, his craving for immortality (man's greatest sin—vanity), we here today would not face the prospect of death. But we must now. I ask you to do so—is it not an alternative?"

"Yes," said Tiy. "We here do not fear death—it is a natural condition since Luemba's folly. But should we not first put it to the others?—there are left almost three hundred of us aboard."

Woot was stumped by the suggestion, and was readying a reply —when Bymba, eyes wide, burst in the cabin. Hoarsely he cried out: "They have killed their medicine man!"

Woot, who had been standing, went back against the wall, his face blank with stupefaction. A great hush fell over the cabin. "Killed? . . ." he said finally—"their medicine man! . . . *Who killed him*?"

"The other cannibals, Master Woot!—led by their captain!"

"It was our only hope," muttered Tum. "He was to instruct us in sailing the ship—the wily medicine man."

"What have they done with him, boy?" Woot said.

Bymba grimaced. "They clubbed him to death—and would have thrown him in the sea had not our people stopped them. His body lies on the deck."

"Round the cannibals up!" shouted Woot—"All of them! Assemble them at that device they look at that tells them the direction of the ship. The time has come!"

"What do we tell the others?—our people," Tiy said, returning to his former concern.

Woot stared at him incredulously—"That the time has come, I say! They know it already—why else did they prevent the medicine man's body from being thrown to the sharks? . . . They saved the evidence of this treachery for all to see! Afterwards I will speak to them, but they know what I must say already."

"They know, yes, Woot," said the woman Buefi—"and the spirits of our elders watch with approval. Our moment in the long tale draws near and we shall meet it well."

The men, except Woot, hurried out now and ascended to the deck, but Woot, Bymba, and Buefi soon followed. They found most of the blacks still where they had left them before going below to confer, yet not a crewman was in sight. Whittier's battered, bloody body lay sprawled at the compass, his eyes open as in life. Woot went over and for a moment peered down into the grisly face, then turned to the others. "He was no better then the rest of them!" he said in a loud voice. "He too was a cannibal, never forget." He then placed a hand on the compass. "It is true we do not know where we are on this terrible and great world of water," he said, "but neither does he now. We are equal. We shall soon be equal to the others also." He raised his voice again. "What say you, my brothers and sisters! Would you rather continue to the cannibals' land and be eaten, or remain here and receive the blessings of our ancestors' spirits who say we have suffered enough? What will it be?"

There was hesitation and murmuring among the crowd. Then a tall, wizened black spoke up. "But to receive their blessings," he said, "we must first appease them—with sacrifices."

At once cries of approval rose from the throng. "Yes!—the cannibals!" called out a woman. "They must be sacrificed—with ritual and custom! Only then will the spirits be satisfied, only then will they receive us into the realm of blessedness where our trials will be over! That is true—it must be the custom of sacrifice! . . . by slow blood, by slow fire!"

Woot hesitated. He glanced unsurely at Buefi, whose eyes now were filled with a mystical stare; she seemed transported, her lips moving silently, feverishly. "Yes, it must be!" Her voice was almost a whisper. ". . . It must be! Their captain now will read no more from his little book. In his agonies he will cry out to *our* gods for mercy!"

Woot then said to them: "So it shall be—it is your wish and it shall be. Prepare for the rites!" A great shout went up.

After they had murdered Whittier, the crew, flailed and beaten by the blacks, were herded into the forecastle and there held prisoners. Stokes was still defiant. There were only eleven of them now and all, except Stokes, sat crouching in wild fear. Cockle raised his head from his hands and stared at Stokes, who ignored him. Cockle, ill and spent from weeks of misadventure and the beating he had just taken, was now almost hysterical. His eyes, hot, plaintive, and almost delirious, clung to Stokes; then he fell to whimpering—"Should we not reconsider, Captain? . . . They are already, I fear, plotting how we shall die. Whittier, too, you recall, said as we bludgeoned him that we would soon follow him." Cockle then turned to the others, his haggard, bloody face supplicating, demeaned. Stokes stared scornfully at him but said nothing, though Cockle still held him in his febrile gaze. Their black guards stirred restlessly, as if disturbed by their inability to understand what was said. Soon McCliff, the linguister, turned to one of them, a giant Hausa, and asked: "Are we going to die?"

"That is not for me to say," the man declared hostilely. "But it is my hope that you are—you are all snakes, hyenas, and cannibals, and deserve to die."

When Cockle heard the translation, he became even more agitated. "Tell them," he said to McCliff pleadingly, "that we will return them to Africa this time; that if they will only spare our lives, we will not again betray them!"

Stokes intervened scathingly. "Your name too is Whittier, I see," he said to Cockle—"and you deserve his fate. Think of it!—I it was who chose you for first mate of this ship. A more ignominious deed I never did. Don't you see that we are going to die, that nothing you can say or do will change that, and that now one ought only think of dying with honor and dignity? Yet you sit whimpering before these savages—debasing yourself and comrades. You are a sorry dog, Cockle, as was Whittier, both of you unworthy of your race of men!"

There was silence. The ever-watchful guards, though unable to understand, were nonetheless avidly interested and stared menacing looks at the crew. Cockle, who sat weakly leaning against the wall, returned his head to his hands, emitted a long, audible sigh, and shuddered.

Stokes now said to McCliff: "Ask them *how* we shall die." McCliff, turning to the Hausa guard again, put the question.

"How would I know?" said the guard. "If I had my way, you would all be bound hand and foot and thrown overboard to the sharks—but even that would not mete out to you what you deserve, you dogs. I venture, however, if you are to die, you will soon know how—maybe it will be by this machete." He raised his cutlass.

Just then Bymba, panting, appeared in the doorway. "Bring them up!" he shouted to the guards, his manner important, authoritative, as he waved toward the prisoners. "There are to begin three days and nights of ritual—the 'customs!' "

"Ah," inaudibly breathed the great black Hausa guard, "so it is to be the 'customs.' That had not occurred to me—sacrifice, the altar, the knife, fire. It is most proper—the cannibals will have three long days and nights to reflect upon their sins. It is very fitting—it could not be better. We also benefit—our ancestors' spirits will then receive us into their midst with pride and gladness. Ah, the rituals will be supreme."

Other guards now moved in and jerked the prisoners to their feet—except for Stokes, the first up, who would not let them touch him. Even Cockle, once on his feet, seemed to regain some of his composure and no longer sighed, though he trembled. Soon they were all ushered up on deck.

Woot still stood at the compass—flanked by Buefi, Popo, Loango, and Tum. Word of the impending rituals had spread through the ship like wildfire; every black aboard was on deck for the announcement of the protracted torture rites devised to facilitate, for others than the victims, the transmigration of souls into the spirit world. But now the great throng standing before Woot had to part far enough to make way for the prisoners being led toward the front and Woot. One of the prisoners, an older man, dirty, disheveled, and bloody, had a rough-hewn wooden leg, yet he limped along behind Stokes with chin high, eyes half closed, as if trying to emulate the captain's cold hauteur—until it was seen that he too trembled. The other prisoners, harried, exhausted, sullen, were also led through the crowd until they had all reached Woot standing at the compass. The skies had cleared, bringing to the sea's horizon a beautiful azure as far as the eye could see; the sun was warm though not oppressively hot. At that moment the *Caper* rose heavily upon a gentle swell only to ride lazily down the other side, its topsails set for the last time by any mortal. The somberness, the awesome foreboding, of the occasion of Woot's summoned assembly pervaded the sea air hovering over the fated ship. Yet many hands were raised to shield intent, earnest eyes from the sun. Woot at the moment stood impassive, his hand resting on the instrument that vouchsafed direction—the compass—as he peered out over the great gathering. He waited.

When finally the eleven crewmen stood before him, he began to speak. But it was soon apparent McCliff, now dour and taciturn, would no longer translate. Woot saw and comprehended. For this Stokes praised the former linguister emotionally: "Yes, it is better, Seaman McCliff, that the rest of us not know what is said by this bloodthirsty savage!" Woot knew that, except for McCliff, he would be understood now only by the blacks. But he made no remonstrance, finding in the fact an emblematic and satisfying rightness. At first he spoke with great calmness, deliberateness: "My kinsmen and kinswomen of the blood of those of the homeland from which we come, I bow to you and crack the token of the kola nut. We shall not see that homeland again, though I stand with my hand on the mechanism made and used by our former captors, the cannibals, to tell them a ship's true direction. But the instrument is no good to us—its use was not taught us by our elders. But those who know how to use it betrayed us—the wretches now stand here before you—and told us after we won the ship that we returned to our homeland, when they knew they were taking us to their own homeland where dire things and misfortunes awaited us as a result of their bloodthirsty cruelty and greed. We from our homeland had never gone to molest them; we did not know they lived on earth until they arrived in their ships to run us down and capture us, even our babies, and wreak on us the most inhuman degradations. Many of us have died at their hands; many more have gone through suffering sometimes worse than death! . . ." Woot's voice was rising. "Now these cannibals before us, the remnants of our oppressors, must be sacrificed!"

"Yes, to appease our gods!" someone in the crowd cried—"to

appease them in order that they may receive our spirits off this hated ship when, as it soon must, our time has come! So on with the 'customs!'"

But Woot was oblivious. Other things clouded his face with anger. "Yet the gods be praised that the ringleader of our betrayors has survived!" he shouted. "He has been first and foremost in the treachery used against us. Ah, but in the rites soon to begin, he shall be last—the better to regale our gods, we shall save him till the very last, after he has been made to wait and witness the 'customs' involving all his evil comrades! Yes, he shall be saved until the third and last night! Thus we shall clear the way for our own redemption! . . . the spirits of our elders most surely will approve!"

"It is so, Woot!" cried Buefi, standing beside him, her head rag now askew. "We pave the way for our own salvation!"

Just then Stokes threw up both arms, almost in Woot's face, and began a shouting tirade in English—"Though I cannot understand a thing you say," he cried, "I know you spew out of your belly a host of lies! We, we"—he was beating his breast with his clenched fist—"of a superior breed of men, will show you how to die!"

McCliff looked appalled. He seized Stokes by the arm. "You do not know what you say!" he said in great agitation—"If you had understood what he said, you would not speak so assuredly! . . . It is good that I have chosen no longer to be linguister—you could not have taken what I would have to tell you!"

Woot raised a hand and hushed the disturbance. "The rites begin tonight!" he declared earnestly, then pointed at the compass—"here on the spot of this instrument, their direction finder. The sun will have gone down and the twilight sky will be painted with the many hues of orange, purple, and pink; the air will be quiet, the sea calm. Nothing will interfere. We shall then attain perfect communion with our elders' spirits through the cries of agony of these cruel and foolish cannibals who have brought us, and themselves, to this fateful pass. In the beauty of the evening we shall rise above our present mean condition and ascend into the higher realm of the spirits. Now go and prepare yourselves. Guards, take the prisoners below!"

But the crowd seemed loathe to leave, and did so slowly. It was as if they sensed the immensity of the acts soon to take place. They speculated too upon their own slow and certain deaths, bellies swollen, racked with the fatal hunger, throats closed and parched from thirst; men, women, children, staggering about the decks half blind and crazed, all at sea in a lost, wandering, specter ship, pilotless and impotent in the storms. It was a somber time and they moped—reflective and solemn. Some wondered what might have been—had they continued the voyage unimpeded by the uprising to their captors' mysterious land. Others refused to consider this, ever, as an acceptable out. Still others thought of their gods, and the spirits of their ancestors, speculating upon how it had happened that these captives on this ship, these sick and benighted African vagabonds of the sea, had, certainly for this time, been so abandoned, forsaken. Yet most were somehow confident the coming rites would purge and cleanse their woes and fears away, giving something more than an equivocal tone to the expectancy of their relief; then they thought of their betrayers, white and black, some of whom at least were now to pay the slow, lingering price of the ultimate penalty, and they seemed somehow appeased.

As the prisoners were taken below, the blacks stood watching, knowing that not long after the prisoners' ordeal would come their own. How long?—weeks, maybe a month or more? The sun was already past its zenith; now it would start its slow, inexorable descent. At long last then would come evening—one doubtless of great beauty—and with it events beginning the final throes of their earthly reality. Slowly dispersing, talking little, they seemed to wish now only for communion with themselves, with their inner, more private selves; they felt this to be godly. So it was as they waited . . . waited for something they could no longer grasp, imagine. Was it peace? Was it knowledge? Was it the grace of ancestral spirits?— of ancient assurances? Or the tragedy of heritage. It could never be known. . . . Thus the *Caper* sailed into oblivion.

*   *   *   *   *

Prostrate in his hospital bed Knight brooded.

*   *   *   *   *

317

The day was grey, misty, chill, the seas running high, as the United States frigate *Valiant,* Captain Ulysses Perlander commanding, cruised in hostile waters thirty miles off Cape Three Points and the Gold Coast. The African early autumn squalls had kept both captain and crew on constant alert, though their duties of patrol for a time would soon be over, permitting them to begin the long run across the Atlantic to Boston and three months or more of the comforts of home life. Nor somehow, despite his usual misgivings and melancholy, were thoughts of Boston altogether unpleasant to Captain Perlander, this though he was a prudent and civilized man who controlled his small and secret enthusiasms as befitted a naval officer given to strict adherence to duty. Indeed his men thought him seldom enthusiastic about anything, rather at times dogmatic, sometimes downright irascible, though they were also aware of a capacity for humaneness in him that they knew he tried to hide. What, however, they did not know was that covertly he was given to the fits and vagaries of a kind of mawkish, though outwardly stark, romanticism. Day or night, as the occasion afforded in his cabin, it was his habit to read Milton and Pope, or to revel in the chronicles of Thucydides.

A rather small, periwigged man, and, for one of his country's best sea officers, habituated to carelessness in dress, he stood on the quarterdeck of the *Valiant* now and stared apprehensively into the clammy mists. Yet though the weather was spiteful, it was not, he thought, violent; he had seen far worse seas even if there was now a wet-ashen, opaque, mystical, quality to the seascape somehow heretofore unknown to him. Now he paced the quarterdeck and, under the curious glances of his officers, experienced in silence his futilities, frustrations, and premonitions. It was the 16th of October, and after almost a year away he had finally to concede, at least to himself, that, yes, he was more than ready to start home. Soon he went below to his cabin, to read again from Milton's "Comus," or, for the hundredth time, from "Paradise Lost." But it was that great man's poem "On the Morning of Christ's Nativity" that he picked up instead and from which he read to himself in a quiet but eloquent voice:

> The aged earth aghast
> With terror of that blast

Shall from the surface to the center shake,
When, at the world's last session,
The dreadful Judge in Middle air shall spread
His throne.

He especially loved these powerful lines. He sometimes thought of those words, "The aged earth," when standing on the bridge of his ship looking out over the vast, limitless waters; he was a religious man and felt the grand phenomenon the earth and its boundless waters represented existed for a purpose; and that man had to one day give an account of his life and trusteeship at the "world's last session." It often caused him to probe, search, his mind and heart and conjecture what, at that crucial time certain to come, his own account might hold for the "dreadful Judge" as He spread his throne. Perlander was therefore a serious, speculative man; yet unduly haughty and fractious whenever suddenly conscious of his small physical stature. But it was always, as now, his mixed feelings about returning home that truly set him apart. It was his wife—his invalid wife; his love for her caused him fits of depression. A decade ago, during the war with the British when he had commanded one of John Paul Jones' ships, Caroline, in Boston, had become ill, the illness turning out to be a virulent form of gradual paralysis which finally rendered her sedentary, a cripple, for the rest of her life. It was a shocking blow to Perlander, who thought her the finest, wisest, most spirited woman—in her way, a beauty too—who was ever likely to be interested in him; a woman who shared with him an unlimited capacity for devotion and love. It was an ordeal now, whenever he returned home, to watch her, wasted and pale, seated in her chair on casters and smiling at him —so happily, it seemed—in a way that moved his heart. Nor were there children to divert her—her illness had struck too early for that—only a maiden aunt and servants. Her sole preoccupation, though it was a passion, had become the anti-slavery cause. She spent her days and nights now writing tracts against what she called "Satan's own holiday" and paying for their printing with her own, inherited, money. Perlander sometimes wondered whether her zeal, her fanaticism, would have been as great had she been ambulatory and healthy. Yet he himself had gradually come to share her views, if not her passion. It was just that he hated slavery.

But he loved poetry. Indeed his unhappiness over Caroline seemed to have heightened his need for it—in a seeming remembrance of her, as if she were somehow dead. Now, at 53, he had allowed it to become a condition of his life—this somberness, melancholy, that sometimes only poetry could assuage; he could well have been a mystic; his officers sometimes even now so regarded him as they watched him standing at the mizzenmast, silent, contemplative, peering out to sea as if he ruminated on some gigantic, philosophical problem involving the fate of the world itself. They would ask themselves what possibly could so preoccupy, disturb, trouble, him; what could make him, granted all his responsibilities of command, seem to want to eschew all normal communication with fellow human beings? He was the ship's great mystery. Yet the men's confidence in him as a leader remained unimpaired, whole.

There came a knock at his cabin door. He raised his eyes from Milton's poetry and responded. Whereupon a midshipman, saluting, entered. "Captain," he said, "the weather remains the same—the mists have not lifted. Are there further orders?"

"None, Anderson."

"The mists are really scary, sir. One can think he sees almost anything. Earlier the mainmast lookout even reported sighting a sail, to windward; but on questioning he thought he'd been wrong; or at least said it had quickly disappeared in the mists, if it was a sail at all. But Mr. DeKoven, lieutenant of the watch, told him to keep a sharp eye out. These mists are weird, sir—it'll be good to see the sun again."

Perlander dismissed him and returned to poetry. Before the interruption, he had been thinking what a strange, yet apt, title for a poem—"On the Morning of Christ's Nativity." Even Jesus, he thought, had at one time been a baby, wrapped in swaddling clothes; but with what a vast new day ahead of him!—though the great good would come only after mammoth betrayal, indignity, suffering, and death. But nativity meant something being born anew, an entity not existing before, some event of shining new promise. Was this what Milton, by his transcendent eloquence, had meant? The riddle intrigued him as he went on reading the rest of the poem—ah, a renascence it was, he thought; a beginning of novel things; the resuscitation of a body perilously close to becoming meaningless. Salvation? . . . great events? . . . history? The rebirth of Christ in the realm of sinful man would perhaps yet come—he felt the sign.

When later he went up on deck he was joined by two of his officers, Lieutenants Basilley and Scott. "We are proceeding cautiously, sir," said Scott, tall, red-headed, animated—"as we must, in these doldrums and mists. An eerie experience, sir—some dunce aloft even said he had sighted a sail; that's what this weather is capable of—mirages! Then in only the past hour the other look-out gave out a fearful cry—thought he saw the sail again. And more!—what looked like, he said, a wrecked and dangling top-mast; he insisted the ship was badly damaged, and somehow floating strange, very strange—almost like a ghost ship, sir."

"What do you make of it?" said Perlander.

Scott at first looked at Basilley. "Well," he answered at last, "it's probably the atmosphere, the mists, sir." He pointed—"Out there now you can see anything you wish. I can't blame the look-outs—they're alert; ha, maybe too alert!"

Perlander asked for a telescope and, putting it to his eye, moved it slowly along the ghostly horizon. He saw nothing but the swirling mists. He turned now to Lieutenant Basilley, barely taller than himself, but dashing in his uniform, with a neat saber scar across the dimple in his chin, and said: "Send up another lookout and let me talk to the one who said he saw the wrecked rigging."

Within minutes the summoned seaman appeared before him, saluting with two inept bare knuckles raised to his forehead. Perlander looked at him—"What did you see?" he demanded of the ruddy tar.

"Beggin' the captain's pardon, sir, I saw a ship. A merchantman."

"How do you know?—what actually did you see?"

"It was limping, sir, like it had been in a battle or somethin'—maybe a battle with the elements. The slings of the fore topsail yard were gone, and the reefed sail was down, with the yard hang-ing all lopsided-like. And not a human soul to be descried upon her, sir—she floated through the seas like an unmanned ghost, a great wanderin' misty ghost. Then all of a sudden she was no more."

"How far was she at the time from us?"

" 'Bout a quarter-mile, sir—and driftin' toward shore, makin' for the Gold Coast, she was, like a homin' pigeon. May nigh be there soon and onto a dangerous, rocky, lee shore—I wouldn't like to be aboard her, sir, in her lost, wayward confusion."

Perlander studied him. "Very well," he said finally, dismissing him—"carry on."

Lieutenants Scott and Basilley had heard the exchange. Basilley gave his captain a deferential smile. "It sounded rather fanciful, sir, didn't it?" he said—"for that apparition of a ship to have disappeared so quickly; and hasn't been seen now since, though we have lookouts in both crow's-nests. In any case, if the weather doesn't close in completely, we'll still be able to sight anything around. I have my doubts, though, sir, about such a vessel."

But all the while Perlander, deep in thought, and seeming not to have heard at all, gazed out to sea. "We are a warship," he muttered finally, "and must not be duped or surprised." He gave his order: "Ready the nine-pounders in the bows and traverse a back-and-forth course parallel to the shore. If the lookout was right, we may encounter this ghost again."

"Aye, aye, sir," said both lieutenants, already moving.

Perlander went below. He sat morosely in his cabin and speculated on the phenomenon the lookout had pictured. He somehow believed him. If so, what nation's ship was it? he wondered—and what in God's name afflicted it? The sailor's account, he thought, had been unpleasant, eerie indeed; it filled him with foreboding, especially the described aimlessness of the ghost ship's course. Perlander now devoted a brief moment to silent prayer, asking, as was his custom, that he, the commanding officer of a man-of-war of a new, proud, and independent nation and, as such, having the lives and well-being of the ship's company within his stewardship, that he be given wisdom and understanding to deal with the vicissitudes of each day's life and duty, and that his heart ever retain the compassion so necessary for favor in the Almighty's sight.

At three o'clock he went up on deck to see if the sun had appeared. It had not, but he found matters otherwise normal—the lookouts were still aloft, yet there had not been a sound from either. Then something unusual, bizarre, occurred. It was the weird light, a kind of vague misty luminosity in the sky. It was doubtless the quintessence of the sun, but how blurry, shielded, how held back behind ashen-grey vapors and cumulous cloud

322

banks. Perlander on the quarterdeck gazed first to port then to starboard, as if yearning in his heart to sight something affirming; to see this ghostly floating image of the very spirit lurking in his lonely soul. He looked quickly about him now and saw that for the moment he was alone—no one to run up to him entreating orders. He turned, stepped to the taffrail, and looked down at the watery wake of the ship. Soon he thought he saw a rippling rainbow in the dark green water. Then suddenly in an aperture in the mists on the horizon he saw a moving hulk, the shape of a ship, its rigging in shambles. Was it real? . . . or was it a mirage, a vision? He clung with a death grip to the rail, his eyes staring, breath coming fast, wondering futilely why there were no cries from the crow's-nests; he longed now himself to give the wild alarm. Then the mist's aperture closed, but even before that the ghost-image had vanished. He felt spent and angered; apparently no one had seen the apparition but himself; it strangely outraged him, as if the lookouts should be able not only to find the phenomenon again but explain it as well. Moreover, earlier the ghost ship had been to windward, which, from the *Valiant's* position then, was to starboard; assuming the same position now it would be to port. It was baffling. Yet it was true, he thought—the ghost ship was helmsmanless, wandering. Stubborn, determined, he took up a permanent position on the quarterdeck, and, using his spyglass, constituted himself a third lookout. But he saw nothing more—though he waited . . . waited . . . waited interminably. Then, just before darkness, the mists began to thicken and a lackluster rain began to fall. Yet he paced the quarterdeck in his obdurate vigil—until complete murky darkness had enveloped his ship and the immense Gulf of Guinea. Finally, wet, hungry, beaten, he went below.

That evening he did not dine with his officers but had food brought to his cabin. He did not feel he had witnessed a phantasm, but that the ship he had seen was real. He somehow sensed above and around its bleak hull an ominous presence lurking, moving, upon the dark waters, yet whose spirit penetrated even to the sequestered air of the quarters where he now sat, brooded, languished. It was the aura surrounding his vision of this ghostlike vessel that mightily disturbed him; it somehow to him meant suffering; there was nothing about the object or the idea that gave any justification whatever for felicity or hope. After he had eaten, he poured a glass of port and lit his pipe, his mind, however, a vacuum in the sense that it yearned for some kind of revelation; it was irresolute, ungratified; there was a vague, unformed craving that something as yet unrevealed be born; that the connecting line of life not be irrevocably cut; that it be somehow sustained, given new tenure; that vigor, freshness, come out of woe and putrefaction. Soon he put on his spectacles and for a time read from Pope's "Essay on Man," then returned to his true love, "Paradise Lost," but on this singular occasion found the latter strangely lacking in fire, stimulation. It was then again he turned the pages to "On the Morning of Christ's Nativity:"

> So when the Sun in bed,
> Curtain'd with cloudy red,
> Pillows his chin upon an Orient wave,
> The flocking shadows pale,
> Troop to th' infernall jail,
> Each fetter'd Ghost slips to his severall grave,
> Fly after the Night-steeds, leaving their Moon-lov'd maze.

He savored the spirit of the lines, their sentience, emotion, caring little, feeling no necessity, for their literal explication—in poetry he was less interested in meaning than in feeling: "Each fetter'd Ghost slips to his severall grave," he reread, his feeling now a continuation, extension, of the malaise felt hours before on the quarterdeck at the moment the ghost ship had vanished. And, as before, there was the wish, bordering on a speculative expectancy, that some new birth would, or might, rectify his strange sense of loss, his psychological disarrangement, at the thought the ghost ship might deliberately have passed him by. Yet there was somehow no proof of its certain representation of death—quite to the contrary; there was involved in some obscure way this thread of nativity, ebbing but recoverable life—rebirth. He read to himself, now in audible whispers, the final stanza of the poem:

> But see the Virgin blest,
> Hath laid her Babe to rest.
> Time is our tedious Song should here have ending,
> Heav'ns youngest teemèd Star,
> Hath fixt her polisht Car,

Her sleeping Lord with Handmaid Lamp attending:
And all about the Courtly Stable,
Bright-harnest Angels sit in order serviceable.

He was somewhat reassured, yet troubled; at last, uncharacter-
istically, he wished for meaning, clearer meaning; a hallowed birth
had been effected, but all knew in this late day and age what suffering, ignominy, and temporary death, awaited this Babe in its innocence and love. What was the meaning, then, the connection? . . .
He went to bed still neither knowing nor understanding. He
rolled and tossed on his Spartan cot and longed for sleep, the sleep
of peaceful knowledge, of genuine repose, not death. He lay in the
dark, feeling the undulating motion of the ship upon the gentle
night swells, the slow-flowing hillocks of the sea. The wind was at a
near standstill, the ship's lethargic locomotion proving it, though
he imagined with some certainty the mists had not in the least dissolved; he felt an oppressive humidity and wanted to remove his
nightshirt but only sat on the side of the cot, chin propped on
hand, eyes staring morosely, musingly, into the darkness. The zero
visibility outside he felt as well inside—inside a bleak, impenetrable sense of impending exigency, or crux, as he lay back down and
wrapped himself in the sheet. Yet sleep did not come until well
past one o'clock.

Then, sometime after three, he was awakened, almost gently, by
something—he did not know what. He lay still, but had almost
dozed off again, when once more he stirred, though only half-
aroused as before. Then silence. Yet he vaguely felt himself trying
to remember his sensation, his reaction. The ship seemed to have
taken, amidships, some kind of broad blow, not abrupt, not violent,
but random and casual, a slight jolt or contact, a nudge. Once
again, though, as if reassuringly, he felt the riding motion of the
ship, then the slipping, relaxing, falling away, before the brief
mounting again. But then amidships there came the gentle blow
again, the jolt, then a kind of intimate nuzzle. Suddenly he was
awake. He sat bolt upright. The ship, he was aware at last, was
in contact with something besides water. He waited, listened, his
heart pounding. Then came the cry above from the weatherdeck
watch, and he heard a mad scurrying, a commotion, a confusion,
before the cry of the watch went out again. He jumped for his

clothes just as an urgent knock came at the door. "Yes—enter!" he called.

The cabin door came open. It was Mr. Harper, officer of the watch, nervously swinging a lantern. "We've been rammed, sir," he said. "There's no damage yet, but another ship is riding our starboard quarter—though we can hardly see her in the thickness of the mists."

Perlander, in a hurry, was putting on a shoe. His had not been a vision, a mirage, he knew now—the ghost ship was real. "Go try to keep close to her, Harper," he said breathlessly—"I'll be right up. *Do not lose that ship!*" His voice trembled with emotion. The watch officer, though leaving, momentarily hesitated, as if to be sure he had correctly heard the bizarre command. "Do not let her get away in this cursed darkness and mist!" Perlander said— "She is a holy ship! . . . we shall never find her again. Stay close up against her, Harper, and use the chains and grappling hooks to secure her to us—we shall secure her and our true salvation! . . . Issue the orders! Prepare to board her!" Eyes afire, Perlander spoke as if in a crazed dream, the watch officer, leaving, staring at him incredulously.

Perlander now could not find his other shoe—in the commotion he had kicked it under the cot back up against the bulkhead. He lit a candle and went to his hands and knees, reaching, stretching, feeling, for it over the rough-hewn floor. He brought up instead an object he had thought lost, had not seen in weeks—a foot-high African sculpture, made of wood and bronze, of a Benin woman seated on a royal chair made of what appeared tiny elephant tusks. Despite all his desperate hurry, he laid the piece carefully on the table and observed it for a moment in the eerie light. Strangely, only now did he realize how much he loved it, what it meant to him—a bridging of epochs and mores—with its dusky colors, red, green, and brown, the rich intricacy of the workmanship, the art. Even forgetting for an instant the crisis at hand, he speculated on the artificer who had created it a century or two before and had then died and passed into oblivion. Was the soul really immortal, fixed? he wondered; where then was that too of the donor of this gift, a friend and fellow-officer, long since dead in combat on another ship of John Paul Jones'? Where also, yes, was that of the tribesman-artist who had created this finely-wrought and portentous talisman on the table before him? Was its creator really in oblivion? . . . or rather perhaps still serving as a link between that time and this, that culture and this, those souls and these. Now came another solid jolt reverberating through the ship and Perlander's startled, harried mind returned to the present. He scrambled for the shoe, put it on, and, throwing on a coat, started above.

The moment he reached the deck, a horrid, sickening stench assailed his nostrils. Everything too was enveloped in the heavy swirling mists. And by now, in the ineffective light of many lanterns, with all hands on deck, the two ships were being lashed together. There was much confusion, excited talk, and running about, as the crew attempted bravely to carry out its captain's orders. Perlander went to the bulwarks and peered through the mists close up at the ravaged vessel. The stink was frightful and there were absolutely no signs of life. She was a ghost, all right, he thought disconsolately —what in God's name had befallen her? "We will not board her until daylight," he said to Lieutenant Basilley at his side—"It will not be a pleasant task even then."

"It's a dead ship, sir," said Basilley—"That's the stink of rotting dead bodies."

"Yes," Perlander nodded gravely, almost diffidently.

"It may have carried slaves, sir."

Perlander turned and stared at Basilley. He had not considered the possibility. "Ah, it may have indeed," he breathed—" . . . *slaves!*" The thought was anathema to him. He had come at last to regard slavery as a moral disease, a plague, an affront to both God and man. Though he had been thus indoctrinated by his wife, he now held convictions almost as stubborn as hers. The thought, then, that the ship may have been a slaver filled him with both fury and shame. He fell into a morose silence. Soon the thickening mists had so enveloped the two vessels that they seemed as one; the crew's lanterns were of negligible utility, as the men stumbled over each other, muttered wary complaints, and tried not to hold their noses against the horrid, repellant odor pervading the air. The two ships rode the swells together as if grappling, tussling, with each other in the restless seas. Though fully aware of his presence, the crew seemed to ignore Perlander now, yet with a deference belying their mystification and alarm at his grisly commands. His officers, apparently of the opinion he craved privacy to meditate, left him

327

alone and talked quietly among themselves, as he, shrouded in the mists, stood at the bulwarks and stared over at the haunted ship. It would be over three hours before daybreak. Yet he began his vigil.

The horrible stench struck him full in the face again. A slave ship, yes, he mused, grimacing. That was likely indeed. What, then, had God wrought?—it was not possible anyone aboard could still be alive; the hulking, ghostly monster, pilotless, unmanned, nonetheless seemed to have been heading for shore—Africa—as if driven by some uncanny force filled with the yearning to return home; drifting, as it were, though still not aimlessly; a mighty wanderer, blind, groping, yet with a sense of retributive direction; of final, homing, victory after all; but now it had been impeded, thwarted, overtaken by the *Valiant* and lashed fast for later daylight investigation. Why had he ordered this thing done? He speculated upon it. Strangely, he thought of the Benin statuette down in his cabin, so moving to him and emblematic, and of "On the Morning of Christ's Nativity." Why had this ghost ship so truly sought out the *Valiant* in these dense, spectral mists—sought *him* out? Was it fated to be? . . . was it a sign? . . . the ghost ship was not the only wanderer; in a real sense so was the *Valiant*—so was he. He sighed heavily; then the oppressive stench made him want to retch; it was the smell of death and putrefaction, all the more dread, appalling, repugnant, in the shrouding mists and mysteries; he felt his life, his fate, involved, and somehow that of some other, a stranger; a nativity it was, in the morning at daybreak; would the mists then clear, the sun return, and all eventuate to have been some ghastly dream? Yet there was this awful stench of rotting flesh and maggots—what of that? No, the ship was genuine, the devastation, dark and baffling, real; so was the presence of foul, stinking death. He dreaded having to board her. Yet he must.

Lieutenant Basilley approached him now. "Sir, why don't you retire below again?" he said. "You will catch a distemper and a fever in this night chill—you are half-dressed."

"No, I'll man the watch," said Perlander. "Send the men below to sleep for these few hours before daybreak—the others and yourself also. It is some other affection I feel; by this venture possibly we shall be saved from further wanderings and, as in the Dantean paradiso, canto twenty-five, returned to the same font where we were baptized—a nativity—and to that fair sheepfold where, as lambs, we slept. Send the crew below, Basilley—much will transpire when next we see light." He turned back to the bulwarks, his face haggard, grim.

When later the deck was clear and Perlander was alone, his mind seemed to turn inward on itself in quest of some divination of what had happened to this ill-fated ship. Though hardly able any longer to withstand the stench, he yet peered restlessly into the mist and murk and over at the ghost ship's deck. Still plying his mind with myriad questions and surmises, he stared so long and hard that in time his vision became faint and blurred, distorted and unreliable. Once he thought he saw something through the greyish haze; he imagined it had been a slight movement, some wraithlike creature, down on all fours, slowly, painfully, traversing that deck —another wanderer. But almost at once he told himself it was all vaporous figment, fancy—or a ghost; the ghost of slavery, he hoped, stinking and dead. Two hours passed and still there was no sign of any faint, pre-dawn lighting in the eastern skies. Yet at last, as he had hoped, the mists seemed slowly on the move; maybe if the skies cleared the sun would burn the fogs away. He thought now, on the deck opposite, he saw the same slight movement as before —a ghost on its knees, smallish, as a child, moving like some phantom across that slimy deck. Then it evaporated before his peering eyes, yet he somehow went on seeing it. It was not large enough to be a mature man, and did not seem to him a smaller animal. Almost another hour passed and the mists began to clear as a faint light took hold in the skies. Suddenly his heart began a fierce pounding. It had reappeared—the specter. It dragged itself to the bulwarks opposite, though hardly able to stand, as Perlander, his breathing coming fast, leaned far forward and held out his lantern to the utmost reach. The specter seemed to stare straight across at him. Then recognition came to Perlander. It was a boy, a black boy, eyes deathly and hollow from suffering yet palpitating like glowing coals. Perlander gasped, unable to believe what he saw. He started to cry out the alarm to the crew in the forecastle but found he could not utter a sound. The haunted, staring eyes opposite him startled, horrified, him. Now he heard the boy's moan, then his weak babbling of something incoherent. It unnerved him and set him shaking. The feeble babbling, the desperate Fanti whispering, he could not understand was: "Kicker-aboo! Kickeraboo! We are all dead!" The boy, Bymba, had then collapsed on the slave ship's death-strewn deck, rolled over on his face, and was still.

Perlander sounded the alarm now. All the time daylight had been fast advancing and, as the mists cleared, brilliant red and purple streaks appeared in the eastern skies. He shouted out again, and Lieutenant Scott came running. "All hands on deck!" cried Perlander—"Arm the men! It is now light enough to board her!" The deck was soon crowded as the armed crew, milling about, pre-pared to carry out the order, for the day had fully dawned and soon the sun would lift itself above the water line of the horizon. But the stench had become almost unbearable, causing the men to try not breathing deeply. Perlander had a seaman bring him three pistols, fully loaded and primed, which he took with him as he led the boarding party across the bulwarks and onto the foul deck of the *Caper*.

Filth, excrement, and signs of riot, chaos, havoc, and devasta-tion were everywhere. Tumid, rotting, black bodies lay scattered over the decks and in the stinking holds below where more than three hundred souls, crazed by two months of horrifying thirst and starvation, had died despairing at last of succor from the spirits of their departed elders. There had also been the inevitable period of berserk violence when, on two occasions, cannibalism had been attempted, only to be put down by the weakened and dying Woot with yet a bloody, murderous hand. "Have you no pride of nation, no esteem of self?" he had demanded in a frail voice of the fewer than one hundred who then survived, after himself summoning the strength to behead one would-be offender. "Only our oppressors, whose tortured, devastated bodies have long since now gone to the sharks, would have perpetrated such an act. It is their way of life. But we shall die free of this taint!"

The boarding party, in its original rushing onslaught over the bulwarks, had neglected to observe that Bymba, though lying un-conscious where he had fallen, still breathed. It was Perlander, re-membering the earlier vision of the hollow, staring eyes, who, when at last returning to the *Valiant*, the futile exploration of the death-gripped *Caper* over, had paused to bend down and examine what seemed merely another body, one more tumescent corpse. But he

330

remembered its undersize and was somehow now not shocked to find the slight breathing, though it was the only sign of life. He was certain, however, the boy would die, yet at once ordered him transferred to the *Valiant* to be placed in a hammock in the sick bay for the ship's surgeon's attention. So it transpired that Bymba was the lone survivor of the now-extinct saga—like Ishmael, rescued by "the devious-cruising" *Valiant* which had found an "orphan" on the deep. A nativity.

When everyone was back aboard the *Valiant*, Perlander, harried, exhausted, still half-dressed, issued the fatal order. "Unleash her!" he cried of the ill-starred *Caper*—"Then stand away!" The men, sensing the solemn act which now impended, hurriedly took away the grappling hooks and chains and the *Caper* was free again. The *Valiant's* sails then were set to catch the dawn's lightsome breezes as the helmsman wore the ship around to head directly away from the stricken vessel. When at last they were separated by two-hundred yards, Perlander spoke. "Heave to!" he cried. "Run out the guns! Now beat to quarters!" It was a ceremony which had begun. Somber, grave, now, he heard the resultant loud roll of the marine bandsmen's drums echoing through the ship and the pipes twittering as the bosun's mates repeated his orders. Soon half the *Valiant's* forty cannon were trained broadside on the hapless *Caper*. Then nothing happened; there ensued a long, momentous pause. Perlander seemed briefly to have lost his resolve, his will to command; he stood there in awed contemplation of the *Caper*, which was once more for the moment a vagabond on the high seas, her insides sullied by heaps of rotting human slave flesh, her rigging, yards, and mizzenmast in shambles; a forlorn sight. Suddenly then he seemed to remember what had happened, grasping again the *Caper's* original mission, the supervening lethal mutiny, the massacre of the crew, and finally, food and water depleted, that fate itself had sent the wandering death ship to seek him out. Now he gave the order. "Open fire!"

The gun crews pulled the lanyards. There was a tenth of a second delay. Then the long nine-pounders belched and roared. At once the *Caper's* topgallant fell amid a shower of nautical debris; also in the cannonading the torn-away topmast had caught against the mainyard and the whole superstructure hung precariously in the air. Yet the ship's deadliest damage had been taken amidships.

She now settled noticeably in the water. Already, though, the gun crews were swabbing, sponging, out the gun bores—preparatory to delivering yet another broadside volley. Again Perlander stood as if bemused, deeply reflective, vindictive, as though he were presiding over the final rites of a grudgingly-admired, yet hated, adversary. It was a slave ship; he could never forget it. Now, on his command, the nine-pounders bellowed again and the *Caper* began to disintegrate. Trash and rubble flew a hundred feet high and the wreckage was in total ruin. "Enough," said Perlander at last, his tone almost one of contrition—". . . Enough," he sighed. The *Caper* was sinking. She had assumed a radical list, with the port scuppers almost completely under water. A small wave broke over her weather deck now, sending cataracting seas directly down the yawning hatchway. Yet now she seemed momentarily to right herself—though the quarter deck was nearly level with the frothy swells—in one last rebellious, piteous, effort. Then, on an even keel, she slipped under—the seas closing over her as her crippled masts slowly disappeared into the deeps of Poseidon. Yet for an instant the sails fairly gleamed under the greenish waters. "Her evil work is done," breathed Perlander—". . . She's finished." The crew stood silent in solemn observance, the vast watery wastes, the very billows, hushed.

Perlander retired to his cabin. He was sleep-weary and overstrained, yet unable to slow his mind to the point of sleep. He stripped and washed, then, in fresh linen, lay down on his cot and wrapped himself in a blanket. The black slave boy would die, he thought, and be buried at sea, having failed his nativity, miscarried in the poignant try to regain Africa, though uncannily the stricken ship had tended there as if with compass-eyes. So the morning had indeed brought birth only to be followed now, alas, by precocious death. Even Jesus had not so suffered. Was it yet possible the ship's surgeon could save this young black Christ?— a miracle was required, he knew, as strangely he reached far over and with some gratification let his fingers touch the Benin statuette on his table. He did not know why he did this—it gave him not only a feeling of aesthetic pleasure, but of refuge, sanctuary; yet somehow also one of impotence and futility. Was it an *objet d'art* which had figured in tribal rites? Did it have preternatural powers? —if so, should they not now be invoked? He sat up and held the statuette away from him in the feeble candle light. What was its essential efficacy, its power? he wondered; here was a woman—a goddess? . . . seated on her ivory throne, eyes reposeful, her severely rigid arms and hands yet at rest; had she just pronounced some final Afric judgment?—ordered returned to its owner, say, some stray calf from the herd, approved a chieftain's suit for marriage to her sister, or herself interceded with the beneficent spirits of her elders in behalf of the unfortunate, the halt, the blind? Who was she? What was she? Whom or what did she represent? Maybe, in truth, she had been merely a slave girl, used by the artist as a model. He knew he would never know.

Yet this statuette, this tribal artifact, typified for him a strange, stoical people, a continent-inhabiting clan with a code of tenets, a system of metaphysics, all its own. Conceivably Europeans and their derivatives might study them with profit, he thought—something he himself had so far not attempted in any depth, although he had smatteringly read of the civilization of Songhay, of the black center of intellect and learning at Timbuktu, of the empire of Kanem-Bornu, and the powerful black states of the western Sudan. It was true he had been fascinated by this, but these successes had proceeded, he had come to believe, from a radically different view of human existence from that held by the West. He was inclined to think Africans, being closer to nature, might somehow be closer to God—closer to the true humane tradition; nor was their folkloric inspiration in any foreseeable danger of drying up; he was convinced the black nations of that continent were still in their great period of the legend-praising of the people, possessed of a rare, mythical, fecundity—intelligence/intuition—all having limitless implications and promise. But could their spontaneous ways ever make the world trust humanity and feeling, or endorse repudiation of the fetish of machines?—though he well knew of black abductors of fellow-Africans on the Guinea coast, and of the tragic blacks aboard the *Caper*, who, after massacring the crew, could not sail the ship back to Africa. What of these matters? he asked himself, floundering; he was not sure, but could it for blacks be the price they must pay in advance to achieve their longed-for instinctive congeniality with the folk, with being and humaneness? —this was of course a matter of the sum total of African cultural values, the essence of the black soul, the racial mark of rational irrationality; pure reason often stopped at the mere surface of things, lacking the capacity to penetrate to that inner essence which eluded the lucid consciousness; it was only intuitive reason that was able to divine what lived beyond the appearance of things, to comprehend total reality.

Hadn't some thinker he had read insisted that man was an irrational composite of metaphysics and history, his greatness inexplicable if he had evolved from the mud and silt deposits of primordial slow-flowing rivers, his misery inexplicable if he now existed in the true image of God? Again Perlander fingered the statuette and pondered these things so crucial, he felt, to his own fate. What had been his own early beliefs on such matters as race, morality, slavery? He was unclear on this. He had once, at the insistence of his wife, signed a manifesto damning slavery. Yet he had never really understood the institution, though he had somehow always hated it and its long history replete with sadism. He concluded the fault was man, the sinister in his nature, the banal, his heel of vulnerability. It was these that had given birth to the curse. Could he himself own a black? he wondered, as if posing some self-righteous test of his own rectitude. He was certain he could not, yet all the while he fondled the Benin statuette; though, in the act, thinking how unusual, bizarre, almost indecent he was. At once in sudden distaste he placed the piece back on the table, considering himself to be in some kind of psychic state of suspension—so much, he felt, depended on the boy and his nativity; were he saved, it would mean much for his own, Perlander's, disturbed quandaries—possibly vindication, reaffirmation, of his own quest for some gift of inner peace, some stillness of the heart. He must talk with the ship's surgeon, he thought just before he slept. If the boy lived, he would take him home to Caroline—he must not die.

Bymba did not die. He lived to reach Boston. He would live, moreover, in many subsequent places and through many troublous times—until his eighty-second year.

*   *   *   *   *

Knight in the hospital bed brooded.

Chapter 3

Saturday morning. She sat in the dentist's waiting room—the office of Chauncey Stiles, a longtime friend of the family—and read, half-attentively, a six-months-old *New Yorker*. "Though adults, we were also children—our landscape was that immense," went on the narrator of the story—"We breathed air, gazed at skies, belched like goats, and wept when it rained—all the while viewing this infinite landscape. And ourselves, fallible, fated, no longer adolescents, were nonetheless cast as mere sibling offspring—watched over by a three-headed dog we gave the name Cerberus, or Niobe without tears, or sometimes Zossima—all children of this dusty landscape. Yet it was only a little league baseball diamond—peopled with children." She paused and let the magazine rest on her knees for a moment—she thought what she read was more fatuous self-indulgence than the mandarin prose it purported to be; it was narrated by the story's retired high school teacher, a grandfather of the left fielder. After the game was over, the children on the winning side, their parents and friends, had come away in great elation, the children's faces beaming, red cheeks aglow, blond hair flying. Ah, how unlike her own two children, Mary Dee thought— Ernestine and Vernon.

Again she took up the magazine, but could not bring herself to continue reading. How she hated waiting on a dentist!—especially a tedious old gossipy busybody like "Uncle" Chauncey—even if it was only to get one's teeth cleaned. She gazed up at the pictures gracing his walls—she could not remember when they had not been there—and smiled to herself about his "arty" bachelor tastes, the pretensions to opera and ballet, his gaudy apartment hung in maroon velvet. The pictures before her were all murky though serviceable reproductions—one, decidedly nondescript, she had never identified; but there were also the two Pissarros and a reposeful bucolic view of trees skirting a field of grain by Sisley. The Sisley made her think of Paris, Raoul, and the fabulous pictures in the

Jeu de Paume—dear, sweet little Raoul. She had not heard from him in months; yet she herself had not written. Much had happened to her in these long weeks of her new life, her new destiny, though she resisted admitting it; she seemed unaware she was no longer the same, would never be. She tried to read again—the *New Yorker's* children were on their chartered bus going home now; they were all very happy; but the strangely poetic narrator, the left fielder's grandfather, sat staring out the bus window, thinking on his lonely widowered life, when suddenly a cheer went up for his grandson, who had collected four hits in the game, including an arching home run. The old man smiled quickly, then laughed with the others as they all returned to their comfortable suburban homes. She thought of Ernestine and Vernon as she put the magazine aside —what a different scene, setting, perspective, these suburbanites and their little leaguers presented! . . . they seemed so foreign to her now, while Ernestine and Vernon were so vital and close. She had seen them as recently as three days ago, for they had become buffers against all the present gnawing unrest in her life—since the recent shocking discovery involving the identity of Knight—shields against her own heart riven with old fears that ironical fate had brought back to haunt her. And it was known now—the hospital's statements were confident—that Knight would live. It was an eventuality her daemon had feared.

Five minutes later she was inside the inner room seated in Chauncey Stiles' dental chair. Chauncey, semi-retired and no longer spry after nearly forty years of standing over patients, at once began his irking prattle. "How's your mother, Dee, in that big old house!" he laughed, though his mirth was accompanied by a wheezing sound in his breathing.

"She's fine," came the attempt at a bright, though untrue, reply.

All the while Chauncey was fitting the circular little cleaning gadget onto this dental drill. "Ha, and your two kids!—your 'wards' —how're they?"

Mary Dee tried to smile. "They're okay, I guess, Chauncey."

"They're not a bit easy to do dental work on, I'll tell you that." Still wheezing, he raised his chin and smiled, his steel-rimmed glasses glinting against the flaccid grey-brown skin of his face. "They alarmed the office with their yelling the day you brought them in here."

"It was their first time in a dentist's chair," said Mary Dee soberly.

"They thought I was going to kill them, I think, or torture them to death—especially the boy."

"Vernon, yes," she laughed. "He's excitable sometimes."

"The girl, though, got ahold of herself right away—after the first outburst—and was soon scolding Vernon for crying."

"Ernestine's the boss—she's always taken care of him. He expects it."

"Has their mother acted up any more—made any trouble?"

"Not recently, after—through the case worker, the social worker —I threatened her a little. But she's really not a bad sort—in her way she likes the children. She's just preoccupied, harried, with a lot of other things—mostly it's trying to get something out of an uneventful, drudging, life, I think. And she likes men." Mary Dee's smile now was acrid. She added, "Ernestine shows similar signs, unless she can be headed off."

"What will become of kids like these?" Chauncey said, breathing almost stertorously, shaking his head—"There're so many of them in the big cities." But the teeth cleaning had begun in earnest and for the moment Mary Dee was spared participation in a conversation grown tedious to her. "They haven't got much of a future, have they?" went on Chauncey—"kids raised in such circumstances. That's why my hat's off to you, Dee. You care. Why, you've become a real crusader!" he laughed again, his glasses still glinting—"rescuing ghetto kids off the street, becoming sort of a den mother to them! Ha-ha-ha! Your father would be amused. He'd be pleased, too, I think . . . well, maybe." His little brush steadily whirred against her beautiful teeth as inwardly she fumed at his chatter. "But sometimes," he said, "I feel these people— people like your kids and their grown-ups—would be far better off down South again, back on the farm or plantation, with no city filth, no rat-infested flats, no dope and crime. It's not heaven down there yet, I know, but it's better than it was—and, for them, a whole lot better now than it is here. But what caused *you* to change, Dee?—you *have* changed, you know." Just then the telephone rang and, having long since dispensed with an assistant or secretary, he stepped aside to his desk to answer it.

All the while Mary Dee had been struggling with her annoyance and impatience. How tiresome this androgynous old man! How dated his talk!—or was it dated? Soon then her feelings toward him began to soften, moderate, and, for no reason she would have understood, her mind reverted to the innocuous *New Yorker* fiction piece, to the blond suburban children in it playing their little league baseball, and to the demonstrable joy of their friends, rooters, and parents. It was completely another world—to her somehow a strange and disturbing world. Maybe, as Chauncey said, she *had* changed, she thought. If so, why?—what had brought it about? Her new activist associates had had much to do with it—she knew that; especially Ornette and Rosabelle Hungerford, even before Knight's shooting. But in her fear, her sense of portent, confusion, she was unaware it had been *since* the shooting, since her shocking, fateful discovery of who Knight was, that she had really changed. What had originally begun as a bitter backlash reaction to her galling rebuff by Philip's world, and all that world stood for, had now, since discovery of Knight's identity, become a low-key, suffused passion directed to the very opposite quarter—in behalf of Knight, his followers, and all his works; the whole concept. Yet it represented goals she was unfamiliar with and about which she was still hopelessly ambivalent and bewildered. In therefore some bizarre, unknowing way now—altogether beyond her understanding—she was drawn to this fabled black man as to some fatal magnet. Yet she feared him, though, having returned from death, he lay vanquished in a hospital bed. She feared him nonetheless—it was in no sense physical fear—he whose burning presence she had not felt since her sojourn in that amorphous other world, Paris of so many long-ago yesterdays; paradise.

There had also been the feverish, idolatrous, activity of Knight's followers in the crisis—this too had influenced her; as well as the outpouring of media publicity directed, as a result of the assassination attempt, at the Black Peoples Congress, the drama of the meetings and fund-raising rallies, the impassioned speeches, all accompanied by Knight's followers' prayers for his total, if miraculous, recovery; to this, moreover, was added Ornette's and Rosabelle's constant exhortations to her—it had all, everything, at last become a deluge, under which she was subdued and powerless. Yet towering above everything was the mighty image of Knight himself —the hero. To her it was beyond any rational analysis—how could she forget, she thought, at Fouquet's, his glowering hate for her, and her own feelings at the time, of foreshadowing and prophecy? All these feelings had returned now, though of late they had been coupled with a strange curiosity, plaguing and mysterious, a fascination, with the *idea* of the man—his fanaticism, the intense, self-righteous mien, his tragic aspect; there was his fame too, ever-growing and in fierce struggle and controversy, his achievements, the image of courage and self-sacrifice, of humanity and compassion; she was hopelessly enmeshed, caught up, in it all, in its confusion and willfulness, its suppressed excitement, as if she were a hapless moth, skirting, toying with, taunting, the flame. But her friends, Ornette and Rosabelle, fanatical Knight followers both, mistook all this, her preoccupied silences, the indecision, the extreme, barely-hidden emotions, for dedication at last to the cause, for an internalized fervor, a devotion, rather than the kind of painful yet euphoric bewilderment it really was. They congratulated themselves—and her. The stage was set.

Chauncey, his telephone conversation with another patient ended, returned to her now and resumed work. "As I was saying, Dee . . . yes, you've changed." He smiled down at her again. "It's like you'd really gotten religion, sort of! But have I got a surprise for *you!*— about myself; but that later. I think your change is great, though, I do—think of it; a girl of your background and breeding, with your education and class, and so forth, comes around at last to feeling for the poor, the unwashed, the pariahs—ha-ha-ha!" He gave his high, cacophonous laugh, which, with the wheezing, could be frightening. "Don't get huffy and miffed, now, Dee, dear! I'm family, you know. I remember you when you were born—I really know you, and when I say you've changed, you've changed. I'm perfectly aware, all right, you've taken up with that John Calvin Knight crowd—your mother's told it to her close friends, of whom I'm one, though she probably wouldn't tell you. But she thinks it's terrible—not that you're trying to help people, but that you have the friends you have now, people, ha, you sometimes bring onto her premises. I know Irene Adkins and she *would* think it's terrible. But get this, Dee, honey"—he smiled elatedly—"I think you're right! Yes, I think your change is great—I'm glad, damn glad, to see it. Your dear family's always been a bit stuffy—even your father—and I'm close enough to all of you to say it."

"Don't bring my father into it," said Mary Dee, pushing his hand away from her mouth in order to speak—"He was *not* stuffy. He would approve of my life."

"You're probably right, at that," Chauncey said—"You could twist him around your little finger, I know. But if he did approve, he'd be right. Honest, I think that. I've long since broken away from most of those dull, unimaginative people we all knew. I've found there are many, many kinds of people, different kinds of people, around who can make life really interesting, vital, new—there *are*, Dee! I know some. You're just finding out, but I've known it for a long, long time. Go on and do your thing, girl!—do what you like to do and to hell with what people say and think about it. That's my motto. Knight's okay with me—I've never seen the man in my life, but I know he's trying to do a lot of good things. Oh my God, why anybody—especially blacks themselves!—would want to kill him is beyond me. Had you ever met him?"

Mary Dee tensed. "No," she said.

"What got you interested in him, Dee?"

"Oh, Chauncey!" she sighed in exasperation—"Who said I was interested in *him*? I've just told you I've never met him! I'm interested in what he's trying to do for black kids."

Chauncey's eyes widened—a new thought had struck him. "I'll tell you what," he said, with his best toothy professional smile, "when Knight goes home from the hospital next week, as the newspapers say he will, let's go and try to see him. As I say, I've never met him, either."

"Chauncey, are you nuts? You could almost as easily get into the White House to see the president. Knight is an important man—especially now."

Chauncey reflected on this. "You may be right," he said—"although I sent him a good-sized check when he set up his headquarters here. He probably wouldn't even remember my name, though."

Mary Dee showed astonishment; then wryly laughed—"I can hardly believe it, Chauncey. You're not exactly known as a spend-thrift, you know—you can understand my surprise to hear you've contributed to the Black Peoples Congress. My goodness, what's happening?"

"Well, it wasn't a fortune I gave, or anything like that—a thousand dollars. But I felt good doing it."

"A thousand-dollar contribution? That's not peanuts, Chauncey —you amaze me." Mary Dee's smile seemed real now, one of genuine gladness—as if she had unexpectedly come upon a compatriot, someone with whom she had now discovered important things in common. "Ah, what if mother knew about *you*?" she said.

"She does," laughed Chauncey. "When she deplored your association with these people, I told her I was a contributor to Knight's organization myself. She was flabbergasted. Yet later she said some good things about Knight herself—she knows he's trying to help people; she's got a heart. But of course, as I say, I've never even seen Knight, except on television. How about it, Dee? . . . let's you and I form a little conspiracy—let's plan to meet him!" Mary Dee felt her trembling heart in her throat—at once the old dread had returned. The strangely distraught but stony expression on her face did not escape Chauncey—"You seem as if meeting him would be distasteful to you, Dee; you really do."

She tried quickly to brighten the look on her face. "I think your idea is harebrained, that's all. It's crazy. Besides, I have no desire to meet Knight in person," she lied—"It's not Knight *the man* who interests me, but what he's done, what he's doing, what he stands for. No, I wouldn't think of trying to meet him."

Chauncey made no immediate comment. He merely asked her to open her mouth again and went on cleaning her teeth. Neither spoke for two minutes or more, though it was apparent his silence was occasioned by his thoughts. But when he had at last finished the job and she had gotten out of the chair, he stood looking at her. As first he smiled, then turned grave. "I must say, I'm puzzled by your attitude," he said. "Even if I have to do it alone, though, Dee, I'm going to try somehow to meet Knight—simply because I think he's an exceptional person, a man of good works whose motives I think are pure, really pure. That's a rarity, my friend."

Mary Dee, though not in context, spoke forthrightly: "I want you to help me with something. I'm planning a get-together, a party, I guess you can call it, for some time next month—in the big room over our garage I've converted into a studio. It will be the first meeting of a committee we're forming to raise, we hope, a sizeable sum for Knight's organization. Will you help us . . . with some of the expense? I know you will, Chauncey."

"Now, don't dodge the issue, Dee." But he laughed. "Of course I'll help you—I'll underwrite the darn thing. Why don't you have

Knight there, though? He'll be recovered by then, probably traveling on planes again. Don't be so negative about him—he might just come, if you go about it right and apply enough pressure."

Mary Dee's strange, distressed tone returned at once. "Oh, Chauncey, do you know who this man is? He's a national figure. As busy as he'll be, besides recuperating, why would he take time to come to something like this—even if it is to raise money for his organization. He's a busy man—an important man."

"Of course. But how did he get to be important? By his natural shyness, his humility, that's how. It comes through on television—it's appealing to thousands. I've studied him from afar—the man's for real. Don't you agree he's essentially humble?"

"Chauncey, you've never met the man."

"But neither have you, right? Imagine, though, someone of his prominence, his notoriety, with all the controversy—from whites *and* blacks—swirling about his head. Imagine a man like that going around everywhere by himself as he does, absolutely alone—driving his own car, carrying his own luggage, going in restaurants and supermarkets, doing his own shopping, with no protection at all, not one bodyguard. I read about him all the time in the black press. Maybe he wouldn't have got shot if he'd had a bodyguard with him. But those thugs who tried to kill him knew he was always alone and that they could do it and probably get away scot-free—which they've apparently done. That's really what I admire about Knight, though—he doesn't try to play the big shot. I believe what I've read and heard, that every dollar that's contributed to his organization goes into his work for the poor, for underprivileged blacks—every dollar. The man is conscientious, sincere, Dee. Why wouldn't he want to come to a gathering of his own supporters who're trying their best to raise money to help him carry on his work?"

Mary Dee sighed, and said nothing.

Quickly Chauncey's jollity returned. "Ha!—and besides, if he were ever to see *you*, he'd jump at the chance to come! Ha-ha-ha! Remember, he's divorced now—he's a single man, Dee!"

Mary Dee stifled an incredulous gasp. "So what," she said grimly. "Chauncey, you're beyond reasoning with. He won't come because I'll never make a fool of myself by asking him."

"Don't you see?" said Chauncey, his eyes never leaving her—

"you seem to fear the man. You act as if meeting him would be very, very unpleasant to you—almost a catastrophe. You really do."

"Chauncey, you're nuts—and for Heaven's sake let's change the subject." But she would not look at him.

"Okay, we'll change it for now, but it'll come up again—I'll see to that. I'm not peeved at you, though—ah, how sad that your father didn't live to see these days." Chauncey grew pensive. "I'm sure—even with his notorious reputation for spoiling you—that he'd have approved of you, of what you've undertaken, as he always did. How he'd admire your selflessness, your compassion—for instance, for those two poor, neglected children! I feel it, for he was the same—you're in his very mold. What a noble man—Horace Adkins! He'd approve of you, Dee—yes. What's more, he'd approve of Knight too. I believe it."

Again Mary Dee was silent, sadly reflective—her thoughts with her father. But afterwards, driving home in her little red Datsun, her mind was on Knight again. She could not rid herself of her fear. She tried to analyze it. It was not physical fear, she knew that; not fear of bodily harm—there was no reason for that. It was rather something which, to her, was even more disquieting—fear of destruction of her image of herself. She feared what she regarded as Knight's uncanny, penetrating, powers to see through her for what she really was. Their two brief Paris encounters had convinced her he could divine her inmost thoughts, inclinations, and motives. The consequence was that he made her appear to herself to shrink in *moral* size. It plagued her without let-up. Even though she did not really know him, she felt he somehow possessed this capacity of someday bringing her down—even though he might not wish to— of revealing her fatal flaws, what she sometimes thought of as her moral bankruptcy. At times she could not think of him without feeling this danger of exposure. It made her feel beneath him— yes, morally. But again above everything she sensed his potential for, wittingly or not, disclosing her in her most unprepossessing light—if only to herself. She thought, however, possible calamity lay in this self-appraisal, or self-knowledge, for it would be with her always. Her demeaning history with Philip, and her continuing, to this day, to pine after him, she considered colossal sins—an abandonment, repudiation, of her own color, and a craving to be with others who rebuffed her. Only Knight, with his outraged Paris stare, had made her feel this. Only he could make her feel it again —it was this eventuality she most feared. Yet she wished desperately to continue to see herself as her father had seen her, as gifted and virtuous. She longed to hold onto old images. The fact that her thoughts, her self-analyses, were forever secret was no comfort whatever. *She* would know. She knew her fear of Knight somehow lay in her own subjectivity—her guilt.

Suddenly, as she drove south on Outer Drive, she found herself almost hating him. He would soon be completely recovered, she realized, and back at his fanatical tasks. Would he be as effective as he had been in the past? Ornette and Rosabelle swore he would be even greater. Despite a complex ambivalence, she somehow hoped they were right. Knight then would be preoccupied, she imagined, with no time for grudges, concerned mostly with his image. That would be good—for what would he be without his image? The thought seemed to trigger a vague intimation, a half plausible reality—about him as a person. Perhaps, she thought now, despite his seeming modesty, he needed all the fame and acclaim he could get in order to maintain himself effectively as a man and leader. But what would he be without these trappings? she asked herself. She was not sure. Nor was she optimistic. Suddenly then the wraith of Philip's remote presence swam into her consciousness—like a cold, desolate wind. Yet it melted her heart. She could not bring Knight within the same thought-frame with Philip. All her past regrets now welled up in her, bringing her to marvel at her capacity for both love and pain. No matter what this great, unknown world of the future held for her, she would never forget Philip—she admitted it to herself bluntly, almost proudly; for no human being had ever brought her such happiness, such profligate joy and ecstasy, before the eclipse, as had Philip. What now was in store for her? she wondered. It certainly could not be Knight. But she paused and caught her breath.

*   *   *   *   *

The rain came down in torrents—a warm, summer rain—as the little man arrived back at his hotel in a taxi from an evening at the theatre. The red-coated, gold-braided doorman came out and met him with a raised umbrella and escorted him into the lobby. There at once he was approached by two men who had apparently been waiting for him. He seemed startled at first, then smiled and greeted them, yet did not offer to shake hands. "Gosh!—you must have something *very* significant to tell me," he laughed to them, but somewhat derisively—for, so far, his relationship with them had been anything but productive. "You've at last broken the case, I take it—you've found her."

"No, not yet," smiled one of the men—the tall, dark, balding one named Gentilenne—"but we've got a lead you may be able to help us with."

"Oh, my God," said the little man. "I've told you everything I know, and then some—some things I've even imagined. What have you turned up, Mr. Gentilenne?"

The man spread his hands in a gesture of near futility. "We obviously can't talk here in the lobby, Mr. Freuhlinghausen."

"Okay, come up to my room then if you like," sighed Marvin in resignation, then mysteriously tittering. The three of them crossed the small, luxurious lobby and ascended in the elevator. On the tenth floor, as they went down the hall to his room, Marvin made mischievous, acrid conversation. "It's unbelievable," he cried, "that a city like Chicago should have practically *no* theatre! Tonight I went to one of the only two shows playing in the Loop and it was awful, simply awful—almost any little San Francisco amateur production could do better—oh, my gosh!" He laughed shrilly, loudly. The two private investigators smiled. They were hardly in his room with the door closed when Marvin turned to the second man— of medium height, but loose-jointed and sloppily dressed—and said: "Mr. Vogel, Knight has been out of the hospital for over two weeks now. He'll probably be back at his desk, or flying around somewhere in an airplane, before we know it—and she hasn't turned up yet?" There was a sinister teasing in his tone. "I can't imagine her being here now almost two months and not contacting the organization's office sometime—or even starting working there again, maybe." Laughing, toying with them, he watched them out of the corner of his eye.

"We monitor the office of the Congress daily," said Vogel, in a not too resonant bass—"There's no white personnel working there

345

at all, and there hasn't been. But why we've come is to tell you about a strange new contact—it may be a lead—that's turned up. Do you know a man named Pryor?—Clarence Pryor?"

"He's a cop—sure. Yes, I know him. I had just got in town at the time, and the papers were still carrying an occasional story about the attempt on Knight's life. But right away I realized there was a lot of investigating going on involving Knight—especially his private life—so I went to the police. I told them I was from San Francisco and was looking for Knight's white girlfriend recently arrived in town—I told this to a Captain Holabird, in overall charge of the case. But he apparently considered this a side issue, even if that, to the murder attempt and shunted me off—quite unceremoniously, I might add—to this flatfoot Pryor, a black guy, by the way, who seemed to know quite a lot for just a patrolman; and a rookie, at that. I learned later, though, this rookie bit was a cover. Pryor is one of the best detectives on the force." Marvin laughed again. "How did you come across him, for God's sake?"

"Our paths crossed in the investigation, of course," said the first investigator, Gentilenne, unsmiling. "You had *not*, then, told us everything, Mr. Freuhlinghausen." He held a steady gaze on Marvin as they all still stood in the middle of the living room of Marvin's fine hotel suite. There was now a silence—it seemed Marvin, for the moment at least, had been put on the defensive. Yet he maintained his smug, triumphant smile—his tantalizing manner.

"What has Pryor told you?" asked slovenly Vogel, in his *basso cantante* voice; yet smiling.

Marvin burst out laughing again and waved them to chairs. "Would you like a drink, gentlemen?"

"Not especially," said Gentilenne, still dour.

"I'm going to order myself a sandwich," Marvin, wily, procrastinating, said—"and a bottle of Heineken's. Will you join me?"

"Not a bad idea," said Vogel. "Tell us about Pryor, though. Is he also working for you?"

Marvin, smiling—almost coquettishly now—still ignored the question and went over to the telephone where he called room service and ordered three club sandwiches and three bottles of imported beer. "Of course he's not working for me," he said to Vogel. "He's a policeman. And a sharp one, at that—I soon learned he was one of the people the police all along have had checking out

Knight's whole establishment from the minute he first brought it to town. No, I didn't tell you any of this—I wanted your investigation to be absolutely independent. I could then check your findings against Pryor's—he's in the 'inside know,' gentlemen, and, I think, if that shooting is ever solved, he'll have a lot to do with it. Pryor's a smart cookie—not at all a rookie!" Marvin squealed, delighted with himself at the rhyme.

"But what have you learned from him, Mr. Freuhlinghausen?" insisted Gentilenne—"that's the question."

"That Griselda's here in Chicago and working everyday, in broad open daylight, right there in Knight's office—*that's* what I've learned from him, Mr. Gentilenne. Ha, ha, ha! But, I'll admit, he told me this only yesterday, and I'd eventually have told you."

"Well, thanks," said Gentilenne nastily—"many thanks."

It only brought more laughter from Marvin, more ridiculing laughter—"Always happy to oblige, gentlemen!" he sang out. "Any time! And when you next take a peek in the Congress' office, look around for a girl about your own swarthy complexion, Mr. Gentilenne—ah, one wearing a big, kinky, Afro wig!"

Both men's mouths fell open. They gasped incredulously at Marvin, then at each other. ". . . Is that girl *white*?" breathed Vogel —"We see her every day. . . . Jesus, she's good-looking! Sure, we see her every time we surveil the place."

"Of course you do," giggled Marvin. "And please take that into account in your next bill for services rendered! . . . Ha, ha, ha! Oh, my!"

"What will you do now?" finally asked Gentilenne, with noticeably more respect—"now that you've located her."

"I will do nothing, of course—for the present, that is," smiled Marvin, so pleased with himself, with his efforts and accomplishments. "You gentlemen can keep an eye on her—the way has been so prepared that *you're* free, as it were, to take up the scent now. Find out where she lives—you know already where Knight's apartment is. She goes to see him there occasionally, in the evening after work—she doesn't stay long, but it's a serious visit. This may, though, eventually all become a problem for Knight—some of his immediate entourage resent her bitterly, on color grounds. He's got a real problem in Griselda, gentlemen—a real problem—ha, unless I come to the rescue and take her away from him." Suddenly all smiles had left Marvin's face. His eyes shone lustrously and a hard, cruel, set expression came on his little mouth. "I *will* be reckoned with, gentlemen—never fear. But I won't go near her now—I think she has come to fear me since she left; it was an awful thing she did to me; so if I suddenly appeared on the scene here right now, she might pull up and flee again; I might never find her then. No, I must bide my time—I must wait until her relationship with Knight has matured, ripened, until they have become in feeling inseparable; that is, if he's capable of such a feeling for her—he's so full of himself, you know. But I'll wait until *she* at least feels so close to him that nothing could make her leave Chicago. *Then* I'll move in—but not until then!" His eyes glistened with satisfaction.

By the time the food came, a strange silence had fallen over the room. Marvin had a fierce grimace on his face, and hardly noticed the waiter in signing the check and tossing a five-dollar bill tip on the tray. "We must not fail!" he said suddenly, softly, to Gentilenne and Vogel. "There is too much at stake, gentlemen." He turned and scanned the room as if suspicious of some unknown, hidden listener. "It has to do with affinity and adulation—with love. I knew a young man in San Francisco—a man of the theatre—who loved Mozart so much, so fanatically, he said the composer was God. He meant it, literally. Some people, if they are sensitive enough— and, my God, the three people I'm talking about surely are—can really feel that way about other people, living or dead. No, no, we must not fail!"

The two puzzled investigators stared at him, then again at each other. Finally Vogel's bass voice ventured: "I must say your logic escapes me—she becomes so attached to Knight that she won't leave Chicago for anything; then, you say, you 'move in.' But how? —to what purpose?"

"You fail to see the true nature of our relationship, my dear sir. But, for that matter, few people do, or can, see it. We're both— ha!—a little bit crazy, you see. . . . We don't react to each other according to most peoples' logic. I have a certain hold on Griselda because I treated her with a tenderness she has never known in her rocky life, never—and never will. But for a while, until she took up with Knight's people, she treated me in a very special way too (ah, or should I say mistreated?); but it nourished, stimulated,

348

roused, my soul!—yes, in an absolutely unprecedented way. No, I shall not have lost my hold on Griselda—for, unwittingly, Knight will in the end help me. His followers will not tolerate his relationship with her for long. It flies in the teeth of everything they all stand for—Blackness. Don't you see? We shan't fail—we *mustn't* fail."

"Well, you've at least found her," grunted Gentilenne. "That was what you wanted, wasn't it?" He began munching his sandwich.

"Of course that's what I wanted." Marvin looked at him in astonishment. But soon he became more subdued. "Ah, but that's by no means the end of *my* mission—*I* can still fail. It must all be handled in a way that will get Griselda not only to return to me, but to go with me to London and induce this young friend of mine —the theatre man, Basil Thorne, a director who's also writing plays now—to return with us to San Francisco, where we three should all be able to live together . . . ah, what do they say? . . . 'happily ever after?' Yes, happily ever after." Marvin's eyes lit up now in a blaze of fervor, transport, and joy that neither of his two listeners had ever before witnessed on a human being's face. "I love them both equally, absolutely equally!" he spluttered, the words rushing, spilling out—"Oh, I know it now! It's just as Basil loved the creator of the *Jupiter Symphony* and of that great work of art for the theatre, *The Magic Flute*! So it is that I think of him, Griselda, and myself—three people so constituted that they are capable of the utmost ecstatic, selfless, yet self-fulfilling love. Oh, I must have them both near me—two of the most exceptional human beings ever fashioned in Paradise! . . . Do you see what I mean, what I must have? Do you understand now my seeking out, at all effort and cost—grail-like, really—this blessed resolution of all my life's pain and suffering? Do you understand it? Yet, as you must know, I can still fail. It's true—I can fail! But it must somehow be prevented."

The other two men, still as puzzled, confounded, confused, as before, also seemed offended, indeed revolted. Gentilenne chewed his sandwich, then took a drink of beer from his glass, but at last shook his head disgustedly. "I'm afraid our services to you are at an end, Mr. Freuhlinghausen," he said. "We can't help you any longer—certainly not with your present plans. All this, I must confess, is very strange to me—it's about a way of life I know nothing of, professionally or otherwise. What in the hell can we do for a man that wants the kind of life you're talking about? . . . Jesus!" Gentilenne almost shuddered, and turned his face away.

Marvin was up now pacing the floor of his elegant sitting room. The heavy damask draperies were swept back and they could see, even through the rain, fog, and blackness of the night, the vague myriad lights of North Michigan Boulevard and the John Hancock Building. He seemed absolutely unaware of the investigators' presence, and kept muttering to himself: "I must have her! . . . I must have him too! . . . there's no other way. I can't help it—I won't be stopped! Oh, God, it is my necessity! . . ."

Vogel and Gentilenne only stared at him in amazement. A pall of embarrassed silence, sadness, seemed to fall over the room.

"I pray to eschew violence," Marvin whispered at last, almost to himself. He had not touched his food, though he stood looking at it, yet not seeing it. He sank in a chair. "I am not a violent man," he said—"*really!*" He turned then to the others—a pleading look in his eyes—"I abhor violence! . . . You must help me—you must stay on the case. We must learn more about Knight and that curious, that outlandish, organization he's put together. In time you'll see how crucial this is! . . ."

*　　*　　*　　*　　*

The Trocadero's air conditioning was erratic. In this sweltering July heat it could not be counted upon, invariably, to meet its required functional standards, though tonight it throbbed and hummed and poured a rush of chilled, fetid air out onto the drinking, the raillery, and commotion taking place in the ghetto dive. One waitress, shivering, wore a sweater over her uniform. In a corner, the poet sat slumped at a table and peacefully slept. Gideon had become a near hopeless junkie—especially since the attempt on the life of his hero. He wrote little poetry at all now, almost none, and sat around brooding, in his wretched flat or at the Trocadero, and hustled or begged money to support his habit. But earlier tonight, at his table in the corner, he began a poem of thanks in praise of

Knight's convalescence and eventual recovery. But soon his chin was on his chest again as he dozed; yet then he would rally for a few minutes when hailed by a friend or when his dreams became so frightening they brought him up with a groaning start.

Occasionally, also, he would be hit by a sudden streak of vengeance. At such times, before lapsing once more into his torpor of despair and indirection, of complete lack of will, he would vow retribution on whoever had dared wish Knight's death, to say nothing of those who had actually attempted to bring it about. One of those moments, those flashing instants, occurred now. He sat up with a start—as if something revelatory, something extremely significant, a clue, had suddenly come to him in his somnolence. He tried to get up from the table, but failed; he was limber, jelly-like, exhausted; the light copper color of his pimply face had turned ashen; he was fairly tall but now so emaciated his pale grey eyes fairly popped—especially now, as whatever it was that had come to him in his dozing jarred him from a kind of mindless lethargy into reality, harsh reality. He lurched forward in the chair in another attempt to rise and this time succeeded. Shuffling, veering, weaving, he headed for the Trocadero's torrid kitchen, where his friend the chef, a huge man named Tiny Glass, presided. It was nine o'clock—midway between dinner and the arrival of the late night crowd—as Tiny sat on a stool against the wall of the cluttered kitchen and studied a racing form. He wore a smudged, soiled, chef's white uniform, a large handkerchief tied scarf-like around his neck, and thick horn-rimmed glasses—through which, on raising his head, he now squinted with displeasure on seeing his nemesis, the poet, enter an unauthorized area of the establishment. "I told you to stay outa this kitchen, boy," he said. "You stumblin' round here and liable to fall up agin that stove yonder—you git your ass burned once in here and you won't be back so soon. And I ain't got nothing to give you tonight, either."

Gideon ignored his talk. "Tiny," he said, almost soberly, "what did Torres Coleman do with that practically new green Mercury he was drivin' around here in the spring?"

Tiny viewed the poet testily. "Say, what's got into your weak and infested mind now?" he said—"I don't know nothing about Torres' business, much less his cars. He's still got the car as far as I know —but it ain't none of my business. Ain't none of yours, either."

"It just came to me. . . . I ain't seen that car for weeks," said Gideon, suddenly wrinkling his face as if a new pain had hit him— "Funny, ain't it?" he added, and gazed steadily at Tiny. "Torres musta got rid of the damn car," he mused now, audibly—"funny I ain't seen it lately." Just then the waitress wearing the sweater, and also a huge auburn wig, entered the kitchen. "What ever went with Torres' new green Mercury, Mabel?" Gideon asked her—"I ain't seen it 'round here lately . . . ain't seen him in it at all. He's drivin' an old beat-out Oldsmobile now—but where's his Mercury?"

"How'n the hell would I know?" said Mabel. "Maybe he got behind in his payments and the finance company come and took it back."

Tiny the chef chuckled: "That sounds reasonable enough—somebody else is drivin' that car by now." Gideon's legs seemed to have weakened now and he looked around for a place to sit down— only to be warned by Tiny: "You can't park in this kitchen, Gideon —I've told you before. Good-bye—I said good-bye." He grinned. Gideon, gloomy, morose, left the kitchen and returned to his corner table, but with his brow wrinkled as if he were puzzled, in deep thought.

Soon more patrons began to drift into the Trocadero. Gideon, still preoccupied with his thoughts, anxieties, misgivings—his suspicions—seemed oblivious of everything around him. Soon, fumbling in his jacket pocket, he brought out an envelope containing a sheaf of worn, soiled newspaper clippings. He began sorting them out, meticulously, on the table, studying, peering, frowning down at them, as if they were cards in a crucial game of solitaire—arranging them in groups again, chronologically, according to their dates. No matter how often he had done this, the whole affair of the shooting remained essentially a mystery—until this now sudden divination. He had not known what else to do except hurry into the kitchen to consult Tiny Glass—but, alas, to no avail. He began his arrangement of the clippings with the first date, that of the shooting—May 18th. He paused now, remembering that this date had also furnished the title for a poem, a long, dirgelike creation, he had written two days afterwards, when it was yet not known whether Knight would live or die. Gideon well recalled the opening lines:

Weep, Black troopers of sorrow!
Weep for the leader fallen.
Weep in your black habiliments
Until the next 18th brings an eye,
Brings a tooth,
Bring's wrong's rectification.

But also now he studied again the *Tribune* clipping, the news account, for the 19th, although he knew it almost by heart. There had been three of them—blacks, it said. At this again Gideon's fury knew no bounds. At least one of them had a hand gun—the one who had used it. And they were driving a "fairly-new, dark-green Mercury." This was what Knight, though bleeding, groaning in his agony, when help came, had whispered to them. "Ah, an eye for an eye!" now whispered Gideon. Hadn't Torres Coleman, again and again, in this very restaurant, for one place, inveighed against "all these nigger leaders talkin' about halfway measures?" Gideon thought. Hadn't Torres shown a deadly impatience, contempt, for any methods of redress that did not involve bloodshed? Hadn't he, Torres, almost screamed it at Talley, the policeman, that snow-bound blizzardy morning early last March, right here in the Troca-dero, when Talley had possibly saved Torres' life, rescued him from Quaker Ferguson's blue snub-nosed revolver? Gideon had been there and remembered it all. He had heard Torres acknowl-edge to Talley that he, Torres, had once been a member of Knight's Congress, but that the organization "had turned chicken, was outa step with the people, with the black man and woman in the street;" that what was needed were leaders who could be depended upon— "street niggers," Torres had shouted, "for they don't fuck around! They see things like they are!—that the only way we can get these honkies off our backs is to '*waste*' some of 'em!"

Accompanying all this evidence surging through Gideon's mind was the ever-present and persistent consciousness of the dark-green Mercury. Its image would not leave him; and soon became an obsession—he could think of nothing else; his certainties soon became set in concrete. He was also aware, however, of the lethal danger to himself of his thoughts, when carried the necessary one step farther—to revelation of the perpetrator's identity. His own life might soon well be in jeopardy—if he could summon the cour-

353

age to do what he knew, if he was true to the cause, he should do, *must* do. The black newspapers had twice made mention of a black policeman, a highly reputed detective, figuring prominently in the investigation. Clarence Pryor was his name. A mere hint to him would suffice. Gideon began to tremble. . . .

*　　*　　*　　*　　*

Though the taxi she was riding in was a rattletrap, Griselda hardly noticed. Her mind was absorbed in other things. Nor did she pay much attention to the evening. It was beautiful, warm, the city alive and noisy, and the sun would not go down for almost two more hours. She could not afford to, but she had rejected the bus outside the Congress' office and hailed a cab—she somehow had the urge to hurry. Chicago had brought change in almost all her attitudes, change of a rather momentous kind. Furthermore, weirdly, whenever these days she thought of her mother, which was not frequently, there were vague, though uncalled-for, doubts that Nancy Hanks really any longer existed. Marvin fared no better. They were both ghosts, ciphers, dissolved in the past. There was someone else now. Initially the change had brought her a feeling of great warmth, which soon burst into a kind of rapture, and at last, for the first time in her now nearly twenty-four years, also into a flood of hard assurance. She had never been sure about anything, but now she was sure about the state of her mind. She occasionally asked herself what had brought it all about, but then dismissed the question as fatuous. The causes were too complex. Anyway, what did it matter? The only thing she knew was that she—or was it her mind?—was at last intact. She felt really whole. Was it some extrasensory communication with Frimbo's band? she wondered. Suddenly the cab pulled up in front of the modest apartment building where Knight lived.

He had been home from the hospital for almost three weeks; had even been downtown, shopping for things like underwear, socks, and shirts. She had begged him to let her do these chores for him but he had only smiled and refused. It was Ferdinand Bailey who always accompanied him. But he was much stronger now, and at

354

times even cheerful, his experience with assassins and surgeons a bad dream out of a murky, hallucinated past. He had also for the last week been coming to the office for two or three hours in the afternoons, though his attempts at resuming the old routine quickly tired him, sometimes made him morose and sad. This alarmed Ferdinand, but only made Griselda bolder, more determined, than ever.

She rang the doorbell in the vestibule and after a moment was buzzed up. In the elevator to Knight's fifth floor apartment she resisted the temptation to take out her purse mirror and examine her appearance. What triviality, she thought—hadn't she just come from work, his work? She shouldn't worry that she didn't look like a mannequin. But then she suddenly became preoccupied, pensive, and began to feel sorry for herself. Soon quick hot tears were in her eyes. Why was this? she asked herself. All of a sudden then she wanted to laugh. Wasn't she happy? Had she *ever* been so happy? Though it was only the second time she had been allowed to visit him, and in both instances by grace of Ferdinand's grudging permission, she meant now to talk to him only of matters of significance—his life, the creed he lived by, his mission. Yet she might even—the thought sent fear into her heart—bring up the subject of themselves, of what lay ahead for them. Leaving the elevator and going down the hall toward his apartment, she blinked back tears and tried to compose herself.

She was of course admitted by little Ferdinand—whom she had seen only that afternoon at the office. Though cool, apprehensive, he tried to be polite, yet she thought his smile full of guile and distrust. "Go in and have a seat," he said, and pointed toward the living room. "Mr. Knight's been trying to shave but the telephone keeps ringing so he hasn't had a chance to finish."

She went in and sat down where she had sat the time before, on the sofa directly opposite Knight's big chair. On the other occasion he had been home from the hospital only four days and was wan, nervous, mostly uncommunicative. She hoped it would be different today and took a deep breath still in an attempt to relieve her tensions. Her eyes wandered around the living room; a stranger could have seen that Knight had not lived in the apartment long—it had been only since April—for some of the furniture, though plain and inexpensive, was new. The rest consisted of miscellaneous pieces rounded up for him by friends. She was impressed by the glut of books in the room—both hardcover and paperback; they were everywhere—on the floor about his chair as well as on an end table and the mantel. A paperback on the arm of his chair, she saw, was *Ghandi, A Biography.*

By the time, a few minutes later, he entered the room, she strangely no longer felt nervous. There was warmth in his greeting, yet she detected a note of caution in his voice, as his eyes avoided hers. He asked if she had eaten, but when she told him she was not hungry, he demurred. "That won't do," he said. "Mrs. Anderson, the lady who comes in and cleans, fixed some dinner before she left. Ferdinand and I were about to sit down when you came. You must eat with us." But she was so absorbed in the way he looked that her assent was barely audible. She had seen him in the office only yesterday, yet she thought he looked very different today at home. He was still thin but his eyes glowed like coals; his mien was grave, resolute. She looked at him in wonder.

The doorbell rang. Ferdinand came in quickly from the rear and pushed the buzzer again. "It's probably Mamie," he said to Knight. "She has some correspondence for you to sign, I think. We've got food enough for everybody."

It was indeed Knight's secretary. "The police have picked up three suspects," Mamie announced grimly, hardly in the door.

"What!" Ferdinand jumped back. "*Thank God!*"

Mamie closed the door and turned to Knight. "The police want you to come to a show-up—to see if you can identify any of them."

Knight frowned at once. The dark skin of his withered face tightened as he shook his head decisively. "I can't—I can't tonight," he said. "I'm not up to it." It was as if he could not bear further thought of what had happened that fateful day.

"Oh, the show-up's not till tomorrow," Mamie said, adding, "Detective Pryor and another cop came to the office just before I left."

Knight was still dour, and shook his head again.

Ferdinand, however, was more excited than ever. "I want to talk to that Pryor!" he said, already looking around for his hat in order to leave. "I'll eat at home later. I knew he was onto something—he's never once given up!"

"I doubt, though," said Knight, "if I could identify a single suspect—it all happened so fast." Again he spoke as if the memory harrowed him.

Ferdinand, eager, officiary, was about to leave. "I must go try to locate Pryor!" he repeated. "I want to see what he's really turned up. All these weeks of ordeal we've had may at last be over. I want to find out who the blasted culprits are he's got!" But then, as if suddenly remembering something, he turned to Mamie Campbell and fixed her with a very purposeful look. "Why don't you stay here, Mamie, and eat with them?" he said. Yet it sounded almost like an order. Knight turned and stalked away—as Ferdinand momentarily lingered to see if his message to Mamie had registered. Then he left. Griselda watched the gnome going out the door. She too had gotten the message, namely, that Knight must not be left alone with her.

Mamie indeed stayed for dinner. But immediately afterwards, within ten minutes of the time she and Griselda had washed the dishes, she left and went home. Ferdinand's ruse in mind, she did so with pleasure.

But Knight knew all too well what had been in Ferdinand's mind. It had to do with the fortunes of the organization, the integrity of the cause of Blackness, fidelity to a sacred undertaking, and seretly he honored him for it. He not only admired him, his diminutive, deformed, faithful lieutenant, who had been through so much with him, and from almost the earliest days of the crusade, but he had a fondness, a deep affection, for him as well. Yet tonight, despite everything, he did not want Griselda to leave. He was tense, ill at ease, about it as they sat in the living room looking futilely at each other. He knew little about her, yet sensed some quality in her, in her life, that stirred his compassion. Now, however, he only talked shop: how he disliked having to go tomorrow to the police line-up, how gratified he'd be when he could resume his full work load in the organization. "It's funny," he said, "how sometimes I find myself wishing the police won't catch those goons who tried to kill me. It would only prolong the confusion in the Congress' affairs. I must get back to work, get back in the harness. Our basic problem is money, you know—we've got to concentrate more on fund-raising, rebuilding the organization financially, that way to make up for the time we've lost these past weeks; months now." It was dark outside as he sat staring out the window.

Griselda had been strangely silent. Even now she made little effort to further the conversation. "Yes, I agree," she finally said. She sat watching him. The subdued light of the living room came from two small lamps, which, from different angles, played on his face, transforming it into something resembling a bizarre mask. He looked older than his thirty-four years. The hollow surfaces below his cheekbones, however, already sunken from his ordeal and the long hospital stay, seemed oddly to receive no light at all, while the chin, nose, and brow were brought into an even sharper, more luminous, prominence. It was an unnatural effect—both masklike and demonic; for an instant, too, enigmatic, almost completely lacking in emotional expression. She still watched him, not afraid but awed; moreover, a mysterious pity for him had suddenly come over her. She moved her eyes away.

But he had turned to her. "You're tired tonight," he said—"I can tell. Why do you work so hard, so faithfully, for us—and at the poor salary we pay you?"

"I believe in the organization's work," she said simply. "I believe in you."

He seemed flustered by the remark, embarrassed. "Why aren't there more whites like you?" he said after a pause.

Momentarily she stiffened. "What's color got to do with it?" She caught herself then and softened her tone. "Really, what has it?"

"Everything," he said stubbornly. "Whites made it that way."

"Color, color! Why is it my husband never mentioned color?"

"Why should he have?"

"He was black."

Knight tried to hide his astonishment. "I didn't know that," he finally said, now in a subdued, almost humble, voice.

"I'm a widow—Alan was killed in Viet Nam. Sometimes now I dream he's a member of Frimbo's band." Knight stared at her uncomprehendingly, yet asked no questions. "His name was Alan Graves," she went on, trancelike. "He was a sweet boy."

"Tell me about it, about yourself, Griselda," he said. "Somehow I never imagined you could have been married. Tell me more—about yourself."

"I can't. It's too horrible."

"What's horrible? That you were living with a rich man in San Francisco—when you came to do volunteer work for us? I knew all that then. There's nothing horrible about that. I want to know the important things."

She did not respond at once. Nor would she look at him. "It was my mother," she said then. "She didn't want me."

"Go on."

For the next hour she told him everything, reciting the chronology of her life—about her mother, about Sima her nanny, the world of opera, the child's sporadic schooling, the community college, the periods of neglect, personal crisis, and rebellion, about Alan, Marvin, the whole history. At the end she seemed torn between despair and relief.

He had sat deeply attentive, at times transfixed. "Your father," he finally said—"what was he like?"

"I never knew him," she said. "I wish terribly I had, but he died when I was small. My mother said I would have liked him, which, if she said that, meant I would have loved him. They were never married." Knight, grave, reflective, said nothing. "Did you hear?" she said, her voice rising again, challenging him—"My father and mother were never married!"

"I heard, Griselda." His tone was full of compassion, rapport, now. "Someday I'll tell you about *my* father," he said. "And my mother who went off and left me with him. It's quite a story too. My dad was one of the most unusual and gifted of men—but in addition a potential derelict. In some ways, in most ways, he was a gigantic failure—yet one of the most unique, yes, gifted, persons you'll ever have heard about. His name was William Goforth Knight. God rest his soul."

"Oh, tell me about him—please."

"No, not tonight—some other time."

At last she rose to go. "I've stayed much longer than I'd planned."

"Don't go," he said, rising.

"Yes, I must. And I'm tired. I'm sure you are too." They stood very close together, squarely facing each other, yet no part of their bodies touched. Then she said it before she thought—"I would stay with you tonight if you were fully recovered."

His heart began a furious pounding, the blood pulsating, his mouth dry. For a moment he could not speak. He tried to take her hands in his, but she refused and walked away to the window where she stood gazing down on the lighted street. "I'll call you a cab," he said finally, his voice husky—"I'm glad you came." He felt they were alike in many ways. Perhaps, he speculated, this was why he had at last begun to feel comfortable—or uncomfortable—with her; he was not sure which. Yet the feeling exhilarated him and he thought this a good sign—until suddenly, ruefully, he thought of Ferdinand. All his commitments, his obligations, then, the vows of leadership, the responsibilities of Blackness, returned to plague him and once more he felt lost.

Chapter 4

1962. Back almost a decade.

It seemed the darkness in winter came swiftly—and now a light snow was falling. Shipmate McCoy had come in the tavern, "Mack's Lounge," early, left, then returned in an hour—absent-minded, out-of-sorts, preoccupied. The other bar patrons observed him, laughed, but thought nothing more of it—his behavior was often erratic these days, especially since his sidekick and mentor Goforth had been ill and finally hospitalized. But there had been word that the doctors would soon let Goforth come home, at least for awhile. It was only emphysema, a few people said. But there had been an operation and now the talk was that the lung condition was something far more serious—Goforth, besides being a heavy drinker, had been a chain-smoker for years. On his return to Mack's Lounge now, shortly after eight, Shipmate had taken a bar seat around the front corner of the bar where he could get the fullest view outside onto the lighted street. After ordering a bourbon and water, he turned around to the window again, maintaining his vigil. It was obvious he was expecting someone. Meanwhile the light snow continued falling.

There was the usual loud saloon talk among the habitués of the place. Tonight the subject had gotten around to politics. "This guy can be president as long as he wants to—forever, man!" someone along the bar was saying.

"No, he can't, neither—the Constitution won't let him!" someone else said.

Mack, the owner of the lounge, was sitting with a handsome, brown-skinned woman in a back corner booth—away from the noise. "It ain't known yet," he was saying to her, "but old Goforth may be in here tonight." He laughed—"Yeah, just out of the hospital this morning and making his rounds tonight as usual, like nothing ever happened. That's the way he'll play it—right out to the end."

Over at the bar, though, the first speaker had continued: "Oh, hell, I know he can't have more'n two terms. Who don't know that? —Christ, we read the papers too. I meant he could be president a long damn time if *we* had anything to do with it. He's got everything goin' for him—he's young, he's sure okay on civil rights, and has got a beautiful wife."

"Hey, man—Jackie, yeah! Right!—ain't she fine? And his old man's rollin' in dough—once cornered the whiskey market. Not only the young guy, the president, but the whole family's like that —on the ball, man!"

A third patron spoke up. "Hell, eight years is enough, though. That'll give him all the time he needs to get the job done—he's got a whole term even after this one. Ha!—and by that time *we'll* have somebody ready, huh? Dr. King, maybe! Ha!-ha!-ha!"

"Hey, yeah!" said the second patron—"we'll have Martin for 'em. But do you think the country's ready yet for a Southern Baptist preacher? *Ha-ha-ha!*"

Meanwhile Shipmate, sipping his bourbon, kept his silent vigil before the window.

Mack, observing, said to the woman, "Look at Shipmate over there—fidgety as a cat. He's the one that told me Goforth may be here tonight. They're almost like father and son, you know. Goforth and his own boy don't get along. He can't do anything with the boy at all—the kid's one of these fiery militants, in his early twenties, that dropped out of college when he was about to graduate to go down South and lead protest marches and sit-ins. The boy's got guts, though—plenty. Goforth secretly admires the hell out of him but won't admit it. But the boy don't try to hide his disappointment, almost disgust, with the life Goforth's led—thinks his old man's thrown his life away on liquor, good times, and women."

"Ha!—what's wrong with that?" said the woman.

"Hey, nothing! So Shipmate—Goforth gave him that name because Shipmate was a messman in the Navy for a hot minute— has sort of taken the boy's place in Goforth's life, I guess. He admires Goforth's mind—Lord, what a mind!—and would sit around spellbound all day and all night listening to him if Goforth wanted to talk that long, as it seems sometimes he does, all right. Goforth could have been a college professor or something like that with no trouble at all—he's read and seen everything there is, about."

"And done everything," the woman laughed again.

"Right! Old Goforth's been around—had a lot of womanflesh. Has also had three wives. And for a third wife ended up—wouldn't he?—with a good religious woman, when he himself is anything but religious. The boy's mother, though, was the second wife. Ha! —just watch this place come alive if Goforth walks in here."

The bartender's telephone rang. He answered it and handed the phone to Shipmate. Shipmate was soon heard uttering into the phone some anxious, chagrined, commiserating remarks before handing the phone back in sheer disappointment. "It was Goforth's wife," he said to the bartender, shaking his head. "Goforth came home from the hospital today, you know. He said he might drop by for a few minutes tonight, but his wife just said he couldn't make it." Shipmate then went over to Mack and the woman. "Goforth can't make it," he said—"His wife just called."

"What did you expect, man?" said Mack—"He's just outa the hospital."

"Yeah," Shipmate said, hanging his head. He returned to the bar and ordered another drink.

Twenty minutes later then a jitney cab pulled up in front of the place and a tall, regal, coal-black man—somewhat emaciated, but of noble, almost grandiose, bearing—alighted and slowly entered the lounge. His clothes fit him far too loosely.

A great shout went up along the bar. "*Goforth!*" Everyone began crowding around trying to shake his hand. Shipmate, now grinning, merely sat at the bar shaking his head. "That woman can't keep Goforth in the house," he exulted to himself—"no way."

Mack rushed over and took off Goforth's hat and overcoat and handed them to the woman. "The old war horse himself!" he cried —"Welcome back!" He threw an arm around smiling Goforth's frail shoulders. "Man, are you a sight for sore eyes! We've missed you, Big Daddy."

"I've missed you'all, too," said happy Goforth, wan but smiling.

Shipmate had finally come up now. "I'd about given up on you," he said to Goforth—"Didn't think you'd make it."

"How're you doin', son?" Goforth said to him, smiling now expansively. "I had to get out of the house—Lord, I've been gone five weeks, ain't it?" He turned and said to them all: "Thanks for the cards—they mean a lot when you're layin' there on your ass, lonesome, frustrated, feeling guilty and disgusted. They mean a lot—I know my wife discouraged visitors but I sure missed seeing you'all." Laughing, he turned around to Mack—"Say, can a man get a drink in this place or not?" Soon he was seated in the middle of the bar, surrounded by saloon cronies of many years, with a sour-mash bourbon and water before him. He held up the iced golden drink and looked at it. "Can't have but a couple of these tonight," he said—"doctors have warned me. No more cigarettes, either. Time ain't long, they say, if I don't straighten up and be-have myself. But I feel all right—just a little weak after the opera-tion, and lost a little weight, that's all." But they all watched him—they could see he had lost more weight than a little. Then he began coughing—a deep, rattling, hollow cough—after which, rather os-tentatiously, he brought out a large fine linen handkerchief and dabbed at his mouth. Still trying to smile then, he glanced at them all, a little forlornly. "What's wrong with you'all?" he laughed—"I ain't dead yet." He raised his drink again—"A toast! I drink to the greatest nigger that ever lived—Martin Luther King."

"*Amen!*"—another shout went up. "Ain't that the truth!" some-one cried—"We was just talkin' about him, Goforth!" The glasses had been raised all around. "Ain't that boy Martin somethin'?" someone else said—"and a preacher!"

"He is that," said Goforth, vigorously nodding his head. "And a young man, a fighter—he's shakin' 'em up down home, ain't he? They talk about niggers ain't got any history—well, he'll make 'em some history."

"You ain't kiddin'!"

"But we had a history long before," said Goforth—"if we'd only recognized it. But sometimes we don't know history when we see it. For instance, I knew Louis Armstrong in the early days—right here in Chicago. I was with him when he cut that record "Gut Bucket Blues," down at the old Okeh studios at Wells and Wash-ington. Ha, that was in the fall of 1925—can you imagine? Where has all the time gone? It was Louis and his 'Hot Five.' That one little record made jazz history—it became famous the world over as a music to be taken seriously, I'll tell you. *That's* history, ain't it? Think of the pleasure, the happiness, that and the other Negro music has brought to millions on millions of people—all over the world, black and white. It raises the question of what the world's all about, don't it? It sure does. I'd rather been Louis Armstrong and made that one little record, to say nothing of the hundreds of others he's made since, than to have split the damn atom and possibly wiped out those same millions. Huh?"

"Teach, Goforth—teach!" someone cried. "We been waitin' for you!"

"Another thing—more history," said Goforth, his breathing faster now and raspy. "My granddaddy, Acts Knight, went all the way from Kansas down to Harper's Ferry with John Brown. That's right. But Acts got away—most of the others didn't, though, and were hanged—and he later traveled with Grant's army, shoeing horses. Lived to 77. Yeah, he knew Brown well. Said there were some great white men in that day—men of vision. Said Brown hated Stephen Douglas worse'n he did the slaveholders—and worse'n Douglas hated abolitionists and blacks. History—ah, our history."

"Yeah, as a kid I heard my own grandmama tell just such things," said another patron, scratching his grey head. "She was a girl down in Georgia when Sherman come through. Said it was a great jubilation time."

"Oh, my, yes," said Goforth. "But it ain't all been that far back. No, sir. There's a whole lot goin' on right today. Take, for instance—"

"Your boy Johnnie—he's in it too, Goforth. Ain't he?" The interrupter, innocent, well-meaning, was the woman with Mack. "I heard somewhere he was in one of the marches, down in Alabama, I believe it was—right?"

There was an embarrassed silence. "I don't know," Goforth finally said, his speech slow, lethargic, almost as if sudden fatigue had overtaken him, or as if perhaps he was being deeply reflective, deliberate, about what he should say. "I ain't heard from Johnnie for some time, you know," he said. "Yeah, he's down there somewhere—was even with King one while. Johnnie's tryin' to prove something to himself—tryin' to solve some of his own problems at the same time he's helping others with theirs, I think. He wants to do somethin' with his life, though—can't blame him for that." Goforth now contemplated his already-empty glass and sighed.

Everyone listened. Johnnie was a delicate subject, they all knew; one that Goforth didn't talk about often. The fact, moreover, that he could talk about him tonight was disquieting to some of them, as if it indicated some feeling of his about his physical condition—his true physical condition. Had he become reckless? They waited. Goforth was restive on the bar stool now, dressed in a quiet business suit which however now fitted him so bizarrely, so loosely, he resembled a scarecrow—with his eyes deep in their dark hollow sockets, his hand shaking as if with some ague as he helplessly fondled the empty glass. "You'all know how Johnnie's disappointed with me," he said—"I don't have to tell you that." He looked at the glass again, then at the bartender.

Sam Dowd, the bartender, long a friend and partisan of Goforth's, appreciative too of the whole situation, turned his back for a moment, then turned back around again with a new bourbon and water, which, offhand, unobtrusively, he pushed before Goforth.

"No, no, Sam," Shipmate said quickly, shaking his head—"Space the drinks a little for him, man. Hey, we don't wanta give him too big a welcome for his own health, do we?" Shipmate, tall, light brown-skinned, about thirty, hunching far forward over the bar, thought finally now to smile.

"Ah, hell," said Sam, "let *him* space 'em. He knows what he's doing." He left the drink where it was.

Goforth's dark, sepulchral eyes lifted themselves up to Sam gratefully. He tasted the drink and put it down gently with still a shaky hand. "I'm watchin' myself, all right, Shipmate," he reassured his surrogate son—"I ain't going to overdo it." He laughed—"You sound like Johnnie's mother used to sound." He paused then, reflective again. "When she left me she said her only regret was leaving Johnnie in my hands—that he'd end up just like me. Well, he didn't, did he? He-he-he!" He tasted the drink again. "Now I think he wants to be some kinda race leader—like King. He's smart enough to be, Lord knows. Ain't he?"

"Sure is," someone said.

"But I've always wondered why Cora didn't take him with her," Goforth, knitting his brow, speculated aloud now. "Johnnie wonders that too—ha. Things did start going pretty good, though, 'tween me and him when I finally quit waitin' tables at the Sherman Hotel and went into business for myself—even if it was only a dinky little restaurant. But I was the proprietor, y'see, and that made a whole lot of difference with that boy—it did until he found out that because of my record (it wasn't nothing all that serious—no penitentiary or anything like that), because of my younger, wild, free-wheelin' days, I couldn't get a liquor license. He was disgusted, and didn't try to camouflage it. Yet I'd had the book learning—I've been a reader all my life—to help him with his school work right up to the time he got a scholarship and went off to college, at Howard. There wasn't a time before that when I couldn't, and didn't, help him with his lessons, and he knows it—even today I'm probably better read than he is. He knows that too."

"Plus the fact you got common sense, plain old mother wit, Goforth!" someone said.

"Thanks—I accept the compliment. All of us have got it. We've learned it from life. Like any nigger of my day, I've been through the mill—'seen the elephant,' as the old folks used to call it. That, plus all I've read over the years, made it possible for me to teach that boy things he'll never forget, that'll stick with him the rest of his life. Where d'you think he got his race pride?—why, from me, that's where. I taught him all about what niggers have been through, their history, how they managed to survive, and so forth. He knows I did. He knows I was capable of doing it, too. Ah, but that's the very thing that bugs him. He thinks that's why I oughta done better for myself, my life—that I've wasted what I had. Just like Cora—the same impatience, quick temper, and all. But the thing about it, the thing that with all his university learning now he can't seem to see, is: *Could* I have done any better'n I have? That's the question. We're what we are, ain't we? You—all of you—are what you are, the way you was born, and what you had to go through with. I believe it. I myself was born to do two things: to understand this world—really dig it—and to enjoy it the best way a nigger can."

Most of his hearers laughed, though some only politely.

"Johnnie don't give me credit," said Goforth, "but I'm the one that gave him his sense of Negro history in the first place. I've taught it to him since he was a little shaver: that Negroes have a history, but that it's a different history, and has to be judged different from the white man's. That it's a grander, more tragic, history, too. Johnnie's saying that now, today—in all them little pep talks he calls speeches he makes around whenever he can get a handful of people to listen to him. He sure does. *I'm* the one that taught him about Africa—about animism."

There were puzzled looks along the bar at this last word. But Shipmate, long inured to Goforth's ambitious, involuted theories, smiled proudly.

"Our greatest achievement," said Goforth, having wet his lips again from his drink, "is the fact that we originated in Africa—where man himself originated. He sure did. You see, we go way back—way back before man got so sinful and greedy. But I won't go into all that right now. On the other hand, I know a lot of my own personal history, too. It's been handed down to me almost all by word of mouth—from Africa times clean down to the present. It's a fact." He struck his breast proudly, though feebly, with his fist. "Yeah, I know my own history—do you? I know my grand-daddy, Acts, went to Harper's Ferry with John Brown and got away with it, don't I? I know his half brother, Aaron, was once owned by Judah P. Benjamin, a rich Southern Jew who later, when Secession came, was Jeff Davis' Secretary of War and was called 'the brains of the South.' But Acts' and Aaron's granddaddy had come direct from Africa—he was the real thing. His last name was Baptiste—taken from the name of his Louisiana master, a big cane plantation owner. Acts and Aaron—my own father used to tell it—both lived to see freedom. They took the name of Knight. But old Baptiste didn't make it to Emancipation. He was a rebel-lious slave and suffered for it. But they never broke him—he was defiant to the end. He had been brought over from the African Guinea coast as a boy, but the slaves mutinied on the ship and took it over—then they couldn't navigate it. He was the only survivor—was rescued by a kind, religious Navy captain and taken to Boston. The poor boy wasn't there but a couple of years, though—he was kidnapped one rainy evening by some slave-catchers and put aboard a ship bound for the sugar plantations of Louisiana. But try as they might they could not work him to death down there; even though sugar plantations were worse than cotton; he lived to be over eighty, but was a slave for the rest of his life—ah, yes, Bymba Baptiste his name. It's history I'm speakin' about tonight. Yeah, Acts and Aaron remembered their granddaddy well—the stooped-over walk from his years of hard labor, the short, kinky white whiskers, the squinty, almost-blind eyes and all. Indeed they remembered him. They remembered their daddy too, but who died young—whipped to death. And my daddy remembered Acts and

Aaron. I remember my own daddy, of course. And I've passed it all along to Johnnie—he's got it now. And maybe he'll have a son someday." Goforth's eyes suddenly blazed; passion came in his wasted face—"Don't you see? It's our *history*, our oral history! Why don't we see it?—glorify it! Why, we gotta be a great people if for no other reason than that we have *survived!*"

"Amen, Goforth!" many shouted. "Teach! Teach, man!"

"Our history's made up of many things—good and bad, happy and full of sorrow," said Goforth. "It's a mishmash, and comes through in a thousand different ways—especially in our music. Take Ma Rainey, for instance—she wasn't called the 'Mother of the Blues' for nothin'. I heard her when I was just a youngster—this was way before Bessie Smith. Until Ma came along, the blues were nothing but black folks' country music—that's all. She made it professional, made it recognized. Lord, you shoulda heard her back in the old days, backed up by the young Louis Armstrong, singin' 'See See Rider'—or 'Tighter Than That,' or 'Blame it on the Blues.' People went wild. She was singin' out of everything that had happened to us, you see; everything—our history. Our animism."

"What?" said someone—"You mentioned that before, Goforth."

"Animism, yeah. That's the name the white folks gave it, though —and what they mean could mislead people. There's nothin' primitive or animalistic about animism—just the opposite. Our ancestors in Africa believed that the spirit of their God could exist not only in man but in anything—a horse, a rock, tree, cloud, bird, anything. Any object, whether it moves or not, whether it's what they call animate or inanimate, can be sacred. That's hard to improve on, my friends—ain't it? We were taught in the 'old country' centuries back that many things could be sacred—what's wrong with that? Nothing. It carries over to this very day, too—you see traces of it in almost everything we do. Lotta people, who never heard of animism, just call it 'soul.' The only thing it is is just havin' a warm feeling for things—not only for man or woman, but for things in general. Yeah, but it had a good side and a bad side, 'cause it lulled us into a false feeling of love and well-being. I don't have to tell you that was bad, very bad—we forgot all about, if we ever knew, the world bein' the dangerous place it is. Before long we had visitors in Africa, didn't we? And the visitors turned out to be cutthroats and robbers. That didn't keep 'em, though, from bringin' their own religion, and later their missionaries. We know the rest—from then on we didn't know what hit us. Soon we were their slaves and they were dividing up our land among themselves. That's the other side of animism, folks. I used to tell Johnnie all these things, even when he was only a little kid." Goforth smiled. "I taught him well—he can't deny that. He'd just preferred I'd turned out to be something more'n a waiter or a failed restaurant owner who wound up being supported by his third—and best—wife. Johnnie's showed he can be tough, all right—especially with me." He had begun to grow dejected now, but, realizing it, he brightened almost at once. "Johnnie's just complicated, that's all—his intentions are high enough. He never got over his mother walkin' out on him, that's all. Cora was tough too—I guess he gets it honestly." Goforth sighed and looked helplessly around him.

It was clear to Shipmate—but who had sensed it all along—that he could never supplant the real son. Yet he felt protective of Goforth. It made him want to steer the talk into more cheerful channels—for instance, to Goforth's wife. "How long did Aquilla say you could stay out tonight, Big Daddy?" he laughed. The others laughed too.

Goforth did not appear to think it funny. "She's only tryin' to look out for me—to help me," he said. "I'm grateful to her—she ain't had an easy time of it with me. Aquilla's been awful good all during my sickness—I ain't going to give her a bad time." He grew reflective, moody, again. "Lord, look where I'd be if I had to depend on Johnnie—he don't even know I've been sick, probably."

Shipmate knew this was not true and that Goforth knew it was not, for young Knight had been informed, through friends, by Aquilla herself. Johnnie had even written to his father when Goforth was in the hospital—though it was a strangely detached, almost curt, letter. All of this did, however, plant an idea in Shipmate's mind. He was already worried, pessimistic, about Goforth's health. He also knew Goforth was constantly agonized by the spiritual distance between himself and young John Calvin Knight. Johnnie, now almost twenty-five, was his only child, and was headstrong, purposeful, self-righteous, morose. Goforth at times loathed these qualities in his son, yet at other times was impressed, awed, by them; then puzzled, sometimes suspicious—that Johnnie's ways were somehow a front behind which lurked gargantuan ambiguities. Yet Shipmate knew Goforth yearned to see his son again—perhaps with a premonition of the shortness of time—and Shipmate felt he himself must try to locate Johnnie, acquaint him with his father's true condition, and urge him to come to Chicago for a visit.

"Johnnie's always been fractious, though, even since he was a little tyke," Goforth said—"Yeah, as I said, he gets it from his mother—Cora. Still, when you get right down to it, he wasn't a disobedient child at all—he was always too serious, ambitious, for that. He didn't fool around—studied hard in school. That's why I can't figure out why he quit college—and within less than a year of the time he would have graduated. But he got all wrapped up in this thing about Negroes and their rights—that's what did it. I don't think he'll ever go back to school now—he's become almost a fanatic. It's a side of him that's kinda crazy—he's really a little 'off' about it. Maybe we all oughta be, though, I guess. That's somethin' to think about too, now, ain't it? But it's an obsession with Johnnie. I began to see it comin' on when he was in high school—when he would get so upset, all excited and mad, when he was studying about Reconstruction times in the South right after the Civil War and Emancipation. It's a funny thing—in his history classes he was always more taken with Reconstruction than he was with slavery itself. He used to ask me a lot of questions about Reconstruction and I'd tell him what all my daddy used to say Acts and Aaron had told him—about the horrible days right after slavery ended. Since then, of course, Johnnie's made a thorough, exhaustive, study of it and thinks it may have been even worse than slavery itself—which it wasn't, but he's about convinced it was. I don't care how bad, how terrible, though, it was, it wasn't worse —*nothin'* was worse—than slavery!"

"It was bad, though, Goforth—mighty bad," again spoke up the grey-haired bar patron. "It was cruel and bloody—Reconstruction was. The South, defeated, their slaves freed, and land laid waste, took out their rage on us. They tried to wipe us out, Goforth— off the face of the earth! There was only the far-off law in Washington to protect us and it was nothin'—there wasn't anybody around to enforce it. We had no way, nothin', to protect ourselves at all—nothin'. We were helpless. Johnnie ain't far wrong about Reconstruction."

Goforth, regarding himself as the expert, was plainly irritated at what he considered the presumption of these remarks. "Reconstruction was shorter!" he said, almost vehemently. "Slavery lasted hundreds of years—Reconstruction ten or fifteen. Sure, it was lawless and bloody, but slavery was the same—and, seems like, lasted forever, an eternity! No, no, there was a big, a huge, difference. But Johnnie always seemed to see somethin' in Reconstruction that sent him into fits, set him afire. I never did understand it—yeah, it would almost send him into convulsions. . . . Yet my daddy did tell about some terrible things that took place during Reconstruction—that were told to him by Acts and Aaron who somehow lived through it. . . ."

*　　*　　*　　*　　*

There was a deathly stillness in the night and stars speckled the vast black dome of sky over the dense forest and swampland of South Georgia. Acts had never before been afraid of snakes but now he knew the peril was real as he groped and stumbled into the screen of wet bushes skirting this random dank depression in the earth. Most of all, though, he thought of the men. But he dare not light a match—they had not given up the pursuit of him but were probably merely waiting for daybreak. Panting, exhausted, his forearm paining from the hound's fangs, he sank down at the foot of a beech tree, surrounded by serried growths of cane and briar, of cypress and gum, and rested for a moment. But he knew he must keep going. Yet where in this black night? . . . Breathing hard, he lay back against the trunk of the tree and waited, but for what? . . . for something he could not quite envision—death? He was not ready to concede that yet. Throughout this night of running, Acts Knight had thought of his younger half-brother Aaron. How had he fared? he wondered. Or was he dead by now?—as Acts realized he might well himself soon be, come daylight. The posse would have more dogs by daybreak—with his knife he had killed their one hound yesterday.

372

So this was freedom, he mused. What *was* this freedom blacks off the plantations had had these four years since the war? Freedom from what?—freedom to *do* what? This was Reconstruction and he did not understand it—how was it different from the slavery blacks had known almost all their lives? He knew one difference certainly—freedom was more dangerous. It was easy now to be beaten to death by a roving band of ex-soldiers, or to be strung up to the limb of a tree, or to get your head blown off by an irate storekeeper or dirt sharecropper. Slavery was safer, surely. There was law then and property value in slaves. Now there was only helplessness and hate. It was a great mystery to Acts. Why was he, his half-brother Aaron, and all the others, black men, black women, even children, the old and young alike, the sick and well, the defiant and the meek—why were they all objects of such scalding, fanatical hate? He thought about it and wanted to pray. He did pray—he addressed God as if He were Aaron—and in silent, songful prayer:

> Don't you want to die easy,
> Don't you want to die easy,
> Don't you want to die easy in that mornin'.
> Don't you want to see Jesus,
> Don't you want to see Jesus,
> Don't you want to see Jesus in that mornin'.

Generations later Acts' and Aaron's descendants would learn what had happened—learn about their history. Johnnie Knight, for instance, in high school and in college, would evolve from long, fevered, and sedulous study his own interpretation of what the Acts Knights and all their kind had experienced, suffered. He would learn the post-war South had been in utter turmoil, that loss of the war in 1865 had brought poverty and calamity everywhere, and that by 1869 the victorious North—almost all by constitutional amendment—had abolished slavery, made citizens of the former slaves, given them the vote, and divided the eleven states of the Confederacy into five military districts in which the authority of the Union army commander was supreme. But Johnnie would also learn that all this was quickly to change—change when, in a deadlocked national presidential election, the South, finding itself in a favorable strategic position at last, would toughly, ruthlessly, successfully, bargain for abolition of military rule in the area and the restoration of white Southern dominance. The federal troops would withdraw—in his studies a vicariously sad, vivid experience for Johnnie—and leave hapless blacks at the mercy of vengeful whites. For Johnnie, scenting history like a bloodhound, there would be an evocation of the utter horror of it come off the book's very pages, despite the historian's quite different, jaundiced, emphases and perspectives. Johnnie would see the Klan riding then, smell the blood of the whip and rope, the acridity of combustibles and burning flesh, hear the outcries and moans; he would study the enactments—the repressive racial laws, the Black Codes— and see the onset of a violent century, a reign of terror, which for him would amply justify a like period of counter-retribution to come. Johnnie, the perfervid, eager youth, would see it all clearly and be entranced by its drama.

The waking wrens and sparrows had begun to chirp now and Acts knew daybreak was not far off though the sky yet showed no sign of light. He suddenly realized his exhaustion had forcibly brought on sleep. How long had he slept? he wondered, sitting bolt upright, seized with fear. Even the singing birds frightened him. But then, like a sudden blow to his hollow stomach, he was aware of his hunger pangs—except for a little bread, he had not eaten for a day and a half. Ah, he thought, it was such hunger that had brought disaster—to both him and Aaron; they had been together and had suffered alike. But he must somehow now find food, he knew, or he would become even weaker. He stood up and peered around him in the dank, weedy darkness, feeling more helpless, alone, more desperate, than he had ever felt before despite—in a variety of both Southern and Northern escapes and adventures— an adult lifetime of brushes with danger and death. He wondered about Aaron, worried about him—for whom he, Acts, had returned South after the war. Aaron was so young and brash, he thought—dangerous traits surely in these times. Yet it was Aaron's daring that had just brought about their escape. From long experience, yes, Acts knew about escapes—Aaron had been too young then—and how uncertain, short-lived, they could prove to be. He had escaped from slavery itself—that was all of ten years ago— and eventually joined up with John Brown and on the very eve of the war gone on to Harper's Ferry where he had escaped again; escaped death by shooting or hanging. That all seemed so long, long ago now; it also seemed that his whole life since then had been one long effort to escape; he knew not what, except death. The long war had been over more than four years now and the slaves were free, yet life was more dangerous for them than it had ever been; it was not a condition easy to understand when immediately after the war hopes had been so high, promise so bright.

So it was, only day before yesterday, that he and Aaron as usual had been on the move, fleeing again. It was early August, a hot and dusty afternoon, and instead of circumventing it, they had stopped in this tiny south Georgia town, a mere hamlet, to ask for some kind of work, quick work, that would get them food and perhaps temporarily a safe place in which to sleep for two uncommon nights in succession. They were exhausted, dirty, bedraggled, tired of running, and had entered this little crossroads country store to offer their labor for food and a place for a few hours' sleep. The storekeeper, a tall, wizened old white man, tobacco juice oozing down a corner of his mouth, frowned and told them at once that he had no work for them and, in more harsh, ominous tones, that it was highly dangerous for them even to stop here. Acts, from experience, was more than ready to accept this advice, but young Aaron, bone-weary and ravenously hungry, bluntly, naively, suggested they be permitted to chop down the horde of weeds overwhelming the yard behind the store in exchange for bread and cheese. "We's ready to work, Cap'n—we's hungry," young Aaron had said. "We ain't lookin' for no charity or nothin' like that." Yet there was no tone of plaint, no sycophancy, in his voice; it was unceremonious, edgy, and, despite the salutation "Cap'n," faintly demanding. He had seen, behind the rough counter, the large wedge of cheese alongside a half dozen loaves of bread.

The old man glared at them. "Don't you worry 'bout them weeds," he said, now threateningly. "You'all jest git your hind-ends outa this store and down that road 'ere."

Acts, experienced, realistic, had started out the door, when Aaron, before anyone could stop him, suddenly vaulted over the counter, seized a loaf of bread, and ran out even ahead of Acts into the road. "You fool!" yelled Acts—but now running, following him.

In the doorway soon the old man raised an enormous pistol. Extending both arms high out toward the two fugitives, squinting hard, he sighted along the pistol barrel interminably before pulling the trigger. There was a loud report. Two dogs came scrambling out from under a nearby house yelping their heads off. But at the erring pistol shot, Acts and Aaron had run off the road, into a line of tall, scraggly bushes, and kept going, as the old man, in reply to the questions of neighbors running out, cried: "Them must be the same niggers that killed Clint Heskins' sow this mornin'!—they just now took a loaf of bread offa me!" He was in the middle of the road now, the huge pistol still held in both hands, peering over at the bushes into which Acts and Aaron had disappeared. "Hungry niggers swarmin' over us like locusts all the time," he said. "Soon we won't have nothin' to eat ourselves." But he held the pistol in one hand now, then finally lowered it and let it hang idly at his side—the pursuit mentally already abandoned.

But at that moment a thick-set, bearded man wearing a black wool hat in the August heat came out of a house nearby carrying a Confederate army rifle at the trail. He seemed unperturbed, self-assured, almost cavalier, as he approached the storekeeper and the others in the middle of the road. "Them niggers have done their dirt, all right," he said to the old man—"They mustn't be let to get away with it, though. I seed 'em comin' down the road 'fore they went in your store, Giles. Likely they're the ones Clarkson Swain caught in his smokehouse. They tied him up after they half beat him to death, then went in and rummaged through the house and took whut money they could find—six dollars. Yeah, but here's the thing—they tied up Jebby, his daughter, too." A hush fell over the group.

"His *daughter*!" someone finally said. "Blade, don't josh us."

"They didn't touch her otherwise—so *she* said. Jest tied her up like her pa. Yeah, that's whut she said. But whut one of the women-folk would own up to a nigger doin' anything to her. We oughta ketch 'em and put 'em through the third degree. I'm going to my boy's place and get old Jonah, my hound. Come on, you'all, let's ketch them two niggers." Little more needed be said—in less than a quarter hour an unofficial posse of fifteen or more men and boys had formed. Soon, with Jonah, the big black and tan hound on Blade's long leash, they set out on the trail of the two brothers.

Thirty minutes later Acts and Aaron, panting, winded, had been resting in a marshy ravine eating the loaf of bread Aaron had torn into halves for them—when they heard the hound bawling. Acts stopped chewing. They both listened. Though the muffled barking seemed far away, neither man would reveal his fear. "This bread's good, ain't it?" said Aaron caustically—by way of reproof for Acts' scolding. "If we listened to you we'd done starved." He was a tall, lanky youth—ebony black, with prominently protruding teeth; yet he walked bent over like an old man; it was not from years of hard labor—he had been only eighteen at Emancipation—but from some kind of back deformity he had had since birth. They heard the hound again now. But it seemed no closer and both tried to hide their alarm. "We got to find us a chicken somewhere," said Aaron, "and roast him over a fire—we cain't starve."

"What you don't know nothin' about is the danger," Acts finally said.

"Deed I do."

"These white folks'll kill you—they're mad and they'll kill you, boy. We got to git outa this countryside, where it's so dangerous, and git into the city—we got to try to make it to Savannah where we can git some work maybe and git lost in the crowds." Acts had a broad, earnest face, now streaked with the sweat of exertion, and a rawboned, though now gaunt, frame. He swallowed another piece of bread and looked at Aaron. "How long kin we live like this?" he said—"all the time goin' from one place to another, huntin' for a bite to eat and a place to lay down outa the rain; dodgin' white folks and tryin' to stay alive. That place we come through day 'fore yesterday—there was three niggers hangin' from the same tree; looked like they'd been there a week, with the buzzards circlin' around in the sky and all and some settin' in the tree. How long we got to live like this?"

"We can make it to Savannah, all right," said Aaron. "It'll sho enough be better there."

Just then they heard the hound—compared to how it had sounded before it seemed suddenly almost on top of them. They scrambled to their feet and started running again. "The damn dog was on our trail all the time," Acts said breathlessly, following Aaron over the rim of the ravine and into a sparsely wooded area. "He's one of them silent trailers." They were soon running through the scattered trees and jimson weeds as the sun moved steadily down the western sky—though the heat was still intense. Acts, his legs now flaccid, weak, from fatigue, wondered how Aaron, with his stooped, deformed back, could run so fast and so long without seeming to tire. They heard the hound again now—he was much closer, possibly already in the ravine. And this time they heard the voices of the posse, though they could not make out what was said.

"We can outrun 'em," Aaron said. But now himself panting loudly, he ran only just ahead of Acts. "They got the dog on the leash yet maybe—they cain't never ketch us with him on the leash. But if they turn him loose then they cain't keep up with him. You got your knife?"

"Yeah. What I want my knife for?" Acts said, running, stumbling.

"To kill that damn dog with if they turn him loose. We'll be all right then."

What, however, instead of the posse, neither Aaron nor Acts saw up ahead through the trees was a scrawny dirt farmer and his son, a boy of twelve, out hunting squirrels. They had spotted a squirrel in a tree and were quietly, stealthily, kneeling in the tall grass waiting for the father to get a shot with his rifle, when they heard the brothers running, threshing through the underbrush, toward them. The father shushed the boy who was about to speak and, remaining very quiet, peered hard in the direction of the noise. Then they all heard the hound bawling as it came out of the ravine hard on the scent of the trail. "He's close," said Acts to Aaron as they ran—"They done turned him loose now." The dirt farmer and his son, both almost entirely concealed in the high grass, first heard, then saw Acts and Aaron approaching on the run. The father shushed the boy again. They had forgotten about squirrels now—here was more significant quarry.

The unleashed hound, now running hard and silent, suddenly appeared, exploded, on Acts' and Aaron's heels. At once it started a loud, frantic, triumphant baying. Acts, pulling out his Barlow knife, wheeled to face the dog; then lunged to seize him but missed. The action mystified the farmer who in the grass had not yet seen the knife. He and the boy watched. The dog, snarling, baying frightfully, now, twice ran a circle around Acts. Acts, however, waiting for another chance, finally lunged again and this time

378

caught it around the rib cage as the dog savagely bit his forearm. But Acts, grunting, stabbed it quickly, repeatedly, until its wailing cries had ceased. Turning it loose at last, Acts let its twitching body fall to the ground. The farmer stood up at once now, and, pointing his rifle at Acts, yelled at him to stand still—but not before Aaron had already vanished in the tall grass. "Nigger, you move and you're dead," the farmer said to Acts, but all the while perturbed, looking around for Aaron. Finally he advanced on Acts, holding the rifle at the ready, his son, though some ten feet behind, trailing him. Suddenly then he heard the boy cry out, and turned to see Aaron, risen from the high grass, with the seized boy thrust in front of him, his head in the vise of Aaron's right arm. "Don't shoot dat gun, Cap'n—I'll break his neck, sure," Aaron said. The panicked boy was slavering and whining and when Aaron gave a sudden, wrenching jerk of the arm the boy cried out in pain. "Throw the gun to my brother, Cap'n," said Aaron, "or I'll kill yo' boy—I swear fo' God. Hurry!" In his fearful confusion the surrendering farmer tossed his rifle at Aaron's feet instead.

At that moment they heard the posse coming—hearing the voices of the men even before they came in sight. Aaron turned the boy loose, grabbed up the rifle, and started running; but in an unlikely direction, at right angles to the route he and Acts had taken—but into denser woods. Frantic, confused, Acts ran the other way. Yet the posse, though seeing them going in opposite directions, raised their guns to fire on them both. Only then did they see the farmer and his son, and, fearful of hitting them, they held their fire and fell to cursing. Thus it was that Acts and Aaron, though now hopelessly separated, had escaped—had stayed alive to instruct their children in their history.

Alone now in the last hour of darkness, Acts thought about all that had happened as he waited in the wooded swampland for daybreak. Where was Aaron now? he wondered. That headstrong boy, armed with a rifle with only one round of ammunition, would surely get himself killed. But their separation had come from their confusion—they were about to be shot at by wizard marksmen and there had been no time to make right decisions. They were trying to stay alive. Now Savannah was Acts' only hope—he was sure it was also Aaron's destination. It was there, he tried to reassure himself, they would be reunited.

At last now to the east a vague dawning light had appeared in the sky. But observing it reminded Acts of his grave, dangerous, responsibilities—he must travel in daylight the better to know where he was, also to get food, yet must somehow avoid those who would want to kill him on sight, be they his present pursuers or enemies to be encountered; come daylight, he must once more face the harsh realities. He had walked most of the night, down an old deserted back road, almost a lane, with weeds growing in the center, but had left it when he realized he could not stay awake much longer. He had been staggering. Now he had no notion of how long he had slept sitting propped against the tree. But the faint light in the sky made him think in terms of motion. He tried to move his right leg but found it numb from cramped inaction, though the pain in his forearm where the dog had bitten him, if untouched for a time, became merely soreness, but when touched, tested, made him wince. He suddenly wondered whether the hound had been a 'mad dog' and whether he himself would soon get lockjaw and die. Then he seemed to realize, understand, he must rid his mind of these debilitating fears and concentrate, even if from day to day, on saving his life; he thought about it for a long time yet became disconsolate, morose, unsure of himself.

He seemed more aware now than ever of the stillness of this indolent dawn—though it was not at all really a stillness; only certain noises did not intrude upon his consciousness, did not count. Indeed the birds were chirping louder than ever—and there were the more plaintive notes from two whippoorwills and a mockingbird; there was also the din of a horde, an infestation, of crickets. Only the fireflies were unheard as they levitated eerily over this dank depression of land, his momentary haven. Again he began to think of his situation—of himself. Acts Knight was his name. He knew that. But he was not sure of much else. He had taken the surname Knight from the slave master from whom he had escaped to go with John Brown. He had since insisted his half brother Aaron take it too—though Aaron for a short time before Emancipation had been owned by the famous Judah P. Benjamin. He thought the same name tended to draw him and Aaron closer together, making them really as full blood brothers would be. Hadn't he come back down south, into violent Georgia itself, to bring Aaron out? This had been fundamental to him. But he dealt only in fundamentals now. His vision, his horizons, ambitions, his life, were all of the simplest, most fundamental kind; raising only such questions as how to escape death or pain, how to get food each day, how from time to time to find a woman to lie with, but mostly how to escape death or pain, physical pain—the pain of a flogging, a shooting, a knifing; he had long since ceased to be concerned with any other type of pain; he had become immune, callous, to all slights, insults, degradations—he had come to believe life had always been like this for him and his kind and would always be. These things were very simple, very clear, to him; taken for granted; he had been totally brutalized. He was not outraged by any great wrong, as wrathful John Brown had preached to them they should be, nor by an insatiable craving for retribution. The Lord God has willed it this way and this was the way it was to be— if only there could be some let-up in the physical pain, the continual flirting with, the nearness to, death, which, however, it seemed, was almost always involved; it was a process at work, the unwitting process of his psychic sterilization; it had transformed him into a piece of wood, a stone, a clod; but he was not aware of this; he thought rather, with blasphemous irony, a higher power to be involved; it was as if the old chant had come in his head:

> Everywhere I go
> Somebody's talkin' about Jesus.
> Me, with my burdens, I hardly cares.
> My knees been acquainted with the hillside clay,
> Somebody's talkin' about Jesus.
> My head's been wet with the midnight dew,
> Somebody's talkin' about Jesus,
> *Jesus*, Lord!
> Me, I sits by the well and stares, while
> Everybody's talkin' about Jesus.

His hunger now brought him to think of the thousands on thousands of his hungry fellow ex-slaves roaming the South, always on the move—men, women, children—thronging the countryside, living on the land; teeming migrants, lame, sick, starved, trudging wearily from place to place, vaguely expectant, hopeful, sometimes going from plantation to town where failure to get food and a roof then drove them back to the plantation where mostly impoverished ex-masters did not want or need them. Their hapless moving and foraging only exposed them to the bitter reprisals of the dirt-poor, white sharecroppers, who showed them no quarter. So far Acts and Aaron had avoided hard crime, any real misdeeds of any kind, shunning even all contacts with whites, except for what seemed the minor incident of the loaf of bread which, strange to say, thought Acts, had now assumed such enlarged, deadly, proportions. But it had been Acts' instinctive appreciation of danger that had always governed his conduct. He had also tried to teach Aaron the various dangers one might have to face. Yet often many vagrant black wanderers were charged with, and made to answer for—possibly with death or maiming—the thefts or similar "misdeeds" of other blacks moving through the area. It was a time of great turmoil and violence, and Acts now seemed dazed, numbed, stoicized, by it all. He only wanted to go somewhere with Aaron where daily, hourly, disaster did not lurk over the nearest hillside or around the next bend in the road.

There was much more light in the eastern sky now. He pushed aside a thorny bush and took a few hesitant steps, trying to decide whether or not to start walking again. He thought when he could see better he might be able to find a few berries to eat to relieve his hunger—he had no confidence in his ability to kill a running rabbit with a rock, and it was rare to find one sitting; he knew if near a barnyard he encountered a chicken, danger or not, he would try to catch and kill it. As best he could in the damp underbrush, he began walking in earnest now and as the light grew he saw that he was emerging from a woodland depression that had recently been under water from heavy rains. As he slowly made his way to higher ground, he constantly thought of Aaron, wondering what might have happened to him, or whether he was still alive. His heart sank at the thought of the possibilities. He finally reached a scrubby, grassy knoll amidst again the cheerful singing of the birds. He looked once more at the heavens—it would not be an entirely clear day, he could see; there were crimson streaks of clouds across a pale primrose sky, and the air was heavy; he could feel it would be sultry hot. From the rise of the knoll he gazed around him, viewing, over a low-hanging mist, the gently-rolling countryside. Though his mind was attenuated and dulled, he knew the direction in which he wanted to go—to the east and a little to the north, toward Waycross and eventually Savannah. He continued walking toward the vague, incipient light in the sky, all the while moving his eyes painfully about him in the hope of seeing a fruit-bearing tree or some berry bushes along the way. Often, however, he would stop and, despite the chattering of the birds, stand for a long time and listen, dreading in his heart that he might soon hear the bawling of the pursuit hounds. Maybe, though, he thought, the posse had given up the chase and gone home. Why, anyhow, had they gone to such lengths to punish the taking of a loaf of bread?—he could not understand what had fueled such vengeful efforts, why they were so eager to kill for Aaron's piddling deed. The soreness in his bitten forearm now intruded itself on his consciousness, diverting his thoughts, confusing his reactions, until he pushed back his sleeve and softly touched the two deep lacerations. He would bathe, soothe, the arm in the cold water of some stream or spring if he could find one. But this only made him aware of his thirst, though everything happening to him seemed like some blurred hallucination, a dream; he was stuporous from fatigue; had it not been for the thirst and hunger he would have fallen to the ground and, despite the peril, slept again; his mind was comatose, his instincts basic, primal; he had been reduced to something inert, that wanted only to eat, sleep, and live.

Thus he wandered for over an hour. It was light now and vaguely he realized he was approaching a road, a highway. And soon there were sounds. Instantly his fears aroused him. He stopped and listened again—he could hear the low murmur of human voices and he quickly squatted on his haunches to lower his profile. His throat was even drier now, his heart pounding. The voices seemed beyond, on the other side of, the highway—in a pasture ravine into which he could not yet see. He crouched perfectly still for minutes, listening, watching, heavily breathing. Then at last he saw someone—a black woman. She had for some reason come up on the road. Stout, heavy-featured, middle-aged, she wore a long thick wool dress with leg-of-mutton sleeves; the dress almost reached the ground and had at one time been dark green but was now faded and almost colorless from the foulness and wear-and-tear of travel.

He stood up now and she saw him. They viewed each other cautiously for a moment, then she retreated back down the slight embankment and was momentarily out of sight. Almost at once though she reappeared, glancing over her shoulder, saying something to someone the rise of the road prevented him from seeing. Suddenly she began beckoning urgently for him to come over to her—to them. He hesitated, but finally, looking both ways, he approached the road, then mounted to it. At once he saw what the women saw, close up—twenty or more itinerant blacks, men and women, young and old, and a few children, lying just beyond the road down in the rough, dewy pasture grass where apparently they had slept all night. Some were still asleep, covered by anything—an old newspaper, a coat, a shawl—that came to hand. The stout woman, however, seemed to have been ministering to someone, another woman, thin, gaunt, near forty, now ill or incapacitated, who lay on her back but with her eyes wide open. The first woman beckoned to him again. He went down the slight incline now and joined her. Of the others lying about who were awake, some propped their chins on their hands and looked wearily, apathetically, at him; one or two seemed suspicious, hostile.

The stout woman stood up from the prostrate woman now and said something to him he did not at first understand. "Is you a man of God?" she then repeated.

"Whut?" he muttered, but somehow dazedly, dreamily, from his hunger and fatigue.

"You ain't by chance a preacher, is you?" At last she pointed to the prone woman. "She ain't had nothin' but fits all night long—needs the devils cast outa her; needs a divine man. *Is* you a preacher?"

Acts shook his head. "No," he said. "Whut's the matter wid her?"

"Ain't nothin' the matter with her 'cept in her head—fits. She havin' fits 'cause the demons is in her—ever since we been on the road, since we been wanderin' all over creation, the devil's been testin' her. Now she cain't hardly walk in the day, and screams all night with her terrible dreams. It's ole Satan and his demons at her since she lost her boy—he was killed. She needs a divine man, a preacher, to cast 'em out."

Acts' jaded mind had ranged off. "I ain't no preacher," he finally said.

"Oh, Lawd," said the woman woefully. "Whut's goin' to happen to her? . . . Oh, Lawd Jesus. . . ."

All the while the gaunt prostrate woman stared up at them, yet seemed completely unaware of their presence. She occasionally mumbled something incoherent to herself, then, mysteriously, raised her hand and with her fingers tapped her chest, and once her forehead. At last she lapsed into a series of random feverish whispers, her eyes now closed. But suddenly then she would open her eyes, wide, gaping, and stare crazily, first at the stout woman, then at Acts.

"She's had a bad time," the stout woman said—"Dey shot her boy de other day. It 'bout killed her too."

Acts, however, gazed at the stout woman inertly. "Ain't you got a piece of bread or somethin'?" he said at last, symbolically holding out a trembling hand.

"Sho I got bread—got plenty bread." She pointed a finger toward the sky. "But it's stored up yonder—in hebb'um. Ain't none down here. I'll be goin' to hebb'um soon, though—plenty bread dere. Ain't stayin' down here much longer. My mammy done gone on, and my sister, and one of my chillum—Ellie—and my man . . . dey all gone on. I ain't tarryin' long, neither—whut I need bread for?"

The prostrate woman now uttered her first intelligible words. "Gi' him that piece of sow-belly to eat, Nell," she said to the stout, standing, woman—"He 'bout to fall."

"You goin' to need that yo'self terreckly," Nell warned her.

"Gi' it to him, I said."

Nell, mumbling, went over to an old battered brown valise on the ground and, pawing in it for a moment, brought out a piece of unwrapped, half-cooked pork. She came back and, grudgingly, gave it to Acts. At once he began tearing at it with his teeth and chewed it ravenously, as the still prostrate woman watched him. "Ah, slavery times is gone," she said now, fixing him with her piercing gaze—"I'll soon be gone wid 'em too, I tell you dat. In slavery times dey didn't hate us so bad as dey do now. Dey laughed den once in awhile. But no more. Dey only frown sumpin' awful an' cuss us now—an' shoot us, or hang us from a tree. Why is dis? . . . Why dey hate us so?"

Acts, however, was too busy eating—white blobs of fat pork oozed from the corners of his mouth as his teeth tore at the hunk of meat held in both hands. Yet he looked at her as he ate but his dull, lifeless eyes were unseeing.

"Dey killed my boy day 'fore yesstiday—Luff," she said. "Luff was only twenty an' de only one of my chillun 'cept one dey didn't sell from under me—an' him, even from a little one, always talkin' about Mancipation. Hummmph! 'Mammy,' he says, 'when Mancipation come we gwine to Atlanta and buy us a house.' Lordy, dis Mancipation was all dat boy talked about. But dey shot him day 'fore yesstiday—he told a deppy-sheriff now he was a free nigger and dey shot him. Why'd dey do way with slavery if dey was goin' to kill us all? Why?" Suddenly she began screaming—"*Why, why, why?*" Flat on her back, she flailed her arms wildly. "*Why?*—I'm askin' you'all!"

"Oh, dere she goes agin," sighed exasperated Nell. She reached down and began shaking the prostrate woman, then slapping her face. "Herta, Herta, don't you start goin' into dem fits agin. I cain't stand it—you yellin' an' talkin' out yo' head all de time."

But Herta was looking at Acts again now, her thin, haggard face in a grimace. "Slavery brought us here, didn't it?" she said at last—speaking only to him, and trying to turn on her side, the better to face him. "We come from Aficky, you know dat—all us. We been here years and years, workin' for de white folks wid no pay—why den dey hate us so? Dey whipped us, dey worked us to death, broke up an' scattered our families—sold three of my chillun from me whilst I cried and cussed 'em. Why dey like dey is? My mammy, 'fore dey sold her way from us, said dey is helpless—dey always been like dis; dey made by the Devil like dis—to go all over de world givin' people misery. My mammy called dem de 'misery people.' "

Acts said: "It's 'cause dey say we ain't no good—dat God done cursed us. But John Brown said it ain't so—he said everybody's most 'bout alike. I don't believe 'im, though."

"Who John Brown?—sounds like a crazy man to me. We *is* cursed."

Acts still chewed the fat pork. "John Brown tried to free de niggers," he said. "And de white folks hung him for it. I sho had been wid him part of de way but when dey tried to shoot us in a barn one night, I got away. I thanks the Master in hebb'um for dat."

But prostrate Herta already appeared unmindful of what Acts was saying; she seemed almost again in a trance; the bitterness had left her ravaged face. "After dey brought us over here from Aficky, dey kept us in slavery times hundids of years," she said. "Dats a long time waitin' for Mancipation. Den after it comes dey kills my boy Luff. Dey de *misery people*, I tell you—it's in dey blood."

Nell stood over Herta. "Sick in de body, crazy in de head," she said, pointing at the prostrate woman. "All de time she talk jes about her boy Luff."

The dawning sun had appeared amidst the streaks of crimson clouds now and, as if emboldened, was slowly lifting itself over the distant Georgia landscape. Some of the blacks lying about on the ground had begun to stir—sitting up and yawning, or raising weary eyes to an uncertain sky. Two or three appeared feeble or ill. "Where you'all headin'?" Acts said to Nell.

"We heerd de Freedmen's Bureau is in Savannah," she said, facing him earnestly now, the leg-of-mutton sleeves of her heavy, long dress making her seem even stouter. "We tryin' to git dere 'cause we got two bad sick people—an ole man dere on de ground and a child; don't know if dey can make it—dey needs de doctor bad. We ain't got nothin' much left to eat, neither."

"Dat's where I'm headin'—Savannah," said Acts. "But white folks back yonder where I jes come from been after me and my brother—wanted to kill us 'cause we took a loaf of bread. We got away, but dey still after me maybe—I don't know where is my brother now. Dees is bad, bad times—sometimes I wish I'da stayed on away from here, but I come back to git my brother. Now I hab lost him agin—maybe he dead already."

"How far back you got away from de white folks?"

"'Bout five miles."

"Dat ain't far enough—you better come on to Savannah den. Maybe dere dey'll feed us—maybe we'll have some place to lay down in outa de rain dere at de Freedmen's Bureau."

Thirty minutes later they were all on the road again, a slowly moving, bedraggled, foot caravan of eleven women, eight men, including Acts, and two children—a boy and a girl. One of the men, old and weak, and the eleven-year-old girl, were so ill they could hardly walk, necessitating frequent stops by the group to enable the two to rest. They would all sit by the side of the road, some munching a piece of bread or any other bit of food they were fortunate enough to have saved, and one of the women would pray aloud for their eventual deliverance. When they resumed the slow march, Herta walked in a deeply self-absorbed silence except for occasional impassioned whispers to herself in which the name of her son, Luff, was brokenly uttered. Otherwise she seemed sleep walking.

By ten o'clock the sun was high and hot. Many were already exhausted and thirsty. Although along the way they passed an occasional farmer's cabin, occupied by poor whites, they knew better than to stop, especially since the hounds on the premises barked so menacingly at them. But finally, much farther down the road and just before noon, they came to what had been a plantation. It was not huge, only moderate-sized, but seemed abandoned. Slowly, solemnly, they trudged up the long, embowered lane toward the house, its three-columned facade rising in a stand of half-denuded and dusty magnolias. There were a half dozen empty slave cabins discernible behind the house but no sign whatever now of blacks about the place. This latter fact caused some apprehension among the travelers, but they continued around to the rear of the house and stood in a large group, ineptly waiting for someone to appear. Dark clouds were already gathering in the hot, humid sky as rain impended.

They waited for two or three minutes. Then at last the backdoor of the house opened and a woman appeared—a tall, pale woman, past middle age, her iron-grey hair long but unkempt and wild. There were narrow stone steps leading up to the door in which she stood and as she looked down on the itinerant motley assemblage, a pet rabbit which had been cavorting about the backyard hopped to the bottom of the steps and, blinking its eyes, stared up vapidly at her. The whole scene then appeared somehow caught in perfect stasis; nothing moved; they all, even the rabbit, seemed forever frozen in place, except for Acts' turbulent inward urges which made him want to catch, kill, and put the rabbit over a fire. He was faint from hunger, as were they all.

Finally, suddenly, however, it seemed everything was animated again. Nell and another woman, the latter also wearing a long, hot, foul dress, went forward to the foot of the steps, but then, looking up uncertainly, seemed unable to speak. The frantic-looking white woman stared down at them. At last Nell spoke. "Missus, we'se tired and mighty thirsty—hungry too—from walkin' in de sun all mornin' long. Please, Missus, kin we have some water?—and any vittles 'round here you might have? We'se goin' to pray for you for it, Missus—we'se goin' to remember you to Jesus in our prayers, see if we don't."

The woman hesitated, her eyes flighty, confused. At last she turned and called back into the house—"Harrison, come here." Before long a tall, ascetic-looking man, his hair almost white despite his unlined red face, appeared in the door behind her. Soon then he stepped out past her and stood in front, facing Nell and the others. "Look at them," his wild-haired wife said to him, irritation in her voice—"They're after food and water."

"Where are you'all on your way to, Auntie?" the man said to Nell.

"We'se tryin' to find de Freedmen's Bureau, Marster," said Nell. "Hear tell it's one in Savannah, but we ain't got no way to git anythang to eat till we gits dere, and no place to sleep when night come down on us—we been sleepin' by de side of de road. We'se hungry and tired—and we got two wid us dat's sick, awful sick, Marster."

The man, who was coatless and wore riding boots, took a deep breath as he surveyed the group. Now appeared two children behind him in the door—a little blond girl and, younger, a wide-eyed boy of eight. "Have some of the slaves come back, Grandpa?" the boy said in awe to the man.

"Of course not," the woman, interrupting, spoke up impatiently. "Be quiet, Seth.

"Grandma," the little girl said, "look how dirty and ragged they are—oh!"

"Be quiet, Jessica," the woman said.

The man now spoke to the blacks. "All right, we can let you have corn meal for bread, and some vegetables, maybe a little meat, for you to make yourselves some soup with—back there on a fire in one of the cabins."

"Oh, we thanks you, Marster," said Nell. "Jesus will sho bless you too, 'cause we has no money. We'se so hungry—the Lord knows it." The others had heard too and began to crowd forward, solemnly mumbling thanks. Then almost suddenly it began to rain —slowly at first, but soon it increased to a cloudburst; the rain came down in sheets. At the white man's direction they scurried down to the cabins and took shelter, while he, his wife, and their two grandchildren withdrew again into the house.

The blacks found the cabin dank, musty, and long deserted, and surmised the slaves had been gone since the ending of the war. The largest of the cabins, where as it rained they were all now congregated, contained an old table, two stools, and a fireplace full of discarded junk and trash, which Acts and one of the other men, after killing a large cottonmouth snake, began to clear out preparatory to building a fire for cooking. In the hardest of the downpour, as the others stood around looking out and waiting, the pet rabbit suddenly ran in the door, through their legs, and stopped—squatting in the corner beyond the fireplace as if waiting with them. At once Herta, her eyes rolling, became very excited. "It's sho a bad omen—it's a hex," she said, pointing. "First a snake, now dis. De rabbit means numbers, great numbers, Lawd—you knows how dey breed and mut'ply. God done sent dis creature as a sign on us. We gwine see *many* of somethin' or other before dis place be's behind us." She raised her eyes to the ceiling beams. "Lawd, you done told us to stop here. Don't send no trouble down on us here, den. Hep us, protect us, Lawd, against the mighty hosts itchin' to come outa nowhere on us. You have give us de sign, Lawd—now hep us!"

Nell looked at Herta talking and shook her head—"Crazy in de head," she said again.

When, in half an hour, the rain had finally begun to slacken, then had stopped, the plantation owner came out of the house again, called them outside around him, and began directing them where to come to get the provisions, some cooking utensils, and firewood for the fireplace. This was met with great gladness and soon the largest cabin and the one adjacent to it had become centers of urgent activity. But Herta, who took no part in any of the work and merely sat brooding on a stool against the square-log wall of the cabin, kept looking about for the rabbit—though it had long since gone and was nowhere in sight outside. Her face in a desperate grimace, Herta cast her eyes darkly about her again and muttered some epithet about calamity, then something about both heaven and hell, and finally the name of her murdered son, Luff.

At that moment two white men on horseback, their rough clothing drenched, came cantering up the tree-lined lane toward the house. They pulled up short when they saw the blacks in the back-yard around the cabins and, in asides, began talking earnestly to each other. At last, with considerable resoluteness now, they rode on up to the front of the house, where one of them, a tall, gang-ling youth, awkward and shabbily dressed, dismounted from his scrawny mare and gave his still-mounted companion his reins. The wet grass he walked through toward the front portico had soaked his trouser legs to the knees by the time he mounted the steps and, in a gesture of grudging respect, knocked politely on the door. There was a long wait and, with slightly more authority now, he knocked again. Soon the wild-haired woman opened the door, at first with a question mark on her face, but then she frowned. The gangling youth respectfully removed his hat, but only after he had pulled a large folded piece of white paper from his pocket. "Good afternoon, Ma'am," he said in his heavy drawl, stuffing his hat under his arm and unfolding the sheet of paper. "This is the Don-aldson plantation?—I take it to be." He consulted the paper, then looked at her again.

"We're the Donaldsons—yes," the woman said, somewhat sharply, impatiently, as she raised a hand to somehow stroke down her tangled mass of iron-grey hair.

"Ma'am, we're canvassin'—for the election Saturday." He watched her. "Is Mr. Donaldson in?"

"Yes, but he's busy now—out back."

"It won't take but a minute, Ma'am. I sho would like to talk with him—mighty briefly. Could I go 'round?" He nodded toward the rear of the house.

"All right," Mrs. Donaldson finally said, but gave him a pains-taking, probing, look as she closed the door.

Neither of the men knew what was taking place at that moment behind the house. The blacks, silent, lugubrious, stoical, were gathered in a rough circle around one of their fallen. It was one of the two sick, disabled, people Nell had spoken of—the old man. Ill for a month now, and after so far barely withstanding the rigors of the journey, he had finally collapsed in one of the cabins and was now unconscious. He lay outside in the yard, though under the sideless shelter of the pump house, where they had brought him for air. He was a mulatto of seventy, of middle height but very emaciated, and almost bald, with the rim of hair remaining above his ears a matted, dirty white. They all knew him as Rodney. Though already on the point of collapsing, he had been standing solicitously over Herta, as she sat slumped in an incoherent daze against the cabin wall, when he had fallen. It had aroused and terrified her and, now bent over him outside, she wailed her anger and grief at what she had predicted would happen to him in the end. "Uncle Rodney's dead! . . ." she cried out—"Look at 'im! He couldn't keep goin' no longer—we all knowed it!"

"Honey, he ain't dead," Nell said to her—"He'll come 'round terreckly." Nell slapped the old man's face as he lay on his back on the pump house floor, but there was no reaction save a slight twitching of the lips. She slapped him again, but somehow always gently; yet then he soon opened his eyes and looked up and around at them all, including the plantation owner. Donaldson had just pushed his way through and was now bent down over Rodney. He picked up the stricken old man's hand by the wrist, felt his pulse, but was noncommittal. Rodney's lips moved again as he still watched them—he was conscious now and was trying to speak; and soon he smiled at Donaldson who he realized was trying to help him. Again now his lips moved, parted, quivered, but no sound came. Soon Herta was wailing again and Donaldson glanced at her disapprovingly, as the others stood mute, helpless, profoundly solemn.

At that moment the gangling, awkward youth from the front of the house, in his loping gait, came around the corner of the house, the white sheet of paper still in his hand. His mounted companion, leading the other horse, at once followed, coming in sight on the gravel track leading around to the back. Everyone, including Donaldson, looked up in surprise; it was somehow a tense moment— Donaldson, a strange uneasiness in his manner, stood up from Rodney and faced the two approaching men, who, however, were now occupied in staring at the blacks; it could readily be recognized the blacks did not live there but as bone-weary travelers had only recently arrived.

"Mr. Donaldson, is it?" the youth on foot said to Donaldson from a distance—"Mr. Harrison Donaldson?" And he glanced at the sheet of paper.

"Yes," said Donaldson, waiting, not moving a step toward him.

Though the rain had momentarily stopped, the few trees, lining the rear gravel path on which the second youth and two horses were moving toward them, still dripped water. There was also an occasional distant roll of thunder, seeming to accentuate the ominous effect of the newcomers' entry. The blacks, their furtive glances going from one to another among themselves, appeared to sense danger though there was little in the overt demeanor of the youths to suggest anything amiss—it may have been the paper in the first youth's hand, giving him as he approached now an air of officialdom, that excited the blacks' fear and suspicion.

When the youth on foot saw that Donaldson did not intend to move, he confronted him with a surly smile—the first sign of any hostility. "Sir, could I speak with you more private-like?" he said in his drawl, and took a backward step as if to draw Donaldson off to one side. Donaldson at last, grudgingly, followed him a few feet away, out of hearing of the blacks, and again stood waiting. "Sir," said the youth, "me and my brother-in-law here are out canvassin' for the Democrats—we was sent out by his father, a member of the Committee . . . the County Central Committee. We are all tryin' to make sure after Saturday the guv'ment of this State ain't no longer in the hands of the Scalawag Republicans, the Northern Carpetbaggers, and the niggers. We know your house here is Democrat but we want to make sure you come out and vote Saturday. We got to take the guv'ment back this time. The Committee aims to do it—whatever it takes. Ain't no question, sir—they aim to do whatever's necessary to git it back. We need your hep."

For a moment Harrison Donaldson's steely blue eyes studied the youth's face. "I'm a Democrat," he then said, coldly, "and mean to vote Democrat. I was in Lee's army at Gettysburg." He started to turn to go back to the sick man.

But the youth, looking over at the blacks now, smiled his surly smile again. "There's where the trouble is, sir—the niggers," he said. "Any would-be voters there?"

"Of course not," said Donaldson.

"They live here on your place?"

Donaldson's red face beneath his shock of white hair grew redder still now. "I'd almost call that impertinence—your questioning me," he said, "though I assume you don't mean it to be. Now, I'm busy—good day." He turned to go again.

"No offense, sir," said the youth, still grinning. "The Committee, though, don't think the county kin have many more of these rovin' bands of niggers comin' through like swarms of locusts, plunderin' and stealin' us blind, sir—or much less that folks oughta be harborin' 'em." He then looked up at his dour, mean-visaged brother-in-law, who, with the horses, had approached closer. Donaldson, though, frowning angrily, wheeled and returned to the hushed, worried blacks. The first youth stood watching him for a moment, but then went over, mounted his horse, and the pair rode off.

By now Rodney once more had lapsed into unconsciousness. Donaldson stood over him again with the others but appeared still to be preoccupied with the nettling experience he had just had with the two canvassers. Frowning, exasperated, he gazed down absently at Rodney, wondering finally what could be done for him. There was no one to send into town for the doctor—there were only himself, his wife, and the two grandchildren on the place—besides, he knew the doctor probably wouldn't come anyway. He felt Rodney's pulse again; it was irregular, weak, ebbing; he was going to die, he thought. He turned around to them. "Where have you'all come from?" he said.

At first they all looked at each other, not knowing how to answer, for they had come from many different places. "I come from Alabammy, Marster," said Nell at last—"Long ways from here, sar." She looked around her. "Susan here too from dar," she said —"and Jasper and Canny. Little Susan she mighty sick too, Marster—she only 'leven years old and walked all de way. Horatio here come from Louisiana—he been beat a whole lot and shot at twice, Marster. Canny, he 'bout blind from bein' pistol-whipped on de head."

Herta spoke up now. "I come from right here in Georgia—dis my home. But soon I be here in de ground."

"Where are you from?" Donaldson said to Acts.

Acts hesitated; flustered. "I come back to Georgia to git my brother, sar," he finally said. "I been in Ohio, in Virginia some, and de eastern part of Tennessee 'fore dat."

"Are all of you going to Savannah?" asked Donaldson.

"Yes, Marster," Nell said—"We heerd de Freedmen's Bureau dere will hep us."

Donaldson pondered this for a moment. "Very well," he said. "You can stay a day or two in the cabins there until you get rested up. My son is a lawyer in Savannah—maybe he can show you how to get help there."

"Oh, thank you, Marster," said Nell, bringing her hands suppliantly together—"De Lawd will sho bless you, I know dat."

Donaldson looked down again at Rodney now. "I don't think, though, he'll make it to Savannah," he said.

"No, look like poor Rodney'll soon be wid Jesus," said Nell. At this Herta began wailing again. "Shut up," Nell said to her—"dat won't hep him none."

"I think you ought to take him back into the cabin now," Donaldson said to them—"and then start preparing your food."

"Marster," said Nell now—with great tact, caution, much fearful hesitation—"was dem two gent'men on de horses lookin' for us?"

"No," Donaldson said. "They were here to see me. Now come and I'll issue you some provisions so that you can cook and eat. But first take Rodney into one of the cabins."

Acts and Horatio lifted Rodney gently, took him back into the largest cabin, and laid him in a corner. Rodney's eyes were closed, his breathing slow, quiet. The others, except Herta and ill little Susan, followed Donaldson to the house for the provisions. Herta took Susan by the hand and moped back to the cabin, where she began a vigil over Rodney.

It was fully two hours before they had cooked the food and eaten, by which time they were so fatigued, exhausted from their long journey and broken rest, that some fell asleep in the cabins while still eating. The rain had for a time dispelled the intense heat, but by late afternoon the skies had cleared and brought back the hot sun which, added to the humidity, made them sweat as they lay sprawled sleeping fitfully on the cabin floor—the women and Rodney in the largest cabin, the men in the one adjacent. It was only at the end of the day when the sun had gone down and twilight descended that they slept peacefully, deeply, in a kind of secure, slumberous repose. Rodney still lay on his back unconscious in the corner and, though they had tried to spoon food through his lips, he had been unaware and could not swallow. Herta nonetheless had sat over him for hours and was the last among them to fall asleep.

Herta was also now the first to awake. It was almost midnight, though she had no idea of time. It was in the dark of the moon and there was a pervading, perfect stillness over the land save for the occasional snoring of one of the women and the universal sea-sound of the chirping crickets. She got up, groped to the open cabin door, and stood peering out into the night of drifting fireflies, while the women slept all about her and the men occupied the cabin adjacent. Though she could see nothing in the darkness except the fireflies, she could sense, reconstruct, the presence of everything as if there had been light—the house, the yards, front and back, the long, tree-lined lane leading from the highroad, the sideless pump-house, the stables and cabins, even the rabbit. The night atmosphere was humid and the heavy, sweet smell of magnolias and honeysuckle saturated the air as she listened to the crickets and wondered what tomorrow, and the next day, and the day after that, might bring. Though she had known only slavery, on a great mid-Georgia plantation, she could still not understand the rigors, hardships, the indiscriminate cruelties, of her four years of "freedom." Slavery, true, had been harsh, brutal, but also sure and predictable—systematic. She had been whipped until, on two occasions, her flayed back had bled with her dark, oozing blood, but she had learned. Knowledge and experience—canniness—had enabled her to avoid a third beating, and all the potential beatings after that; she had discovered how to cope. But "freedom" was a very different matter—unique and dangerous, a vast unknown, with no guidelines, where also hunger and lack of shelter were the order of the day and the blight, the curse, of uncertainty dogged one's footsteps night and day. She lived a life of turmoil and fear now, of pain and heartbreak, to say nothing of constant illness brought on by the weeks, the months, of privation and want. Presently she had little will, desire, to continue this life of the hungry, wretched nomad, especially since the cold-blooded murder of her son, who had only insisted to his murderers that now he was free. So now she spent most of her time in a state of complete fantasy, of visions, morose reveries, as if by design shunning all contact with hard reality.

During slavery she and her man had been field hands in their youth, but at nineteen she was sent up to work in the big house, to do the heavy kitchen work and help the two cooks. But she had been miserable there. She so missed being with Elias everyday that she deliberately performed so blunderingly, ineptly, that after three months she was sent back to the fields. There, soon pregnant by Elias, she went through the perfunctory "marriage" ceremony with him which the slave drivers and overseers called "jumping over the broom"—to which makeshift union was born a first child, a boy, Luff. Three children followed, though the middle two were eventually sold and the last child died. But Luff lived to say, at twenty— and only day before yesterday—that he was a "free nigger," and had died for it. Her eyes were dry in the dark, her face hard; she had cried all it was possible to cry. There was left only her numbed, perplexed, questioning mind; and her hysteria. But the chief and tragic element in her present outlook was its confining narrowness, and the unrealism, naivete, of it; this figurative wearing of blinders. She knew so little about anything, conceptualized nothing. The world was immediate, the domain of primary sensations; tactile before intruding. She was merely assured by her mother that she had been born; and there on the plantation, near Macon, in Crawford County, Georgia; but that her father was soon thereafter sold with a shipment of brawny black men being sent to still harder labor in Louisiana. This was all, however, of little consequence to the child Herta. She was interested only in her mother who fed her. But soon came another early and powerful awareness. It was the immense and fateful difference one's physical appearance made in this life on the plantation. The great gangs of workers, men, women, and children, marching to the fields each morning at sun-up were somehow always black, ragged, and shambling; and, ironically, sometimes singing. And they were invariably cowed, dominated, by men whose appearance was very different from theirs, from hers. Their skins were pale white or rough rutted red, their hair stringy, their voices of command shrill and loud. Some carried guns. Others whips, which they used on slightest provocation. These were her large and omnipresent impressions as she stood bewilderedly on the threshold of her life and as she emerged into it. This was, for all she knew, the way things had been immemorially. It was ordained and, according to all she had seen, fitting, even just. Into adolescence and beyond, this was her world; it had probably always been this way, would always be, she believed; there was no point in quarreling with it; rather, one had best spend one's time in getting something to eat, in staying clear of whippings, and in doing as little work as one could get away with. There was no history, no experience; no standards by which to intellectualize such abstract concepts as freedom, morality, justice; it would have been ludicrous. She could not have, had her life depended upon it, defined slavery; would not even have recognized a slave, herself included. They were merely all creatures put here for some purpose not entirely clear to her and were to live out their allotted time and then, as did everyone, die—vanish, rot in the ground. There was only the main fact, the necessity, at hand—existing.

Ill little Susan, lying near the door on the hard-packed dirt floor of the cabin, now stirred and began to moan. Soon she was coughing her deep, hollow cough again—she had slept far too many nights in the chill dewy grass of roadside pastures, and, weakened now, racked with a burning fever, was on the verge of consumptive pneumonia. Malnutrition, moreover, had distended her abdomen as if at eleven she were eight months pregnant. She moaned again now and turned and lay on her side, her eyes staring death-like into the pitch darkness. Herta, her own eyes open for hours and accustomed to the darkness, went over, bent down to the child, and stroked her brow. "Now, now, baby," she gently whispered, "go back to sleep. You need yo rest."

"Auntie, water! . . . I wants water! I'se thirsty—my throat is parched, Auntie."—the child's voice raspy, fretting, desperate.

"Baby, ain't no water in here," said Herta. "We had de water when we et—ain't none now."

"Water, water, Auntie! . . ."

Finally Herta, stepping over the sleeping women, groped to a crude shelf low on the wall and found a crock they had earlier used in the cooking. Two women lay snoring at her feet. She took the crock and went outside to the pumphouse. The night was silent, black, and starry now; she had never experienced such perfect nocturnal stillness. She stood and listened, as if expecting to hear some inconsequential, random noise break the ominous silence. She heard nothing. Yet she was somehow aware of her tense, pounding heart. She still stood there listening, but at last pumped water into the crock, returned to the cabin, and gave the feverish child water. Strangely now, though, the two women had stopped snoring. Only the quiet, regular breathing of the other sleepers could be heard. Herta sat down on the cabin floor now, preparatory to lying down to try to sleep again. How much longer would they be permitted to stay here? she wondered. And then how many days of walking and starving would it take if they were lucky enough to reach Savannah? What would happen there? She found herself not caring. Luff was to have been arriving there with her, for they had begun the journey together. She could only think now of the shallow grave where he was buried, after hurried, impromptu, fearful, graveside rites performed by an itinerant black preacher-laborer. She had been wild with grief. But now she felt only numbness, torpor, a vast uncaring stoniness of the heart. She lay down now, resting her head on her arm, and waited for sleep once more, all the while half listening to the mechanistic whirr of the crickets as the night silences engulfed them all and kept mute their fate.

There came then another, sudden, sound—a light swift swooshing through the doorway; then past her, over to, it seemed, the cabin wall. It was followed almost in the same instant by a second sound—yet the same. She sat up, frozen with fear. She heard no further movement for a moment. Then came a slight restless stir as if that of some small animal or animals over against the wall. She wondered if the cabin had been invaded by some creatures of the fields or forest. She lay perfectly still, until she heard the slight stir again and then a faint, timid whining. She got up at once and lit the candle Donaldson's wife had given them with a few matches. Then she saw. Over against the wall squatted the rabbit. But it was accompanied now by a black and tan hound pup not more than three months old. Both rabbit and dog seemed uneasy, cowering. But Herta was relieved. She held the candle far forward and studied the two creatures. They were clearly pets of the household, she could see, and were well acquainted with each other. But they still sat strangely cowering in the corner near unconscious Rodney, the pup occasionally whining again.

It had awakened Nell. "What you lit de candle for?" she said to Herta.

"Dat rabbit just run in here," said Herta—"a puppy wid him."

"Whut dey doing running in here?"

"How's I to know dat?—go back to sleep." Herta blew out the candle. Everything was quiet. Heaving a sigh, she lay back down, rested her head on her arm again, and before long, sleep, labored, fitful sleep, came at last. Now in the black stillness of the night there was only the vague chanting of crickets and the occasional drifting fireflies.

The stillness seemed to intensify with the slow passage of time, or it was as if the crickets' noise had gradually abated as Herta slept. The pup continued to whine but so softly Herta was not awakened—the whines, however, had taken on a low, piteous desperation now, as if the pup shivered and shuddered as it uttered them. At last Herta sluggishly stirred. Had it been the dog or the outside bodeful silence? But she did not soon move again; she lay exactly as she had lain before; she had never experienced such black unearthly stillness; even the pup's whines were infrequent now. Then she heard the sound. It was far distant and seemed in her half somnolence a light clatter or rattle—as if the faint, far-off warning of a deadly rattlesnake. She lay very still—curious, half-uneasy, questioning. The strange, cadenced clacking continued; soon her limbs froze with fear. Slowly, though still far away, the rattle increased now and the cowering pup whined again in the darkness as if trembling with its same old fear. Suddenly then Herta sat up; glimmers of recognition came in on her—the sound. She knew it at last. It was the clatter of distant horses' hooves— many, purposeful, resolute, galloping on the hard highroad— slowly, but inexorably, approaching.

Her heart pounding, she stood up now, as if the better to listen. But the horses seemed all of a mile away and at once she seized on the hope she had heard amiss—that the sound was receding, not growing. Soon, however, she knew it was gaining—the riders, whoever they were, were coming this way. It was only a matter now of how long. For a moment it appeared she would panic. Then suddenly Nell stood beside her. She had heard too. Yet neither spoke at first. But the still-distant intonation of the hooves on the pike was not that much louder, so far; there was no dramatic, no imminent, heightening of the alarm; yet the tension mounted—it was the sound's steady and unrelenting portentousness, the feeling, conviction, it was not ordained to go away, that it must soon engulf them. Herta stood trembling now. "Is our time come, Lawd?" she whispered, as if unmindful of Nell beside her. "Protec' us, Lawd ... hep us! You hab told us you would not f'sake us for long." She knelt on the cabin's dirt floor now and prayed in desperate whispers.

In the darkness Nell, herself with a trembling hand, reached down and touched Herta's shoulder. "De Lawd's gonter look after us, see ef He don't," she said, trying to reassure Herta as well as herself. "We don't know who dem horses is, comin'—soon dey'll ride on by, I bet, and den we kin sleep some more. Mark my words."

But Acts stood in their door now. He too had been awakened by the epochal sounds. He did not enter at first but stood on the threshold; then, shifting, indecisive, he turned and faced outside again, lifting his face to the night, eyes in the darkness glowing, chin jutted, ears acute, straining, listening. From experience, habit of peril, his heart raced and his breath came fast—the sound in his ears of the echoing hooves was unceasing. He went into the women now and was recognized by his voice. "Don't know who dat is comin'," he said, "but we best wake everybody and go to de woods till we find out—might be Klan nightriders."

"I knows dat—oh, Jesus," said Nell.

"Den our time is done come, ain't it?" Herta whispered aimlessly, more to herself than to them. "I'se been ready, I has."

"But we got de sick dere!" said Nell, anguished, to Acts—"Rodney and little Susan. We cain't run off and leave dem behind."

"I kin carry de child myself," Acts said. "De ole man, he nigh 'bout finished anyhow—we hab to leave him. Wake 'em all up in here while I go rouse de men. Hurry." He ran out toward the men's cabin.

At once Nell began running about among the sleeping women, prodding, shaking, pulling them; calling out: "Wake up, you'all!—somebody up de road! . . . Hear de horses comin'? We got to git outa here fast—might be nightriders. Ef dey is, look out—ef dey don't shoot us, dey'll whip us to death. We gonter cross dat field back dere and git into de woods. Listen! . . . hear all dem horses comin'?"

The women, startled, awakened so suddenly, hardly knew where they were. They jumped up, and, now hearing the dogged horses' hooves, began scurrying about in the dark for their few paltry belongings. In the confusion someone stepped on the pup, which let out a piteous yelp and ran out the door, followed by the rabbit. By now the men were coming out of the adjacent cabin, and, herding the emerging women in their midst, headed, running, for the

401

open field behind the cabins leading to the woods. Acts carried the whimpering sick child Susan in his arms, and Nell and Herta ran alongside him. The horsemen were noticeably closer now—less than quarter of a mile—and what had earlier seemed by the sound to be their galloping had turned out, at least presently, to be an inexorable trot. Yet there were clearly more of them now than had originally been thought—had the war still been on they would have been guessed to be squads of cavalry. Lying prostrate in the women's cabin, old Rodney, deserted, left all alone, opened his eyes to the darkness and, his mind hovering between unconsciousness and consciousness, breathed a fitful sigh. For the first time then he heard the horses coming. Suddenly he was conscious, aware, but could not move or speak. He sensed the strange emptiness in the cabin and with a sinking heart wondered where everyone had gone. Where had he been?—what had happened to him? He tried to speak, call out, but was slaveringly mute. The clattering hooves were closer.

Harrison Donaldson's wife had awakened him only moments before. The plantation house was quiet, dark, as they lay in the bed listening now—to the noise of the cantering horsemen approaching. "Who in Heaven's name is it?" she said—"There're so many of them...."

Donaldson had sat up. The riders were close now. But he was interested in detecting whether they would finally pass his place; ride on by. Yet in his heart he sensed, almost knew, they would not. "Most likely the Klan is out tonight," he said simply, wishing not to further frighten his wife, yet to prepare her.

"Oh!... the darkies!" she said—"They're after the darkies back there! That's it—I know it! Those two canvassers! ... those skunks! They went back and told about the darkies!" She sprang out of bed and went to peer out the front window of their second-floor bedroom. "You shouldn't have let the darkies stop here—it's only worse for them. And maybe for us too." Donaldson knew she spoke the truth. He jumped up and began to dress. "Ah, there they are," his wife said, still at the front window. "Some have lanterns—yes, I see their white robes! Oh, Harrison, they're coming up the lane!"

There were thirty or more of them—white-robed, hooded, Knights of the Ku Klux Klan. They were, in fact, turning off the highroad now and approaching up Donaldson's lane. Soon a few had stationed themselves in the front yard but most of them cantered around to the back where the cabins were. There was much talking among them but no loudness. In front of the cabins now, many dismounted, a few with lanterns, and began to search the cabins. They found no one but Rodney, whom they roughly carried out and threw on the ground near the pump house where, now groaning, he had lain before. "He's the only one what was in there," said one of them, pointing to limp Rodney—"Looks lak he's 'bout dead already."

"They heard us comin'," said another, the giant leader—Hedgepath, the Kleagle—"and lit out to the woods back there. They ain't fur—we'll find 'em. Tell Curtis and them around at the front to rouse that nigger-lovin' Donaldson and bring his hide out here to stand trial. Come on, you'all, let's find them niggers. They ain't fur—cain't be." Most of them remounted now and rode off behind the Kleagle toward the woods.

Acts and the others were indeed not far. There had not been time. In their harried flight they had only been able to cross a corner of the field and reach the sparse strip of woodland flanking a former expanse of cotton ground. But, fearful, they had not stopped. Yet when they heard the Klansmen's horses leave the cabins to press the pursuit, they considered for a moment hiding in the underbrush at the edge of the woods, but Acts and two others of the men warned against stopping. "Come on!" cried Acts, panting from the exertion of carrying the sick child—"We got to git deeper in dese woods. Dey maybe cain't find us in de dark then lessen dey got hounds. Ain't no time to stop now!" The feverish child was still coughing and whimpering, her eyes half closed as she moaned and clung with both arms around Acts' neck. He tried to quiet her to no avail. They all pressed on in the darkness through the trees and undergrowth, the sound of the pursuing nightriders ever in their ears. Once Acts turned and beyond the foliage saw the light from the oncoming lanterns. "We got to keep goin'," he said—"else dey'll catch us sho." Two of the black men had no shoes and in the mad rush had cut their feet on jagged rocks, roots, and briars. One of them, Dandy by name, a tall, timid youth of nineteen, his hair matted and body reeking stench, already limped badly. Acts recognized the danger of having a straggler in their midst but knew no remedy for it. The women, however, except for the child, seemed, of all, the least hindrance to the flight. Led by Nell, they kept up with big Jasper—he had come with her and some of the others all the way from Alabama—who led the way through the woods. But Dandy, his bare feet a bloody mass, had become panicky. "Oh, Lawd, my feets're all chopped up!" he cried, grimacing in pain. "Deys bleedin' bad—cain't go much fudder!" Acts turned and remonstrated with him—"You stop and dey got you," he said. "You wants to git shot? Dem nightriders'll shoot you, boy—after dey done half beat you to death." But as the others ran on, Dandy stopped, sat down, and began nursing his feet. The others, not yet missing him, pressed on, for the pursuers were in the woods now and had fanned out over a large area, a few with lanterns, but most without. Their talk, communication, had at last grown loud as they called out to maintain contact and to keep from shooting each other. Dandy, hearing their onrush toward him, crawled behind the base of a huge oak tree, the only object of refuge he could make out in the darkness, and then all but collapsed. He began a fervent praying—"Oh, Lawd, don't let 'em ketch me and kill me!—please, Lawd!" Then, almost hysterical, he buried his face in the earth and grass at the base of the tree—just as the source of the precipitant noise he had heard, a dismounted Klansman leading his horse with the reins in one hand and a lantern in the other, broke through a clump of wild berry bushes and confronted him. Dandy had looked up and they both saw each other in the same instant. The now unmasked Klansman, the knight, his white robe reaching nearly to the ground, was so startled at the sight of Dandy he almost upset the lantern in setting it down with the same motion with which he drew his huge pistol. He called out loudly to the others: "*Hey!*—you'all! Here's one of 'em! We've found 'em, brother knights! Come!—come look!" He turned to trembling Dandy—"Stand up, nigger! Git up from there! . . . and heist your hands in the air high as you kin get 'em—or I'll blow yo burry head off!" Quaking Dandy shot up both hands high over his head as he scrambled up and faced the knight. "Don' shoot me, Marster!" he pleaded—"I ain't done nothin'! *Please* sar, don' shoot me!" But soon they were surrounded by other knights, armed, robed, some also no longer hooded, others still mounted, but most now on foot. Lanterns jostling, they dragged whimpering Dandy into a nearby clearing where the giant leader of the knights, Kleagle Hedgepath, booted, spurred, a sharpshooter's rifle in his hand, strode out of a thicket and stood over the kneeling, cringing boy for a moment, looking down at him and curling his lip in detestation. "Nigger, where'd the rest of 'em go?" he demanded and put the muzzle of the rifle to Dandy's head—"Ah'm fixin' to pull this trigger! . . . which way did they go?" He jabbed the rifle barrel into Dandy's ear—"Ah'm givin' you two seconds!" But Dandy was already stammering and pointing in the general direction in which the other blacks had fled. Hedgepath turned vehemently to the others. "Let's go round 'em up, brother knights!" he yelled— "Somebody stay back and hold this one till we see ef he's tellin' the truth. You guard him, Sims," he said to a short, stout knight standing behind him—"Ef he tries to break and run, kill him!" With that they hurried off in search of the others.

The Klansmen, six of them, who had been left back at the Donaldson house had quickly surrounded the place and, by their thundering knocks on the doors and their yelled imprecations at Donaldson, summoned him to appear outside. When still half-dressed, he did appear in the back door with a lantern in his hand, they saw he also carried a pistol in the other hand. Curtis, a hooded knight from an adjoining county whom Hedgepath had left in charge, did the talking—"Drop that gun, Donaldson, and come out here! Yere surrounded an' outnumbered—you'll only git yosef killed and yo house burnt down around yo family's heads. Turn nat pistol around and give hit to us." Donaldson, tall, ruddy, glowering, his shock of white hair bristling, the ironic features stern and dyspeptic, finally complied, coming down the back steps and into their midst. Curtis took the pistol and threw it thirty feet into the high grass, then turned angrily on him—"Where's them niggers you been harborin' around here?" he said.

Donaldson's eyes narrowed. "Who are you?" he said—"I know what you are, but *who* are you?"

Curtis ignored the question. "We're goin' to make an example outa you, Donaldson," he said, and turned to the others. "Tie him up, and see ef he'll answer some of our questions without bein' so high an' mighty."

A tall, lean, mountaineer Klansman, a knight named Tullenbeck, stepped up with a long squirrel rifle in his hand. But instead of

Donaldson, he confronted Curtis—directly. "Cut out all yo God-damn ceremonies," he said to his fellow-knight. "Niggers turned loose on us by Yankees, carpetbaggers, and scalawags too, and overrunin' everythang—sassin' us with their damn freedom talk, stealin' our hogs and chickens, molestin' our women, jes plain run-nin' amuck, and you talkin' about questionin' this scalawag here, who's been harborin' a drove of 'em right here on his place, talkin' about questionin' him about where these niggers have gone to now. Hell, they run back in them woods there when they heerd us comin', that's whut they done—you don't have to ask him that. Then when he gives you his lip, you tell him you goin' to make an example outa him. Well, whut kinda example, is what I want to know. Better come up with somethin' good—else I'm puttin' a piece of lead 'tween his eyes; that'll be an example." He brought the rifle waist-high.

"Now, wait a minute," Curtis, overcoming his astonishment, said to the mountaineer. "Ah don't give the orders here, but neither do you. You don't do nothin' till you git orders from the Kleagle—you made an oath when you jined up. We'll hold this scalawag till the Kleagle and the others come back."

"I'm no scalawag," Donaldson said hotly—"I'm a Democrat like the rest of you."

Curtis turned on him with vehemence—"Then whut you doin' harborin' all these niggers the Yankee Republicans turned loose on us?"

"They're trying to get to Savannah where they can get food and shelter and a doctor—there're some sick among them. They'd had no food and we fed them—and let them stay the night in the cabins back there. They're there now."

"No they ain't," Curtis said. "They all run, except one. He's layin' right there, dead—or damn near." He pointed to old Rodney lying on the ground.

"He *is* dead!" said the mountaineer Tullenbeck, raising his rifle hip-high. He took two steps to where mute, quivering Rodney lay with his eyes still open and fired a bullet point-blank into his brain. He wheeled then and trained the gun on Donaldson. But stunned Curtis and the others at last leapt forward, wrestled the gun away, and subdued him.

"*You fool! . . . you lunatic!*" yelled Curtis—"You'll answer to the Kleagle for this!"

406

"He would'a killed the nigger 'fore I done it," Tullenbeck said, his tall, skinny frame leaning forward malignantly in Curtis' direction. "See whut he does when he brings them niggers back—ef there'll be any of 'em still alive."

Donaldson turned to them now, his eyes gleaming with horror. "*Who are you?*" he cried. "What do you mean to gain by murder? —riding in the night, with your faces covered. You're the Klan, I know—but who really are you?"

The disarmed mountaineer broke loose and rushed him, jerked off his white hood, and, livid with rage, thrust his bared, hawklike face in Donaldson's. "Take a look, you traitor!" he said. "Ah'm a Southern patriot!—Ah fit, and was wounded four times, in the war! *That's* who Ah am!" With that he swung his fist and knocked Donaldson down.

There was a scream from the back door of the house and Donaldson's wife, still in her night clothes with a wrapper on, her grey-streaked hair affright, came running. Donaldson saw her as he scrambled weakly to his feet. "Go back, go back, Martha!" he cried out, trying now to run to meet her, head her off. "I'm all right!" he said—"Go back in the house! Do as I say! . . ."

"*You vermin!*" she screamed at the white-robed knights. "You murderers! Leave him alone!—I'll go back and get a gun and kill you all! Leave him alone, I say!" She ran to Donaldson's side.

But Curtis now yelled to the knights—"Take 'em both, brothers, and tie 'em up! They'll stand trial when the Kleagle comes back! We'll go search the house now—might be niggers or scalawags in there! Tie 'em up first—they'll find out pretty soon we mean business!"

Donaldson and his wife were overpowered and, their wrists bound behind their backs, were taken back into the house.

Meanwhile, deep in the woods, Acts and the other fugitive blacks had seen their pursuers' lanterns, had heard the loud voices and all the threshing forward through the trees and underbrush toward them, and become fearful the noise of their own flight would give focus to the hunt and betray them. He and big Jasper, with whom he had now taken turns carrying the sick child, called a short halt to let the exhausted ones rest a moment and to parley among themselves about what they should do. Nell insisted they should press on, and two of the men agreed. But they were the stronger ones and soon found themselves in the minority. The others spoke of the noise of their continued running; they wished to find, as best they could, some natural hiding place in the woods where they could stop, remain perfectly quiet, and hope they would not be discovered. They could not know that the boy Dandy, apprehended and threatened with death, had given his captors directional information which had greatly, disastrously for the fugitives, narrowed the pursuers' area of quest. Otherwise Acts and the others might well have chosen flight in a radically different direction. But now they had decided to take their chances and stop soon and hide.

Less than five minutes later they found a thick, overgrown area of tall, parched weeds and murdock, situated on a slight upward incline into a rough corridor of trees where also had fallen dead pine limbs and trunks that made any approach both tedious and taxing. There in the high weeds they all huddled into the smallest group possible and, exhausted, minds drugged by constant fear, they sat awaiting whatever was to come. The night was clear and still, the moon down, though galaxies of stars flecked the immense black sky; a damp chill from the dew had also fallen upon everything as insects whirred and fireflies drifted. The fugitives were soon very cold as they all sat bunched together even closer now, cringing too each time they heard the not-so-distant voices of their pursuers. Herta, her mind completely isolated now from the others', had already begun to whisper and mutter again, to ask herself when and how it would ever all end, as she thought of her dead son Luff and ceased to care about the present; she wished in her heart to have it all over with, even if they were to be in the end found by the nightriders. Nell reached and put a hand on her arm and tried to warn, then mollify, her; yet Herta only stared fixedly into the blackness.

She was ripe with fantasies. She saw the Klansmen, the knights, as grinning, evil ghosts and had a vision of them gathered around Luff's blood-spattered and disfigured body—though his killers had not worn robes. The Klan's white habiliments, however, seemed to give the image of her son's immolation a wild, ethereal aspect; the evildoers were called knights and truly deserved, at close range, to be examined—their purposes, motivation, the causes leading to them as a phenomenon, their bloodthirst. Why did the knights ride at night?—yes, they must be studied; they had ridden through her little west-Georgia town six months ago, spreading fear and havoc, superstition, maiming both blacks and suspect whites, whipping black women, shooting black men. A perfect terror. Why? They, the black victims, had all then taken to the road, where they saw hundreds upon hundreds of others similarly afflicted, joining some, eschewing others; but ever since, staying on the road—as wayfarers, mendicants. Again why? The question had never left her. She felt now it would never be answered; she had given up—her feelings were those of complete resignation. She was tired now and only wanted it all to end. She could not, however, conceive of death. She had seen much of it, both in slavery and now, yet she could not envision herself dead, and did not really want to die; she merely longed for a peace she knew in her heart this world, her world, did not and would not afford her and her kind. How, though, could things be changed short of death? In her fantasy-filled dementia she descried a need for crisis, a new departure, a confrontation—one which would defy, stare death down. Passive confrontation, yes—it had its virtues. Those around her, she felt, lacked purpose, direction—nourished hope when none was justified; thought in terms only of two mutually-exclusive alternatives: continue to run, or stop and hide. She conceived of this as too simple; it flew in the face of realities; and did not take into account the thinking, the ways, of the knights. It was ineffective. To the knights, however, indifferent forthrightness could be a stranger, but to herself a weapon of immense effect. Strangely, her weariness, fatigue, began to leave her; her body had become a network of taut energies; her bizarre mind a melange of psychopathy and whim conjuring up numberless possibilities, then certainties, of promise and deliverance—and all the while laying tragedy's groundwork.

Soon the noise of the pursuing knights came through without let-up, though the fugitives could not help trembling even more on considering what it would be like had the Klan had bloodhounds. However, the distance between pursuers and pursued had alarmingly diminished and the latter understood it was they themselves who would soon be tested. Suddenly the ill child, Susan, began to whimper and then cry again. "Stop dat!" whispered Nell fiercely. "We got to be *still!*—don't you hear 'em comin'?" But Susan continued making the same frantic sounds as before, until Acts, who had carried her much of the way from the cabins, put his arm around her in an attempt to soothe the pain in her distended belly and her fears. Once more everything became very quiet—even their labored, nervous breathing could scarcely be heard. Acts sat gazing up at the stars, wondering where his half-brother Aaron was at that moment. Was he alive? Was he unhurt?—or was he lying along some lonely roadside bleeding to death? He prayed he was alive and well. Yet would they ever be reunited? The sky, tonight a great, black, jeweled dome of heaven, gave him such a conception of the vastness of life and of the world, of their impersonal, unfeeling, immensity, that he despaired of ever, among the countless people on earth, seeing Aaron again. As a human, a man, a black man, he felt himself smaller than an ant or bug. He was nothing, absolutely nothing, he was convinced—a creature despised by the totality of his surroundings and hunted down like a rat. Why was this? he kept asking himself. In his fruitless speculations he finally laid it to his birth; something at that time, or before, had gone wrong; it had in fact gone so wrong he did not care to know what it was—was in mortal fear of this fated knowledge. It must indeed, however, have been something earth-shaking. Some great, primordial affliction had been ordained against all those now cowering in these bleak, stygian, and lonely south-Georgia woods where it was not known whether the next quarter hour would or would not bring death. The world was so boundless, immeasurable, held so many matters in the dark realm of the unknown, that he felt he knew no more about its workings, its mysteries, than a squirrel in a pine tree. He only knew it held much unhappiness, at times terror, and that, for some kinds of people, it always had—that it was dangerous for some merely to exist in it.

Now he heard and felt Herta rummaging in the canvas bag she carried with her containing her few wretched earthly belongings, as she muttered and mumbled to herself all the while. Soon she took something out of the bag; a garment, very light in color, a covering of some kind; or a sheet?—he could not make out. She folded it in her lap now and went on with her low, ruminative maunderings. The threshing, stumbling, pursuit noises were ever closer now—the knights could be heard calling out to one another, their tones, however, strangely free of vengeance and invective; no cant, death avowals, no blasphemy of their quarry; yet there was a dogged, fateful, confident purpose in the air not unsensed by the motley band of fugitives—all as Herta sat fingering the folded white raiment in her lap and whispering her fantastic night musings.

Another lantern came in sight—this time close; a bare thirty yards away. A thorn bush then collapsed under a knight's heavy-breathing, onward tread toward the huddled ones as a shower of fireflies went up in a wild gesture of escape. "Keep on goin' *in*, Ogden," someone in command behind him (it was Hedgepath) said —"I bet the niggers're settin' right in here somewheres lak a covey of quail 'bout to git up. Keep goin' in, boys—yere liable to stumble on 'em any minute now and git the livin' daylights sceered outa you!" There were a few laughs.

The blacks were hushed, quiet, their hearts pulsing in fear. Herta stirred once, as if she would get up, but then desisted and became quiescent again—still mumbling. They sat thus for a few moments. Suddenly then she arose, held out the folded white sheet from herself with the tips of her fingers, and let it unfold to the ground. She tossed it over her head then and draped it down and around her body to her ankles. Big Jasper, sitting closest to her, staring at her, scrambled up in astonishment and shock. She had taken two steps in the enemy's direction when he dove for her over one of the other women, but missed—just as she slipped away to emerge from their hiding place and make her way down through the brambles toward the now assembling white-clad knights. "Oh, Lawd!" whispered Jasper in terror—"she done gone crazy!" "Hep us, Jesus!" said Nell—"Oh, hep us!" Acts was on his feet now. "We got to leave!" he said—"run! Come on!" He picked up Susan and made off through the bushes to the rear. The others had scrambled up and in wild panic and disarray now ran to follow. But Acts, the child of eleven in his arms, had struck out in a new, different, direction from the others and was soon swallowed up in the night.

The knights were close now. They had moreover been rejoined by some who had been beating the bushes off to the left, to form a pursuit group with new, clearer, more focused directions—the boy Dandy had pointed out the way well. Some were still mounted, their white hoods pulled off, others were leading their horses through the trees, high grass, and thickets only fifteen yards now from where the fugitives had scattered. Yet the moment somehow seemed precarious for the knights; it was like the stars in the heavens had receded, grown pale, shed their romantic luster as the

411

pursuers' bumbling, unwitting, congregating took place. Once they had gathered, they seemed strangely helpless, immobile. Their few lanterns glowing, they stood in a cluster and conversed, though it was like a powerlessness, paralysis, had overtaken them. "We're right on the line of direction the scared nigger boy pointed out to us," said Kleagle Hedgepath. "We got to fan out agin now and go forward abreast—that way we cain't miss 'em." They had all agreed and were about to disperse—when by the weak lantern light they saw another sheeted figure approaching through the thicket out of the eerie-yellow darkness.

It was coming from where they had just meant to go—straight ahead of them; coming down through the tangled high weeds and briars from a general area into which they could not yet see. "Who's that?—Is that Joe?" said Hedgepath to the others, holding up his lantern. The white-cowled, white-robed figure approaching walked with an unhurried and indifferent gait. At last one of the men brought up his rifle. "Put that damn gun down!" said the Kleagle—"It's Joe . . . *ain't it?* . . . ." The last words were riddled with doubt.

When Herta had approached within twenty-five feet of them she uncovered her head for all to see. An inaudible gasp went up. The same man raised his rifle again. "Hold it!" Hedgepath said to him —"Whut in God's name is this?"

Herta had reached them now. She confronted them. "Marsters, I hab come to jine you," she said, in the same indifferent, composed way.

"You nigger bitch!" exploded Hedgepath—"Where're them other niggers?—show us! Grab her, brothers—she'll talk when we put the whip to her. You black sow, where'd your other niggers go?"

"Deys gone, I reckon, Marster. I come to jine *you*—see my white robe?" She displayed the sheet by wrapping it still tighter around her, as if she were frigid cold.

"Who's got the whip?" said the Kleagle—"Grab her."

Three knights seized her and stripped the sheet from her. She seemed unmindful—too eager now to speak: "I hab come in my white robe—which I'll sho nuff wear in heb'um soon—to jine you and git Luff back. Luff, he my boy, Marster—he already jined you. Show me to Luff—he got a white robe too now, praise be to Jesus!" At that moment someone, not the Kleagle, swung the whip. Herta caught its full force on her back and shoulders and was knocked to her knees. She looked, stared, up at Hedgepath, though, and was struck a second time, yet kept her reproachful eyes steadfastly on him. "Marster, dem streets paved wid gold where Luff is —take me dere." She was struck again, on the face and neck, bringing the blood, and though she tried to get to her feet was struck three times more.

"She's out of her head," said Hedgepath. "Where're them other niggers?" he thundered at her—"Take us to 'em or you'll die under that lash! . . . Where ere they?"

"Deys gone, Marster—I put on my robe and come here to jine you where Luff is, ain't he?"

She was still on the ground when she was struck yet again, her face now a mass of blood. "Hold off," said Hedgepath at last. "I thinks she's crazy—sho talks lak it. We won't git nothin' outa her —she's looney as a bedbug. Let's swarm up that incline of weeds there and round up the rest of these niggers and take 'em back to the house. That nigger-lover Donaldson will answer fur this—he'll git some of the same whip, all right. I ain't none surprised 'bout him—when them two boys that wuz canvassin' for the election come back to town last evenin' and said he was harborin' all these niggers here, I wusn't one whit surprised; he's that kind, yet claims to be a true Southerner and a Democrat. We'll see, then, how *he* takes the whip. Let's go now and git the rest of these niggers and git back and have the trial—daylight'll be here 'fore you know it. Come on." He pointed at Herta on the ground. "Somebody take charge of this old bitch till we git back. Come on, now, let's go!"

Hedgepath's posse of Klansmen, however, did not arrive back at the Donaldson house until almost 3:00 A.M. But what the Donaldsons and their six captors saw returning was a grisly sight. Blood, a welter of blood—but none of it the knights'—had been shed in order to capture the few blacks now seen returning in the Kleagle's custody, and, except for one child, most of them were women. Only two black men returned—the timid boy Dandy and the half-blind Canny. It had been a cold-blooded and ruthless encounter—the embattled blacks in the thicket, though unarmed and helpless, had fought back with tree limbs and fists when surrounded, and Nell, Jasper, and Horatio had been bloodily massacred. Acts, however, and the other, the ill, child with him, were never again seen by them after the wild break for cover when

413

Herta, wrapped in the white sheet, had wandered off to join the Klan. Now as the beaten and bleeding captives, escorted by the mounted horde of knights, all of them hooded now, entered the Donaldson backyard again, there was much wailing and crying among the women and much reviling of them by the Klan. In the low yellow light of the lanterns the captives were made to sit on the ground surrounded by the standing, hooded knights to await whatever further punishment was to be meted out by the drumhead court about to be convened. All the while the women, trembling, in shock from their ordeal, were wailing now more than ever—except for Herta, who, though her face was a mass of dried gore from her whippings, sat mute, detached, out of contact with surroundings, all as the horses stamped impatiently and swished their tails in defense against the night insects.

When the Kleagle, his white robe dirty, bloody, as he dismounted, saw old Rodney's body lying near the pump house, he looked directly at the Klansman mountaineer Tullenbeck. "It's the hardest dern thing in the world," he said to him, "fur you to follow orders, ain't it? That trigger finger of yours is gonna git you in a heap of trouble one of these days—when you ain't dealin' with niggers. Now, go bring that Donaldson out here to stand trial." The stringy, saturnine mountaineer went off.

After earlier tying up Donaldson and his wife, their captors had taken them back into the house to stand guard over them, as the two grandchildren, now awakened by all the commotion, ran in and out of the room wildly crying out in fear and confusion—they had never seen the Klan and its bizarre white robes before. Now, on the Kleagle's orders, man and wife, their wrists still bound behind them, were brought back out through the back door and made to face the assemblage of black captives and Klansmen. The wild-haired wife Martha came out in an incoherent rage, tossing her head about, cursing and reviling the knights, and professing undying allegiance to the "true South" and against such "vermin" as her captors hiding their faces under hoods. The hooded Kleagle, encountering her for the first time, seemed for the moment unprepared, taken aback, indecisive. At last he went up to Donaldson. "She's your wife," he said. "Handle her or I'll sho shut her up myself."

Donaldson's eyes flashed in outrage. "Who are you?" he said, his tone contemptuous, insolent. "Identify yourself—even one of your men here had the conviction to take off his hood and show his face. Why don't you? Who are you?—do I know you?"

"You're agonna know me in a minute!" Hedgepath shouted— "You'll never forgit me!" He turned to a Klansman—"Prefer the charges, brother Advocate."

"Kleagle," said the little man, stepping forward, his soiled hood radically askew, his horse's reins in his hands, "this man, this Donaldson here, knowin' mighty well the awful fix our beloved South is in, how it has been invaded, and humbled, disgraced, by northern Yankees and all their kind, knowin' how they have freed the niggers, includin' his own, and set them agin us, encouragin' them— lazy, dirty, bent on crime, diseased, shiftless—to run amuck, rob, steal from us whut little we had left after the war, molest our women, and bring general havoc to our region, full-well knowin' all this, he takes in a rovin' bunch of these niggers, feeds 'em, lets 'em sleep in his cabins, in short, rests 'em up good so they are stronger to go out and do their dirty work all over agin. He knowed these things, yet he went ahead and done what he done. We have caught him in the act and have sho brought him to account for it. He must answer now for what he has done, and answer to the people he done it to—which is fittin' and proper. We reckon he is an intelligent man—he's a plantation owner—and sho knowed better. Now he must answer. I have give you the charges."

The Kleagle nodded a firm affirmation and turned to Donaldson. "What is your answer!—speak up!" he cried. "How do you plead? —it better be somethin' special!"

Donaldson threw his head back arrogantly. "What is there to say?" He was speaking mostly to Kleagle Hedgepath. "I find my wife and myself in the hands of lawbreakers. You do not—none of you—recognize the law. I have not violated *it*."

"The hell with the law!" now shouted the gangling mountaineer Tullenbeck. "Hit has failed the people—has let 'em down. *We* ere the law now!"

Donaldson ignored him. "I fed these hungry Negras," he said, again to Hedgepath—"They had been on the road with little food. Yes, I did it. I told them they could stay in the cabins there till they could rest up and then go on. I did it—it violated no law."

"*God* is our judge!" cried Martha Donaldson—"not you! My husband is right!"

The Kleagle studied the pair, and finally looked around him, again indecisively—though ceremoniously as if to make up for it. He started to speak then, but was interrupted. Herta, squatting on the ground only ten feet from Rodney's corpse, had begun a loud moaning, which soon became a kind of low, guttural, wordless song. She then began to sway, slowly, sideways back and forth, her eyes closed, yellow teeth just barely parted, a stark expression of rapture, transport, on her blood-caked face, as the sound, coming up from deep inside her chest cavity, soon attained an even heavier volume, billowing and swelling; a plaint of desperation, longing, of deranged grief. Hedgepath tried to be heard over her now violent keening—to no avail. Soon in a frenzy, she clambered up, lurched two or three paces, and fell, sprawled, across Rodney's body, the left side of whose head had been partially blown out by the mountaineer's rifle blast. "Luff! Luff!" she screamed over Rodney, "Where yo white robe? Where yo white hood? Where yo gun? Where yo rearin' horse? Where is dey, Luff? Don't pay no mind to dem wings and golden slippers!" Again she screamed—"*Luff!*" Then she dove forward on her stomach and kissed Rodney's intact right cheek, her lips yet coming away bloody. The other women soon took up the loud, sing-song moaning which in the night's stillness could be heard for a mile. The knights, by their furtive uneasy glances behind their hoods at each other, showed their deep concern over this outlandish noise of sorrowing paranoia. "Oh, Jesus, come take us!" one of the women now wailed out in a piercing, far-carrying cry—"Oh, *J-e-e-e-sus!*"

But Hedgepath would not be outdone, diverted. Grabbing up a lantern and holding it high, he began to shout out the (his) arbitrary sentence of the drumhead court: "Before we deal with these yellin', crazy niggers—which, I warrant you, won't be long—this traitor here, *Mister* Donaldson, this great Southern gentleman, patriot, and loyal Democrat, will, in the presence of Missus Donaldson, receive on his bare back twenty-five hard lashes with the whip! Tie him to that tree there, brothers!"

Donaldson, hearing the sentence, seemed strangely immobile, paralyzed. He looked around numbly for his wife, only to find she

—her hands still secured behind her—had silently slipped to the ground in a limp faint. The mountaineer, Tullenbeck, and two others seized Donaldson now and dragged him thirty feet to a strong oak sapling at the edge of the yard and with a piece of rope began to tie him at the waist securely to the tree. The black women's clamor, which seemed directed at nothing or no one, grew even more in intensity; they were crying, moaning, wailing now, at the top of their lungs. It was general bedlam. Hedgepath, though still stomping about and shouting his orders, could be seen by his manner to be distraught, alarmed, confused. He looked at the short, squat knight waiting with the whip to carry out his sentence and seemed sorely troubled, as if it were the strange response of the black women that so plagued, puzzled, him—now filled him with prophetic fear.

The uproar finally became so great the lanky mountaineer began to berate Hedgepath—for his indecisiveness, bluster, his ineptness. "Whut're we here fer?" he said disgustedly, turning to the other knights. "Why're we lettin' these niggers make all this noise? —alarmin' the countryside. Everyone of 'em shoulda been dead long 'fore now. Whoever thought the Kleagle would let this happen? What's come over him?—he's a different man! You brothers ain't any more surprised than me, though. Whoever seed such a situation?—shouldn't *never* been! The Kleagle cain't handle it— we need a *new* leader!" The knights, a few irresolutely dangling their lanterns, many still mounted, stood in a rough semicircle around the Donaldsons and other captives and seemed inert, incapable of reacting to Tullenbeck's taunts, his tirade, except to look at its object, Hedgepath, to observe his reaction. The ritual moaning was at its highest pitch now. Hedgepath glowered at the women, then, clearly frustrated, glanced reluctantly at the mountaineer; but no words came. Suddenly then he sprang over to the knight holding the whip and snatched it from him, then wheeled and faced them all defiantly. "You might need a new leader, all right," he said, quivering, speaking through almost clenched teeth and nodding toward the mountaineer, "but *he* ain't it!" With that he took one step forward and slashed Tullenbeck across his hooded face with the whip. Unarmed Tullenbeck, aghast, took, fell, a step backward, his hand wandering to his face; but he made no sound— there were only the plangent and mournful sounds of the women going out into the far-echoing night. Hedgepath, grunting now, swung the whip again, sending it across the mountaineer's neck and shoulders. He swung the third time with all his might and Tullenbeck seemed to wilt under the blow, though, strangely, almost pliantly, not resisting the sinking, then prostrate, fall that came thereafter. At once then he scrambled to his knees and, his hood now on the ground, stared up at Hedgepath with a sudden vague, confused, ecstasy in his face. "Don't whup me, Kleagle!" he groaned at last, begging now with a wild, harrassed, almost feminine rapture in his eyes. With another heaving grunt Hedgepath came down on him again. "Aw, don't whup me no more, Kleagle!" Tullenbeck cried. "*Kleagle, aw, please!*" His breath came in short, spasmodic gasps, his eyes looming large, piteous. "Aw, Lawd God, Kleagle!" The semicircle of gaping knights, without knowing it, began slowly moving toward, closing in on, the spectacle, having completely forgotten now the waiting Donaldsons and the moaning blacks. Hedgepath's next savage cut of the whip brought a still more anguished cry, almost a scream, from the mountaineer, which, blended with the cries of the ever more loudly-mourning women, rent the night air. "Aw, Kleagle! . . . *Kleagle!*" cried Tullenbeck. "Have pity on me! . . . My Gawd, my Gawd!— look at whut you're adoin' to me! Have mercy, have mercy! Why, aw why, do you whup me so!" Tullenbeck continued wailing, now crying tears, as Hedgepath, panting, sweating under his hood, went on flailing him savagely without letup. The knights stood awed, transfixed, themselves caught in a strange excitation by Tullenbeck's screams.

Donaldson, tied to the tree, stared in horror at the rite, as his wife, only now recovered from her fainting, sat, still dazed, on the ground. But the blacks seemed not to have witnessed, or cared about, what was happening. The women, now joined in their dirge-like chant-noises by Dandy and Canny, the two remaining black men, had averted their eyes from the knights' rapt involvement with the new scapegoat. The hooded men, craning forward to see the savage whipping, were obsessed, mesmerized; under the Kleagle's lashes the mountaineer's rapturous pleading could be heard over all the bewailing of the blacks, as the whole scene was caught now, suffused, in the lanterns' sallow yellow light. It was a macabre tableau. The Kleagle, at last pausing in the whipping to catch his breath, glared down at the mountaineer writhing on the ground before him. Panting, he turned and looked over at Donaldson. "Untie him," he ordered, dropping the whip, "and send him and his wife in the house." It was done at once—as the mountaineer still lay staring up pathetically, almost expectantly, at Hedgepath. Again the Kleagle glowered at him. "Git up!" he shouted. The mountaineer began whimpering. "Git up, I say!" Hedgepath then turned to the other knights. "It's enough, boys," he said, almost too loudly, for his indecision was already returning —"We have learned 'em *all* a lesson they'll never forgit for the rest of their lives, I bet. Mount up—I guess we're headin' home. . . ." But he seemed unsure of himself—hesitant, contemplative, full of doubts. "Mount up. . . ." he finally said again.

The mountaineer, dazed, limp, sated, his back bloodied through his robe, was helped onto his horse by the others and they soon all rode off into the night. Before long, far down the pike, the cadenced hooves of their horses could be heard echoing just as before, though now receding, as the blacks' oblivious, mournful dirge went on and on into a seeming eternity.

Chapter 5

Goforth's health failed to improve. Six weeks after his return home and his visit to his night drinking friends in Mack's Lounge the doctors ordered him back in the hospital for a few days of new tests. He had lost ten more pounds and was weak, debilitated, but kept telling his wife Aquilla he expected to be better soon once the bad winter weather had gone and spring brought its blessings. So during the last weeks of winter he sat at home with her and read and watched the few television offerings of interest to him—yet always thinking of Johnnie. His son had been much on his mind the last few weeks; he was not certain of all the reasons for this; his own health doubtless had much to do with it; he knew his days were numbered, that his disability was lung cancer, and that, although the doctors had not said so, the prognosis for even six more months of life was not good. Yet he in no way panicked; seldom did he brood, mope, or feel sorry for himself, and in the main was as cheerful, as normal, as the situation could be expected to allow. He had always lived precariously, had taken life as it came, had always told himself death was a part of life, so that now, despite brief periods of secret despair, the prospect of his leave-taking at sixty-six failed to frighten him. His only agony was his relationship with his son.

He sometimes thought it might have been different had there been, besides John Calvin, other offspring from his three marriages. It had apparently from the first, however, he thought, not been meant to be and he had long since accepted it. Yet Johnnie's estimate of him was like bitter gall to him. He moreover could not shirk or shed his feelings of guilt. Why had he not foreseen this? Why had he not earlier recognized the obligations of fatherhood? The truth of the matter, he knew, was that he did foresee; he did recognize. Yet he had seemed powerless; he had indeed been powerless. It was as if he had been driven by some dogged, mechanistic impersonality to do what he had done—to light up cigarettes pack after pack, to drink far too much whiskey, sleep with an array of women, go from one mediocre job to another, seldom, if ever, saving any money, and, except for the reading of books, heedlessly squandering his time. One of the reasons for this tinsel life was his utter attractiveness to women. Tall, handsome, quite black, with a bold, cajoling, fun-loving, devil-may-care charm, always trim and neat in his cheap but dapper suits, he spent his wages on the entertainment of his women. Yet there had been this freakish contradiction, this lifelong reading routine—his one good habit. He had early discovered that women were somehow fascinated at hearing him talk, expatiate, on the myriad subjects he had informed himself on in an absorbed and zealous reading of all the newspapers, magazines, and books he could lay hands on; he especially loved politics and history—Negro history, and art as well, especially Negro music, and was quick, particularly with these impressionable women, to open conversation on any subject that in a recent book had caught his fancy—all on the scant foundation of a high school education acquired it seemed eons ago, in Frankfort, Kentucky. He had sought so eagerly to make an impression—especially on women. Their favorable reaction, however, was generally short-lived; their admiration for his rustic intellectuality, his curiosity, the store of sporadic information, soon faded; they sensed they were somehow pandering to a strange psychological need he had. It was almost always the same: his insubstantial life was found out, and the women, certainly the shrewder and more worldly among them, ended up calling him, though not to his face, a fraud, a faker, a big-word-spouting fourflusher. Yet they seldom hated him, even if for a time he had deceived them. They merely lost interest in him—except for the women who married him thinking they could reform him. This especially had been the case with Cora, his second wife and John Calvin's mother. Now it was Aquilla.

So in what was to be the last year of his life now he sat at home, in the small but comfortable apartment Aquilla had provided for him, and thought back on his life, speculated on what, while there had still been time, he could have done to change, improve, save, it. He was always shocked, then, to find he did not actually wish it had been different. He had derived too much pure hedonistic pleasure from it to wish it had not happened. He only craved his son's understanding. Yes, that was it, he thought—John Calvin should have had more patience, tolerance, should have made an effort to see what he had had to contend with. But even to him, Goforth, this did not ring true for long; he was not satisfied with his own rationale and became confused, frustrated, unhappy. These were the times he most valued his infrequent evenings with his friends in Mack's Lounge. There at the bar, nursing a weak bourbon and water, he could laugh, argue, reminisce, regale them on a variety of topical matters or subjects more substantial, all to their delight and the alleviation of his own tension in this gregarious mode of escape. But now as he weakened, went downhill, these nights became less and less frequent. Instead he sat at home reading, watching television, talking to Aquilla, or awaiting a visit from his younger friend and admirer, Shipmate McCoy.

One evening in April Shipmate stopped by to see him and brought along a half gallon of butter pecan ice cream which he, Goforth, was known to like. Shipmate, however, had other designs in mind as well. He had long noticed his mentor's slowly but steadily worsening condition and felt he could also read his mind. He sensed Goforth's suppressed anguish over John Calvin and meant to draw him out on the subject tonight; maybe something could yet be done, he thought; perhaps Goforth, tacitly or otherwise, could be persuaded to go along with his plan to try and locate John Calvin and exhort him to come see his father. It was a matter, however, about which young Shipmate did not have good feelings. Although he had never known John Calvin well, he did not like what he knew and liked far less what he had heard—that young Knight was an arrogant firebrand, brooding and temperamental, an impractical visionary and dreamer, who could be selfish and callous to boot. From all this Shipmate always got a decidedly bad reaction and what he now sought to do, in view of his unlimited admiration for Goforth, was in many respects a sacrificial step he nonetheless hoped would bring some final measure of contentment, perhaps even happiness, to Goforth in the equivocal weeks ahead.

Aquilla admitted him into their apartment. She was a tiny, very light-skinned woman, an octoroon, and wore her lank hair, dyed jet black, combed straight back, tight, severe, and secured in a knot at the back, topped with an arc-shaped comb. She had been a widow, though not an impoverished one, when, nine years ago now, she and Goforth were married, and ever since, morally pressed by the dictates of her church, the African Methodist, she had sought to run, dominate, his life. She meant to save him. But Goforth had presented problems; he had still thought he was young.

"It's Shipmate!" Aquilla called to him over her shoulder as his stand-in son entered. She laughed to Shipmate—"Your friend's been inquiring after you. Come in, come in." She stepped back and Shipmate saw gaunt Goforth in pajamas and robe seated in his big chair in front of the TV set—more and more, especially since his illness, Goforth had come to appreciate "his" home, as he called it, this apartment, one, the topmost, of three in the building Aquilla's dead husband, a retired postal clerk, had owned and left to her.

"What you say there, boy?" Goforth, grinning eagerly, greeted his caller. "What you got there?—a fifth of sour mash bourbon?"

"No, it's ice cream," said Shipmate, smiling. He gave the bag to Aquilla.

"A sorry pass I've come to—friends bringing me ice cream." Goforth watched as Aquilla left with the bag for the kitchen. The clear, mild, jonquil evening was fast fading and soon the moon would be out. Through the windows they could see the beauty of the sky as well as the street below where noisy children played. "You wouldn't even take that little galfriend of yours ice cream!" said Goforth. But his mirth seemed to Shipmate spurious, contrived. Shipmate sat down and they appraised, then smiled at each other. "You're lookin' good, boy," Goforth said—"Them chicks won't leave you alone, I bet. Ha! ha! You better enjoy it while you can." Shipmate only smiled. Soon Aquilla reappeared, with a tray bearing three plates of ice cream, spoons, and paper napkins. "Oh, Lord," sighed Goforth, his eyes following his wife again—"Baby, we ain't going to eat it already, are we? . . . While he's still here and you have to give him some?—we won't have none left." He laughed again, the sound, coming up out of his remaining one lung, gravelly, hollow. Suddenly he coughed and reached for a tissue of Kleenex. Shipmate and Aquilla, averting their eyes, began talking, exchanging idle irrelevancies, as Goforth tried to quell his coughing. When at last he had succeeded, he seemed weak, spent, and for the brief-

423

est moment sat glum and despondent. But suddenly then he looked at Aquilla and laughed. "How about a bourbon and water, baby?" he said—"just one. Oh, come on."

"No, Goforth—you had your two drinks before dinner. No more now till tomorrow." Aquilla sensed, however, his inward agitation and distress, but knew whiskey would not help him. She was glad now Shipmate had come. After they had all eaten their ice cream, she took the tray of plates and left the two men to themselves.

Goforth now sat eyeing Shipmate for a moment, suspiciously; it was as if he sensed Shipmate was bent on discussing something serious, perhaps unpleasant, with him; he seemed wary, put off, by the prospect, and at once resumed his raillery. "Did I ever tell you 'bout the time as a young man I found myself in Terry's Fork, Mississippi after sundown—when the signs at the outskirts of town had warned against it? Huh? *Ha, ha, ha!* Man, oh man! It was somethin'—those crackers made it hot for me! If I hadn't had brains, and used 'em, I wouldn't be here this evening to tell it!"

"Goforth," said Shipmate, interrupting—calm, almost impassive —"I was thinking about trying to locate Johnnie and having him come up here for a few days."

Goforth leaned forward slightly in the big chair. There was a belligerent pause. "You were thinkin' about doing *what*?" he said. Yet he had sensed it; in his unconscious, had expected it. There now was brought down on him a cataract of memories, ancient, racial, familial—flooding his mind, heart; the flesh, blood, his very loins, were being addressed by this man, this friend, only slightly older than his own son, the central figure in it all; this younger friend who had broached his son's name out of selfless motives yet in a way to bring only pain. "You're thinkin' of doing what? . . ." the words came again, his lips staying parted, though he would not look at Shipmate. Then he was inundated by a great wave of sorrow. "Doing what?" he repeated, trying to check, exorcise, it. Shipmate watched his now gaunt face, the holes for eyes, sunken, ravaged, shadowy even in the stygian skin. His heart went out to this his surrogate father, his friend who had dared and lived; he would gladly have adopted him as his sire and sent feckless Johnnie on his callous way—his, Shipmate's, own father had died in a dice game knife fight and left his mother with four children, shoeless, their noses running snot, their clothes fouled with their feces. To

424

him, then, Goforth was a man, responsible, caring, against great odds even loving; though tortured now.

Shipmate tried to laugh. "Yeah, Goforth, I'm thinking about it —sure, why not?" He sat back in his chair. "Johnnie ought to come."

"You don't even know where Johnnie is. Why, what an idea— Christ! He probably wouldn't come anyhow." Goforth faced Shipmate now, his eyes appealing for some contradiction. "You know I'm right." His gaunt fingers on the arm of his big stuffed chair played over Aquilla's crocheted doily as he glanced nervously at Shipmate again.

"Oh, I think he'd come," Shipmate said.

"Why should he? I'm a wreck now—my life's caught up with me, boy." Goforth's face then went into a grisly, bragging grin. "When I had my wings, though, I was a flyin' sonofabitch!" He did not laugh, though; he was defiant.

"Tell me, Goforth, have you got regrets?"

Goforth stared; a stare of jagged impatience, riled, irascible; the question was a hard one, impossible—almost impertinent. Finally —"No, I don't regret nothing . . . till I think of Johnnie." Quickly then his eyes glazed over, his lip quivered. "It's Johnnie—most of it's because of the kind of boy he is. That's it—I know it. He's always had, even from a kid, this cuss-ed, this unreasonable, streak in him. It could come and go—he could have the highest thoughts sometimes; when he was in high school, say, and doing a term paper on Frederick Douglas; oh, he'd have the noblest thoughts; he'd catch fire, seems like—you should have read some of his papers, and him just a kid; yeah, upright, lofty, thoughts; full of race pride; full of courage, determination, for all niggers. He believed in 'em, you see, way back then even. Oh, Lord, and when I'd tell him about his ancestors—about old Bymba Baptiste, and Acts and Aaron Knight, even my own daddy, and my first wife's cousin, poor Parret Webb, just a kid, who had come back from the army in World War I only to have such a short and tragic life ahead of him, and some of the others back there—and all they went through in our bloody, cruel, nigger history, he would break down and cry; yammer just like a calf—in pity and outrage, especially about young Parret; all the time vowing someday to get even—just like a simple kid would. He didn't know, of course, and still don't, that

425

the way you forget all this, the way you put it out of your mind and keep it out—ha! ha!—is with liquor, with good-lookin' fast women, and good times! You don't think about all the bad things then; you ain't got time—look at niggers on Saturday night; balling, boy; livin' it up; why do you think they do it, huh? It's simple. Otherwise it's no use— you ain't never going to get even with the white man; he's too far along; besides, when you get close enough to him to get even, you start takin' on his ways; then where are you? You've lost again, ain't you? Ha!—you sure'n hell have. But Johnnie don't see this; never has. A strange boy—Lord, have mercy! He's just as strange today, too; maybe more so. No, he ain't coming to see *me*." Goforth stopped for a moment now, reflective, breathless in his silence; studied, deliberate, yet confounded. "There's another side to Johnnie, too," he said then, "besides all his noble thoughts for niggers, and that's his mean side. He's got an awful mean streak in him, and a bad temper—I only whipped him once but he didn't open his mouth for a week; he's quick to feel sorry for himself and can sulk for days. He can be heartless, though, to anybody, even to his own mother—though he worshipped her till the day she died, even if she did go off without him when she left me. He hated her for that, yet loved her at the same time. He was mixed up even back then—and still is. It's a fact, Shipmate."

"Don't you like Johnnie, Goforth?" Shipmate said.

Goforth sat up; he gaped at him. "What makes you say a thing like that?"

"You say he's mean and he's heartless, and feels sorry for himself a lot—those're unkind words, ain't they?"

"And they're true—everyone of 'em."

"You must not like him, then."

"Oh, hell, it ain't that." Goforth's face showed his distress. "He's my son—sure I like him. Don't you understand that? I've talked about his faults—to you. Why, don't you know I wouldn't do that with anybody but you or Aquilla?"

Shipmate grinned. "Yeah, and in bars—like Mack's Lounge, for instance."

"Not much I don't, though—only sometimes when I get to feeling down about him and me, after I've had a couple of drinks. But Johnnie's got a lot of good qualities. For one thing, he's got his head in the clouds all the time. Some people wouldn't like that about him—but I do; he's got a vision about the way things oughta be, and that's good. Even I had a vision once—ha, for about five minutes. But Johnnie's serious—that's what I like about him. I never was—and he ain't twenty-five yet; think of what he may be by the time he's thirty-five. Sure, I see all these things—they're plusses, ain't they? Maybe before long he'll marry some nice girl, that's got her feet on the ground, and she'll bring out all the good in him maybe and get rid of a lot of the bad—I don't know. Maybe he'll have kids—yeah, a son of his own; that'll wake him up. You can't tell, though, can you?—things don't always turn out like they ought to."

"Johnnie's main trouble, as I see it, is that he thinks he's bet-ter'n most people," Shipmate said—"I've seen that in him."

"You're right—it's a fault. But then how do you explain his out-rageous love and sympathy for the masses of niggers, street and field niggers, that ain't got a quarter and don't stand for nothing—how do you figure that? Huh? It's genuine; not only that, it's a passion."

"Yeah, yeah," Shipmate said; he was perplexed.

"I believe it's because he sees what niggers've been through that makes him feel that way about them. That's why, as a kid, he used to blubber so when I'd tell him about slavery times as it had been told to me. That boy could never hear enough about it—never. His mother used to say he was neurotic. I don't believe it; he's just sensitive, and hates to see people oppressed—what's wrong with that? Nothing, Shipmate, nothing. Yeah, I'm proud of him. Be-sides, he's my son, ain't he? Why, he's made more out of himself at twenty-five—down in the home country fighting them crackers about niggers' rights—than I would at a hundred. You're going to hear from Johnnie in years to come—I won't be here to see it, but you will. Mark my word." Goforth paused then, as if some new thought, possibility, had overtaken him. He seemed loathe to utter it. But at last—"Or else," he speculated aloud, "he'll bring a heap of misery down on them closest around him. . . ."

*   *   *   *   *

The month of May had come and almost gone; now spring would soon give way to the heat and glare of summer. But Goforth's condition had slowly, if sometimes imperceptibly, worsened by late May and Shipmate had already had two letters to young Knight, who had been rumored to be at an address in Prichard, Alabama, returned for want of an addressee. Johnnie could be located nowhere. Then suddenly his name appeared in a Chicago black newspaper. There had been, the news story said, a series of mass arrests of black marchers and protesters in Louisiana and Georgia, and—behold—John Calvin Knight was among those being accused by some more strident blacks of counseling a moratorium on efforts to desegregate deep South public accommodations. The professed motive was not strategic but tactical, to allow time, the theory went, for the embattled insurgents to refinance and regroup, a stand which, as to Knight, played into the hands of his numerous enemies in the movement (they too had apparently experienced his brash, ambitious, highhanded methods) and fostered the innuendo that he and others of like mind had lost the will to continue the fight. As his detractors anticipated, Knight, though not the leader of the rump group, nonetheless issued for it a characteristically vitriolic, intemperate, denial of wrongdoing when found by black reporters in his seedy hotel in the ghetto section of Monroe, Louisiana. This was how Shipmate finally reached him by telephone. When told of his father's condition (he had known of the earlier surgery), he, surprisingly to Shipmate, said he would come at once. At heart, however, Shipmate refused to see his motive as entirely pure; his father's illness could add to the plausibility of his temporary retirement from the fray. Such thoughts, though, were sedulously kept from Goforth, who, with justification, would in any event have refused to accept them—mindful of Shipmate's bias.

The news, at last, that Johnnie was coming seemed not only *not* to cheer Goforth, but to plunge him into deepest despair. What he had so long yearned for was finally coming to pass, yet now he was virtually unhinged, filled with the direst misgivings; with the result that the day before Johnnie was to arrive he lapsed into an impregnable silence that neither Shipmate nor Aquilla could coax him out of. The truth was that Goforth, who so desperately, pitiably, had wanted a reunion with his son, was now in mortal fear of the meeting. It loomed to him as a crisis—the crisis of his life. How, he wondered, would he deal with it?—and in his steadily weakening condition. He became morose, and himself self-pitying; hence, twenty-four hours before, came the dismal, stubborn silence. Shipmate seemed to understand it all—that Goforth was reacting under the circumstances as he might well be expected to react— in abject fear. But Aquilla was greatly alarmed—she called the doctor twice. The doctor, however, when he learned Goforth, throughout his silences, was as usual seated in his big stuffed chair staring fiercely out the window, told Aquilla to calm herself, that nothing untoward for the time being was imminent. Yet Aquilla kept nervously scurrying back and forth through the apartment performing all kinds of nonsensical, unneeded, tasks she used to allay, cast out, her own persistent fears. Meanwhile Goforth, a great, gaunt, deathlike, silent Sphinx, sat glowering out the window.

But it passed. By early Friday afternoon, Johnnie's scheduled arrival time in town, Goforth, inexplicably, in the final hours, cheered up. He began to talk, and in a surprisingly jocular vein, about the time he had won a bet with Johnnie, then fourteen, over their disagreement about the number of U.S. Supreme Court justices who had dissented in the Dred Scott case. "Ha!" he said, almost spitefully, "I taught that boy a lesson he ain't forgot yet, I bet—never to argue with *me* about nigger history. He never did after that, I'll tell you." Aquilla was elated. But soon then, sitting peering out the window again, as if at that moment he were looking for Johnnie to come walking up the street, he fell to musing—into a somber, deeply reflective, state.

Moreover, there was a seemingly minor detail that concerned, troubled, him, though neither he nor Aquilla—both out of fear, but of different kinds—had discussed it. Did Johnnie on his visit plan to stay with them, or, possibly, in a downtown hotel? Goforth, aware of the larger implications—Johnnie's current attitude toward him—hoped his son would occupy the small spare bedroom, where, however, Aquilla, since his illness, now slept. She, on the other hand, hoped, because of Goforth's illness—his night coughing, the hawking up of diseased sputum, his sweat-drenched nightmares—that she would not have to surrender her present room. If she had to, she thought, she meant to sleep on the living room sofa. Goforth was aware of the problems, the complexities, yet hoped Johnnie had at least planned, even if, on learning the facts, he did not carry through, to stay with them. He needed to be reassured that Johnnie was willing to remain on the spot, live, as it were, for his few days in town in the bosom of the family, be available, day or night, for long, reminiscing talks of earlier times —this way, hopefully, to try to heal the breach between them while there was yet time. If Johnnie, with no prompting, had actually meant to come stay with them, had wanted to maximize the time available to spend with his failing father, had really journeyed on a mission of painful love, it implied much, thought Goforth—much indeed.

But alas when Johnnie alighted from a bus from downtown, rang their doorbell, and, after trudging up the stairs, presented himself to Aquilla at their apartment door, he carried no luggage at all—nothing, not even a briefcase. But Goforth and Aquilla were so excited, surprised—Johnnie had not phoned—that they did not at first notice. There was only a hullabaloo of gleeful commotion. Goforth's voice miraculously assumed its old volume. It almost boomed. "Oh, Lord! . . . Hey! Looka here! Hey, hey, boy!" In his robe he rose majestically, if weakly, and embraced his son. Young Knight wore a fierce kinky beard. But his rumpled clothes were dark and somber, somehow conservative. Facing his father, he seemed at first subdued and diffident—nervous; yet above everything his callow youth showed through his hirsute face. "Hey! Ha! ha!" cried Goforth—"What's that stuff on your face? Oh, Lord, look at him, Aquilla!" But young Knight now only showed his shock at his father's appearance. At once then, however, he smiled, gravely, and at last laughed, as he returned Goforth's embrace. Next he kissed Aquilla. But Goforth was still whooping it up— "Them rednecks ran you niggers clean outa Louisiana, didn't they?" he shouted. "Ha! Oh, boy!" But at once the exertion sent him into a fit of coughing. Sinking now into his big chair again, he reached weakly for a Kleenex. Knight stood looking at him, amazed at his condition; then gazed questioningly at Aquilla as Goforth, making a deep hollow gravelly sound, at last cleared his throat.

Aquilla seemed reluctant to return the stare and merely stood there, diminutive, almost Caucasian white, a tiny ornament, like a Christmas tree bauble, affixed to the tight ball of black hair at the back of her head. At last, though training her eyes now on Goforth, she said to young Knight: "You can see your father hasn't been a bit well. We're sure glad you came, Johnnie—it'll help him." Knight backed up and sat down on the sofa.

But Goforth soon rallied. "In spite of all that stuff on your face, boy," he exclaimed to Knight, "you look great!—you always was thin, and ate like a bird. But you look good! Say—ha! ha!—who dissented in the Dred Scott case?"

Knight laughed. "Curtis and McLean," he said.

"You'll never forget that, will you? I bet you won't! Ha! ha! Now, tell me this: If I know the circumference of a circle, how do I get the diameter?—tell me that."

"Multiply the circumference by point 31831," Knight laughed.

Goforth turned gleefully to Aquilla. "You see?" he said—"this boy ain't forgot a thing I taught him! He's known these things since he was just a little shaver! Now, John, how many gallons in a cubic foot of water!"

"Seven and a half," said Johnnie.

"Hey! Go to the head of the class! Sharp as a tack—always was! We're proud of you and glad you're home. Now, once more: Define 'moribund' for me."

Johnnie laughed again. "Do you want the proper definition or your definition?"

Goforth sat up, arched his back, and merrily bucked his eyes. "*Well*!—is there a difference?"

"I think so, Dad." Knight was genuinely amused.

"Go on, give me mine."—Goforth had already burst out laughing.

"You used to say 'moribund' was what Negroes were."

The answer sent Goforth into gales of gravelly laughter. "What a memory!" he cried. "John, you got a head on you—you remember everything I told you! Yeah, it's a fact of life—niggers are moribund! Ha! ha! ha!"

Thus the hilarious getting-acquainted-again talk went on for almost an hour. But it was not until Knight said in passing he would be in Chicago until the following Wednesday that Goforth realized he had no luggage. He sat up at once. "Where're your bags, John?" he said.

"I'm at the Hilton Hotel. What was the point in my inconveniencing you and Aquilla?"

Goforth started to stand up again, but finally refrained. "Incon-

venience us!" he said—"what'n the world are you talkin' about?"
He swallowed hard and made a grimace. "You go get them bags
and bring 'em in this house." Goforth's order brought a concerned
look on Aquilla's face.

"No, it's better this way," said Knight, though placatingly—"I'll
only be sleeping in the hotel. I've got to see a few people while I'm
here but I'll be here in the apartment the rest of the time."

"Oh, hell!" moaned Goforth.

"Let Johnnie do it his way, dear," said Aquilla, her motives dual.
"He knows he's welcome."

But before long the conversation had gone on to myriad other
subjects. Soon Goforth, almost suddenly oblivious, grinned broadly
as he said to Knight: "Bet you can't remember a single damn line
from W. E. B. DuBois—from his 'The Song of the Smoke.' Ha, I
got you now!—look at him, Aquilla!" Knight had hesitated, then
laughed. "Laughing ain't going to make you remember!" cried
Goforth.

Knight, sensitive, tender, to the challenge, sat trying, straining,
to remember any lines from the poem. ". . . I can't recall how it
begins," he finally said—" . . . but somewhere in the middle of it
I remember:

> I am the smoke king,
> I am black,
> I am darkening with song,
> I am hearkening to wrong;
> I will be as black as blackness can,
> The blacker the mantle the mightier the man,
> The purpl'ing midnights no day dawn may ban.

Aquilla broke into applause—"Oh, isn't that fine!"

Goforth grunted, then guffawed—"It's fine, all right, but I can
recite the whole thing! Ha! ha! But that ain't bad, John—ain't bad
at all. Next to your boy Martin Luther King, Du Bois is the greatest nigger we've produced. Huh?"

On the sofa Knight stirred uneasily, but then smiled—yet it was
an insistent smile. "The word is 'Negro,' Dad," he said evenly.
"Can't you say 'Negro' instead of 'nigger?' "

A hangdog look came on Goforth's face. " 'Negro,' then," he
finally said, as Aquilla smiled. "These two *Neee*groes, King and

DuBois, rank right along with each other—yeah, DuBois is great, all right; no question."

"Right—he's a great old man," said Knight—"He's ninety-three now, I think; living in Ghana." Then with a twinkle—"I thought you also liked Booker T. Washington."

"Well, I don't talk him down, I'll tell you that—like you young cats are always doing. He did some good too, in his day. They were bad days he operated in, awful bad—dangerous days. Down there where you just now came from you might today get whacked across the head with some redneck cop's night stick, but back in those times you could get hung by the neck to a tree limb with a piece of baling wire and your testicles sliced out. You'all got a picnic today."

Knight gravely shook his head. "No, no picnic, Dad," he said.

"Well, I'm just comparing the two times—you mentioned Booker Washington, didn't you? You should'a heard my granddaddy, Acts Knight, tell about the Ku Klux Klan on the rampage down in Georgia during, and even after, Reconstruction—there were over a half million of 'em in the South. They made it hot for the niggers, I'll tell you—er, the *Neee*groes—and some good white folks too. Acts and his half-brother Aaron, running from them cracker posses, got separated—and Acts carrying a sick child in his arms who died—and didn't find each other again till almost six months later, in Savannah. It was tough then, dangerous—you think it's bad down there now but it's nothing, nothing, compared to those days; and not only in the South—what poor Parret Webb went through happened in *Ohio*, and as late as World War I. Also remember down in Alabama Booker Washington founded Tuskeegee Institute in 1881. Why, you could lose your life trying to educate niggers—Negroes—in those days, let alone trying to drink a coke down there now in some white man's drug store. Think of those things, boy!" Goforth's voice was full of urgency.

Young Knight nodded gravely again, reluctantly, a fierce, pained expression, visible despite the beard, on his face. "Yes, I know—I know," he said, his voice vague now, far away, reflective, bitter. Suddenly he lurched forward on the sofa—"But *why*?" he blurted. "Why?"

Goforth and Aquilla stared.

"*Why, why*, is our history what it is?" Knight said. "Why has

433

everybody—even we, ourselves—wanted to brutalize, kill us? Why, Daddy?"

Goforth, who at first had been merely surprised at the outburst, now felt a sudden surge of nostalgia and emotion. His son had once again addressed him as "Daddy." It brought back a flood of memories—the seemingly limitless times when together they had done the homework little Johnnie had brought home, and when there had always been that same incessant, oft-repeated question: "Why, Daddy?" Goforth was numbed. He sought now to contain himself, hide, suppress, his emotion. He sat back, pausing, then suddenly laughed—"Ha! John, the answer to your question is that we're *moribund*. That's why! Ha! ha! ha!"

But neither Knight nor Aquilla laughed; they rather seemed puzzled. "What do you mean? . . ." Knight said.

Goforth, however, sat musing now. He seemed not to hear. He had begun noticeably to tire.

Aquilla got up. "Goforth, dear, it's time for your afternoon nap, now," she said. "Come on."

"Yeah, I'll go lay down awhile, I guess," said Goforth weakly, and turned to Knight—"Aquilla's got a big beef rib roast for dinner back there; we knew you'd be here, boy. I'll go take a nap—I want to be ready for it, and a couple of bourbons besides. Then after dinner I want to hear all about the niggers—the Negroes—carrying on down home. It's something—they're sure acting up, ain't they?"

The stage was thus set for young John Calvin Knight's five-day visit with his father in the latter's last months of life. Shipmate McCoy joined them all for dinner that evening and, afterwards, at almost ten o'clock, dropped Knight off downtown at his hotel. As they drove toward the Loop in Shipmate's jalopy of a car he realized again the relationship between the two of them had at best always been tentative, insecure. He had never felt comfortable with Johnnie Knight because he knew Knight had really little respect for him—he was aware in Knight's eyes he lacked ambition and would never amount to much. Moreover Knight, he knew, applied the same yardstick to his father—Goforth had lacked ambition, Johnnie's concept of it anyway, and as a result had been doomed to failure from the start. Yet what they all recognized in Johnnie as this crazy, fanatical, ambition of his, was, they also sensed, not

434

entirely for himself alone, no mere simplistic conceit; it was more complex than that, pervaded somehow with a messianic selflessness where Negroes were concerned, thereby all but diluting completely any claim made for it as mere ambition. Shipmate knew he did not fully understand it all and doubted Knight himself did. Knight sat there now beside him in the moving old car, engrossed in his thoughts; musing, but saying little. Shipmate somehow resented this and vowed himself also to say little, which finally brought Knight to sense the strain in the air.

"Dad looks bad, doesn't he?" he said—"I was surprised. I'm glad you got ahold of me."

"Yeah," said Shipmate, using the dashboard lighter to light his cigarette; that was all.

"He told me, at least two or three times, what a friend you've been to him."

Shipmate nodded, caring not at all whether in the dark Knight saw even his nod.

"Yes, I know you think I should have been here all along," Knight said.

Shipmate now gave an impatient, irritated, little laugh. "Well, maybe," he said, "but that's your affair, ain't it?"

Knight seemed suddenly in a dreamlike state. "Ah, you're so right—it is my affair," he said at last. Yet the hostility in Shipmate's laugh had nettled, angered, him; he could not conceal the resentment in his own voice now. "There's more to it than that, though," he said—"It's not all that uncomplicated. What I'm trying to do down South is important, I think. Before that I'd been away from here getting a university education. Then I involved myself in the Negro struggle." He turned pointedly to Shipmate—"Everybody hasn't done that. It's been an investment of my time and efforts in something that's got promise—a future. It's not a *dead issue*! I had to set some hard priorities for myself, but I did it."

"Sure, it's your affair, as I said," nodded Shipmate—"You've set your priorities. I ain't in your situation—I can't test myself against you, because my father died when I was a kid. But if he was living today and in Goforth's shape, I guess I can't say what I'd do—can't say for sure. You see, though, my father, I don't think, would ever have felt about me like Goforth feels about you —he idolizes you."

435

Knight turned on him in a fury. "Then why did he fail—why did he fail me? Why?—a man of his gifts, his born ability!"

"Fail *you!* What're you talking about, Johnnie? Who in the hell are you not to be failed?—Goforth may have failed himself, but nobody else. He, too, though, thinks he failed you. Jesus, that's the worst part of it—he feels apologetic; he's so ashamed, feels so guilty. His remorse is an awful thing to watch—it's killing him as much as the cancer."

The air was electric, tense, now; they rode on for a time in silence, though Knight's anger had quickly subsided in the face of Shipmate's clear sense of outrage. When they reached the hotel he invited Shipmate to come in and have a drink in the bar, though Knight did not himself then drink, but Shipmate found the proper excuse, early job hours, to decline, and let Knight out—each of them, in the end, leaving the other thoroughly puzzled, confused.

Later, Knight in his hotel room had taken a shower before the full import of what Shipmate had said penetrated his inmost centers of awareness, feeling. He then stood naked toweling himself, angry at Shipmate for having so spoken, angrier still at himself for having given the undoubted justification. Yet he felt no true remorse. In these earlier days of his life, his career, there were no doubts—absolutely; he had studied and knew himself, was sure of himself, and above all else had set his course, seen his mission. Still he was not without compassion for his father; moreover, there was much yet to be learned from him that could be put at the service of the struggle—authentic black legend, invaluable vicarious experience, oral history. He told himself, despite all, he loved his father—in some ways, really honored him. What more, under the circumstances, could anyone, including Shipmate, want of him? He put on fresh pajamas from his val-pak and now, brushing his teeth, preened before the bathroom mirror. There was the same messianic, demonic, light in his eyes he had somehow never become aware of, which told his subconscious self that it was he who had been ordained to redeem the Negro race, to uplift and inspire it, especially the young; to right the wrongs, avenge the squandered blood of the race—a race that would be "moribund" no longer.

His lunch with his father next day was preceded by the most pointed, practical, yet insinuative, question Goforth could have asked. Grinning—"John, how in the hell do you eat these days?—

436

ha!" They were seated in the tiny dining room before being served by Aquilla.

Knight stared at him—"How do I eat? . . ."

"How do you pay for it, how do you live, boy?—ha! ha! ha! You're staying at a downtown hotel, ain't you?"

Knight smiled. "I'm splurging, really—just this once. I get bare subsistence money, when there's that, from the organization—from the coordinating council of N.C.J., the Negro Coalition for Justice. I'm a staff member, an organizer."

"I see." But Goforth's mind had taken flight to the larger implications; he sat pondering. ". . . for Justice, eh?" he breathed. "Niggers—Negroes—finally wanting something they never had, eh?" he chuckled. "Justice—well, that's all right; they've sure yearned for it long enough, ain't they? . . . prayed for it, even down in the canebrakes and cotton fields in slavery times. Lord have mercy—yes, way back then, back when there wasn't any hope; as the song says, back 'in the days when hope unborn had died.' Slavery times—Acts Knight didn't like to talk about them much; made him have nightmares afterward. Slavery was a strange thing—think of it; think of yourself owning another human being. Remember I told you George Washington owned three hundred and seventeen . . . er—Negroes when he died? And Jefferson—and some of the others, like Madison, had plenty of 'em too. Think of yourself, boy, owning another human being—it gives you goose pimples, don't it? Whew! I ain't the most religious man in the world but when I think of coming up before my Maker on Judgment Day after being responsible for what I made happen to the souls of people I *owned*, like hogs and cows, it gives me the shakes, I'll tell you. Ah, but this country's paying for its sins now, huh?"

"I'm not sure," young Knight said—"It may be too early to tell. This country surely doesn't mean to pay for them if it can help it. We ourselves have got to *act* to get our rights."

"Son, what you civil rights boys and girls don't understand," said Goforth, "is that we Negroes were put here on this earth to suffer, be kicked around and brutalized. That's why we're here—I believe it. Just like an individual, a race of people can bear a curse too—did you ever think of that? Lord, how else do you explain our history? The Negro in the street understands it—he senses it. It's you college boys that don't see it—that there ain't no

437

answer to this thing. The Negro just keeps on living the best he can—making do, having what fun he can, and forgetting the rest. Sure, street Negroes understand this—it's the code they live by; it's their way of life. They dig the curse, huh?"

Knight was shaking his head and grimacing. "And still you say DuBois and King are great men," he said—"How can it be? What they've done, what they stand for, the sense of dignity they've brought us, are all absolutely in vain, right? You don't believe that, Dad, and you know it—why have you spent your life studying Negro history?"

Goforth, his heart sad, yet forced levity. "Why, Johnnie!" he laughed, "don't you know? It's *interesting,* that's why! The history's intriguing!—fabulous! Niggers too—Negroes—are fabulous! Ha! ha! ha! Yeah, they're downright fabulous!"

Knight seemed not even to have heard him. "DuBois and King are examples to us all—they didn't let their lives whip them, did they? They *dealt* with life. They're an inspiration to everybody—including you, Dad—simply because, unlike so many others, they refused to take the easy way out."

Goforth's jaw dropped

"Yes!" cried young Knight—"You, Dad, you let it whip you."

"Oh, Johnnie!" remonstrated Aquilla—"That's not so." She had served all three plates and had herself just sat down, only to go now into a fierce pout.

Goforth seemed to have aged, become more gaunt, ravaged, in the instant. His face long now, hurt, he dabbed at his lips with his paper napkin. Finally he said nothing. It was the moment he had feared since learning Johnnie was coming. He felt powerless now to deal with it, this inevitable, cruel, challenge. It was the crisis, *his* crisis; the moment he had feared, dreaded. Soon a big tear coursed down his face and he weakly rose and left the room.

"Oh, Johnnie, look what you've done," said Aquilla, her voice full of distress. She jumped up and followed Goforth into their bedroom—leaving Knight seated at the table, the food uneaten.

Goforth did not reappear that afternoon and, despite Aquilla's tearful protests, Knight finally left and returned to the hotel. After eating a sandwich in the hotel grill, he spent a dismal afternoon in his room trying to read—but to no avail. He made three phone calls then, in an attempt to reach two friends in the N.C.J. move-

438

ment, but failed in this also. Finally he called Aquilla and askcd about his father, how he was feeling; but he did not apologize; he felt he had spoken the truth, that his father had let life overcome him without a struggle, and that he ought not now be allowed, unchallenged, to preach defeat to others—even if he was ill, very ill, in this he must not be indulged; there was too much at stake. On the phone Aquilla, clearly still distressed, urged him to return for dinner, telling him Goforth had only in the last two days become self-pitying and temperamental, that she was sure by dinner time he would have emerged from his tearful bedroom sulk and most likely become his cheerful self again. Knight said he would come. But after hanging up he was suddenly aware he wanted to leave Chicago and return down South; he realized he was already restless, and knew why. He had met a girl down in Alabama, about whom he now thought constantly.

At dinner, however, contrary to predictions, Goforth was not his old self at all. He was mostly subdued, uncommunicative, and, looking ever more gaunt, ate little. It was not until dinner was over and the three of them were in the living room that he asked Aquilla, in a kindly yet harried, almost wretched voice, to leave them. He then faced his son at once. "John, most of the afternoon back there in the bedroom my mind's been on you, just you. But my hardest job was making up my mind—I didn't have the guts at first—to tell you about . . . about yourself. Yes, son, yourself. I might have acted a fool most of my life, but, if I do say it myself, I ain't a hundred percent fool. I made up my mind today to tell you, for your own good, what it is I see when I see you—you my son."

Knight had stirred uneasily in his chair. He watched Goforth, and finally smiled. "I'm sure," he said, "there's much you see, Dad, you don't approve of." He waited then. At last—"What is it you see?"

Goforth was deliberate, resolute, dogged—"Yeah, you're right. What I see ain't all good, surely. I see a young, very young man, not yet twenty-five, brilliant but inexperienced, with no compassion. None whatever."

Knight vaguely shook his head. "I hate to think that's true."

"I fear it is, John—you ain't got the nature for compassion."

"Why do you think I've been down South, then?—for almost a year now."

"You've been down South for the highest motives; I grant it; I don't question it a bit. You want to help your fellow . . . Negroes. Ain't no question but what that's a high cause."

"You say, though, I'm not capable of compassion."

"What feeling you've got for people, John, is all in general—you love Negroes as a group of people; millions of 'em, maybe. But that ain't necessarily compassion. Compassion is when you can look at another person, some lone person, an individual, and see both the bad and the good in 'em and then see if the good don't really after all outweigh the bad. What's wrong with you is you can't give a guy a break. People get caught in life, trapped by certain things, circumstances, they can't do nothing about, and if you got compassion you try to see this and make allowances for it. But you can't do this, John; you'll never be able to do it—it ain't in you. You know why?"

Knight's eyes had never left Goforth's face—"Go ahead, Dad." But he was breathing hard.

"It's just because, like everybody else, you're caught too. Only you don't know it. That's why I'm telling you. I'm your dad; if I can't tell you, who can?—you ain't got a wife. Yeah, you too are caught in circumstances you can't do anything about and the reason you can't have compassion for a person is because your mother before you wasn't capable of it. She didn't have any for me and she didn't have any for you—she walked out on you just like she did on me, didn't she? So, yeah, John, you get it honest—you've been like this from the beginning, from the time you were born down there on 49th and Champlain right here in Chicago. Ah, and you'll probably be like that when you die, too, if I, or somebody certainly, don't turn you around. But it's a shame; it makes me feel bad just to think about it. Here, you want to be a great leader, a race leader—oh, I can see that's where you're trying to go—yet you got no compassion. So you'll end up loving niggers in the mass and probably hating them individually. What kind of leader is that?"

"I deny what you've said, Dad." Knight was very earnest now. "I know what triggered all this—I'm sorry, very sorry, I had to say what I said to you today. It upset you and I wish it could have gone unsaid, for you're my father; but that's the reason I had to say it—if it had been somebody else, it probably wouldn't have mattered to me; I could have kept my mouth shut, maybe. But Negroes have got to stop feeling sorry for themselves; they've got to stop looking for excuses for their failures. It won't work, Dad. That's why we're all in the fix we're in—excuses, excuses! We've got to get tough, hard—you call it lacking compassion—and do whatever's necessary to become strong, strong in every way, so we'll no longer be mistreated and kicked around like we've been for so long. I *had* to say what I said to you."

"Sure, you had to say it," said Goforth, bridling. "It wouldn't have been in character for you not to. You *had* to, you see. Sure. Oh, boy! Oh, boy! That's how we get strong, eh? Lord, what'll you do when women start coming into your life?—and I sure hope they will, and pretty soon. How're you going to be a husband, John?—huh? Just how are you? . . . Tell me, have you got a girl-friend?—I never hear you talk about women. You *like* women, don't you?" Goforth, intent now, almost breathless, leaned forward in his big chair as if he were unsure of what the answer might be.

"I like women," Knight said simply.

"Have you got a woman?—a girlfriend?"

"I've met a girl down in Mobile I admire very much—I like her, yes."

Goforth pondered this, and studied Knight. "Maybe marriage would help you," he finally said—"I don't know. You mean to get married someday, don't you?"

"Yes."

"What's this girl's name?"

"Velma. Velma Bailey."

"Yeah?—what kind of girl is she?"

Knight tried to smile. "She's . . . well, she's pretty—a dark brown-skinned girl."

"You met her on the marches, eh?—is she a civil righter too?"

"She hasn't been all that active, no. It's her father who's been. He's a Baptist minister in Mobile. He won't let her get too active —he's been shot at twice, at night."

"Is she a girl you could marry?"

"I've asked her to marry me someday. She's said she would. It'll have to wait, though—she knows this. I haven't got any money or any real job. But maybe, at least when the present phase of the struggle's over, when the N.C.J. is on a sounder footing, I can marry her. She understands; she's no clinging vine type—she's a strong-minded person; almost headstrong sometimes, I think."

Goforth heaved a great sigh and lay back in his chair. "It's good news, John," he said. "Lord, that's what I've been wanting to hear—some girl in your life." He brightened for the first time during the evening. "And maybe if marriage won't change you for the better, a son will. Ah, a son—maybe someday you'll know how I felt the first time I laid eyes on you. There in the hospital you were all wrapped up to the ears and in a nurse's arms—and sleeping; sleeping your ass off! Lord, did you sleep right after you came in this world!—like getting here had been a terrific struggle, that tired you out, exhausted you. Ha, ha! But I don't think you've slept since—growing up, you was always fidgety, on the go; and still are, looks like."

Knight said nothing.

"John, what do you want? What's eating you? Am I right?—you want to be another Martin Luther King or something, don't you?"

"Oh, how's anyone going to be a Dr. King, Dad? No, I want to take part in the struggle—make a contribution to it, if I can. Negroes have been through so much. You yourself taught me that—told me our history. It's had it's effect on me, I'm sure."

"Do you hate white folks, John?"

"Most of them."

"They're caught too, though, remember that—everybody's caught."

"I've met a few Southern whites I feel good about—who in spite of all the pressures and dangers have been on our side. Some are very decent people—very brave."

"They're caught, though," said Goforth. He cleared his throat and gazed out the window down onto the lighted street. "Ah, but maybe when you get a son, you'll escape—who knows? Maybe you'll learn compassion. But I have had bad dreams about you just the same. This unwillingness, downright refusal, on your part to try and see the other fellow in the midst of all his peculiar circumstances, bogged down in them maybe, whatever they might be, before passing judgment on him is, as I've said, a fatal flaw that may bring you down if you ain't careful—may bring tragedy, to yourself as well as others, if you don't mend your ways. I'm asking you to think about it. One thing, though, has been cleared up for me since today back there in the bedroom: I had wondered why I wanted you to come home so bad—sure, I'm sick, had an opera-

442

tion, and don't know from day to day what's in the cards for me; I knew all that and it was only natural I'd want to see my son, my only chick or child in the world. But I found out today, as I thought it over back there, what had really been in the back of my mind. It was to warn you. Yes—that's it; to warn you. So I've done that now. Johnnie, don't forget what I told you. I've had this feeling, yes, of uncertainty, fear, for you. Maybe now it'll go away. Ah, let's hope so, Johnnie. . . ."

Knight, as he had planned, left Chicago by plane on Wednesday to return to Monroe, Louisiana. Before he went he came to say good-bye. Aquilla, seeing father and son together for what she sensed was the last time, could not restrain her tears—she left the living room. Goforth had dressed for his son's departure. He wore a dapper tan suit, which now hung in folds on his wasted frame, and a red sport shirt open at the collar. He was jolliness, loquacity, bombast, personified. Knight recognized it was an act and was reflective, almost distant, in order to hide his own devastated emotions, his sadness.

"When're you coming back this way?" Goforth demanded, laughing. "Soon, I hope! Maybe you'll bring a wife with you next time— what's her name? . . . Velma? Yeah, Velma! Ha, ha! Maybe I won't be laid up so bad then—the four of us can get out and see the sights and have some fun next time, huh?" He looked at Johnnie and for an instant his mouth fell open as if he were seeing him for the first time. Agonies of the spirit overwhelming him, knowing he would never see him again, he swallowed and once more broke out laughing. "Say, who's the only nigger that ever called Woodrow Wilson a liar to his face and got away with it?"

Knight smiled. "William Monroe Trotter," he said.

"Boy, I taught you plenty, didn't I? Ha, ha, ha! Pass it down, then—pass it down to *your* son!"

Then Knight left.

Goforth died on July the fourth.

443

Book III

Canticle

Chapter 1

Ornette Hungerford led the way down the littered sidewalk, with Ferdinand Bailey and Knight, who now seemed completely recovered, behind him. No one particularly hurried, for the night was mild, though it was early autumn, and there was just enough wind to stir up the dust particles and debris along 47th Street and send them flying up against the garish signs over the storefronts, pawnshops, and taverns. The street lights shone pitilessly on the scene and the acrid, smoky smells from the fish and barbecue joints were everywhere. Knight was smiling.

Graciously, he greeted the passersby who recognized him—a goodly number—and even stopped to shake hands with a few. But big, serious Ornette stayed 'close to him, protectively—it had been only five months since the attempted assassination—proud of his recent promotion in the organization and the new intimacy with the leader it brought, while little Ferdinand laughed and chattered with evident pleasure at Knight's popular reception. It was like old times. "Most of them know you, recognize you, all right, John Calvin," he exclaimed, grinding his teeth in glee. The three of them were on their way to dinner at Stout's, a much-frequented soul-food restaurant on 47th Street, where Ferdinand loved the collard greens, ham hocks, and the free-and-easy atmosphere. "Say, I'm hungry!" he said to them in anticipation.

But now they were approached by two ragged black men, one staggering, the other carrying an opened quart wine bottle in a paper bag. The latter asked Ornette for money; it was for food, he said. Ornette only grinned at him, but Knight shook hands with the man and said, "If I thought it was really for food, I might give you something. But there are a lot of important things needing what little money I've got."

"Whut you come shakin' my hand for, then," the man bristled, his battered, unshaven face thrust toward Knight's, "if you ain't gonna put nothin' in it?"

"I shake many hands," Knight smiled. "I do it as a friendly, a brotherly, greeting, that's all." Ornette now stepped up beside him and looked soberly at the two derelicts, who then, muttering, went on. "Somehow we've got to learn how to win people like that," Knight said, in a kind of mild self-reproof, watching the pair go down the street. "If we've got any enemies or doubters, it's among people like that. We've got to get closer to them somehow." Ferdinand and Ornette, devoid of suggestions, made no reply.

Shortly, when they were only a block from Stout's, Ferdinand laughed, "I'll bet Rodya's been here for an hour already." In addition to dining, they were to meet at the restaurant Rodya Belloes, a young man, Jewish, who had been proud to tell them he was a graduate student in political science at the University of Chicago and in the committed process of writing his Ph.D. dissertation. His subject: John Calvin Knight and the Black Peoples Congress. Knight was grudgingly fascinated by him, by his inquiring, meddling, mind, his tenacity, and, though appearing to be inaccessible, aloof, looked forward to the interviews he occasionally gave Belloes. "There's no shaking the guy off!" Ferdinand said. "Are you up to him tonight, John Calvin? Oh, the questions he can ask! We ought to make him pay the dinner check!"

Knight, trying to scoff, laughed. "Rodya hasn't got any money. But, Lord, is he persistent—and a nuisance. He's making a record, though, of what the movement is trying to do. That's good, maybe."

"Yeah, but I wonder how accurate it'll be," spoke up Ornette, frowning. "How did this guy get on your trail anyway, John Calvin?—he won't give you any peace. What's his story?"

"He kept coming into the office, pestering Mamie Campbell and the staff—till I had to see him. I was going to get rid of him, but I got to talking with him, questioning him, and found out he knew things about us, about the movement, that even I didn't know. He carries around a headful of statistics that would jam a computer. He's using us, maybe, for his own purposes, but what *are* his purposes? He's going to write up a study he's making on us, that's all—to get a Ph.D., he says. But probably nobody will read it afterwards anyway, so what if he does do a hatchet job? He can't hurt us."

Ornette, walking at Knight's elbow now, thought this over. "You know a whole lot more about these things than I do, John Calvin," he said, "but it seems to me that even if he can't hurt us, we don't stand to gain a thing by talking to him. You don't think just because he's a Jew he'll be any lighter on us, do you?—he's white, ain't he?"

"He's made me think about the movement, and about myself," said Knight—"He asks hard questions; his questions are a kind of test; they make you think. The other day he asked me if I really thought blacks could be helped."

Ornette swelled up in resentment—"That's a damn insult," he said.

Knight seemed oblivious. "Last week he asked me if I'd ever thought about why blacks would want to shoot me."

Ferdinand laughed again. "Did you tell him you *had* thought about it—plenty—John Calvin?"

"I did—yes." Knight then turned to Ornette. "He asked about you too, Ornette—why I'd asked you to come on the Central Planning Committee. And knew your wife's name, Rosabelle, and that there'd been a recent addition to your family, a boy, named after me—John Calvin Hungerford. He knew these things."

"This white boy's dangerous, John Calvin!" Ornette said. "You oughta check him out, investigate him, before you keep tellin' him more and more of our business."

"I watch it," Knight said—"I'm careful not to tell him anything the public doesn't know already. It's the questions he asks, though, that makes him unusual—he's so excited, so downright carried away, by what we're trying to do for people; that's it. I keep thinking why on earth didn't some bright black boy or girl, maybe working on *their* Ph.D., think of doing a study on us. It's a pity—here I am spilling my guts to a damned, opinionated, condescending, white boy who just came barging in on us and who'll write it all up and get his doctorate for it." He shook his head. "It doesn't make sense."

They had reached their destination. Stout's Restaurant, cluttered and old-fashioned, but clean, popular, and well-patronized, was nearly full tonight. While Knight went to the men's room to wash his hands, Ferdinand and Ornette waited briefly for a table to be cleared for them. But Rodya Belloes was nowhere in sight, and

449

later as they were all taking their seats, Ferdinand still laughed, "I was wrong—our nemesis has been unavoidably detained. Where *is* Royda?"

"He'll show up—don't worry," Ornette said sourly. Knight smiled.

Amos Stout, the restaurant's owner, hearing Knight was in the place, hurried out from somewhere in the back to greet him. A large, affable, dark brown-skinned man in a business suit, he informed them of the two specials of the day—ham hocks and collard greens, and red beans and rice. "And, Mr. Knight," he said, "I got plenty buttermilk to go with 'em—I know you like it."

"Wonderful, Mr. Stout—wonderful," said Knight, as they all began to order. Then Stout went off.

As they waited for their food, Ornette turned to Knight. "John Calvin, you've heard me speak of a girl who's a friend of Rosabelle's and mine . . . a very fine artist, a painter—Mary Dee Adkins?"

Knight thought for a moment. ". . . Have I? I'm not sure."

"I told you about her garage studio, remember?—where there's also some of my pictures."

Ferdinand, again laughing, interjected, "That you have, Ornette —about your pictures—half a dozen times!"

"Yes, I remember now," said Knight—"She's active with us, you said."

"She is, and she isn't," Ornette said seriously. "Before you got hurt, she seemed *very* interested. We were even going to form a committee by having a party in her studio to plan a fund-raiser for the local operation here. But a sudden change came over her when you got hurt—as if she was nervous and scared, or thinking about something else all the time. Rosabelle thinks it's because she was so shocked by the attempt on your life that it really put her out of business for awhile. But I'm not so sure it's all that simple—she's a strange, sensitive, very high class girl; a very beautiful girl too, and from one of the finest families in the community."

"We need some of that kind too," Ferdinand said—"Don't let her get away, Ornette."

Knight seemed only vaguely interested, but said to Ornette, "Yes, you've mentioned her more than once before—she's really impressed you and your wife, I can see that. It's true—people like this can help us too."

"Right, right, John Calvin," said Ornette, "—she's got great potential for the movement. Rosabelle's about talked her into getting active again—into forming this committee. If to get it started, we do give this little get-together at her studio, maybe you and Ferdinand could stop by for awhile to greet us. It would be a great encouragement, an inspiration, for everybody."

But before Knight could answer, Rodya Belloes hurried in the front door. He was a tall, very thin, sallow, bespectacled youth in his middle twenties, who wore his dark curly hair almost shoulder length and lugged a bulging briefcase.

"Ah," sighed Ornette disconsolately the moment he saw Belloes.

"It was inevitable," said Ferdinand.

Belloes' eyes had quickly swept the place and landed on Knight, and soon, rumpled, disheveled, unkempt, he stood over his quarry at the table—ignoring Ferdinand and Ornette completely. "Good evening, Mr. Knight," he said eagerly. "I'm late—my little car broke down again." At last he glanced at the others. "May I sit down?—though I had a sandwich not long ago."

"Do," said Ferdinand, in a tone of sarcasm—"Do sit down, Rodya."

Belloes, as he sat down, caught the derision and at once set about defending himself. "If I had been lucky enough to get a few interviews with Mr. Knight in his office, say, I wouldn't have to trail you around like this. I realize I'm a pest. But what I'm doing is important, extremely important."

"Oh, I didn't know that," said Ornette.

"Oh, yes, you did, Mr. Hungerford," smiled Belloes—"and stop baiting me, both of you. You, of all people, know the importance of what I've undertaken. There's never been a force at work in this country quite like your Black Peoples Congress. The Congress is something unique, special, and what makes it so, of course, is Mr. Knight."

"Really?" smirked Ornette.

This was merely the beginning of minutes more of such testy banter among Ornette, Rodya, and Ferdinand, and kept impatient Rodya from starting his questioning of Knight. Frowning, scratching his head through his long, curly, matted hair, he could hardly conceal his displeasure. Then the food came.

"Won't you have some dinner, Rodya?" Knight said, a little queerly, whimsically, and smiled. Rodya looked at the corn bread, the steaming red beans and rice, the collards and ham hocks, the cold beer and Knight's buttermilk for a moment. "I think I'll just have a coke, if you don't mind, Mr. Knight."

Ornette stared at him incredulously.

As Knight beckoned for the waitress, Ferdinand smiled jeeringly at Rodya. "It's too bad, too bad, that Mr. Stout hasn't got any chicken soup, or lox and bagels."

"I don't eat any of that either, Mr. Bailey—I'm a vegetarian. I catch the banter, though, the slightly anti-semitic ridicule—but I'm not religious either."

"You act so damn superior, Rodya!" exploded Ornette. "You *need* some bringin' down."

"Why fight?' said Knight good-humoredly. "What maddening questions do you have for us tonight, Rodya?" He was already eating.

At once Belloes brought up his large briefcase to his knees, opened it, and, after rummaging around in it interminably, pulled out the sheaf of battered papers he wanted. "When we had to stop last time, Mr. Knight, you were about to discuss your childhood—the role of your mother."

Ferdinand looked dismayed, apprehensive. Ornette frowned again.

"It was uneventful—my childhood," Knight said at once, but with bitter sarcasm detectable in his voice—"Except that when I was ten my mother went off and left me and I never saw her again, ever." With his ballpoint pen Rodya was writing furiously.

"Why go into all this, John Calvin?" remonstrated Ferdinand—"It's embarrassing; also demeaning."

"Go on, Rodya," said Knight.

"Why did she leave?" Rodya said, pen poised again. Ferdinand and Ornette looked disgusted.

"Essentially because she could no longer stand my father—who somehow was never able to get himself together. He drank and chased women; consequently, he seldom had any money when he got home. She finally got enough of his irresponsibility and left." Knight now glared at Rodya. "She *could* have taken me with her," he said, through almost grating teeth, "but she chose not to. Yes, somehow . . . somehow she chose not to. Almost ever since I've wondered why. It wasn't until I was lying up there in the hospital bed in pain this summer that it finally dawned on me why." He laughed, now showing his perfect white teeth. "It was simple— ha, ha, ha! She didn't *want* me—she didn't want me any more than she did my father." Rodya wrote like a zealot.

Ferdinand, though eating, sneered. "This is political science, eh?"

"It ain't even sociology," said Ornette—"It's phony psychoanalysis. Maybe even psychiatry. Jesus, John Calvin."

"Next question, Rodya," said Knight grimly, taking a drink of his buttermilk.

"What eventually happened to your mother?"

"She died—oh, she died."

Rodya hesitated, concerned at last about decorum. ". . . I know, Mr. Knight—but how? . . . and so forth."

"She married again, much later, and died in childbirth. Ha!— how about that? But she loved this guy very much, her young husband—eleven years her junior. You see, she had found love at last —and wanted to give her lover-husband a child. So she did, and died for it—at forty-four."

"John Calvin!" spluttered Ornette, throwing down his napkin— "Christ!"

"Let him continue," said Ferdinand, now sadly shaking his head. "It's a purgative."

"So you see, Rodya," said Knight, his eyes crazily burning, "all along I've had a half-brother. But he's not around—he doesn't freely circulate. He's in the crazy house—where sometimes I think I should be. His brain was damaged in the ordeal of birth in which my mother died. Ever since, he's been a resident inside the grey walls of a Michigan State mental institution. So much for my childhood, Rodya."

Rodya soon lifted his head from his feverish writing and spoke in utter exasperation. "Oh, Mr. Knight, can't you see how much better job I could have done if you had let me use my tape recorder! What I'm able to get down like this is only fragmentary. You are relating a powerful ingredient in this whole phenomenon of the black torment, the black struggle. It is a potent clue—it must be traced, explored, followed out to the end. You must help me, Mr. Knight!" Rodya quivered with excitement. "Oh, if you had only let me use my tape recorder—can't you see? I can't get all this down as it should be. What you're saying is tremendously important—empirical. Now, listen to me carefully, very carefully, Mr. Knight: How was it that this experience—your abandonment by your mother—was eventually transformed into your present intense dislike of white people?"

Ornette was now plainly beside himself—"John Calvin, can't you see he's making fools out of us all! Don't you see how he claims all knowledge for himself and treats you and the rest of us as clowns! How can you let us be shit on by this little . . . this . . . oh, Christ!"

"Ornette, I can see you don't have the least confidence in me," Knight said sharply. "For you everything sits right up on the surface—you can't for the life of you comprehend something that doesn't wave a red flag in your face. Rodya is one of God's chosen people."—Knight's words dripped sarcasm—"While we are among the people cursed and written off by God. What do I have to fear from Rodya's questions? If he has the sense he thinks he has, and that of those he comes from, those he really represents—the all-knowing world of Whiteness—he will not regard us as people he can deal with so condescendingly. We have no stake in any of this. It's a matter of letting him see it for himself—then he'll never forget."

Ornette was writhing in his seat. "John Calvin! . . . he's practically told you, last week, you were confused—a fuzzy thinker—"

"Now, wait a minute," Rodya said—"just let—"

"It's a fact," said Ornette—"He meant, of course, confused in your role of leadership. Why, he don't regard you as a real leader —only a nigger leader! Wake up, man!"

"Oh, God," whined Rodya, almost to himself, writing wildly, frantically, now—"They wouldn't let me use my tape recorder! Don't talk so fast! . . . you people—you're all talking too fast! Now, hold off a minute, all of you. What did you say the other day, Mr. Knight?—about how your abandonment by your mother made you hate white people? The connection . . . I missed that . . ."

Knight was cool, sinister, malevolent. "I didn't go into detail, Rodya. What connection do *you* see?"

Rodya's pallid face was flushed now as he wrote on, excitedly. "Can't you see, Mr. Knight—you've already said it! As a child you were abandoned. Don't you see?—you were *not* chosen! But you have just said blacks were cursed by God—completely written off! Don't you get the connection? . . ."

Ornette shouted (as people around them turned and gaped)—
"No, he don't get it! He—*we*—ain't got the intelligence! Everything must be explained to us—'very, very, carefully.' Now, *you*
tell us the connection!"

"Calm down, Ornette," Knight said.

"Yes," said Ferdinand, "cool it. This is all a crazy, insane, cha-
rade anyway. And the nuttiest of all of us is Rodya."

"Mr. Knight, Mr. Knight," pleaded Rodya, "the connection is
very clear—because you were abandoned, you somehow illogically
deduce blacks, generically, are abandoned. So this underlying conviction has been the fuel for your preachments, your exhortations,
to blacks: 'We are abandoned, we have been abandoned from the
very beginning, there's nothing we can do about it, so let's pour
the fire of our wrath on the heads of our abandoners!' Right? Oh,
it's so plain, Mr. Knight. It's *this* attitude, this burning conviction,
that has met with such a flaming response from rank-and-file blacks
—and with justification. They feel abandoned, and ought to—for
they are, and have been, abandoned. Yes, by man and by God.
Your movement is really a marvel—in that for the first time a
black leader has emerged who has a direct, kinetic, fuel line to the
great masses of submerged blacks. Your personal experience out
of your childhood has undergone a bizarre but gigantic transformation, metamorphosis; no racial experience you have ever had
can match the trauma you experienced in the abandonment by your
own mother. It has now served as a link to all those millions of
blacks who have this same burning, raging, feeling but from different, yet the same, cause. It's dynamite, Mr. Knight! It's so powerful it has confused you. You haven't been able to deal with it.
Your speeches—and I have read most of them—are filled with
confusion. But then your hearers too are confused; so they listen
to you with an understanding, a compassion, an affinity, a fervor,
that only a Napoleon, or a St. Paul, or a Savonarola, if not the
monster Hitler, could call forth out of a people. Yes, you are an
idol of the people but this is the reason!" In his excitement Rodya
had dropped his ballpoint pen on the floor; now he bent down and
vaguely felt around to retrieve it, his breath coming fast.

Ferdinand angrily shook his head. "I never heard such claptrap
in my life," he said.

Knight spoke with great agitation. "I once went in a restaurant like this one, in Paris—I was in Paris for a couple of months last fall—where an American black, an expatriate, attracted a motley assortment of non-whites, from all over the world, to his food establishment, a business he'd founded by money he'd gotten when discharged from the army after World War II. The food was 'Black' food. It was by coming to know many of the men and women, blacks, who frequented this place, people from all over, spawned by centuries of the Black Diaspora, that—contrary, Rodya, to what you say—I may have lost my confusion forever. It was there I really learned about Blackness—as a concept, that is —and the scales fell away from my eyes. Throughout my stay in Paris, I became an angry tiger, hating, *with my mind now*, everything white. I became a fanatic! Our troubles, don't you see, come with our enchantment with Whiteness—with the baubles of our oppressors, the meretriciousness of their goals, their rapacious tendencies, their cruelty. It was there, in Paris—not in Montgomery, Alabama—that I became a true leader, if I'm ever to become one, and lost all my doubts. Blackness is a state of mind, Rodya— a higher, an exalted, state, once it's achieved. Having achieved it, I have had simplified, solved, many of my problems as a man and a leader. Yet—it's strange—I did not arrive at this state only by thought, by cerebration, *only* by the mind, but by feeling and by faith. So it is now my religion—I feel it, I believe it, I preach it. As an individual I am nothing, but as an instrument I am much, in that I have touched this the vital spark among the people—the folk . . . yes, the street niggers, if you will! For in them lies the true salvation!"

Ornette was crying. He pulled out his handkerchief and blew his nose. Ferdinand was reminiscent, again sad. Ornette stood up, stuffing his handkerchief back in his hip pocket, and said to Knight in trembling, almost tearful tones: "That's why I follow you, John Calvin—that's why my wife follows you too, and all our kids. You have found the answer for us. Everyone has spurned our people; now we must believe in ourselves—our Blackness!"

"Yes, yes!" said Knight, even more excitedly now, "but I have not gotten this message across, or else they—my own people— would not have tried to kill me. I must return to them, make the message clear, and redeem myself!" His fist struck the table. "This I will do!"

456

Rodya had long since stopped writing; he sat glumly, with down-cast eyes. "I know now . . ." he said falteringly—"I know now your confusion is infinite. It has no bounds. It comes from desperation and bodes no good. It is all a phenomenon; yes. My study will prove it. It will be a masterpiece—a path-breaking master-piece."

Ornette half stood up again—"How you gloat!" he shouted at Rodya, as diners around them turned and frowned. "I oughta throw your ass out in the street! You're only here to examine, torment, us—so you can come up with a lot of statistics and half-baked, phony theories that prove only that you're a young upstart fool with a lot of secret contempt in your heart for blacks!"

Mr. Stout had at last had the disturbance called to his attention. Warily, unctuously, now, he came through to the table, smiling down at Knight. "Has somethin' gone wrong here, Mr. Knight?— I heard the loud talk. I knowed there hadn't been any drinkin' at your table—'cept for a couple of beers."

Knight dismissed him impatiently, summarily—"Everything's all right, Mr. Stout. We'll be going pretty soon—don't worry, don't worry!"

Rodya had scooted back from the table, in obvious fear of Ornette. Quickly then he began stuffing his papers back in his briefcase, preparatory to making a hasty exit.

Ferdinand spoke up again—"Rodya, don't feel badly, don't be afraid. You just don't understand the significance of the study you've undertaken. You can't possibly fathom it, nor will you ever be able to—unless by some magic you suddenly became black. But you must not abandon your research—call me and I'll even try to make it possible for you to see Mr. Knight again. It's for his benefit as well as yours. Maybe."

Soon, on this note of inconclusiveness, the dinner meeting ended. They all seemed confused, resentful, troubled.

*　　*　　*　　*　　*

Inevitably, if indirectly, Griselda was affected by all this. Knight, throughout the coming days in the office, was cool to her. His attitude persisted. She could not understand it—the marked change in his manner—and was secretly, inwardly, wretched; then angry, frustrated. She finally, to herself, began to blame it all on Ferdinand Bailey, for whom she had now formed an intense dislike. It was his plotting, she thought erroneously, his machinations, that had brought on Knight's coldness, his neglect of her, his busyness and preoccupation. Although Knight, in their till-now still burgeoning relationship, had never completely let down his guard, he had nevertheless maintained a relaxed and friendly attitude toward her. But now she could see, and feel, the sudden change. It could only be something, she thought, her enemy, this awful, this sinister, dwarf, Ferdinand, had done or said about her, some lie, calumny, now abroad in the office—indeed an attempt to drive her out of the organization. She became almost paranoid about it, and was resolved to resist; also to gain, if possible, more information; to get to the bottom of the mystery. Then suddenly she forgot all this, for at night she began to have dreams—wild, terrible, dreams.

As for Knight—had she only known—his change had come about as his most immediate reaction to the dramatic session with Rodya Belloes at Stout's. The experience, in his opinion, had served him in a very beneficial way. It had once more reminded him of, evoked for him, his original covenant—with blacks as well as with himself—to live austerely in the cause, resist temptation, and above all to live and think Black. He knew, however, he had not always done this, even recently, nor been true to these undertakings; that he had vacillated, or at times been enticed—if not overtly, certainly in his mind—from his vows, from the true doctrinal paths he had early-on acknowledged to be the only way of truth for himself as a black man struggling to know himself, identify himself, and thus be saved. In this there were many obstacles in his path, he knew; he had to contend with them each day of his life. But by far the most formidable threat lay in the omnipresence of Griselda Graves. Every time he saw her now, looked on her trim, lithesome figure, the swarthy beauty of her face, the sensuality of her mouth and teeth, he recognized her for what she was—the symbol of his potential defeat, his utter collapse and infamy, his betrayal of the folk, those whose uplifting had been his true mission. He had suddenly, with great force, become aware of it again the night in Stout's, not so much by anything Rodya had deliberately said or done, but by what Rodya's persistent taunting had conjured up in his, Knight's, own mind. His heart had filled to the brim with guilt, yet his resolve had been newly strengthened. Then something happened to Griselda. Was it illness—physical? Or had a fierce, blurred mysticism overtaken her?

It happened on the last day of September. At about two-thirty that afternoon, Mamie Campbell came running out of her office calling for Ferdinand Bailey. But both Ferdinand and Knight were still out. Learning this, Mamie turned back, grabbed her coat, and hurried toward the door. As she passed the receptionist, a tiny girl wearing a "corn-row-tight" hairdo, she, Mamie, explained: "Griselda just called. She went home sick from lunch. I'm going to go see what's happened." With that she left.

Ten minutes later she drove up in front of the very plain apartment building in which Griselda rented a small flat. She had never been there before and had difficulty finding the name in the vestibule. When she did find it and had pushed the bell, she was only buzzed up after a long, suspenseful wait. It frightened her, for Griselda seemed to have been in great pain—abdominal pain, she had said—when she called the office. When Mamie reached the second floor apartment she could already hear the attempts inside at unlocking the door—there were frantic sounds of tussling with double locks and a rattling and unlatching of door chains. Then the door came open and Griselda, in a robe, and wearing her Afro wig, stood there staring out, a strange, wild fright in her eyes. Mamie quickly entered and closed the door. "What in the Lord's name is the matter, Griselda?" she said—"Is it something you ate?"

"It's something I *dreamed* I ate."

Mamie gaped at her.

"Oh, Mamie, it's been like this for a week—I've had these awful dreams. Dreams about Frimbo and his little band of saints, about old Cleet—"

"About *who*?"

She went on obliviously. "—also about having a child by John Calvin. Yes, all these things and more—many, many more. Oh, it's true—all the time now I dream about having John Calvin's baby, a son. Then today I had shrimp de jonghe at that little restaurant, Gary's, down the street from the office, and got these awful stomach pains."

Mamie, astounded, uncomprehending, only stared at her. At last she said: "Griselda, I don't know what you're talking about—I haven't got the slightest idea. Did you really eat shrimp de jonghe or did you dream it? You're talking out of your head, girl. Have you actually got the belly ache, stomach pains, *now*? Or did you just dream last night your stomach hurt—this is the weirdest thing I ever heard of."

Griselda, a dazed, bewildered look on her face, pulled Mamie over to the small sofa, where they both sat down. "My stomach . . ." But she paused, her eyes searching Mamie's face. "My stomach, it hurts now . . . I think."

"You *think*," said Mamie, in both pity and exasperation. "Oh, Griselda—what's the matter with you? . . . I'm afraid for you, honest I am."

Griselda shook her head foggily. "I don't know what happened— it started, I think, about a week or so ago; when John Calvin stopped talking to me. Why did he practically stop noticing me, Mamie?" She turned and looked Mamie full in the face. "For then I started having these dreams, dreaming I was going to have his baby, sometimes that I was already in labor, and that these awful stomach pains were hitting me, it seemed, from head to foot. A change has come over John Calvin, I tell you." She seemed to shiver as she said it. "Mamie, look, you're my only friend—you know you are. You know, all right, what's been going on—you're no fool. You've known all along how much I love John Calvin."

Mamie threw up her hands. "Oh!—don't say such a thing."

"It's true! Oh, you know it's true! And he loves me, in a way. He's never said it, of course—he would never say it. He loves me, though."

"Griselda, you mustn't talk like that, girl!"

"Men are such bastards. Now, for some reason, he hardly recognizes me, my presence. Something's come over him, Mamie. It's unsettled my mind, I think. My mind isn't too strong anyway, you know—I've been through so much. But I dream all the time I'm pregnant by him. Then I go getting these labor pains after eating that shrimp de jonghe today."

"Griselda, *are* you pregnant?—have you been to bed with John Calvin?"

"Oh, no, no!—I haven't. I've wanted to—I would if he asked

460

me. He's been here twice, you know, but nothing like that's ever happened. When it comes to that he's mortally afraid of me!"

"But are you pregnant?—have you had sex with anybody else?"

At once Griselda became sad, reflective, guilt-ridden. "Not since in May—on my way here to Chicago. But he was only a kid, a boy." She sighed deeply. "But I was so desperate then. I hungered for someone to be near, to be close to me—I was so lonely. Why is this, Mamie? Why am I like I am? . . . Why do I have such a weak hold on life?"

Mamie was watching her. "Does your stomach hurt now?" she said.

Griselda did not answer. There was perfect silence—as if she were testing, assessing, the true state of her feelings. "Why, no . . . I *don't* feel it," she said, her eyes wide with wonder. "It's gone— I don't feel a thing—at least for the present. Ah, maybe it was Frimbo, maybe it was his little band of saints—my brothers and sisters in the spirit—who had something to do with it, with my relief. And maybe it was you too, Mamie—you came at once to my rescue; yes, you are my one true friend. Oh, how well I remember, back in San Francisco, how I hated you when you almost refused to see me, how smug and cruel I thought you were. And to think now how wrong I was. Yes, it's been you as much as Frimbo who's helped me—I know it, I acknowledge it?"

"I think you need rest, Griselda. You should take some days off and just rest, relax—read a book, look at television, sleep."

"Oh, no, no! I don't want to sleep!—I'm afraid to sleep. . . . it would bring back the stomach pains, the labor pains, of carrying John Calvin's child. You know of course about his child, his little four-year-old son who died—well, I've wanted to give him another. I've wanted to heal *his* pain, don't you see? We have much in com- mon—we were both spurned by our mothers, you know, and will always bear those scars. He needs me but he won't admit it—he won't let me help him, as much as I've tried. I've begged, pled with him, to let us consummate our love, but he somehow stonily re- fuses. He has such discipline, such will power, you know—although there've been times I've seen him shaken, weakened, watched him go to the brink, but he has somehow always turned back in time. Yet I dream all the time I'm pregnant by him. Lately he all but ignores me—which then makes me dream I'm carrying his child.

461

Mamie, Mamie!—he's made me forget Alan . . . dear, sweet Alan, my husband. It makes me feel so terrible, so trashy! What has come over me, Mamie?—what's happening to me? Am I sick! Yes, yes, I can tell it by the look on your face! I *am* sick! I'm mentally ill. For God's sake, don't tell John Calvin!" The wild look had come back in her eyes. But there were no tears. Her face was cold, stony, though her mind fought hysteria. She merely folded her hands in her lap now and was quiet.

But Mamie, after a half hour, returned to the office. At once then, somehow summoning the courage, she closeted herself with John Calvin Knight and told him everything.

*   *   *   *   *

For the rest of the afternoon Griselda watched television soap operas—something she never did; her nerves were in shambles. Later she ate a dinner of canned soup, crackers, and hot, very hot, tea, dreading to see night come, a time when eventually she must sleep. For a week sleep had been excruciating for her and she was determined tonight to fight it off as long as she could. Then a bizarre awareness came over her: she wished, of all things, for a drink—whiskey. It might settle her nerves, she thought, though she knew two drinks would make her drowsy and soon she would be asleep and into the frightful dreams again. But it was idle to think of whiskey; there was none in the house; she did not buy it these days; it was too expensive for her little budget, for since she had taken this apartment, tiny and plain as it was, she was constantly put to it to makc ends meet. The Congress paid her only bare subsistence.

She asked herself why she didn't leave the organization. With her skills she was certain in Chicago she could get a far better job in the corporate world. Yet if she left the Congress, why stay in Chicago at all? At once then she was forced to recall why she had come to Chicago in the first place. It was *because* of the Congress, she told herself, though somewhat shiftily—knowing this was not true but that it had been John Calvin Knight, to her the great and glamorous leader, who had been her lodestone. She remembered the days, even back to her childhood, when she associated all kind-ness, all warmth and affection, indeed love, with Negroes. In this she thought especially of her Negro nanny, Sima, whom later her mother would summarily fire. Sima was love embodied, and her, Griselda's, feeling on receiving love would remain with her forever. Then came along Alan to reenforce this. The impression, the fal-lacy, had persisted until her original encounter with the Black Peoples Congress, till her first experience with the cold, unrespon-sive people in the San Francisco office—even with Mamie Camp-bell, eventually her only friend. She told herself now she must face the truth. The Congress had brought her mostly misery. She was dismayed by her own reluctance, her virtual refusal, in this situa-tion, to associate Knight with the Congress. She knew she strained to see him as something wholly apart, somehow wanting always to hold him blameless, when in her saner moments she knew this was error. In fact on his second and most recent visit she recalled how she had sat beside him there on her little second-hand sofa—it was hardly larger than a love seat—and tried to muster the courage to tell him of her misgivings, those she already harbored, even before his recent coldness. Yet she could not summon the will to do it. He was in too gloomy a mood as it was, for they somehow fell to talking about his dead son and she had witnessed his struggle to hide his grief and outrage. Yet then she had suddenly, before she thought, asked about his wife. But he seemed impassive now, sur-prisingly stoical, toward the subject. Velma, he said, had, after vindictive alimony demands, finally agreed to divorce him; that he had been single now for two years. Fear had risen in Griselda's throat as he said it and she had dropped the subject at once. Otherwise she felt he might think her question calculated, design-ing. But he seemed unmindful.

For the short time he had remained, they talked only about rou-tine office matters and about the mail still coming in deploring the recent trial and jury acquittal of the three men—Torres Coleman and two others—charged with the attempt on his life. From the start, however, chances of conviction were slender, for at the show-up he had been unable to identify Torres, much less the others. This made the acquittal highly likely, despite the defendants' creaky alibi. And when the not-guilty verdict came, Knight had now told Griselda, he was strangely relieved; he did not wish, he said, to know who it was who tried to kill him; this way, he laughed, he could always maintain to himself it was a case of mistaken identity, that his assailants' bullets were meant for someone else, that neither he nor the organization had such depraved enemies. Knight then chuckled: "Even though it isn't true—and it isn't—it's good for one's morale." Then, leaving, he had hesitated, looking deeply into her eyes. He put his arm around her waist and she was pliant, unresisting, as he drew her to him, still watching her. Suddenly then he seemed to come to himself. He smiled, dropped his arm, and bade her a courtly good-night. She remembered she had felt a kind of thwarted, unfulfilled, happiness—yet hope.

But now things were altogether different; something had happened with Knight. She saw him only in the office, where he was cool, preoccupied, pointedly indifferent. It left her mystified and desperate. She went now and made herself another pot of hot tea—it would keep her awake, she thought. Between eight and nine o'clock she tried to read a magazine, with only sporadic success. She was waiting for nine o'clock and a Bob Hope TV Special. Soon the show came on with riotous hilarity and before long she was wanly smiling at Hope's jokes, their deft timing, the irreverent sorties at public figures, the comic flippancy. Soon she was absorbed, smiling frequently, and once she even laughed aloud.

Then at 9:35 the telephone rang.

At once her heart began to pound. Practically no one—only Mamie Campbell and Knight—possessed her phone number, she knew. She was sure, in the light of events, it was not Knight. Maybe Mamie was calling, to find out how she felt. Soon the phone had rung three times before she got up and went to it. Breathless, she lifted the receiver warily, barely uttering—"Hello . . ."

"Griselda? . . ." The man's voice was high, lilting, vaguely sinister.

A sudden frozen pause—it was her inability to reply.

"Griselda? . . . Is that you? . . ."

"Oh! . . ." She nearly collapsed.

"It *is* you! . . . ah, yes!—Oh, my sweet!"

Only a numb stricken silence.

"Ah, yes!—you recognize my voice, all right! . . . though it's been a long, long time, months, since you ran out on me. . . . Eh? You sound scared, though you haven't uttered but one sound. You have no cause to fear *me,* my sweet! I've re-entered your life only to help you, to save you from the sordid mess you've got yourself in. Speak, speak, Griselda!—call my name!"

". . . Where are you?—how did you find me? Oh, Marvin—have pity on me!"

He caught the anguish in her voice. "Why do you think I've trailed you, my sweet, if it wasn't to help you, protect you, to take you back where you belong? I'm sure you realize that! . . ."

The only response was a bloodcurdling scream as the phone fell to the floor.

Suddenly Marvin was yelling, yammering, into his phone. "Griselda? . . . *Griselda!* Are you there? I thought I heard the phone fall—have you fainted or something? . . . Griselda! . . ."

Though still faint, shocked, silent, she had at last bent down and retrieved the phone, again placing it to her ear, yet scarcely breathing to prevent the slightest sound.

"Griselda, is there someone with you? . . . Is that why you can't talk? Say something, my sweet!"

"I'm alone," she said heavily, her voice ghostlike in the phone.

"Then talk to me, Griselda. I'm not coming there tonight. I want to learn about you, about your well-being and comfort, how you're faring—ha, in your missionary work."

"Are you calling from San Francisco, Marvin?"

"I'm calling from within five miles of your apartment, no more —from a downtown Chicago hotel where I've been living."

"Oh! . . ." A long pause. "You're in Chicago? . . ."

"Yes, my sweet—where I've been for well over a month now. Ha, ha, ha!—surprised?"

"Oh, Marvin! . . ." Her voice then trailed off ineffectually.

"I could have put my hand right on your shoulder, my sweet, any time within the last three weeks I'd wanted to. I preferred to wait, though—wait till you got enough of this crazy, wasteful life you've been living among these misguided blacks; wait till you wanted to return to a normal life. Now, from what I've learned, that time may have come, right? That's why I've called you. I've put a lot of time, effort, and money into finding you, my sweet— and why? It's been to save you from yourself, from your masochistic, almost suicidal self. This, of course, is all aside from my own need for you, a need you are all too aware of, that once you

465

spurned. Oh, Griselda, we must become reunited; it's vital to us both! I've written the same to Basil Thorne in London. We are three unique human beings, far superior to the average run of men and women. You must, yes—for your own sake as well as mine—return with me at once to San Francisco. I can make you happy there now. I failed before because I didn't know you like I've come to know you since you went away. I can make you happy now—oh, Griselda, I know it! Then when Basil comes—he has not said he won't—we three will have a life that can only be described as idyllic! . . . oh, it's true!"

"Marvin, Marvin, what on earth has Basil Thorne got to do with *us*? Oh, I've dreamed lately that you want to hurt me, that you have some unnatural, ghoulish compulsion to do me harm. Is it true? Marvin, oh Marvin!—I've come to fear you! Why have you traced me, followed me, like this?—why, why?" She was seized by hysteria.

"Ah, poor, poor, Griselda—me harm *you*?" clucked Marvin cunningly. "Is there anything, anything whatever, in our past relationship, our marvelous mutual experience, to warrant your fears? Nothing!—absolutely nothing!" Here a hint of anger came in his voice. "Your mother was sometimes right, after all—you've seldom ever in your life recognized what's good for you. You've almost invariably chosen those paths certain to bring you unhappiness, if not downright misery. I've come to bring you back to sanity, to take you out of all this, into a life befitting your essentially fine character, your natural patrician bent. Oh, Griselda, you *must* be able to see that! You must return with me to San Francisco!"

Griselda began to tremble; she was on the verge of hysterical crying now. "Marvin, I don't want to talk to you any more tonight! I'm too nervous—you've surprised me, upset me, so!" Then she thought of an artful ploy. "Where are you?—where can I reach you . . . if I need you?"

"Oh, now, now—none of that, my sweet! You don't need to know where *I* live. I know where *you* live—that's sufficient—and where you work, and the people you see each day, your associates, and where you go, and so forth. I even know about your new wig. I know all these things. Ah, I also know about your boss, Griselda —ha, about your idol, he of the feet of clay. I haven't been resting, you see—I didn't come here for nothing, my sweet. Griselda, you'll understand it sooner or later, that I came here for *you*. Now I'll let you go—I won't pester you any more tonight. But think about what I've said, think about the condition you're in now, and whether you want to spend all your immediate future like this— with these frenzied, rudderless, ill-starred people. Think about it and I venture your good sense will come to the fore and you'll listen to me. So, for the time being, good-night, Griselda. Try to get some sleep, to clear, refresh, your mind; then tomorrow think over seriously, sanely, what I've said. So again good-night, for now —good-night, my sweet. . . ." Then she heard him hang up. She began to menstruate, bloodily.

*   *   *   *   *

Black night. But he had resort to his diary. For him over the years—even in high school—it had been a source, a means, of release; also of guidance and instruction. Knight now wrote of himself: "I am determined to keep my mind free for the tasks at hand, though it seems the farther I go, the more obstacles, the more difficulties, are thrown in my path. But the mark of greatness is strength. So be it." In his pajamas, he sat at the small, lighted table in the bedroom of his apartment, the open ledger-like diary before him. His little bedside AM-FM radio had been playing soft music, but a moment ago he had gotten up and turned it off as its clock showed 10:50. Yet he was not sleepy; his mind was in torment. He wrote: "I feel, despite my years of bewilderment and perplexity, that soon I shall emerge into, as it were, a clearing, where many past worries, doctrines, those damned thorny obscurities, will be made plain to me. The way, the direction, for the folk out of the wilderness will at last be shown to me and other perceptive men and women. I somehow feel an evolution, not a revolution, is taking place." For the first time in a long time now he wanted a cigarette. During his hospitalization he had not smoked and, as a result, since then was determined not to resume. He had expected the first months of deprivation to be severe, but to his surprise and gratification they had not been at all. But now he wanted to smoke, badly, and he knew why. His mind was not on what he wrote in

467

the diary. It was rather on what Mamie Campbell had told him today when she returned from Griselda's flat.

He had never been so taken by surprise. Nor had he ever seen Mamie so upset. He was also somehow astonished to realize she would dare discuss so personal, so intensely personal, a matter with him. He had been embarrassed and secretly angry, and had taken the easy, albeit cadlike, way out. He had said: "Griselda is neurotic." Now he was sorry he had said it, though he believed it was true—despite in her case the extenuating circumstances. He was assailed by another fear: What if Mamie told Ferdinand Bailey? It could mean serious trouble. Ferdie had his quirks and conceits, he knew, but anything, ripe or potential, posing a threat to the organization brought out all of Ferdie's solid and sensible qualities, his strengths, though his ire and cunning as well. Moreover, Ornette Hungerford had been brought onto the Central Planning Committee, into the inner circle, and he and Ferdie, fellow zealots, had become inseparable colleagues. He, Knight, could, with all too little difficulty, envision Ornette's puzzlement, if not hostility, even outrage, at seeing this white woman, though ostensibly only a typist, assuming so prominent a role in the national office of the movement. But to think of Ornette's reaction if he ever learned what Mamie now knew, that none other than the founder and leader of the movement himself, he who preached such fierce Blackness, was involved in a liaison with this woman—the mere thought unnerved Knight, filled him with an unsettling fear; and he knew it was with justification. He clearly saw now the problem was one he could no longer ignore—it would get no better, only worse.

Though the light over his writing table still burned, he had long since ceased to write. Once more he sensed that familiar feeling of futility coming over him and on these occasions invariably formed a low opinion of himself. It was, he knew, his inability to define certain important things he had to deal with that so harrassed him, for throughout the time he had been regarded a leader he had been plagued by this incapacity to define what the basic, the true, direction of the movement should be. During the early, the organizational, stages of the Congress, this had been somewhat less of a problem. The goal then was building a constituency, augmenting the number of the faithful, and preaching the rhetoric. But the rhetoric of what? It was his impassioned demand for relief of hunger, of poverty, privation, all of them regarded by him the natural offspring of racism. But now with legion adherents throughout the country an accomplished fact, the time was fast coming, if not already arrived, when basic principles of direction—the future—must be defined and articulated. Yet here he was, as it were, paralyzed, helpless, unable to see through the doctrinal fogs. Was this paralysis finally becoming evident to those around him—or to even a larger audience? Was this why they had tried to kill him? He could not say; he could only feel his fears.

The really exacerbating ingredient, though, was Griselda. Here too, in addition to the continuing threat to the movement her presence posed, there had been this fatal incapacity to define. In this case it was a definition of his feelings. What were they—toward her? He had often pondered it, to no avail. Didn't, however, this very fact rule out love? But, even here, he was not sure. There was of course the undoubted, undeniable, physical attraction. It had been there from the beginning, though he had early sought to bar it from his consciousness. Yet now he was mortified to have to admit even to himself there had been times he had downright lusted after her. This was before he was hurt, shot. Now he fantasized his embarrassment at the prospect of being naked before her, with the long, grisly surgical scars crisscrossing his abdomen—where before his body had been so unmarred, so whole.

But these considerations were physical. What, if anything, was there in addition? In San Francisco he had, against all seeming good judgment, approved Mamie Campbell's proposal that this strange, beautiful newcomer be allowed to volunteer her office services. This had been the first step. Why had he taken it? Even then he had not taken it before he had seen her in person—he knew now, in view of what he considered the rash folly of the step, her proffer of services would otherwise not have been accepted. But once inside the organization, she had grown on him—as she had, with the exception of Ferdie, on the rest of the office as well. Then came the move to Chicago—here had been the grandest of all opportunities to change course, be rid of her. But it was her power over him—he dare not deny it—that got her hired in Chicago, causing his new local associates, aghast, to wonder what on earth was happening. Yet he did the deed, answered Mamie's question, approved her tacit proposal, as the others looked on in bewilderment. So this was in sum the evidence. How then did he feel toward Griselda? He still did not know; he could only tell himself it was without doubt something beyond the pure physical—but what? And her mind—what was the state, the condition, of her mind? She seemed at times demented, unhinged, given to hysteria—at least he'd had these fears since Mamie's description of Griselda's talk of horrible dreams and pregnancy. It was all confusing to him. Yet, he thought, the very fact of this indefiniteness, unsureness, should enable him now to cast her off with subjective impunity—with no hurt to himself. Could it really be so simple? He knew he did not want to hurt her—she had known enough unhappiness in her young life. So, he asked himself, was this where matters finally stood? Then the sudden compulsion hit him. It was too powerful for all his rhetoric, his lofty vows, to call him back. He went to the telephone—at five minutes before midnight—and dialed her number.

The phone rang once, twice, three, then four times—to no answer. It seemed to go on then ringing interminably. At last someone timorously picked it up; there was a hesitant, fearful, whispered answer—". . . Hello."

"Hello," said John Calvin boldly, feigning self-assurance. "Knight, here. Don't shoot me for waking you—I know it's midnight. Forgive me. . . ."

"Oh! . . ." A long pause—of relief. ". . . I wasn't asleep. . . ."

"Griselda, is it really you?" laughed Knight. "This is John Calvin—remember me?"

"I wasn't asleep—never mind. Yes, of course I know who it is." Yet there was still a vestige of the breathless fear. Another pause, then—"I was afraid to answer."

"Afraid? I thought it took you so long because you were asleep."

"How could I sleep? . . . oh, God!—how could I sleep *ever*?"

". . . Has something happened?"

She gave a feeble laugh. "Yes, something's happened—you called." But she was still shaken.

"Ha, I call—that's an event, eh?"

"Well, isn't it? You must somehow have known, though, how badly I needed the call. So yes, it's an event." All the while she was trying to contain her hysteria.

Knight could not know what she meant; he was relating everything to what Mamie Campbell had told him. Yet he sensed there might now possibly be something in addition—her voice had been so cowering, so filled with fear. "It's crazy for me to call you like this," he said—"in the dead of night. I was sitting here thinking, though, trying to define my thoughts, arrive at some conclusions. I didn't get anywhere."

"Arrive at conclusions about what?"

"You."

"Oh! . . ."

"Yes."

"Do you want me to come over there, John Calvin?"

"Tonight?"

"Yes."

"Lord, no—of course not."

"Why don't you come over here, then?"

Knight hesitated. But not for long. "Okay . . . I will," he said, but hung up the phone slowly, reflectively, with a racing heart; he had felt his breathing quicken, his throat go dry, at the invitation. He realized he hungered for her, for her body, and resigned himself to what he thought tonight the inevitable. Where were his resolutions now? he asked himself ruefully as he dressed—where were his covenants with the people? Yet, feeling a strange, animal, excitement, he went down, got in his car, and drove over to her flat.

Later the bolts and chains clanged and rattled again as she unlocked the door and let him in. She wore a housecoat but this time not her Afro wig, at first looking very strange to him with her straight, dark hair cascading down her shoulder blades. He closed the door and, all resolve vanished, forgotten, reached to do something he had never done before—take her in his arms and kiss her. She strangely froze—conscious of her condition—and stepped back from him. It surprised him; then offended him. Quickly, to divert him, she smiled—"You know, it's the first of October already, as of thirty five minutes ago."

"What's that got to do with us?" he said glumly, but then also tried to smile.

"Nothing, I guess." She looked at him again. He had never seemed so handsome to her as he did tonight, in his sober business suit and quiet green necktie—though actually he was something less than a perfectly handsome man; his steady, sometimes pierc-

471

ing, gaze was too often a glare, giving him an unprepossessing air of self-importance, self-righteousness, almost petulance. All this, however, she seemed now altogether unaware of in her idolatry of him. "I'm sorry I have no refreshments to offer you," she said— "no whiskey, or even wine. Would you like some hot tea?"

"Nothing," he said, and sat down on the little sofa. Standing across the tiny living room from him, she finally sat in a straight chair almost against the opposite wall. Yet there was little distance between them. All the while he had been giving her his steady, fierce gaze. "I can't get accustomed to you without your Afro hair-do," he said.

She made no reply; it was as if what had happened to her earlier in the evening, Marvin's phone call, had recurred in her thoughts; she seemed still out of touch, absorbed, inwardly quailing, from her recent fears; though she stared at him, her mind was elsewhere.

"Where is your wig, Griselda?" There was a trace of harshness in his voice.

"In the bedroom," she said.

"Please go put it on."

"Why?"

He did not reply; he only held his gaze on her.

"Why?" she repeated.

"Okay, never mind. I have no right to insist."

"If it will make you feel better, I'll go put it on, John Calvin." She got up and left the room.

His emotions ran strong, though they were myriad, confused, a hodgepodge of motives; he also felt foolish and almost wished he hadn't come. Above all, he condemned himself for having revealed his hang-up, fixation, so flagrantly, nakedly, in asking her to resume her guise of a black. For it diminished not a whit his violation of his aims, his vows, he knew; his vaunted racial principles. Yet when she returned, smiling, the Afro wig deftly, becomingly, in place, he felt much easier. He took a deep breath. "I'm really confused about you," he said—"but you know it all too well."

"Yes—yes, I do." She sighed then. "I think it's more accurate, though, to say you're confused about yourself."

"Maybe it's the same thing," he said.

She sighed yet again—"Yes, maybe it is."

"What is it you want of me, Griselda?"

472

She thought for a moment and smiled. "Wouldn't it have been more chivalrous to let me ask that question of you?" she said.

"Yes, yes, you're right—Okay, I'll assume you've just asked it. What is it I want of you? . . . h-m-m-m, let's see." He thought for a long time while she watched him and waited. Soon his thoughts were in total disarray; he felt cornered.

"Let me help you," she said, "though this is not really an answer, only a clue. Isn't it that your life—and work—would be less complicated if I weren't around?"

He pondered what she had said. "But that assumes I have no feeling for you." He frowned as he spoke. "No admiration . . . no affection, no gratitude for your faithfulness to us all, the organization. I don't concede that. It would be callous and unprincipled."

"I'm not saying you care absolutely nothing for me; only that, irrespective of your feelings, I—my presence—make things more difficult for you. It's very simple—if I were black, the difficulty wouldn't exist. I indict you for that, John Calvin."

He was silent, but could not conceal his distress. He glared guiltily at the floor.

She threw up a hand in a gesture of futility. "We've been over all this before," she said—"It's no use." She was silent for a moment. "Would you prefer I left town?" she finally said. "I can, you know." At this she became pale and began to tremble. "I can, you know!" she cried, her voice full of anguish; she bit her lip—"I've been asked to. I have . . . there are others."

Knight, watching her, seemed more confused now than ever. He was reluctant, however, indeed afraid, to ask her to clarify. He rather spoke what was on his mind: "Griselda, I realize I'm helplessly confused—I've admitted it to you. But I know I'd be unhappy, in fact miserable, if you weren't with us, weren't in the organization, weren't in the office each day. I'm not confused about that."

"Then why have you acted toward me as you have the past week? Why, John Calvin?"

"I've told you how confused I've been—and foolish too, maybe. I won't act that way again—it was dumb."

She tried to hide her gratification but could not. "I will stay if you want me to," she said very submissively now. "I want nothing but to be near you and your work."

473

They both sat silently, not knowing what further to say. Finally she went and made a pot of tea and they had tea and crackers. But soon he withdrew into himself and they seemed strangely afraid of each other.

Later, back in his own apartment, he wanted to tell himself, convince himself, some things had been settled, the air had been cleared somewhat, that things might now be better. Yet there was somehow still an aura of doubt, inconclusiveness, over everything; he could not escape it; it would not go away. He tried hard, strenuously, though, for the time being, to put all his former concerns behind him and go on with his work; realizing, however, only time would tell. Next day he went out and bought himself a new suit and a few evenings later took Griselda out to dinner. It was only then—they were in a sequestered downtown restaurant where he would hardly be recognized—that she told him she meant to get another apartment and another phone number and pledged him not to ask why. Things at last seemed better to them both.

That night, after he had left her off at home following their dinner, she wrote him a letter, and next day slipped it to him as he left the office to catch a plane for Baltimore. He read it on the bus to the airport. "Dear John Calvin," it went, "I've never told you how you saved my sanity the night you came, after midnight, to my apartment. I was on the edge of terror and you snatched me back. I shall always be grateful to you for it. I must confess, however, I still find life a burden at certain times—the times when I feel out of rapport with you. I've become very dependent on you— dependent, really, on what I like to think, in your own peculiar way, is your love. There can be no possibility of doubt in your mind about the feeling I have for *you*. It has its grave dangers for me, though; it makes me so vulnerable, so easily hurt, possibly destroyed. It puts me at your mercy, the mercy of your whims, your unpredictable, sometimes harsh, and temperamental character. Please always bear this in mind and try to think sometimes of *my* well-being—so few people ever have—and be nice, be kind, to me . . . even if, in my frantic nature, I don't always deserve it. I beg this of you, John Calvin. You know I believe in you, in your ultimate destiny of greatness, and I tell you again how grateful I am to you for saving me. I hope I shall never have to be saved again. Please think of me now as your sweetheart, your only sweetheart. I shall bless you for it. Griselda."

474

Knight later sat in the airport lounge, at the departure gate. After he had read the letter for the third time, he slowly folded it up again and, deeply absorbed in the thoughts it provoked, returned it to his pocket. It had embarrassed him greatly. It made him uneasy, almost miserable; it brought on the feeling that it had increased his burdens no end—infinitely. He flew off to Baltimore utterly wretched again.

*　　*　　*　　*　　*

During the month of October Knight visited five cities where he hoped soon to found new branches of the organization to add to the twenty-three already in existence across the country. The present local organizations were all in the larger cities having heavy black populations, each branch with its own local leader, steering committee, and constituency. Knight was eager, indeed avid, to extend the organization into even the medium-sized cities now and talked constantly to Ferdinand and the others in the office of expansion, expansion, always expansion. It was as if he felt large memberships, sheer numbers, would somehow ease the necessity to at last come to grips with the thorny doctrinal, philosophical, questions involved in the matter of the direction in which he should be leading the Congress. He was all too aware of his perplexity, his indecision, in this and it haunted him; he also sometimes felt his wish to hide these shortcomings smacked of utter dishonesty.

The Central Planning Committee of the Congress was made up of the twenty-three local leaders and a few others (at-large) and met periodically at the national headquarters, until now in San Francisco, to chart policies and programs and give attention to the crucial task of raising money with which to carry on the work of the Congress. Such a meeting, the first since the move to Chicago, was now scheduled for the second week in November, at which time Knight also planned to stage a mass meeting, a mammoth rally, of the Chicago membership and followers. His purpose, among other things, was to impress the visiting leaders, fire them with enthusiasm and zeal, by example show them what was possible back home with their own organizations. Ferdinand, Ornette, Mamie, and many others in the Chicago organization were

475

already busy planning the big event. Similar great plans had been made before, in the early past spring, including preparations for a giant rally and parade into the downtown section, the Chicago "Loop," but everything had been aborted, thrown into confusion, utter chaos, by the attempt on Knight's life. So now, though there would be no parade, efforts were being redoubled to assure an outstanding, if belated, grand meeting.

Knight, however, had already begun to worry about what he would say in the great fiery speech always expected of him at these huge rallies. He could say the same things he had always said; it would be safe and was still likely to be effective; hadn't he built the organization to its present strength largely on these speeches, this rhetoric? Yet he did not feel easy; he could ill afford to be regarded as having gone stale, he knew, of no longer being creative and resourceful, now as merely repeating himself. Besides, there were members in the various branches across the country, by no means unintelligent people, who weighed carefully what he said and did and were not reluctant to speak up when his expressed views differed sharply from their own. Indeed there was one local leader specifically, Jesse Lumpkins of Cincinnati, who had all the earmarks of a real trouble-maker. He had a penchant for questioning almost everything, especially any proposal he thought insufficiently Black, and was sometimes not too tactful about it. This seeming distrust irked Knight but he took pains to conceal his dissatisfaction. He shuddered to think of Lumpkins' reaction were he to learn about Griselda.

The month of October was the busiest ever for the national headquarters. Hosting its first meeting of the nation-wide Congress since leaving San Francisco placed a burden on its inexperienced local staff that gave even Ferdinand and Mamie, both true veterans, a rash of anxieties. Nor were their responsibilities in any way lightened by Knight's having to be away so much. On the other hand, Griselda, as a result of recent developments—i.e., her midnight visit from Knight, unproductive, unconsummated, experience though it was—seemed unusually reticent; though she was the soul of retiring friendliness and cooperation in the office, she was yet noncommittal about anything of importance. It was clear to Mamie Campbell, who of course knew much, that Griselda was watching, disciplining, herself, was determined to keep a low profile, had by no means entirely rid herself of her insecurities. Knight was on her, Griselda's, mind constantly and there were still too many times when she felt the latent hysteria she harbored coming dangerously near to surfacing. She would suddenly find herself dissolved in desperate whispers, making little supplications to the saints in Frimbo's band, beseeching of them an inner peace she had seldom if ever known. At other times she was assailed by feelings of deepest guilt that she had fled Kansas City that night without going to the police and telling all, about how old Cleet had been murdered—he who, in the short space of an hour, had in the vague realm of psychotherapeutics done so much for her. Yet she was still shocked to recall Cleet had said Knight was "one of the biggest liars and fakes to come along since Marcus Garvey." She had never understood this, had in fact never heard of Marcus Garvey—maybe Cleet, as his acrobatic young wife Della had insisted, had indeed been senile. But she, Griselda, knew she would always remember him as a human being very much in touch with the mystic spell of some strange, profound spirituality, some harbinger of hope.

By mid-October Ferdinand, Ornette, and Mamie were working long hours on the great November national meeting. Rosabelle, Ornette's wife, was also actively involved, as now was much of the inner-city black community. Ornette and Rosabelle, despite five children at home, were, as they had been for months, donating their services to the movement. Ornette still made a tolerable living for his family by selling life and property insurance, but Rosabelle, since the recent birth of their fifth child, had not yet returned to her job as a supermarket cashier. Yet they were somehow able to make ends meet and still give much of their time to the work of the organization. When their sacrifices and dedication were brought to Knight's attention, he had sought to recognize this devotion to the movement by elevating Ornette to membership on the Central Planning Committee. Ornette, his honest face beaming, his hulking frame swelling with pride, had never been more pleased. He would now, as a member of what he loved to refer to as the "C.P.C.," be able to help make policy. This was at least how he viewed his future role. He was tremendously pleased and proud; it was the opportunity, the honor, he had coveted since originally joining the movement. Yet he now posed an ironical problem which sometimes caused Knight to doubt the wisdom of ever bringing him into the inner circle of the Congress. It was that Ornette had strong opinions. This was not all; he held them with a savage, unrelenting tenacity and belligerence. Surmounting even this, he at once began badgering, beleaguering, Knight with a host of new ideas, grandiose, expensive programs, plying him with every tenet in Ornette's fanatical creed of Blackness. Knight, though patient, long-suffering, saw now he had made a mistake. Then one day at lunch, in Ferdinand's presence, Ornette had dared mention Griselda to Knight. "Griselda sure can turn out the work, John Calvin," he said, "but when you get right down to it, ain't she really a liability? I'm always having to go into a long story to blacks who have been in the office, explaining—like, 'Yeah, she's white, all right, man, but she's a stronger supporter of the organization than you are, I bet.' Then I laugh. But it don't go down all that well with 'em—they can't figure it out." Even Ferdinand, no sponsor of Griselda's certainly, looked shocked, not so much at the thoughts expressed but by Ornette's temerity, presumption, his lack of respect for Knight, the very gaucherie of the act. Knight's eyes had popped with surprise, then anger. He stared at Ornette as if unable to believe what he had heard. Ferdinand intervened—"Ornette, Griselda doesn't happen to be your responsibility, old man. The only thing you have to do when—and *if*—her name comes up is say nothing. She's my responsibility, mine alone, until John Calvin has something to say about it, and as yet I haven't heard anything from him." The lunch went on to the end in near silence, after which Knight stalked out and left them both.

Afterwards, however, he wondered if the incident hadn't been handled, by both himself and Ferdinand, somewhat clumsily. But they had been taken completely by surprise, he thought, and had over-reacted—all of which he considered understandable. It probably would have been far better, though, he thought—given the delicacy of the subject and his, Knight's, own vulnerability regarding it—to have merely let it pass. For it was clear now Ornette was convinced he had been right and that he had been insulted to boot. Lately he had poorly concealed his feelings; he sulked. It was not a good situation, thought Knight—in fact, everything considered, it frightened him. All he needed, he told himself uneasily now, was for Ornette, in his awkward, unsubtle way, to start talking around in the Central Planning Committee, asking embarrassing questions, speaking in innuendoes, arousing suspicions, generally stirring up trouble—which might eventually point in the direction of the leader himself. It was disquieting.

The upshot of it all was that three days later Ornette, at least now smiling occasionally, once again at times showing more of his agreeable side, reminded Knight of what Ornette described as Knight's "promise" to attend a certain party. It was the affair, Ornette reminded him, being given to launch the newly-formed fund-raising committee, and was to be held the following Friday evening over Mary Dee Adkins' garage, in her artist's studio. Knight, slightly remembering, listened attentively; he was sure, however, he had made no promise to attend; besides, he knew absolutely nothing about this young woman Ornette had so earnestly, extravagantly, extolled; in addition, he was not even sure he would arrive back in town in time for the function. Yet he knew he wished to favor, placate, Ornette; it was important. So he finally decided he would make it his business to get back in time to be present. Then in the inevitable crush of business and travel he gave the matter no further thought—unmindful the occasion would change his life.

Chapter 2

There was something unique, she thought, matchless, unalloyed, about the blue heavens of October. What a rare color!—so pristine, pure, even limpid, depending on one's mood. Such a sky, she knew, had intrigued, bedazzled, painters for centuries. Gazing at this grand, cloudless, blue firmament out of her second-floor bedroom window, she thought of Raoul; but suddenly realized, in her entrancement, she had stopped work, had ceased her sad, tedious chore. It was Saturday morning and she was rummaging through months, years, decades, of accumulation of papers and bric-a-brac —newspaper clippings, snapshots, books, letters, pins, buttons, a teen-ager's tarnished costume jewelry, and, thrown carelessly across a chair, even the ancient Halloween getup of a nine-year-old child —herself. She conceded at last most of this precious miscellany must eventually find its way into a trash can. It would be silly to try to take it along—the new place, the modest (by contrast) condominium apartment into which she and her mother would soon be moving, would not be large enough for it. She looked at the mid-October sky again; it was a blue that Raoul, always the master technician, had often remarked on. It was in Paris, when with him, that she had first been brought to appreciate that no painter ever had, or ever would, put together pigments in a combination achieving this magic hue—this magic blessing. Speaking of Raoul, she had just tossed, discarded, his last letter, of two months ago, into the wastebasket along with other items she was saying good-bye to. However, it had contained nothing important, she told herself— only frivolous scraps of gossip about a way of life that for her was dead now, a finished book. She refused to think about it; she had closed her mind. But she was unaware fully of the bitterness that remained; none of which of course involved Raoul; yet at times a bitterness so intense it almost overwhelmed her. She turned now, though obliviously, and gazed out again at what Raoul would have remarked upon as the composition of the primary pigments of a beautiful azure sky.

So it was that now she spent parts of her evenings and Saturdays throwing away precious mementoes, in effect, bits of her very life from a time when it was all joy, sure optimism, naivete, delight, innocence—absolute self-assurance. Soon she came across a man's lone onyx shirt stud. She wondered how it had gotten among her effects. But though she did not recall ever seeing it before, she well knew it had at one time or another adorned a tuxedo shirt worn by her father. It had been only since the final break with Philip that she had thought constantly of her father, and with feelings of deepest guilt. Even during the time surrounding his death, her attention, she knew, had been divided—even her grief. It was a scandal, she thought. And in the months immediately following his death, her sense of his loss had, in the partial diversion, division, of her mind, been shamefully mitigated by the sense of the loss of another, someone so utterly unworthy. Maybe all that had since happened to her was retribution; even in the case of her mother—whose condition had not improved and who still at times was a burden. Yet she, ultimately the loyal daughter, had somehow developed a new love, a compassion born perhaps of mutual sorrow, for her mother. They talked to each other more now; there was at times greater understanding between them, to the point that Mary Dee had no longer so violently objected when shown how necessary it was that, to cut expenses, they put the grand old house, overly large and expensive, up for sale and buy an apartment. Mary Dee had tried to appear calm. Yet it had really been only resignation.

A real boon, however, had been her painting, the new burst of creative energy, and the five new pictures she had to show for it. There was also the time, the attention, she was able to give to her new friends, especially Rosabelle and Ornette, and the Black Peoples Congress. But sometimes it was as if she stubbornly insisted on misleading herself—that her secret bitterness was not the cause of, had nothing whatever to do with, her recent diligent efforts with the Congress. Yet at other times the true awareness almost surfaced, only to have her mind then, her will, at once suppress it. Her "little" brother Ronald—he was really a strapping youth now —away at the University of California at Davis, had learned of her new interests and was surprised, also mystified, but glad; he himself showed signs of activist leanings, to the lengths even of theoretical Marxism. Her sister Jocelyn, however—she too was still away, at Williams, an eastern college—so extravagantly admired, idolized, her older sister that anything the latter decided, any action she took, found unquestioning favor with Jocelyn. If Mary Dee had taken up with new, somewhat strange, unlikely, friends, it must, in Jocelyn's mind, be eminently good, exemplary. Neither Ronald nor Jocelyn of course could have understood what spleen, torments, vengefulness, motivated their sister.

Only "Uncle" Chauncey Stiles, the dentist friend of the family, sensed, suspected, something very fundamental was amiss, something, however, he could not isolate or fathom. But to his snooping, old-maidish, suspicious sensibilities, Mary Dee's recent zeal for the poor, her embracing of these new "friends," like the Hungerfords, seemed, the more he thought about it, somehow forced, unreal, at times ridiculous. He continued to watch her, study her talk and actions, in an attempt to penetrate the mystery. First there had been her cloudy, cryptic attitude about Knight. Now it was her intense, too intense, adherence to the very center, indeed the apparatus itself, of black militancy. Then one day she told him how she hated white people, and that even the so-called better ones were "a deceitful lot, deceitful as hell." "Dee, Dee," he had laughed, clucking in mock disapproval—she was getting a ride home from her job with him in his well-kept, shiny, but ancient Lincoln—"don't be coarse; it so unbecomes you. You know you don't believe all that. It's so simplistic, dear—ha, ha, almost corny. Your careless remark overlooks complexities. You're anything but an ingenue, you know—you're a worldly-wise intellectual."

She had replied before she thought, emotion welling in her voice: "I'm nothing of the kind—I'm a woman."

"Oh, my God—if I had said that, you'd be furious, dear, just furious! Ha! ha! ha!"

She had finally made herself laugh with him. "Oh, Chauncey—you bachelors. Stop badgering me."

Then, suddenly, he said: "Did you talk to Ornette yet about getting Knight to come to your party?" She stiffened—at mere mention of the latter name. There was a pause, as Chauncey, getting the green traffic light, pulled off and turned the corner. "Did you?" he repeated.

"No," she finally said. "But it's not a good idea anyway—heavens, Knight wouldn't come."

"How do you know that, Dee? Well, *I* called your friend Ornette."

She turned to him in astonishment. "You did *that*? . . . What did he say?"

"What could he say?—he said he'd try."

She sat frozen in silence for almost the rest of the way home. This recurrent suggestion had always been anathema to her. She was even more shaken now that the idea, the possibility, encroached nearer, and still nearer, toward reality. It was unthinkable, she told herself, that she would ever have to meet, confront, this man— who had behaved so boorishly, so hatefully, toward her. There could be no doubt whatever about his identity—he was the very same man. She had not merely relied on having seen, at the time of his shooting, his picture spread over the front pages of the newspapers. She had in addition craftily queried Ornette on Knight's recent foreign travels. There could be no mistake; he had been abroad, and in Paris, at that crucial time—exactly a year ago. Yet, she thought, he very well might not recognize *her*. But at once she could not bring herself to believe this—it would have been, even if unwittingly, a blow to her ego, she who had been throughout her life so often told how striking, arresting, beautiful, how unforgettable, she was; no, a crisis seemed almost inevitable.

That night at home after dinner, alone up in her room, she had wanted to write to Raoul, but she wouldn't let herself do it. She had even begun the letter, yet after ten minutes had torn it up— it had turned out to be a confession and she hated confessions. She had told him too that she had come to hate white people and, except for those on her job, no longer had any contact with them; that she now worked with an organization, a black organization, that stressed, glorified, blackness; that its leader—whom, she wanted to tell Raoul but didn't, they both, incredibly, had seen in a Paris restaurant—taught blacks across the country a new truth: the virtue, the fundamental efficacy, of Blackness. The man and the organization had wrought wonders, miracles, she wrote feverishly; it was the wrathful bitterness he communicated to the people in his speeches, recounting their long history of brutalization and suffering, that somehow made them proud and gave them hope. But it was hope of a new kind; it lay in the attainment of a new sense of selfhood, black selfhood. The leader was able to do this largely by reminding the people, the folk, endlessly, of what they had been through; their racial history. It was perhaps the history itself that worked the miracles, for there was something magical, though bloody and horror-filled, about this history—Africa, the Middle Passage, slavery, the plantations, the whip and branding iron, war, *de jure* emancipation, horrifying Reconstruction, the howling lynch mobs, the hangings and gasoline burnings alive, the massively imposed Jim Crow. The leader had also written about it all and she had read his works, every word, and, lo, the paradox of it was that what he preached somehow made her, too, proud. She confessed it. If it could happen, of all people, to her, how telling, how powerful, must it be to his more typical followers who had never known the world's good things, its pleasures and advantages, as she had. Ah, yes, she thought, she had known those pleasures for a time and they had brought her to her present sorry pass where, to use Knight's own biblical expression in his writings, the scales had at last fallen from her eyes.

Then, as if suddenly coming to herself, she tore up the letter and tossed the fragments in the wastebasket. She sat sadly musing for a moment. She had just then gotten the feeling she was forcing herself to think these things, capturing others' ideas, convictions, and holding them hostage; self-generating her zeal. Idly now, absorbed, she picked up the soiled pamphlet of poems lying among the scattered effects of her rummaging; long forgotten, they had turned up the prior Saturday when she was clearing out closets and dresser drawers preparatory to the move scheduled for January in the new year. She glanced at the pamphlet now, reluctantly, remembering all too well the blizzardy morning seven months ago and that wretched place, that greasy "Trocadero" restaurant, where the poems had been thrust upon her by their weird creator himself —one Gideon—a lunatic idolater of Knight. The whole experience, even at times the ragged, neglected children Ernestine and Vernon, brought back a deluge of bad memories—for, sitting in that foul, detestable place, she had constantly thought of Philip and Paris. For the first time now, she read one of the poems:

> I am the fire,
> Saith the Leader,
> I am the Rock,
> To bring down Armageddon;

Blasting his honky minions
And spraying his blood
On my mustache in flames.
All hail to our man, then.
Our MAN!

She cast the poems also in the wastebasket and gazed across at herself in the dresser mirror, her mind wandering, jaded, gloomy. Then she returned to reality, sudden, inescapable reality: the party, the committee party, was all set, she reminded herself. Certain key people in the local movement were invited, some thirty-five of them; the garage-studio had been readied—for its first and last party—and a number of paintings, both hers and Ornette's, put on prominent display. Ornette's colorful mural was of course a fixture. But Knight had not been invited—despite Chauncey Stiles' protestations, she had seen to that. The very idea of Knight's coming always brought her a shudder. Still she sensed she could not be sure what Ornette might do—he was so stubborn in his purposes, and wily too; so hard to out-maneuver. At once it brought back the old feeling of presentiment she had experienced when, in the restaurant with Raoul for their last luncheon, she had seen Knight the second time in Paris. The feeling was not easy to define—a vague mixture of fear, foreboding, prophecy. Yet it was also capable of inducing in her an almost eccentric urge for bravado. She told herself, insisted to herself, she was *not* afraid. What, she thought, was there to be afraid of? Still the uneasiness, the sense of dread, persisted, hung over her like a low autumn haze. She accepted it, yet at the same time sought to free herself of it—to no avail.

The telephone rang downstairs. Though there was an extension in her room, she knew her mother, who always raced to the ringing phone, would answer it—it was as if Irene Adkins awaited, craved, something to happen in her ever backward-looking, empty life. But soon she called upstairs and Mary Dee picked up the phone.

"Hello . . . Ms. Adkins?" asked the callow, male voice.

"Yes."—warily.

"You don't know me, Ms. Adkins—my name is Rodya Belloes. I'm doing a study, a research project, on the Black Peoples Congress and John Calvin Knight—it's for my Ph.D. dissertation at the University of Chicago. I know you've come to be active lately

485

in Mr. Knight's movement and I'm calling to find out if you'd be willing to answer a few, a very few, questions for me. It wouldn't take five minutes—just three or four questions. . . ."

Mary Dee froze. "What about?"

"For one thing, about what Mr. Knight should be stressing in the speech he'll make next month at the national meeting here. What should he be emphasizing, as the theme of the meeting—or as the direction of the movement for the future?"

"Who *are* you? . . ." There was scalding anger in her voice— she knew from his speech he was white. "Are you a newspaper reporter?"

"Oh, no, ma'am! I'm a student, as I told you—a U. of C. graduate student. . . ."

"I don't have any information you'd want! I wouldn't tell you anyhow—what do I know about you?"

"Please, Ms. Adkins—I'm trying to get all the information I can on an extremely important subject. It's important, Ms. Adkins. It will be an influential contribution toward interpreting the goals of the organization to the public, to a wider public. Mr. Knight knows this; he's granted me four interviews already."

"Then go back to him and get your answers; don't come bothering me. How would I know what he ought to say?—I'm not his speech writer."

"I've asked him, two or three times, what he plans to say—but, Ms. Adkins, honestly, I don't think he knows. He seems so puzzled, so indecisive, about everything."

"Oh, that's incredible—I don't believe it. But if he doesn't know, *I* certainly don't. Now excuse me—that's all I have to say."

"Wait, wait, Ms. Adkins—please don't hang up yet. Don't speak so deprecatingly of yourself—you're a very gifted, a very brilliant, young woman. I know all about it. And you've finally begun to make quite a few friends in the organization—they admire your quiet sincerity, your genuineness. But what they value most is your mind—I've found this out too. I'm sure you've thought a lot about the organization—you must have—and about the direction it should be taking. Please think about this again for a moment—then tell me what you think should be the theme, the motif, of Mr. Knight's address at the big mass meeting next month. You must have given this some thought—maybe not so much the speech itself, but the real substance of the matter; that is, a definition of goals, clear goals, for the organization."

Mary Dee's anger had in no way subsided. "Yes, I *have* thought about it," she said, her voice ringing. "If I were Mr. Knight, I'd preach, I'd constantly preach, *xenophobia* to black people. . . . I'd—"

"Oh, my God," breathed Rodya—"wait a minute! . . ." There was a pause—she sensed he was trying to write it all down. "Ah, yes," he said—"xenophobia. I wonder, though, Ms. Adkins, if we both understand the word in the same way—you would, in other words, preach to blacks the fear and hatred of foreigners, i.e., of whites. Right?—ah, xenophobia. . . . Beautiful, beautiful. . . ." He was still writing.

"Exactly—you have it! Yes, by all means that's what I'd do. That's what Mr. Knight should be talking about—xenophobia— *that* should be his theme!" She slammed the phone down. Soon however, angry and frustrated, she thought: "But what's so new about that? . . . nothing—though not using the word, it's what he's been preaching all along, isn't it? . . ."

* * * * *

Marvin returned to his hotel—the elegant Plaza Royale—after a day spent in the pursuits of both business and pleasure. He had first had conferences at the offices of his private investigators, Gentilenne and Vogel, then at two o'clock had gone to a matinee concert by the Chicago Symphony Orchestra. His investigators had again located Griselda, after her fearful move to a second apartment, but they had so far been unable to learn her new telephone number. This Marvin especially wanted—he was very upset; he did not wish to call her at work. The truth was, however, she had not yet had a new telephone installed in her present flat, and was undecided when, if ever, she would—she meant this time to thwart him. Marvin's frustrations knew no bounds, and yesterday, as he not infrequently did, he had called Nancy Hanks back in San Francisco, despite the fact his calls always seemed to frighten, irritate, her. "You never cease to amaze me," she had said, impatiently, as if Griselda's telephone number was so trifling a matter her, Nancy Hanks', time ought not have been taken up with it. "But it's plain —she's afraid of you, Mr. Freuhlinghausen. You've scared her out of her wits—why don't you leave her alone for awhile?" "Oh, my God!" spluttered Marvin, ". . . leave her alone! How on earth can I?—just answer me that. Why have I practically moved permanently to this big uncouth town if I could leave her alone? Why would I have hired a couple of Mack Sennett private detectives, whom I pay handsomely, and whom I weekly threaten to fire, if I could leave her alone? Why, why, Mrs. Hanks?" Nancy Hanks had sent a heavy sigh into the phone—"Poor Griselda. . . . I almost feel sorry for her; she *is* my daughter. You've frightened the life out of her with your slavering pursuit. Yes, sometimes I feel sorry for her. Yet I'm convinced it's better for her that she return to you—she'll really be less unhappy in the long run." But Marvin wailed—"Oh, how silly it was of her to move to another street, another flat, just to escape me! Why, I knew where she had relocated within forty-eight hours." Nancy Hanks sighed again, "Poor Griselda . . . poor thing. . . ."

In the hotel Marvin mused on all this as he went down the hall toward his suite. It was almost dark outside now, a cloudy, autumnal gloom, though the soft, sumptuous lights along the hall cast their glow down the length of costly Oriental carpet he walked on. Then, well before reaching his suite, he encountered three scarlet-uniformed Hispanic busboys. They were removing tables of soiled dishes, food remains, empty liquor and champagne bottles, and rumpled tablecloths from a large suite (Number 1020) along the hall. As he passed, he glanced in. At once he paused—curious, startled. The door was flung back wide; all the guests were gone; only the elaborate parlor was directly in view; but what had startled him was beyond the parlor. It was the weirdly revolving patterns of light, myriad, many-colored, ever in motion. The light seemed emanating from a source unseen, perhaps from a bedroom remote and out of view. The sight amazed, almost frightened him; then somehow it sent a thrill through him, through all his salacious faculties; at first his throat went dry, but soon it was exuding hot saliva as his imagination went out of control. He stood now staring, gaping, past the playful busboys into the parlor, at the vividly whirring, cascading, dancing, reflections on the rear walls and ceiling.

The images cast were fluid, ever-changing, demonic, and seemed made up of a thousand radical hues—red, green, purple, yellow, blue, orange, white, even sable, then red again—all variegated and iridescent, dappling all the exposed surfaces of the resplendent suite. It entranced, enkindled, him; soon he was in a furor; he wriggled past the busboys now and entered the parlor. When they saw him thus transfixed, standing again as if stuporous, they laughed—apparently the experience was not new to them. "Ah, the light, the wonderful light, eh, señor?" said one of them—"We like it too; that's why we always turn it on; some sight, eh?—some show! This is not the most expensive suite in the hotel for nothing, señor. As you see, even the daytime parties are grand."

Marvin, unmindful, still stood in the middle of the parlor, an absent, rapturous smile on his face as if he were all alone in the room. Soon he took a few hesitant steps toward the nearest bed-room, the apparent source of the slowly whirring, gaudy light. At the threshold, he stopped dead still—as the busboys, watching, laughed again. What he saw astounded him. Everything was mir-rors, myriad mirrors. They were everywhere—except on the great bed; the walls and ceiling were a constantly refracting series of glass panes, glass shafts, both clear and opaque, all intricately placed, ingeniously arranged, below, around, and above him. But he was puzzled—what was the source of this unholy illumination? Stepping inside, he began to look around him. Then he saw. He understood. It was a large, low, revolving light fixture, its lenses ever-changing and multi-colored, bearing a complication of adjust-ments and gadgets, the whole complex machinery fixed securely into the floor in a far corner of the bedroom, its movements and gyrations sweeping up and around the walls and ceiling of varie-gated mirrors. He was ecstatic; the eerie, erotic atmosphere it all created made him again salivate; soon he was rushing around like a madman, looking, gawking, stooping to examine the complicated gadgetry, touching, feeling, the mirrors, all the while breathing, exhaling, a frenetic excitement. But now one of the busboys came in. "We must turn the light off now, señor," he said, smiling— "We must lock the suite and leave." Whereupon the boy bent down and turned a switch, plunging everything in the bedroom into total darkness.

"Oh, my God!" Marvin cried out, in a kind of howling lament.

"The darkness, the darkness!—after that beautiful light, those beautiful patterns of light, now darkness! Oh, once more—please, please, let me see the gorgeous light once more!"

"Señor, we had no business turning it on in the first place. But we also love to watch it going round and round, throwing all those beautiful colors onto the big bed—we turn it on every time we're in here; but it's a violation. Now we must go." The boy led the way out of the darkened bedroom into the parlor again, as Marvin, groping, protesting, mumbling, slowly followed. Soon they were all out in the hall again, the suite door locked. "Good-bye, señor," another of the boys smiled, wheeling a table of dishes down the hall toward the rear service elevator—"You should have that suite yourself, señor," he laughed.

Marvin suddenly struck his forehead with the heel of his hand— the thought was a revelation. "Oh, Christ! . . . you're right, you're so right!" he said breathlessly, now hurrying to follow the three boys. "I *should* have it!—yes, yes! But the manager of this hotel— that awful Mr. Dennis—is a bastard, a real bastard. He'll never let me have it—never. I had a frightful row with him when I asked that a piano—just a little spinet piano—be put in my suite. After much wrangling, he finally did it, but he sure didn't want to—got nasty, downright nasty, about it. No, he'll never let me change to that heavenly suite. Oh, I know it, I know it!—he won't!"

"Señor, pardon me, but it's a very, very expensive suite."

"Oh, what the hell do I care about that? I must have it—I must, I must! What a divine bedroom! Oh, Griselda must see it!"

"Good luck, then, señor." The boys went on.

Marvin, trembling from his excitement, hurried down the hall, got out his key, and let himself in his own suite now. He went directly to the telephone and called downstairs for the manager. Mr. Dennis had gone, he was told—a fact, however, that much encouraged him. He asked for an assistant manager. Soon a Mr. Abel, so identifying himself, came on. Marvin's voice was husky from his agitation. "I'm Mr. Freuhlinghausen, in suite 1041," he said— "I've just been in suite 1020 down the hall. I like it very much— oh, a lot! Is it at all possible that I could exchange this one for it? . . ."

Mr. Abel was slow to reply. "I'm afraid not, sir," he said at last. "How long will you require it?"

"Oh, for some time—I don't know how long exactly . . . weeks, maybe."

"Mr. Dennis would have to approve an indefinite occupancy like that, sir. He's gone for the day—why don't you see him tomorrow morning?"

"I want the suite tonight!" Marvin almost shouted; but not from anger; he was pleading. "Let me have it tonight and I'll take it up with him tomorrow!"

Mr. Abel still hesitated, though not unimpressed by someone who could afford indefinite occupancy of 1020. "Well, perhaps you could have it for tonight," he finally said—"but just tonight. After that you'll have to see Mr. Dennis."

"Oh, thank you—fine!" said Marvin breathlessly. "Now get maid service up there, will you, please?—the suite's not made up. Thank you—thank you, Mr. Abel. Oh, one more thing—I'll need a couple of men to move my little piano down the hall. That will be all. Thank you, thank you!" He hung up in great joy and went at once and made himself a Scotch and soda.

He was of course thinking of Griselda. But his thoughts both excited and saddened him. It was such a long, melancholy story— his life with (without) her. How could he contact her now?—it seemed almost hopeless. At once he began cursing Gentilenne and Vogel, his operatives, for what he thought their failure to come up with her new telephone number—neither he nor they could know she had not even decided on a phone. He must go find her himself now, he thought; some way, somehow—and tonight. It was a compulsion, a necessity. What was a suite like 1020, with all its magnificence, its garish beauty, color, and madness, without Griselda? He thought of their life together in San Francisco—it seemed so far away and so long ago now. He had at least known spells of happiness then, no matter how sporadic; now his misery was constant, unremitting, complete. His drink in hand, he began pacing the floor and feverishly talking to himself.

What most mystified him, however—and intrigued him too—was John Calvin Knight. He, Gentilenne, and Vogel, had left no stone unturned to learn, to know, everything possible about him. This even included sending a spy into his camp, one Bernard Faxson— alias Rodya Belloes. By his wily, brash persistence, Faxson (who was, however, in fact a college student, though not at the University of Chicago)—to the amazement of them all—had penetrated so effectively he had almost become Knight's confidant. Somehow, though, this had significantly changed some of Marvin's attitudes—especially toward Knight. Heretofore, despite knowledge of Griselda's involvement, he had often read of Knight's activities and accomplishments with secret admiration. Marvin himself, first hand, knew something of the rebuffs of society. Here was a brave, fiery, committed black man and leader, he had told himself—a dedicated man; above all a smart man. Now this episode—Rodya Belloes. He somehow felt only disgust now for what he considered Knight's unthinking negligence—and naivete. What kind of leader was this? he thought. What could Griselda see in him?—what was she thinking about, to have become swept away by someone so dense, so ineffectual? Was it sex? he wondered then. He was not sure—yet the possibility had to be reckoned with. It was a paradox that he was not at all repelled by—this was life, he thought, the life of today; besides, to understand it, one had only to know quixotic, driven, Griselda; a person *sui generis*. Otherwise, he could not fathom her attachment to Knight—unless it was her unwitting mite of black blood calling out to its counterpart for union. Someday, in all likelihood very soon, he would have it all out with her— they would meet and discuss this whole strange business. That time might still be tonight, if he could only find her, persuade her, say, to have dinner with him—in his new, if perhaps temporary, suite. He knew by his terrible feelings of agitation, urgency, he had no choice—he must somehow reach her. He half bent over now in his agony, almost as if he were going to pray; but then, almost tearfully, he snuffled and stood up, his nose running, teeth chattering. He fled finally to the telephone again. "I'm moving!" he cried distractedly to the desk personnel downstairs—"I'm moving into suite 1020! I told you I need someone to help me with my piano!"

Two bellmen soon came and moved him, tiny piano and all, into the suite of mirrors. Then, still tingling with his excitement, the suspense, and somehow the dread, he went down to the lobby level, ordered his rental car from the hotel's garage, and drove off into the foggy night.

* * * * *

Griselda was not happy in her new apartment. She had taken it in utter, frightened, haste. Moreover, it had cockroaches; yet it somehow appeared clean, and was bright and cheerful. She had bought exterminating powders for the insects, but to no avail; the roaches only seemed to proliferate. Yet at times these were almost welcome distractions—for her thoughts were almost always on Knight. Then suddenly Marvin had thrust himself again into her life—causing her thus to flee. She thought often of Marvin now; he loomed in her mind as a menace, yet she could not have said specifically why. It was all in her feelings, her intuition; at times when she thought of him, her flesh took on cold creeps. She could not, however, forget his strengths too. In San Francisco he had housed her in an apartment where cockroaches were certainly unthinkable, bought her beautiful clothes at I. Magnin's, and provided her with a smart, new Porsche to drive. He was not all bad, she so often told herself—if only she could rid herself of this strange fear of him. She thought him essentially crazy.

Nor did she feel right in an apartment, any apartment, without a telephone. Yet who was there to call on a phone, or who would be calling her? Mamie Campbell, maybe. Then she stopped trying to fool herself. There was Knight, unmistakably Knight—he was the real reason. In the other apartment he had called her occasionally, but now, except for a smile and a "hello" in the office, she was completely cut off from him. When he had broken his pledge and asked her why she no longer had a phone, she had laughed and said she couldn't afford one. It was a problem he could never have imagined—no one in the organization knew of Marvin's presence, absolutely no one. Nor was there anyone, not even Mamie, she could talk to about him. At last her thoughts seemed dull, strung out; it was ground her mind had traversed so many times before; and soon somehow she began yawning. She had been home from the office since six; now it was only eight-thirty yet she was already nodding sitting in the chair; she knew she would soon be in bed and asleep, for last night she had slept poorly. Then came the sudden, loud, jarring sound—the doorbell.

At first she panicked and ran into the bedroom—as if to hide.

493

But then, slowly, tentatively, she returned to the tiny living room, her eyes wide with fright. Could it be Knight, though? she wondered. She was certain it was not Mamie Campbell—at night; and no one except those two knew where she had moved, or that she had moved at all. Then she speculated it might merely be someone down in the entrance pushing the wrong bell. She finally started over to the intercom—just as another long, loud, persistent ring made the little flat vibrate. Almost panicking again, she decided not to answer. But what if it were John Calvin? she thought. At last she spoke into the intercom—"Yes? . . ."

"Griselda! . . . Oh, I'm so glad I caught you home! This is *Marvin!*" There was a pause. "Do you hear?—it's Marvin!" He was unsteady; while waiting to be moved out of his suite he had had four Scotches. "I must see you tonight, Griselda—it's important! May I come up?—will you go out with me? We must talk—it's terribly important, Griselda!"

Thus her worst fears were confirmed. "Oh, no, no! . . ." she said, trembling. "No, I can't see you! . . ."

"*Griselda!*—may I come up? I want to talk with you!—*please.* . . ." His voice was almost tearful now.

"No, no, you can't!" she cried. "Go away, go away!" Then there was a click in the intercom—the conversation was ended.

At once he began ringing again, repeatedly, furiously. But there was no response—only a final silence. Soon he was cursing, then crying. Then in a fit of vengeance he pressed the bell and held it ringing for thirty seconds—until a man from the second-floor apartment adjoining hers came down to see what was wrong. A stocky black man, about forty and wearing glasses, he opened the stairwell door and looked out curiously at Marvin. "What's going on?" he said—"Who're you looking for?" Then he frowned. "Must not be anybody home in the apartment you keep ringing—you trying to raise the dead?"

Marvin flew into a rage. "She *is* up there!" he shouted—"She just answered—I talked to her! Oh, she's up there, all right!—let me go up and knock on her door, will you? Please, please—it's important!"

"*She* must not think it's important," the man said, frowning again. "No—you can't come up. If she'd wanted you, she'd buzzed you up." He moved to close the door.

Marvin lunged and threw himself against the door, preventing its closing. "She's my wife!" he almost screamed—"I have a right to see her! Stand aside!"

"Your *wife!*" The man blinked.

"Well, almost," said Marvin—"anyway, I have the right to see her."

The man now studied him out of the corner of his eye—suspiciously. "Say, what is this?" he said, now resisting, bracing himself against the door with both hands—"I'm goin' up and call the police." He finally managed then to close the door, leaving his intruder spluttering, cursing, crying, outside. Finally Marvin rushed out into the street to his car.

He was back at the Plaza Royale within twenty minutes, sick with grief and disappointment. He went up to 1020, his new suite, turned on the madly-whirring colored light in the bedroom, and again stood gazing at its myriad reflections on the walls and ceiling, as tears of wretchedness, utter misery, coursed down his cheeks. He was grieving for many reasons, he knew; yet mainly about Griselda—his Griselda. Why had she so cruelly, so heartlessly, rebuffed him, turned him away? he asked himself, really loathing himself. He was desperate and lonely now; he had never felt so all alone in his life. What good was this gorgeous suite, that he had come upon so accidentally and gone to so much trouble to get, he thought, if there was no one to enjoy, revel in it with him? He was not only grief-stricken about Griselda but furious with her as well, for not coming with him, not trusting him, though this was the history of his whole life—unqualified rejection, by everyone, by even his parents when they were alive. But he was as furious with himself as with anyone else, and, though he stood transfixed observing it, even the bedroom's revolving light was now no comfort to him.

Soon he could stand the desolation, the loneliness, no longer and went downstairs to the posh little bar and lounge off the lobby, where he took a seat almost in a corner. As he ordered still another Scotch and soda, he remembered he had not eaten, and called the waiter back and ordered a rare roast beef sandwich in addition. Later as he sat eating, patrons came and went, or some lingered over drinks in quiet or mirthful conversation, as the clock over the bar showed 9:30. Not for a moment did anyone take notice of him, of one who so desperately needed noticing. The lights were low in

495

the lounge but he could see all the happy, eager faces about him; it made him more miserable than ever. Again then he thought of his beautiful suite upstairs, going to waste with no one but himself to see it. He felt bitter now at Griselda for refusing to come out with him, or even to talk with him, or let him come up to her flat. Why did she fear him so?—yes, it was plainly fear. Except for his few childish displays of petulance or his one ridiculous, laughable, attempt to physically chastise her back in San Francisco—all clearly provoked by her—he had never threatened her or talked in a way to frighten her. Yet tonight there was almost terror in her voice when she learned who was ringing her doorbell. He could not understand it. But then something began slowly to dawn on him—his true feelings, his latent, as yet unsurfaced, longings about her. They were strange—dark, mad, perhaps dangerous and forbidding. He could not define them; he was only vaguely aware of them; but maybe—doubtless—she sensed them too. They partook of violence, though he hated violence—the sight of blood made him swoon. He feared violence directed against anyone, but especially against himself. Sometimes he dreamed, in terrible nightmares, of being attacked in his bedroom by some random young man with a knife. He always woke up screaming. Yet he knew violence was another name for life—for the world. Not everyone escaped it. They were the unlucky ones—fated pawns, victims.

Now a well-dressed, middle-aged, man, a businessman, accompanied by a woman much younger than himself, came in the lounge and took the space next to Marvin. He could see the man was furtive, shy, not entirely at ease, as he ordered drinks for the girl and himself. Then he began to talk, or rather respond to the girl's questions—How did he like Chicago? Did business often bring him here? Where was he from? It was clear to Marvin now they had just met. When the drinks came, the man would laugh nervously, then quickly sip his drink, as if trying to bolster his courage, attain a jaunty poise. The girl—from what Marvin could see of her, pretty—laughed often, as if trying her best to put the man at ease. Soon she began to hum a tune in his ear, which seemed to please, titillate, him greatly, after which Marvin's eagle eyes saw her hand lightly stroke the inside of his thigh. "I'll bet you're the cuddly type," she said to him, and giggled. The man, his face now a cherry red, also laughed—"I'll bet you are too," he said huskily. Whereupon Marvin, before he thought, let out a guffaw; then, guiltily, dove his eyes in his plate—as the girl glowered at him and the man fidgeted nervously. Marvin at once returned to munching his sandwich.

Five minutes later he saw another girl—she was alone—pass the door of the lounge and glance in. Without the slightest hesitation—it was inauspicious, preordained fate—he quickly rose and beckoned to her. But she kept on going and he could not be sure in the darkened surroundings whether or not she had even seen him. Yet a thrill went through him; he began, as was his habit, freely to salivate; he loved accosting strange women, having that way met Griselda, though he had not often done so—even if, as now, they were prostitutes. But soon then, outside the lounge in the hotel arcade, he glimpsed the girl again—in animated, and familiar, conversation with a dour-looking, if cheaply handsome, young man, the temperamental, hot-headed, Latin stereotype, wearing a crudely ornate suit with bell-bottom trousers. As they talked briefly the young man seemed giving her orders, and then, alone, she came into the lounge, looking vaguely about her as if for a seat. But Marvin somehow sensed now she had caught his earlier signal. He rose again and threw up his hand. She seemed ignoring him, however, at the same moment she was making her way, as if a robot, straight to the exact spot where he expectantly stood. "Hello!" he beamed at her—"Thank you for joining me! I waved at you as you passed the door a moment ago, but at first I wasn't sure you had seen me."

She laughed—"I saw you; only I had to speak with a friend." Yes, your pimp, thought Marvin. She wore a thin blue, attractive, coat over her pants suit. And her dyed auburn hair was just long enough to be carried back over her delicate ears, making her almost pretty, except that her mouth was too small; but there was an animation about her, a fire in her eyes, that very much appealed to him. When they had sat down, she eyed him, now at close range, rather critically—appraising him. At last, cautiously settling back, she looked away and seemed to shudder—Marvin's affluent clothes and elegant manners could in no way hide the quaintness, distortion, the ugliness, of his lewd little body. Finally she tried to smile at him—"Do you live in the hotel?" she said.

"I do indeed!" he still beamed—"Ha! ha! In the most gorgeous suite in the whole place. But let me order you something—may I?"

497

She hesitated. "Well, maybe a small liqueur of some kind—a Cointreau?"

"A Cointreau—fine." He beckoned for the waiter. After he had ordered, he turned to her again—"Tell me, what's your name?"

"Sally."

"I'm Marvin, Sally." Then at once he began a long, rambling monologue on his personal misfortunes that nothing appeared able to stop—everything pent up in him seemed to pour out in a desperate, manic, flood. After three or four minutes of this, he added, "I'm so lonesome I could scream! Do you ever get lonesome, or feel you don't have anybody that gives a damn about you?" Then giving her no chance to answer, he plunged on: "That's my situation—don't you see? A sorry spectacle, me—cut adrift without a friend in the world. That's my lot, you see! . . . a wicked, tragic, lot!"

The girl, her eyes snapping impatiently at his maudlin self-pity, put up her hand to stem the torrent and get in a question. "So you want a little fun, eh?" she managed to smile, still watching him critically.

"I want company, I want companionship, and friends—just like other people!" he went on mawkishly. *"That's* fun, isn't it?" The girl did not answer—she only gaped at him. He continued, "I have this beautiful suite, you see—with no one, absolutely no one, to share it with me! Oh, you must see it!—it's beautiful, with the weirdest lighting! . . . all manner of colors, of shapes, and images, almost like fairies and hobgoblins, on the walls and ceiling! It's a riot—it's mad! . . ."

The girl seemed almost ready to yawn. "Yes," she said—"1020."

"Oh, you know it—you've been there! . . . Oh, I see! Gosh! Have you really been there?"

"Sure—who hasn't." She lit a cigarette.

"But I'll bet it didn't have a piano when you were there—now, did it? Well, it has one now—I saw to that; at least a spinet. I rented one—oh, I must have my music when life gets to be a drag, as it is now most of the time."

"So you have a piano," the girl said, pettishly—"What else is new, Marvin?" She had long, dark—authentic—eyelashes; they often blinked or flickered as she talked, and especially when she was displeased with something or someone; they did so now, giving her face a kind of mobile comeliness, refinement, it did not have in repose. "Why did you invite me to your table?" she said—"You beckoned me over."

"Why, gosh, I wanted your company, Sally—why not?" He gave his brilliant, eager smile.

"I thought you wanted to have some fun—up in that suite of yours." The eyelashes flickered as she also tried to smile. "Oh, Marvin, why don't you go on up, and let me join you in a minute?—how about it?"

There was a momentary hesitation; his smile gave way to the briefest, fateful, reflection. There was somehow a wavering, a prophetic reluctance, as he stared in seeming wonder at her face now and his lips moved slightly, inaudibly.

"What?—" she said, with impatience.

At last he sighed. "Oh, why not?" he said. Still reluctantly, though, as if almost pulling himself away, he looked around again for the waiter—as the girl at once returned outside to the arcade and her waiting boyfriend. Soon Marvin, pensive, thoughtful, now, was in the elevator on the way up to his fantastic suite—his rendezvous.

Although he had had much to drink in the past three hours, he entered 1020 in a sober, almost meditative, state. There were times, as now, during his most painful, desperate, his most searching and confused, bouts with his psyche when alcohol had little or no effect for long. Rather, as if, on entering the suite now, to steel his resolve, as would a knight donning protective armor, he quickly closed the door behind him and ran and put on his red silk brocaded smoking jacket. But he hugged it to his body as would a woman swaddled in mink. Then he went in and turned on the bedroom's bizarre light. THE LIGHT. It of course transformed the suite though strangely this time not his heart. He glanced at himself in the dresser mirror, now a sea of swirling colors, and took a hairbrush and quickly brushed down his thin hair; then as if in his fantasies trying to augment his poor height, he stood on the balls of his feet and preened. In the mirror he was merely a tubby little harlequin grotesque, as he sighed and his heart beat wildly. Now to calm his agitation he went out to the little piano, situated almost in the middle of the parlor, sat down, and began to play, a Stephen Foster tune he loved so well—"I Dream of Jeannie with the Light

Brown Hair." He was trying to keep his mind off Sally—and the considerable contrast. He knew of course she was a whore, and he hated, abhorred, whores—male and female alike. Yet Sally was not his first, though in all there had been few, very few; but he feared them; and they almost always brought temporary impotency on him—followed then by frightful bouts of guilt and contrition. He tried humming the song again now, accompanying himself lugubriously on the spinet. Then came the knock. And his heart began pounding more frantically than ever. He got up and, though walking, felt the sensation of floating across the room.

When he opened the door, Sally, instead of facing him expectantly, was somehow staring to her left down the hall, as if of necessity temporarily parting company with someone intimate; a friend, protector. Nor did her face show any pleasure as she finally turned to Marvin.

"Come in!" he beamed. His heart was heavy.

She smiled wanly, stepping in; she too seemed somehow pensive, frightened. "Hello," she said, and would not let him help her out of her coat but took it off herself and placed it on the arm of the sofa. She sat down.

"Well!" said Marvin, and then could think of nothing more to say. Finally—"How about a drink?"

"No, thanks." But now she gave him her sweet, artificial smile. "Do you want to have a party?" she said.

"A party! . . . what do you mean, dearie?" He had insistently gone and hung up her coat.

"A party for two—*us*." She tried to laugh. "I see you have the green, red, and purple lights on back there. Wouldn't you like to see me undress in your fancy bedroom?"

Marvin almost blushed. "Oh, gosh! . . ." he said, and fell silent.

"Then, what do you want, Marvin? Downstairs you asked me to join you—you said you were lonesome. I'm good company—I know I'm *very* good company." Then came the void little laugh again.

"Oh, I'm sure you are—that's why we're here, isn't it? I want to play my piano for you, sing to you—talk to you."

"Oh, that's so time-consuming—I'm not inexpensive, you know."

"I'm sure of it, Sally—but *how* expensive?"

"We could go back there"—she nodded toward the bedroom of

whirring colored lights—"and have scads of fun for fifteen minutes. For just fifty bucks."

"Fifteen minutes!" said Marvin. "I want you for longer than that."

"*How* long, Marvin?"

"Oh, for maybe half the night, I don't know."

Sally almost gasped; unconsciously her eyes flew toward the front door, as if for help, or consultation. "That's impossible," she finally said—"besides, you wouldn't want to pay that much."

This somehow sent Marvin into a manic fit of laughing. "Oh! Ha! ha! ha! Oh, gosh! How do you know how much I wouldn't want to pay?—Ha! ha!" He looked at his wristwatch, then reached in the inside pocket of his jacket and took out his wallet. "It's now 10:45," he said. "You get a hundred bucks, as you call them, an hour—how's that?" He took out, and exhibited, two crisp, new, fifty dollar bills.

Her eyes studied his face for a long time, for seeming evidence of his seriousness. Again then the eyes moved unwittingly, for a fleeting instant, toward the door, as if she sought permission. At last—"I don't think it would work. . . ." she said, though still hesitating, then finally sulking.

"Oh, Sally, you're going to stay somewhere tonight—why not here? I want to play and sing for you—talk to you. How about it?"

She stared incredulously at him. "Then, you don't want to go to bed with me? . . ." she said.

He laughed again, uproariously—"Oh, why don't we just play it by ear, and see what happens? Now, take this." He reached over and placed the two fifty dollar bills on her knee. "This will take us to 11:45—okay?"

She took up the money at once, but then, trying for more casualness, slowly, methodically, folded the bills twice and held them, tightly, in her hand. All the while, however, her eyes were searching his face, as if trying to fathom his very being. He could see she was nervous and confused; almost shaking. For a moment he felt sorry for her, and for himself. He smiled at her—just as she said, "You're wealthy, aren't you?"

"Oh, not really," he laughed. "I just throw a lot of money around—it makes it look like I'm wealthy. Next year I'll make up for it probably by living on potato chips." He apparently thought

501

this clever, funny, for he tossed his mammoth, heavy head back and gave a long, strident laugh. She gaped at him in horror. When he saw her shocked expression, he was at once subdued. The experience was not new to him. He grew reflective, downcast, now. "Would you like me better, Sally, if I were wealthy?"

She thought about it. "I came from a poor family," she murmured. It was her only answer.

For a moment they were both silent. Suddenly then, laughing, he jumped up, went to the piano, and began playing and singing, his quavering, sentimental, falsetto voice carrying almost beyond the door of the suite and out into the hall:

> Down in some lone valley and in a lonesome place,
> Where the wild birds do whistle, and their notes do increase,
> Farewell pretty Saro, I bid you adieu,
> But I'll dream of pretty Saro wherever I go.

Soon, in his fervor, his potato-shaped little body was swaying from side to side as he pounded the spinet and sent his high voice virtually scaling the walls. He sang three stanzas of the song in all, then stopped, pulled out his handkerchief, and dabbed his moist brow. "Oh, that's such a lovely, sad song—popular in early American colonial days. I love the old American songs, don't you?"

Sally, however, was concerned with other matters. She uncrossed her legs, as if she was about to stand up. "What time is it?" she asked, glancing toward the door. "I may not be able to stay very long."

"Sally, come, come—at a hundred dollars an hour?"

She seemed exasperated. "Is this all you want me to do?—listen to you play and sing?"

"Would you rather go to bed with me? Ha-ha-ha! Now, tell the truth!—would you? Not the way you were looking at me a moment ago certainly!"

She paused and reflected on this, discomfort in her manner, as she occasionally glanced at him as if taking the measure of his contorted little figure and gargantuan head; again she shuddered. "Sometimes I get the impression you're not interested in women," she finally said in a diversionary move.

"Ah, now wait a minute," said Marvin—"And you didn't answer my question. But, yes indeed, I like women, and men, and all human beings. They all intrigue, fascinate, me. I love the study of mankind, you see." He was deeply serious now and went over and sat on the sofa beside her. "I'm a typist by profession, you know; but I often think if I had it to do over again, I'd have been an anthropologist, or a philosopher maybe—if not a classical musician. The study of mankind and his relationship to the universe is absorbing and important—did you ever think of that?"

"I only had a year in junior college," she said, and strangely smiled.

"Oh, what difference does that make? It's so fundamental you don't have to be erudite to see it. Pope said the proper study of mankind is man!"

She sat up. "I'm Catholic," she said at once, proudly. "The pope speaks the truth—he's a very educated and wise and good man. Ah, the Holy Father. . . ."

"I know, my dear; only I was speaking of Alexander Pope, the English poet."

This brought an almost ill expression to her face. But soon she recovered and said, "The Bible says, 'What is man that Thou art mindful of him?' That's in the Psalms, I think."

"A great question, yes—I've heard that but didn't know its source; a very great question. What I'd be interested in as an anthropologist is tracing man to his earliest beginnings to try to find out how he got to be like he is today. He's a sorry spectacle today, you know—all of us are. Look at me. Look at you. It's not a very pretty picture, we must admit. Do you think I wanted to be like I am?—not on your life. But what could I do about it?—and I'm not only talking about the way I look, my physical self. I'm also talking about my mental make-up—it's bad, very bad; the worst part of me. Do you ever ask yourself *about* yourself, Sally?"

"No. I'm definitely not like you—I think well of myself. Why shouldn't I?"

Marvin smiled and shook his head ruefully. "Why should you?"

"What are you referring to?—the way I make my living?" Her eyes thinned to slits.

"Although ancient, it's not exactly an exalted profession, is it, my dear? I'm by no means any blue-nose or wet blanket, understand, but what's it like to have a man climb in bed and on top of you that you've never seen in your life thirty minutes before? That happens, doesn't it?"

She virtually snapped at him. "You damn right it happens, but your mind's closed to those things—you don't think about them." She looked pointedly at him then. "Don't tell me *you've* never been out on the town—even on a midnight cruise, maybe. I'm no fool. Yeah, you've cruised a bit, I'll wager."

At this a sudden pall seemed to fall over the conversation. Marvin did not respond. He seemed at first offended; then he tried to smile; but his lips seemed dry, turgid, the smile at last somehow sinister. "The trouble with you," he said, "is that you've seen so much filth, so much degradation, you ascribe it to everyone else you meet. I'm a man who's lived a respectable life," he lied—"now you insist on insulting me."

"Well, you talked to me as to a whore. I've had my problems, sure; my setbacks, bad luck, and all. But I'm a human being." Her eyes snapping again, she turned away in a huff. "What time is it?" she said.

Marvin only looked at her, dolefully.

She half stood up. "What time is it?" she repeated—"don't you owe me more money by now? Huh?" But the thought somehow brought sudden laughter from her.

This strange turn of attitude startled him. "It's not anywhere near 11:45 yet," he said, though rather meekly, and without looking at his watch. At this, staring straight at him, she kicked off her shoes. Then, letting out a little peal of bravado laughter, she stood up, took off her suit jacket, and next got out of the pants to the suit. "Hey!—what is this, Sally?" he laughed nervously, his eyes big. Soon then he was trembling, for in thirty seconds she stood before him stark naked. "*Sally!*—oh, God!" Shivering with excitement, he ran to her, touching her body worshipfully, in wonder; fondling her. "Oh, God, Sally! . . ."

"Hurry!—go run a tub of bath water," she said breathlessly, her eyes enkindled.

"A tub of bath water?" He directed a piteous gaze at her. "—for what?"

"For you to take a bath in, Marvin—that's what. I'll leave if you don't. What time is it?—maybe I'll get in the tub and bathe with you. Go run the water and take your clothes off—you speak of what sinful people we both are; we'll cleanse ourselves, then, right? Sure we will—'wash me and I shall be whiter than snow,' as you Protestants say. We'll both be baptized, Marvin—see? . . . by each other. Come on, let's go." She took him by the hand and led him back through the bizarrely-colored whirring lights into the bathroom, where she began running water into the giant marble bathtub. "What time is it, Marvin?—you'll soon owe me another hundred. Give it to me now—before you take off your clothes."

Marvin felt his emotions rise even more, the blood under his skin surge, the top of his head grow hot. Still trembling, he quickly got out his wallet and gave her two more fifty dollar bills, which she placed on the closed toilet seat. "That'll take us to 12:45, my dear—don't forget," he said seriously, tenderly. "You know we're both insane people, don't you? . . . *absolutely insane.*" Then he began tearing off his clothes. By now the steam was billowing up out of the huge tub. "Run some cold water in!" he cried in ecstasy— "we won't be able to get in it!"

"Oh, Marvin!" she said—"this is the biggest bathtub I ever saw in my life! Oh, my! Oh, my!" She began running cold water into the hot, though the steam continued billowing; then she looked up; her jaw fell. Marvin was naked. Through the steam he looked like some kind of embarrassed satyr, his bulbous, distended, little body a blue milk white. With awkwardly crossed, spread, hands he was somehow trying to shield from view his tiny genitals. "Oh, my God! . . ." breathed Sally—"Oh, my God!" she said. "Marvin, come here and let me look at you."

"No, no, I won't!" he said, his lips protruding in a peevish, stubborn pout—"You're just making fun of me, that's all. What if I'm *not* endowed as well as some men—I have other strengths, sensibilities. Now, you stop it." He stood not far from the tub, enveloped in the billowing steam, his hands still cupped over his groin.

"Oh, come here, Marvin," she said, in exasperation now. She had reached down, felt the temperature of the water, and was running still more cold water in. Finally she climbed in the tub. "Come on, now, Marvin—I won't look. Honest—I'll turn my head the other way till you get in." At last, with hesitant, mincing step, and still with his hands covering himself, he sidled up to the tub and lifted over one foot, testing the water with his toe. Sally, already

505

standing thigh deep in the water, watched him. "It's okay—it's fine," she said. Finally he climbed in and at once, to hide himself, started to sit down. She lunged for him—"My God, Marvin, don't sit down—you'll drown yourself!" He looked at her helplessly, and at last remained on his feet, though now in the huge tub he stood navel deep in the water.

All the while the myriad-colored lights from the bedroom were spinning, cascading, circling, casting their bizarre reflected colors on all the walls and ceilings of the suite. The bathroom, no exception, was a veritable marble fairyland of revolving tints and tones, the billowing steam, though thinning, clearing away, had yet caught in its cumulous all the pastel hues redolent of a rainbow. Marvin and Sally stood like stones, or pillars of salt, naked and transfixed in the deep water, and for a moment were caught in the luminosity of the now soft, now harsh, gyrating colors. "Oh, look!" exclaimed Marvin—"the lights, the blessed lights! They look like they're about to swallow us up—*look,* Sally! That's why I so adore this suite—I saw it today for the first time but asked for it as quick as I could get to a phone. Oh, it's magnificent!—look, look! . . . at the colors, all the colors, the whirling colors! Why, it's like a rainbow! Ah, like the rainbow bridge—the entrance of the gods into Valhalla!"

"Why're you so carried away?" said Sally—"A minute ago you were talking about what terrible sinners we were."

"We are, we are!—maybe almost beyond doing anything about it; beyond redemption."

"Speak for yourself, will you?" Yet Sally reached for the big bar of soap in the marble niche above the tub. "Here, Marvin, soap my back good—bathe me, scrub me all over. Come on."

At first Marvin's face had still shown excitement, but then there had appeared a sadness at the mention of sinners. He finally took the bar of soap from her at the same time he reached a wash cloth off the stack of towels at the edge of the bathtub. He began to soap her body then, all over, as she stood there docile, unsmiling, humble, almost contemplative. Soon he was vigorously washing her down with the dripping, sudsy wash cloth, as she braced herself to endure, withstand it, all the while gritting her teeth as if she were deriving some kind of discomfort, even pain, in the process. Suddenly she cried out, "Harder, harder, Marvin!—use more soap! 'Wash me and I shall be whiter than snow'—right? Oh God, you

Protestants!" Marvin, in his exertions serious, intent, emitted little groans and grunts of involvement as he performed the soapy ablutions. "That's it! . . . yes, harder, harder!" she breathed excitedly. Soon, from his selfless efforts in all the steam, wetness, and exertion, he was perspiring. He had begun to tire. At once she seemed to sense it. "Want to rest?" she said—"I'm not clean yet, though," she added ruefully. He did not reply, but only stood there panting, his arms at his side, observing her curiously. "Why are you looking at me like that?" she said, her voice now suddenly full of distress.

"It won't work," he said, shaking his head.

"Oh, yes, it will—don't stop."

"It won't do any good. I'm tired."

"All right then, let me bathe you," she said, and took the soap and wash cloth from him.

"It won't work," he said again—"it won't work for me, either."

"Oh, shut up." She began soaping him vigorously—"How do we know it won't?" She was now applying the wash cloth with all her energy and soon he was covered with billows of lather, even to his neck, face, and ears. "You'll be 'whiter than snow,' you Methodist, before you know it," she said. But suddenly she stopped, and, barely smiling, added, "Say, don't you owe me some money by now?—what time is it?"

"*It is damn later than you think!*" a voice said—a strange, a new, voice. They froze, then looked at each other. Suddenly both whirled to face the open bathroom door. There stood the pimp.

"*Dominic!*" Sally cried, and began trembling like a leaf. ". . . Oh, God . . ."—then her voice fell to a hush, an awed, fearful, now almost conspiratorial whisper. "How did you get in here, Dominic? . . ."—still trembling.

The tall, dark young man in the garish suit and maroon suede shoes ignored her. He was scowling at Marvin—who recognized him. Then he saw the two fifty dollar bills on the toilet seat and came in and snatched them up.

"Dominic, what're you doing in here?" Sally tried to smile as she said it, yet still trembled. "How did you get in here?"

The pimp curled his lip. "Who the hell couldn't pick a lock like that?" he said, still ignoring her as he stared hostilely, malevolently, at Marvin—who in his paralyzing fright seemed to have turned to a rock. At last he too began to shake. But the trespasser had turned to Sally. "Get out of that tub and go get your clothes on," came his summary order to her. Marvin remembered the flashy suit, the wide lapels, and flare-legged trousers—all accouterments of the panderer—as Dominic put the money in his pocket.

Sally, already climbing out of the tub and grabbing a huge bath towel, tried to laugh—"There's another hundred in the next room, Dominic. Oh, he's been generous, very generous."

Dominic only glared at Marvin. "I want money!" he said to him. "Do you hear me? Money—*more* money!" Marvin, standing alone now, still navel-deep in the sudsy water, was shaking so hard he could not answer. Dominic called into the parlor where Sally had fled to her clothes—"Get his wallet! . . . bring his wallet in here! And turn out those God-damn freakish, whirling lights—I hate them!" He faced Marvin again, studying him. "How much money have you got?" he said—"Come on, you got more than any two hundred."

Marvin, though trembling, was finally able to say something. "You're going to rob me. . . . is that it?" Yet his voice was not weak. "Is that what you want—money?"

"You must be deaf, you weird, repulsive, little bastard! Sure, I want money!—that's all I've been saying!"

"You have no right to rob me," said Marvin, a little curiously, self-righteously, yet somehow meekly. Then he lifted a foot to climb out of the tub.

"Wait a minute, now!" Dominic ordered. "You stay in that tub." He turned and called over his shoulder again, *"Sally,* bring the damn wallet!" When Sally finally appeared she was all but dressed —only her jacket was still unbuttoned and as yet she wore no shoes. But she had taken Marvin's wallet out of his hurriedly castoff clothes and now handed it to Dominic. "Go back and bring that wet towel of yours back in here," Dominic said to her. As she spun around to obey—though not without a puzzled look on her face— he quickly went through the wallet. There were three hundred and fifty-four dollars left in it, three hundred of which he took and stuffed in his pocket, and when she returned, the frightened, quizzical look still on her face, he gave her back the wallet. "Now, go put it back in his jacket," he said, "and hang his clothes in the closet—be sure and make everything *neat.*" Her eyes had grown large as she watched him. She hesitated. "Go clean up that room!" he said—"Remember, nobody's been in here!"

At once she faced him, her mouth open. "Oh, Dominic! . . ." she said, then desisted—"What are . . ."

"Go!" he said. His hair was dark and pomaded, the face, except for a few pockmarks, nondescript and sallow, the hands very large and grasping, his frown hammy, melodramatic. But there was a crazy, heated expression in his eyes. "And close that bathroom door," he said to her.

She seemed quivering with a strange terror. ". . . Oh, Dominic— come on, let's get out of here," she pleaded. *"Come on!"* She turned and looked at Marvin standing belly-deep in the water. *"Dominic, come with me!"*

"Get out," he said, but did not look at her—nor at Marvin either. He appeared for a moment to have become inept, indecisive. Whereupon he reached in his vest pocket and took out a tiny envelope containing white powder.

"Oh, Christ, Dominic!—please, don't start that." But her pleas were somehow losing force; there had entered a tone of near hopelessness, resignation, in them.

Now, as if the tiny envelope were a snuffbox, Dominic took a pinch of the white powder from it, dramatically tossed his head back, and sniffed the dust hard, deep, up his nose. At once he repeated this, then carefully folded the little packet and returned it to his pocket. Already a new—a low—fire had come in his eyes.

"Oh, *please!* . . . Dominic!" she said once more, and glanced at Marvin—"He hasn't done anything, Dominic."

It was only now that Marvin seemed to grasp the gravity of the situation. His hands began to move about nervously as he looked at the somehow-now-crazed young man who had been sniffing cocaine; then, as if for help, he looked at Sally. ". . . What's . . . what's going on here?" he finally said. Then a pleading, almost distraught, look came on his face. "Take the money," he said to Dominic, trembling—"Take it all. Then go—please go. We'll just forget everything—okay?" He tried a brave little smile. "We've had enough fun for one evening, eh? . . . let's just call everything even and let it go at that . . . right?" But already Dominic was pushing Sally through the bathroom door. Nor was she any longer resisting, but was allowing herself to be pushed. She would not look at Marvin. Suddenly, though, he cried out to her in a long, pitiful wail— *"Sally!* . . . where are you going? . . . !" But in the next instant she was gone and Dominic had closed the bathroom door behind her.

Now he turned to Marvin—who was helpless, naked, shivering from fear, in the water—and for a moment coolly observed him. Then the melodramatic, far-too-sinister, frown returned on his face, as Marvin looked frantically pained, then questioningly, at him. "What do you want with me, Dominic?" he said at last, trying to bring a slight note of hope, even daring, into his voice.

Dominic stood towering over him. "You creep!" he said to Marvin now, "you filthy little creep. You dirty, sleazy, little freak, you. You're not fit to live!" Marvin's hands had ceased to move about now. He hung his head, almost as if conceding the truth of all the names he was being called. But then somehow, Dominic's very last words ringing in his ears, he seemed to assume a strange dignity in his trembling, naked, ridiculous bearing in the water. He made no reply. Dominic's corny frown now became an even more ludicrous scowl. "You're not fit to live, I say!" he repeated, shouting. Then he dramatically tossed his left shoulder back like a vaudeville villain tossing aside his black cape. Still not a word from Marvin— who looked only sad now, again almost guilty. "You get your freakish kicks out of humiliating people!" said Dominic, the fire literally blazing in his eyes—"people you consider beneath you, those you consider dirt! Well, I'm an anarchist, myself! I say to the wall, the firing squad, for your kind and your cruddy money, your filthy wealth!"

"I beg your pardon," finally said Marvin, utterly bewildered, "but I have humiliated no one."

At this, Dominic, taking a quick step forward, drew back as if to strike him with the back of his hand, but then desisted. "You! . . . you making the girl get in the bathtub with you!" he said—"making her wash your putrid little body! What do you mean you have humiliated no one!"

Marvin shook his head sadly. "I had bathed her before she insisted on bathing me," he said—"Sir, that's the truth. It was a kind of ritual, a rite."

"Augghhh! When I look at you I want to puke. You lie! You're not fit to live, I tell you!"

Marvin was reflective. "I feel she and I wanted in some way to help each other by this," he said, though unsurely, almost as if trying to convince himself he was right. "Yes—she kept saying, 'Wash me and I shall be whiter than snow.'"

Dominic had stepped closer over him.

510

"You're going to kill me, aren't you?" Marvin said—"you're going to drown me. Then why did you turn out my lights in there? . . . why? Please open the door and go turn on the lights, will you?" Then he began to whimper—"I don't want to die! . . . Life hasn't been very good to me, it's true; it's been a living hell much of the time; yet what's the alternative to it? Death's certainly no alternative—I don't believe in God, I don't believe in an after-life, so death is bad, very bad, for me; it's an infinite, horrible, black void that terrifies me! Oh, Mr. Dominic, I don't want to die!—you can see I'm scared almost to death as it is, can't you? *Please* spare my life; yes, my miserable life! . . . and go turn on those lights in there. I beg you not to kill me—in fact, I'll resist, I'll fight you, sir!" Dominic curled his lip in scorn. Marvin then began to cry—"Are you really going to kill me?"

All the melodramatic frowns and scowls had at last vanished from the pimp's face. He stood even closer to Marvin, his face white, masklike, impenetrable. He did not answer.

Marvin, still standing belly-deep in the water, wiped a tear off his cheek with the back of his hand and snuffled. "You won't even answer my question," he said.

Dominic could get no closer. Already his knees were against the tub.

But Marvin's eyes had drifted away now, far, far away, seeing nothing but oblivion; yet somehow he suddenly appeared more self-possessed, stoical, seeming now almost cool in the acceptance of his fate. ". . . Griselda," he whispered (almost as if she were there) though in a dry, matter-of-fact, way—"Griselda, why did you do it? Why did you turn me away?" Again then he looked up at Dominic looming over him, and repeated, "You won't even answer my question."

But now there seemed little remonstrance from him with the ebbing of his life; there would not really be fighting; it was as if his supineness flowed out of some ready-to-hand fatalism—though he was by no means at peace, nor welcomed this end; yet he faced it with a strange lethargy, incapacity, fatigue. It was too bad there was not time to hark back into the residue of his memories and dwell, dawdle, upon them; time had now collapsed all that like a deflated accordion; yet there persisted this palpitating presence of almost total recall; as it were, a data bank disgorging its long-held stores, its secrets. Yet his life had, in a way, been large—not happy

511

but large, his living a matter of some consequence, though he had not willed his life, or his death. Sometimes he thought he could yet hear his foetal screams, the rebellion, bitter and outraged, against the prospect of birth. But not now against death. Born to wealth, culture, high expectations, indeed demands, he had become a typist. Yet a champion. But before that at Stanford he had been interested in theatre, the university theatricals; he purloined scripts and, studying far into the night, learned whole parts, only to be told by the professor he was not quite right for the part; then later, behind some sets, his presence unknown, hearing the laughing pedagogue ask two students if in fact the part existed he was right for. It was the end of the theatre idea. Then came the try at music, the tortured, protracted piano study, the cautious hopes for a career. To no avail. Then the long months of despairing of all things artistic. He became, yes, a typing champion. It was no effort, absolutely no effort; after which came the establishment of a thriving business, again with no effort—the things not coveted came readily; those craved, not at all. Then, a successful businessman, he had seen Basil Thorne, to whom—it was an irony—the theatre came so naturally, move into his life; and into his apartment. Basil taught him many things—among them the certainty that Mozart was God. Yet—another irony—it was also Basil who revealed to him the art of Ray Charles. This was the odds-off accident that on that fateful night of music had brought him to the feet of Griselda. Now he had known her for a year—he had lived for a year; yet in the end he had frightened, repelled, her, and she had run off after an arrogant, zealous, do-gooding black; it was the one drop of alien blood in her veins seeking its complement; she was pulled as if by some great stubborn magnet and he had come home only to find her fled, the apartment ringing in empty silence, her Porsche parked outside. So it was that in his prodigal pursuit of her he had now come to the quietus of a fatuous, silly, soapy water grave; forty-five years of life, almost all of it hell; the foetal kicks and screams had been prophetic and right; but at last now he felt a certain ennui, no matter that he saw and recognized the valley of the shadow, the Reaper in the guise of a cheap, crazed, narcotized, anarchist pimp. He hadn't the heart to fight him. The first stage, therefore, the telltale lassitude, was already upon him and he did not choose to resist. It

512

was only Griselda now that constituted both his failure and remorse. But he had made his convenant—and in the end would step
forward to meet the Pimp of the World as if greeting him in fond
embrace. . . .

Chapter 3

A few days later Ornette Hungerford was in one of his less pre-possessing, if not ugly, moods—Ferdinand Bailey called them his "ornery spells." Ornette was still a problem for them. His nasty attitudes were almost always provoked by Knight's or Ferdinand's rejection of one of his super-ambitious, sometimes ill-advised, schemes for the organization. On such occasions then he loved to bring up, even taunt them with, some of their own plans and projects that had floundered or failed. Today the three of them were in Knight's office, when Ornette suddenly diverted the subject. "Say, whatever happened to your kosher boy, Rodya—the Ph.D. man?" he said, grinning testily at Ferdinand, though all knew the remark was meant for Knight. There was no immediate response. "He ain't been around for some time, has he?" Ornette went on—"or at least I ain't seen him."

Ferdinand laughed—"Just for that he'll show up today, prob-ably. He'll sweep in here any minute now, his briefcase banging against his legs and his notebook out to take down John Calvin's answers to those outlandish questions he can ask."

Knight sat back in his desk chair, thinking for a moment. "It's been over a week, hasn't it?" he said, "since Rodya's been here. Sure, he'll show up, all right—any minute."

"It'd be okay with me if he never showed up again," said Ornette. "I can't figure him out—I never could. What do *we* get out of this deal, out of the thousand questions he asks? We tell him our guts, don't we?"

"No, we don't," said Ferdinand. "We only tell him what we want him to know."

Knight smiled. "The last time he was here was to tell *us* some-thing, for a change—not ask. He said he called your Miss Adkins, Ornette."

Ornette gaped. "He's called *Mary Dee?* About what?"

"You know Rodya. About anything." Knight laughed. "He was

very excited—she'd told him I ought to preach xenophobia to the people." Knight watched him mischievously.

"Preach what?" Ornette said.

"He had to explain it to us. If I'd ever heard of the word, I'd forgotten it—so had Ferdie. When he told us what it meant, though, it was clear we'd been preaching it all the time—from the beginning. It's strange, ironical, she'd come up with that."

"What's it mean?" Ornette was aroused. "Lord, has that girl got a mind—what a fertile brain!"

"It means we should stay to ourselves, do our own thing—keep whites out of our affairs. Of course Rodya—wouldn't he?—gave the dictionary meaning of the word. It means fear, distrust, even hatred, of outsiders—for us, meaning whites. Xenophobia, yes—keep them out." Knight laughed—"We've been teaching it all along, only we've never given it such a high-falutin' name."

Ornette was vastly impressed. "That Mary Dee is something—Lord, is that girl smart."

Knight was whimsical. "So is Rodya."

"Naturally," Ornette said; "wouldn't he be? How do you spell the word? Z-E-N-A . . ."

"No." Knight spelled it correctly.

"Oh—I thought it had something to do with Zen."

Ferdinand broke out laughing—"Maybe it has, after all."

"No," said Knight seriously, "it has nothing to do with the anti-rational, or with Buddhist or Oriental thought. It's very rational; in our case, very practical too. It simply means blacks must stick together—an old cliche, but true—that we must solve our own problems, together; that we must keep whites out; whites' priorities are different, and always will be. Our movement has taught this from the beginning—we don't need any newcomer telling us this." Already, however, now thinking of something else, he turned to Ferdinand to ask about some routine organizational matter.

But Ornette's mind had not budged. "Ah, xenophobia . . ." he breathed, much engrossed, impressed. "There's something in that word, there is—I feel it. But it should be spelled differently—like Z-E-N-A-P-H-O-B-I-A. We could use it—it could be a great rallying cry. . . . Yeah, *Zenaphobia!*—keep whitey out! Oh, that Mary Dee!—what a fertile brain." He turned to Knight impetuously—"You must meet her, John Calvin! You'll *never* be the same."

But Knight, his thoughts still elsewhere, had not heard the prophetic words.

*   *   *   *   *

Throughout the week following the night of Marvin's futile attempt to see her, Griselda had lived in a kind of frozen, debilitating fear. Yet, strangely, though the fear was real, indeed oppressive, it was still somehow less than total. Her thoughts were sometimes at cross purposes. But what was she in for, she asked herself, if any night she could be jarred from her sleep by someone downstairs violently ringing her doorbell?—by someone, this man, who, her personal experience ever reminded her, was not all the time sane. He was in fact, she felt, little of the time sane, driven by a possessed psychosis his utter loneliness had created and then turned into fantasies of manic, aberrant, sex, if not violence. Like herself, she knew, he was obsessed with loneliness, its eternal accomplice and prey, and had doubtless been a distraught, a vulnerable, man the night she turned him away. Now at times she was sorry. But at other times she was afraid—afraid of him and what she somehow sensed he was capable of doing to her, mentally as well as physically. What had he wanted of her that night? she wondered. Maybe he'd had some startling news to tell her. She felt, however, it was inevitable she would encounter him again, and finally consent to talk to him. She took no particular note of the fact that she seldom read newspapers these hectic days; her awareness of what was happening in the world about her came from her television screen. But even on television she had failed to hear the brief, very brief, item of local news a few days ago—that a man had been found dead in his hotel bathtub, apparently of a heart attack while taking a bath. She had not heard. For, besides, what mostly occupied her thoughts these days, and nights, was John Calvin Knight.

This news void, however, had been contrary to the experience of Mary Dee Adkins. On her lunch break at the office the following day, she had seen the small item in one of the daily newspapers. But she had only paused when she saw that the Plaza Royale hotel figured in the story. Suddenly then, four lines down, she had

516

glimpsed the fateful words that sent her heart into a furious pounding—"in the suite of mirrors" was the way the tiny story described, specified, the site of death. She read it breathlessly now. The death of course did not interest her; it was mention of the hotel room, the suite, in which it had occurred, the memory of it, that brought on her rush of shame and emotion, the return of all the old guilt feelings, love-misery, and humiliation from which she now so often suffered.

The rest of the day was ruined for her. She could not liberate her thoughts from what, in retrospect, she regarded as that soul-sick, blissful, degrading night in this same bizarre "suite of mirrors." The mortification had become an obsession with her, especially now since her attempts at involvement with a new way of life, with the Black Peoples Congress. These old memories, moreover, inevitably, had soured her personality on her job, where almost all her associates were white, to the point now she was already looking for different employment. Her life had therefore taken a sharp turn, she well realized, yet it was ironical that it lacked, she knew, anything approximating the purpose, the focus, it had had before, when as each day dawned there was one thing only that mattered: whether or not the day would bring a letter from Philip. Now she had destroyed his few letters, bitterly torn them into desperate tiny bits before discarding them in the trash can on the back stoop—the final chapter, she thought; the end.

On the other hand, John Calvin Knight that evening at home was still wrestling with his stalemate, his irresolution, the problems of his scruples. It all somehow involved Griselda, of whom he could not rid his mind. There was also, however, the nagging responsibility of next month, of hosting the annual meeting of the Congress' Central Planning Committee and its followers from across the country, that plagued him as well. He had yet to hit upon anything new, convincing, dramatic, to propose to them that might stimulate them to even greater effort. This inability to come to grips with many basic questions affecting the organization, including the philosophical direction it should be taken in, frightened him. Time was short—there was less than a month. There was also money to be raised for next year's effort. The national fund raising drive was to be launched with the huge rally at the Amphitheater, where he hoped by a landmark speech to create the kind of enthusiasm, fire, as well as a show of organizational strength among the masses, that would influence many black businesses, large and small, to give money, to have confidence that to invest in the Congress was to invest in themselves. He knew that the speech he would make on the occasion of the rally would be crucial. If he failed, nothing occurring in the whole week of meetings could dispel the pall. It was also likely he would draw the criticism of such potential dissidents as Jesse Lumpkins, C.P.C. member from Cincinnati, who continued to view his, Knight's, leadership with a watchful, jaundiced eye. Knight was worried and, for the first time, was consciously aware he was worried—shaken, discouraged. And all without justification, he was convinced; which now caused him to regard his malaise as a suspicious, telltale, morbidity. Was he losing his hold on himself? he wondered. What was he really worried about? Was he tiring from his decade of effort?—had he lost his enthusiasm, his zeal, his ideas? Was his leadership—inwardly—flagging? If so, why? One conceivable cause had occurred to him, plagued him, before. It was of course inextricably, maddeningly, entangled with his relationship with Griselda, with his attitude—whatever that was, for he constantly vacillated on it—toward her. It was his fear, his covert suspicion, of his own hypocrisy. Did he now really believe what he had preached all these years—about Blackness? Was he a true xenophobe?—as the Adkins girl had said he should be? Suddenly he was morose, disconsolate; he had that very moment become conscious of something, he thought, that proved him beyond any doubt the hypocrite he had become convinced he was. Tonight, all along, he had wanted to do this thing, he sadly realized. He was helpless; he could not contain himself; it was a necessity. Finally, at long last, he did it. He went to the telephone to call Griselda. He took out his notebook, read her number recorded there, and was about to dial it—when he remembered she had moved and had no telephone. He cursed the fact as he went and got his topcoat. He had not been to the flat where she had recently moved but she had insisted he take her new address; now he emerged from his building to go to his car feeling strange, guilty, in the role of tracing her whereabouts. It was 8:30 and as he drove off in a night of slow-falling rain, the wet pavement sent up reflections of the street lights and their glare came through the windshield into his harried eyes.

But constantly, doggedly, in his mind was his dilemma. What was this thing he was doing?—though driving, he felt like a groping, guilt-ridden sleepwalker. What was pushing, what was pulling, him? Where was he going? Why? He reproved himself for his weakness—again the old feeling of himself as falsifier, deceiver, came over him and aroused his disgust. What if the faithful followers were to see him now? . . . on his quest, on the prowl—Ferdinand, Ornette, Jesse Lumpkins? They would judge him, he thought, for what he was—a fraud. But he drove on.

When, ten minutes later, her loud doorbell sounded, Griselda's first impulse was to scream. Yet she did not. Heart racing, fatalism at work, she sat perfectly still, knowing, believing, it was Marvin; that he would ring again and again and that, despite her cold fear, she would this time let him come up. When the loud ring was repeated, she went to the intercom and answered. Knight identified himself. But she seemed strangely inert, her mind grooved, really unappreciative of the fact it was he, though on another level she clearly recognized his voice. Yet she somehow still envisioned Marvin standing down there in the vestibule, impatient, fuming, half-high on his Scotch, feeling sorry for himself, angry, maudlin, crazy —and very dangerous. She felt more than certain that when she decided to push the buzzer, he would come bounding up the stairs and into her flat. He, Marvin, was *there*. And before she could think another thought, she said to Knight over the intercom, "I'm sorry, John Calvin, I've got company tonight." From downstairs there was an incredulous pause, after which, glowering, he replied, "Excuse me," and wheeled and left the vestibule. When she realized what she had done, she grabbed her keys and ran down the steps to overtake him, call him back. When she found the vestibule empty she ran out into the street in the rain, in time to see him up near the corner unlocking his car door. "John Calvin! John Calvin!" she cried out, running toward him. When he heard her, then saw her, he stopped and watched her coming. He was almost sneering. "I said 'excuse me,' " he muttered as she reached him—"Now, don't stand there without a coat in the rain. Go back to your company." She was not wearing her Afro wig and her hair had gotten matted and stringy in the rain. His consequent gaze was severe, disapproving. The wig had become his fetish.

"Oh, John Calvin, I don't know why I said that to you!" she cried. "I must be out of my mind!—there's no one in my apartment! For a moment when you rang I really thought I had company—you know, the man, my boyfriend, in San Francisco. It's strange, so strange! I could see him down there in the entrance . . . *like a ghost!* It was weird! Come back, come back, with me—please, John Calvin! . . ." A crazed wild look in her eyes, she grabbed his arm, whispering, "You must come back with me!—I'm afraid, I'm scared! It was Marvin's ghost! . . ."

Knight, uneasy now, staring curiously at her, finally locked the car again and followed her back up to her apartment. When many hours later he left, the rain was over and the sun was up, strong and bright

* * * * *

Mary Dee at last had sent out the little handwritten invitations to the guests to her party. The time had come and somehow she dreaded it. But she had ordered beer, two jugs of wine, and from the house had brought out to the garage studio a large cut glass bowl, treasured by her alarmed mother, for the spiked Hawaiian punch. After the committee meeting was over, the business transacted, there would be sandwiches, coffee, more mingling, and talk. Ornette had wanted to help pay for the refreshments but she had refused—it was her party (with Chauncey Stiles' underwriting) and she had invited the people in the movement, committee members of course included, whom she wanted to be present. This of course did not include Knight. She could not have explained her developing attitude toward this man whose name was so much on the tongues of the people she had met in the organization. They saw him in a way radically different from the frightening impression forced on her by their two brief Paris encounters. His followers always spoke of his honesty, his rigid, almost fastidious, honesty. Others attested to a variety of virtues; that he was kindly, considerate, sometimes even gentle, with a crystalline intelligence, fierce anger, and the courage of a lion. She was willing to concede he merited some of this extravagant, if sometimes naive, praise, but she could not forget her reaction in Paris to his behavior that afternoon at the sidewalk cafe—at Fouquet's. Seeing her squired by two ostensibly devoted white men, he had sat staring a violent hate at her. The other time, at the little Canary restaurant, with neither her nor Raoul's awareness, he had sat far back at a table in the corner and observed with his cold, implacable eyes her final luncheon with Raoul. At last, having watched, studied, them to the full, gathering then all his hauteur about him, never once deigning to notice them now, he had stridden past them and out of the place.

She could never dismiss how she felt that day, realizing she had unwittingly sat there all that time under his unwholesome gaze. She was as frightened, she recalled, as she had been the first time, at Fouquet's. She had also been filled with a strange sense of dread, as she felt even now; but of wonderment. Where had she gone wrong about him? she asked herself. But maybe he had changed, fundamentally changed—which, however, she could not bring herself to accept. Or maybe his bitter, boorish behavior had been a cover-up for more basic failings—a streak of defensiveness perhaps, a lingering unsureness of himself. No matter, she did not wish to meet this man again, she told herself. But almost immediately then she would vacillate, wondering, despite her own negativism, what there was about him that had so impressed, overawed, inspired, the thousands of submerged ghetto blacks across the country who blindly followed him. He must have something—magnetism, a mind, stamina; and he had been engaged in activities that were dangerous, courage-demanding, enough to get himself horribly shot, almost killed. What manner of man really was he? These and kindred questions concerned, intrigued, her—what, for example, if they were to meet again, would be his attitude toward her? Or would he remember her at all? The closer came the evening of the committee party, the higher mounted her interest, curiosity, fear, fascination, as well as bafflement—to the point where she almost wished now she had acceded to Ornette's suggestion and invited the "great leader."

Ornette, however, had not told her of his recent disenchantment with the leader, of how Knight made a habit, as Ornette had put it to Ferdinand, "of spilling his guts to this young Jew that keeps saying he's from the University of Chicago but may be straight from the 'enemy'—from the C.I.A. or F.B.I." Nor had he ever mentioned (he dare not think of it) what he described to himself as his real "bone in the throat"—Griselda. To him, this woman, her strange, vague presence, flew in the teeth of everything the movement stood for, including one of its most vaunted tenets—respect for black woman. And all this assumed the weird relationship between her and the leader, whatever it was, had never been consummated—an assumption on which Ornette would not have liked to stake his life. Yet he was true to Knight, in the main still believed in him, and revealed his concerns, worries, his narrow areas of disagreement, only in the office to Ferdinand and Mamie. Only rarely —and then hesitantly, distressfully, about Griselda—had he ever mentioned such matters to Knight. Of course in the case of Griselda he had been promptly, angrily, shut up.

All this was why Mary Dee figured so prominently in Ornette's thinking. She must be used, he thought; she must be impressed into service in the cause. There was too much at stake—the very movement itself. How could Knight fail to react positively to this rare, gifted, this beautiful girl—to whom, secretly, Ornette himself was by no means impervious. But in his faithful fervor for the organization, the cause, he had tried manfully to will, suppress, stuff his feelings back down deep into his subconscious and hold them there. He was anomalous—Ornette the fanatic, the embryo eccentric, above all, the powerful true believer. He believed in Knight still, in the Black Peoples Congress, and in the pure African race. He also believed in himself. Nor occasionally, moreover, was it unusual for him to envision, fantasize, himself as "leader." After a few drinks one evening at home he had let the idea slip out to Rosabelle. She had wheeled and looked at him aghast—"Who's going to feed these children?" she demanded, which closed the subject. Yet in spite of all obstacles, difficulties, he was, where blacks were involved, the dreamy absolutist. It was his life—he lived the cause. Therein, however, ironically, lay his vulnerability. But also his prophetic strength.

*　　*　　*　　*　　*

Griselda was happy, unreservedly happy, at first. But soon it became an urgent, apprehensive, complicated happiness, if happiness it was at all. There were good days and bad days. This great love that had so overpowered her months ago in San Francisco, and had been through so many doubtful and tortuous phases, had at last on that recent rain-filled night burst into fruition, consummation, virtually searing her soul with ecstasy. Yet the physical bliss of the event had only served to heighten the spiritual, indeed moral, turn of her feelings. She thought constantly now of Frimbo and his little band of saints. She searched mind and heart for ways to purify herself, cleanse her thoughts, motives, and actions, so as to be estimable, worthy. She tried to monitor her mind now, bring it under a rigid control, in order that the whole of her existence might be chastened. She felt this man Knight in every way deserving of the effort, for in his paroxysms in her bed, in her arms, that night he had said things to her she would never forget, words signaling his deep involvement with her but also his doubts, the misery and confusion. She must lead him gently, she told herself. It was her mission now to help him. She believed to do this she must be cautious, retiring, unobtrusive, thus true to herself as well as to him; she must not push him, but give him time—yet opportunity. But above all she must first prepare herself, somehow bring order, self-denial, purity, into her own life.

On the very first day following the decisive night, Mamie Campbell in the office could note a difference in Griselda's behavior. The change persisted for days. Although she had never been talkative, Griselda now lapsed into long periods of absorbed, other-worldly, blissful silence. Even as she typed, or helped Mamie prepare requisitions, or assembled materials for organization publicity, she seemed in a happy, grateful trance. But the most telltale sign of all was her manner whenever Knight appeared. She seemed not to recognize his presence, his existence, at all. She would not look at him or even in his direction. It was noticeable not only to Mamie, but to others as well, including watchful Ferdinand. But Ferdinand misread what he saw. He wondered if Griselda wasn't now finally showing some deep, secret resentment of Knight, for a reason unknown to any of them. He was of course encouraged, hopeful—anything causing a rupture between those two had his blessing.

But Mamie, herself a woman, construed what she saw in more intuitive, if realistic, terms. It was mainly that Griselda's refusal, or at least failure, to acknowledge Knight's existence was accompanied at other times by her constant dreamy preoccupation. It was as if for hours she barely knew where she was; she worked as though she were an enraptured automaton. Mamie knew something significant had happened. Then, on the third day, Griselda came to work not wearing her Afro wig. Her own long, dark hair fell straight, cascadelike, down her supple back. In the office everyone stared as if a white stranger had entered. In addition next day, the wig still at home, she wore a bright carmine sweater with skirt, modish low shoes showing off her shapely limbs, and had her nails tastefully lacquered and eyebrows neatly plucked. People coming into the office stared at her in awe, confusion, at last distrust. Mamie in dead earnest now wondered what really had happened.

Knight's attitude had been one of quiet nervousness—until Griselda's radical change in appearance. Now he seemed panic-stricken. Ferdinand, ever observant, saw too that Knight, even when in town, spent less time in the office than before; used any pretext to be elsewhere. In truth Knight was again utterly confused. He was also now a harried man, with the national meeting fast approaching and so much to be done. Of course most pressing of all was his speech. He had not even yet begun work on it. He knew why—he did not know what he would, or could, say. His mind, his faculties, seemed to have atrophied; no really useful ideas came. Each night in his apartment he would sit at the little table in his bedroom, large pad and a pencil before him, poring over notes he had written to himself from time to time in an effort to generate new ideas—but without success. It all only made him realize what a turmoil his life was in; this was now exacerbated by the fateful lapse with Griselda. Groaning, muttering, to himself, he began pacing the floor.

Before long he found himself up front in his living room, staring out the window down onto the lighted street. His mood was black, desperate. The true origin of his difficulties, he realized, was his self-doubt, the lack of certainty he could attain in his work his original goals. Nevertheless, Griselda had become a symbol of something inseparable from his basic problems—to him, especially now since their grave peccadillo, she symbolized his essential dishonesty. It, moreover, appalled him that he could not avoid this belief, conviction. Yet, despite everything, he knew he could not even now vow that a repetition of that recent night would never take place, for he recalled it with a rueful, earthy, stormy pleasure that haunted each recurrent memory. He had never experienced a woman so crazed, tornadic, in bed. She had cried out her long-pent-up love for him in high, harsh, frightening tones. But it had somehow only heightened his lust for her and he had borne down on her ever harder and faster, their frantic breathing, sighing, outcries, abating only after the soaring final release of passion. Afterwards she had cried—softly, briefly. Then she raised herself in bed on her elbow and studied him. Soon she snuggled against him, soothingly exploring, caressing, the surgical scars crossing his abdomen, as she called him a great, a courageous, man who had suffered so much for others. In retrospect, it had been a moving moment for him; yet now he could only view the experience as a lapse, a fearful mistake and indiscretion. In their sensitiveness, they had not spoken to each other since. He knew though this could not last. What then, he wondered, would he say to her when she finally approached him again? He did not know and had no way of predicting. His weakness now only angered, saddened, him and, muttering again, he left the living room window and returned to his bedroom and the speech.

Sitting at the little table, the light from the brass lamp glowing on the pad of paper, he slowly, painfully, began to write: "We seek self-fulfillment through self-identification, my friends! We *glorify* blackness! It is our badge of strength, pride, and hope! We also wear it as a proud mantle, a reminder of what it has cost us in suffering and blood—so that we will never, never, forget it or our enemies!" But the words were hollow to him, ashes in the mouth, and futilely he tossed aside the pencil and sat morose, brooding, again. The words were the same; they were merely what he had said to them time after time before; there was nothing new to be found in this vein; it would arouse no one; would in fact leave them cold. He needed a new, a ringing, message, and racked his brain for insight, for power to truly create—to no avail. Yet he took up the pencil and in a few moments began to write again: "We need anger! We need righteous anger to arouse us, my friends! We only have to review our history. In Mother Africa kidnapped by our own kind and brought out of the bush to the white invader on the beaches. Put on the horror ships and those who survived disgorged at last in America and sold as slaves. Centuries of slavery now—

525

families split up and sold apart into oblivion, women raped by masters, runaways caught by bloodhounds and flogged to death! Hope yet unborn already dead! Then 'freedom!' Then *freedom*, my friends! But what kind of freedom? Freedom, and Reconstruction, and the nightriders! Whippings, shootings, terror, starvation, and the holocaust of the galloping consumption—death! Then World War I, to make the world safe for democracy and the lynch mobs! Hear me, hear me! Yet nothing, through it all, could crush our *blackness!* It enabled us to survive! It was and is our strength! And at all costs we will preserve it!"

He winced as he wrote the bombast. Yet this time he did not put the pencil down. He rather sat musing; vaguely, historically, reminiscent. There was much truth, he told himself, in what he had just written. The exaggeration was only in the way he expressed it. Soon he began to feel as he had felt months ago in the hospital bed, his mind again conjuring the sensation of slowly receding into an unlit past, a dark and murderous past. He recalled now—intermixed with much his father had told him—the experience of the hospital visions, and felt the promptings of the vicarious, yet luminous, memories of the race, the black race, as once more they rather ponderously unfolded before him . . . treading inexorably with heavy step through the reaches, then the portals, of time. Mythic memories, grand and sad, receding, re-emerging, now faint again, now all too painful and distinct—wearing down the rational consciousness. Soon they had moved downstage and become, as it were, the fateful present only decades removed—now no longer receding, no longer the shadow of history. Only ghostly reality. . . .

*   *   *   *   *

Ghostly reality indeed—the Red Summer of 1919 and the saga of young Parret Webb.

"Cindy, that water hot yet?—it's sure biling by now, ain't it?" The husky female voice came from out in the yard behind the shack located on the outskirts of the little town. "Bring it on here, Cindy!"

"Yeah, Mama," the robust girl in the kitchen called back—"it's just now comin' to a boil. I'm comin' with it." But she lifted the large pail of boiling water off the kitchen stove with great caution, and as she made her way to the door managed to hold it well out from her body despite its weight.

In the backyard in 90-degree July heat her mother, Minnie Webb, a large black woman, stood over an iron pot of hot, soapy water, floating shirts, underwear, socks, and nightgowns. She raised up from the washboard as her daughter approached. "I shoulda built a fire out here, maybe," she said to Cindy, "'stead of in the kitchen, but this washing ain't big enough for that. But tomorrow when you and Parret go get Mrs. Stewart's washin', then you'll see a big one for sure—it'll take both you'all to bring it." Gingerly, she took the hot water from Cindy and poured it with caution into the iron pot. From her exertions, as well as the sultry weather, sweat ran off her face into the hot water.

"Pshaw, Mama," Cindy said, "you ain't likely to get Parret to go fetch no white folks' washing—you know how he is now."

Minnie Webb sighed at the mention of her son's name. "Girl, don't you go bein' so hard on your brother," she said. "That army just spoiled him for awhile, that's all—he'll come around tereckly. Things was so different over there in France." She had hardly uttered the words when from up the graveled street they heard the noisy chug and sputter of an ancient combustion engine. Soon an old Model-T Ford, bearing 1919 Ohio license plates, came into view—it had come from the center of town—with two Negro youths riding in it. "Oh, Lord," said Minnie uneasily, "speak of the devil and his imps will appear. It's Parret and Sam, ain't it?"

"Yes'm," Cindy said, also watching the car—"What they doing back so soon?" The car stopped, but only the stout, squat youth, in shirtsleeves and denim trousers, got out and came toward the house. "Sam ain't comin' in," Cindy said.

"He ain't leavin', neither," said Minnie, looking hard at the car.

Her son Parret seemed barely to notice them as, trying not to appear to hurry, he went instead toward the house and his friend Sam, tall, ungainly, with large staring eyes, remained behind the wheel of Sam's decrepit Ford. At once Minnie, flinging soapsuds off her hands, left the washboard and went to intercept Parret before he reached the house. "What you want, son?" she said—"Now, you

527

just wait there a minute." Parret, low-built, muscular, black, stopped and, arms hanging loose at his sides, waited. But already she suspected he'd been drinking whiskey and in a few steps more smelled it on his breath. Her anger flaring, she yelled before she thought. "You'all been hanging round that tacky nigger saloon again, ain't you?—*ain't you,* Parret? Huh?—oh, yes, you have!"

Cindy had followed her. "Come on, Mama—leave him alone."

Parret, frowning, nodded to his sister. "You better tell her somethin'," he said.

"What you want in the house, Parret?" Cindy said.

"I come to get a clean shirt—me and Sam are driving over to Hoopton." But his eyes were uneasy, shifty.

"You be back here by suppertime, boy," Minnie warned as Parret sidled away toward the house. "You and Sam chasin' after every little black gal in this county—and botha you drinkin' whiskey like you was forty-year-old men. You going to run off the road one of these days in that rattletrap old car and kill yourselves."

Parret seemed fidgety, impatient. "I had some whiskey but I ain't drunk, Ma," he said—"neither is Sam." But still retreating, he soon disappeared into the shack of a house.

Minnie and Cindy had scarcely returned to the wash pot when Parret emerged from the house carrying a folded clean shirt in his hand. He went to the car, climbed in, and Sam drove off. Inside the shirt was Jake Webb's, Parret's father's, .38 caliber Smith and Wesson revolver. Parret had lied—neither he nor Sam intended to go to Hoopton. Where they did intend to go was back to the center of their own little town—Gem City. It was urgent.

Gem City, in southeastern Ohio, boasted in 1919 a population of 5,850. There were two good-sized industries in town—a metal roofing plant and a huge dairy—and many of the workers and their families had come during the war boom. Jake Webb, head of a family of five, was one of them, though he had only come from nearby Hoopton, and had gotten a job cleaning out cow barns at the dairy. Now Jake, though a tough little man, was laid up in the hospital with a leg broken in two places when he was thrown from a horse. But Minnie and Cindy carried on, taking in washings— as they did anyway twelve months a year—to supplement what Jake did or did not bring in. It was Parret who posed a problem for them all. Age twenty-two, out of the army only four months—

hc had been overseas in a segregated stevedore battalion—he was headstrong, contentious, and hated Gem City. Jake, his father, understood him and in his wry, noncommittal way supported him as he listened to Parret's embittered tales of hostile treatment American Negro troops in Europe received from American white troops; of the fights, humiliations, the recriminations. It had not only unfitted Parret for further army life but for return to civilian life as well. Even his friend Sam, who had not left home, harbored much the same attitude. They also both hated the menial part-time jobs they were limited to in Gem City. Parret really longed to join his big brother, Claude, a bellhop in a Cleveland hotel, but so far Claude had not encouraged him to come, and their mother, Minnie, had taken a harsh stand against it. "Parret needs lookin' after yet," she told her husband Jake—"He's too rash and uppity for his own good; for his own safety too, in these troublous times. We gotta keep him here in Gem City 'til we can talk some sense in his head —and get him outa this habit of talkin' back to white folks, especially the police, like he does."

Gem City's constabulary consisted of eighteen policemen and a chief. The rookie of the force was one Stanley Cutts, age twenty-three, and home from the army only a little longer than Parret. Stanley, ever since a teenager and high school football star, had been a favorite of the white townspeople. Tall, slender, fair-haired, extremely likeable with his slow, ingratiating grin, he was lionized on his return home from France—his only wound a little shrapnel left in the calf of one leg. At once he was offered several jobs, one or two of them with real futures. Moreover, he was soon to be married, to his high school sweetheart, Estelle Fenner, the girl who had waited for him two years. Both of his older brothers urged him now to take the lathe-foreman job he had been offered at the roofing plant, but he put them off. The difficulty was that Stanley loved uniforms. His army uniform gave him a sense of importance, well-being, fed his vanity, as nothing else could. It also stirred his patriotism. He dreaded now having to take it off and store it in moth balls—the tunic with its proud sergeant's stripes, the wrapped leggings, the smart overseas cap worn always at a rakish angle—and don drab civilian attire. And what would be the effect on his affianced? he wondered—would her eyes lose the soft glitter he had seen whenever she looked at him resplendent in his uniform? It worried him. Consequently, within a month of his arrival home he had taken the police examination, after that the ten days of training, and then been sworn in as a Gem City policeman—replacing the adored brown uniform with the next best thing, a blue one with brass buttons. Soon afterwards then came the big wedding in the Carmelite church, and now already by July his wife was pregnant. The townspeople, neighborly, nosey, romantic, seeing themselves when young, loving Stanley and Estelle, truly rejoiced.

Parret Webb loved his khaki uniform also. This was when he had just come home, and although he was far less motivated by patriotism than Stanley, he still felt when wearing it the same cocky sense of importance, the same vanity—when the smiling girls at the Negro Baptist church eyed him approvingly, he loved it. What titillated him more than anything, however, what gave him the greatest, most perverse pleasure of all, was the hostile looks he drew from some of the townspeople, men lounging about the town square or in front of the stores and saloons. This was when, sometimes with civilian Sam, he would walk past these loiterers with his inevitable little swagger, the slight hauteur. He could not help it, could not restrain himself; it felt too good. "It's killin' these peckerwood sonsabitches, ain't it?" crowed Sam when they were out of earshot and laughing—"They can't stand it." Yet what, only a moment ago, they had overheard from these men still reverberated in their ears. One red-faced man, mildly, jokingly, remonstrating with another for his caustic talk and racial slurs, had said, "But he's wearing the uniform of the United States, ain't he?" The other, spitting tobacco juice, glaring, replied, "I don't give a Goddamn if he's wrapped in the American flag, he's still a nigger!" The remark rang yet in Parret's ears. But again it made Sam laugh— bitterly. Then they would keep walking—until, down by the railroad siding, they had reached The Plantation.

Berry Bell's tiny saloon, The Plantation, was the only public place of its kind—liquor-dispensing—in Gem City that a Negro could enter. But Berry laughed about this—he had a monopoly. Berry was also a politician, a Negro politician, who faithfully delivered Gem City's seventy-five or so Negro Republican votes each election—there were no Democrats—and for it got occasional round trip excursion tickets to Columbus for his followers, a seat on the platform, back row, at county-wide Republican rallies, and the tacit go-ahead from the town constabulary to run a Saturday night dice and poker game in the back of The Plantation. In his small way Berry had prospered. But then, alas, the shadow of the Volstead Act moved over the enterprise, over everything, and he soon learned that his place, like all the other saloons, must go out of business—Prohibition would come in with the new year. He was frantic, distraught, and spent most of his time worrying, moping, trying to think up ways to survive; he had never imagined such a calamity befalling him. But it was during these final months of The Plantation's existence that Parret and Sam spent much of their time there. In fact, it was hardly noon on that fateful hot July day in question when they entered to find Berry Bell at a back table in earnest conversation with two strange white men. Otherwise, except for the bartender, Hogarth, the place was empty. The white men were drinking; Berry was not. Parret and Sam gaped at the spectacle—they had never seen a white man in the place before, certainly none drinking, and it surprised them. But soon, after a couple of drinks themselves, it began to nettle, then anger them. Why didn't these white men go to their own places to drink, they muttered to each other, to their own rigidly segregated saloons where Berry would not dare stick his head. They of course could not know the men were there strictly on business; that one of them was Jerry Rudd, the tough hill country bootlegger, who was at the moment reassuring Berry, instructing him on ways he could stay in business after Prohibition and be well supplied.

But soon after Hogarth, the bartender, had served Parret and Sam third drinks, their angry talk began to get louder, far less controlled. Finally, inevitably, the white men's attention was diverted, drawn to the bar—in time to hear Parret, his back to them, say to Hogarth and Sam, "When're one of them peckerwoods back there goin' to invite Berry into a saloon of *theirs,* I wonder? Huh?"

"Don't hold your breath till they do," said Sam, his voice almost as loud as Parret's.

Hogarth said nothing. As bartender he had the continuing responsibility of maintaining the peace.

"Berry's a chump, havin' 'em in here," Parret said, turning around now and glaring at the men.

"They're talkin' business," Hogarth said. "Keep your shirt on, soldier boy—you ain't in Paris now."

531

When soon the conference at the back table broke up, Berry, too preoccupied with business problems to have been much concerned with what was happening at the bar, led Rudd and the other white man toward the front door. As they passed the bar, Rudd, tall, gaunt, red-faced, turned to get a good look at the customer—Parret—who had been so loudly castigating them. Their gazes met, both hostilely. Then Parret blurted out, "Yeah, it's time you'all left—let the doorknob hit you in the back!" Rudd suddenly stopped, his red face now blanched white, and glowered at Parret.

Berry, at last forced to take notice, said sternly to Hogarth, "Don't give soldier boy any more to drink—some folks just can't handle their liquor."

Parret looked scorn at him. "Some folks can't handle their peckerwoods, neither. They let 'em shit on 'em, then ask 'em to come in and have a drink. Okay, then ask 'em to take you up to one of their places—yeah, to Bud Detweiler's saloon—for a drink. Go on, Berry—ask 'em!"

The second white man now began pulling stubborn, resisting Rudd out the door. "Come on, now, Jerry—hit sure ain't worth gittin' upset about . . . come on, come on." Rudd said nothing. He only jerked free of his companion and glared again at Parret. But in a moment they left.

Berry Bell in other, better, times had been a man with a ready smile. He was famous for it, among both whites and blacks. But now his worries had affected him and he looked harried, nervous, somehow insignificant. As soon as Jerry Rudd and the other white man had gone, Berry got out a handkerchief, took off his horn-rimmed glasses, and blew on them. As he polished the lenses, he squinted at Parret and Sam at the bar. "I'm gonna do something," he said out of the side of his mouth to them, "I ain't done in a long time—ask a customer to leave. You'all are trouble-makers; you ain't good for my place; or for this town, neither—you ain't good for colored folks in this town—"

Parret had already interrupted—"You wanta know something, Berry, colored folks in this town been asleep for years; asleep on their rights."

"Sleep or no sleep, we was doin' pretty good before you come back here and started all your foolishness. We got some bad, some evil, white folks in this town—as bad as down South—and looks like what you're doin' is tryin' to rile 'em up, get 'em on the warpath. Everybody'll suffer then, especially colored folks. I don't want you'all in my place no more—when I see you I see trouble. When you finish your drinks, you can leave."

Parret stood up at once. Sam then did the same. "Don't have to finish 'em," Parret said, going in his pocket for money to pay Hogarth. "We'll find another place to spend our money in."

"It won't be no saloon," said Berry—"not in this town. From now on you'll drink your liquor at home, or in your car, or in the street or some place—not in no saloon." But Parret and Sam were already going out the door.

Parret, his jaw set, chin stubbornly on his chest, marched ahead of Sam across the gravelly little street to Sam's Ford. He was grim, silent.

"Where you goin' now?" said Sam, apprehensively.

"Get in—I'll show you where I'm goin'." As Sam got in the car, Parret went around to the front, used the crank to start the motor, then, amidst the sputtering and backfiring, climbed in beside Sam. "Drive up to Bud Detweiler's saloon," Parret said.

Sam swung around to him. "You losin' your mind?"

"No. I'm *usin'* my mind. Somethin' niggers ain't done in this town since they been here. All these places are public places, ain't they? And we're members of the public, ain't we? We're black, sure, but still members of the public. Ain't no law in this state sayin' they *can't* serve us in a public place, is there? You damn right there ain't. We just ain't had the guts to go get our rights, that's all. You got the guts to go in Bud Detweiler's or not?"

"Sure I have," said Sam, but quietly now, almost pensively, as he drove the Ford onto paved streets now and toward the center of town.

They were two brash, though dangerous, boys—hardly men at all—reacting to strange, cruel, phenomena whose unjust history and complexities they had not lived long enough to know or understand. The only thing they knew was that they were human beings, yet not treated as such; they felt this a condition unjustified, yet rectifiable. They—especially Parret—considered themselves truly men, and that not to try to change these evils was to reduce themselves to craven, gutless things. They had not read books on the subject, nor heard inciting speeches; the only redress they understood was violence; that state of mind, moreover, did not extend to consequences.

Sam was a bastard—illegitimate. Yet he knew his putative father —Otis Sykes, an itinerant jackleg preacher—and as a twelve-year-old boy had even sometimes gone fishing with him on his occasional returns to Gem City to lead revival meetings. Sam suspected nothing until one day Sykes exhorted him to consider going into the ministry himself when he grew up. Sam, however, demurred, saying that when he reached twenty-one he wanted to go to Detroit and become a molder in a foundry there where he had heard they paid fabulous wages to men in this trade. Of this Sykes was at once supportive, even vowing when the time came to give him the money to learn the trade and get a job. Sam knew for sure then. He asked his mother if he was not right and, after evasively looking away, she had burst into tears. Somehow though Sam felt better, knowing. But Sykes died when his son was not yet sixteen and that was the end of that. Soon Sam had dropped out of school to help his still-unmarried mother provide their livelihood and his dreams would now forever go unfulfilled. At present he worked part-time as a horse handler in a Gem City blacksmithery. Yet he had never rid himself of his restlessness; he still hoped somehow to escape the town, but there was always his self-pitying mother to think of. He felt trapped.

Primarily, on the other hand, Parret's attitude was one of indignation. He was indignant—and mortified—about his family's poverty, his father's chronic failures, about his mother and sister having to wash the fouled linen of white folks, and about his own defeat. His paranoia about his own life, as well as that of Negroes everywhere, explained much of his general bitter malaise. The eighteen months he had just spent away from Gem City—in U.S. Army camps, then in England and France—had been disastrous for him. He saw how other people lived, even during and after a terrible war. The luxury, affluence, and privilege, all with their accompanying callousness and contempt for people like himself, shocked and mystified, then outraged him; made him capable of almost any act. Naive, he did not understand the world or its capacity for evil and at times considered the life he lived an insult.

The Ford was moving up Pine Street now. Parret turned and looked at Sam, silent beside him. "You know damn well it ain't Detweiler's liquor I want," he said. "I only want his bartender to set them drinks on the bar in front of us. We won't be wantin' 'em but we'll drink 'em just the same—then pay and walk out."

Sam nodded and kept driving. He was somehow thinking of his mother—he did not know why. Finally he said, "Suppose they won't serve us?"

There was a long pause as Parret fought the question, tried to come up with an answer. "They'll serve us, all right," he said at last, though it was a mere assertion, vacuous and makeshift. "When we walk in that place—you and me—I tell you, they'll serve us!" But his excited determination seemed self-generated.

They were in front of Detweiler's now before they knew it. Situated on the corner of Main and Pine Streets, it was the largest saloon in town, though this was of course relative, as the others could justifiably have been called little more than "holes in the wall." Flanking the front door, the two large windows were plate glass and there were brass rings in the cafe curtains, but the curtains were much the worse for wear and unsightly. Nor apparently had the windows themselves been washed for months, though the window on the left as one approached bore in large, now flaking, gold leaf the one word: DETWEILER'S. The Post Office was in the same block on Main Street and across from the Post Office was the police station.

Sam stopped the Ford across from the saloon, but on the Pine Street side. As he turned off the ignition, he heaved a heavy, nervous sigh—he was afraid. Parret's heart too was drumming from agitation and uncertainty but outwardly he seemed calm, prepared. Yet both, looking straight ahead through the car's windshield, continued to sit there—as if trying to summon the courage to do what they had come to do. Finally Sam, hesitating, said, ". . . What we gonna do if they won't serve us?"

Parret bridled. "You already asked that," he said—"and I told you they'd serve us."

Sam's face had a hangdog look, as if showing contrition for doubting that Parret's avowals were anything less than guaranteed truth. "Okay," he said—"sure, I guess they'll serve us."

"Let's go, then," Parret said, and opened his door.

Still Sam lingered, somehow thinking again of his mother. "Suppose, though," he said, "they raise a big fuss before they serve us, git hostile-like?"

Parret turned on him savagely. "You're scared! Scared to death!

You go on home, then—I'll go in there myself!" But Sam was already climbing from under the wheel and soon both of them were crossing Pine Street on their way to their destiny.

At barely dawn that morning Stanley Cutts, rookie policeman and on the way eventually—in six and a half months—to becoming a father, had been aroused from sleep by his pregnant wife's fitful retching into the slop jar. Estelle, pale, woebegone, feeling sorry for herself, groaned and heaved indelicately. When at last, however, she slowly returned to bed and Stanley's sleepy arms, he embraced her, patted her back, and whispered sweet, sympathetic nothings in her ear. Outside the sky was clear, but though their rented little frame house was cool and pleasant now, it could already be seen the day would be sultry. But Stanley was soon asleep again and Estelle tried to lie still to quiet her stomach. She thought of the months ahead and fearfully wondered what it would be like to have a baby; though her mother, who had had five, laughed and assured her that after the first one it was nothing—that she would have many babies for Stanley.

At 6:30 the alarm clock went off and Stanley, yet stirring sleepily, reached and turned it off. But he lay there for a few minutes more, hating to get up—that is, until he thought of his new blue uniform. It hung in the closet, as if waiting. His eager expectancy of wearing it again always eased his daily reluctance to get out of bed while sleep still beckoned. He got up now and built a fire in the cook stove, washed and shaved, then, insisting Estelle stay in bed, prepared to get his own breakfast. The sun was up and the morning beautiful. Already old Harley Reed next door was out in his garden with his hoe tending his pole beans and sweet corn before the heat came and enveloped everything. Stanley was already thinking about his friends, the "boys" at the police station, and the jokes they made about his new uniform—only yesterday, as the men of the day shift, his shift this month, were leaving the station to go out on their beats, Oscar ("Slider"—from his baseball days) Wente himself, the chief, had grinned and remarked for all to hear how careless, sloppy, Stanley was getting lately about his uniform, when everyone, including Slider Wente, knew Stanley would not so much as tolerate the tiniest bit of lint on his immaculate blue habit. So, still in his nightshirt as he put the coffee pot on the fire, he smiled with good humor and satisfaction as he thought of his colleagues;

he looked forward to each day's duties, with the fun that went with them, and basked in the popularity he enjoyed not only with his associates but with the townspeople at large.

He breakfasted now on homemade buttered bread (baked by his mother), a half dozen strips of bacon, three eggs, and a pot of strong, hot coffee. Then he returned to the bedroom to put on his uniform, as Estelle lay watching him. "Feel better?" he said to her, carefully holding out the blue jacket for inspection, and admiration.

"A little," she said, then gave a slight, quizzical, laugh. "Oh, it's going to be hot in that uniform today—can't you leave the tie and jacket off?"

"Sure, if it gets hot enough."

But Estelle knew it would never get that hot. In a few minutes, as he prepared to leave—it was 7:40—she got out of bed and followed him to the door. "Bring home some lemons, will you?—we'll have lemonade with supper."

"I'll bring home anything you want," he grinned—"including me." He took her in his arms, held her close to him, and kissed her on the forehead. Then he left.

He waved at old Harley Reed in his garden and kept on down the street, his stride brisk, military, the blue uniform and gold-braided stiff blue cap magnificent. He passed Biddie Dawson now, the widow, a friend of his mother's, in her sunbonnet as she tended her petunias before scrubbing her front porch. "Now, don't you look nice!" she said to him—"just like you were going to be in a parade somewhere. My, my!" In the next block, little Jimmie Wayne, his empty dinner pail in hand, was just getting home from working the night shift out at the plant. "Say, Stanley, how you like that policeman's job?" he laughed—"Remember, I knowed you as a little shaver when you was fishing for bass with an old cane pole. You ain't forgot that, have you? This job you got now is different from the army, I bet—you didn't have it so soft then. A runt like me couldn't never be a policeman, could he? Ha, ha, ha!" Just before good-natured, smiling Stanley reached Main Street he encountered the Reverend Winfield Pike, the Methodist minister, leaving his house. "John Karns is bad sick, Stanley," he said, shaking his head—"very bad sick. Doctor's about give him up. His wife wants me to come see him, pray with them—that's where I'm headin' now, at this time in the morning. But it ain't never too early

537

to do the Lord's work, boy." Stanley then continued down Main Street to the police station where he entered and signed in at five minutes before eight.

Neither Parret nor Sam hesitated any more when at last they found themselves face to face with their destination—the screened front door of Detweiler's saloon. With Parret leading the way, they entered at once—as if to hesitate would destroy their already lagging resolve. Though there were over a dozen men standing along the bar, no one at first seemed to see them. Another marvel was that in that instant the two invaders saw only what most surprised, startled, bedazzled, them—it was as though they would stop in their tracks—for high over the bar, for almost its entire length, was affixed to the wall an enormous oil painting, ornately framed in gilt, of a bosomy, half-naked woman, her blond hair in ringlets, coyly reclining full-length on a couch and smiling down at the patrons. To Parret and Sam it all the more confirmed, exemplified, the premises as alien territory. Now they were also aware of voices, activity, emanating from the back room where still more patrons were having lunch with their drinks, out of view of the bar. Next it appeared almost as though the two had actually reached the bar before anyone saw them. Then, as if epiphanized, everyone seemed to see them in the same split second.

Parret was the first to stop and put his foot up on the bar rail. In doing so—merely performing the random, trivial act—he suddenly experienced a sense of power he had never known, or imagined, before. It was heady to him. Sam came alongside him now, but they looked at each other only in the expanse of mirror behind the bar—they felt like a thousand other eyes were upon them. One of the two bartenders, however, big Jody Sims, nearest them, at first seemed not unduly perturbed; he did not panic; for he vaguely knew who Sam was, and had heard, though not kindly, of Parret Webb and his ways. He faced the two now. "You boys lookin' for somebody?" he said, altogether excluding Parret from the gaze he trained on Sam.

Sam froze; could not talk. But Parret talked. "No, we ain't lookin' for nobody," he said.

"What you want, then?" Jody's beefy face was still bland, curious, unbelieving.

Where Parret now, in partial answer, produced the big one dollar bill from, no one could have said for certain—it was as though, Houdini-like, it had suddenly sprung from the palm of his hand. "We wanta couple of drinks," he said, his voice tense, husky, his face showing the hopeful, nervous urgency of what he undertook.

Jody screwed up his nose. "Now, you boys know better'n that." He again addressed Sam. "Whut the hell—"

Sam, in a vague echo, interrupted, "Yeah, we wanta couple of drinks." Then, in his agitation glancing at what Parret's slight-of-hand magic had produced, added, "We got money."

"I don't want your damn money," said Jody, arching one eyebrow, his voice rising for the first time. The bar's business had come to a standstill now.

"Our money spends," Parret said. But somehow he looked around malevolently at the others.

Jody said nothing. He merely turned and reached down two glasses, then poured a shot of whiskey in each and shoved them toward Parret and Sam. Whereupon Parret released the dollar bill onto the bar. Jody took it, returned sixty cents, then, also malevolently now, leaned an arm on the bar and, as did the customers (some even, still chewing food, emerging from the back room), waited to see what would happen to the two drinks—it was as if the drinks were strychnine and had raised a mighty curiosity over whether they would be actually consumed. The customers hadn't long to wait. Parret, first pocketing his change, lifted his drink and tossed it off neat, his face a mask. Sam of course then did the same. Jody, crouching now as if he had been stealthily lurking in wait, removed his elbow from the bar and seized first Parret's empty glass, then Sam's, and, one at a time, hurled each violently to the floor. The customers at the bar, covering their drinks, ducked as glass fragments flew fifty feet.

At this suspended moment in time a loud, drunken cry, a bellow, came from the direction of the back room. They all turned to see a customer standing in the back room door, a roast beef sandwich still in his hand, and yelling profane obscenities. It was tall, gaunt Jerry Rudd, the hill country bootlegger, whom Parret and Sam had within the hour encountered at The Plantation. Rudd was yelling at Jody the bartender. "Whut the hell you tryin' to do?—git rid of your white customers?" he cried. "Breakin' glasses ain't gonna do no good! Where's Bud Detweiler?—I wanta complain!"

"Bud's in Columbus," someone said, then, ironically, laughed.

"Whut the goddam hell you laughin' at?" roared Rudd over his shoulder; he was red-faced, mean-and-evil drunk. Advancing now on Parret and Sam, he first hurled his sandwich at them, parts of it flying off Sam's shoulder.

Sam, wide-eyed, observing developments, had already stepped back from the bar. "Come on, let's go," he said to Parret. "To hell with 'em—we got our drink. Come on!" But Parret had not moved and was glaring at Rudd. But soon he too left the bar and, unhurriedly, followed Sam toward the front door.

"You *better* git your black asses outa here!" Rudd, again in unsteady pursuit, yelled at them.

Neither Sam nor Parret reacted. They walked to the screened front door and Sam, ahead, opened it and stepped out. But Parret had barely reached the threshold when Rudd, now overtaking him, drew back his big-booted foot and kicked Parret in the backside with all his might. Parret went tumbling, hurtling, headlong through the open door and landed out on the sidewalk on all fours. Before he could get up, two customers had seized Rudd, wrestled him back inside, and slammed the screen door.

Sam pulled Parret up off the sidewalk. "We'll git that redneck son of a bitch one of these days, see if we don't," Sam said.

Parret turned on him as if he would fight him. *"One of these days?"* he cried, incredulously. "Take me home!—come on! Now! Take me home!"

Sam's eyes searched Parret's face. "Whut you fixin' to do?—whut you wanta go home for?"

But Parret was already running toward the car.

Less than ten minutes later Stanley Cutts and another, older, policeman, named Barker, entered Detweiler's and, greeting customers as they went, headed toward the back room where they customarily ate a sandwich and drank a bottle of strawberry or orange pop at noon. The grim merriment among the customers, however, was still rife as all the talk was about the incident they had just witnessed. But Stanley and Barker, the latter a big towheaded man, soon munching their sandwiches, wanting not to be bothered, listened without comment—though occasionally smiling and nodding their heads.

"You sure did miss it, Barker!" one customer persisted.

Barker grinned—"Yeah, that's what I understand."

"But it was Jerry Rudd that turned out to be the bouncer," the man said—"not Jody, the bartender. Jerry kicked 'em out in the street—saved Jody the trouble! Ha! ha! ha! You shoulda been here!"

"Not necessarily," Barker smiled—"I might've had to arrest Jerry. Where is he?" He looked around the back room.

Someone else answered. "He's out front at the bar again—still drinkin'."

Stanley Cutts sat eating his sandwich, often smiling as he listened attentively, in admiration, to Barker. Barker, twelve years his senior and a veteran on the force, had, so to speak, taken Stanley under his wing whenever they chanced to work, as now, the same shift. Stanley, on the other hand, never looked, or felt, so callow, so "green" and young, such an unfledged rookie, as when with Barker. Even Barker seemed to sense this, for he would sometimes tell Stanley that police work was nowhere near as demanding, or as dangerous, as what Stanley had just experienced fighting overseas in real war. One day he said to Stanley, "Law enforcement in a place like Gem City—except maybe on a Saturday when some of them hill country boys come to town—is a snap compared to some big places, like Columbus or Cincinnati. You got a different type of people altogether in Gem City; a lot of church people, quiet, law-abiding folks—they're all a policeman's friend; they don't resent a policeman like they do in many places. Take your own case; you got a lead pipe cinch—most of these people have knowed you since you was a kid goin' fishin' barefooted. *You* ain't got nothin' to worry about." Hearing Barker say these things always gave Stanley, who was already apt and eager, an ever-growing sense of confidence and ambition; his admiration for Barker knew no bounds. "You'll be the next chief," he told his mentor—"when Slider retires." Big Barker let out a guffaw—"Yeah, and by that time I'll have a long, white beard." Stanley loved to talk to Barker. But today, as they sat eating in Detweiler's back room together, they could hardly talk to each other at all for interruptions from the talkative, gregarious customers anxious to reenact for them the expulsion of the two blacks. They bore it, however, with good-humored tolerance.

Stanley said, "White beard or not, you'll—"

541

There came a strange, sudden hush up front—in the bar. They heard the shot then—almost simultaneous with someone's yell, *"Hey, look out!"* . . . followed by a mad scramble as if people were running for cover. Then another shot. It was then ironical that the first of the two policeman out of his chair and pulling his pistol was Stanley Cutts. Running ahead of Barker now, he charged through the door into the bar—only to collide with reeling, retreating, Jerry Rudd . . . just as two more shots were heard. Both Rudd and Stanley then fell—though one of the shots had missed entirely. The other bullet, however, had struck Rudd in the thigh, a flesh wound, passed on through, and tore into Stanley's abdomen, shattering liver and other organs. All Stanley's adulthood vanished; he screamed in agony as he hit the floor, his pistol skittering across and hitting a brass spitoon.

Policeman Barker, himself now silhouetted in the door, at once saw his own predicament. Parret, gun in hand, still only Rudd on his mind, was in full view but with most of the bar customers behind him—his chance protective backdrop. Barker knew if he fired he might hit not Parret but someone else. He dropped to the floor then, on top of Stanley, just as Parret fired again at prostrate Rudd and missed. But before Barker could rise far enough to shoot, Parret had bolted out the front door where Sam awaited in the already moving Ford.

"Did you git him?" said Sam breathlessly, the old car careening on a corner.

"Yeah . . . he went down," Parret said, panting, the smoking pistol still in his hand. "A damn policeman went down too."

"Whut?"

"There was two of 'em—in the back room. The redneck was runnin' from me and run right into one of 'em just as I shot—both of 'em went down."

"Lord, let's git outa here."

"Yeah," Parret said, "take me to Hoopton—I can ketch a train there and go up to Cleveland. They won't git me there. We better hurry—they're goin' to be after us." He put the pistol in his pocket.

"Yeah," breathed Sam—"the police've got a couple of them big Buick touring cars. They're fast."

On Detweiler's barroom floor Stanley's bleeding was all internal. Had it not been for his wild threshing about, screaming, and crying

542

no one could have been sure he'd been shot. But they gathered around him now—Jerry Rudd, drunk, with only a flesh wound, was completely ignored. Already Jody the bartender had sent someone a half-block up the street to the police station to fetch Chief Slider Wente. When Slider, tall, lanky, and red-headed, came running in, everyone turned frantically to him with a plethora of unsolicited advice: "Better put up road blocks, Slider," they said—"The niggers was in an old Ford, but it'll run. They'll be done gone if you ain't quick."

Slider, having just seen his pitiful rookie prostrate, the resplendent blue uniform sullied with the grime of the floor, the eyes affright, the legs threshing in spasms of pain, he flew into a towering, bitter rage—at his would-be advisers. He began yelling, "*God damn it to hell!*—ain't you bastards got sense enough to get him to the hospital! *Fuck* the niggers!—I'll have them in ten minutes! Call the hospital! . . . have 'em send that thing they call an ambulance up here! God damn it, get this kid to the hospital!—*quick!*" Jody hurried to his telephone on the wall behind the bar, as Slider ran back out and up to the police station again where he summoned all his men, with orders to seal off the town against the fugitives' flight. He then called the sheriffs of the three adjoining counties for additional help. Within fifteen minutes the manhunt was on.

The roadblocks, however, were too late. Sam, with the old Ford's accelerator lever yanked down all the way, had already negotiated the town limits and, with Parret sitting grimly beside him, was now well into the countryside—on the way to Hoopton. It was nearly two o'clock and the July sun's heat was stifling, oppressive. And though Sam had said nothing about it, he was beginning to worry about his frothing radiator. He knew he had enough gasoline but he wished now he could stop somewhere and cool the radiator with fresh, cold water. But there was neither time nor opportunity. They were on a strip of blacktop road that soon entered a stand of maple trees and foliage where thick weeds grew along the highway. Parret was cool, self-possessed, almost optimistic. He had not reckoned, however, with Slider Wente's acumen in calling for help from neighboring counties. It meant of course pursuit might be coming from ahead as well as behind.

"You know train times in Hoopton?" Parret asked.

"Naw. You'll have to hide somewhere till the Cleveland train

543

comes." But Sam was thinking again of his mother. He had never been so aware before of his dependence on her and the realization was somehow now linked with his premonitions. He did not believe Parret could escape for long. "You think anybody got killed?" he said after a moment.

"I couldn't tell. Everything happened fast—*fast*. I hope so—I hope that redneck bastard that kicked me is dead. Why would he wanta kick somebody because they went into a public place, just like everybody else, to buy a drink? It don't make sense. Yeah, I hope the bastard's dead."

"You gotta figure out how to git away now," Sam said, but his doubts were grave and mounting. The old Ford's chassis and tin doors fairly shook, vibrated, under the strain of its 35 m.p.h. maximum speed; and there was no knowing how long the radiator would hold out. "I think there's an early evenin' train," Sam added, hunched over the wheel, the fear swelling inside him.

Parret turned and looked at him. "You goin' with me, ain't you?"

Sam hesitated. "I would maybe if it wasn't for my mother—I oughtn't to go off and leave her."

"Hell, I got a mother too, but I'm leavin', ain't I?—niggers ain't never gonna be nothin' in this burg. Bad as down South. In France you could go in any damn place you wanted to, long as you had the money—hell, you didn't git kicked like a dog for it."

Sam did not reply. He was thinking of Parret's refusal to see that his chances of flight were poor, almost nil. Sam was also aware of the difficulties of his own situation, and that returning to his mother would by no means be the end of them. Realizing he would be pursued as vengefully as Parret made him tremble; the peril of it almost immobilized him, made him desperate; soon he was utterly confused. He tried to drive faster but this was not possible. If he made it to Hoopton and let Parret out, he thought, what would he, himself, do then? If he returned home he would without doubt be arrested. Then maybe he should take his chances with Parret. But again—there was his mother. His confusion now bordered on panic.

"I think about my mother too," Parret said again, defensive, self-righteous, insistent, almost as if reading Sam's mind—"and about my sister, and my old man. You don't think, do you, it made me feel good to come home and see them still livin' like they are—my mother and sister washin' white folks dirty, stinkin' clothes, and

544

my old man shovelin' cow shit out in that goddam dairy. But, sure, I hate to leave 'em—they're my folks; only ones, except my brother, I got, ain't they?"

But Sam was still trembling. "You think you killed anybody, Parret?" he said again. "If you did, everybody's after us—right now—to kill *us*."

"I don't reckon I killed anybody. I think I musta at least hit one of 'em, though—that son of a bitch that kicked me, the one I was tryin' to hit. Or the policeman."

"Jesus, I hope it wasn't the policeman," said Sam.

"I sure wasn't shootin' at him."

"That won't help none—if you hit him," Sam said.

Parret did not respond, for suddenly the Ford's engine had begun to wheeze, then sputter, and misfire. In the intense heat the radiator was boiling. Sam's hands were flying everywhere over the few available instruments, trying anything he knew to keep the motor alive. Yet the car seemed about to stop. He finally pulled off onto the road shoulder in a wooded area but wished he could have waited for a covert lane or side road to use. It was not to be. And as the heat had halted the car, so his mortal fear had paralyzed his ability to function. He got out, lifted the hood, and stared blankly, futilely, at the churning radiator. Parret still sat in the car, as if above all such mundane things—that is, until he saw the big car facing them down the road ahead, full of uniformed men, coming full speed toward him. With a tight-throated "Come on!" as his only words of warning to Sam, he took a giant leap from the Ford and, landing across a ditch, raced into the woods and disappeared.

Sam, now hearing the car, froze, his back still to it. The big car of deputy sheriffs from neighboring Halder County skidded to a halt. "It's them, all right!" somebody yelled. Life came to Sam's body then; the back and thigh muscles flinched and twitched, the blood, like purple electricity, coursing through them to his brain, then down the tributaries into his utter fingers and toes. He leapt behind the Ford, then, high and flying, cleared the ditch—as a big deputy dropped to one knee in the middle of the road and took a bead on him with an Emden rifle. "Stop!" the deputy shouted, as well as some of the others. "We're the law!" he yelled—"Stop or I'll shoot!" There could have been in the sultry stillness no failure to hear him; yet Sam heard and did not hear him; it was as if he listened only for his mother's call. There were two shots then, and, just short of the woods, he fell forward into a bed of violets. All of the deputies, six of them, their guns at the ready, were swarming across the road now—when a big green Buick touring car full of Gem City policemen, Slider Wente driving, sped up from the other direction and came to a quivering halt. "We already got one of 'em, Slider!" a deputy sheriff called as the police chief came running forward and was led to where Sam was lying face down in the flowers. They turned him over; both rounds had entered his back, one going clear through, and he was breathing his last. ". . . Ma! . . . tell my Ma—" he uttered feebly—"Ma . . . Ma!" Then, his eyes still open, he expired.

"Which way did the other one go?" Slider now cried out, suddenly aware his job was only half-done. "He's the one that done the shootin'."

"He made it into the woods there," a deputy said, pointing, "but he sure cain't be far."

Slider waved his arm forward. "Okay, boys—fan out! These woods ain't big, but be damn careful—he's got a gun and knows how to use it. Come on, let's go!"

The sun was hot on the tops of the trees, but at a slightly lower level the thick, embowering—protective—leaves afforded, if not a coolness, a more temperate, bearable, warmth to someone hiding in their midst. Parret was very still; still as a ghost, hardly allowing himself to breathe. He had been shocked, dismayed, to discover the wooded area so small, a mere rectangular patch of trees one could have loped through in three minutes. It was a very dangerous place, he realized, to try to hide in, especially when his pursuers had seen him enter and were numerous enough to surround the plot and ferret him out. To try to fight them, he knew, with only one bullet left in his pistol, would be futile. For the first time then he considered surrender. The idea revolted him. Were things this bad? he thought—this hopeless? He refused to concede it. They might not find him after all; his ruse might succeed; for he now sat perched high in a tree of his own necessarily quick choosing. At first, on entering the woods, he had frantically run about in every direction, seeking in vain any vista leading to what might be a greater depth in the trees. When he found there was none, he began, as a last desperate resort, to look for a tree with thick enough leaves and foliage that if climbed would hide him—so far as he could tell, his pursuers had no dogs. Again he began a frantic search, wishing furiously he had more time—he could already hear the loud voices; then he heard the two shots and, understanding all too well their probable result, knew he could wait no longer. In less than a minute then he had scaled a tree, one in his haste chosen less for its foliage than its low, accessible limbs, and was soon as high as the strength of the limbs would give support. He clung there now in a fork of the tree, wilting from heat exhaustion and weak from fear. He had never in all his life known such fear, for he felt, almost knew, the worst had happened to Sam and that he would soon be next. Why hadn't they captured Sam? . . . at least why hadn't they tried?—he would not have resisted; he had shot at nobody. Why did they have to fire a gun?—twice. Parret's mind was chaotic now, his panic total.

Slider Wente, ignoring the county deputies' higher jurisdiction, had now taken complete charge of the hunt. But his four policemen and the six deputy sheriffs had hardly left the road near which Sam's body lay and entered the tiny woods when another car of Gem City policemen, Barker driving, arrived from town with the horrible news that Stanley Cutts was dead—Barker said he had died just as they got him to the hospital. The word, called out loudly, vehemently, to the dragnet of men deployed throughout the tiny woods, had an electrifying, stunning, sick, effect upon them all. "Oh, my God," breathed Slider, stopping in his tracks, then, rifle still in hand, staggering, falling back, against the trunk of a tree. "What'll I tell Jack and Melvin, his brothers?—they was the only ones, the only damn ones, that didn't want him to come on the police force anyhow. Oh, my Lord! . . ." he moaned, "this is awful—and his poor wife in the family way. Jesus Christ . . . Stanley, the poor kid, didn't have a chance—the nigger shot him in cold blood." Slider's commiserating men now had gathered around him as if Stanley Cutts had been his son. "It's awful! . . ." he went on, as if in a daze—"*awful*! Ain't nothin' like this *ever* happened to Gem City!"

A burly deputy sheriff nicknamed "Highball," his shirt under-arms wet with sweat stains, came up now. "You gonna stand 'round here sheddin' crocodile tears all day, Slider?—or are we gonna go git the other nigger? He's hidin' in here some place—we'da

547

seen him if he'da lit out across that open field yonder. He's in here, all right. Come on, let's git goin'!" At last Slider, still mournfully shaking his head, straightened up from the tree and wandered off behind his men.

Despite the fact Parret and Sam had discussed the possibility that the policeman could have been hit, when Parret up in the tree heard the loud, shocking, incredible, news, he could not believe it. He had not killed a policeman! He refused to accept such a fatal turn of events; it was unreal. Yet soon he felt and knew in his heart it was all too real, too true He also knew now his fate was sealed if they caught him. And all the time they were coming closer—closing in. Panic rose in his throat almost as if he would cry out. He looked down at the ground, then all about him. The leaves of the tree in which he hid were not nearly dense enough to entirely conceal him; especially in the fork where he sat. Moreover, although his trousers were dark enough—blue denim—his shirt was white; for better concealment he must somehow find a spot with more leaves, he thought; though he knew now there was not time to climb down and look for another tree. Soon he began climbing out on the limb of the fork where he had sat, to a place where the foliage looked slightly heavier. But the limb was not large and he was horrified by the thought of crashing to the ground in their very midst. Yet slowly, carefully, he crawled out on the limb, though a distance of less than six feet, and then better arranged his legs and tried to take a grip on the limb that, hopefully, his hands could hold for the duration of the fateful test he knew he faced. Voices were all around him now, yet no one had come in sight. Suddenly then he saw one of them—Barker—and his heartbeat almost stopped. Barker, though some distance away in the scattered trees, was carrying not a pistol, not a rifle, but a 10-gauge Winchester shotgun. Nor were Barker's eyes scanning the ground; they were instead fiercely sweeping the leafy limbs of all the trees. Breathlessly Parret watched him, his heart pounding against his ribs, his throat dry as dust. Then suddenly Barker was gone, out of sight, though only shortly before two deputies had appeared, both with pistols on their hips and rifles in their hands. Intent, bent forward, as they almost crept, they seemed more interested in searching out the ground than the trees, examining all bushes and clumps of growth, all weeded ground depressions, and any other likely spots capable of concealing even a child. Not once did Parret see either of them lift their eyes to the tops of the trees. Then he heard Slider's loud voice, not close, yet not far, admonishing, almost scolding, everyone to keep a sharp lookout also in the trees; for, said Slider, it might be from one of these maples "we might flush that nigger bastard."

What Parret could not know, however, was the change Barker, not Slider, had made in his, Barker's, tactics. On purely a hunch, he had returned to his former spot now and instead of moving about in the area had decided to take up a covert station, remain perfectly still, and just wait and watch, and see what happened. Unseen by Parret, Barker was now no more than a hundred feet from him, standing quietly under a maple sapling that had foliage enough but was too small to hold a man's weight, his fierce eyes searching every tree in sight. But because presently there was no one in view, Parret, if only for the moment, breathed a little easier. He stirred slightly, to get a more comfortable posture in the tree, but made no sound. Barker was unaware. Everything was quiet except for the not-far-distant voices of Slider and the others. Barker, however, sinister though outwardly impassive, stood quietly under the sapling, his hard eyes without letup roving the tree tops. Soon those implacable eyes had become inured, habituated, to the single color green, other colors distinctly distracting, alerting, them. This was the strange phenomenon that within less than five minutes was to mean Parret's undoing.

Barker at first thought what he saw in the tree his eyes had now come to rest upon was a bit of sky, a patch of white cloud, but it raised no suspicion and his eyes passed on to other trees. But soon his gaze returned. To his surprise, and interested curiosity, the white patch of cloud had not changed, had not moved, metamorphosed; it seemed stationary and eternal. Barker, shotgun in hand, watched it intently now. When he still saw that nothing ever changed, he concluded he wanted a better view, and left the cover of the sapling and moved out into the open—where now agitated Parret saw him. Parret's first impulse was to pull his pistol and use the last bullet on this his tormentor, but quickly realized this was fancy, fatal fancy. Now he saw Barker looking what seemed directly at him and he became faint with fear. Barker just stood there like a staring-eyed stone, or a dog on the point, his breathing coming fast as he moved once more, not closer but farther to his right. He was almost sure now. Yet he waited—waited to see some inevitable movement. Suddenly then he came to his senses— he was out in the naked open, he only now realized, and his quarry had a gun. He stepped back at once to the cover of the sapling, then, putting two fingers in his mouth, gave a loud, shrill whistle. The response was immediate—"See somethin', Barker?" he heard Slider Wente, who knew the whistle well, call. He did not answer; he only waited for Slider to come. He trained his gaze on the tree again, holding it there, literally piercing the spot. Soon then on the limb he could see a denim leg, and he stopped looking. When Slider and the burly deputy sheriff, Highball, entered the little clearing, Barker, still saying nothing, merely pointed. It was all over.

Desperate, Parret Webb had sat there—his heart pitifully thudding, jumping—and witnessed it all. He too knew it was all over. He was certain now he would meet what he knew had been Sam's fate—after shouting something at him once or twice, they would shoot him out of the tree. He was sure he would soon lie mangled and bleeding, torn open by the shotgun's blast, the pain making him gasp and groan, as these men stood in a circle around him watching him die. In this swiftest of interludes his mind went to his family, his thoughts compressing, crowding, days, weeks, years, into seconds. He would see them no more now, he thought. He especially longed to see his father, one person whom he admired and loved, now in the hospital with a broken leg. His father had seldom ever criticized or scolded him, never tormented him as had at times his mother. "Keep on and you'll break that boy's spirit," Jake Webb, Parret recalled, had once complained to his wife— "when he'll need all the confidence and guts he can get, facin' what he's gonna have to face. Let him alone—he ain't a girl, y'know, and don't try to make him one." He knew his father understood what it was to be a Negro male—male, not man, thought Parret—in this country, South or North. Here a Negro male could never be a man, he told himself, with great, almost tearful, bitterness and desperation; soon then he was almost catatonic with rage; he hardly now knew where he was; he only knew he was cornered like a rat by his lifelong enemies and that, unless he abjectly surrendered, they would kill him. It had all been reduced to a very simple proposition—surrender and be hanged by a judge or die now. In full view then of all the gathering lawmen, he crawled back from the limb and sat where he had before in the fork of the tree, gazing down at them.

Slider Wente stepped forward. "Okay, boy," he said—"throw your gun down here, then you can come down. We've had enough shootin'. Carry out my orders and the worst that'll happen to you is you'll be taken back to town and put in jail to stand trial for murderin' a police officer. If you don't obey my order, then I myself am gonna shoot you outa that tree with Officer Barker's shotgun. Okay, now, which'll it be?"

Strangely, demonically, Parret began a slow swinging of his legs in the tree. He said nothing, but bent his head in reflection as if studying Slider's proposal. At last licking out his blood-red tongue, leering savagely down at them before heaving a great sigh, he snatched out his pistol and shot himself in the head. He toppled to the ground with a sickening thud in their midst. They were stunned. ". . . Jesus God!" Highball said. Slider ran to him and pulled him over on his back. Parret was bleeding profusely from the upper neck but was still conscious. In a feeble voice then, gnashing his teeth in rage and mortification, he began cursing them, then himself, for botching the job. He had failed to bring the pistol high enough and instead of shooting himself in the temple as he planned, had sent the bullet into his neck just below the ear, inflicting a ghastly, but not immediately fatal wound.

Slider, picking up Parret's empty pistol, quickly sent one of his men to the car for the first aid kit. Now, as best he could, he dressed and bandaged the wound, then made quick preparation to get his wounded captive safely back in Gem City and the jail. He also sent a detail of men to retrieve Sam's body and take it back in the deputies' car to a room in the police station used, when infrequent occasion arose, as a morgue. In another situation, Slider would have been swelling with pride, with boasting egotism, but now when he realized that none of this would bring back Stanley Cutts he was depressed, almost maudlin, at times also savage, and grimly had little to say. As Parret groaned in agony now, they carried him to the big green touring car and threw him on the back seat. Soon they saw his lips moving; he was trying to speak, but they sullenly ignored him. Finally he was able, despite the pain, to make a slight vocal noise. ". . . Take me . . . take me to my Pa," he said—"hurry . . . hurry, to my Pa! . . ." But they were already on the road now, speeding to the jail.

In Gem City the news of Stanley Cutts' killing had spread like wildfire. The town was in turmoil, an uproar. Stanley had been brought from Detweiler's saloon to the hospital at the same time a hurried call had been put in to Hoopton to procure the services of the county's best surgeon, a Dr. Spooner. But even before Spooner could leave Hoopton, he received another, countermanding, call—that Stanley was dead. A wild scene at the hospital ensued when Estelle, Stanley's pregnant wife, arrived accompanied by her mother and father. Estelle, screaming, then sobbing, over Stanley's body, insisted he was not dead, that he could not be dead, that she and her parents would continue to pray over him, all night if necessary, and that he would not die. But Stanley had been dead almost since they had brought him in. Yet at the hospital for almost an hour after Estelle's arrival there had been utter chaos, bedlam, as, still screaming and sobbing, she wrung Stanley's limp, dead hands, smothered his pallid face with kisses, and called him all the endearing names she had so often used in their love-making. All to no avail. After yet another hour of these scenes, her tearful parents finally led her away.

Stanley's two older brothers, Jack and Melvin, had gone bass fishing over in adjoining Halder County that morning and only learned of the terrible family tragedy on returning home that afternoon about four o'clock. Besides their families, five or six of the Cutts' men friends awaited them, to give them more details and to confer on what should be done now. One of them was Neal Livermore, a sheet metal worker and religious fanatic, who had also been in the army but had seen no fighting; had not left the country. When Stanley's tearful brothers had had time to partially recover from the initial shock, outrage, and anguished sorrow of the news, Livermore, an average-sized but scrawny, febrile man, whose eyes glowed like coals, spoke to them for the others on Jack Cutts' front porch. "They got the nigger in jail now," he said. "He had tried to kill his self, shoot his self, when they had him cornered, but didn't quite make it—though I understand he's hurt bad and probably won't live. But we ain't interested in that; we're Stanley's buddies and the Bible says, 'An eye for an eye, and a

552

tooth for a tooth,' don't it? The nigger must pay the price for what he done. He ain't entitled to live. But you boys, the family, stay out of it; we'll handle it—there's twenty-five men at least in this town that'll gladly jine us and do the job."

"No, no, I'll go with you myself!" blurted Melvin Cutts, in tears again. "Oh, God!—what a shame, a filthy shame! . . . poor Stanley! Jack and I tried to talk him outa bein' a damn policeman!—oh, that poor sap, our kid brother! . . . little Stanley! You God damn right I'll go with you!"

"So will I," said Jack Cutts at last, though gloomily confused, as if he still did not completely understand that it had all actually happened. "Yes, I'll go . . ." he said.

"No, it ain't fittin'," said Livermore firmly, shaking his head. "You'all have got your responsibilities—this ain't a matter for the family. You stay home, both of you, and look out for your loved ones—and Estelle, that poor girl. We'll take care of the other—tonight." With that the men tramped off.

But Melvin and Jack Cutts themselves, though still reeling from shock, soon left—to go see their dead brother's widow. Before they got near Estelle, however, they found the rented little house full of people—friends, neighbors, mourners, commiseraters, the curious, an assortment of townspeople and hangers-on—while in the bedroom Estelle's parents were still trying to calm her, soothe her, persuade her to lie down and rest; all to no avail. Moreover, the impact of what had happened to her had brought on Estelle a savage attack of hiccups which so far they had been unable to stop. Though her mother and others had tried all the well-known rural nostrums on her, nothing worked. Even after Dr. Cobb, the Gem City doctor, had come and given her a sedative, the hiccups persisted and her hysterical condition remained little changed. She continued to wail, moan, whisper to herself, and then would once more break into a wild fit of crying. And when Melvin and Jack Cutts entered the bedroom, pandemonium really broke loose. Estelle's father, Harlan Fenner, his face livid with rage, jumped up and seized Melvin by both shoulders, glaring into his eyes, shaking him savagely. "We'll mete out our own justice!—I'm telling you! . . ." he spluttered. "No damn spineless, lily-livered judge will ever get this case! . . ."

"Harlan . . . Harlan, don't worry," Melvin said, finally disen-

553

gaging himself, his lip trembling, a frantic look on his face—"It's all being taken care of. You just stay out of it. We've got enough grief—oh, poor Stanley, poor Stanley!" Melvin put his hand to his eyes and broke down and cried again. "God damn it! . . ." he quavered, tears running down—"It'll be done, all right!" His brother, Jack, looked on with a long, mournful face.

Estelle, still hysterical, hiccupping, now threw herself on Melvin's breast and sobbed bitterly. "Oh, bring him back, Melvin! . . ." she cried—"Pray to God to bring him back! . . . Poor, poor Stanley!—he'll never get to see our baby! He wanted a boy *so!* Now he'll never get to see his little boy! . . . Oh, God! . . . *Oh, God!*" She let out a chilling scream.

Half an hour later Neal Livermore and his five henchmen arrived to pay their respects to the young widow. They were calm, composed, now; for they had just come from their leader in the plot, one Augustus ("Gus") Rudd, brother of the wounded Jerry Rudd. There all tactics and plans had been discussed and perfected—plans now only awaiting nightfall. Livermore talked to Melvin in low, deadly assured, tones. "The main thing," he said, "is for you boys tonight to stay with the family—you and Jack. And keep Estelle's daddy, Harlan, with you—he's fit to be tied; he's too reckless. You'all just look after them and keep everything under control. We'll take care of the rest."

Outside the little house people continued to come.

As soon as Chief of Police Slider Wente and the others had returned with Parret Webb to the Gem City jail, Slider found himself facing yet another problem, one hardly less pressing than had been that of Parret's apprehension. How would he be able to keep his prisoner in the jail and not surrender him to be taken to the hospital? It both perplexed and distressed him—Parret was bleeding and in terrible pain. But there were at least three reasons Slider wanted him to remain in his charge. One derived generally from his fierce pride as an arm of the law—it was his determined objective to retain in his own self-confident hands total control. The second was his awareness that, despite the bleeding and excruciating pain, Parret could walk—Slider did not want him trying to escape. The third had to do with the townspeople—he did not like the turmoil, anger, the widespread excitement, that Stanley Cutts' killing had created; though as yet he detected no air of actual

554

violence; but all the talk and uproar worried him; still he did not want the prisoner to die on his hands—in his custody.

He sent for Dr. Cobb. Cobb came to the jail, took one look at Parret's wound, and said he would have to be removed to the hospital. Slider, hearing the pronouncement, wished he hadn't called the doctor. Yet he relented. But in doing so he ordered all the precautions taken he could think of. And at all times there was to be a policeman standing guard at the door of the private room the hospital would put the prisoner in. Moreover, one ankle of the prisoner would be manacled to the foot of the iron bed and the key returned to Slider. Yet, despite all the precautions, he still disliked the idea of relinquishing his prisoner. He brooded over it; even after everything had been accomplished and he had gone home briefly to eat a hurried supper, he felt a premonition.

Crowds of the curious had gathered in the heat outside the jail when it was learned the killer had been caught and returned. There was also widespread rumor that during the capture he had been shot by the police and was so badly wounded he would not live through the night. The rumor had a mollifying effect. But when the crowds saw the prisoner, alive and apparently alert, being taken from the jail on a stretcher and put in an ambulance bound for the hospital, their mood changed. Some became angrier and louder, though they were still outnumbered by the essentially curious. The crowd soon moved the short distance to the hospital where it was augmented by more of the curious but also by some vociferously hostile. Many women, some with their children, were in the crowd, not a few of them vocal in condemning the prisoner and all his kind. The crowd continued to swell, until by dusk it numbered in the sweltering heat almost a thousand, for Gem City had seldom if ever in its history experienced an event of this magnitude. Though most of the people milled about on Adams Street in front of the hospital, the curious, and still swelling, crowd actually surrounded the building. The conversations were various, sporadic, heard in fitful snatches, while the people speaking or listening stood at the same time craning their necks to see; as if the wounded prisoner might any minute come out and address them, plead his innocence, or Chief Slider Wente might mount the hospital steps and tell them the rumors were all groundless, that Stanley Cutts was alive and well, home eating supper with his

555

wife. It was impossible to tell what the crowd was waiting for, or hoping to see; they themselves could not have said.

"They were in Detweiler's," one old man with white whiskers commented, "—the colored boys. Can you imagine?"

"Why, sure—they was wrong to begin with," another man said authoritatively, mopping his brow with a red bandanna. "They got their own place, ain't they?—that Plantation saloon place down where most of 'em live. Neither one of 'em, though, will ever see inside Detweiler's again. They killed one of 'em in the capture, and the judge'll make short work of this here one."

"Well, they shot two white men, didn't they?" someone else said, "—and one of 'em a young officer of the law, who was killed. Down South both of them colored boys would be dead by now, not just one."

A big red-faced woman, holding her little boy by the hand, interrupted. "What do you mean?—colored boys," she said. "They're niggers! . . . two nigger killers!"

The old man with the whiskers looked ruefully at her. "You ain't lived around here long, have you?" he said. "We don't use that word much—it's coarse, vulgar. We say 'colored.' We fought on the Union side in the Civil War."

It was almost dark now, yet the still-growing crowd showed no signs of dispersing; when the street lights came on, the throng appeared, in fact, to have reached almost two thousand. No event was scheduled to happen, or expected, yet they stood there surrounding the hospital, unperturbed, immovable, patient, though talkative—as if they too had a premonition.

Earlier that afternoon, not more than twenty minutes after its occurrence, the shooting in Detweiler's saloon had become known to Jake Webb in the hospital—though after that for over an hour little else came except wild rumors. But in none of these was there the slightest indication his son Parret was involved; nor for that matter Negroes at all. As his broken leg and other disabilities suffered in his accident mended, he and two other Negro men lay in a room well sequestered from all white patients at the very end of an upstairs corridor. Their first information had come from a white window washer who told what little he had heard of the shooting at Detweiler's, saying there had been a quarrel, then the shooting, and that the two wounded men had just been brought into the hospital—there was no word yet on the perpetrators. Jake and his roommates, however, had already detected uncommonly feverish activity on the floor below and, though they were far out of touch with things, knew something was amiss. Then one of them, Charlie Rivers, had a visitor, his sister, who said she had heard that a policeman had been killed, and that the shooting had been done by "two colored boys." None of the men could believe this—what would a Negro be doing in Detweiler's? Until early evening then there was no more word of any kind. But as evening approached they began to see the sweating crowds gathering outside the hospital and they knew something deadly serious was afoot. Maybe Charlie Rivers' sister had been right after all. What Jake could not have known, however, was that at that very moment Parret was in an isolated, guarded room downstairs, having been brought in through a side door, and that, his ankle manacled to the foot of the bed, he lay bleeding, faint, in intense pain, and moaning, sometimes whimpering, for his father. But soon then the hospital was sealed off by the authorities, foreclosing all further communication between patients and the town—including Minnie Webb's frantic, screaming, hysterical efforts on the street outside to get in to tell her husband it was *Parret their son* who was in mortal danger of his life.

As darkness descended on the heat, and the crowds still showed no signs of going home, Slider Wente called his available policemen together in the station—there were only sixteen of them now, for one was dead and another, named Childs, guarding the prisoner's room in the hospital—and in the crisis gave them their official duty instructions. "These people will leave after while—when they get good and ready," he told them confidently, though his face showed his anxieties. "So don't worry about 'em—just don't do anything to get 'em upset, that's all. If any trouble starts it won't be down here in the center of town but out in the neighborhoods. The colored people might even try to start somethin', or some drunk hillbilly, or anybody. I've already asked Mayor Wayne to close down all saloons tonight—that old deacon and Prohibitionist of course jumped at the chance. So you'all just circulate out on your regular beats and keep peace, law, and order—I'll try to do the same down here. We'll ride this thing out, see if we don't. We'll all be mighty sleepy tomorrow, though. Still, how could I sleep anyway with Stanley on my mind." He dismissed them and they left for their assigned areas. Afterwards Slider slumped in a chair and, sighing, for a moment held his head in his hands.

Gus Rudd, a childless widower, lived by himself just outside Gem City on the old Scudder turnpike. When word reached him in the afternoon that his brother Jerry had been shot, and by a Negro now in custody, he got back on his party-line telephone and called a number of men in town he knew—among them Neal Livermore. But knowing at least six or seven nosey neighbors were listening in on the phone conversation, Gus spoke cryptically, using mostly code words. He asked the few men he reached if they'd like to drive out to his place for some spring-water chilled, delicious watermelon; then he rang off when Livermore assured him he'd round the others up and be out before dark. Gus then got in his ancient Essex and drove into town to the hospital.

A tall, red-faced, evil man, about fifty, he had served two stretches in the state penitentiary, both for bootlegging, but the last one was also coupled with a conviction for the fatal stabbing of a Negro customer who owed him money and was late paying. Some of the Negro's imprisoned black friends, however, greeted Gus on arrival to do his short time for the killing with all manner of deadly reprisal acts. First, one day in the carpentry shop, he was set upon and nearly beaten to death. Two months later he received a seriously-intentioned, though superficial, stab wound. But they repeatedly assured him he would still never go home alive. Finally, on the third try, the authorities moved him upstate to another prison. Gus, however, never forgot. His scalding hatred of Negroes had grown over the years until it had become paranoia. Now they had shot his brother.

He got in to see Jerry, and out, just before they sealed the hospital off. Though the visit was brief, he gained a full account of what had happened in Detweiler's. Jerry, in bed with the flesh wound in the thigh, talked volubly. "It was the low-built, muscle-bound one that was after me," he said, "—not the tall, lanky one."

"I know it," said Gus, "—the tall, lanky one is dead. Thank God they didn't kill the other one, that shot you. He'll wish to hell they had, though, before the night's over."

"Ain't nothin' too bad for him," Jerry said, "—the black son of a bitch! Nothin'! And in tryin' to get me he kills that young boy that hadn't been on the police force six months—and the kid with a pregnant wife. It's terrible!"

"We'll see to that nigger," Gus said, and got up. "You take it easy, now." In a few moments he had gone. He wanted to get back home before Livermore and the others arrived to eat the cold watermelon.

Later downstairs in the hospital, Parret, still in his denim pants and grimy white shirt, but barefooted, lay with his eyes closed. However, having feebly managed shortly before to urinate into a bucket an orderly had put under his bed, he was now, despite the closed eyes, wide awake and thinking. Earlier an intern had probed for the self-inflicted bullet in his neck, but unsuccessfully. Nevertheless, afterwards, he had dressed the painfully throbbing wound and stopped some of the bleeding, though Parret was weak and in torment. The noise of the milling crowds outside in the sultry night heat could be plainly heard, as the policeman, little Billy ("Onion"—from the shape of his head) Childs, still sat guard in a chair just outside the open door of the room. But except for the policeman, Parret lay there now alone, his right foot manacled to the steel bed, his pulsating head swathed in bloody-pink bandages. His thoughts, however, were sharp and clear. He was searching, racking, his mind, for some way to locate his father in the hospital, get word to him that he was there and in bad, terrible, trouble. He had even considered asking the callow, awkward young intern who had treated him, but not yet given him a gown, to go find his father and deliver the message, but was afraid to trust him, for throughout the time he had worked on Parret's wound he was so rough and stonily hostile that Parret could not possibly mistake his feelings. He knew it would be useless to ask him.

About eight-thirty Slider Wente paid a visit to the hospital. He came directly to Parret's room and, perspiring freely through his blue shirt, glancing occasionally in at Parret from the hall outside, he talked in low tones to Onion Childs, his man on guard at the door. "Things'll quiet down before long, Onion," he said—"Wish I had a spare man to send in here tonight to spell you, but I ain't got nobody. We'll handle it, though—I ain't thinkin' about sendin' out no-wheres for help. The people in this town are our people; we all know each other. If we can't handle 'em, a bunch of outside damn deputy sheriffs—most of 'em strangers—sure can't. The

559

crowd'll be thinnin' out before long, when they find out there ain't nothin' more going to happen here tonight. They're curious—yeah, some of 'em are mad as hell about Stanley, but they'll be goin' home pretty soon." Onion nodded comprehension, if not complete agreement. Slider looked in at Parret again. Their eyes met for a moment, but no longer. "I'll be back before long," Slider said to Onion—"I'll bring you a sandwich." Then he left.

Parret lay there, besides the merciless pain still worrying, fretting, almost frantic, about how he could reach his father. He needed his father, he desperately knew, and was hopeful, somehow even confident, he, Jake Webb, could do something—he did not know what—to help him. He had confidence in his father, and admired him far more than he had ever indicated to him—a fact he now recognized and regretted. They had never formed the habit of talking at length to each other, yet there had always been a kind of stoical, reticent, supersensitive communication between them they well understood and appreciated. Parret knew his father's life had been a long, endless struggle against grinding poverty, and that he had not succeeded. With only a fifth-grade education and no hope now of ever elevating his family above a bare subsistence level, Jake Webb, his son knew, though still working at his miserable dairy stable job, was merely going through the motions. Parret knew he had given up. Yet his father, though sometimes grim, uncommunicative, never complained; but when once he had left the family shack to go to work or out on some other business, he seldom ever smiled; his austerity, reserve, his egregious, outlandish, dignity, were the only possessions he had been able to retain and he seldom failed displaying them—to the displeasure, frequently the hostility, of many Gem City whites.

Parret had always regarded all this as indisputable proof of his father's strength; he admired him for his stubbornness, his bitter pride, against such odds. Now he needed him, wanted him; it was a necessity; he wanted most of all, however, to talk to him, state his case, explain how it had all happened, why he had had to use his father's pistol in the situation; he was sure Jake would understand. Parret recklessly, rashly, needed someone to understand his feelings; he was fully aware that a man, indeed a policeman, had died in the fray; he comprehended the enormity of his act, and that the crowds milling around the hospital were not picnickers.

560

Earlier in the day he had despaired of his life, had tried to obliterate it, and had failed miserably. But now he had changed; he no longer regretted having failed, though he lay racked with pain from bungling the job.

He wanted to live now. He had high hopes of living if only he could see his father. It was as if he felt that by listening to Jake he might somehow receive into his own mind and purpose his father's strength, wiliness, his sense of endurance. Yet he was not sure Jake would fully understand why he had let the situation get out of hand—to the extent of killing a policeman. Would his father think him stupid? But he would explain everything to Jake, describe his feelings at the time—at being kicked like a dog by this filthy, drunken white man. His father would understand, all right; he too, during a much longer life, had many times experienced the same feelings, and with cause. But Parret wanted the opportunity to explain everything to him; it was as if the whole horrible situation would all be resolved if he could only get to his father, impel him to see that what he, Parret, had done was necessary—absolutely necessary. It was urgent. Parret for the moment had become unmindful that it was not his father who wished his death, but others. Nothing had been resolved as to them. Suddenly then in the bed he felt a hot tear moving down his cheek and at once turned his face to the wall, fearing the worst, that the policeman guarding him might see him crying. Oh, where was Jake his father? he cried out inside himself—if only he could talk to him things again would be all right. Then before he could think, forgetting all his pride, he raised up on an elbow and looked pleadingly at Onion Childs. "Mr. Policeman!" he called weakly—"my father's somewhere here in this hospital too; come here with a broken leg. Could you try to get word to him . . . to come see me? He don't even know I'm in here."

Onion Childs turned and glowered into the room at him. "So what?" he said. "No—you ain't seeing nobody. I'm here to see to that. You should have thought of your old man before you shot Stanley Cutts down."

Parret turned his face to the wall again and said nothing. But soon, with great agitation and violence, he tried to spring off the bed—"I'll go find him myself!" he cried, his eyes wild, lips twitching. He had of course forgotten the manacle. The policeman, however, not moving, only sat waiting. The leg chain anchored to the foot of the bed brought Parret up so violently he lurched forward and almost sprawled on the floor, causing his neck wound to start oozing blood through the bandages again. Grating his teeth, cursing under his breath, he finally dragged himself onto the bed again and lay there limp, exhausted.

Onion watched him, and became thoughtful; though saying nothing. He was impressed, however, almost awed now, by Parret's violence and passion; his utter desperation. The black bastard was really upset, wasn't he? he thought—about seeing his old man. But he should have thought of things like that before he did his dastardly deed of killing a white man. What in the hell could his father do for him now anyhow? Not much—that was for sure. Under the hot ceiling light swarming with insects, Onion could still hear the milling, sweating crowds outside; the very fact of their presence made his blood race. These were people, he thought, like himself, like his family and friends, all anxious about the outcome of a matter, a terrible outrage, the like of which this town of his birth had never experienced. These were good people, moreover, and he only wished he might now walk away from his present tedious duties, of guarding this black scourge on the innocent people of the community, and join them.

But Parret then suddenly spoke again. "If I'm goin' to die, I wanta see my father!" He turned his incandescent, tormented, eyes on the policeman.

"Who said you was goin' to die?" inquired Onion. "That'll be up to the judge. But I sure know what I'd do if I was in his shoes." He seemed unable, however, to take his eyes off Parret; his fascination with his prisoner's suffering riveted him.

"If you was any kind of policeman, any kind of *man*," Parret said, "you'd go get my father—even in the war both sides had the Red Cross!" His voice was even more irascible, pained, yet weak. "No, you're like all the other white folks 'round here—you'all got hearts like rocks. It was a helluva mistake I made—ever comin' back here!"

"What you done don't entitle you to one damn favor," the policeman said, "—not from me anyway. The man you killed was my buddy—he's dead now, all because of what a worthless bastard like you went and done. What had he ever done to you?"

"Plenty." But Parret, now reflective, spoke softly, almost in a whisper.

"Don't hand me that!—you didn't even know him; probably hadn't seen him more'n half a dozen times in your life."

"I've seen many like him, though—and like you—all my life. You'all never gave me any peace—never; you've always had the upper hand and liked to make people suffer; that's what you'all like to do more'n anything in the world—make people suffer; just like now, you won't even go tell my father I'm right here in the same building with him. That's how you make yourself feel good—by makin' people like me suffer."

"Oh, shit," Onion said in disgust. "Don't hand me that, I say!" But he would not look at Parret now, and for the moment said no more; he had become thoughtful again.

"If I was a white man," said Parret, "you'da had my father in here soon as I asked you—no matter what I'd done. But it makes you feel real big—and you wearin' that uniform and badge too—to lord it over me. You couldn't stand to treat me like any other man."

Onion suddenly turned on him, both anger and anguish in his sweaty face. "I'm treatin' you like you are—a damn criminal! Look what you done!—you forget that! You killed a close buddy of mine, I tell you! . . . He hadn't done nothin' to you. You just shot him down! Now you come askin' for favors!"

"I wasn't shootin' at the policeman," Parret said. 'Nobody'll believe it, but it's true. I was shootin' at a man that had kicked me, kicked me like I was a damn cur dog—because I went in that place, a public place, to buy a drink."

"That's a damn lie. . . ." But Onion's voice lacked conviction. "It's a damn—" At that moment a frowning nurse came in with a pitcher of water. When she had deposited it on the stand by the bed and was going out again, Onion slowly got up and followed her down the hall, saying something to her Parret could not hear. He did not soon return.

Parret cursed him under his breath. How he hated them all! he thought. Why had God made white men so evil?—it was a question he had often asked himself but had never unearthed an answer to it. He hoped he would some day, some fervently-dreamed-of day, when he had lived through, survived, the present ordeal and he and others like him were strong, that he would be able to do something about it. Thoughts of his mother and sister came in on him now, flooding him with familial memories as well as fears for their present safety. They had learned of his tragedy by now, he was certain, and his heart went out to them in their helplessness—he did not have to be told his mother had made every frantic, pleading effort possible to get in to see him and his father. The thought brought pain as harsh as that of his wound. At last he thought of his guard, the policeman. Where had he gone with the nurse? he wondered. He speculated it must be all of nine-thirty by now, perhaps ten, and he had become gradually aware that the noise of the crowds outside had considerably diminished. Were they at last going home? he asked himself, experiencing some slight sense of relief. Yet, despite the pain, he felt exhausted, drained, now; he wished only to sleep, but knew the pain would not permit it unless he was administered a drug—which he did not expect; they had not done it so far. Five minutes passed. Soon he heard voices coming down the hall toward him. He listened, his heart strangely pounding. Then a little cry escaped from deep in his throat—one of those voices approaching he recognized. It was his father's! Then in came the wheel chair—pushed by none other than Onion Childs.

"*Pa!*" cried Parret.

Parret's cry came at the same instant Jake Webb uttered: "*Whut's happened to you, boy?*"

The policeman glumly wheeled Jake, whose left leg was in a heavy cast, over to Parret's bed, left them together, and returned to his chair outside the door.

But in those brief, fateful moments everything had come to Jake Webb in a flash. His hospital roommate Charlie Rivers' sister had indeed been right—"two colored boys" were parties to the shooting and Jake now realized with unbelieving horror that they had been Parret and Sam. He saw too the head bandages and the blood. Moreover, a policeman was dead. His popping eyes stared incredulously at Parret and his mouth fell open but no words came.

Parret saw that his father understood everything. "Pa!" he cried —"I wasn't shootin' at the policeman! . . . I was shootin' at the guy that had kicked me! . . ."

But again Jake was looking at the bloody bandages swathing Parret's neck and head. "Did they shoot you!—are you hurt bad?"

he asked breathlessly, leaning forward in his wheel chair which he had already pushed hard against the bed. "Who shot you, boy?" His voice had dropped to tenderness.

"Nobody. . . . but they was going to, Pa! They was going to shoot me with a shotgun. I had climbed up a tree to hide in—in a woods, outside of town—and they found me. They had already killed Sam and I knowed they was going to kill me, even if they did try to get me to come down; so I was goin' to beat them to it—I shot myself. I didn't do a good job, that's all."

"Oh!" breathed Jake. ". . . Thank God."

"The bullet's still in my neck. It hurts, Pa—they ain't given me anything for the pain." Parret's lip quivered as if he would cry.

Jake was frantic—he suddenly wheeled the chair around and propelled himself to the door where Onion Childs moodily, nervously, sat. For the first time in a long, long time Jake was humble. "I want to thank you, Mr. Officer," he began, "for comin' and gettin' me. It was sure enough a mighty good deed for you to do that; an act of mercy—sure it was. He's my boy. He ain't had nothin' for the pain, though—could you please, sir, get the nurse to give him a shot of somethin' for the pain?" Jake's eyes shone, mirroring his desperate, pleading, predicament.

For a moment Onion only stared at him, though it was a reflective, indecisive, stare. Then without a word he again got up and went down the hall. But almost at once he returned. "The nurse says before the doctor left he told her not to give him *anything*." Onion, mopping his face, then sat down again.

"Oh, Jesus," Jake said.

Onion stared at him fiercely now. "He'll be back tonight—but he's the same intern, and a hometown boy, that saw Stanley Cutts die,' he said grimly. "I know damn well how he felt."

Jake, his face long, agonized, wheeled himself back to the bed. His sense of powerlessness and frustration, of defeat, had rendered his body weak, limp, now. He sat looking at Parret for a moment, trembling with emotion as he reached over, affectionately, and touched his bandaged face, in this futile way to try to assuage, soothe away, the pain—when a mighty crash of flying wood and glass rent the air. It was the first-floor front window up the hall disintegrating, at the same instant Onion Childs jumped to his feet and pulled his pistol—he could see too now, next to the smashed win-

565

dow, the big, locked, front door just before it also came in with a terrible splintering implosion, giving way to the wild force of what seemed some kind of battering ram. On impulse Jake Webb, though he could see none of it, tried to stand up from his wheel chair, but the shock, the fright, had all but paralyzed him. One more shattering blast of the ram brought the front door off two of its three hinges and two men stepped through, handkerchiefs tied over their faces from nose to chin. At once two or three more, also masked, then possibly five or six, came through behind the first two, all seeing, yet somehow ignoring, Onion and his trembling pistol pointed at them. Onion yelled: "Stop! Stop, I say!—in the name of the law! . . ." Still another half dozen men, masked like all the others, poured in through the torn-off door now, as what remained of the crowd outside the hospital immediately set up a fearful din. They had got their action at last. "Stop!" yelled Onion again at the intruders, his voice high, yet hoarse. "Stop, I say! . . ." —still brandishing his pistol as they poured down the hall toward him.

The ringleader obeyed Onion, momentarily, though partially-masked Gus Rudd, tall, red-faced, sweating, yet full of cold watermelon, paused on reaching Parret's room and briefly studied Onion. Then the others, who already now surrounded Onion, for a moment did the same. "Put that pistol away, son," Rudd said to Onion. "This don't concern you. We've come for the nigger." Rudd then looked in at the bed from which Parret, eyes wide, paralyzed with fear, had now sat up—and where Jake Webb had spun the wheel chair around in front of his son's bed, protectively, to face the invaders. Rudd said to Onion, "You gonna give him up peacefully or are we gonna have to take him?" He then brushed by Onion and entered the room.

"I'm the law!" cried Onion, but trembling as he followed Rudd —"I ain't givin' him up!"

The words were hardly out when a masked man behind Onion grabbed his pistol arm and forcibly held it pointed up at the ceiling, while two other men wrestled the pistol from his grasp. But they then made the mistake of turning him loose in the room—with his bare fists he began fighting them like a tiger, almost knocking one of them down before they took him seriously. "He's my prisoner!" he cried to them in desperation—"I'm the law! . . . You have no right—" A wild scuffle followed—until finally they subdued him and two of them were assigned to hold him, his arms pinioned behind his back, in the corner. "You bastards! . . . you scum!" he yelled, still fiercely struggling—"I'm an officer of the law! . . . you have no right!"

But already Gus Rudd had lost interest. He was heading for the bed—there to meet Jake Webb, a small man, who had somehow managed, despite the cast on his leg, to get out of the wheel chair and now stood confronting red-faced Rudd. "Git outa my way, you little black bastard, you," said Rudd, stepping sideways to elude Jake—"before I put that other leg in a cast!"

But Jake clumsily shifted with him—to head him off. "He's my boy," he said huskily, almost imploringly—"he's my son."

"He's whut?" Rudd then swung. His fist sent Jake half sprawling over the chair, blood drooling from his mouth. The others surged forward now—but intent on Parret. Parret, however—wild, cursing, vengeful, his head in the bloody bandages—was trying to get out of bed to get at Rudd. Then he remembered the manacle—at the same moment Rudd saw it. Rudd let out an angry howl—"Jesus Gawd! . . . they got his leg handcuffed to the bed, to the foot of the bed! What a rotten fuckin' trick!"

Masked Neal Livermore rushed up to see. "Damned if they ain't!" he said. "But the kid policeman must have the key." He turned around to Onion in the grip of his two captors. "Unlock the leg iron and make it quick," he said.

Onion's eyes blazed in triumphant anger—"Chief Slider Wente's got the key, not me! I wouldn't give it to you, though, if I had it!"

Jake Webb, still stunned from the blow to the face, was struggling to get back in the wheel chair, but his leg in the cast made this difficult. At last he struggled to a sitting position in the chair, only to find no one now noticed him. Cursing, breathing hard in the stifling heat, the men had all crowded around Parret and were raining blows on his already bleeding head, though Parret had not once uttered a cry. "Wait a minute, there, God damn it!" yelled Gus Rudd at the grunting, cursing men. "Hold off! . . . Stop that! You'll beat him unconscious! Hold it awhile, will you?—we don't wanta knock him out!" His tone was impatient, harried, almost outraged —as if he addressed stupid, unthinking children who lacked appreciation of the foresight and sacrifices of leadership.

Meanwhile, dogged Jake had wheeled the chair back toward the bed they all surrounded; suddenly then he began fighting, clawing at their backs, to reach Parret. At once they turned their wrath on him—the blows they now withheld from Parret fell on Jake with fierce, cursing vengeance. "You black nigger bastard!" one of them said, giving him a vicious blow. "You're the one that whelped this black ape murderer—you learned him everything he knows! . . . didn't you, didn't you! . . . We oughta take you along too! . . ." He grunted and swung on Jake again; then the others joined in; soon Jake had been beaten out of the chair again and, his face a mass of blood, lay in a crumpled, unconscious, heap against the wall. In the melee the bucket under the bed was upset, strewing its contents across the floor where Jake lay fouled in his son's urine.

They had all returned to bleeding, incoherent Parret on the bed now. First Parret's eyes glowed and shone; they seemed then to dilate with a sudden fright; it was the realization that death now was almost certain, that it had not long to wait. Rudd, standing over him, jealously, issued another warning to the others. "Don't nary one of you hit him another lick, now! Hold off!—just take it easy, won't you! Your time's comin'!"

"Tell us this then, Gus," someone said irreverently—"How'n the hell you gonna git that leg iron off him?"

"Without the key, it ain't comin' off," said Rudd. "We gotta try somethin' else."

Neal Livermore pushed through again. "We gotta break this damn bed down—break it apart," he said, "and take the foot of it with him. We cain't take the whole bed." Then grasping the foot of the steel bed in his huge hands, he began straining and heaving with all his might.

"Wait, Neal!" said Rudd. "Don't force it—you'll spring the frame and it won't never come apart. Here, you'all, hold the bed down and let me try to lift the foot part out."

Soon three of the men were holding the bed—with wild, threshing Parret still on it—as Rudd, sweat running off his face onto the sheet, tried to disengage the foot of the bed from the steel grooves securing it to the rest of the frame. At last, after much coaxing and straining, the foot of the bed suddenly came loose, letting the rest of the steel bedstead—half-stuporous Parret, clutching at thin air, on it—crash to the floor, as a low, suppressed cry of satisfaction

568

went up from the others. "Okay, let's git goin'," Rudd said, and grabbed Parret under both armpits.

When Parret, the bed falling free, at last realized what had happened he let out for the first time a wild little cry of terror, his eyes flying back in his head, his hands raised and fingers fluttering. Part of it was the stabbing pain from the bullet lodged deep in his neck, and then he stared over at his father lying unconscious, blood coming from the half-open mouth, and lost all control of himself—uttering a high, almost startled, crazed, moan. *"Oh, Jesus! . . . Pa!*—goodbye, goodbye! I'll never see you again, Pa! I'll—"

Rudd had turned him loose and two other men were already dragging him, but feet first now, through the blood and urine and out of the room. A third abductor hurried close behind, carrying the foot of the bed behind Parret like a bridal train, as Parret's piss-sodden back slid roughly along the floor, for each of the two men dragging him, now almost running with him, each had one of his bare feet tucked under an arm. Soon, the rest of the masked men following—leaving raving Onion Childs disarmed and helpless—they were all up the hall and plunging out through the front door. When the smaller, but re-grouped, crowd outside saw the prisoner, a great shout went up. "They got him!" many cried—"They got him! . . . look, look!" They surged forward as if to greet the heroic captors.

But Gus Rudd and Neal Livermore, in the struggle their makeshift handkerchief masks barely concealing their identity as, like mitered bishops, they brought up the rear, at once saw their problem—their two men, cohorts, trying to reach the street, had dragged the captive recklessly, heedlessly, into the crowd. Some of the onlookers were already cursing, striking, or kicking at the prostrate, bleeding prisoner and Rudd and Livermore now had real fears they might not be able to save him from the crowd for their own purposes. They fought now to get to the head of the rough semblance of a column, all the while shouting to the crowd, "Let us through! . . . let us through!—How can we carry out your will and do justice if you won't let us through? Make way, make way!" Rudd's loud, hoarse shouts could be heard despite the din. There was some compliance; some of the crowd began to give way, move back. Then Rudd saw a short, porcine-like man, with a shock of straw-colored hair, push to the front edge of the crowd, an ax handle in his right

569

hand. Rudd yelled at him—"Git back, you fool! . . . You want to knock him unconscious! Git back, I say, or I'll kill you!" Rudd produced a large pearl-handled revolver, but, mindful of the crowd, did not point it. Yet the man lunged and struck a grunting, vicious blow with the ax handle down at Parret's head—which now in being dragged over the rough pavement had lost much of its bandaging—missing only partially, though Parret's shoulder caught the heaviest force of the blow. Parret gave a sudden loud grunt, then another strange shrieking moan—as Rudd furiously shoved, hurled, the assailant back into the crowd. "You damn dummy!" Rudd yelled at him again—"But we ain't goin' to let riffraff like you spoil this!" Then, running forward abreast of his men, he cried out to Livermore—"Go start the cars! Let's get outa here—I'll clear the way here now! You be ready with them cars—we'll be there in a minute or two!" The column, led by Rudd, now continued fighting its way through the crowd—dragging Parret on his back and trailed by the cohort carrying the bed-foot, all under the hot yellow light of the street lamps. Soon they were clear, heading toward the caravan of dilapidated automobiles lined up, waiting, in the next block. Arriving, they threw Parret and the bed-foot into the backseat of the lead car, a man with a gun seated on either side of him, and the seven cars made off into the sultry night.

The whole abduction had been accomplished in less than ten minutes and harried Police Chief Slider Wente, getting only belated word at the station, arrived on the scene too late. He was beside himself with mortification and rage when Onion Childs related the incredible details. Both of them, panting and sweating, ran back to the station to get Slider's car. But Gus Rudd had foreseen this contingency—there was no air in Slider's tires. Almost berserk now, he stood in the middle of the street waving his arms and shouting lunatic imprecations, as Onion grimaced and wrung his hands. They both then ran back to where the crowd had drifted into the town square—Slider meant now to commandeer a car and somehow pick up the trail. Yet he knew time was running against him; that his adversaries would move fast to carry out their purpose. Going from person to person, it took him almost fifteen minutes to get a car capable of the rigors of such a search and pursuit, only then to have to concede to himself he lacked the faintest notion, or clue, as to where the abductors had taken his prisoner. He was almost in tears —disgraced, humiliated, before the world.

Two and a half miles outside, east, of town there was a farm, and a farm house, called "Hollyhocks" (formerly after its beautiful flowers), whose owner, a spinster lady and failed Catholic, Idela Hazel Stallings by name, had died, at 70, during the year—on the thirty-seventh weekday following Ash Wednesday. There was nothing about the farm or its environs to be regarded as exceptional, much less ostentatious, save its barn, its big, red, hip-roof barn. Compared to the barn, which had been Idela Hazel Stallings' pride and joy, the house was negligible. On the broad side of the barn facing the road she had even had her three initials painted—in high, white, rather ghostly, letters. Now her nephew, Clint Stone, and his family, during the period of the probating of the modest estate, occupied and farmed the premises. It was to this farm that Gus Rudd and his party were now at full speed heading—all with Clint Stone's prior knowledge and consent. Yet at no time during the night would Clint ever leave the shelter, sanctuary, of his house.

Across the road from the buildings, but a part of the same premises, was a rolling meadow. Here, also by prearrangement, at a spot no more than a hundred yards from the road, awaiting Rudd and his entourage, were eight men, likewise wearing handkerchief masks and equipped with three lanterns. Shortly after dark a few of them had gone to Clint's red barn and brought back several armfuls of straw. From a nearby thicket others had procured a quantity of dead, dry, twigs and branches. Their final foraging task then had been to purloin a half dozen or more parched chestnut rails from a dilapidated rail fence close by and to break them into two-by-fours. Out of these prosaic materials they had built a pyre. It needed only igniting. Now they waited.

Though the moon was not yet up, the sultry black sky was full of stars. Neal Livermore was driving the lead car, an old Pierce-Arrow touring car, with Gus Rudd seated beside him—the other three in the back. Parret, bandages gone completely, the festering neck wound slowly percolating blood, though he was fully conscious, was somehow gasping for breath, for air; yet there was no physical obstruction to his breathing. It was the trauma of what he had been through. His deepest psychic faculties, though not his rational mind, were adversely involved, faltering, and now affecting the physical functions. It seemed to him his lungs would soon collapse. Barefoot, wearing what was left of the denim pants and grimy white shirt, reeking of sweat and urine, he leaned back between his two masked guards in the back seat, the steel bed-foot between his knees and the seat ahead, and threw his head forward, then to one side, spasmodically, crazily, and made a now gurgling, now dry, then half-choking sound, this all soon followed by a wild attack of shivering and trembling. He knew full well now he was soon to die. Only he did not know how he would die. He hoped it would be quick. The four white men rode silently, except that occasionally Rudd would pass some remark to Livermore, though in a low, almost inaudible, oddly casual voice. The four seemed self-possessed, solemn, calm, save for frequent anxious glances out to the rear, at the headlights in the stirred-up dust, to see if the other cars were keeping up.

At times now, strangely, as though in a dream, Parret wished to talk to, confide in, his captors; to tell them of his hours of physical agony, the beating, the manhandling, by the crowd, of his father's bloody subduing; it was somehow as if they were his rescuers, come in the nick of time, now whisking him away from some horrible experience and taking him to friends, who would treat his wounds, care for him, nurse him back to health. Once, eyes wide in wonder, almost in reverie, he turned to the big, sweating man in overalls on his right and opened his mouth as though he would speak. Yet, when he met the foe's animal glare, no words came. He withdrew again into himself and his pain. They were well outside of town now, and on either side of the country road Parret from the headlights of the car could see the growing corn already shoulder high, beyond that a field of alfalfa, and above it all the brooding purple sky flecked with stars. Suddenly, without warning, he cried out—"Where're you'all taking me?"

The men started. They seemed surprised. Rudd turned around and gaped at him.

"What're you'all going to do to me?" Again Parret was trembling, from fear, but also from a manic, inner agitation, almost religious in nature though not prayer.

"Nigger, we're goin' to bring you to account for what you done," Rudd spat. "You won't be curious long."

But Parret, now staring crazily out of the side of the car, seemed not to hear him. Rudd turned back around and faced the front.

Parret again was thinking of his father—it was odd, seldom now of his mother or sister. In the hospital he had wanted so desperately to see his father; and had finally got his wish. Why had the policeman done him this favor? he wondered. Should he have thanked him? He was not sure—anyway there had not been time. But now it would all soon be over, he knew. They would hang him from a tree. He would then die; be dead. What was it like to die? he wondered. What *was* death? Where would he go?—to heaven? Suddenly he was shocked to realize his omissions—in all the hours of turmoil, bloodshed, and struggle he had not once remembered to pray; not even when earlier in the day he faced death in the tree. Now he prayed; he closed his eyes tightly and prayed, whispering, murmuring, to the Old Testament God—Jehovah—about whom he had learned in Sunday School. He asked that he would soon go to heaven. There he would begin a new, a possibly beautiful, life, if what he had been taught about God and the Bible was true. He believed it was true. He continued to pray, until for a time he no longer trembled, but then soon, bent forward, slavering, no longer in reverie, he began to moan again from the terrible pain of his wounds. His captors sat stoical, self-absorbed.

When later Rudd's caravan of cars, their headlights piercing the night dust and heat, at last approached the Stallings farm, they saw their masked colleagues standing waiting almost in the middle of the road—except for one who, on seeing the line of lights coming, had run down to the pyre and hurled, dashed, his lighted lantern onto the dry straw, twigs, and branches, spewing kerosene and fire over everything including the parched fence rails topping the pyre. A wild conflagration ensued, and by the time up on the road the caravan had come to a halt and the men had climbed out with their prisoner, the whole sky was alight.

By daylight next morning the appalling, grisly news had spread over at least four counties, and within hours the curious, estimated at not under three thousand, came from as far as thirty and forty miles. There was, moreover, extensive newspaper coverage. The *Hoopton Sentinel's* front page carried one of the more balanced and unsensational accounts, though its graphic pictures made up for the lack. One picture showed a part of the trampled meadow, another, a close-up, showed the charred torso of the victim—no arms left and only a stump of a leg—cold now, already putrifying, after the roasting. Following a big to-do about the huge crowds that had descended the following morning, the *Sentinel* gave, in part, an unidentified eyewitness' account of the chief event: "By then the flames were ten feet high. When the murderer was asked if he had anything to say, he remained silent. Instead, he seemed to be staring up at the big red barn across the road, like he was looking at the big lettering there, the three big white initials; it was strange—he kept looking, staring, until the men grabbed him. Two of them picked him up, while a third carried the foot of the bed chained to his ankle, and they threw him on the fire. He gave a hoarse, guttural, piercing cry that seemed audible for a mile. As the flames licked his clothes and seared his flesh he gave a mighty leap and dragging the foot of the bed with him tried to run toward the fence. But he was instantly seized, a rope put around his neck, and he was thrown back onto the flames. Twice more he attempted to get out of the seething furnace and each time was beaten back with fence rails, until finally all was still and only the sickening smell of burning flesh remained. The murderer had paid an awful penalty for his crime."

In an adjoining column, the *Sentinel* gave still more space to the huge crowds that came the following day: "The body had not been removed. It was still there, plain as day, in the ashes. But everyone, though pressing forward in the crush to see it, was quiet and orderly. There was no loud talking, no profanity, and the utmost deference was shown to the ladies who came to the scene. Men stepped back as the ladies came forward, or some were led to other points of vantage, where they could obtain the best view of the burnt Negro. During the night a mist had fallen, enveloping the nearby creek and even the fields beyond. Later the timid rays of the sun were powerless to dispel the misty greyness, for the spirit of death seemed in the very air. . . ." Thus, after a few other comments, the *Sentinel's* account ended.

* * * * *

Knight, still at his bedroom desk in the dead of night, worked slowly, painfully, on the speech he would make at the rally—burdened with his tragic sense of history. What a history it was, he thought—he who since the earliest days at his father's knee had absorbed its tragedy into the very pores, fiber, of his being. He could never forget Goforth's fanatical insistence: *"We Negroes are what we were made!"*

Indeed, Martin Luther King, Jr. himself had referred to blacks' history as "our long night of suffering." A decade ago, Knight well recalled, he had heard the great leader use the phrase one afternoon in a short speech to a few followers on their release, King included, from an Alabama jail. The phrase seemed to him now even more apt, if possible, than his father's way of saying something very similar. Dr. King, he thought, particularly in choosing the word "night," had made the concept vastly compelling—*night* of suffering. John Calvin was suddenly filled anew with a mystical awe, a reverence, for this man, now a martyred hero gone to his reward, whom he had followed through so many marches, encounters, and confrontations when the issue of victory or defeat hung in the balance. He meant someday to probe, study, King's words in their deepest significance and try if he could to relate them to his father's prophetic saying. There was a connection here, he was convinced, that would reward the sedulous student. They would be studies of great importance— these "night" studies—and capable, he hoped, of clearing away his present bewilderment, indirection, and inner turmoil. He returned earnestly to his speech.

Chapter 4

"Mary, have you ever flew over—"

" 'Flown,' you mean, Ernestine," Mary Dee said.

"Have you ever flown, then—over the lake, or over the ocean?" Ernestine, spotlessly dressed, was staring out at Lake Michigan on the right of their moving car.

"Over both, yes." It was Saturday and the three of them, Vernon on the front seat between Mary Dee and Ernestine, were riding in Mary Dee's Datsun up Lake Shore Drive. The sun was bright, the lake was blue under a sky of blue, and the afternoon bore the crispness of autumn.

"Whew—eee!" said Vernon, also very dressed-up, turning to Mary Dee in happy awe—"over all that water? . . ."

"Shoot, airplanes don't care nothing about flying over water," Ernestine said—"they do it all the time."

Mary Dee sighed, despairing for the moment of mentioning grammar again.

"Where'd you fly to, Mary?" asked Vernon, again in wonder, then, for no obvious reason at all, laughing.

"Oh, she told us that," Ernestine said pettishly—"to Paris, Vernon."

Mary Dee herself had forgotten—unable, as to the children, to imagine a circumstance in which Paris would have come up. Yet she knew Ernestine's acuity and did not contradict her. "Yes, to Paris," she said to Vernon—"and some other places in Europe too. Also to the Caribbean, and the West Coast—California."

"Whew-ee!" repeated Vernon. Age nine now and in the fourth grade, he wore a natty tan suit, under a heavier corduroy sports coat, and sturdy shoes, all from a bargain basement store but clean and attractive, topped off by his jaunty, checked, maroon cap. It was apparent he was a happy child—especially today, out riding, in his view of life, with the most magnificent and beautiful human being he had ever met, in reality or in all his Elysian dreams. He turned and gave Mary Dee a mooning, idolatrous look, then laughed inscrutably again. "Mary, take us to where the little airplanes come in from the lake," he said.

"*I* want to go up in the Sears Tower," countered mature Ernestine, now twelve—"It's the tallest building, y'know, in the whole world."

"We won't have time for the Sears Tower today," Mary Dee said. "But we can stop by Vernon's airport for a few minutes on our way back. I've got to go now and buy some things I'll need for a party."

"A party?" Ernestine was immediately interested. "I never did go to a party."

"You will someday, when you get older," Mary Dee said— "There's plenty of time."

"You gotta have pretty clothes to go to a party," Ernestine said, wistfully now, but at the same time giving Mary Dee a half-furtive, crafty, glance.

"You've got pretty clothes," said Mary Dee. It was an unwary reply.

"Can I come, then, Mary?—and Vernon too? He's got nice clothes now too."

Mary Dee, duped, sighed again. "The party's not for children. It's for some people in the organization."

Vernon, though wedged between them, began bouncing on the seat. "*We're* in the organization!" he laughed.

"Sure," Ernestine said—"Mama says we're in the organization just like she is."

"That's true in a way," said Mary Dee—"but you and Vernon are junior members yet. The party's for getting together some of the adult members to form a committee to raise money."

"Oh," Ernestine said, pausing to think this over. Then: "Is Mama coming?—she ain't a junior member."

Vernon laughed again. "She ain't got time—she's busy working!"

Vernon spoke the truth. His comment, moreover, was made with obvious pride—his mother had a job. The case of Pinetta Carter— so John Calvin Knight, had he personally known of it, would have said—was a graphic, almost ideal, example of what the Black Peoples Congress was doing: rehabilitating people. At nineteen, Pinetta, as yet unmarried, had been pregnant with Ernestine. The boy involved, one Lemuel, however, also from a penniless family,

577

married her with no qualms, no remonstrance, whatever—it made no difference to him; his life, his squandered, empty existence, would go on unchanged. He had no job and expected none, with the result that Pinetta went on the public assistance rolls and became one more ADC—Aid to Dependent Children—mother. Three years later Vernon was born, and soon thereafter Lemuel uneventfully disappeared into the dark depths of the ghetto, not to be heard from since. But it had changed nothing; had he remained, the lives of the mother and two children could anyway have hardly been worse, more wretched, squalid. There were years of this until Mary Dee, with Ornette and Rosabelle Hungerford's help, had brought the organization's apparatus to bear on Pinetta Carter's case. Now Pinetta had a job in a neighborhood cafeteria operated by an organization member, had moved into a better apartment with her sister, and the children were clean and decently enough dressed; and far happier. What, however, was even more significant was the change that had come about in Pinetta's personality. Much of her negativism, her surliness, was gone now as she gained some measure of self-respect and became, moreover, herself a member of the Congress. The organization's influence on her, its literature and teachings, had considerably changed her life—all of which was soon reflected in the lives of her two children.

As Ernestine and Vernon kept up their chatter, Mary Dee continued to the Loop, made some delicatessen and other purchases, and on the way back stopped briefly, reluctantly, at Meigs, the little lakeshore airport used by the small planes of businessmen wanting not O'Hare but the quick convenience of downtown Chicago. It brought back bad memories to her. For a short time the three of them sat in the car in the parking lot watching the Cessnas and Beechcrafts take off and land. "Sometimes the planes fall in the water!" observed Ernestine, with excessive enthusiasm.

"No, they don't, either," Vernon said. "The people would be killed—wouldn't they, Mary?"

But Mary Dee sat staring out over the lake into space, her mind far away on that evening which now seemed so long ago—though it had been only seven months—when Philip had sat beside her here, in this car, in this lot, on his brief visit to Chicago to see her. Here he had taken her in his arms and hungrily kissed her. And afterwards had come the night of the bliss, and ignominy, of the hotel bedroom of mirrors. Her life had changed radically since that night, she knew—doubtless *because* of that night, for her desperation and bitterness had sent her into the Black Peoples Congress. But nowadays she often asked herself if she would ever be happy again. Maybe that wonderful year in Paris had been, in retrospect, the most unfortunate happening of her life. Its consequences, aftermath, had affected her in a way she had never been fully able to understand. But that was all behind her now—she was trying so hard to exorcise it all from her heart and consciousness and to look forward to the future and whatever it held. She was often furious with herself, however, for not having been more easily able to do this. What did this future hold for her that was really meaningful? she once more asked herself—though the question always brought difficulties. There was the work she was doing with the organization, certainly —that, she knew, was meaningful. Proof of it was these two children here beside her, she thought. Their lives had been changed, she hoped improved, by the trick of circumstance that had brought the three of them together on that frigid, blizzardy morning last winter. But she had been able to change their lives only because the organization was involved that had changed her own. There could be no doubt about the meaningfulness of this, she told herself; she was thankful her life surely now stood for something.

Yet at other times when she looked into her future and saw only these things, she could not avoid, could not turn her eyes from, the true bleakness they held for her. Would she, for instance, ever marry? And what of her mother, the new apartment, her brother and sister, and so many other matters dangling in limbo? These were all unanswered questions pertaining to a future she seemed unable, helpless, to see into very far. Where here was there happiness for her—real happiness? It filled her, simultaneously, with both anxiety and, strangely, ennui; there would be no more of the excitement she had known before—ever; there could be no ecstasy in her life again. The prattling children beside her could not distract her or dispel her feelings. Suddenly she realized she was wretched again—with her, not an unfamiliar state of mind, and one that always finally brought its own ennui; its desensitization.

"*Please* let us come to your party, Mary!" said Ernestine. "We can help you serve—we can bring out the food you bought. Can't we, Vernon?"

"Yes, yes!" Vernon said, his laughing eyes eager, bright.

Mary Dee, still gazing out nostalgically across the expanse of blue lake, made no reply. She had hardly heard. Soon she started the car and headed back to take the children home.

* * * * *

Was it a metaphoric coincidence? she wondered, when later she thought back on it. If not, it was at least significant: that Friday, the day of the party, was also her last day on her job at Aico & Aleshire's. She had given them a month's notice and when the time finally came she was glad to go—knowing she was a different person from that who had taken the job, though she could not have been specific about in what way; she could only approach it in vague generalities; but she sensed a definite difference, and her intuition was a major part of her make-up. She promised herself the next job she sought would be more in keeping with the way she felt these days, though she lacked the slightest notion of what manner of job it might be. Anyway she wanted to rest for a month, think about herself, about her life and the direction it was taking, and to spend more time painting. Her intuition told her, however, that she had reached a point of new departure, though without intimating to her that Friday's party would somehow symbolize it.

She spent late Friday afternoon readying her second-floor garage studio behind the house—which had already received a thorough cleaning from housekeeper Mrs. Grier—and placing three of Ornette's blatant, fierce, paintings in more prominent positions. He would want that, she thought. Then just before dark she took the car and went and got Ernestine and Vernon, who had given her no peace until she consented to their coming. Yet she had not, finally, been at all reluctant—this kind of gathering, with such a conglomeration of people coming, was a new experience for her and she was anything but comfortable, and showed it. The presence of the children might help, and Chauncey Stiles, the dentist, would be there. In addition Ornette and Rosabelle, who themselves had suggested the names of many of those invited, were constantly reassuring her that everything would be all right, that there was

580

absolutely no cause for concern, that all the invited guests, save Chauncey Stiles, were organization people, active members, all friendly and well-disposed. Ornette was also aware she might be nervous over the possibility of Knight's coming. But Knight somehow had not crossed her mind—besides, she had not invited him, and had she thought of him at all she would never have considered he might come uninvited. Moreover, although Ornette had invited him—actually urged him to come—he, Ornette, himself could not have been sure Knight would arrive back in town in time to be there even if he had decided to come at all. As for Mary Dee, she had forgotten Knight completely.

The guests began to arrive shortly after eight—though Ornette and Rosabelle, considering themselves co-hosts, had come early—and were admitted by Ernestine, who had insisted on tending the door but who was now less sure of herself despite wide-eyed Vernon's constant station at her side. Growing tall for her almost twelve years, Ernestine wore her best dress, a white, red, and black affair with prim, starched, white collar and cuffs and her hair in a neat Afro. For once, however, she was daunted; instead of with a smile, she greeted the guests with irresolution, a stunned awe, backing warily away from the door as they entered; retreating, hypnotized, Vernon ever beside her. Two men and a woman, in their late twenties, had been the first to arrive. One of the men was a bearded giant, and his friend, not much smaller, and coal-black, had a shaved head, yet wore a suit with a vest. Both were fierce-looking. Yet the woman, in long African garb, was only slightly less so, though she smiled at the children as she entered. Mary Dee, Rosabelle, and Ornette came forward to welcome them, all six giving each other the "soul" handshake, an upright, perfervid, grip Mary Dee had never quite mastered.

"Preston!" Ornette said, greeting the mammoth, bearded guest— "How you doin', man?"

"Okay, Ornette." But the giant was looking across the room at Ornette's color-splashed, polemical mural. The room was large— above the Adkins' coach house-garage—and extended over the entire area of the elongated structure below. The walls and ceiling had only a few months before received two coats of fresh white paint, and the floors were bare, as was mostly the room itself, except now more chairs had been brought from the house for the occasion. The room's saving grace was its mural and pictures—Mary Dee's and Ornette's arresting creations were everywhere. The difference, however, the obvious contrast, in the talent and training of the two artists was evident throughout. Ornette's pictures were bolder, cruder, more extravagant in their colors, with less attention to detail, his settings and subjects invariably political. Mary Dee's paintings were also energetic and colorful but showed more finish, sensitivity, and skill, yet possessed a vivid power and emotion of their own. Almost immediately the giant Preston went around viewing all the pictures and the mural, while the others stood and talked and Ernestine and Vernon went to bring the guests plastic glasses of punch.

The two Carey sisters (they were actually half-sisters), in their middle thirties, were the next guests to arrive. Bess, the older of the two, deep brown-skinned and only recently married (though people still called her a Carey), had the reputation of an organization firebrand. The other, Vonita, light-skinned and unmarried, was said now to be slowly going blind. Ornette, seeing them enter, was surprised; then nervous, fearful. He hadn't been aware Mary Dee had invited them, for had he known, he would never have given her the names of the giant Preston and his friend with the shaved head, Freddie Phillips, to invite. The Carey sisters hated Freddie with a vengeance. Freddie and Vonita, though he was much younger than she, had been what Vonita, before misfortune involving her vision struck, had regarded as serious sweethearts. In fact, she had given Freddie money—"a loan," he had called it, with which to start a small dry cleaning place. But most of the money was never repaid, nor had the business ever gotten off the ground. Then it was found her eyesight was dangerously failing, and a short time later that it would probably soon be gone. Freddie had become alarmed; then gradually, albeit clumsily, had set out, plotted, to cool the relationship. At last he had precipitated a quarrel between them that allowed him to escape the anticipated marriage altogether. It was only then his true intentions, motives, were understood by the two sisters and, realistically or not, they panicked; their fury knew no bounds. Bess, herself ironically just married, was outraged and grief-stricken for her ill sister—half sister. Ornette, knowing them both, and how erratic, volatile, they could be, saw a potentially explosive situation developing at the party. He realized now what a mistake it had been, through lack of communication between himself and Mary Dee, to have invited both Freddie and the sisters. And to make matters worse, not only were both Freddie and the sisters there, but Freddie had brought his new girlfriend, Nan Bacon, the fierce-looking young woman in the long African garb. When suddenly Freddie saw the sisters he was first startled, then unsettled, furtive, scared, and was grateful to see Ornette go over to monopolize them in conversation until more guests arrived to swell the numbers and prevent an embarrassing, possibly hostile, encounter. Though Vonita, her sight truly impaired, the images for her vague and indistinct, had not seen Freddie, Bess of course had; and showed it, by her seething silence, as Vonita talked animatedly to Ornette. At last in a few minutes seven or eight more guests arrived, who for Ornette temporarily eased the situation and he asked busy, now excited, Ernestine for some punch.

By 8:40 at least twenty-five guests were there—the widest possible miscellany of members, though most were youngish, opinionated, and committed. Mary Dee moved among them. She naturally knew, from her work in the organization, those she had invited and some of those Ornette had suggested she invite. She circulated among her guests with a seeming familiarity and ease that falsified her true feelings. Inwardly she was joyless and her heart was not in the occasion. Besides, she could not help thinking of her mother, whom that afternoon she had asked, urged, almost implored, to come to the party with her and meet some of the people she, Irene Adkins, had so often fumed about when seeing them using her driveway to go back to the studio to visit her daughter. Though Irene had sometimes lately spoken with greater tolerance toward "these people," as she referred to them, and their admittedly good aims, she had never become entirely inured to Mary Dee's association with them or with her daughter's new friends and life in general. And today somehow she had shown particular petulance at what she considered Mary Dee's effrontery in asking her to come mingle with them—Irene had not actually said it, but Mary Dee, by her mother's smoldering manner, could not avoid sensing it. It had depressed her; though, even while still then in the kitchen with Irene, she could not have said why; it was perhaps because, no matter how she tried, she, Mary Dee herself, had yet to become acclimated to her new life—though she would never have admitted it even to herself. She would have felt far better tonight, secretly strengthened, not so tense and uneasy, had her proud, patrician, if fragile and vulnerable, mother been at her side. Instead there were Ornette and Rosabelle, Ernestine and Vernon—when only Irene Adkins' presence could have made valid, bearable, this curious occasion. At last she began to realize how badly she had needed her mother. Yet her mother had denied her—almost repudiated her. Now, however, somehow affable, smiling, a glass of punch in her hand, she moved among her guests, already grown in number to at least thirty, and suppressed her emotions. Chauncey Stiles had also arrived now, and talking to him eased for the moment some of her tensions. Suddenly, with a twinkle, Chauncey said, "Is Knight coming?"

Mary Dee stared at him—as if she had never heard the name before; during the entire evening she had not once thought of Knight. "Of course not," she said. "Why would he come? Besides, he wasn't invited." The subject, however, had brought more uneasiness, an explicit apprehension, in her mind.

Chauncey laughed and looked inquiringly over the loquacious people around them. "Have you talked to Ornette about it?" he said.

"No, Chauncey—tell me, why is it so important that Knight, as busy as he is, come to a little meeting we're having to get together a committee to raise money? Am I missing something?"

"For one thing, I want to meet him! I admire the man for the work he's doing. Isn't that reason enough?" Chauncey scanned the talkative crowd again until he saw Ornette; then, waving, beckoned him over. "Have you heard from Knight, Ornette?" he said when Ornette, wearing a handsome, emerald green leisure suit with his sport shirt open at the throat, had pushed through to them.

"No," Ornette said to them—"he's not due back in town 'til tonight; what time I don't know. I was going to wait a little while, then phone his apartment—even if he did plan to come, he couldn't find the place. I'd have to go pick him up."

Mary Dee was surprised and shaken. She abhorred the mere idea of Knight's coming. Then she remembered, gratefully, that her studio had no telephone. Her anxieties for the moment eased, she again moved among her guests.

Meanwhile, Ernestine was having the time of her life. Mary Dee, who had allowed her and Vernon to serve a few glasses of punch to indulge them, now told them if they liked they could go get themselves sandwiches—the guests were not to eat until after the business meeting. Within minutes of the time Vernon had eaten a big sandwich, he was asleep in a chair in the corner. Seeing him, Mary Dee felt guilty for letting him and Ernestine talk her into bringing them—until she realized what a major event it had become for Ernestine, who now mingled freely with the guests, talking, asking questions, giving opinions to anyone who would listen. Ernestine was one minute awed by these people, fascinated by them the next, then suddenly overjoyed; she had never met anyone vaguely resembling them, no one before who talked to her as if she were an adult. The guests crowding the room—there were in all finally thirty-seven—indeed presented a variegated sight. There were black women, brown women, and women half white with hard red hair, most, but not all, of them young; the same was true of the men; all at various levels, from high to low, of formal education and all dressed with the originality, daring, and confidence of true free spirits. It was a serious, dedicated group, however, all fervent admirers of John Calvin Knight; people who had raised the concept of Blackness to a fetish. Tonight they were together as blacks in a cause, yet in an agreeable, affable mood, and enjoying themselves. After months, they had now largely overcome their initial misgivings about Mary Dee. Time, and her simple, unadorned honesty and straightforwardness, had won them over. Now she had proven herself to the point that it was she who was enlisting their aid in organizational fund-raising. They were therefore comfortable in the role of guests on her premises.

The conversation, or "cocktail," hour had gone on for forty-five minutes, when Mary Dee and Ornette agreed it was time to begin the business meeting. But Ornette was still thinking of Knight, and not until then had he realized there was no telephone in the studio. "I should go somewhere and call John Calvin," he said to her, reflectively—"He really told me he might come."

Before she thought, Mary Dee, fearfully, had put her hand on his arm—as if to stay him; there was an unwitting, anguished, pleading, look on her face. "Let's forget it, Ornette!" she said, distress, foreboding, in her voice. "We don't need Knight! Besides, he will distract the meeting if he comes."

Ornette was watching her. "It's funny," he said—"you've never met Knight and never seemed to want to." He laughed. "What's the matter? You afraid of him or something?—even before you meet him?" On impulse she started to speak, then desisted. Ornette still watched her. "I don't get it," he said. "But may I go up to the house and use your phone?"

"Oh! . . ." Mary Dee's hand had unconsciously gone to her face now. "There's no one there, though, to let you in—mother's in bed by now, I'm sure. Oh, forget Knight, Ornette! . . ." The pleading had returned in her voice.

Ornette was watching her closely now. Finally he shook his head. "Go start the meeting," he said, and disappeared into the crowd. As Mary Dee, tense now from all her anxieties, went over to an unoccupied corner of the room to call the meeting to order, Ornette found his wife Rosabelle and said, "I'll be right back— I'm going out somewhere and find a phone. I want to see if John Calvin's home yet." Then he went out the door—but not before Mary Dee had seen.

"Mary Dee, are we going to get started, honey?" a girl said, taking a seat on the floor along with many others—including eager, agile Ernestine.

It was not clear Mary Dee had heard. Nervous, almost trembling, yet with a vague smile on her face, she stood there trying to summon strength for her voice, fearing it might quaver. The crowd, seeing her now, began to grow quiet and look for seats. Still more sat on the floor. Soon only one remaining, though not loud, voice was heard, on the other side of the room, in what seemed a spirited, reluctantly-ending, conversation. It was the voice of Freddie Phillips, of the shaved head, finishing discussion of some point with another guest, as his girlfriend, Nan Bacon, at his side hung on his every word. He seemed unmindful that the two Carey sisters had just taken seats in chairs nearby. The almost blind sister, Vonita, finally hearing the familiar, unforgettable, hated, voice, at once froze, then, as if it were sonar-equipped, lifted her face toward the ceiling, listening, straining to verify. It was that voice, all right, that despised voice, she knew, her anger immediately boiling. She nudged her sister Bess. "You hear that? . . . ain't that that sonofabitch? Huh? You can see him, can't you? It's him, all right, ain't it?"

Bess sighed. "Yeah, it's him," she said. "I saw him when we first came in. I wasn't going to say anything to you about it, and get you all upset. He shouldn't be here! It ain't right! That no-good bastard oughtn't even belong to an organization like this—they ought to throw his ass out. It's a shame!"

But Mary Dee was speaking now and everyone, including Freddie Phillips, had become quiet. The men, leaning against the walls or squatting on the floor, however, were so struck by her beauty they could hardly keep their minds on what she was saying. She wore a quiet navy blue pants suit, but with a flaming orange and cerise silk scarf at the throat.

"Jesus," soliloquized the giant Preston, standing in the back of the room, "what a woman."

Mary Dee had begun shakily. ". . . Thanks for coming," she said first. "I thought it would be good . . . if we could get together like this some evening and try to find . . . some new ways, if possible, of going to the community for money. This hasn't only been my idea, but others' as well—I know I've talked with Ornette and Rosabelle about it a lot. So how do we go about it, how do we do it? I'm sure many of you have had more experience in this sort of thing than I have. That's why I've wanted us to get together and try to explore it all . . . and share our ideas with each other. . . ."
She paused now, her mind for the briefest moment leaving, flying outside the room, as she wondered where Ornette had gone, how long he would be away, and—her fearful heartbeat quickening—whether he would soon come walking in with Knight.

Meanwhile, the Carey sisters sat rigidly erect, in their anger hearing little of what Mary Dee said. Bess Carey would then suddenly train her eyes on the back of Freddie Phillips' shaved head and, her lips moving, glare her outrage at him. As Mary Dee continued speaking, Ernestine unobtrusively, almost stealthily, began crawling farther forward, nearer her. Soon, pride, possessive pride, plain on her face, she was on the floor directly in front of Mary Dee, listening with rapt attention to her every word. Vernon still slept sprawled in the chair in the back of the room. Dentist Chauncey Stiles sat rather off to himself, in a chair against the far wall, where, eyes roving, he seemed more interested in watching the reactions on the faces of the listeners than in what the comely speaker was saying.

"It's sort of been my feeling," Mary Dee continued, "that we should form teams of, say, four or five people each—small teams." She looked around. "Please feel free to stop me whenever you have questions or comments—or when you don't agree. The teams would of course be recruited from the ranks of the organization. This would be the responsibility of the committee—this committee, if we decided to form one permanently. Then long prospect lists would have to be made up—this would be a big job, I realize —and the hundreds of prospects classified roughly according to their reputed means and their record of community involvement." Mary Dee smiled. "Does that sound sensible or am I talking through my hat?" A half dozen hands went up. "Yes—Quanita," she said, calling on a tall, ungainly girl sitting on the floor in the midst of the crowd.

The girl scrambled to her knees. "Mary Dee, we got to go after the dicty society niggers first. But they ain't never had a history of community involvement, so how're you gonna group them by that? We got other ways of finding them out, though. Then we don't go begging them, either. We go threatening them—right?" The crowd laughed. But, instantly incensed, Chauncey Stiles was already on his feet, waving to be recognized. Mary Dee, however, so quickly facing an awkward, explosive, situation, conveniently overlooked Chauncey and called instead on the giant Preston leaning against the wall. "Yes—Mr. Preston."

"Quanita's not talking sense," Preston said.

"Yes, I am, too," snapped back Quanita.

"You ain't talking sense because you don't know any society niggers." Preston's hulking frame leaned out from the wall toward the girl. "There ain't many of the kind you're talking about left anyhow. They need the respect and support of the black community; not only to make a living, but to be somebody—so they're involved too."

Other hands went up, but angry Chauncey Stiles, though still ignored by the chairperson, began shouting his retort. "You talk about what you call 'society niggers,' " he said to them all, heatedly—"well, there's one right *there!*" He was pointing, jabbing the air, over their heads directly at Mary Dee. "You've been listening to one right here tonight, my dear," he said to Quanita. "She's your hostess! I'm proud of her because she's cultured and brilliant *and* cares about black folk!"

"Right on," said Preston, no trivial admirer of Mary Dee himself.

"Right on!" said others.

Mary Dee's face was stinging from her embarrassment and confusion. She was furious with impulsive Chauncey for bringing her into what she thought a fatuous discussion.

But then, further breaking the tension, Rosabelle Hungerford gave a loud laugh and herself pointed at Chauncey. "You too, Dr. Stiles!" she said. "You're another one—you're a society nigger and we love you! Ain't we all black folks together?"

"Right on, girl," someone said. Chauncey, surprised, also embarrassed, sat down at once.

The planning and discussion now resumed in earnest, and though there was still much exuberant talk from the floor, Mary Dee, gradually feeling surer of herself, soon gained a control of the meeting that kept the discussion reasonably channeled and productive. Soon thirty minutes had passed. She next brought up the important question of what arguments the soliciting team members might best use when approaching prospective givers. On this she well knew the Hungerfords' views and asked Rosabelle to say something. Rosabelle spoke while remaining seated on the floor. "I wish Ornette was back—he could say it better than I can. But it's simple. It's the children. If we take time to think about why *we're* involved in the organization, it always boils down pretty much to one thing—the children. We're trying to make it better for them, for they're the future of black people. I don't say children are the only pitch we should make, but I think it's sure the best one." Throughout Rosabelle's remarks, Mary Dee was reflective, occasionally glancing down at alert, involved Ernestine, then back toward the rear of the room where Vernon slept. She knew these two children were Exhibits A and B in support of what Rosabelle was saying, and at the first opportunity she herself began to speak, seconding much of what Rosabelle had said. She was in the middle of a sentence—when someone, puzzlingly, applauded. She looked around—wondering who, and why. Then she saw it

589

was Chauncey, whose chair was by the open door at the top of the steps leading up from the first floor, who was smiling and applauding. He had apparently seen something or someone the others as yet could not see. Now he stood up and applauded enthusiastically—as Knight entered through the door, followed by Ferdinand Bailey, then Ornette. When Knight was seen and recognized, a wave of applause swept the room as everyone, smiling, applauding, stood up.

Knight smiled gravely, wearily, and put up his hand to get silence. "Please," he said—"I insist on not interrupting the meeting. Will you please go on?" Two chairs were quickly made available for him and Ferdinand and they sat down.

It seemed as if Mary Dee had lost her voice. For a moment she stood immobilized. At last a few words came. ". . . We were discussing possible methods . . . of fund raising," she said. "Rosabelle said that she thought . . ." She paused again. "Rosabelle said the children were the best talking point for us. . . ."

Knight's piercing eyes, on the speaker, had suddenly begun to burn. Lips slightly parted, breath bated, he was staring at her now. It was a fierce, incredulous stare. Then his jaw dropped in total recognition—and disbelief. Yet he was sure—as sure as he was of his whereabouts. It could be no other—there could not be two such women in the world. He sat dumbfounded—mystified. Then Ferdinand beside him discreetly moved his head no more than three inches toward him and whispered—"Ah, John Calvin, so that's Ornette's black *Jeanne d'Arc,* is it?"

"Black!" Knight for no apparent reason turned on him and seemed about to utter still another imprecation, when he managed to regain control of himself, yet still sat staring, almost glaring, at Mary Dee.

Ferdinand said, "Do you know her?"

Knight did not answer—his heated eyes only remained on the speaker.

Ferdinand, though surprised by the leader's strange behavior, was even more puzzled by it. In this he was not alone. Ornette, standing against the far wall, his evening's mission accomplished, had observed Knight's reaction, and was also puzzled—it looked troublesome. He continued to watch him, wondering what was up.

Mary Dee, however, though still shaky, had recovered at least a measure of her composure and, firmly keeping her eyes away from Knight, still talked of children. "It was Rosabelle and Ornette I first heard talk about our children—"

"—Wait a minute, Mary Dee," Ornette, laughing, spoke up. "You had already sort of adopted two kids of your own before you ever met us. Tell it like it is, now!" Knowing about Ernestine and Vernon, everyone laughed with Ornette, who had never been more pleased with Mary Dee, for at last now he had embarked on his ultimate mission—that of matchmaker.

Knight sat transfixed. But how beautiful this woman still was! he thought grudgingly.

Mary Dee resumed. "How could we possibly find—for anybody, ourselves included—a stronger motivation than children provide?" she said to them. "If what the black children in the devastated ghettos of the great cities have suffered won't move the people we go to for money, then I can't think of anything that will." Though she was nervous, excited, scared, her voice had somehow taken on a clarion ring that carried to the farthest corners of the large room. "Yet we all know a lot will depend on *our* people, the people in the organization, who will have the hard job of carrying the message to the prospects we'll be trying to reach. We must carry a message of dedication, hope, and love."

Before he thought, little Ferdinand Bailey was half out of his chair. "Yes, yes, that's it—that's right!" he said. "Oh, how beautiful, sister!—how beautiful! *That's* our message to black folks—hope and love!"

Ornette, over against the wall, was beaming. Ferdinand, he knew, was a natural ally. Together they would somehow bring it off. He watched Knight now, whose eyes had not once left Mary Dee's face. Ornette had never seen his leader so stunned, affected, mesmerized, and attributed it to Mary Dee's beauty, her presence, and articulate intelligence. Yet this did not entirely satisfy him. He was determined now to talk to Ferdinand tomorrow, to find out, if he could, the cause of Knight's strange, perplexing, behavior.

Mary Dee talked very little longer—she had really wanted to stop the moment Knight walked in. Now again she asked for any questions or comments from the audience, this time about the choice of canvassers. Instead, almost at once, Bess Carey was on her feet. "It's wonderful," she said, "that Mr. Knight himself could pop in on us like this. What a surprise—what an honor. Me and my sister, Vonita here, are glad because for some time we have wanted to ask Mr. Knight a question or two about our organization, the Black Peoples Congress. . . ."

Things got quiet. Ornette was watching the situation though not concealing his impatience. "Miss Carey," he said "Mr. Knight just got off a plane, but, tired as he was, still kept his promise to pay us a visit. Maybe he don't feel up to any questions tonight, sister."

For the first time now Knight seemed to stir from his smoldering trance, his fierce inertness, and, trying to smile, turned to Bess Carey. "No," he said, "I'm always available to try to answer questions about the organization. What's your question, sister?"

Now, however, that Bess Carey had license to speak, she was so nervous she seemed unable to. There was a long, embarrassing silence. Finally—"I don't quite know how to say it, Mr. Knight . . . but ain't this organization got some kind of standards? Just can't *anybody* get in here, can they? Or if they do, and keep on doing wrong, turn even worse, ain't there some way for them to be called on the carpet for what they did, and put out of the organization—so they won't spoil its good name and the people in it?"

Everyone sat puzzled; they looked at each other. Knight, pondering the mystifying question, slowly stood up—as if biding for time. He studied Bess. "I'm not sure I understand the kind of situation you're talking about, sister," he said. "Could you give an example?"

But Bess only sat there, seeming to debate now whether to answer. Vonita, beside her, turned her half-seeing eyes to her sister—waiting. But no words came—Bess now seemed merely stubborn.

Finally Knight said, "If you can't think of a specific case at the moment, then let me try to answer you in general. The organization is made up mostly of good people, dedicated people, like yourselves; that's why we've been able to do some good things for black people, though there's still a mountain of work yet to be done." As he talked, Bess Carey's doleful, unplacated, bitter eyes were again trained on the back of Freddie Phillips' shaved head. "But we must remember," said Knight, "we don't turn anybody away—we're an organization of the people."

"Yeah," glowing Ornette spoke up—*"black* people."

But Freddie Phillips was also watching everything—he saw what was developing. Having been apprehensive, fearful, since he came in with Nan Bacon on his arm and seen the Carey sisters present, he sought now to intervene and possibly divert from himself a potentially bad situation. Brushing his hand lightly over his shaved head, he laughed at Ornette's fervent remark. "Why do you talk so Black, Ornette?" he said. "You got a white chick workin' right in your front office."

Knight stiffened. Ornette's face clouded up, but before he could say anything, Knight, alarmed, hurried on. "We're trying to reach the *people*," he said, too energetically, almost vehemently—"the people as they *are*. So we mustn't be too quick to judge them, for not one of us is perfect. The organization must have a moral code, that's true, and try to persuade the members to live by it, but we shouldn't be too quick to judge—that's a big undertaking. Don't you agree? . . ." He sighed nervously.

"Right!" someone said.

But Bess Carey had recovered her aplomb; she was respectful but persistent. "I know the organization's not a church, Mr. Knight. But we got to have some standards, don't we?—and see that the members live up to them. Ain't that right?" The puzzled audience was getting restive, impatient, now, and Ornette was still glowering at Freddie Phillips. Mary Dee, however, unobtrusively, had moved to a chair near Ernestine and sat down. Knight was clearly nervous, upset, now—Griselda had come up in the discussion and, not knowing whether the same subject was also on Bess Carey's mind, he was afraid to probe her further or again ask her to be more specific. Also dark, unwarranted suspicions rose in his thoughts now; he wondered if he hadn't been victimized, invited by Ornette and this astounding (avenging?) Adkins girl into a trap. He was groping for something to say, when Bess suddenly, stubbornly, repeated: "Ain't that right, Mr. Knight?"

Knight lost his composure. "Oh, sister, why don't you come to the office sometime and we'll thresh it out between us," he said, unable to keep irritation out of his voice. But then he tried again to smile—"We shouldn't get so serious, should we, at what I was told was to be a party; please, let's not forget the party part of it." He laughed vacuously and looked around him.

593

"Right," said Ornette—"let's break it up, folks, and get this meeting over with. Mary Dee says there's some sandwiches and beer, also wine, for us when we finish." Seeing the nodding of heads, frowning Bess Carey looked thwarted, resentful, but stopped her questioning for the time being.

Mary Dee dutifully rose now and went up to preside again, hopefully to end the meeting—Knight's eyes following her intently. There could be not a scintilla of doubt, he told himself; it was the identical girl—and just as breathtaking as ever; what a sight to behold. He gave another troubled sigh. Mary Dee now quickly resumed the business of appointing solicitation teams and arranging future planning sessions, then in less than five minutes had adjourned the meeting. But the social hour had hardly begun when Ornette came and took her by the arm, her fearful heart racing, and ushered her over to where Knight stood with Ferdinand greeting followers and well-wishers, among them Chauncey Stiles. Ornette pushed through. "John Calvin," he said excitedly, "this is Mary Dee—Mary Dee Adkins—you've heard me talk so much about! You saw how she ran that meeting, didn't you?" He gave a loud, self-congratulating laugh.

At first Knight's face was stricken; then he smiled, shiftily, nervously. "I did," he said, reaching out to find Mary Dee's hand, then giving it a wary shake. "Nice to meet you," he managed—"Ornette has spoken very highly of you." He turned and introduced her to Ferdinand as myriad, confused, thoughts went scurrying through his brain—he was doubly sure now she was the same person, the Paris person; how could he ever forget? He was almost equally sure she also remembered him. It was her manner now, her futile effort to be oblivious, at the same time blandly pleasant, earnest, even respectful. What, he wondered—what on earth—could have happened in her life in the interim, what could have so affected her, to bring her into Ornette's and Rosabelle's orbit? Into his, Knight's, orbit? It was a crazy world, he thought—she now a member of this, *his,* organization of *Blackness!* . . . when he knew how she had loved, reveled in, the world of Whiteness. Almost at once then he gave a troubled, inward sigh, thinking of himself and Griselda—of himself as a person living in a glass house yet throwing stones. There was also, he thought, on this subject, the perilous escape he'd just had in this very gathering tonight—all of which reminded him that strange things could, and often did, happen to people whose perennial curse it was to get their goals confused. But what a woman, he thought—what an extraordinary, beautiful, talented woman. A black woman!—a lump almost came in his throat. He was stunned, bowled over, by her now and for a moment lost his composure. Finally glancing around at the walls, smiling in desperation, he said to her: "Your pictures are eye-catching—Ornette has mentioned them."

"Some are his," she said simply, and smiled. She easily sensed his confusion, his perturbation of spirit, and somehow knew why. This calmed her somewhat, eased her nervousness, her fear. There could be no mistake, she thought. He remembered her. She could see it had shaken him. Strangely, it made her feel glad—triumphant, avenged. Once more she smiled as he said something, again nervously, she did not quite hear—something, she was sure, quite innocuous. Just then Ernestine came up and said the guests were gathering at the food. Mary Dee, thankful for the interruption, excused herself and, taking Ernestine, went to make sure everyone was invited over to the two refreshment tables along the wall. Suddenly now Vernon was awake and standing at the first table with the other guests crowded around for the food and drink. Mary Dee's thoughts, however, were on Knight and her friendly smiles for her new friends gathering at the tables soon grew set, false, preoccupied. Yes, he remembered her, well remembered her, she thought, almost gloating, her vanity soaring—though their two Paris encounters had been brief, they were only a year ago and he recalled them well; she felt it in her now mixed-up emotions. Yet his recognition did not surprise her; what did was the absence of evidence of any lingering aggressive hostility toward her; he seemed now only confused, uneasy, withdrawn, perhaps too somehow embarrassed. She felt an inward victory she had never anticipated. Her anxieties, tensions, about him had vanished and somehow she did not expect them to return.

Within ten minutes the social hour, the party, was in full swing. Everyone had had a sandwich or two and a glass of beer, wine, or punch; the talk was animated and free—except, that is, for the Carey sisters, who sat mostly off to themselves as they ate their sandwiches and pouted. Mary Dee had received so many compliments about her chairing of the meeting that, despite everything—

including the mammoth ambivalences of her life—she felt, if not happiness, a kind of smug gratification, undefined satisfaction. Though not yet in active collusion, neither Ornette nor Ferdinand (the matchmakers), however, was at all pleased that Mary Dee had spent so little time talking to Knight before hurrying off to attend to the guests' food. Each had in mind trying to do something about this. Soon then, and with little subtlety, Ornette, followed by smiling but equally purposeful Ferdinand, again took Knight over to where Mary Dee stood surrounded by admirers. But it was Ferdinand, now somehow beaming, who spoke first—to Mary Dee. "It certainly would be nice, Miss Adkins," he said, showing his teeth—as Knight was drawn into side conversations with others around them—"if you and Mr. Knight could get together sometime, before our big national meeting next month, and talk over what you think we ought to be proposing to the Central Planning Committee in the way of strengthening our women's program—to get more women active in the movement, do you see? That's not to say many aren't already active, but we need more; many, many more. What we need is a variety of programs in order to attract a greater variety of women—don't you think so? You could be so much help to him . . . to us." Ferdinand was soon so ingratiating he was almost bowing and scraping.

But before Mary Dee could answer, Ornette, who, over all the other talking, had been trying to hear what Ferdinand was saying, broke in and said, and again with little ceremony, to Mary Dee, "This is a natural, if I ever saw one in my life—you've got to get to know John Calvin, Mary Dee! The man's a genius and you're a genius! That's why I say this thing's a natural! Think of how much you can do—and I'm talking about on a *national* level—for the organization. Just think of it, girl!"

Mary Dee did not know what to say—to either of them. True, she was taken aback, yet not much so—having always been told by her father, and others, how intelligent, resourceful, how effectual, she was in everything. It would have been by no means difficult for her, in an expansive moment, to believe she was capable of leading the Congress herself, and better than Knight. She therefore seemed to receive Ferdinand's and Ornette's commendations with a poise, a thoughtful aplomb, that mystified, perhaps even dismayed, both men. Finally she said, "I'm not sure I should . . ."

—she paused to correct herself—"I'm not sure I'd like to become more active than I am. My mother's health is uncertain; we're moving into another, smaller, place; besides, I want to paint more." She laughed—"And there are Ernestine and Vernon. . . ."

"Oh, Mary Dee!" Ornette said, twisting in exasperation— "What're you saying? I never heard you talk like this before!"

Rosabelle had now come up and had just been kissed on the cheek by Knight before both turned around to the others. At once, unwittingly, she injected a new subject in the conversation—the skyrocketing prices of food and their consequent hardships on the black poor. The ensuing conversation, in which Knight uneasily joined, gave Mary Dee, who chose to be silent, her first real opportunity to watch, studiously observe, him. She liked his quiet, modest, almost somber, mode of dress—his business suit. He also seemed tired, drawn, from his travels and responsibilities— which to her made him no less attractive. But it was his eyes—his evil Paris eyes—she could not abide. They were hard, piercing, almost cruel—too much so, she sometimes thought, really, for authenticity. Could it be that he feigned a hardness, therefore a decisiveness, he really did not have? She felt, in any case, he was a complicated, maybe unhappy, man. But perhaps, it occurred to her, this was the secret of his sway over the thousands of submerged blacks in the ghettos across the country—his seeming role, especially since the attempt on his life, of the tormented near martyr. Yet, right or wrong, she saw him as a kind of bifurcated personality, with both a positive and a negative side, all, however, eventually combined in and exemplified by his unforgettable, his emblematic, truculent Paris stare. It was indeed what the stare represented, whatever that was, that she had sometimes so feared. Yet she could not forget she stood in the presence of a powerful and famous man, though a stranger coming in the room would not have so recognized him—among his followers his manner was so quietly engaging, his smile so reserved though sincere, his greeting so freely given to all, high and low alike, that he would easily have passed for merely another of the organization's trustworthy members. This, his unassuming way, his accessibility, she knew, was another source of his strength with those closest around him as well as with the thousands of the faithful throughout the land. Despite, therefore, all her former doubts and misgivings, her old

597

fears, she realized he was a strange, yet intriguing man—though she could not like him; which brought her to what she regarded as the transparency of Ferdinand's and Ornette's motives, their zeal in trying to throw them together. It irritated her—she knew Knight was single now—yet somehow also interested, magnetized, her. She wished to put it out of her mind.

Very little further of consequence was to happen at the party except that the two Carey sisters finally got Knight off to himself long enough to whisper to him about Freddie Phillips' perfidy. Knight listened attentively, sympathetically, until Bess—with Vonita leaning against her, listening—finished, then asked the two perplexed, unhappy women what they would have him do. Bess answered without hesitation. "He should be put out, Mr. Knight—he ain't fit to be in the organization."

Knight thought for a moment, and finally shook his head. "But what if he needs the organization?" he said. "True, as we heard you say during the meeting, we're not a church, yet many people have been changed, for the better, by joining with us; we've given them a different, a new, outlook on life, and in many cases—by coming to understand true Blackness—their lives have been edified, improved. If this young man has acted as you say—and I don't have any reason to doubt you—he's probably the kind of person the organization can help. This is a serious business we're in, sisters—trying to show blacks that, despite all the outside pressures against them, because they're black, they can still afford to be magnanimous to each other."

"You'll never teach Freddie Phillips that!" hissed Bess.

"Now wait—he probably didn't feel he could afford to be like that; therefore he reacted as he did—out of fear, maybe. Fear of what? Fear of further handicapping himself—with all the other strikes he's got against him as a black man. But perhaps the organization, in time, can show him he has *strengths* too as a black man—strengths he didn't know he had."

The Carey sisters were less than satisfied with Knight's rationalizations, though they listened and made little further remonstrance. "Maybe so, Mr. Knight," Bess finally said, "but you don't know Freddie Phillips like we do. You heard him yourself, right in the meeting tonight, bring that up about that white girl you'all got working in the office. That's the kind of man he is—a snake."

Knight could not conceal his frightened discomfort. Then Bess hesitated, before blurting it—"We helped him *out,* Mr. Knight . . . moneywise!"

"Oh . . .you helped him that way—I see," said Knight. He seemed stumped. "Well, I can imagine how you feel. . . . Did he pay you back?"

"Only part of it," Bess said. "Y'see, Mr. Knight, it raises the question of what kind of organization we got—and what kind we oughta have. We read a lot in our literature about how blacks oughta stick together, and so forth; how they oughta look out for each other, depend on each other—be Black, and so forth. But suppose a member don't care nothing about this, don't never intend to live up to it?—we don't have no way of dealing with him, do we? I don't know too much about these things—sure not as much as you do, Mr. Knight—but it seems to me like this is a great failing of our organization. It makes it look like sometimes we don't know where we're going—or if we do, that it maybe ain't in the right direction. Does anybody in the organization, you leaders, ever think about things like this?—about where we're going?"

". . . Yes." But Knight said it uneasily. "There's a limit, though, isn't there, to what we can do about personal, private, acts, even misdeeds, of members. It's too big a job . . . we just can't police them, sister—don't you see? It would be impractical."

Bess nodded, with irony. "Yeah, Mr. Knight," she said—"if you think tryin' to make people do right is impractical."

Knight was frowning, agitated—"It's not that, sister—" But Ornette intervened, having come across the room to get Knight and take him home. On this slack, irresolute note therefore the conversation with the troubled Carey sisters ended. But although Knight later persuaded himself he had been right, what Bess Carey had questioned about the organization's direction stayed on his mind—overshadowed only by his thoughts, his utter amazement, indeed shock, at seeing Mary Dee again.

Ornette in his big second-hand station wagon took Knight home, then Ferdinand, before delivering Ernestine and Vernon—Vernon asleep on Ernestine's shoulder—safely home to their mother. All in all, Ornette considered it to have been a successful evening for the organization, for the cause—possibly, hopefully, a new beginning. He was bent, certainly, on making it so. In this he thought Mary Dee a godsend. As for Mary Dee herself, she went to bed feeling exhausted—and uneasy.

During the next few days Knight thought of little else except this astonishing new girl who had come on the scene, *his* scene— though how could he regard her as new, he thought, when he had seen her no more than a year ago in circumstances he had at least then considered dubious, if not compromising? He craved more information about her now—yet whom could he ask, he wondered, without betraying his deep interest in her? It was embarrassing. But who was, who really was, she?—this extraordinary person he had seen in Paris in a setting he did not even now like to recall? He remembered his blazing, unreasoning, anger at the time. He had recognized her even then, however, as a woman of class—it was apparent in everything she did, in her every gesture. Ornette, he recalled, sometime ago had said she was a Chicagoan. What then had taken her to Paris? What, moreover, had thrown her in with white men of obvious standing, men of affairs?—what truly had been the relationship? He thought it an amazing case, though one which could only further complicate his already equivocal existence. It called for caution—he was certain of that—and patience. But already he thought of his life as somehow changing course.

*   *   *   *   *

All during the week of Mary Dee's studio party, when until Friday evening Knight was out of town, Griselda had had strange feelings. She looked forward as usual to his return but wondered now how she would be able, as busy as he would be in the immediate future—with the national meeting soon to come—to purloin for herself more of his time, his attention. What most concerned her, though she felt it must change for the better, was his obvious disinclination—his fear?—to commit himself. He was still elusive. She felt she must somehow deal with this; she did not know just yet how—it must be subtle, adroit—but she saw the clear necessity. All week, especially during his absence, she had thought about it. It was this that had given her the strange, inexplicable feeling that a turning point in their relationship was approaching. She disliked the prospect and tried as best she could to put it out of her mind—though it persisted almost as a presentiment.

Then there was the matter of Marvin. Hardly a day, or night, passed when, fearfully, she did not think of him—expect his unwelcome, dreaded, reappearance. Where was he? she wondered. What had happened to him? Had he finally become discouraged and returned home to San Francisco? This she could not believe; it was so unlike him; he was too crazily persistent, tenacious, for this. She merely expected him, any time now, once more to intrude himself in her life, her plans, her other nagging worries. She was resigned to the prospect and considered it only a matter of time. But when? how long?

There was to be little waiting—significant events were set in motion simultaneously. The Monday morning of the week of the national meeting—with delegates that weekend having arrived from all over the country—Nancy Hanks walked in the headquarters office. Griselda could not believe her eyes and almost fainted. For a moment she could not get her breath. ". . . Mother," she said at last, though weakly, still breathlessly, yet somehow already with censure in her voice. "What—" The words would not come, though she had hurried over to Nancy Hanks at the railing separating office personnel from waiting visitors.

"It was the only way I had of trying to locate you," Nancy Hanks said gruffly. Despite her weather-beaten face, she was not unattractive—in her severely prim but expensive grey coat and her red and green turban. "It's important, Griselda—did you know that Marvin Freuhlinghausen is dead?"

Griselda stood staring. ". . . Oh, my God! . . ."

"It's true. You didn't know?—hadn't he contacted you? He died here—he had come here to find you and bring you back."

Griselda's eyes were wide, still as if with fear. "Marvin dead? . . ."

"He died in his hotel room—of a heart attack. It's been three weeks—you didn't know?"

"Of course I didn't know!" Griselda said petulantly, but at once then melted into what seemed almost tearful contrition—"He had finally found me, all right . . . but I had refused to see him. . . . I wouldn't see him. He begged me, but I wouldn't."

"But it's important, Griselda. You were mentioned in his will—substantially."

Griselda's face, however, was still long and sad. "I don't care—I don't want it. I don't deserve it—I'll refuse it."

Nancy Hanks bristled with anger. "Just listen to you! . . . You will not! It only proves what I've always said—you've never had the slightest notion of what's good for you. If there's any step you can take inimical to your own interests, you'll take it. My God!—I can hardly believe sometimes you're my daughter."

Griselda sighed. "Nor can I."

"Oh, nonsense! You've got to get on a plane with me and go back there ready, if necessary, to be in court if complications develop in probating that will. Don't be foolish!"

Griselda had not realized it, but their agitated voices, though not loud, were yet attracting attention. The other girls in the office, as well as some of the visitors, clients, though unable completely to overhear, were nonetheless observing them. When finally Griselda became aware, she leaned forward and, in almost a whisper, said to Nancy Hanks, "We can't talk here, Mother! . . . we're creating a scene. I'll come to see you—where are you staying? We can talk then—oh, you shouldn't have come here! . . ."

"How else did you expect me to find you?" Nancy Hanks then turned and for the first time let her haughty gaze sweep the room. "If you must know it," she said in her gravelly *mezzo* voice, "it's not all that pleasant to have to come out to a place like this—I would have much preferred finding you somewhere else. Anyway, I'm at the Conrad Hilton hotel and I want you to take the day off and come down there with me—now. We've got to talk. Whether you realize it or not, this is important."

"Oh, I can't leave here today, Mother! . . . This is the first day of the national meeting, the organization's most important day of the year. Maybe this evening I can come. . . ."

Obdurate Nancy Hanks looked at her watch—it was 10:45. "No, you're coming today—I'm not going to let you out of my sight. I'm going to help you in spite of yourself." Pointing to the line of seats for waiting clients, she said, "I'm going over there and take a seat and wait for you—I'm not going to budge. If someone asks me what I want, I'm going to tell them I've come to take my daughter out of this place—out of this awful place that

602

teaches nothing but race hatred. That's what I mean to tell them."
She turned then to go sit down—whereupon Griselda, riven with
fear and distraction, ran and got her coat and, followed by her
frowning, self-willed mother, left the office.

*   *   *   *   *

Ornette Hungerford, in the interim days between Mary Dee's
studio party and the start of the week of the national meeting, had
not been idle. In addition to the many organization tasks he had
undertaken in connection with the national meeting, he had had
at least three conversations with Ferdinand Bailey—about, of
course, Mary Dee. They had agreed completely. She must be given
—even if it had to be thrust upon her—a heavier, more important,
role in the affairs of the organization. The way must be cleared
for her to work more closely with Knight, to contribute her undoubted abilities to the leader—thus to the cause. There was also
the matter, the possibility, as yet unmentioned, perhaps at this
early juncture unmentionable, that the leader and this remarkable,
gifted girl might in time become friends. Though Ornette and
Ferdinand never engaged in speculation so sharply focused, it was
all tacitly understood between them. They also agreed upon a
division of labor. Ferdinand would seek, circumspectly of course,
to influence Knight to assign Mary Dee some relatively important
tasks, though not before fully acquainting him with her proven
talents and dedication, her family and background, as best he,
and Ornette, knew it. Ornette, on the other hand, assisted by Rosabelle, would deal with Mary Dee. With all the tact at their command, they would set out to persuade her of her potentially crucial role in the life, direction, and growth of the organization—
"the cause," as Ornette always thought of it. That, they agreed,
would be the strategy.

What, however, the conspirators failed to take into account was
the intelligence, acumen, of the two people they sought to influence. Both Knight and Mary Dee, though in no way in communication, saw through the intrigue almost before it began. The only
difference was in their reactions. Knight, though not entirely aware

603

of his feelings, welcomed the plot. Mary Dee's reaction was almost exactly opposite.

*   *   *   *   *

Yet Ornette's very first victory was in talking Mary Dee into sitting up on the platform the night of the big rally that closed the week of the national convention. After four days of successful meetings, discussions, and panels, the mass meeting was to be the grandest occasion, many veteran members, including Ferdinand, vowed, in the whole history of the Black People's Congress. As it turned out, an estimated three thousand people were packed into the 43rd Street Amphitheater Hall that night. Enthusiasm, emotions, ran high. This was especially true when, early in the evening, the children's chorus, dressed, not in white, but black, sang the moving spiritual "We Are Climbin' Jacob's Ladder." Tears glistened in many eyes as the sweet young voices, voices of innocence and hope, carried out over the crowd and even up into the steel girders buttressing the high domed roof of the hall.

Mary Dee, quietly seated in the second row of rostrum seats and, where Ornette and Ferdinand had meticulously placed her, immediately back of Knight, listened without being totally, unreservedly, moved. Somehow the old rage swelled again within her. Blacks were always the victims, she thought—why weren't they ever, *ever,* the victors? Again she looked over at the children's chorus, trying to find, identify, Ernestine and Vernon—she hoped Vernon was awake—as the tender, yet somehow triumphant, music of travail and faith searched out the hearts and consciousness of the hushed, rapt throng. But in anger and frustration her fists were clenched till the blood ran thin and cold—the blood-wish of vengeance and retribution. Why, why, why?—why must *we* always be sufferers? Would it, *must* it, always be thus? She was somehow now blind with an unreasoning rage—until it hit her: She did not belong here, she thought. She belonged elsewhere—she did not know where, but not here. Everything in this mammoth, packed hall was foreign to her. She was not of these credulous people. Then almost at once a great wave of guilt and mortification came over, inundated, her and once again she was frustrated, bewildered, wretched.

Knight, solemn, impervious, though somehow alert and gravely smiling, sat directly in front of her—she could not avoid noticing his poor, botched, haircut, but, she also recognized, he was the soul of immaculate neatness. Yet, though now her view of him was confined to the back of his head, she could never forget his eyes, those hateful, hostile, Paris eyes . . . that day on the *terrasse* at Fouquet's—ah, on the blissful, romantic, Boulevard Champs Elysées, only a year ago, when she had not really been a part of the world, but of heaven. Why then, she thought tonight, was she here? She told herself it was to try and help change things, to make the world better, more just. But she realized this was a lie. Rather it was, she knew, to vent her personal spleen and bitterness.

Suddenly, in her abstraction gazing out over the audience, her eyes momentarily came to rest on what appeared to her to be a young white woman. It surprised her. This could not be, she thought. Yet her inquiring eyes soon affirmed her first impression. The girl, slightly, very slightly, olive-complexioned but with Negro hair and very pretty, sat in the center section about a dozen rows from the front, her burning eyes trained, it seemed, on her, Mary Dee . . . until she realized those eyes were rather on someone directly in front of her—John Calvin Knight.

It was very noticeable, for now the center of attention was on a young poet—Mary Dee recognized him with a shock—who was reading, exhorting, from his manuscript of poems about "the beautiful man-leader." She could see, however, his efforts were wholly lost on the girl—who now, except for her thick Afro hairdo, looked quite white. But the poet raved on—as the girl's eyes burned into Knight. Mary Dee now, though, turned and watched the poet—she could never forget him, from the sleazy Trocadero restaurant in last winter's blizzard, when he had forcibly thrust his doggerel upon her and the two children—and saw now his lunatic fervor had in no way abated. Knight, sitting in the midst of his family of Central Planning Committee members from across the country—there were at least forty people seated on the platform—also watched the poet, as the wild, livid poems heaped praise of the gods on himself as leader; but then he somehow seemed embarrassed, as perhaps he wondered what his father

Goforth would have said. Yet at the end of the fiery recitation a great shout went up from the audience, followed by heavy applause.

Ferdinand sat on Knight's right, Ornette on his left. Ornette was both excited and impatient. He was to speak following the next musical number—for the self-appointed purpose, as he had heard the old folks in his family say of their assistant pastor, of "warming the meeting up" for Knight, for the pastor, who would then be introduced by Ferdinand. But the poet Gideon had almost upstaged him, he ruefully thought, stolen his thunder, and he wanted to take over the meeting as quickly as possible. The musical number, next, was a solo sung by a blind girl—a tall, slender, sallow yellow, young woman who was led to the microphone by her piano accompanist, a boy of no more than high school age. As she sang "His Eye Is On The Sparrow," which her high, fervent voice made sound like an anthem, her own eyes, slate-colored and dead, moved up, up, in her mesmeric manner, it seemed, to the very steel girders high above. The audience watched her, listening, enthralled. But Ornette watched the audience. *It* was his interest— its temper, its mood. Though with little or no experience in speaking before crowds, Ornette had a natural instinct, a gift, for sensing the extent of a black audience's receptiveness, what it wanted to hear, and not hear, what it would tolerate. He had listened with rapt attention that morning to a speech made from the floor, to a much smaller audience in a panel discussion, by Central Planning Committee member, and sometime-dissident, Jesse Lumpkins of Cincinnati. Of late Knight and Ferdinand had considered Lumpkins, an older man, in his late fifties, dangerous, a potential troublemaker, because of his independence, his sharp tongue, and habit of taking what they regarded as ill-considered, even rash, positions on many issues affecting the organization. Ornette, however, had a secret admiration for Lumpkins—especially for his rough, ungrammatical, eloquence in mettings in which he had heard him speak. That morning, as now, it was also the audience that Ornette had watched. He was greatly impressed. The audience loved Lumpkins' gutty, earthy, "down-home" delivery style and applauded him lustily. Ornette had sat watching, taking lessons, unable to avoid contrasting the effect of Lumpkins' gut power and vehemence with Knight's more academic, reasoned, if at times passionate, manner. Ornette could find no role model in Knight and when finally it now came time for him to "warm the meeting up," he remembered Jesse Lumpkins.

"Friends!—brothers and sisters in the cause!" he began breathlessly, but at once became more confident and strong—"How I've hated to see this night come! Oh, yes, yes! We've had such a great week together—a week of hard work, but one of accomplishment and fellowship, of working together in the cause. Yes, yes, I wish it could go on forever! But it can't, my friends! We must go back now, go back to our respective tasks of putting into action the plans and programs we've labored so hard on here all week. Yes, now *real* duty calls! We must return to the vineyard, so to speak! We've been up on the mountain top, brothers and sisters, but now we must come down in the valley and get the hard job done—yes, get it done! . . . and take the work of our great leader and our organization to the people!" Big, strong, standing center-stage before them, Ornette now raised his fist. "Yes, *the people!*—for that's where our strength comes from!"

"Amen!" cried Gideon the poet, momentarily jumping up.

"Yeah!" went up a shout from much of the audience.

Mary Dee had turned to watch Ornette. She could see his excitement, his glory, in this self-appointed role to which he seemed so naturally fitted. He continued speaking and as the minutes passed his voice became harsh, strident, more impassioned, but she could see both the fire and the joy in his eyes as, fist raised high again, he exhorted them to more strenuous effort, more faithful, fanatical, devotion to "Blackness." "We need to see ourselves in a new, a brand new, way—in a *Black* way! We need to shut out everything else! *Everything!"* Another great shout of approval went up from the audience. Knight's eyes were on the speaker now. He watched him as intently as Ornette himself had watched Jesse Lumpkins that morning, yet did not applaud with the others when the great outbursts from the audience came. He rather seemed reflective, contemplative; even, at times, sad. Then his consuming eyes went past Ornette and out over the huge audience, the sea of faces—there they were, the thousands of black poor, and not so poor, their earnest, restive, countenances turned up toward Ornette as if from this fresh, new, eloquent, young leader they derived a truly magic nourishment, especially when he raised his fist and cried, "We need to see ourselves, my brothers and sisters, just like the white folks see us—*Black!*" Another great shout went up from the crowd—as now Knight's eyes in utter astonishment and fascination, perhaps also grudging envy, seemed glued on Ornette, for it had been months, if not years, since he had heard any such hysterically emotional response to his own platform utterances. Again, not applauding, he seemed sad. It showed in his manner— and Mary Dee noticed. Then for a moment, unconsciously, his left hand groped to his right breast where in his inside jacket pocket rested a folded sheaf of papers—his speech, on which he had la- bored and struggled for weeks. It was a critical occasion for him and he sensed it—yet he somehow looked fragile, weak. Soon he felt faint.

For five minutes Ornette's voice fairly boomed over the loud- speaker system. He was perspiring freely now. Then his muscles tensed and his breath went short as the excitement inside him seemed on the verge of exploding. It was as if he thought the meeting itself had now reached its climax—that everything follow- ing would be anticlimatic. He wheeled and, as though it were a magic wand, waved his right hand high over his head in a gesture of command to some mysterious, unseen, subordinate; a phantom. High up behind the rostrum then and over the heads of the plat- form guests, just as the houselights dimmed, a screen, a movie screen, lit up. At once now from a projector heretofore unnoticed in the center aisle, one giant word, its letters at least two feet high, flashed up on the screen—"ZENAPHOBIA!"

Knight started, and spun around—surprise and questioning an- ger on his face. Ferdinand Bailey, beside him, almost sprang from his chair in trying to wheel around, along with all the other gap- ing platform guests, to see. "What's Ornette been up to now?" Ferdinand cried to Knight. Mary Dee, having no inkling yet "Zen- aphobia" was Ornette's deliberate misspelling of her word "xeno- phobia" in order, he hoped, to make it more easily pronounced, was as mystified as the others—but not for long.

"*Zenaphobia!*" shouted Ornette, pointing up at the screen, sweat running off his face—"*Zenaphobia!*" The surprised, puzzled, audi- ence sat hushed. "Do you know, brothers and sisters, what that great word up there means?" he cried rhetorically. "Well, let me tell you!—let me tell you about it, and where it came from . . . and who thought it up!" He turned now, a big grin on his face, and looked over at Mary Dee. Her heart began pounding, though she did not know why. "Yes, now, what does that big word mean?" he yelled—"I don't have my dictionary with me tonight but I can tell you! I've looked it up. It means be *your own* man and woman! —be true to yourself and your race, your Blackness! Know the outsider, the white man, for what he is—the enemy! Depend on *yourself!* Stay away from him—keep him out! He is a contaminator! We ought to know—we've suffered from him long enough to know! So keep him out! *That's* what Zenaphobia means!" The applause was instant, loud, and prolonged, though some were still puzzled. Then it hit Mary Dee—with the sudden force of an electric shock. She realized now it was "xenophobia" Ornette spoke of. But why, she thought, had he turned and given her the grinning, all-knowing look!—they had never discussed xenophobia. "We must do our *own* thing!" Ornette went on loudly. "Develop ourselves—be *Black!* Be proud! Be angry! Keep the white man away from us!—he's done us enough dirt! Keep him away, I say—ostracize him! Eat, drink, breathe, and *think* Black!—yes, till it becomes a *state of mind!* It will save us! It's called *Zenaphobia!* That's its name! It will cleanse our minds, give us a new outlook— yes, a new state of mind! *Zenaphobia!* Let me hear it, then!"

The thundering response came up like a whirlwind—"ZENA-*PHOB*-IA!"

Ornette, panting, paused now and smiled—then turned again and looked over at Mary Dee. "Now, my friends, I'm going to introduce to you the person that came up with that powerful idea!— one of our most serious, yes, devoted, young members, the epitome of all a black woman should be; smart, cagey, hard-working, yet compassionate and kind; and above all, dedicated to Blackness!" Fear, and a furtive guilt, seized Mary Dee; she shuddered. "Yes," cried Ornette, "and although she don't know that I know it, *she's* the one that came up with the theory, the wisdom too, of Zenaphobia! And because of her other work in the organization as well, she will soon, I'm dead sure, be moving up—where she will be of even greater service to our leader, John Calvin Knight— closer to him, a lieutenant, his adviser and colleague. It's bound to happen, brothers and sisters!—I predict it! She's ready—and capable! I know she's quiet and retiring, don't care for publicity, but I want her to stand up and let you see her—so you'll remember her as one of our great and advancing members!" He turned with another beaming smile—"Miss Mary Dee Adkins!"

Mary Dee could not move—she seemed frozen to her chair. In the audience, necks craned to see who was meant, yet no one stood up to be seen.

"Mary Dee!" cried Ornette—"Stand up and let the brothers and sisters see you!" Now Knight and Ferdinand, sickly expressions on their faces, turned around—as if to verify Mary Dee's actual presence. This seemed at last to arouse her and she got weakly to her feet. When the audience saw her, they broke into wild applause. Though she sat down at once, the clamor continued. "Stand up again, Mary Dee!—let 'em see you good!" exhorted Ornette. Once more, briefly, a shy, embarrassed smile on her face, Mary Dee stood, to loud and prolonged applause. Griselda in the audience, her breath coming fast, her heart, strangely somehow, sinking, leaned far forward in her seat the better to see, to search, the face and motives of this unfamiliar, captivating woman about whom she suddenly now felt a fateful premonition. The beauty of the standing, rising, star dismayed her, and she sat back for a moment and tightly closed her eyes.

Knight had turned around to the front again and now, quiescent, stoical, stared out over the audience, though seeming to see nothing specific, concrete. Worried Ferdinand leaned sideways and said something to him, but Knight ignored him and seemed communing with himself.

Meantime Ornette had taken up a guttural chant. Looking up to the lighted screen before clenching his fist again and holding it up and out before him in a form of salute, he began to bellow in heavy rhythm: "ZENAPHOBIA! ZENAPHOBIA! ZENAPHOBIA!" Soon the audience was on its feet, returning the clenched fist salute, as its cadenced, hoarse shouts of "Zenaphobia!" rent the air and seemed shaking the very foundations of the hall. As the din kept up, fervor swept the audience almost out of control. Ornette ran to the front edge of the stage now, his fist ever high in the air, and once more tried to lead the chanting shouts, but now many in the audience had left their seats and were rushing down the aisles toward the stage, where they massed in front and continued the wild cadenced delirium—"ZENAPHOBIA! ZENA-

PHOBIA! ZENAPHOBIA!" The thunderous chanting in unison, the rigid upthrust fists, the receptive frenzied faces, could only be likened to the Nuremberg rallies. Mary Dee, eyes wide, watching in awe, was plainly frightened. Moreover, she had never seen Ornette so violent, hypnotized, so wild and carried away, as by this new taste of leadership and power. She somehow felt he would never again be the same, and in this was confirmed in looking over at Rosabelle—sitting next to Mamie Campbell on stage—who watched her husband's frantic peregrinations with a strangely sober, almost dubious, gaze.

When fifteen minutes later Ornette, excited, perspiring, triumphant, had at last sat down, and the din and bedlam had subsided, then finally stopped, the audience again took their seats. Ferdinand Bailey now, nervously, apprehensively, got up and went to the lectern and, somehow with a brave smile, adjusted the microphone down to his dwarfed height. After waiting a full minute for the already drained and sated audience to quiet down and become attentive again, he at last cleared his throat to speak—to begin his introduction of Knight. But the crowd was still unsettled, many yet in happy side conversations about Ornette, and Ferdinand had twice to repeat his salutation—"Friends! . . . Brothers and Sisters!"—before making himself heard.

Meantime Knight had taken his speech from the inside pocket of his jacket and now sat trying to appear composed, if not serene, though he felt a stifling sense of dread. But in it all there was something far deeper. It was not what he would say when he spoke that troubled him, but how he felt, what he *was*, as man and leader, that produced such painful doubts. Tonight, he knew, would be crucial—Ornette, though he might not even have realized it himself, had smelled blood in the guise of a power coup and had loved every minute of it. Many things would—must—be settled tonight.

Ferdinand was now fully launched into his usual fiery—and loyal, devoted—introduction of his leader that he so loved to make in bringing Knight before a large audience. Tonight, however, the ritual was somehow unusually moving to Knight, for he realized, even now more than ever, that Ferdinand was his closest, indeed in many ways, his only friend. "Brothers and Sisters," Ferdinand was saying to them in his high, earnest voice, "when the national organization last met—that was spring a year ago in San Francisco; Lord, how time flies—little then did we dream that that could have been, for many of us, the last time we'd ever see our leader John Calvin. The rest you know—the insane attempt on his life, and so forth. But the Lord, only the Lord, decided it was not John Calvin's time yet, that he was too sorely needed amongst us, needed by the *people*, the benighted and downtrodden, needed to carry on the mighty work he had long ago undertaken under God's own imprimatur!"

"That's right!" someone on stage behind Ferdinand cried— "Speak the truth, Ferdie!"

"Now, thank God, his health has been restored and he has called us together—better late than never, my friends—from all over this great but sinful land, from wherever in it our black brothers and sisters yearn for freedom and justice! We've had a wonderful week together and now the time has come for us to part for another year, but not before our leader, new-born with fresh determination after his brush with cheated death, has told us those things, conceived in his own brain and heart, that will give vitality and direction—our own north star—to our efforts in the coming year! I'm so proud and honored once more then to give you our leader! . . . *our Messiah!*—John Calvin!"

Ornette, never more sincere and moved in his life, was the first on his feet leading the applause. At this the audience then stood and gave Knight a round of steady, prolonged, though no longer frenzied, applause. Ornette was not pleased—as he listened to the applause that far too soon subsided. He was angry. He rushed to the front of the stage once more, applauding till his hands stung; then, bristling with outrage, he faced them, rigidly at attention, and raised his clenched fist again in his former salute. Though hoarse now, he began shouting, croaking, chanting, as loudly as his lungs could furnish power—"ZENAPHOBIA! ZENAPHOBIA! ZENAPHOBIA! Damn it, brothers and sisters!—let me hear it for our leader, for our leader, for our leader!" Almost in tears now, he resumed his frenzied, raucous, cadenced chant—"ZENAPHOBIA! ZENAPHOBIA! ZENAPHOBIA! . . ."

Almost immediately the packed house took up the rhythmic beat of his impaired voice and soon the place again was rocking. Now Rosabelle rushed to Ornette's side and joined in his exhortations to the crowd, which by now was already at a peak of chanting frenzy. When under the momentum of the couple's vehement leadership the pandemonium continued without them, they went over to the lectern where Knight, his speech in his hand, now humbly stood. They stationed themselves on either side of him, before each of them raised one of Knight's reluctant arms in a gesture of victory. The house went wild. Finally Knight returned the now useless, inadequate, inapplicable, speech to his pocket, disengaged himself from Ornette and Rosabelle, and began feebly waving the people to take their seats. It took him fully three minutes to succeed. The din was deafening. When it had finally stopped and everyone was seated, Knight stood before them a humble, grateful man. He tried to begin talking, but choked up and had to wait. Griselda, on the edge of her chair, watching from the audience, was also near tears—she wanted to rush up onto the stage to him, comfort him, tell him of his greatness, how much she loved, worshipped, him; then she was shocked to realize this would be the very madness that would bring him—them—disaster. She moved back in her chair and put her face in her hands.

Finally Knight began to speak. "I hope you will bear with me," he said to them—". . . I hope you will listen to what I have to say, and without applauding; though there will be little to applaud about." Mary Dee's eyes were upon him; she did not know what to make of him—this strange, troubled, tormented man. He seemed to her to have at least two distinct presences, two personalities— one fierce and cruel, the other humble and indecisive. Her eyes left him now and wandered out into the audience. Soon again she saw the strange, comely girl, by color so conspicuous in this throng, who, save for her immoderate Afro hairdo, looked white. But now the girl's face was distraught, almost tearful, as her eyes went up ever lovingly to Knight. She puzzled Mary Dee, stirred her curiosity. Who was she? she thought. But Knight now, to her sudden realization and surprise, was saying: "My dear friends, I come before you a confessing sinner." She was transfixed. "Oh, I haven't stolen any money," he said—"ha, haven't raped anybody; haven't even consciously lied to you. None of that, brothers and sisters. My sin is greater than that. My sin is that I've kept from you my doubts. My *doubts*, friends!" He paused now, seeming not to know how to explain it. A hush had fallen over the huge crowd.

At last Ferdinand, hiding his concern with a half playful, indulgent, laugh, said loudly to Knight: "What are they, John Calvin!"

Knight turned and studied him almost as if he had never seen him before, and even when, turning back around to the front, his answer came, it was not responsive. "My doubts," he said to them, "have run so deep they've been a cruel burden to me. I'd like to be able to say to myself, and to you, my friends, that that's why I haven't shared them with you, but it would be a lie. My doubts, I can only think, somehow come out of our history, our suffering—as Dr. King put it, 'our long night of suffering'—but beyond that I'm afraid to speculate. Our history and our suffering, you know, are one and the same thing—they can almost be used interchangeably. Our suffering—our history of suffering, if you will—has been so terrible, so outlandish, so extreme, it has caused me to doubt the very existence of God."

"Oh! . . ." a whisper of reproof went through the audience.

"Did God early abandon us in our history?—or did He himself *decree* our history?" Knight's eyes were feverish, wild.

"Oh! . . ." Faces turned to one another.

"Why has more suffering been inflicted on us than on any people in the history of the world? Why is it? If there's an answer, for me it's remote—deep, deep, as it were, in the recesses, the shadows, the utter backwaters of time. But if we don't know the answer, how can we put together a strategy for survival? Recently, especially since I was shot, this has been my most perplexing doubt—and it affects the very direction of this organization. It's a great mystery—we see on every hand the results of our suffering, what it's done to us, made of us, as human beings, yet we don't know why we were chosen to bear this terrible history."

Mary Dee watched Knight with burning, piercing eyes. She had become so involved, engrossed, in what he was saying she had almost forgotten where she was. Her emotions overflowed. Her eyes were stinging. She too, and recently, had thought similar thoughts—and about her own life as well. She considered the question of "why" both relevant and profound—critical. She also for the first time thought Knight himself profound and listened now with absolute absorption, rapport, and sympathy. It was as if he were speaking directly to her. The central question he raised—of "why"—had become almost personal.

"I learned from my father," said Knight, "that we blacks are what we were made. If people think we're strange, or irrational, that we often act outside of logic, if we seem filled with hate and rage, which is the case, it's because we were made so." However, he spoke into the microphone with seeming moderation, as if loathe to unduly raise his voice; it appeared deliberate. Indeed, he soon said, "I speak to your minds now, not to your emotions, though I know they can't for long remain separate. But, you see, I raise the question again of my doubt—as I told you, I come before you a confessing sinner. Let me share then my doubt—is not the 'xenophobia' you've shouted here tonight more a symptom than a cause? I ask you. And are we not looking for causes?—the 'whys'? God knows we know from tragic experience the symptoms. Please apply your *minds* to this." But he had still spoken temperately.

A woman in the audience, seated near Griselda, had gone to sleep. There was yawning and restlessness in various other parts of the hall. Knight sensed it and was filled with angry frustration. For a moment he considered taking the written, more familiar, trite, and inflammatory speech out of his pocket, but at last decided against it. Yet as he continued speaking, and the apathy spread, he somehow grew bitter, anguished, considering himself a dupe and unappreciated. His extemporization became more heated, barbed, then, and criticism soon crept into his tone. "I will not detain you much longer," he said with unconcealed sarcasm. "But why did I ask you to refrain from applauding me as I spoke?—a request you've so dutifully obeyed. Why did I rather imply I meant tonight to speak to your *minds*? It was because of the enormity, the hugeness, of the doubts I've raised here in full confession!" His emotions, his hurt and anger, had mounted to the point he had began to feel weak, faint, again. With both hands now he seized the sides of the lectern as he spoke. "Here tonight I have raised the one, the vital and overriding, issue affecting our organization!" he cried out now almost helplessly, shaking his head crazily and grimacing. "Hear me, brothers and sisters!—is 'xenophobia' the answer? Hear me!" But his voice had so weakened he could hardly speak. ". . . hear me . . . is *Blackness* really the answer! . . ."

"Yes—it is!" said a stern voice behind him on the platform. He turned around to see the portly, grey-haired man standing. It was

Jesse Lumpkins—frowning, outraged. Lumpkins continued standing, defiantly.

The now-awakened audience was nevertheless ambivalent, confounded—in their hearts agreeing with Lumpkins, yet knowing, respecting, admiring, Knight. There was silence—and tension. Knight, gripping the lectern desperately now, turned back around to the audience, ignoring Lumpkins, who finally sat down. "It's an issue, my friends, we can no longer ignore!" he said, almost maudlin distress in his face. "Can we overcome by withdrawing into ourselves?—by chanting 'xenophobia?' Is this our strategy for survival and victory?"

"What's *your* strategy?" shouted Lumpkins.

Knight, though keeping his quivering lips near the microphone, turned around to him again and said weakly, "I have already confessed, Jesse."

"Confessed what?" Lumpkins had stood up again.

"That I have no strategy—only doubts. . . ." With that Knight seemed to wilt. Then he slipped to his knees behind the lectern, and finally collapsed prostrate on the floor.

Ferdinand, Ornette, Rosabelle, and Mamie Campbell all rushed to him. "Get some water!" Mamie cried to Rosabelle—"Loosen his collar, Ornette!"

Knight was on his back now on the floor, Ornette feeling his wrist pulse. Ferdinand rushed to the microphone—"Mr. Knight has fainted! . . . Is there a doctor present?"

The entire audience was standing now. All eyes were on the stage. Ornette, after loosening Knight's shirt collar, bent down to him again. "How do you feel, John Calvin?" Knight, conscious, though barely so, looked up at him and tried to speak, yet seemed unable. Soon two physicians were on the stage. They examined Knight, after which they had him lifted and laid across three chairs, while someone went to call a fire department ambulance.

Mary Dee sat stunned, shaken. She had developed, and quite suddenly, a terrible compassion for Knight, a deep-felt admiration for what she considered his sacrifices and essential integrity. There was also the fact she had loathed, abhorred, the audience's wild, frenzied "xenophobia" demonstration. It had frightened her out of her wits and she was horrified to have finally realized it had all come about by her chance use, in a moment of petulance, of this provocative word when talking on the telephone to an annoying student doing research on the Congress and Knight.

Suddenly now she saw another commotion on the stage, only thirty feet from where she sat. A young woman, by appearance white, and excited, gesticulating, was standing over Knight as he lay across the chairs. Suddenly then she remembered the Afro hairdo and at once recognized her as the strange girl she had seen in the audience. Since his seizure, Knight had not talked, but now, the girl keening over him, fright and mortification at exposure plain on his face, he was trying vainly to discourage her anguished, almost distracted—and far too intimate, familiar—entreaties. Though Mary Dee, in the general commotion, could not hear what the girl was saying, she could see and with no difficulty interpret, understand, what was taking place—it was clear to her the girl was distraught, almost hysterical, over Knight's sudden illness and collapse. The relationship was obvious for everyone—including astounded, unbelieving, Jesse Lumpkins—to see. Mary Dee would think about this in the days to come, for it explained much of what, on a far vaster scale, had taken place in the hall tonight.

When the ambulance came, Mary Dee still watched the girl, who, though suffering Ferdinand's and Ornette's shocked, baleful gazes, left, along with Mamie and Ferdinand, behind Knight bound for the hospital on a stretcher. Mary Dee could not help it —inside her now she felt toward the girl a slowly simmering rage. Meanwhile, the audience—confused, frustrated, inarticulate—at last began filing out of the great hall into the chilly November night.

Thus ended, on this symbolic note, the national meeting of the Black Peoples Congress.

617

Book IV

Crucible

Chapter 1

But well before the night of the big rally Griselda had known all along she should stay out of sight, especially far away from Knight, during the week of the national meeting. She had perfectly understood the peril to him—with all the Central Planning Committee members in town and crucial discussions under way about the future direction of the organization. She had vowed to herself to contain, discipline, herself—her feelings—and refrain from even trying to communicate with Knight. Yet she could not help hoping he finally would want to see her and would seek her out again as he had on the night, recently, when she had so willingly, desperately, given all of herself to him. Then Nancy Hanks had arrived on the scene and everything—plans, vows, resolutions—quickly changed, vanished into thin air.

Still feeling the surprise, the shock and dismay, at seeing her mother that morning walk into the organization's office, Griselda, under threats, had returned with Nancy Hanks to the latter's downtown Hilton hotel. They had wrangled on the bus all the way there and as soon as they entered Nancy Hanks' room, Griselda turned on her mother heatedly: "If you think I'm coming back to San Francisco to live—ever—you're wrong. My life is here!"

"And *what* a life!" Nancy Hanks, throwing off her coat, said. "Here a man you lived with, who adored you, dies and leaves you the principal beneficiary in his will, leaves you stocks the lawyer says will appreciate in value, but are even now worth $80,000, and you say you can't leave Chicago—ha, and I guess your true-love—long enough to cooperate with the lawyers and go through the probate proceedings necessary to get this windfall! You're demented, Griselda! Well, this time you'll do as I say!"

"Sure, sure, you want to get your hands on that money—why else would you come all the way to Chicago looking for *me*? You hadn't done it before! Now you want me to go grubbing after

Marvin's money—when I treated him so abominably. I treated him awful, simply awful—I have no right to his money!"

"Don't feel so contrite—he didn't leave you everything." Nancy Hanks spoke scornfully. "There was of course a cash bequest to his British friend, Basil Thorne. I'll bet that young man won't stand on any ceremony in collecting his share. I don't care what you charge me with, I, as your mother, simply won't sit by and see you act so dumb, silly, so gauche. What in God's name's come over you since you took up with these misguided black people—or should I say, this misguided black man? What do you see in Knight? On the bus talking about your newly-adopted life you sounded like some kind of visionary or soothsayer. Frimbo! Who in heaven's name is that? . . . Is it another name for Knight, or what?—is he some kind of messianic seer? Is Frimbo the one who's got you hating money so? Honest to God, Griselda, it's true —you're demented. You pain me!"

"I know it. I've always done that."

"But on reflection maybe it was I who, though not meaning to, put a curse on you." Nancy Hanks, having just sat down, sighed and waved Griselda to a chair. "Sit down," she said—"I want to tell you something about that . . . something I've withheld from you all your life, that's very relevant, I think, to this penchant, this insistence, you have of identifying yourself with blacks."

Quizzically, Griselda looked at her, but instead went over to the window and gazed down through the crisp November sunlight at the traffic on Michigan Boulevard, then across at the beautiful fall flowers in Grant Park.

"Sit down, I say, Griselda."

Griselda, still facing the window, did not move. "What is it you have to tell me?" she said. "I'm sure it's not good news—you never bring good news."

"It's simply that the affinity you somehow feel for blacks comes honestly. Your father was part black."

Griselda turned around. "What do you mean?"

"I mean you yourself have black blood."

Griselda stared at her.

"Your father's maternal grandmother was an African slave in the Caribbean."

Griselda came over and eased down in the chair now, her eyes not leaving her mother's hardened face. Finally she said, "Is this what you just meant by saying you had put a curse on me?"

". . . Well, maybe I didn't mean a curse. . . ."

"Oh, that's what you meant, all right."

Nancy Hanks bristled. "The word was poorly chosen. Listen, I was your father's mistress knowing he had black blood, and would certainly have married him had he been able to get free of the wife he already had. So if I put a curse on you I put one on myself too—voluntarily, of my own free will. Your father was a noble, exciting man. As I say, the word was poorly chosen."

For a moment Griselda sat in a deep study. "It's anything but a curse," she finally said. "It's a blessing. I can't have much black blood though—you can see it's hardly discernible. I wish I had more. At last, Mother, you brought good news—and I don't mean about money."

Nancy Hanks shook her head. "It's incredible—Griselda, really, I fear for your sanity. You're poor, I'm poor, yet you hate money."

"I don't hate money. It's just not important to me. I don't care about living the kind of life most people like. I dig Frimbo. Also I like to be a part of something, some big project, maybe, where a lot of people are involved in trying to help other people, trying, for instance, to help lessen their load, their unhappiness. I'm happier when I'm doing something I think's worthwhile—like working with the Black Peoples Congress. I've known a lot of unhappiness myself, so I know what it's like. My life was a nightmare—I was at my wit's end until I got involved with these people, with this organization. Now I learn, at this late date, that *I'm* part black. What if John Calvin knew? . . ."

"Tell me about this Knight," Nancy Hanks said. "Is your relationship with him personal? Isn't it Knight himself—rather, than the organization—you're really involved with?"

Griselda hesitated.

"Are you in love with him, Griselda?"

"Yes." The reply was quiet, musing.

"Of course. I knew it. I just wanted to hear it from you. Is it returned?"

There was another pause. "I think so."

"You think so! Don't you know?"

"I'm not sure that *he* knows. There are many complications. It's not easy for him."

"I should think it isn't!—the way he's always inveighed against

623

whites. I don't see how you ever got accepted by these people in the first place."

"But they finally did accept me, in a way, and it saved me. I was in a terrible state. They saved me—I need them now more than they need me."

"This is absolutely unfathomable. It's crazy! Griselda, you're my daughter but a real weirdo."

"You may think that, but I make sense to myself. It all falls into place—especially now since I know I'm part black; not much black, but enough for it to have meaning for me, enough for it to be a symbol of something far more significant and important to me. Yes, Mother, you finally brought good news."

"If you consider that good news, you're welcome. At least, though, I hope it will furnish you with enough sanity to return with me to San Francisco to talk to the lawyers and help in the probate of that will—so that maybe you'll have something besides Frimbo and Knight, something that will *jingle in your pocket*. Honest to God, Griselda! . . . I've never—"

"Okay, I may come—if it won't take long. But my work is here —I hate that place. Except for my time with Alan, I was miserable there. Yes, I'll come, but only to get that money, for I know a place where it's needed, badly needed—where it'll be used by an organization that's trying to give people hope. Yes, Marvin's money will be put to the highest use, I assure you—one I think really he himself would approve of. Despite his foibles, his near insanity, Marvin at heart was a very idealistic man. I'm almost sure he'd approve."

Nancy Hanks, a combative, incredulous, look on her face, leaned forward in her chair, her hawklike eyes piercing Griselda. "What on earth are you talking about?—what are you planning to do with this money? Griselda, don't tell me about some damned hare-brained scheme you've suddenly thought up—to give this money to Frimbo, or Knight, or the black poor, or to anybody except yourself and those close to you."

Griselda smiled—a bitter, satiric smile. "Those close to me are the very ones I have in mind, Mother—those who've really been close to me. Yes, I'll return to San Francisco with you just long enough to go through the legal red tape necessary to get poor Marvin's largess to me. Poor, poor, Marvin—it's incredible that he's dead. I can't believe it. I didn't know he had a heart condition; he never mentioned it, and you know he was always feeling sorry for himself, complaining about his ills. It's something my mind can hardly accept. But I know—for he was a true visionary—that he'd approve of what I'll do with his money. It won't be wasted."

Nancy Hanks shook her head in utter futility and exasperation. "Oh, my God—what a burden you are to me sometimes. Yes, it's the curse, I think."

When two hours later, Griselda returned to the office, she went directly to the washroom and stood gazing at herself in the mirror. She bent forward and scrutinized her face closely, minutely. It looked the same, she thought, despite her mother's astounding revelation—though now she did think she saw, though in the vaguest way, a slightly deeper coloration of the skin, a faintly duskier hue, of which she'd earlier not been aware. Yet her mother had shocked her—what she had revealed was almost beyond believing, even more incredible, if possible, than Marvin's death. She pinched her cheek now, to see if the color reacted. It did—the spot grew rosy, then rosier, yet somehow darker than she had imagined it before. She believed her mother now—this was proof, she thought, of what she had said. But there had not yet been time for her, Griselda, to fully react to the disclosure; she was still bewildered, though it had possibly already begun to change her way of viewing her life. She imagined it better enabled her to think, and feel, black.

It all emboldened her. She felt less defensive—about the organization, as well as Knight. She was even determined for the rest of the week of the national meeting to hide no longer—she would move about as freely as others, take her proper place in the week's events, and do whatever she thought she should to help make the meeting a success. She would even go to the rally. It was something she had not dared dream of, but now she would go and hear Knight's great speech. Moreover, she would sit as far up front as possible. Now she thought of Knight again. Would she tell him what she had learned—about her blackness? The thought frightened, shocked, her—by all means not! She could not possibly do it—anyway, he would not believe her. Besides, he would think her either crazy or designing. She must keep the secret locked inside herself—and also the secret of her new-found financial ability to help the organization. But she realized now her love for him had reached a new high, a rising tide that threatened to engulf her and her extravagant expectations. She must therefore, she thought, be careful, cautious, anything but headstrong or impulsive. Yet it was something she was not sure she could do, though she sensed danger and disaster.

*   *   *   *   *

After the debacle the night of the rally, Knight had been kept in the hospital for two days of tests. However, when nothing was found to afflict him save physical and mental strain and fatigue, he was discharged. But he feared the embarrassment not only of returning to the office but of even going home to the peril of the telephone. Also, at times now, he seemed not to know where he was or what he was doing; he became discouraged, realizing what a blow his leadership had taken as a result of Griselda's behavior —her maudlin, hysterical, public display of her love. Her carryings-on had continued even in the ambulance to the hospital, all in Ferdinand's and Mamie's presence. Mamie, though alarmed and trying to quiet her, was, knowing many of the facts, not at all surprised. But Ferdinand was mortified and angry—his worst fears had been confirmed.

Of course neither Ferdinand nor Mamie could know that Griselda had become a very different, a wholly new, person since her mother's arrival and revelations. Also, throughou* the whole week of the national meeting, and despite all the activity and other distractions, she had undergone pain and contrition over Marvin, grieving for him now, and somehow feeling the condition, the apparent heart ailment, Nancy Hanks had said had caused his death had been brought on by his distress and helplessness over her and her refusal to see him; and his act of leaving her much of his estate, even though he had no relatives, only heightened, exacerbated, her anguished feelings—if there had been any doubts about how he felt about her, she thought, they were demolished by this his last and magnanimous act.

Yet nothing lessened her passion—now her boldness—where Knight was concerned. She came to see him both days he was in the hospital, luckily at the time encountering neither indignant Ornette nor long-suffering Ferdinand, and talked to him about what she referred to as "our future." Knight at first had grimaced as if in pain, but then, and really for the first time, began to feel sorry for her—for it amazed even him to think that throughout all these lonely hospital hours his only thoughts had been of Mary Dee Adkins. The realization, bringing guilt, made him now almost tender to Griselda. The first day, Monday, he was home, she phoned at noon to ask if she might come see him, that she must very soon return to San Francisco, for possibly two weeks, on business. He was vague, unenthusiastic, seeming somehow otherwise engaged or preoccupied, and, though he was not curt, finally begged off. He said he would explain later. It made her wonder.

The truth was that Ferdinand had earlier been there to pass on to him information Ferdinand, for obvious reasons, had feared telling him the weekend Knight was hospitalized. It was the ominous, disquieting news that Jesse Lumpkins, and another Central Planning Committee member, Vilas Lee, from Richmond, Virginia, had stayed over following the national meeting and rally for the purpose of having a conference with Knight. It could be no secret, Knight realized at once, why the meeting was being sought. He also knew he had no choice but to assent. The meeting was arranged for 3:00 that afternoon and Ferdinand was asked to be present and to bring Ornette. At 3:15 Ferdinand arrived with Lumpkins and Lee but said he had been unable to contact Ornette, though he had left the message about the meeting with Rosabelle. But Knight barely heard, for, admitting the two C.P.C. members, he was so visibly nervous he could hardly talk.

Ornette, however, was not idle. He was at Mary Dee Adkins' house—seated, for the first time, in her parlor. He had come quickly after phoning her and now found himself in a setting in which neither of them felt comfortable. He, unaccustomed to such elegance, such staid luxury, could hardly conceal his feelings of resentment. Nor could she, in her very secret heart, easily accommodate herself to the sight of Ornette seated in her father's great wing chair. Irene Adkins, on learning who was coming, had shown her objection by beating a hasty retreat upstairs, leaving Mary Dee to suppress a nervous sigh as she admitted Ornette. Entering, he barely looked at her. Her casual, sweatered, beauty only added to his discomfort. He was grim. "I want to get your okay on something, Mary Dee," he said.

She had closed the door and gone and sat in a delicate Italian chair at one side of the dead fireplace, at least twenty-five feet from him. "Okay on what, Ornette?" She tried to smile.

"What would you say to coming to work for the organization—to do program staff work—if they'd pay you some kind of salary?"

"Oh, gee." She looked at him as if to verify his seriousness. "I've never thought about anything like that—I haven't had any experience in that sort of thing at all."

"Who has? It's all new; new to everybody—including Knight."

"How is he? Is he out of the hospital?"

"Yeah—he came home this morning. Aw, Mary Dee, can't you see?—that's where all the trouble is. You saw it all the other night at that rally! He needs help. He needs more people around him who can really *help* him. You saw what happened—there in front of all those people!"

"Yes—he fainted. Didn't he?"

"Hell, I don't mean that! You saw that woman rush up on the stage and make a public scene over him."

"Who was she?—yes, I saw it. I thought she was some crank."

"She works in *our office*. I'm not kidding! She followed the organization here from San Francisco—a damn camp follower."

"Oh, don't say that about her." But Mary Dee studied him. "Isn't she white?"

Ornette almost stood up. "Of course she's white! Christ! That's the whole trouble!—John Calvin has let her get too close to him. I don't know *how* close, but you can see they're by no means strangers. That's the whole thing—it's bad, it's fatal, for the organization. Something's got to be done about it—fast!"

Only now, however, was Mary Dee reminded of Ornette's and Ferdinand's matchmaking antics the night of her studio party. At once she became cold. "What are you going to do?" she said, watching Ornette.

"Whatever we can—that's why I'm here. You could do a lot to change things! John Calvin needs someone close to him . . . to advise him, and—"

628

Her sarcasm interrupted him. "You mean a woman, don't you?"

". . . Well—he needs . . . *Yeah!*"—Ornette blurted it—"A woman! A *black* woman!—somebody who cares about the organization and its image, its image in the eyes of the people it's trying to help. What happened on that stage the other night was a disgrace. I blame John Calvin for it more than I do the woman—sometimes he makes me think he's weak, downright weak. He can see the harm in this—he's no dumbbell. Suppose you pushed yourself like she has into one of their organizations; got close to their *white* leader. You don't think they'd sit around and let you get away with it, do you? They'd get rid of you—some way."

Mary Dee said nothing, though secretly she agreed with him.

"Let's face it," Ornette said—"the organization's in a crisis. Some of the members of the Central Planning Committee are jumping up and down after seeing what happened up on that stage Friday night—they're no fools; they know what's maybe been going on! Jesse Lumpkins, a C.P.C. member, is even threatening to pull his Cincinnati organization out of the Congress—this could have a chain reaction, could start what would be like a run on a bank! Knight by his weakness is endangering the whole Congress —we need to get that woman out of the organization fast, and surround John Calvin with people who care about what we're trying to do for black poor people. Mary Dee, you can see that!" There was almost pleading in his voice.

But suddenly somehow Mary Dee was furious at him—at his presumption. "I'm not sure I see it at all," he said. "Where do you see me fitting into a miserable, chaotic situation like this? You say you want me to do what you call 'program' work."—she could barely conceal a sneer—"What kind of a 'program' have you got in mind? Not the white girl's, I hope."

Ornette almost lost control of himself. His loud, angry voice brought alarmed Irene Adkins, though out of view, to the top of the stairs. "Hell, I can see you ain't interested!" he said—"You ain't got the stamina, girl! You ain't got street guts!—you ain't a real, a committed, black woman, anyhow! Here we got a white woman—the enemy—who's not only infiltrated our organization, but its leader too! . . . and none of us are able to do a damn thing about it. Some of us don't even want to do anything about it!" He got up to go.

629

Mary Dee did not move from her distant chair. Unflinching, she said, "You haven't been forthright with me at all. You're not really serious about this 'program' bit, and you know it. Instead you see me as a kind of companion—if not new girlfriend—of Mr. Knight's. Isn't that it, Ornette?"

He stood glaring at her. "It's true it's not any *society bazaar* I'm asking you to take over," he said, sarcasm dripping.—"No, nothing like that! It's stronger stuff than that! But I can see plain as day it ain't your cup of tea. Forget it, Mary Dee—I'm sorry I took up your time. Forgive me!" His topcoat already grabbed up, he turned and started to the door. By the time she had finally got up to follow him, he had gone.

She was shaken. As she turned back around, her furious mother stood in view on the stairs holding a letter in her hand. "Oh, I don't know what's come over you!" Irene Adkins said. "But that ruffian will never enter this house again as long as *I* hold title to it! What's happened to you, Suky?—Good Heavens! . . . don't you have any feelings for your family, your household, what they've stood for, the memory of your father—any of this? I thought that burly brute would strike you! And all this happening the very day Mrs. Grier brings up this letter to me, from your sister—from little Jocelyn!" Holding up the opened letter, Irene Adkins' lip quivered as if, in her brandy, she would cry. "Its from Jocelyn, your baby sister, who's setting an example for you!—an example you should have emulated long, long ago! . . ."

"Mother, what in the *hell* are you talking about?"

"Oh, my goodness!—how gross you've become since you began associating with these roustabouts! Your father would turn in his grave!" Irene Adkins, weaving on the stairs, started down.

Mary Dee was on the verge of screaming. *"Mother,* what's happened about Jocelyn?"

"I'll tell you what's happened about her—she's engaged! . . . engaged to be married!—that's what! . . . and to that extremely nice young man, Geoffrey Hurd, whose been coming out from Boston to see her at Williams. Oh, it's wonderful news!—my sweet, sweet, little Jocelyn, who never, unlike some, gave me a minute's anxiety or worry in her whole life. Oh, I'm so happy for her—I at least have *that* much to be happy about. She's bringing him home with her week after next—at Thanksgiving—to meet us."

"Well, I'm glad," Mary Dee said at last, glumly—"Yes, he's a nice boy, from all I've heard. It *is* good news. . . . I agree, I'm sure he's a nice boy."

"Oh, he is—of course he is! And his family—it's a very old, free colored, family in Boston. They've had a modest merchandising and import business there for years. And one of them—an uncle of Geoffrey's—is a surgeon. Your father knew him at one time, from the medical conventions. Oh, this is such wonderful news! Jocelyn has already written your brother. I know Ronald will be just as happy, as proud, as we are. Ronnie's the only male of the family left, and, thank goodness, will soon be able to take charge." Irene Adkins had descended and now sat down unsteadily in a chair. "You won't have to worry with things much longer, Suky. Despite all his silly Marxist talk, Ronnie will develop into a very sane, responsible man—I'm sure of it. Ah, just think—my little Jocelyn engaged. How wonderful!" Irene Adkins now rose and hurried back to the kitchen to have Mrs. Grier prepare her another cup of "tea."

Mary Dee went up to her room and closed the door. The very thought—marriage—sent her mind spinning, then ready to explode with anger and despair. It was not for her, she thought— marriage. Never, now. She had once dreamed of it as though it were some shining celestial state of being taking her into an almost certain paradise. But all too soon the dream was shattered— obliterated. All was over. She stood staring out the window.

*   *   *   *   *

From the Adkins' house Ornette had gone straight home. Rosabelle, after vainly trying to learn why he was in such a brutal, ugly mood, gave him Ferdinand's message about the three o'clock meeting. It was almost four when Ornette arrived at Knight's to find Jesse Lumpkins angrily walking the floor and excoriating the leader to his face. "I ask you, John Calvin," Lumpkins said, his tone expostulating, "do you love blacks? You must, I keep tellin' myself, or you wouldn't have spent the last ten years tryin' to turn this country upside down for 'em! I was one of your first, your original, followers—you know that. You came to Cincinnati in 1965 and made a speech no one that heard it will ever forget, I'll tell you! My wife bawled like a baby, and it was all I could do to keep from doin' the same myself. You was a firebrand in those days! Afterwards I brought my little raggedy committee to see you—in that run-down motel where you was staying on Canter Street—and we pledged our support to you, everything we had and could beg, borrow, or steal. You probably don't remember these things, but I remember them all well."

Knight, sitting back in a corner of his living room, his face drawn, dejected, nodded agreement: "I remember them, Jesse."

"Then," said Lumpkins, "you asked us—I'll never forget it long as I live—if we had *'stayin'-power!'* Those was your very words. We said we had. You asked why we thought we had. Then I told you about my father, how he was pistol-whipped by a Mississippi sheriff till he was a vegetable the rest of his life—twenty-three years! And how my mother, that poor woman, then had to try to raise us—and fed us on grits and greens. Some of the others also told you things like that—some worse'n that. You asked us then to join up with you, and that we'd never regret it—that we'd turn things around, fight these crackers, give blacks new hope. Dr. King was goin' strong then, but you said we'd take up if and where he left off. You remember it, don't you, John Calvin!—*do you hear me?"*

Sitting near Ferdinand, Knight's face seemed pinched with pain. "Oh, Jesse, of course I remember it—I remember it all."

"All right then—what happened? What happened, John Calvin? You owe it to me, of all people—tell us what happened! You make a speech the other night—before fainting dead away—telling us all about your doubts, about how we should re-check our thinking about Blackness, and so forth; hinting Blackness might not, after all, be the answer. Then you faint and up runs this white gal and almost takes you in her arms! . . . *John Calvin,* it curdled my blood!—I saw all the work I'd done, all the stairs I'd climbed looking for new members, all the quarters, nickels, and dimes, I'd raised, and all the rest! I wanted to kill you!—God bein' my judge, I did! Now, as a member of the Central Planning Committee, I demand to know who this white woman is, how she got into the organization, what your personal relationship with her is, and whether or not you're goin' to get her out of the organization.

That's what me and Vilas here, speaking for the C.P.C., want answers to from you."

Ornette, admitted into the apartment by Ferdinand, had carefully tiptoed to a chair near Knight, opposite Ferdinand, and sat down. He was all eyes and ears—his feelings mixed; he revered Knight, yet was driven to distraction by his doings. He turned and looked at Vilas Lee, a heavy, rotund, light brown-skinned man who was nodding affirmation of everything Jesse Lumpkins was saying. Lee was also an organization veteran and Ornette sympathized with his present perplexity, his investment of time and effort in the organization, and his sorely troubled spirit, for Ornette felt the same.

"The young lady's name is Griselda Graves," Knight began saying in a rather numbed, singsong voice—he seemed almost in a daze—"She came to us in San Francisco and worked for nothing. She's extremely intelligent, capable, and loyal. When we moved the office here, she soon followed. Based on her prior record of service, I authorized her to be hired. As I say, she's loyal, but she doesn't agree that our efforts and public statements should be directed only at blacks—she has so much faith in what we're trying to teach that she thinks we're wrong, and unjust, in confining it to blacks. She says, in effect, blacks don't have a corner on misery."

"Oh, John Calvin! . . ." wailed Ornette now, unable any longer to remain silent, smiting his forehead with the heel of his hand—"don't be naive!"

Imperious Jesse Lumpkins, however, waving Ornette to silence, said to them, "Wait, wait—I got another question for him. The girl really acted up the other night, didn't she? She gave the impression—to me at least, John Calvin—that you two had some kinda personal thing, personal relationship, going. Huh? Is this impression correct?"

Knight made the mistake of hesitating.

"Is it correct?"

". . . No," he said at last, but weakly, the lie implicit in his manner.

At once, abruptly, Jesse Lumpkins stopped pacing the floor and turned and sat down, as would, in a court of law, a victorious cross-examiner.

633

The room was silent, tense. Even in the eyes of Ferdinand and Ornette, Knight sat convicted.

"There is only one remedy, John Calvin," now said Jesse Lumpkins—"Fire this woman tomorrow! Get her out of the office, out of the organization—and, I hope, out of your mind, your life! Oh, we need you, John Calvin—you're our *leader!*" At last Jesse Lumpkins' voice quavered with emotion. "Have you lost sight of your mission?—*your great mission?* If so, I want to know it! Why don't you speak up—why don't you explain things to us? We want to believe you! . . . oh, God! . . ." Portly, grey-haired Jesse Lumpkins, dentures ill-fitting, eyesight weak, hands coarse, gnarled, from hard manual labor, then broke into tears. At last, in a tremulous voice, he said, ". . . We still love you, John Calvin. . . ."

"Yes! . . ." whispered Ferdinand, choked with emotion.

It had started tears in Ornette's eyes now. There was a moment of universal and embarrassed silence. But Ornette soon regained control of himself, saying to them, "This is enough for today, brothers—don't you think? We'll straighten this thing out—Ferdie and I. Give us a chance. We'll talk to John Calvin—he's been under a lot of strain, involved in staging the national meeting and all. It's a heavy responsibility, Jesse. Let's hold off a week or two —let me and Ferdinand talk with him. We'll give you a full report —you can bet on it. This thing can be worked out—John Calvin's been through *so much* in the last six months! We're lucky he's still alive. Now he's a nervous wreck—he really ought to have the next six months just to rest and get a hold of himself, get himself together. Listen, Jesse and Vilas, let Ferdie and I work on this thing for a week or so—we'll let you know what happens, how things come out. We'll give you a full report on the phone. Trust us. Alike, we're all dedicated to the organization, ain't we? Jesse, you and Vilas go on back home, now. Next week I'll bring you up to date on how this thing's coming along. It *will* be resolved, believe me—I'm talking about the girl." Ornette had spoken bluntly, grimly. Now he turned to Knight, who sat again in a kind of somber, bleak stupor. "John Calvin, we'll all get out of here now and let you take a hot shower and get in the bed and get some much-needed rest. How about it?"

Knight raised his weary eyes. "I'd very much appreciate that," he said.

Soon they all filed out. When down on the street Lumpkins and Lee had gone and Ornette and Ferdinand were also parting, Ferdinand, in a low voice, said thankfully to Ornette: "You saved the day! . . . thank God, Ornette, you saved the day—and maybe the organization too!" They clasped hands.

*   *   *   *   *

Nancy Hanks was itching, frantic, to leave Chicago and get home to press the probate proceeding. She had twice talked by telephone with the San Francisco lawyers, who assured her the legal complications requiring her daughter's cooperation and testimony were as real as when she had gone off to Chicago to search out Griselda. Nancy Hanks, moreover, daily grew more alarmed at the mounting expense of her continuing hotel stay. Yet, with $80,000 and more at stake, she was unwilling to let Griselda again out of her grasp.

On the other hand, Griselda, who had not been able to see Knight since his release from the hospital, and having been able to reach him briefly by phone only once, was determined not to leave with her mother until he would see her and they had talked. Also, in her naivete, she felt in his condition he might have need of her, that it would be callous, inconstant, of her to leave without some kind of explanation to him and her assurances of a prompt-as-possible return to Chicago. Since her short Monday morning phone talk with him she had phoned his apartment repeatedly, only to get no answer. She could not of course know the reason was that Ornette and Ferdinand, after the critical Monday afternoon meeting with Jesse Lumpkins and Vilas Lee, had, with her in mind, prevailed upon Knight to move in temporarily with Ferdinand. Though Knight had made a show of reluctance, the real fact was he welcomed this opportunity for a period of inaccessibility, hoping in the interim Griselda might have left, if only for the two weeks' stay she had mentioned, for San Francisco. He had not even gone to the office since his hospital release. Griselda, with the daily, almost hourly, pressure on her from her mother that they leave at once, coupled with Knight's strange eclipse and her failure so far to reach him, was frantic, near panic.

After two days and nights of vain attempts to reach him, she sought out Mamie Campbell—going in Mamie's office that morning and closing the door. "I've been trying to reach John Calvin," she said, the worry and distress plain on her face, "but he doesn't answer his phone and he hasn't been in the office. Do you know where he is?—has he gone out of town so soon after getting out of the hospital?"

Mamie sat at her desk observing her. "I don't know where he is," she said—truthfully, for at this point Mamie knew no more than Griselda—"He's probably hiding out somewhere, away from all telephones for awhile, till he gets to feeling better. When Ferdie comes in, though, I'll find out—he'll know." There was then a pause, as Mamie's eyes remained on Griselda. "You know, though," she said, "if I were you I'd let John Calvin alone for awhile. That was kind of an unfortunate scene you made there Friday night, at the rally—it's upset a lot of people."

"Why has it upset them, Mamie?

"Lord, girl, don't you know?—can't you see?"

"Yes—I'm not blind, nor, I think, all that dumb. But I did nothing wrong. That's what I want to get John Calvin to recognize —that's why I want to see him, talk with him. Mamie, I want to *change him!* Besides, I've got to return to San Francisco soon, real soon, to take care of some business, but I don't want to go without first seeing John Calvin."

"Okay—but try to be a little saner, steadier, can't you? Not so impulsive and upset. You don't want to make problems for him— or for yourself either—I'm sure. I'll try to find out where he is and let you know."

Griselda still went out perplexed. She felt harried, put upon, abandoned even by her friend Mamie. Also, any minute her mother would be calling again, furiously urging her to hurry and pack so that they could leave at once.

Later that morning Ferdinand Bailey phoned Mamie to tell her there would be a staff meeting that afternoon, but not in the office. They would meet in his apartment, at two o'clock. Knight and Ornette would be there, he said, and asked her to arrange to come —that it was important. Mamie, immediately sensing the difficulty, the purpose, agreed to be there.

Ferdinand's apartment was nicer, if slightly smaller, than

Knight's—also in a better black neighborhood. Ferdinand, when he could find time for it, was a camera buff—this was evident from the appearance of his unusual living room. There were photographs everywhere, in both black-and-white and color, some blown-up and leaning against the wall, others up on one wall. Most of course documented the activities, doings, of the organization over the years and portrayed a variety of localities, scenes, and personages, high and low; at least a half dozen candid shots were of Knight—one of them of a much younger Knight in an impassioned speech to an audience in Chattanooga. Also a beautiful ornamental Japanese screen, which Mamie Campbell adored, graced one corner of the room, and, like Knight's place, there were books in evidence.

Mamie on her arrival for the meeting was admitted by dwarfish Ferdinand—who seemed in false high spirits. But Mamie, knowing his mood, sensing his worry, apprehension, was almost certain some very crucial matter would be discussed; she also guessed, knew, what it would be. When, she thought, had there ever been a staff meeting held outside the organization office? When she entered the living room Ornette had not arrived and Knight was not in sight. She sat down on the sofa which doubled as a day bed and smiled at Ferdinand. "What's up, Ferdie?" she said.

"*Sh-h-h-h!*" His forefinger flew to his lips to silence her at the same time he nodded toward the bedroom. Mamie knew then that Knight was in there. Ferdinand came over to the sofa. "It's about Griselda! . . ." he whispered—"We've got to talk to John Calvin about her. . . . Oh, I dread it! But it's got to be done—somebody's got to do it. That's why I wanted you here. I told Ornette to keep his big mouth shut and let you and me do most of the talking. He promised. Ornette gets so upset; he's like a bull in a china shop—and you know how insulted and stubborn John Calvin can get. So you and I have got to try to handle this thing—there's a big hullabaloo brewing in the C.P.C. about Griselda and we've got to deal with it, try to head it off!"

"What should we say to John Calvin?"

"Lord only knows—we'll have to play it by ear! . . . But finally, *finally,* Mamie, we've got to tell him that Griselda must go!"

Mamie was troubled—and almost incensed. "This is a fine thing for *me* to be taking part in," she said. "I brought her into the

637

office, you know—back in San Francisco. John Calvin just went along with it—but not too willingly. Ferdie, I pass."

"No, you don't, either! The welfare of the organization's at stake. John Calvin's let her get too close to him—you can see, from the other night, it's developed into a bad, a dangerous, situation!" Little Ferdinand, the pitiful hump on his back looming larger than ever under his informal green and yellow pull-over sweater, was whispering so vehemently, excitedly, that little sprays of saliva escaped his lips, reaching Mamie's face and causing her to draw away. "Oh, Lord!" he went on distressfully, "what a mistake John Calvin's made—letting her get that close to him! . . . I didn't realize she was so aggressive."

"Ferdie, it takes *two* to tango, you know." Mamie was not smiling.

"Oh, I know, but—"

The doorbell rang. It was Ornette and the whispered tête-à-tête ended.

Now Knight entered the living room from the bedroom just as Ferdinand admitted Ornette at the front door. Knight, in shirt-sleeves, seemed rested and composed and spoke almost cheerily to Mamie and Ornette. "Ferdie's got some cokes back there," he said—"Will anybody have one?" It was only now the tension in his voice was detectable.

"No, thanks," said Ornette—"I need somethin' stronger than any coke." Mamie also declined and Knight sat down on the sofa beside her.

"Sit down, Ornette," ordered Ferdinand, taking a chair himself. "To get right to the point, folks, we've got to try to figure out how we deal with this issue Jesse Lumpkins has tossed in our laps like a hand grenade. If we don't, everybody's going to get hurt, I'll tell you that. To make a long story short—and I've told John Calvin this— I think Griselda's lost her usefulness to the organization." Ferdinand stopped—waited. No one said anything. "It's true, she's a very nice person," he went on—"intelligent, conscientious, a hard worker, and, in her way, loyal to the organization. But she lets her emotions get away from her. Maybe we shouldn't be blamed too much for letting her start with us, back in San Francisco, but when we came here, and she followed us, that should have been the tip-off. *Why* did she drop everything

638

and come here? Well, we pretty much know now—or at least can make a good guess—that it was because of John Calvin. She had *fallen for him.*" Ferdinand stopped again now—and waited.

Finally Mamie said, "I don't feel good about this thing at all. What if she did fall for him?—what's so outlandish about that? John Calvin wouldn't have so many thousands of people across the country his trusting followers if he didn't, by his personality, distinction, his magnetism, or whatever you want to call it, inspire this kind of fierce loyalty and hope—yes, even love. Griselda, though she's young, has had a very hard time, a troubled life—*I* can see her becoming emotionally involved with John Calvin's compassion and idealism and the way he's held out hope to thousands of people. I can see it."

Throughout the time Mamie was talking, Ornette in a suppressed frenzy was twisting in his chair, shaking his head, and grimacing. Finally he could restrain himself no longer. "But, Christ, Mamie—she's white!" he said. "She's the *enemy!*"

"Just a minute, now, Ornette." Ferdinand's hand went up in warning. "Remember your promise. But, Mamie, if the organization weren't involved, maybe what you say might sound reasonable—sure, might make a little sense. But the organization *is* involved. Here we are preaching Blackness, black self-reliance, race pride, black assertiveness and militancy, the whole bit, and then in front of over three thousand black folks Friday night, including all the members of the Central Planning Committee from across the country—the elders of the organization—a good looking white girl rushes up on the stage when John Calvin faints and starts making over him like crazy, bending down to him and crying hysterically, just like she was his wife. Can anyone say the organization's *not* involved?"

Ornette heedlessly spoke up again—he was ruthless, his jaw was set, and Ferinand knew better than to try further to keep him quiet. "Mamie wasn't at the meeting Monday when Jesse Lumpkins and Vilas Lee came to John Calvin's apartment," Ornette said. "They had come spoiling for trouble—no doubt about it—but we asked them to hold off and give us a chance to go into this thing ourselves and see if we couldn't come up with some kind of solution. These are good, *sincere,* men, I tell you!—Jesse and Vilas." He had turned now and was speaking directly to Knight.

639

"But, John Calvin—and you must forgive me; you know we all love you and would follow you into the fire—but you, our leader, you who was at least a party to precipitating this whole thing, this incident, in the first place, sat there right through that meeting and hardly said anything until you were asked, or challenged, to talk. I couldn't understand it!—can't understand it now. Now here it's the same today—here we are sitting talking about something we don't know a fraction as much about as you do. Yet you sit there and say nothing. It's not criticism, John Calvin, I'm expressing, so much as downright puzzlement. . . . *Have* you been seeing the girl outside the office? . . ."

"Ornette! . . ." Ferdinand said.

"Well, *has* he? Ferdie, you said she carried on in the ambulance, and later when you got to the hospital, worse than she did up on the stage at the rally. *Has* he been seeing her?"

Though Knight's face was a kind of rough, dark mahogany mask, he looked stricken. "Of course not," he lied, then remembered too late that Mamie Campbell knew better. His hand began to shake.

Ornette noticed. "Well, John Calvin, the organization's definitely involved, dangerously involved, ain't it? And you're the leader of the organization. Besides that, you know more about what the true facts are than anybody here. Do *you* see a problem about Griselda? And if you do, what solution have you got?"

Knight's eyes were blazing now—"Ornette, are you cross-examining me?" Ornette's mouth fell open. "The only solution," Knight, subdued, finally said, "is that the girl must eventually be persuaded to give up the organization."

"Who's going to persuade her to do *that*?" said Mamie Campbell.

"I will," Knight said—"at the proper time, and under the proper circumstances. She's leaving town, possibly this week, for awhile—she's returning to San Francisco on business. While she's away, we can—I can—write to her, explaining things, the delicacy of the situation, and so forth. In that way we may be able to spare her feelings some."

Mamie Campbell looked at him aghast.

"Did *she* tell you she was going to San Francisco, John Calvin?"

Ornette said, his eyes almost boring holes into Knight.

"Yes."

"When was that?—since you got out of the hospital?"

Knight flew into a rage. *"God damn it!*—I won't have you cross-examining me, Ornette!"

"Ornette, shut your mouth!" cried Ferdinand.

Ornette at last sat stammering, whispering, babbling incoherently to himself. "Yeah, it figures, all right," he said half-aloud, his voice dripping anger and sarcasm. "It figures. He's still in contact with the chick." He turned to Ferdinand and Mamie—"I feel sorry for the *girl* now, no foolin'. She can't help it because she's white. But John Calvin could!"

Knight sat glowering at him. "Sometimes, Ornette, I think you're disloyal to the organization," he said—"to its leadership!"

"Not to both," Ornette snapped—"there's a difference."

"All right—then to *me.*"

"Oh, John Calvin, I don't want to be disloyal to you!" Ornette spoke in great distress. "Don't *make* me!"

"Please—let's stop going into personalities!" cried Ferdinand again, his fear more evident than ever. "There's too much involved." Yet he turned to Knight. "But what do you think we should do, John Calvin—in dealing with Jesse Lumpkins and the C.P.C.?"

"Just let me handle it," Knight said impatiently. "I'm leaving tonight for New York for a few days. By the time I return, Griselda will probably be in San Francisco. As I said, I'll write to her and try to explain the whole thing. I don't want to injure her —any more than she's been injured already. She deserves better."

"She sure does," said Mamie.

"I know all that!" Ornette said. "But the organization's been injured too! What about the organization?"

"That doesn't happen to be your responsibility alone, Ornette!" said Knight—"*yet.* So keep your shirt on!"

Whereupon Ornette went into a stubborn, silent pout. In this atmosphere the meeting soon broke up and Knight made ready to leave town.

Back at the office thirty minutes later, Mamie, although she had promised her otherwise, was reluctant to say anything at all to

Griselda about Knight or his whereabouts. She felt sensitive, guilty, and went in her office and closed the door. Yet hardly five minutes had passed before she heard the timid knock and knew it was Griselda—who entered with a dejected, almost distraught, look on her face.

Mamie feigned a start—quickly smiling and cheerful. "Oh, yes —I forgot! John Calvin's gone to New York."

Griselda, having closed the door, stood as if glued to the floor —studying Mamie. "Were you able to find out how long he'll be gone?" she said.

"For some days, I think, Griselda—a week, maybe. You said you had to go to San Francisco; why don't you go ahead—ha, and forget John Calvin?" Mamie's eyes sparkled falsely as she laughed.

"You're withholding something from me, Mamie," Griselda smiled, then sighed. "But that's all right—I'll go on out to San Francisco, get it over with, and come back." Slowly she turned to go, shunning further mention of Knight.

"Griselda,"—Mamie called to her, but then lost her nerve. Griselda turned around to her, though, and waited. ". . . Griselda, I wish I could talk to you. But my thoughts are so mixed up I don't really know what I think, much less what I want to say. You're a nice person, a very nice person—everybody knows that —a sweet person, really. You deserve not to be hurt. . . ." Mamie then stopped—she was floundering.

"What's going to hurt me, Mamie?—*who's* going to hurt me? You're withholding a lot—I can tell."

"It's only because I don't know how to say it—nobody *wants* to hurt you. Every day you've been with us, even back in San Francisco when you worked for us for nothing, you've turned out the work of two people—you've helped us that much. Nobody wants to seem not to appreciate it. But don't you ever get the idea, or the desire, to start making a life for *yourself?*—living more for yourself and not so much for others? Wouldn't it be more sensible, more practical, if you gave it a try?"

Nervously, warily, Griselda had begun to sidle away. "You talk in riddles, Mamie—but I don't want to hear any more, at least not today. You make me feel uncomfortable when you talk like that." She started toward the door.

Mamie got up from her desk and came around to her. "Griselda, listen to me—don't be so quick to come back from San Francisco. Take it easy—stay out there for awhile and get a good rest. You and I can keep in touch and I'll let you know how things are shaping up here—how does that sound?"

Griselda turned on her—desperation in her eyes. *"Mamie!*— tell me what you're trying to say! Out with it and stop beating around the damn bush!"

Mamie's face got long. "It's that . . . some of the Central Planning Committee members are on John Calvin about you— because of what they think was revealed by the way you lost control of yourself and acted the other night at the rally. They think there's something between you and John Calvin, and that it's bad, very bad, for the organization. That's as clear as I can make it. You asked me to speak out and now I have."

Griselda was looking down curiously at her own feet, pondering what Mamie was saying. "But you had intimated as much before," she finally said. "You're really telling me I should stay in San Francisco—not come back. Isn't that right?"

"Oh, no, Griselda." But Mamie knew she lied. "I only want you to protect yourself, your dignity as a person, until we see what develops—that's all."

"Is this why John Calvin left town?"

"I don't know why John Calvin left town."

Griselda thought this over for a moment, then, without another word, opened Mamie's door and went out. She returned to her little desk outside, sat down, and began writing Knight a letter. She wrote for about five minutes, then sealed it, and returned to Mamie. "Will you give this to John Calvin for me when he returns?" she said. Mamie took the letter, sighed, and said nothing. Griselda then phoned her mother at the hotel and said by early evening she would be ready to leave.

"It's about time!" said Nancy Hanks. "And for God's sake, Griselda, get rid of that horrible Afro wig!"

Griselda did not reply.

643

The next week found the Adkins' household alive with preparatory activity—Thanksgiving was only a few days away and there was much yet to be done. But Mary Dee could not help observing her mother's new personality, attitude—one of feverish elation; she could not remember, certainly not since her father's death, a period when Irene Adkins was so excited, seemed so free of misgivings and care, so absorbed in her family. Moreover, her son Ronald, on learning of his younger sister's engagement, promised to catch an economy-fare flight from California and be home for Thanksgiving when Jocelyn and Geoffrey, her affianced, were to be there with the family. He also knew it would be for them all their last Thanksgiving in the grand old house. It was the only somber note in the otherwise happy planning. Mary Dee had tried hard to accommodate herself to the thought of leaving, moving, yet the nearer January came the more she regarded the decision to move as calamitous, a surrender, a tragedy. She tried now to give herself up to the contagion of happy excitement and anticipation around her and, despite everything, was willing to do whatever she could to help and humor her mother. It sometimes relieved the depression, at least during the day. Nights were another matter.

One afternoon early in the week, Rosabelle Hungerford phoned but gave no indication whatever she knew about Ornette's visit to Mary Dee and their clash. It puzzled Mary Dee— but maybe, she thought, he had not told Rosabelle. She acted decisively—even before Rosabelle could get to the purpose of her call. "Rosabelle," she said, with barely a laugh, "I hope you aren't calling about the same thing Ornette came here to talk about the other day."

"Yes and no," Rosabelle laughed warily. "It's about the organization but not John Calvin. Ornette gets carried away with himself, I know—he's impatient and headstrong. He's a very sincere guy, though. He told me about coming there, but I'm calling to ask you to a women's meeting at the organization's office day after tomorrow—we need you and your good, hard sense; we need you too for your proven organizational ability, and because we know you care about the part women can play in what the organization's trying to do. Mary Dee, you just *can't* say no."

Mary Dee was somehow strangely flattered, and moved, by Rosabelle's straightforwardness, her sense of urgency. "Okay, I'll come," she finally said—"although I'm very busy preparing for a family Thanksgiving reunion. Besides, you're certainly overestimating what I can do, but I'll do what I can. What happened about the girl Ornette was so angry and upset about?—the white girl."

"She left town."

"Oh, so quickly?"

"Yes." Rosabelle, however, seemed uncommunicative on the subject and carefully omitted mention of Griselda's planned return. "But that has nothing to do with us, Mary Dee—with what I called about. I'm just happy you're willing to come and give us a hand—you've never been in the organization's headquarters, have you?"

"No."

"It'll be pretty quiet probably Wednesday—certainly not jumping like it was during the time of the national meeting. And John Calvin's in New York—so like this the women can have a better, not so hectic, meeting. Two o'clock Wednesday, okay?" But Rosabelle, conspiring with Ornette, failed deliberately to tell Mary Dee that Knight would return next day—Tuesday. To Mary Dee, Knight would not be in town the day of the meeting and in this she found considerable, though not unmixed, relief.

There still lingered, however, vestiges of her old curiosity about Knight. Later that afternoon, as she was helping Mrs. Grier put up kitchen curtains, she found herself thinking about his curious, but for her emotion-charged, remarks to the audience the night of the rally. The more he had exhorted them to apply their minds, rather than their emotions, to what he was saying, the greater the emotional impact it had seemed to have upon her. She had thought he spoke the truth. She had also been moved by the courage and poignancy of what he called his confession to them—his doubts. It once more aroused dormant questions she constantly harbored, doubts which always recurred, yet which in the end her rage invariably returned to conquer. It was the *experience,* she thought, which continued to block the path of rationality—blacks, because of their experience, found it impossible to be objective. She ad-

645

judged Knight an exceptionally intelligent man, but, like most intelligent blacks, a man torn between the fierce passions flowing from racial history, on the one hand, and on the other, the logical processes of his mind. In this she knew she shared a kinship with him. She too had experienced.

Yet, in view of all this, she wondered how Knight could possibly have gotten involved with, of all people, a white girl! It boggled the mind—the man, she thought, must have been deranged. Then Philip's image came swimming into her suddenly sensory vision and her heart turned over; for a moment as of old she was caught, suspended, in this aura of both bliss and agony; she too had transgressed. But she was not Knight; she had not, as he had, traversed the length and breadth of the land preaching Blackness. There was a difference. Ornette, in his anger and outrage, was right, she thought—this woman should almost be flogged out of the organization. She thought the only flaw—an outlandish flaw— in Ornette's current attempt to improve things was his fatuous wish, his purpose, to use *her*, Mary Dee, as a pawn, as bait to lure Knight away from his white girlfriend. How demeaning! Before she thought, she had let out an angry, cynical laugh—aloud. In the kitchen she was atop a short stepladder at a window; her laugh prompted Mrs. Grier, below her handing up a brass curtain rod, and herself too heavy to mount a ladder, to ask, "What you laughing about, Mary Dee?"

Mary Dee's laugh at once turned even more sardonic—"Oh, I think I'm going batty, that's all," she said. "Maybe the family reunion will restore a little of my sanity." She continued her chores. Why, she wondered now, rather suddenly, had Rosabelle when she called been reluctant to talk about Ornette's angry blowup in the Adkins' household? Rosabelle, it certainly seemed, had she not been asked, would never have mentioned the incident—she had only meant to talk about the women's meeting. Mary Dee thought this strange. At last she became suspicious—what, if anything, was up? she asked herself. Knowing Ornette, however, she was certain he had not given up. Was there collusion afoot here between husband and wife? An hour later, when she had gone upstairs to take a shower, her suspicions still goaded, intrigued, her. Soon she was certain Ornette and Rosabelle were somehow working together —but to what end she could not divine. Yet what, or who, else could it involve but Knight? Would it transpire that Knight by pre-arrangement would—as he had at her studio party—show up at this meeting? He certainly wouldn't, he couldn't, if he was out of town—yet *would* he still be out of town?

The upshot of it all was that she soon looked up the phone number and called the organization headquarters. A female voice answered. "Is Mr. Knight in?" Mary Dee said, meaning to hang up if she said "yes."

"Just a moment, please," the girl said.

The call was put through to a male voice, but Mary Dee knew it was not Knight's. "Mr. Knight's office," the man said.

Suddenly she recognized the voice—Ferdinand Bailey's. She had not expected this, had not rehearsed for it. She hesitated, then stammered—". . . Is Mr. Knight in?"

"I'm Ferdinand Bailey, Mr. Knight's administrative assistant. Possibly *I* could help you—unless it's personal. . . ."

There was an awkward pause—silence.

"May I ask who's calling," Ferdinand said.

". . . He's not in, then?"

"I think . . . I think I recognize this voice!" Ferdinand, surprised and elated, laughed. "No, Mr. Knight won't be back in town until tomorrow—Tuesday. Now, shall *I* tell you your name? —ha, ha! It's—"

"Mary Dee Adkins." Her answer was quick—in order to maintain her dignity—and stern.

"*What?* . . . Oh, my heavens! What a mistake on my part—I thought it was Miss Peavoy, Miss Billie Peavoy. How *are* you, Miss Adkins? It's certainly good to hear your voice even though I didn't recognize it. How are you? What a fine meeting you had that night at your studio!—how is the fund drive developing? Real well, I hope. . . ." Ferdinand was fairly prattling.

Mary Dee had been cursing her ineptness and her ill luck; now she sighed the sigh of the defeated and the damned. "We haven't had time to really get underway yet," she said lamely, trying to rid her voice of the chagrin at having tricked herself. "But immediately after Thanksgiving, we'll start."

"You must let us know here at the headquarters if we can assist you in any way. You may *now* have been calling Mr. Knight for some such assistance, or other information. . . ."

". . . Well—I had learned of a women's meeting to be held at the headquarters this week," Mary Dee said. "Is it true that it's Wednesday? I thought I'd call to make sure," she lied.

"Miss Adkins—ha, ha!—I'm sorry to tell you I haven't the slightest notion. But hold on for just a moment—I'll go find out." As he put the phone down, however, Ferdinand remembered that Mamie Campbell was not in the office. He then went out and asked the girls working in the front office, but no one knew. He was told only it was Rosabelle Hungerford's project, her meeting; that she should be contacted for further information. At last Ferdinand returned to the phone and told Mary Dee what little he had learned. "I'm sorry I can't help you more, Miss Adkins. Just let me have your phone number, though, will you?—I'll have someone, possibly Rosabelle herself, call you."

Mary Dee almost gasped. Then she realized it was too late to further hedge; she surrendered completely and gave him her phone number.

"Well, thank you!" Ferdinand said happily, writing it down— "You'll get the information in plenty of time. I'm sorry Mr. Knight's away—although he couldn't have answered your question either, I'm afraid, he'd have been glad to talk to you, and *especially* glad you had called. I hope you'll come into the headquarters again soon, when he's here—maybe, in fact, he'll be in the office when you come to attend the meeting—and we can all have a chat."

"Thank you, Mr. Bailey," Mary Dee said, wearily, and at last hung up.

Now, by her own dissimulation, she knew, a veritable host of problems had been created. Why had she mangled things so dreadfully? she asked herself almost in disgust. Ferdinand, in great glee, would doubtless call Ornette immediately and tell him she had been so bold as to call the office for Knight; whereupon Ornette and Rosabelle would know she had lied and would wonder what she could possibly be up to. Mary Dee now began to despair— until suddenly it came to her that Ornette and Rosabelle would realize Rosabelle had also been caught in a lie, about Knight's still being out of town on Wednesday. It was plain they had meant for Knight to be in the office the day of the meeting. It made Mary Dee feel slightly less defensive. But there was still a multitude of questions, problems, she knew, left in the wake of her bungling. Yet soon she was determined to play it straight, not give up a foot of ground or show the least defensiveness—she had no need to, she told herself. Wasn't she volunteering her services?—couldn't she walk away from these people any moment she felt like it? She knew she could. Yet, on another level, she knew she could not. She declined to search her consciousness for the answer to such a thorny, complicated question. She only knew she would not let herself become a dupe—she would confound everybody and stay away from Rosabelle's meeting completely. Besides, Wednesday was Thanksgiving Eve and she'd be in the midst of the family reunion. She felt better now—almost smug.

* * * * *

Knight returned from New York, as scheduled, on Tuesday and came to the office in the mid-afternoon. The first thing he noticed was Griselda's absence—and her covered typewriter—but he was afraid to ask Mamie about her for he had the feeling Mamie was in less than perfect sympathy with him in his difficulties, especially where they involved Griselda. He went looking for Ferdinand then, but soon learned he was out—he had wanted to make sure from Ferdinand that Griselda had indeed left town so that he could move back into his own apartment. But then Mamie saw him pass her door and she brought Griselda's letter into his office. "Griselda gave me this for you the day she left," she said. Embarrassed, Knight took the letter but then did not seem to know what to do with it. He finally put it in his pocket. "Also, Rodya Belloes was here yesterday looking for you," Mamie said. "He said he'd probably come back today."

"I don't want to see him—I don't have any time to waste on him," Knight said. "I knew I'd soon be hearing from him, though —he's long overdue." He then glanced at the stack of accumulated mail on his desk and Mamie left. The moment she had closed his door, he took Griselda's letter out of his pocket, tore it open, and began to read: "Wednesday. Dear John Calvin, I'm leaving for San Francisco this evening. But I don't feel good about it—I'd

649

have much preferred seeing and talking to you before I went. But you left town saying nothing at all to me. It has all left me with an inescapable feeling that you've been trying to avoid me—that you're still upset about my behavior at the rally. If you are, I'm sorry. But if it's caused you problems, as it probably has, with some of the members of the organization, I must say honestly I'm somewhat less than sorry. I'm a human being, with feelings like others, and I did no wrong. I knew only too well what you'd been going through that week, with the endless work and preparation for the big national meeting on your shoulders—I knew the strain you were under—so you can imagine how frightened, really scared to death and appalled, I was seeing you up on that stage suddenly slump to the floor. I didn't know whether or not you were *dead*. And all this after I'd heard you say those wonderful, moving, things about your doubts, and also your misgivings about that wild xenophobia demonstration that I hated so. I loathed it. I was moved to tears by what you said, and I honestly felt, as I do now, that I'd had at least something to do with bringing you around to saying those things publicly. Oh, John Calvin, you were magnificent in your courage and sincerity—in the *truth* that you spoke. I was so moved and proud. Then you fell to the floor and I thought you were dead. You can imagine my panic—or can you? I'm not sure, really—especially now that I sense you've been trying to avoid me. We must talk it all out, once and for all, when I return. But in the meantime I want you to write to me before I get back— I need letters from you, letters of reassurance. I'll send you my address as soon as I know where I'll be staying. John Calvin, you mustn't start vacillating again, you *mustn't retreat* from the stand you took so beautifully that night up there before that big audience. Everything—your image, your self-esteem, as a man, as much as my own happiness—depends on your maintaining, standing by, the position you took that night. These are all things I wanted to talk to you about before I went away, but you left without so much as a phone call or scribbled note to me—nothing. It's made me afraid, afraid maybe you've become a backslider not only about me, but about me *as a symbol*—I'm thinking about the larger things, things you talked about at the rally. Write me as soon as you get this and tell me I'm wrong—you'll no doubt, by the time you read this, find another letter among your accumulated mail containing my address. Please write to me at once. I need—so badly, John Calvin—a letter from you! You know of course I love you. (Signed) Griselda."

Knight was greatly disturbed by the tone of suppressed hysteria in the letter. Also at once he began going through the stack of mail —searching. He found not one, but two letters from her. They were fat letters and, knowing they were tediously long, he sighed and put them in his pocket along with the letter he'd just read. All the while, concomitantly—as he had during his entire stay in New York—he was thinking of Mary Dee Adkins. How could he find a pretext to make, then widen, contact with her?—come to really know her? How would she respond—he was nervous, uncertain, about this. The whole complex dilemma had plagued him throughout his absence—it was a paradox, almost an implausibility, that he had thought of little else except this extraordinary girl he had first seen and hated in Paris. Now the hate had vanished into thin vapors, disappeared—leaving . . . he did not know what. He only knew his heart had taken on a fainting, sinking—mooning—feeling every time he thought of her.

When five o'clock came, the office staff stopped work and prepared to leave. But Knight planned to stay on and catch up on some of the neglected matters on his desk deferred by his absence. It was at this juncture that Bernard Faxson, alias Rodya Belloes, walked into the office. Mamie, already in her coat to go, came back to tell Knight that "Rodya" insisted on seeing him. "I told him you couldn't see him today," she said, "but he won't leave—he says it's too important."

Knight shook his head resentfully, rose, and went up front to face "Rodya"—to tell him he meant business and would not see him. At once, however, he was surprised by the tall, lanky youth's changed appearance. He was no longer unkempt, and wore black shoes and a business suit; moreover, his hair, though not short, was neatly trimmed, and his dark, beaked face clean-shaven. His manner was sober, quiet—serious. "I know you don't have time to see me," he said to Knight—"Mrs. Campbell told me that. But what I have to tell you, Mr. Knight, is important enough for you to *take* the time."

Knight somehow was angered by his cool, self-possessed manner, and became hostile, stubborn—determined not to be tricked into another interview. "Who do you think you are?" he said heatedly—"that you can come barging into this office any time you feel like it and expect me to drop everything and do your bidding? My answer is *no*—I won't see you."

"Mr. Knight," said Faxson, suddenly now almost humble, penitent, "you have figured, even if indirectly, in an investigation of murder."

Knight stared incredulously at him—failing even to notice Mamie, who had not heard, as she departed and left him standing in the outer office with his caller. "Of course I've figured in an investigation of murder!" he said—"and not indirectly, either. I was almost the murder victim."

"Oh, I'm not talking about the attempt on *your* life," Faxson said. "I'm talking about a perpetrated, accomplished, murder. But I have many things to tell you." His voice was low now, subdued; he gave Knight a quick, oblique look of remorse. "As you did at your big rally recently, Mr. Knight—I was there and heard you—I too want to make a confession. You must hear me—it's no triviality."

"What on earth are you talking about, Rodya?"

"My name's not Rodya, Mr. Knight. It's Bernard—Bernard Faxson. All the time you've known me, I've been in the employ of a private detective agency; but I'm not a professional. I was a special employee, a special investigator, picked because I'm in fact a university graduate student, though not at the University of Chicago. I was employed only for this case. But, after interviewing you a couple of times, I began to realize I was being drawn more and more to your career and accomplishments and to the phenomenon of the organization itself. I was taking it all to heart, very much to heart. I found what you were trying to do was so fascinating, challenging, important, that I had become involved personally. Everything, including my investigative mission, was getting pretty mixed up by then—when a mysterious death brought the assignment to an end."

Knight's lips parted; he still stared. Finally he said—"Come back in my office." He turned and Faxson followed him. When they had sat down, Knight for a moment studied the youth's face. "Well, don't think, Rodya, that—"

"Bernard—Bernard Faxson."

"Don't think for a minute we didn't suspect you as an infiltrater," Knight said contentiously. "We only told you what we wanted you to know. And I'm sure you'd have soon been found out by Ornette Hungerford, who was even more suspicious of you than the rest of us."

Young Faxson, sitting across the desk from Knight, leaned forward as he spoke. "But by that time I wouldn't for the world have done anything against you—I had become partisan; as I learned more about your aims and objectives, I became emotionally involved, and at heart your adherent. That's why maybe I shouldn't feel guilty now—because I was never really against you and at the end definitely a sympathizer. I'd have told on myself eventually— I know it, I feel it."

"Do you expect me to believe that?"

"Yes, I do—I certainly do."

"You've come here to 'confess,' as you put it—is that right?" Knight was scornful. "Is that the reason you've been camping on my doorstep—to 'confess?' "

"No, not that alone—though that's surely part of it. What brought things to a head was death, sudden death—almost certainly murder."

Knight was staring at him again.

"The man who retained the services of the detective agency, which then employed me, was found dead in his hotel room—in a tub of bath water. It was thought he'd died of a heart attack, but the agency, the two private investigators, he'd hired to investigate you and your organization didn't consider their employment quite ended by his death. They abandoned their original mission—which was pointless with their client dead—and began investigating the facts and circumstances surrounding his death and later turned over what they found to the police. As a result, the police have in custody a woman, a prostitute, who was seen with him the night of his death. Now they are looking for her vanished pimp—whom under grilling she finally implicated as the perpetrator. It's only a matter of time now—they'll have him very soon."

Knight was shaking his head impatiently. "What's all that got to do with the organization, with me?" he said. "What were you trying to find out from me?"

"This man, who's now dead, wanted to know everything, really *everything*, about you and the organization. This was because his former mistress was working for you, working right here in your office. It was Griselda Graves, of course—who created that scene at the end of your rally. He felt she was deeply attached to you, personally—to put it mildly—and he wanted to know everything that went on, every detail. I was paid to be painstaking and thorough, and I was. But then the more I found out about you and the organization, what you were trying to do for people, I began to lose my objectivity—this was true even though, or maybe because, I disagreed with some parts of your rhetoric."

"Ah," said Knight, ". . . Griselda. What was the man's name?"

"Marvin Freuhlinghausen. He was crazy, paranoid, about getting her back and returning with her to San Francisco."

Knight was silent. But at last nodding his head in affirmation, he said, almost to himself, in a whisper, "This is a strange, a *lunatic,* world!"

"Yes, it is, Mr. Knight—I agree. And in many ways—not only in the situation I've just described, which prompted your remark, but in many others. It must be very hard for you to maintain your idealism in such a world. Do you ever, in moments of difficulty, say to yourself the world really has no purpose?"

Knight was agitated, thoughtful. "No. I believe it has purpose—though I'm sometimes puzzled by what it is."

"Isn't that almost the same thing?"

"No—the fact that the purpose isn't always clear doesn't necessarily mean it doesn't exist." But Knight then frowned, seeming troubled by his own rejoinder.

"Mr. Knight, you often refer in your speeches and writings to the suffering blacks have experienced. Has this suffering had a purpose, do you think?"

For a moment Knight hesitated, as if his thoughts were in disarray. "I'm not sure," he said. "This is a question that needs study —long, deep, serious study. I hope some day to have the time, and inclination, to do in-depth reading and research on the question, to think about it—really study it."

At this, young Faxson regained some of his old ardor. "Oh, Mr. Knight, I think that would be great! Conceivably, it might help resolve some of the doubts you expressed the night of your rally talk. The two may be inextricably linked. Studying the question, probing for a purpose, if any, may reveal that such subject matter and the effort to understand it constitute only the tip of the iceberg. What's beneath the surface, the *big* part, may in fact represent the plight of numberless people of all kinds, everywhere, humanity itself— *all humanity*. Any study of your question, Mr. Knight, I think must reckon with this possibility. It may turn out, as your doubts may be said to suggest, that your organization's exclusionist rhetoric may be, ideologically, off the mark, as well as tactically unrealistic."

"Oh, Rodya—or whatever your real name is—you talk like you know so much, like one of your university professors! You sound like a pedant. But you haven't lived long enough to be so wise. Besides, you're talking just like a white man could be expected to talk. You haven't—you *can't* have—the faintest notion of what Dr. King was talking about when he spoke of the 'long night of suffering' that blacks have been through. None whatever!"

Faxson's high, querulous tone had reverted to that of his Rodya days. "Oh, I know, I know, Mr. Knight! But how presumptuous of you!—you would exclude me, and others like me, from the chance to learn about it. Also, we might be able to tell *you* a few things."

"I don't believe it!" said Knight—"Not unless you've experienced them, which you haven't. You see, that's the difficulty! How can you ever learn it if you haven't *experienced* what Dr. King speaks of? It's impossible. The question is so easy for you—in your position you can decide it in ten seconds. But for me the answer will come, if at all, only after long preparation, seclusion, and study. You're white, Rodya. We're black. Your decision, as I say, is easy. Ours is not only difficult, it's torturing. Although there are times, like the night of the rally, when I waver, I can nevertheless see that xenophobia, as a current remedy, a temporary expedient, so to speak, is a perfectly logical, natural, thing. What worries me is whether it will consistently serve us—over the *long* haul. That's my only concern. It will require, as I've said, long, arduous study."

Faxson, more eager than ever now, almost combative, edged forward in his chair. "Mr. Knight, I've confessed, fully and freely, my perfidy in my relations with you and your staff—my disguise. I'm sorry that all those weeks I did such a thing. But now I've humbly confessed. I've wanted to rid myself of my feelings of guilt—I've had a terrible urge, almost torment, to do this. I could have stayed completely away from you after Marvin Freuhlinghausen's death, for the game was up. But I had to come and confess to you. Don't you see—*can't* you see?—the significance of that? I'm sure a man of your intelligence can see it. So let me ask you: May I have your approval to become a member of your organization? I think I could be an asset."

Knight, who had been sitting erect, threw himself back in his chair with a strange, unnecessary, violence. "Oh, God, not that!" he said. "You don't know the crisis I'm going through already!"

"Ah," said young Faxson, breathing heavily in his involvement, "you mean a personal moral crisis, don't you?"

Knight glared at him. "No."

"But you hadn't considered it in that light, had you?"

Knight was angry. "Hell, no—of course I hadn't! I've got a crisis in the *organization*—though it's about Griselda Graves."

"How well I know it, Mr. Knight." Faxson spoke almost triumphantly. "And now *I* come along, right?—to make matters even worse, get you in deeper trouble. But I'm sure a man of your foresight sees the question—the 'crisis,' as you call it—for what it is. It's *moral,* Mr. Knight."

Knight now was almost quivering in his anger. "Don't you, a white man, dare talk to me about morality! I won't hear it! . . . it's revolting! No, you won't become a member of this organization! Indeed, you won't!" Then Knight said it before he thought—"Nor will Griselda Graves any longer *be* a member! If this is xenophobia, so be it!"

Young Faxson slowly shook his head. "Sad, sad," he said—"and now Griselda. She was so faithful, so sincere. There was a time recently—as a thorough investigator I know all about it, of course—when you thought well of her. There was a time—of an evening, Mr. Knight—when you would spend long hours alone with her in her flat. You didn't wish to expel her *then*. But that's what precipitated your 'crisis.' "

"You have made me—by your facile accusations—see things, possibly for the first time, in a far, far, clearer light, Rodya! You have shown me *how* to be a xenophobe—a better xenophobe. Yes, yes, it's true!" Knight's fist came down on his desk—"And I thank you for it!"

Faxson's voice now dripped irony. "No, no, Mr. Knight, it wasn't

I. I can't take credit for it. That credit must go to someone *new,* a female someone, who has very recently come on the scene—a person, equally lovely, who has made it a little easier for you to turn Griselda out. By these means then you will meet and ride out your so-called 'crisis.' Ah, but at what cost, Mr. Knight—what cost."

Knight, his ebony face fierce, hard, impermeable, abruptly stood up, signifying the meeting was over.

"After all those interviews, Mr. Knight, this may be our final, our parting, encounter. I have no rancor. I understand considerably more than you think."

Knight's lip curled in scorn. "Well, that's mighty white of you. But you understand *nothing.* Until you've lived our history—which of course is not possible—you and all the others like you will *always* understand nothing! Even if you, a university man, undertook a lifelong study of Dr. King's almost inspired way of putting the question, the problem—'our long *night* of suffering'—you still could not so much as get an inkling of it. Never! You can't possibly envision the blackness of that night."

Young Faxson, who now had also stood up, spoke softly but defiantly—"Remember, I am a Jew." With that, he walked out.

For a moment Knight wanted to call him back, but did not. Later he wondered why he had wanted to do that—was it to say that, despite everything, he understood? He was not sure. But he knew he had always had a grudging respect for "Rodya's" seeming idealism and, above all, his almost astounding precocity, which he had never seen more effectively displayed than this evening, but he too had a feeling they would not meet again. Yet he was not sorry, but only thankful to "Rodya" for bringing him to realize there was no middle ground—that he must be a xenophobe until the studies he hoped someday to undertake might show him a different path. He somehow felt strengthened by "Rodya's" visit; he thought himself fortunate it had occurred. It was six-thirty now and he tried to calm himself enough to resume work but his mind was in such turmoil he knew he could work no more that evening. He was preparing to leave and go home—when his phone rang.

It was Ferdinand. "John Calvin, I *thought* you might be back, and slaving away, after-hours, in the office!" There was all the characteristic good humor and enthusiasm in Ferdinand's voice tonight and Knight was glad to hear it. "If you haven't eaten, John Calvin, I'll pick you up and we'll go to Stout's for some good down-home cooking. Say, listen to *this*—Miss Adkins, Miss Mary Dee Adkins, no less, none other, called the office the other day for you! Honest! She left her phone number."

There was a shocked pause on Knight's end of the line. ". . . What did she want?" he managed to say.

"Oh, I'll tell you when I get there!—I'll pick you up in a half hour."

Slowly Knight hung up. He was already whispering to himself—"Incredible . . . incredible. . . ."

*   *   *   *   *

That same evening, about seven o'clock, Ornette came home from his mode of livelihood, selling insurance, in a mean, unhappy mood. But the moment he walked into the large, haphazardly-furnished apartment and was greeted by his four-year-old daughter, Sojourner, he was a changed man; becoming rollicking, high-spirited, irreverent, yet at times thoughtful, almost pensive. Throwing off his coat, he picked Sojourner up in his arms and looked directly into her large, earnest eyes. "Hey, there," he said—"Hi!"

She did not reply, though she was studying his face—her mood contemplative, reserved, prim.

"What's the matter with you?" Ornette said. He protruded his lips—"Give me some sugar-plum-sugar." Sojourner permitted herself to be kissed, yet soberly observed her father—who had never seen her so uncommunicative, almost reproachful. Finally he carried her into the kitchen, where Rosabelle was watching a casserole, topped with pork chops, in the oven. "What's wrong with this little chick?" he said to her—"What's she so down-in-the-mouth about?"

Busy Rosabelle did not even turn around from the stove as she replied—"She hasn't got over hearing you say you were going to change her brother's, little John Calvin's, name. She doesn't know, or care, about your falling out with Knight—she doesn't even know we named Johnnie after him. She's only interested in her brother

658

who's not old enough to speak up for himself—she objects to his having his name changed. She couldn't care less that you're no longer one of Knight's most ardent admirers."

Already, though, Ornette's thoughts had shifted. "That Mary Dee bugs me as much as Knight," he said—"I don't understand her either, lately."

"It's not easy," said Rosabelle. "I told you on the phone what happened today."

"I can't figure it out. If she knew from you about the women's meeting at the headquarters tomorrow, why afterwards would she call the office and ask *them?* If she forgot, why didn't she call you back?"

"Beats me. They didn't know at the office anyhow, and had to call me to find out. But Mary Dee didn't forget—I'd bet money on that. We don't know what it was, but she had a reason for calling the office. You ought to ask Ferdinand if he knows anything about it. Mary Dee's no fool—she's plenty smart."

"Well, you'll have a chance to be with her at the meeting tomorrow," said Ornette—"you may get some clues. I'm pretty sure John Calvin will be in the office at the time—maybe in some way you can get them together for a few minutes. I'm going to call Ferdie too, to see if there's anything he thinks he can do. Now that Griselda's gone, we've got to push this thing—hard. Ferdie agrees. Oh, but my patience with John Calvin is getting thin—and then thinner. Mary Dee's acting up too. I told you how she performed when I was at her house last week. It made me think she and John Calvin deserve each other."

A half hour later the family—Ornette and Rosabelle, three of their five children, and Rosabelle's widowed mother, Mrs. Ransom, who lived with them—were seated around the dining table eating. The baby, John Calvin, was asleep, and the oldest child, Frederick, age eleven, was still out on his newspaper route. "Why're you gonna change Johnnie's name, Daddy?" asked Nathaniel, the seven-year-old son.

Rosabelle laughed. "Oh, instead, Nat, your father may change his *mind*—about Johnnie."

"And your father may *not* change his mind, too," said Ornette.

Nathaniel, a serious child who, with his expansive forehead and prying, overcurious, eyes, resembled his mother more than his father except for the identical broad nose, looked at Ornette. "Why, Daddy?"

"Well, I'll tell you why. I want all of you'all to grow up to be somebody," Ornette said. "I want you to be proud you're black. Mr. Knight—John Calvin Knight—at one time stood for all these things. He preached, *and practised,* them. But now I'm not as sure about him as I was. That's why, Nat, I don't want to saddle one of my sons—little Johnnie, back there asleep, who had nothing to say about what his name would be—with a name for life that he can't always be proud of. Don't that make sense?"

Nathaniel resumed quietly eating and seemed unsure of how to answer.

Rosabelle, again laughing, intervened. "Let's make a proposition to your father, children. How about us suggesting to him he hold off for awhile on his decision and see what happens in the meantime. Mr. Knight by that time may have again proved himself to be the kind of leader we all want him to be. It may be that he just needs help—he's under a lot of strain much of the time. Yes, help might do it. In fact we're—your father and I, and Mr. Bailey— we're thinking of ways right now that might help him in his associations, in his friends, the people he sees, and things like that."

Harriet, eight years old, wearing glasses, spoke up then. "What did Mr. Knight do, Mama?"

". . . Well, we won't go into that—it's too long and complicated anyhow."

Ornette was staring at Rosabelle. "Why don't you tell 'em!" he said.

"Oh, for heaven's sake, Ornette, let's get on some other subject— can't we?" Rosabelle's face showed her concern. Also her mother, a grey-haired, slight woman in her sixties, now looked alarmed. She liked and admired Ornette but dreaded his explosions of temper.

But Ornette did not further pursue the subject and the crisis passed. After dinner he even helped Rosabelle with the dishes. "Tell me this, baby," he said, handing her a sauce pan to wash, "how do you think Mary Dee's gonna react to John Calvin?"

Rosabelle turned around from the sink and looked at him as though the question had never occurred to her. "Lord, I don't know," she said.

"Mary Dee knows what we're up to, y'know. She won't be surprised. She's already formed an opinion of John Calvin, though; we just don't know what it is yet."

"Why don't you ask what John Calvin's reaction will be to *her?*"

"Okay, what will it be?"

"Again, I have no idea, Ornette. Maybe it'll depend on how deeply he's already got himself involved with Griselda. She'll be back, you know—you're not rid of her yet, not by any means."

"If he lets that chick come back in the office, I'll start a fight on him he'll never forget! I'll go *public,* you see if I don't—just watch me!"

"Ornette, you've got to have more patience—we've got to try to *help* John Calvin, not hurt him."

"He's hurting the organization, ain't he?"

"Well, maybe—yes, I'm sure he is. But have you thought about what the movement might be without John Calvin? There just might not be a movement very long—consider that."

Ornette studied her; soon he was staring. "I ain't so sure about that; I ain't sure at all. Nobody's indispensable. Only the movement is. The movement will go on—there're those of us who'll see to that."

Rosabelle was gaping at him—in wonder, incomprehension, then vague uneasiness, discomfort. Finally, however, as if recovering, she said, "But we gotta try our best to help him, like we've been— what's Ferdie think about the chances of John Calvin and Mary Dee hitting it off?

"Oh, hell, you know Ferdie—he's a confirmed optimist. He thinks it'll work out just fine—he would. But I'm not all that sure. It's because of Mary Dee. I can't figure her out—come to think of it, I never have. Why did she ever choose to join the movement, Rosabelle?"

"Well, you and I can take credit for some of it—we talked to her, remember? Then those two children—Ernestine and Vernon—had some influence on her feelings, I think."

"Well, I hope you're right. But remember, Mary Dee's a silk stocking through and through—don't forget that. It just ain't *natural* for her to like street niggers—a leopard can't change its spots, Rosabelle. Tell me, just what was it about the organization that made it such an attraction to her? I still don't get it. And what she thinks of John Calvin, the *leader*—so-called, anyway—of the street niggers, is anybody's guess."

"It's also anybody's guess about what he thinks of her."

"Yeah, that's right. You know, I'm getting to believe this whole idea we got about bringing these two together, all cozy-like and everything, is plain crazy. It could somehow boomerang."

"Oh, you're for walking away and leaving everything to Griselda —is that it?"

"Aw, hell," groaned Ornette, "this thing's so damned mixed-up, I don't know what I'm for—or against. I can tell you one thing, though, things can't stay the way they are; they're gonna change— something's gonna happen."

Chapter 2

Wednesday—Thanksgiving Eve—Knight, tired, drained, left the office at noon and did not return. Rather he spent the afternoon in his apartment, in the attempt at least to catch up on his sleep. Much or most of his life had been troubled-filled and stressful, yet, customarily, he had been able at night to sleep, even if, in a host of unique situations, there had not been adequate time at hand for sleep. He had nonetheless managed—had gone to sleep quickly and, in the time available, slept soundly. But now since returning from New York and reading Griselda's three letters awaiting him, and having to consider the hopeless problems they posed, he could no longer sleep for more than two hours at a time. In bed at night he rolled, tossed, and fought nightmares until dawn, then during the day was so leadened and fatigued, his mind so frayed, he could hardly function, much less do effective work. The letters from Griselda made it clear she intended, indeed fully expected, to return as quickly as her transaction of the "business" in San Francisco would allow. It was only in the third letter, however, that she had revealed the nature of the "business." Knight could hardly believe what he read. And now in possession, since "Rodya's" visit, of far more critical information on Marvin than Griselda had, he was stunned by this new, weird, development.

Griselda in the third letter had gone on to elaborate, with a sense of mission, fervor, on the necessity that she return to Chicago as soon as humanly possible in order to explore with Knight plans—and she did not fail to set out at great length a number of her own—for the best use to be made by the organization of the $80,000 plus which she would derive from the probate of Marvin's will. Knight was dizzied by the problems the letter raised. He thought Griselda manic. Despite the fact his critics in the organization had given him a virtual ultimatum to get rid of her, here she was now devising all manner of fanciful schemes and projects for the resuscitation, rejuvenation, of the organization, together with the ways and means to broaden, intensify, her own input and participation in its long-range affairs and destiny. It was not only an impossible situation, he thought; it was a catastrophe. He was so harried and confused he had no capacity for weighing alternatives. He only knew something must be done—and fast. He of course could not realize Griselda had withheld from him what was, at least to her, an even more critical piece of information—her mother's revelation of her, Griselda's, part-African ancestry. No matter how long she wrestled with this new and, in her mind, potent disclosure, she could not bring herself to decide what, if any, use there was to be made of it. She therefore divulged it to no one.

Not the least of Knight's trying difficulties in the whole matter, however, was his wish, authentic and sincere, his seeking for some way, to avoid hurting Griselda. But the prospects now dimmed daily, almost hourly. Although he agonized about it, he knew what he wanted to do, yet did not want to do—namely, write Griselda a very painstaking, lucid, yet compassionate, letter explaining the bad, almost hopeless, situation that had developed in the organization, and why; and finally ask her not to return—that she deserved to be spared the acrimony her further attempts to serve the organization would provoke. Yet he could not overlook, forget, what the organization could do with a transfusion of $80,000—his emotions and inclinations, therefore, to say the least, were not unmixed. He knew, though, harboring in his mind such contingencies, speculations, illusions, was dangerous—this could be no solution; only more trouble. All these thoughts, he told himself, should be conveyed to her; yet, so far, he had been unable to write such a letter. A further fact had by no means lessened the complications: throughout, and despite, all the mounting difficulties, his mind had ever been on Mary Dee Adkins. His thoughts of her could not be erased—especially since he had heard, from elated and hopeful Ferdinand, that in his absence she had phoned him at the office, then left her number. At least for the moment this had strengthened his desire to find the confidence, the resolution, to write the letter to Griselda that he knew he must eventually write.

Now the red sun had sunk below the horizon and soon darkness would descend. He sat in his living room trying somehow to force himself into a quiet, peaceful mood. He felt it a necessity. He seemed not to understand this was impossible as long as he was unable to bring himself to do something, this time not directly involving Griselda, he very much wanted, longed, to do—that is, return Mary Dee's call. He thought about it, yet could not summon the courage to do so trifling, inconsequential, a thing as take the few short steps to the telephone. Yet he tried to reason himself into doing it. *He* would not be the initiator, he tried to tell, reassure, himself. He would be *returning* a call. Yet he sat there unable to move.

Instead he was soon looking across at the photograph of his dead four-year-old son, John Calvin, Jr., that he had recently found the heart to bring out and place on the end table. He had taken the picture himself, with a camera borrowed from Ferdinand. The boy, even so young, had his father's piercing eyes, yet their potentially forbidding effect was offset, mitigated, by an angelic smile. At that very moment, though no one of course had known, the small body harbored, silently, lethally, the riotous white blood cells of leukemia. Why had it been Johnnie, *his* son? he had a thousand times asked himself. What had he, the father, done to deserve this ungodly blow—the worst yet of his thirty-five years. Moreover, there could be no other explanation for the failure, dissolution, of his marriage—his wife, Velma, had eventually turned into a person so different and strange, so cold yet insecure, he soon, despite himself, could only regard her as a rank stranger. But now, to his egotistic wonder and disbelief, she had remarried—to a widowered clergyman, her clergyman father's friend and age peer. Knight speculated on the chances of his ever having, getting, what he most wanted, coveted—another son; he considered it hardly likely, for in his view, and mold of character, this required a wife—no casual relationship would do. And that was the rub. He thought of Griselda. The shock of the idea produced a reflex action: he painfully shook his head. Unthinkable—no matter how he felt about her, or she him. It would destroy him, and should. Hardly mindful of it, he got up and began pacing the floor.

Shortly after seven o'clock he went to the kitchen, fixed himself a drink, then broiled a steak. Outside it was dark. As he sat eating, he still thought of Griselda. The problem seemed eternal. He was racking his brain for a way, a tactful yet honest way, to compose the letter to her that he knew he must soon, very soon, dispatch. Again he felt the deep sense of guilt. Although he knew he had been to a degree pursued, he also knew he should have had the strength, resoluteness, to turn away. He tried then to analyze, as best he could, what had been his true feelings toward Griselda. He could not come to a conclusion. The vague total of them he sensed consisted of a number of distinct parts: admiration for her, for her character as well as her beauty; also gratitude; but exasperation too, especially with her talk of Frimbo; then pity and wonder; and of course lust, but also somehow love. Yet how were any of these things to help him now—in writing the letter? In utter frustration he could not say.

When he had finished eating he went into the bedroom to his little writing table, put on the light, and in longhand began to write a rough draft of a letter to her he might use. Yet he could not concentrate. A portion of his mind, his inclinations, wanted to take him to the telephone to call Mary Dee. But he somehow kept on writing: "I could use the old cliches, Griselda, and say this is the most difficult letter I've ever had, or ever will have, to write. Yet it would be true. What makes it difficult, I guess, is that I hate so much having to see myself truly—as I really am—in this situation. I get a very unattractive view of myself and it disturbs me. I already know, and well, what you think about this whole matter— that I should assert such authority as I have and open up the membership and affiliation privileges of the organization to everyone, black or white, who comes, to all who see merit in our work and want to become associated with it. In your case, you couldn't possibly have been more faithful, more conscientious and hardworking in behalf of the organization—and now in addition you offer us that huge sum of money we need so badly—you could not, as I say, have been more dedicated, committed, had you been black. You can see how hard it makes it for us. . . . for me. . . ." He reread what he had written and, shaking his head, crumpled up the sheet of paper and tossed it in the wastebasket. He detested what he was saying—it sounded, he thought, wheedling and phony.

Finally he made a fresh start: "The veteran members of the organization, especially those on the Central Planning Committee, have always seen the organization as a vehicle for the development of things Black, black pride in accomplishment, black history, black tenacity and militancy—yes, black chauvinism, if you will. That's how they see the organization—*their* organization. It's been the way I've seen it too—until I met you, until you started working with us. Your influence on me, Griselda, has been considerable—I admit it. That's what's got not a few of the people in the organization, senior in service, people who've been with me from the early days, who've looked primarily to me, as leader, for the formulation of Black doctrine, these people see me now as slipping, backsliding, and attribute it to your influence on me. As I say, the influence is there, only they vastly overestimate it, for I must tell you that, despite my occasional vacillation, I still see things as the old heads and the rank-and-file members see them. I see Black! Oh, Griselda, it would take me hours to give you all the reasons, to point out to you why it is that blacks so distrust whites, how they feel they must create their own institutions, because white institutions, where we're concerned, are basically perfidious. It's true—all this spelled out might take us from dark till dawn. No white person, Griselda—including you—can ever adequately understand it. You are not black. Therefore much of what I'm saying will sound bigoted to you—it's only natural. . . ."

Knight stopped writing, sighed, and tossed the pen aside on the table. He was unsatisfied, discouraged. He couldn't, he thought, say any of this—besides, he was getting no closer to the point of the whole thing, no closer to what he had to use the letter to *do*, than when he had begun; he felt he was merely posturing, marking time, flinching from saying what eventually he must say. The letter *should* start off, he perseveringly told himself, by saying straight out: "Dear Griselda, I hope you will find that the reasons I give later on in this letter will tend to justify what I must now, painfully, with a heavy heart, ask you to do—namely, not return to the organization, not return to the office." He winced and shook his head wildly, distressfully—this would not do! It was too harsh! It would be brutal! He could not say this. At once, as often in recent days, he remembered what his father, Goforth, had accused him of—lack of compassion, tolerance. No, he could not write such a letter. How then *would* he communicate to her what he must say?—it had somehow to be done. But he was too confused and disconsolate now to pursue it further.

Soon he returned to the kitchen and poured himself a second drink. It was after eight o'clock. He took the drink up to the living room, got a book, and sat down to read, realizing, however, as he often had, how empty his private life was, how lonely, as now, he was so much of the time. It was a miserable state and he deplored it. So now—though he considered in the long run the gesture futile—he began to feel himself impelled to do what so far, ever since arriving back from New York, he had lacked the stamina to do: go to the telephone and return the crucial call. Finally, halfway through the drink, he got out the phone number Ferdinand had given him and dialed Mary Dee.

*　　*　　*　　*　　*

Meanwhile on the same afternoon—Thanksgiving Eve—at the very hour coinciding with the women's (Rosabelle's) meeting at the organization headquarters, Mary Dee, who had long since determined not to go, was waiting at home with her mother and Mrs. Grier for her brother Ronald's arrival from California. He had only thirty minutes before called from O'Hare to say his plane had just landed and he was in the terminal; that after picking up his bag he would be home by three o'clock. But Jocelyn and her boyfriend, in the east, had said they wouldn't arrive until early evening, around six. Irene Adkins' excitement and elation knew no bounds. Mary Dee, however, who all week with Mrs. Grier had been readying the house for the festive weekend, was somber, subdued, reminiscent. She could hardly bring herself to believe the grand old house, harboring so many memories, was to be sold. It was for her a bitter cup, and, she knew, the end of a way of life she had cherished—she had somehow all afternoon been thinking of her father and happier days. They were great days though she had not at the time so regarded them. She'd been presumptuous, headstrong, self-centered, assuming the world was the way she had entered it and would always be so; that—hadn't her father's pampering proved it?—she could have anything she wanted, with no questions asked. Then two years ago in Paris she had found this shockingly untrue and had not yet recovered. She had entered that critical period in her life (Paris) in a frantic, almost panting, search for happiness, never realizing happiness is more readily won when not pursued, that it is only known when lost; that one cannot say "I am happy," only that "I was happy."

668

It was almost four o'clock, not three, when Ronald, bag in hand, came up the walk and onto Irene Adkins' front porch. He was five feet-eleven, 180 lean pounds, a tawny, golden brown, with a neat Afro. Mrs. Grier was the first to sight him, and, crying out to Irene Adkins and Mary Dee, went running to the front door. Ronald, who in addition to his university studies had a job in Davis, California, had not come home at all during the summer, so they had not seen him in eight months. Now there was much joyful commotion, including a few tears from Irene Adkins. When all the hugging, kissing, and rejoicing were over, Ronald explained his lateness by saying he had taken the bus instead of a taxi—not only from O'Hare into town, but from downtown out to the house. That way, he said, he easily saved ten dollars. His remark almost embarrassed Irene Adkins. Imagine, she thought, her son having to pinch pennies like that—she had for the moment forgotten Ronald's at least professed socialist leanings and that the dollars themselves he saved were, conceivably, not his only motive. He had seen poverty first hand, he claimed, among California's migrant farm workers during his recent efforts, along with other students, in behalf of the grape and lettuce boycotts, and thought, even if one had them, the ostentatious display of material goods was boorish, in callous bad taste.

With Ronald there, everyone now looked forward to Jocelyn's arrival later in the evening. Irene Adkins followed her son up to his old room and sat in a straight chair watching him, talking to him, as he unpacked. Ronald, knowing what she had been through since his father's death, and how jittery and vulnerable she was—he was also aware of the brandy problem—was tender with her now. He listened attentively, sympathetically, to everything she was so eager to tell him, though hardly ten minutes had passed before she brought up Mary Dee and her new life, her new friends. Irene Adkins' voice now dropped almost to an agitated murmur as repeatedly she darted furtive glances in the direction of the open door. "Ronnie, she's *very much* involved with these people!" she whispered. "She even had them—one night, in droves—back there in that big room over the garage she's made into a studio. And the other day, listen to this, one of them—a burly, very crude fellow— was *in this house*! Yes—sitting down there in the parlor big as anything, and talking so loudly and uncouthly to her! I don't know what's happened to Suky! They call themselves members of the Black Peoples Congress."

"Oh, that's a well-known organization," said Ronald, surprised and relieved. "They used to be headquartered in San Francisco—I know a couple of guys who're members. You've heard of John Calvin Knight, Mother."

"I think I've read about him—yes."

"Well, he's head of it—he founded the organization. It's nation-wide, with branches and members all over the country. It's now headquartered here in Chicago."

"What does *Suky* find in it, though?—she has nothing in common with those people."

Ronald laughed and shrugged. "Maybe she's decided to change her lifestyle, Mother. You know Suky's always had pretty grandiose ideas about herself—a lot of them put in her head by Father. Well, maybe she's finally come around to seeing how wacky some of those ideas were."

Irene Adkins looked hurt. "I don't see anything wrong with the ideas she had."

"Oh, maybe they weren't all that wrong, Mother," Ronald laughed apologetically. "But there are at least alternatives—maybe she sees some of the alternatives now. Come to think of it, though, this *is* quite a change for Suky. Does she talk much about what she does in the organization?"

"Oh, no, no—hardly at all. But she doesn't talk much about anything—to me, at least; or anyone else. And she seldom ever goes out—for instance, on a dinner date, or to a party, or anything like that. Young men, highly respectable, eligible, fellows, most of whom you know, call her up all the time. But she always finds some way to put them off, and in the end declines."

"Well, Suky's got a mind of her own—she's always had."

"Oh, my, yes. She was terribly upset when I brought up the matter of selling the house. Although I think she's finally become reconciled to it, the idea still makes her gloomy, moody. But we've got to do it, Ronnie—this house has become a white elephant."

"Yes. It's not a pleasant thought, though. But, sad to say, things have changed and we don't need a big house any longer. An apartment is a much more sensible idea—and less costly."

"Oh, Ronnie, you're so wise, so mature, for your age—I feel so much surer of myself after I've written and told you all about the business matters I've had to undertake. I was so glad when you answered about the house and said you agreed with me. I'll be happy when you come home for good. It will be such a relief to have a male in the family again—even if my little girl Jocelyn won't be here—and I know Suky is glad too."

"This, as you know, is my senior year, Mother," said Ronald. "I'll be home in June—ha, looking for a job."

It was well after dark when Jocelyn and Geoffrey arrived from O'Hare, yet they were in good time for a delayed dinner. Jocelyn, though not as comely as Mary Dee, was an extremely attractive, feminine, girl who extravagantly admired her older sister. Geoffrey, a tall, brown, rather erect and serious young man, was trying his hardest to seem more lively and agreeable, seeking to make the best possible impression. Tonight Irene Adkins was so thrilled and excited that the idea of lacing some tea with brandy did not once occur to her. This did not go unnoticed by Mary Dee—confirming her theory that it was isolation and loneliness, the breakup of her family, that caused her mother to drink. But tonight, with her family, her children, seated with her around the dining table, she was happy, and her happiness made Mary Dee for a time forget her own troubles—until in the middle of dinner the telephone rang.

Mrs. Grier came out of the kitchen and answered it. There was a pause, then—"She's having dinner," they heard her say. ". . . Can I give her your name? . . . Oh, yes—just hold on a minute, will you, sir?" Mrs. Grier stepped in view and looked at Mary Dee. "It's Mr. Knight," she said.

Mary Dee at first looked blankly around her, then froze in her chair; she seemed unable to move. Finally she made a motion as if she would push back from the table and get up. Yet she desisted. At last, her voice weak, she said to Mrs. Grier, "Will you take his number?—and tell him I'll call him back." Mrs. Grier complied.

As well as the others, Ronald had heard and Irene Adkins had heard. He was impressed; she was totally, woefully, unimpressed. The dinner went on, but Mary Dee at times sat almost like a stone statue, eating her food and only occasionally, mechanically, joining in the talk. What had come over Knight? she asked herself. Why was he calling her?—as if she didn't know, or had forgotten, the opportunity, license, through Ferdinand Bailey, she had so handily given him. He had moved quickly, she thought, once she had so unwittingly, ineptly, given him the pretext to call her—Ferdinand, she was certain, who, laughing, delighted, had so victimized her, had hardly been able to await Knight's return to tell him she had called; had, moreover, left her phone number. But what, she wondered, would Knight, had she gone to the phone, have said to her tonight?

Now she suddenly realized her predicament—he would merely have said he was returning her call. It was that simple. He could have been perfectly cool, self-possessed, about it had he wished—so well protected. The next move then would not have been his, but hers. Yet, in her heart, she could not bring herself to believe Knight capable of such shallowness, deviousness—she could not forget once more his moving statement to the huge audience the night of the rally, nor his tormented concern, openness, modesty, his courage and honesty. Whatever he was, no matter what traits he had that she hated—as in Paris—deviousness was not one of them. Yet at last she concluded she would not call him—it was, despite everything, too risky. So why take the chance? Embarrassing, awkward, as it would be not to call him, she felt it her only recourse, if matters were not to be made even worse. She still, however, abhorred her role as the defensive one of the two of them, a role she was not accustomed to play. But maybe he wouldn't have put her on the defensive after all, would rather have been gracious, courtly, understanding. Now she almost regretted not having gone to the phone. Her curiosity mounted as she speculated on what might have happened, the kind of person he might have turned out to be, had she talked to him. Maybe he'd have said something in addition to a mere acknowledgment of her phone call. What, though, in addition *could* he have said? Her curiosity was now rampant; yet she resolved not to call him.

Across the dining table Ronald had been watching her. Now, a twinkle in his eye, he did nothing to improve matters by observing that not everyone, he was sure, joining the Black Peoples Congress started at the top and got phone calls at home from the leader himself. Irene Adkins looked appalled. But Mary Dee controlled herself, made a very necessary effort at nonchalance. "As a matter of fact," she smiled, "it's the first time he's ever called.

And I'm almost certain he's got something he wants me to do," she lied—"some assignment or other, that will be difficult, probably impossible, but also very time-consuming." She laughed— "That then is what you may, if you like, call joining at the top." Everyone, except Irene Adkins, also laughed.

But this soon centered the conversation in earnest on Knight. Both Ronald and Geoffrey began to speak favorably of him— about what he had done for inner-city blacks, his organizing ability, his intelligence, zeal, and vision. Geoffrey had heard one of his speeches in Boston and praised his courage and sincerity, and the broad appeal he enjoyed among the masses of blacks. The longer they talked, the more Mary Dee felt she had underrated Knight as a man, ignored his well-earned fame, failed in general to give him his due. Now, in addition to her ravenous curiosity, she was suddenly aware of the offense she must have given him by failing to take his call in response to her own. But it had all happened so suddenly, she thought; she had been so unprepared. Besides, she was frightened, and also loathe to talk to him within earshot of listeners.

The upshot then of all her confusions, waverings, her resolutions, was that after dinner was over and the others had moved into the parlor, her resolve long vanished, she went and found the scribbled phone number Mrs. Grier had left on the phone stand— she saw at once it was not the organization headquarters' number —then quickly went upstairs to her room. Heart pounding, the piece of paper gripped in her hand, she closed her bedroom door and went and dialed the number. At once she got the busy signal. Trembling from her qualms, she sat down for a moment—waiting. Three minutes later she dialed again. Again the busy signal. Two more attempts produced the same result. But by now her fear had become so great that the last time she dialed she found herself hoping, praying, she would again get the busy signal, which she did. She had lost her nerve completely, and knew the conversation would have been a disaster for her had she reached him. She returned downstairs.

Later that night in bed—it was an inexplicable occurrence, an aberration—she spent most of the time in wistful, bizarre, unhappy, dreams. She later felt they'd been largely occasioned by a midnight chat she had had in her room with Jocelyn before both retired.

673

Jocelyn never tired of asking questions about Paris, and had spoken of school and a female professor she had who was French—born in Avignon—but who made occasional deprecating remarks, though not in class, about, of all places, Paris. Jocelyn, having gotten her extravagant impressions of Paris from Mary Dee, had been surprised—if not dismayed, certainly confused. Mary Dee, listenening, had immediately sat up and taken notice.

Jocelyn went on: "Professor Poincaré—she's a remote descendant of the great French mathematician, and also of his cousin, the politician—says Paris is no longer the romantic city it used to be; that the government hasn't the will to protect it from the inroads of the profiteers defacing it with skyscrapers, motels, hamburger places, and all manner of other gauche modernizations and gewgaws. She says the Champs Elysées will soon look like lower Broadway or Times Square, and that, if it does, the French will deserve it."

"Oh, she's crazy!" Mary Dee seemed taking it personally. "What a terrible thing to say!" Then realizing she was over-reacting, she calmed down. "Paris has always been great—*and romantic.*" Her heart went into the statement. "It always will be—despite what your cynical professor says. The woman is nuts, Jocelyn."

But she felt uncomfortable even later as she went to bed—the part of her talk with Jocelyn about the French had somehow been a seed, or spark, producing reflections, visions, memories, good and bad, of Paris. Then in bed asleep the dream hit her with such force it woke her midway through it. In the dream, one evening in Paris she was riding with Philip in his Citroën. They had been to the Comédie Française and were driving down, not the Champs Elysées, but the Rue de Rivoli toward the Champs Elysées—when he said to her: "I saw this street for the first time in a movie. It was about Paris during the war—the World War II German occupation. My father, my brother Randy—Kermit Randall—and I saw the movie one summer on Martha's Vineyard Island. I was sixteen, I guess. It was about spies and espionage, about torturing information out of people, and all that—you know the whole bit; a grisly business. The Gestapo, I remember, had captured—just off the street at random—a French Negro, a mulatto, who clearly hadn't succeeded in getting out of Paris before it fell. The Nazis were hustling him down this street—I remember the street sign, *Rue de*

Rivoli—beating him as they went, until he was bloody all over. The movie then got pretty gruesome and my father was disgusted and wanted to leave, though he finally didn't. But later, when we came out, he attacked the picture and said that, although Hitler was indeed a madman and committed many heinous crimes, he did not reflect the true German attitude at all; that the picture was made by Jews and misrepresented, slandered, the German people, who were a manly, civilized race and had been trying to save the world from being mongrelized by people who didn't have the morality, nor the discipline and culture, to make things work." Philip then laughed.

Mary Dee turned to him. "What did you, or Kermit Randall, say to him, Philip?"

Philip laughed again. "We didn't say anything. You don't talk back to my father."

"What would you say to him if he said that today?"

Philip paused and thought. "I know I'd be angry as hell—and he could tell it by looking at me and would probably shut up."

"What would you *say*, Philip?"

"You don't talk back to my father."

"Oh! . . ."

Her outrage had awakened Mary Dee with a start—shaken, trembling; then angry and sad.

Throughout the next day, Thanksgiving, despite all the family reunion activities and goings-on, her thoughts remained on Philip. She wondered what his present life was like, now that he'd completed his Paris studies and gone home to stay. He was no doubt a junior executive already, an architect in some big Philadelphia firm —via his father's clout. His father had also probably already picked out a girl, a Mainline bud, for him—to be his wife. Philip would hardly resist—at least not vocally. You didn't talk back to Father. She thought of how this devastating young Apollo, and what he represented, had altered her life. Though last night's dream—or nightmare—had been shocking, it was true; true to life. It was Philip. Yet Philip had character, she told herself adamantly—she was certain of it, and that it would eventually come out, assert itself, some day—when his father had passed on to his Nordic Valhalla. But she felt that Philip would have been different had he been reared in another setting, uninfluenced by his tyrannical bigot

675

of a father. She was sure of this, for she knew Philip—knew him in ways his family did not, in ways it was impossible for them ever to know him. She knew him at his best and his worst, and at his best he was glorious. This was truth—for they had experienced too many transfiguring, noble, moments together. He had enkindled her soul, then broken her heart. They would not meet again now— she felt this, and accepted it. But no one, nothing, in or out of a dream, could convince her that Philip was bad—basically bad. She thought him tragically misguided. Yet he had left her embittered for life. Ornette was right, then. Rosabelle was right. Ferdinand Bailey was right. John Calvin Knight was right. Knight's stare of hatred in Paris she now understood, and forgave. Finally, at two o'clock that afternoon—a chilly but bright Thanksgiving Day—she called him and this time he answered.

*　　*　　*　　*　　*

The night before, however, Knight, on Mary Dee's refusal at dinner to take his call, had never in his life felt so humiliated. He burned with shame, then anger. And though during the next hour his feelings somewhat subsided, he still wondered what had happened. She had called him first, then had declined his call in answer. Yet, he asked himself, would she still call him back? He hadn't long to wait. Only four or five people had his unlisted phone number, so that when, shortly after nine o'clock that night, his phone rang, he jumped, almost leapt, to it to take the expected, eagerly awaited, call—only to hear from San Francisco Griselda's plaintive voice. It was therefore Knight's and Griselda's ensuing fifteen-minute phone conversation that had resulted in the repeated busy signals Mary Dee had gotten when after dinner she had tried to return his call.

Knight, now caught by surprise, had heard Griselda's voice with a sinking heart. He sat down in the chair at the phone, aware that all his troubles had returned. He was sure he knew what she would say, or rather ask: Had he gotten her letters and why hadn't he written or called? Instead, after mutually nervous brief greetings and pleasantries, she asked him for money. This was a second sur-

676

prise for him—she had never done this before. She explained her funds were embarrassingly low as a result of the expenses of the trip and her present stay in this small but nice hotel. Then again she gave him her telephone number and asked that they hang up so that he could call her back and have his phone incur the charges. He of course agreed and added he would wire her a thousand dollars immediately. Yet, after they had hung up, it took him all of three minutes to phone her back. He was stalling for time in order to collect himself and his thoughts, to decide what to say to her about their situation—and how to say what he had been unable to write. He knew now somehow he must. Finally he dialed her number.

"My God!—finally," she said, and tried to laugh. "I was getting ready to call you again, even if I am broke. What took you so long?"

He was honest. "I was thinking," he said.

"What's come over you, John Calvin? Out with it—tell me everything that's happened. Maybe then I'll see why you're trying to avoid me." Her attempts at jauntiness sounded false. There was almost hysteria in her voice.

"It's going to cause a big to-do in the organization if you return," he said simply.

"Who's pressing it?—Ornette? . . . Ferdie?"

"Ornette and Ferdie are very loyal to the organization, yes. But it's really some of the older members on the C.P.C. who are making such an issue of it. It's gotten bad."

"Well, we must resist them, John Calvin. We mustn't run from people who think like that—they're misguided. We know better, so we mustn't run."

"That's just it, Griselda—they're *not* misguided. They know what's best for the organization. Some of them helped found it. I'm the one who's been remiss." Knight's voice was unsteady, distressed, husky.

"What are you going to do, then?"

There was a pause; he was floundering. "I must stand with them," he said at last. "I owe it to them, and to the organization."

"But I want to come back, John Calvin—what will happen if I come back?"

"It will make bad matters a whole lot worse—very much so. It

677

will create an intolerable situation—Griselda, you must not come back."

She did not reply to this; there was silence in both places.

Then he made the mistake of saying: "I'll try to make it up to you somehow."

"Make it up to me!" she screamed in the phone. "How can you *ever* make it up to me! By your spinelessness you have dishonored, desecrated, me!" Now he could hear her crying as she said: "Well, go tell your followers *this!*—that the lowly little typist you had in your office that they thought was white, and should be thrown out, is not white at all. Go tell them—and tell yourself, John Calvin —that I am black! For it's the truth! My father's maternal grandmother was an African slave in the Caribbean! Do you hear me, John Calvin?—say something!" She continued crying; he could hear her.

He was stunned. "I don't know what to say, Griselda," he finally said. "I'm surprised of course—it's incredible. But what difference does it make?—how does it change things?"

"Oh, don't you see how wrong you are?—my color made a world of difference *before.*"

"I'm sorry—I'm sorry."

"Oh, John Calvin, there's no need for you to lie. You're not sorry. You want to be rid of me and the sooner the better. I'm not trying to appeal to your sympathy. I'm telling you what's in my heart. How can you forget that night, in my bed, when you told me that in finally doing what we had just done we had made each other complete, whole, when before we had lacked something essential and life-giving. You had said it in response to what I'd said about how you, and somehow the organization, had come to be my moorings to life; that before, especially since Alan's death, I had had nothing to seize and hold onto, nothing to give any meaning to my existence, that I'd been just a floater. Then that night you said by what we'd done we'd made each other whole. Oh, I thought what you said was so beautiful, so lovely. Do you remember?

Knight said nothing.

"Were you lying?"

"No," he finally said. "I believed it."

"But you no longer believe it—is that it?"

678

Anguish in his voice, he embarked on a speech. "You don't understand!" he cried. "It was a lapse on my part—a terrible lapse! I'm human like anybody else—I'm not perfect, I'm no robot, I have feelings!"

"Physical, yes, John Calvin."

"But it was a lapse, I tell you! I betrayed my responsibility to a task I undertook early in life—a commitment to help uplift blacks. I strayed from my duty. It's clear now to the organization leaders too that I've strayed. They of course place most of the blame on you, without even knowing you. I would tell them differently if I thought it would do any good, but it wouldn't. My only recourse is to return to what I know to be my duty, my calling, my true way of life, hoping to have profited from this experience. Oh, you can see what I must do!" But Griselda, without his knowing it, had already hung up in the middle of his speech. "Can't you see? . . ." he said ". . . Hello . . . hello, Griselda?" At last he realized what had happened and returned the phone to its cradle.

Yet he sat there, inundated by the agony of the experience. Suddenly then he dialed her back. When she finally answered, he said: "Why wouldn't you hear me out? I was trying to get you to see *my* side of this too! . . ."

"I see your side, John Calvin—I bear you no ill will. I guess I was being unreasonable, selfish—and pretty unrealistic too. I assume it's because I hate so returning to my old life, the life of a floater, with no longer any moorings—I'd been through so much of that."

"Griselda, we must remain friends—we *must!* We too have been through a lot together. First thing in the morning I'll wire you the money."

"Oh, no, no!—heavens no. Don't do that—don't you dare. I'd send it right back. I can get money from my mother until the probate proceedings are over—poor, poor, Marvin. But asking you for money made me feel closer to you, sort of dependent on you. That's why I did it. No, no, I'll make out. I'll send Mamie Campbell my key and ask her to send me what few clothes I left in that furnished flat. But somehow I keep thinking of Marvin. . . ."

"Griselda, I want to—" But he hadn't the courage to tell her Marvin's death was murder. He desisted.

679

"Good-bye, John Calvin," she said. "I wish everything good for you. I honestly do. Good-bye." Then before he could say anything she had hung up.

He did not sleep till nearly daybreak.

So later that day, Thanksgiving afternoon near two o'clock, when again his phone rang, he still had not shaken himself free of his feelings of misery and guilt over Griselda. He seemed in a daze of preoccupation, of deep self-absorption. In the bathroom shaving when he heard the phone, he assumed it was Ferdinand, at whose place he was later to have dinner, and went in to answer lackadaisically. But when he picked up the phone, said "Hello," and heard in reply the female voice, which he had not heard often enough to recognize, he was alert, curious. He had long since forgotten Mary Dee.

"Is this Mr. Knight?"

"Yes."

"Mr. Knight, this is Mary Dee Adkins . . . Rosabelle's and Ornette's friend—you may recall."

In his sudden surprise and excitement Knight's face, one half of it still lathered, felt prickly and hot. Yet, easing down onto the chair at the phone, he somehow remembered to keep his aplomb—after all, she had not taken his call.

"Yes, of course—how are you, Miss Adkins?" He spoke pleasantly enough.

She seemed to want to rush on, her voice nervous, inept. "Thank you very much for returning my call last evening but we were in the middle of a family reunion dinner and with the noise and all I thought it would be better if I called you back rather than try to talk then. But later in the evening I would get the busy signal each time I called you." She was almost breathless.

"Well, I'm sorry." Though excited and elated, he said nothing more, making her come to him.

"I won't keep you," she said, still nervously, "but I'm between jobs—I've had a job for some months as a commercial artist, but it got uninteresting and I left—and Ornette and Rosabelle have been reminding me that until I find something else that's suitable I might think of giving more time to the organization, as a volunteer staff person in the office perhaps . . . I don't know how that strikes you."

Knight was thinking fast. This explanation did not sound quite

680

right to him—was this why she had first called? But he too was getting more nervous now, and anxious that he not offend her, scare her off; yet wanting somehow to punish her. "It strikes me fine," he said—"as very magnanimous. But I'm on the road so much that I'm not the one who knows most about these things— Ferdinand Bailey and Mamie Campbell in the office are more conversant with staff arrangements than I am. As I recall, Mr. Bailey talked to you when you called, but of course he didn't know why you were calling, so couldn't advise you. Why don't you let me ask him or Mrs. Campbell to call you and discuss it with you? It's, as I say, though, a very magnanimous gesture on your part. We're grateful."

Mary Dee seemed taken aback by this. She had expected a more eager, enthusiastic, reception, and an affirmative decision on the spot. "Well, thank you," she finally said. "I'll be glad to talk with either of them. . . . Good-bye—"

He held her. "Except briefly at the rally, I haven't seen you since the fine gathering that evening in your marvelous studio. I can't forget all the wonderful paintings—they were something. I enjoyed being there very much. How are your committee plans developing?—they really sounded promising that night."

"We'll be starting very soon—next week, I hope. Well, thank you—I'll talk to Mr. Bailey or Mrs. Campbell when they call. Good-bye."

"Thank *you*. Good-bye."

It was how things had begun with them. It was a new phase, a sharp turn of events, in the lives of both. Knight had soon, very soon, recovered from all his qualms and remorse over Griselda and returned gladly, safely, to the fold of Blackness in all its manifestations and attitudes. Ferdinand elatedly called Mary Dee, had her come into the office for talks with himself and Mamie Campbell, and soon Mary Dee had been taken on, not as a volunteer, but as a paid staff member to develop programs—though at only a hundred dollars a week, which was less than a third of what she had received at Aico & Aleshire. But she had not come to work for the organization for money—she was grimly motivated by experiences and memories far stronger than money. Therefore she was not at all dissatisfied and looked forward to throwing herself into the redemptive work of Blackness with resourcefulness, energy—and vengeance. But Knight, as a person, did not interest her. It was his work and what he represented, the organization, the people, she wished to contribute to. It was a challenge she rather welcomed. Though not without occasional ambivalence, she hoped things would somehow work out and began her new duties without consulting, or even telling, her mother. She meant to be unfettered, purposeful, hard— to even old scores.

There were only two people who were less than enchanted with all this. One was Mamie Campbell. Try as she might, Mamie could not forget Griselda and even herself harbored some sense of guilt over her departure and what she suspected had been the manner of it. The other, surprisingly, was Ornette. Of late he could hardly bring himself to trust Mary Dee, though he tried to react well to the new arrangement and to cooperate as best he could. But he had never forgotten their encounter in her parlor. Knight, however, was secretly beside himself, euphoric, about it all. He fairly glowed inside and now traveled to distant cities far less frequently than he formerly had. Mamie observed this, and so did Ornette. But Ferdinand was oblivious, optimistic, rapturously happy. It was because he sensed Knight's happiness and for the glowing future was convinced it augured well.

*   *   *   *   *

Within less than a month what was thought to be further changes in Knight could be seen by the people in the office. He seemed to some a new man, now in full command, with once more a firm grasp on organizational affairs. On the surface this appeared to be true. At staff meetings he presided with considerateness but also with a show of authority, displaying little hesitancy in ruling against at least two of Ornette's fanciful proposals for increasing the organization's membership. He indicated vaguely he had other ideas about how it should be done. His behavior many times was strange, nervous—affected. Mary Dee seldom said anything in these meetings, only listening attentively to the other discussants. Yet Knight, in most of his nervously-aggressive remarks, seemed to talk directly to her, at her, in almost total disregard of Ferdinand, Mamie, and Ornette, as if only she could really comprehend what he was saying. It embarrassed her. Her uneasiness stemmed also from Knight's lack of tact in the way he did it; it was so noticeable—his ignoring of the others. The result was that she deliberately stayed away from the next staff meeting. She was not at all unmindful of the paltry salary they paid her and felt freer to do as she pleased. At the following staff meeting, however, held late one afternoon, she was present and spoke freely, openly, with confidence, on a number of subjects—all with Knight's undivided, riveted, attention on her. She was pleased with herself. The meeting ended well. Then when she went down to get in her car to go home, she discovered it was gone—stolen. Angry and upset, she returned to the office, where Ornette glumly offered to take her to a police station and report the theft, but Knight intervened and said he would take her himself, as he knew certain of the police officials, who would expedite the investigation. At once he had become solicitous of her, almost hovering; and earnestly trying to reassure her, played the car theft down, saying his own car had twice been stolen but both times found and returned by the police, practically without a scratch. Soon he ushered her out of the office as the others looked on.

In his modest Pontiac they drove east on 47th Street, then north on King Drive. It was mid-December, early evening, and the air was chill and dry; so far there had been little snow. Knight was silent, absorbed, Mary Dee the same, as darkness fell and the street lights came on. She was not only morose about her missing car but that Knight had seemed to use, seize upon, the incident to become more personal, get closer to her. It made her uncomfortable. Yet she could not dislike him; she really felt a strange compassion for him. During the past few days she had begun to sense his growing dependence on her. Now, in almost everything he did concerning the organization, in every decision he made, he seemed—despite what passed as his insensitive self-assurance—to look to her for support, approval. She was sure too the others—Ornette, Ferdinand, Mamie—saw it and wondered what was going on, what it would all come to. While Ferdinand was still clearly happy about the way things were developing, the other two seemed uncertain, skeptical. Mary Dee could not escape realization of the possibility she existed in the middle of an adversary situation. Yet, if she could, she wanted to help Knight. She wanted him to resume his old Black fanatical ways, the fiery advocacy, aggressiveness, the vindictiveness and spleen against whites. Though she sometimes vacillated on this subject, as of course he did himself, she always returned to her first thirst for blood, to the need, the compulsion, to wreak vengeance on her former tormentors, the Philadelphia Wilcoxes and all their kind everywhere, and to try, if only symbolically, to somehow even old scores. To this end she regarded Knight an instrument—*the* instrument. She must therefore help him. Yet beyond this she had no other interest in him; certainly not as a private person, a man. It was what, with her help, indeed her goading, he could be made to accomplish that propelled, engrossed, her. There was a vast difference in their motives, though possibly neither was aware.

When, at 29th and Prairie, they reached the police station, Knight boldly took her in and asked the big ebony-black desk sergeant for a Captain Youngblood. The sergeant, however, took one look at him and broke into a wide, idolatrous smile. "I think you're Mr. Knight," he said—"Mr. John Calvin Knight. Sure you are."

Knight seemed embarrassed. "Yes," he said.

"I'm Sergeant Talley. I'm a member, a member in good standing, of your organization—so are my wife and kids." Talley beamed. Suddenly then the shock of recognition hit Mary Dee. This, she realized, was the policeman who had quelled the violent disturbance in the Trocadero restaurant the morning she had rescued Ernestine and Vernon from the blizzard and taken them into the wretched place for breakfast. Talley said to Knight: "We're all glad as can be to see how you bounced back from your brush with death last spring. And they had to go and turn those hoods loose—I knew them all, a bad bunch—that tried to kill you. Really, couldn't you identify any of them, Mr. Knight?"

"Obviously not," said Knight, some coolness in his smile.

"The police department did a mountain of work on that case," Talley said. "They studied you too, almost as much as they did the clues on the suspects. They know all about you, Mr. Knight," he laughed—"from A to Z; your travels and all—even to Paris. What brings you here, though?"

Knight had tensed at the word "Paris." But now he said: "Sometime ago I met Captain Youngblood from this station. I've come to see him to make a report of the theft today of this lady's car. This is Miss Adkins of our office."

"Youngblood's gone for the day," Talley said, though admiringly eyeing Mary Dee. "I can take the report myself—I'll be glad to." He turned and produced a clipboard and was soon asking Mary Dee for license and engine numbers, a description of her little red Datsun, her address, telephone numbers, and other details. Knight stood by protectively, watching as she brought out various cards and documents from her purse to aid in answering Talley's questions. While waiting, Talley said to Knight: "You got a fellow in your office that's really a crackerjack—Ornette Hungerford. My, is he devoted to the organization! He spoke at our lodge meeting not long ago. He's a real asset to you—dedicated."

"Yes, he is." But Knight was watching Mary Dee, as if yearning in some way to help her; there was an anxious, possessive, expression in his eyes. "What are the chances soon of recovering Miss Adkins' car?" he said to Talley. "Mine's been stolen twice but both times you got it back for me the same day."

"We never know," said Talley—"it all depends. Many times we don't get those results." He now smiled in Mary Dee's direction. "We'll do our level best, though. But I see here she's got a good insurance company—that's always nice, just in case." He still eyed Mary Dee—humorously, quizzically. "Y'know, Miss Adkins," he said, "I keep tellin' myself I've seen you somewhere. I just can't figure out where. But maybe I'm wrong." He laughed and scratched his head. "Whew, but you wouldn't be all that easy to forget—that's what I keep tellin' myself. Ha, ha!"

Mary Dee felt her face stinging. But she smiled: "You could very well have seen me somewhere, Sergeant—I've lived in Chicago all my life."

Talley's familiarity incensed Knight. He frowned and shifted from foot to foot impatiently as Talley asked Mary Dee a few more questions about the car, then filled out a form and had her sign it. "We'll get this information out right away, Mr. Knight," he said, "and as soon as we get any response, we'll contact Miss Adkins."

"No, contact me," said Knight, and insisted on giving Talley his two phone numbers. "I'll follow through on it with you—you don't have to bother Miss Adkins." He had touched Mary Dee's elbow and was starting out with her, when he thought to turn around again. "Thanks a lot, Sergeant—it's very kind of you," he said. "I hope you'll stop by the office when you're near and see us." Then they left.

Outside they had hardly got in the car when Knight asked Mary Dee to have dinner with him, somewhere downtown or anyplace —he seemed agitated, nervous, impetuous. She declined—saying her mother expected her home, to a dinner they had jointly planned. At once then she realized her mistake. The excuse had created an enormous vacuum—in which an invitation to him to come home with her to dinner was so natural. It was embarrassing. Yet she did not feel up to it—or to him. She also feared to invite him. It would only involve her more deeply. Knight, sensitive, feeling the slight, sulked as he drove her home. But soon his behavior, by her considered childish, annoyed, nettled, her. Paris—even had Talley not mentioned it—inevitably came to mind. In view of the long history of things, she thought Knight presumptuous—she could never forget his conduct in Paris at Fouquet's, or later at the little Canary restaurant when she was with Raoul. Certainly she had experienced his insults. Now, she thought, though he was not quite wheedling, he had the effrontery to sulk. What did he expect from her—thanks? "Sergeant Talley mentioned you were in Paris," she said suddenly, unable to veil the taunt—"When was that?"

He turned on her fiercely. "You know very well when it was," he said. "You saw me. Twice."

"So you remember, I see," she said, almost bitterly. "Well, I must say, you've changed quite a bit since then—your attitude." At once she was remorseful, remembering all he had been through in the interim, and, knowing his present state of mind, she became subdued, silent.

Strangely, he made no reply. He took her home, but though he had been on the premises the night of her studio party, he now had to ask directions to her house. She gave them in a quiet, reflective, voice, and on arrival, as they sat in his car for a moment before she went in, he said, "You'll probably have your car in a day or two, but on my way to the office in the morning, shall I pick you up?"

She looked at him in the dark of the car, then gazed up sadly at the big, lighted house. "No," she said. "I won't be going to the office tomorrow. The movers are coming to talk to my mother, and I want to be here. We're moving after Christmas, you know."

He turned to her. "Where?"

"Not too far—on the near north side, but in an apartment."

When she moved to get out of the car, he stopped her by his sudden, unexpected, remark. "I think you saved me," he said. "Me, as well as the organization. You arrived in the nick of time. I was collapsing under all I'd been through and would soon have lost leadership. I'm very grateful to you."

Shaken, embarrassed, by what he had said, she could only murmur, "I'm sure you're wrong."

He seemed hardly to have heard her. "I was very unhappy," he said, musing. "It wasn't so much the attempt on my life. It was my wavering, the temporary loss of faith—in the organization's mission—that almost finished me. I was miserable."

"What do you know of misery!" she suddenly cried out. "This time next month I'll be gone from this house! Think of it!—the house I grew up in; all its memories . . . of my father, of school, my early painting; all the happy times with my family and friends. It's all gone . . . it's all gone now and will never, never, come back! And you speak of misery! . . ." Her voice had grown hoarse.

Speechless, he had then watched her get out of the car and go up the walk to her house. But later in his apartment that evening as he prepared food to eat he was not unhappy. Hope had somehow risen.

Chapter 3

Valentine's Day. She was chic in her bright new red coat from I. Magnin's. It was late afternoon and the light, yet extremely rare, snow in the chill grey air was swirling about the bridge. Though Alcatraz could readily be seen, neither Belvedere nor Sausalito was so easily descried. She lifted her face to the elements as if to sniff, savor, the sporadic snow, then with her beautifully gloved hand she touched for a moment the cold steel of the girder and railing which were in color a brazen burnt orange. This, she thought, did not seem at all a *Golden* Gate. Now in the middle of the limitless span she peered blindly back toward the south in the direction of what she knew or guessed was Huntington Park, where she and her mother now lived in quite dramatically improved circumstances. Indeed Nancy Hanks had thus described them that very morning as the two of them were having breakfast in their marvelous new apartment. Things were better.

But things were over. They were ended, she thought—the daughter. All's well that ends. Why else this trial mission today, this reconnoitering and rehearsal, on the bridge? Till another day —soon. Or a night. She thought back on other times when she had viewed this now inscrutable scene, a vast blue placid vista in summer when seen from a car, bus, or room window. Many times as a child and adolescent she had witnessed, studied, it. It was even yet more exciting at night . . . then especially in the mists, the autumn mists, and California fog. As at the beginning of it all, she still felt its eerie indistinctness fading out the pointillism of a million city lights. Ghostly, yes! . . . a great specter to the spiritual wanderer. She had been searching but only black nothingness had been found. So the search was ended now. She had even settled matters with Frimbo, having only two weeks before flown to Kansas City and belatedly told authorities what she knew about old Cleet's death; his murder. She seemed surprised when they preferred no charges against her and told her she could return home as long as she kept them advised of her whereabouts. She could see, however, few efforts had been made to apprehend Cleet's murderer, and wondered if her lengthy statement had a chance of renewing interest in a case where the victim was a black nobody and the occurrence almost a year past. Yet she had returned west, home, with some of her guilt lifted. But what if they found killer Lonnie and brought him to trial? Who would be there to testify against him and in Cleet's behalf? She would not be there. And Lonnie's mistress-aunt would never implicate him. So there would, could, be only an acquittal—even if there was a trial at all. Yet her own guilt, though not entirely dissipated, had been somewhat eased by her going—after that, however, she had abandoned Frimbo, for in these final months had he not abandoned her? But now, all's well that ends. She had also destroyed her wig.

She turned up her face again to the lightly swirling snow, then once more touched the railing of the bridge and held onto it tightly, fearing now even to look over, though she was barely able to see the bay which seemed a mile straight down beneath her. She had searched, yes, and she knew now in quest of a fatuous grail. But she seemed to have realized all this sometime, somewhere, in the long, long ago, in the vaguest past. Now the realization had returned, but with greater force than ever. How futile, how vain, it had all been. Sometime, somewhere, yes, in the past she had told herself—predicted?—that she must one day make this decision; must make it in order to attain, to *become*. Left unfulfilled, there could be only the same anxieties, torment, that fearful dread of the heart, instead of the bold mission of becoming. Even in what seemed the remotest of yesterdays she had felt all these promptings and foreshadowings. This was even before Marvin. Now he too was no more, though about him her dogged guilt persisted. Would it ever, never, ease? She did not know and there was not much time; the guilt would probably outlast her and such posthumous benefactions from him as her chic red coat. Now there was only the Golden Gate; the gate to what? To becoming. So this rare day of swirling snow was Valentine's Day. She had sent the other him the final of final communications, mailed two days ago and addressed to "The Honorable John Calvin Knight." She had meant the irony in the salutation, though it was a Valentine card she had made herself—six inches tall and four inches wide, inside it merely the crayoned words: "Happy Valentine, and many, many more. Griselda." Now she reconnoitered and rehearsed on the bridge. Possibly within the week, or the month—who knew?—she would become. *"Oh, John Calvin, John Calvin! . . ."*

In the thirty-five years of the structure it had been accomplished 603 times, she had read; indeed eight months ago there had been a *twin* accomplishment!—two Asians, man and wife, hands clasped, had jumped; thus becoming. But, due to bad or hurried planning, the feat had been attempted from the north tower and the landing had been, not mercifully into the cold bay waters, but on the pavement of a road near the rock-strewn shoreline between the Pacific Ocean and San Francisco Bay. This must be avoided. The incident had brought public proposals that an eight-foot high barrier replace the present three-and-a-half-foot railing along the skyway's catwalk, but this was still in the discussion—debating—stage. Some objected to its four-million dollar cost. There was, however, an ominous installation, already in place and effectively used— closed-circuit TV. Even now, in the swirling snow, she could feel the cameras on her as she nervously—fear of heights constricting her bowels—reconnoitered and rehearsed her way along this ribbon of celestial sidewalk. Her investigations had informed her that TV cameras, nestled unobtrusively over the high roadbed under each of the two bridge towers, roved restlessly both the north and south sections of the bridge and their zoom lenses could bring you in instantly and fix you like a fly. Guards, already boasting of a seventy-five per cent prevention record, could then come running and maybe reach you before you could reach the barrier, the parapet. It was a crucial, fiendish, business and must be accomplished stealthily—and at night. *"Oh, John Calvin, John Calvin! . . ."*

*   *   *   *   *

Also Valentine's Day. He sat in his office with the door closed, having lost, regained, then lost again, his nerve for what seemed a dozen times that morning. Two months now of the most mooning, frenetic courtship, in which he had completely lost control of himself, and he was still riven with fear over whether—and if so, how

—she would accept his gift, a meaningful, though not-too-expensive, yet very personal, Valentine's gift. It was a brooch. He knew it was, to be sure, an old-fashioned gesture, but he wanted it that way; it would denote his utter seriousness—as if, he thought, she wasn't already aware! Once more he took the handsome little box out of his desk drawer, opened it, and studied the modest ornament inside—garnet, heart-shaped, set in sterling silver; not elegant, not extravagant, but honest and tasteful; an avatar of his sincerity. Though her office, now immediately adjacent to his, was quiet, he knew she was in there; yet he could not muster the courage to pay her the crucial visit. From his fear his stomach felt queasy and the hand holding the box had slight tremors.

How could all this have happened? he wondered. Yet he did *not* wonder. He knew. He had discovered one thing; and he believed it mightily. It was that he had fallen in love with her the very first time he saw her—that afternoon at Fouquet's in Paris. Hence the savagery of his reaction—seeing her in the company of two white men. Even now he could feel again his blind, unreasoning fury and told, assured, himself his reaction that day had, paradoxically, been quite rational, entirely explicable; it was the result of love on the spot; now "love at first sight" was no longer a myth, a canard, to him. It could happen, he thought. It did happen. Yet that day he had vented his feelings on her, not on the men with her; that was the strange, unnatural, perhaps unfair, part of it, he felt now —though he had never been able to get her to talk about those men except to say they were friends at the art school where she had studied. His questions had noticeably nettled her; it was as if she felt them presumptuous and ill-mannered, almost blasphemous. He had never forgotten it, her reaction, and had felt extremely unpleasant, almost as though he had committed, if not a felonious crime, a most serious misdemeanor. He had often since speculated about this her swift, taut, defensive reaction; the cause of it. Yet he knew his Paris conduct to have been loutish. Now she was making him pay for it, dearly, by her almost unexceptional refusals to hear his heart's plaints, his pleas for her love and understanding. Two months of this.

He felt low and demeaned by his own actions and she seemed embarrassed, frightened, by his uncontrolled, almost eccentric, behavior—he in fact wondered why she still stayed with the organization, though he could sense her strange zeal, passion, for it, if not for him. When her stolen car was never found, he offered to have the organization replace it with a brand new one, but she had declined, saying her insurance was entirely adequate. She had gone out socially with him four times, twice to ideological-type public lectures, once to a black jazz concert, and once to dinner, but had steadfastly confined conversation to organizational and doctrinal matters and declined his invitation to dine, potluck, in his apartment, begging off on the pretext she and her family were still busy trying to get settled, comfortable, since they had finally sold their large house and moved into the condominium apartment.

It made him grim, desperate. On impulse now he put the little box in his pocket, left his office, and in the instant found himself standing at her open door. From their own offices, Mamie Campbell and Ferdinand Bailey could see him plainly, standing there in manifest fright. Mary Dee finally looked up from a sheaf of papers she had been going through and marking with a pencil. "May I come in?" he uttered hoarsely.

"Of course," she said, her mouth agape; she seemed surprised, then wary; yet she smiled, tentatively, still with pencil in hand. There was the usual noisy activity in the outer office, the sound of clattering typewriters abounding. "Come in," she said, again tentatively.

He entered, closing the door behind him. "May I talk to you for a minute—I want to ask you a favor." He was earnest, nervous, as she watched him and he gazed helplessly into her face. She wore a tweed skirt and white blouse, the matching tweed suitcoat on a hanger on the hall tree behind her. Her hands, the fingernails unlacquered and immaculate, were as beautiful as her face, as she finally relinquished the pencil and sat back uneasily in her chair. He had already sat down. "I want to give you something," he said, his voice quavering. "I want you to accept it knowing there are no strings attached—absolutely none." She still looked at him, the tentative smile, however, gone, the wary look returned. He took the box from his pocket, opened it, and placed it on the desk before her. She leaned forward slightly, still warily, and looked at the brooch inside; then her lips parted again, but she did not speak, nor did she touch the box. Once more she looked at him. "Dee, don't refuse me this," he said, his voice almost pleading. "Please take it."

692

"It's beautiful," she finally said. "Oh, but I can't—"

"Dee!"

"I wish you hadn't done it. You make things so hard for me. I've tried to be honest with you, John Calvin."

"I know you have. I know too I've been an awful nuisance. You've all but told me, warned me. But I can't help myself. I'm helpless, Dee."

She gazed at the sheaf of papers on her desk and said nothing. Finally—"I don't know what to say; you know that. I don't like to appear unappreciative, or disrespectful—we've been through this before. As I said, I've tried to be truthful. I *do* want to help you— in your work."

"Oh, I know that—you're practically donating your services. I made you let the organization double your salary, so what does it amount to now?—two hundred a week. Stupendous! Considering your ability and dedication, the hard work you do for us, it's almost an insult to you. Now you tell me you want to help me in my work. Dee, you're already indispensable to us—to me! I've told you I'm helpless." He reached and got the box and made her take it. Sighing, she looked at the brooch again. The garnet heart, a deep ruby red, looked well in its sterling silver setting. "It's beautiful," she repeated sadly. "You mustn't misunderstand me, though, if I agree to take it. I'm *not* a prude, I don't feel at all compromised, for I respect you in every way, but it's just that I want to be fair, honest, with you—you deserve it."

Erratically, with great force, he scooted forward in his chair. "Tell me, Dee, is there someone else? Do you love someone?—are you engaged to someone . . . out of town?"

She was sadly reflective and gazed far away. Then suddenly her irritation showed. "You continue to want to ask about my personal life," she said. "Suppose I were to do that to you, a man of your standing and reputation?—you wouldn't like it. Neither do I, John Calvin, although I have none of your eminence. If I'm being dogmatic about it, you must forgive me. Please be tolerant with me." Then in great anguish she said it, impulsively, before she thought: "I've been through so much! . . ."

"What do you *mean*, Dee?" With his hand on her desk, he steadied himself. "Tell me!—what is it you've been through, what is it that makes you like you are?"

She sighed again and said nothing. At last she reached and got the box, took out the brooch, and pinned it on her blouse. Then as if resigned, defeated, she sat staring out the window. Both now sat in silence—until there came a knock on her door. It was one of the office girls distributing the day's mail. She gave Mary Dee three letters and a magazine, then turned to Knight. "I'll put yours on your desk, Mr. Knight." When she left, they resumed their stoic silence. But soon Knight got up, his face long, and returned to his office.

His mail was stacked on his desk as he sat down and began perfunctorily going through it. Then, halfway down the pile, he saw the piece of San Francisco mail addressed in that most familiar of handwritings and his heart began to pound in a wild, guilty contrition. He tore the envelope open and read on the makeshift crayoned card: "Happy Valentine, and many, many more." *Oh, John Calvin, John Calvin!* . . .

*   *   *   *   *

Ornette Hungerford, glum and disconsolate, astounded Ferdinand Bailey a week later by coming into Ferdinand's office and telling him he thought he, Ornette, was neglecting his family, was devoting far more time to the organization than he was to selling insurance, and that as a result his wife Rosabelle wanted to return to work, get a job. Ornette added he might resign his staff duties with the organization. Ferdinand, wide-eyed, unprepared for this, quickly got up, closed his office door, and motioned Ornette to a chair. "Oh, I'm sorry to hear this," he said—"Goodness gracious."

Ornette was impatient, exasperated. "Well, it makes sense, don't it?—I ain't going to let my family starve."

"Oh, Lord, no—of course not, Ornette." Dwarfish, hunchbacked Ferdinand squirmed higher on the three cushions he kept in his chair to give himself more height at his desk. "You've got a wonderful family—a wonderful wife, Ornette."

Ornette testily sucked his teeth. "I ain't much needed around here any more anyhow," he said. "Our girlfriend Mary Dee has taken over. That scheme you and I cooked up to get her and John Calvin together sure worked, didn't it? He forgot that white chick Griselda five minutes after *our* girlfriend came on the scene."

694

Ferdinand only gaped at him.

"Ferdie, if Mary Dee walked out of this office today, left the organization entirely, John Calvin would collapse like a rag doll. All that cocksureness and firmness he tries to show are phony. You can see how dependent he's become on her—in just months. He won't do anything without her; checks everything with her first. *She* gives him his ideas—in her modest, tactful, slick, way, of course—and a lot of times vetoes his. You've seen it, Ferdie. If this keeps up, she'll be running the organization soon."

Ferdinand was frowning now. "I remember last fall," he said, "how you were all upset about how close Griselda had gotten to him. Now, no sooner than we get rid of her, you take out after Mary Dee the same way—when you and Rosabelle were the ones who brought her into the organization and got her active. What's happened among you three?"

"I wish I knew," Ornette said. "It's just something you feel. I think sometimes she's almost as bad for him as Griselda was—in a different way maybe, yet still the same. He's so dependent on her. Ah, Ferdie, he's love-sick—don't you see it?"

"No, no—it's just that we're *Black* again now. If love is the result of that, then so much the better. But there's no more vacillation, no more doubts—the organization's *Black*. And Mary Dee's the one who's brought it about. She's *Black,* fiercely black, Ornette."

Ornette shook his head. "Well, you may have it all figured out, but I ain't," he said. "It don't make sense, Ferdie—her being all that Black. It don't ring true to me. Hell, what did white people ever do to her? Nothing—except maybe ogle her good looks. And her whole life's practically been in the white world, or in a world very much like white—ha, as close as her family could make it white. She's never been kicked around by honkies like the rest of us. Then why's she, as you call it, so fierce? Where's her motivation come from? It's a weird situation, Ferdie—it's something I feel."

"I think your feeling is irrational."

"Maybe so, but I'll tell you what ain't irrational—that from now on, I'm going to start supporting my family. I'll be rational about that."

"Ornette, you know we need you. We've got to work this out—I'll talk to John Calvin. We couldn't get along at all without you."

"Don't make me laugh," said Ornette. "Every idea I come up with is practically ignored. You people don't need me. And you don't need my wife, either—she ought to be stayin' home looking after the kids."

"So you've suddenly lost interest in poor ghetto blacks, have you?—people who need you so much. Sure, your family comes first—but I don't believe you'll ever turn your back on the poor niggers you've been fighting so hard all these years to help. I just don't believe it, Ornette."

Again Ornette shook his head. "There're going to be some changes, though, Ferdie. I can't keep on like this and still go home and face my wife and kids—they'll have no respect for me. What can John Calvin do for me anyway?—nothing, except maybe talk about paying me something; which I don't want. I won't take money from the organization. I just can't spend as much time with it as I have in the past. You and I always got along okay, Ferdie —I hope that'll continue." He got up to go.

Ferdinand's face was long, distressed. "It mustn't end up like this," he said. "We must talk, Ornette. You can't walk out on us— we need you."

Ornette paused for a moment; he said nothing. Finally he left.

*　　*　　*　　*　　*

They had long since moved—were in the new apartment—and it was already late March.

"Mother, why won't you join us, eat with us?" Mary Dee said. "Otherwise, he may think something; be offended."

"He won't be offended in the least," Irene Adkins said. She was standing in Mary Dee's bedroom door. "He's coming to see you, not me." She was stern, almost obdurate, and, considering her habitual fragility, vulnerability, seemed unusually strong and clear-headed tonight. "I'll have my dinner before he comes and be out of the way."

"Mother, you're determined not to recognize him, aren't you? I know you so well—you refuse, absolutely refuse, to acknowledge him, his position . . . his national reputation, accomplishments, all he's done for blacks. You just won't, will you?"

"That's not so. I can't understand the *personal* relationship that's developed between you two, that's all. I know Mr. Knight's position, what he's done. What I don't understand is you."

Mary Dee, seated before her dresser mirror, was emphatic. "That's no news," she said—"you never have." But as soon as she said it she was sorry.

"What a harsh, unjust, thing to say." Irene Adkins partially withdrew from the doorway.

"I'm sorry, Mother—I didn't mean it." Sighing, Mary Dee turned to the door, but Irene Adkins had gone. She felt contrite, knowing her mother's concern, anxiety, of late for her—since she had become so involved with the organization and Knight. She got up and followed Irene Adkins up into the parlor. "Mother, John Calvin will be here in an hour. Please help me—I want you to sit here and talk to him while I'm putting dinner on the table. It will make him more at ease—he's a very tense, nervous, man." Irene Adkins, pouting, had sat down on the beautiful sofa. She said nothing. Finally Mary Dee—it was Saturday evening and Mrs. Grier had left at noon—went in the kitchen and looked in the oven at the lamb roast. Why was her mother so intransigent about Knight? she asked herself; yet she knew at once; had always known. It was a mother's fear for her daughter's well-being, her future happiness, and Mary Dee was somehow grateful.

Though she and her mother had been in the apartment since mid-January, Mary Dee had not yet gotten accustomed to it, did not like it, and felt she never would. Irene Adkins had also at first not been entirely happy, until Mrs. Grier, whose housework had been considerably lightened, began praising the efficiences of the place in such glowing terms that Irene Adkins soon changed her mind. The apartment was attractive—six large, bright rooms, a serviceable kitchen, and two baths, all on the twelfth floor of a handsome near-Northside condominium building. Although Irene Adkins had had to sell her large house for less than she had bargained, she soon found, since moving, that her expenses were somewhat less burdensome than formerly. This made her even more confident the move had been right. But she missed the old house and all its memories and made a secret vow never to return to the area, never to see the house again. Yet she knew her memories would never allow her to enforce this vow. She sensed, however, Mary Dee's misery over the move, her restlessness and depression, and could only attribute her recent taking up with Knight to the emptiness of her life. Mary Dee worried her. She could not, moreover, understand a man as complex as Knight interested in her daughter, and therefore viewed him with misgiving, if not suspicion and hostility, despite his position and fame. It was a complication.

Knight arrived for dinner shortly before seven and was admitted by Mary Dee. Irene Adkins, however, soon appeared, to whom he was formally presented, and for a short time she joined them in the living room. The air, though, was tense, uneasy; there were awkward pauses in the conversation. But Knight, courtly, in attempted good spirits, though nervous and uncomfortable, soon turned from Irene Adkins and, smiling, said to Mary Dee: "Police Officer Talley's people finally found your car—your little red Datsun."

"Oh, no!—where?"

"Abandoned in a vacant lot on 45th Street—I'm afraid it's totally banged up—stripped and worthless. A strange thing, though: the trunk was full of our literature—pluggers and handbills about the national meeting last fall, the big rally in the 43rd Street Amphitheater."

"The handbills were mine," Mary Dee said—"Ornette and Rosabelle had me delivering them around. Oh, my, but the car's a total loss?"

Knight nodded—"I think so, yes."

"You did right, Suky," said Irene Adkins at last, "by going on and buying a new car. I never thought you'd ever get your little red Datsun back—or at least in a condition to use it again."

Knight then said to Mary Dee: "The only other thing they found in the car—it was in the glove compartment—that might also be yours was this." He pulled a notebook, considerably scuffed-up now, out of his pocket and handed it to her. "When I saw 'Ecole des Beaux-Arts' printed on it, I was pretty sure it was from your student days—in Paris."

"Oh! . . ." Mary Dee stifled a cry. "Yes, it's my sketchbook—my Beaux-Arts sketchbook. I so hated losing it." Uneasily, hurriedly, then she put the notebook down on an end table, but almost at once picked it up and took it back to her bedroom—all the while wondering if, fearing, Knight had looked through it. As she returned to the living room, she was all but certain he had.

It contained not only pencil sketches she had made during her various goings and comings in Paris with Philip but, inside the back cover, there was a love message Philip had written to her one day as they sat at a sidewalk cafe table in Montparnasse. For sad, nostalgic, reasons she had always kept the notebook with her, on her person, or sometimes in the glove compartment of her car. It had been the only thing she had really lamented in the theft of the car. Now she feared, was almost sure, Knight had read it and her secret anger, outrage, flared. How dare he! Introduction of the notebook had given the evening a bad start.

Fifteen minutes later Irene Adkins—having insisted on serving herself dinner before Knight's arrival—had gone to her room and left the pair alone. Her action and its import were far from lost on Knight, and, by the time Mary Dee had put dinner on the table, he sat eating mostly in preoccupied silence. Mary Dee, her face a cold, blank mask, tried to maintain conversation as best she could, but Knight seldom responded. At last as she ate, she too fell silent.

"This is only my second time in your home," he said at last, with the devious intention now of seizing on some other excuse for his moroseness, "so you must forgive me if I still feel a little strange —and like a stranger. Maybe—I don't know why—it's got something to do with the very first time, some months ago now, you phoned me at the office. Remember that?—I was in New York and you talked to Ferdie. You'd never called me before and I've never understood why you took the initiative and did it—out of the blue. I know you've already said it was to get a job with the organization, but, frankly, I've never believed that. Really, why did you want to talk to me that day?"

"I didn't," Mary Dee said simply. "I wanted to find out whether you'd be in town the day of the women's committee meeting Rosabelle had called to be held at the headquarters. I found out from Ferdie that you would, so the day of the meeting I didn't go." She smiled. "It was during the time, you'll recall, that Ornette, Rosabelle, and Ferdie were trying so hard to promote our friendship. I meant not to cooperate at all and was trying to avoid you."

"So that was it." Knight gave a sardonic smile. "Little has changed, though—you're still trying to avoid me."

Mary Dee spoke seriously. "You're having dinner in my home

again—at my invitation. That doesn't seem as if I'm trying to avoid you, does it?"

"You won't believe that I started not to come tonight. But then I decided to come on one condition to myself—that once and for all I'd talk things through with you. I don't have to tell you I've been in a pretty bad state about you for months now—you know it, of course. You know it well."

"Eat your dinner," unhappy Mary Dee said to divert him— "You've hardly eaten a thing. Drink your wine. Isn't it good claret? I got it for the occasion."

"Ah, the occasion," he said with irony.

But she kept him off the subject for the remainder of the meal.

Later they sat in the parlor listening on her stereo to Paul Robeson singing "No More Auction." Knight had given her the record the week before, though she was playing it now for the first time. The stereo instrument's volume was down, but Robeson's deep bass voice, confident, determined, full of pride and nobility, yet poignance and hope, filled the room. "What men and women have influenced you most?" Mary Dee suddenly asked. "Is Robeson one?"

"I don't know," Knight said—"I've never thought about it. I know Dr. King has. Robeson, though, is a great, a very great, black man—he's proven he has the courage of a lion. But more and more I'm coming to see—and I guess nothing could be more ironical—that my father's influence has probably been greatest of all."

"How did he influence you?—what did you learn from him?"

"Patience, tolerance—if I've learned them. At least he counseled that."

"But how tolerant can we, as blacks, afford to be?" she said with sudden impatience. "Whites have made us suffer so—we must somehow make them suffer in return! Blacks must get even!"

Knight said nothing at first; he was pondering what she had said. "I guess if it motivates blacks to do other things," he said, "constructive and lasting things, then it's all right to feel vengeance. It's certainly understandable—that blacks want, as you put it, to get even. Only—"

"We *must* get even!" Her fists were clenched. "We must teach them a lesson!"

Knight watched her strangely, suspiciously. "Only," he continued, "we must have other weapons as well—tenacity, shrewdness, clear heads, knowledge, courage. We mustn't, so to speak, put all our eggs in one basket. Right?"

"No matter, we must pay them back!"

Knight's eyes remained on her; he was puzzled, dubious. But then, his voice soft, emotional, almost imploring, he said: "I need you so—really I do. I need your determination, intelligence, your strength—you're a strong person. You'll never know what you've meant to me in the past few months—you *can't* know. It's been everything, your presence—your physical nearness to me—in the office; also of course your advice and counsel, your support. I think it was one of the marvels of the world that brought us together—though the first time I saw you, in Paris, I hated you, of course. God, how I thought I hated you. And for good and obvious reasons. But look at me now—I'm completely at your mercy, mooning like a schoolboy. I think about you day and night and realize now I'd never known love before. Tell me—tell me, Dee . . . Is it misplaced?"

Mary Dee's face showed her utter distress. "Oh, don't say that, don't ask that! It's unfair. How would I know that? It's unfair of you to ask it!"

"Why is it unfair?—look, we've been working together, closely, for at least four months now. You've become indispensable to the organization—and of course to me. And now I'm very emotionally involved. It's not only your character—I think you're the loveliest, the most beautiful, most capable and appealing woman I've ever seen or ever known of. What could possibly be more natural than my falling in love with you? . . . what could be more natural even than my wish that some day you might be my wife, might bear me a son, another son?—I lost my little boy Johnnie, you know. Yes, it's true—I think of your becoming my wife, of our having children."

Mary Dee took a sudden deep breath, almost a gasp, as if someone had dashed her with ice water. But at once then she tried to calm, control, herself—hide the shock his statement had given. Softly, Robeson now was singing "Didn't My Lord Deliver Daniel?" She spoke evenly: "I can only say I respect you tremendously for what you've accomplished. You can't doubt that—otherwise, would I be in the organization? So your confidence in me—in the work I try to do for the organization—is certainly not misplaced."

"Oh, how you circumvent and hedge, Dee. That wasn't my question—you know it. I won't press it further for now. Please think about it, though—try to understand it. And I'll try not to mention marriage again soon—for fear next time you might faint dead away." Knight's attempt at humor was flat.

Afterwards, when he had left and she was alone in her bedroom, she sat reading again the message Philip, on that sweet afternoon in Paris so far-off, reminiscent, never to be experienced again, had scribbled in her now poor battered sketchbook: "You're spoiled but I know I'm to blame for it. You're like I like you, though. So please stay the way you are—forever. Please don't change, ever. Don't tamper with our love—then it will never die." At once she dissolved in tears.

Yet by eleven o'clock next morning, Sunday, she had phoned Knight and talked for fifteen minutes, about nothing—in her desperation somehow trying, hoping, to use him to break Philip's unyielding hold. Knight, elated by the call, of course misunderstood it.

*   *   *   *   *

By the time a fortnight had passed Knight was even more optimistic, encouraged; he saw the bright light of hope—especially when, early one evening following a day at the office, Mary Dee, after his importuning, agreed to come by his apartment and cook dinner. After she called her mother, they went to a supermarket to shop, where she got spaghetti, garlic, grated cheese, and had the butcher grind a small piece of sirloin for the meat of the spaghetti sauce. Then, at her suggestion, Knight made a second stop and bought a bottle of red Barolo wine. He was beside himself with joy and as they entered his apartment he leaned forward, rather comically, and kissed her lightly on the mouth. "I'm out of my head about you," he said. "Don't toy with me—don't hurt me. I'd kill you," he laughed.

She froze. For a moment, despite his laughter—and for the first

702

time in what seemed ages—she sensed the old fear, dread, the foreboding, she had felt on those earliest encounters with him in Paris. He had seemed so evil, ominous, so malign then; now he was just as different—humble, solicitous, kind, almost gentle. She thought it therefore so out of character for him to say such a ludicrous, such a crazy thing—that he would kill her. Yet it had shocked her.

Now in the kitchen he fixed drinks. It was the first time she had been to his apartment, but she felt no uneasiness, rather seeing him as the perfect gentleman type, a trait, ironically, which had for her, in him, no special appeal. She had even not much minded his kissing her—it.had been rather pleasant, for she sensed his happy emotions and felt vaguely flattered. Of late, however, she constantly asked herself the question: what future was there for her in this growing relationship with a man who even now was much of a mystery to her? Yet—and she thought this the important thing—would it in time bring her, enable her, to exorcise the unhappy past, the love-misery, the heartbreak? Would it heal her hurt? If so, then it could only be considered a blessing from God.

As she cooked the spaghetti he sat with his drink watching her. "You don't seem the kind who could cook at all," he said, laughing again. "But clearly you can."

"That's hardly a compliment. Why shouldn't I be able to cook?"

"You were brought up with servants, weren't you?"

"*One* servant. And she ran, still runs, the whole family, everything, including teaching me, making me, cook."

He watched her, and was suddenly serious, emotional. "It's a joy just watching you—watching you do anything," he said, awe too now in his voice. "How on earth did you happen into my distracted, mixed-up life?—an empty, though, terribly empty, life. . . . How is it you're here, right here in my kitchen, cooking dinner? It's a miracle, that's what it is! Does it mean anything to you at all to realize how much happiness you've brought me in just a few weeks?—how much hope? . . . accepting an inexpensive little bauble from me, a Valentine memento, inviting me to your home, and now cooking dinner in my apartment. Does that mean anything to you?—it's meant everything to me. It's changed my life, forever—no matter what happens to me my life will never be the same. Sometimes this gives me happy fits, other times it frightens me. Nobody has ever had such impact on my life as you—nobody. Really, does that affect you at all?"

At the stove stirring the simmering spaghetti sauce, she shook her head with some impatience. "I don't know how to answer that," she said, and would not look at him. "You ask hard—also embarrassing—questions. I guess one is always glad to make others happy."

"How cautious you are!"

But a wholly unrelated thought had hit her. She turned around to him. "Much of what I am," she said, "can be found in my painting—in even my drawings and sketches." Watching him, she seemed uneasy, shifty. "Tell me, did you look at any of the drawings in my sketch book they found in the Datsun?"

"No," he said. "I didn't take the time. Should I have?"

She gave a great inward sigh of relief. "Not necessarily. But I must show you some of my work sometime."

"You must, since you say much of what you are is in it. I must study it, know it. Are you at all interested that I learn something about you?"

"I guess my ego, if nothing else, would say yes." She gave a small artificial laugh—"Of course I want you to know me better." At once she regretted saying it.

His dark face lit up in a smile. "You're a perfect joy, Dee. Does the fact that I'm crazy about you bother you? . . . or frighten you?"

Her fear, however, was of his questions. She said nothing.

His eyes took on a half-dreamy gaze now. "Do you know what it's like . . . to be in love with somebody? Have you ever been in love—really in love?"

Although shocked, shaken, by the question, she looked him squarely in the eye. "I guess not," she said, yet wondered how convincingly she had lied. Suddenly then she wanted to go home. She was miserable. His ineptness, she thought, had spoiled everything. Afterwards, as they sat eating, she thought only of when she could go home.

Yet the following week—it was April now—she went with him to tape a television talk show he was to appear on, after which they went to dinner in a good downtown restaurant, the relationship continuing as undeterred, inexorable, as before. Thus she persevered, administering this self-therapy, assuaging old wounds, telling herself she was somehow not unhappy.

In May he proposed to her. He begged her to let him buy an engagement ring. She was tortured, evasive. She said she wanted to think about it more, that of course she was flattered, that he knew she considered him a great and selfless man. She also said she wanted to talk to her mother. She was being honest; all that she told him now was sincere, true. Yet, considering his marriage proposal, she somehow felt clean, chaste, again. It was a feeling she could not recall having had since before she, even though not a virgin, had left home for Paris. She sadly realized the feeling had its rewards.

That evening she told her mother. At once Irene Adkins broke into tears. "Oh, Suky!—I don't know, I don't know! . . . *must you*?" She had had three cups of laced tea. "He's not really your kind. . . . Must you?"

"No, Mother," Mary Dee said, with pity and forebearance—"it's not a must. I only want you to think about it tomorrow."

"What will happen to *me*, Suky? . . . Had you thought of that? Had—"

But Mary Dee, contrite, confused, had escaped—left the room.

*   *   *   *   *

Memorial Day—rather Memorial Night—with a full May moon hovering low over San Francisco Bay. Still furtive, though having escaped detection, she stood on the bridge's skyway catwalk, her mad, insensate face, a face possessed, turned heavenward, and breathed in the acrid night air made heavy with the dank smell of ocean water. It had been three months of irresolution and failure for her, but now the sands had run out. She gazed at the moon, then at what seemed a mile straight down, the shimmering Bay waters; and, holding onto the catwalk's railing, walked, groped, ten feet farther forward. It was her first time here at night—and, night or day, her last. She began to pray—for strength and courage—for there had been so many, repeated, failures. Five in all. Was it then at long last to be tonight? She knew what the answer must be. Between quick, deep breaths she sighed—a heavy, frightened sigh. The sands, yes, were depleted. She gripped the railing tightly— in the moonlight her bare knuckles were stark and white, but the insides of both hands now bore the Golden Gate's dry, brazen-bright, orange paint, emblem of a bizarre anathema, a curse. "Oh, John Calvin, John Calvin! . . . Oh, Marvin! . . . Oh, Mother! . . . Oh, Alan! . . . Oh, life!"

But—to go back—it had not begun this way. For weeks there had been hope. Unwittingly, her mother had almost saved her— by a rare, unprecedented, display of filial love. Marvin's bequest, in the situation certainly no impediment to filial love, had turned out to be slightly larger than estimated—just under $92,000. Nancy Hanks took a cheerful, commodious Huntington Park apartment for three persons, brought with her her friend and companion, lithesome, attractive Lily Heller, the music shop proprietress, and embarked on the sincerest of efforts at warm domesticity for the three of them. Her daughter Griselda reacted by sleeping. But the first stage, immediately after Chicago and Knight, had brought trauma, torment, and utter sleeplessness—followed, however, by long periods of heavy, drugged, sleep, her mother having scrounged the prescription. But after a month of nostrums and deep apprehension, Nancy Hanks had taken her to a psychiatrist. After two sessions, Dr. Kemmer said the patient was catatonic, this syndrome, he said, being encountered most frequently in schizophrenia, with muscular rigidity and mental stupor, sometimes alternating with great excitement and confusion—with sometimes, moreover, intermittent suicidal longings. Nancy Hanks was shocked, frightened—contrite. Then one day her daughter, silent, morose, trembling, came home with bright orange paint on the palms of her white gloves. Nancy Hanks was mystified, yet afraid to inquire. Now the ordeal was hers also. She took to smothering her daughter with affection, but with a cold, forbidding, response.

Nancy Hanks persisted. There was a confrontation one morning in the kitchen after Lily Heller had left for her music shop. "Griselda, we must talk," Nancy Hanks said, nervous and overwrought. "You've never been like this before. Would you prefer to return to Chicago?—if you do, I won't stand in your way. I'm worried about you—your health. You won't confide in me at all—maybe if you talked to somebody, it would help. Tell me, what's bothering you?"

Griselda sat stolidly at the kitchen table munching a piece of toast and sipping black coffee. She ignored the interrogation.

"You seem deliberately out of touch with everything," Nancy

Hanks said. "You show no inclination whatever to communicate with anybody, not even Dr. Kemmer. Why then won't you talk to me?—I'm your mother. You know I care about you, have affection for you, as my daughter, my only child." Griselda gave her an indifferent, cynical gaze. "You're ill, Griselda—do you know that? . . . you're ill and I want to help you." Nancy Hanks bristled. "Is it that John Calvin Knight? . . . Oh! . . ."

"No," said Griselda softly, almost as if in a daze.

"Then what is it?"

"Life."

"What? . . ."

Griselda finally added, "John Calvin was just one more symptom." That was all. When Nancy Hanks could get her to say no more, Nancy left the kitchen, just as Griselda, in a fierce whisper, said once more—". . . Life."

Yet within two weeks things had taken a turn for the better. Nancy Hanks often took hot milk to Griselda's room in the evening where together they sat and watched television and where sometimes, though not always, she got Griselda to talk. Nancy Hanks missed no opportunity to show all possible understanding, affection, and love, and when Griselda felt like talking Nancy Hanks was careful not to question her about Marvin, or Chicago, or Knight, or try to steer the conversation into crucial, painful channels. Gradually, though sporadically, Griselda began to respond, to talk more. One evening, with complete earnestness and sincerity, she asked Nancy Hanks, "Why are you being so nice, so loving, to me these days, Mother? Is it because I've come into some money, or is it that you really find it in your heart to love me?"

Nancy Hanks showed shock and offense, at first, but then gained control of herself and, sighing, said, "It's the latter, Griselda—love—and I'm being truthful with you. Of course, money's no idle matter with me—I've never had much of it. I've had to live as best I could, helped out, as you know, by fees I've received as a voice teacher. It hasn't been an easy time. But money's one thing and my feelings for my daughter—her health, welfare, her happiness—are quite another. I hope you believe this, for it's true. What's more natural than a mother's love for her daughter? It's the purest, most tender, love." It was a paradox that Nancy Hanks was sincere; what she had said she believed herself.

This long-withheld, heretofore unheard-of, avowal of love, however, seemed to have a strangely positive, therapeutic, effect on Griselda. She often appeared immersed now in a comforted, dreamlike, state, and began occasionally to seek her mother out, engage her in conversation, ask her questions, especially advice, and furtively broach subjects calculated to bring repetitions of Nancy Hanks' expressions of solicitude and affection. One day Griselda even related what she thought a ridiculously funny incident that had occurred in Chicago—a rare office spat betwen Ornette Hungerford and Ferdinand Bailey, neither of whom, she said, she liked—and derived obvious relish from telling of the episode, once throwing her head back in a shrill, bizarre, laugh. But Nancy Hanks, miraculously gentle, caring, kindly, laughed with her. Next day, a Saturday afternoon, they went to a movie together. Later that evening at home, only the two of them present, Griselda suddenly, impulsively, embraced her mother and put her head on her strong shoulder, delivering a little cry—"Oh, you're my only friend now . . . thanks for what you've done for me these past few days." Nancy Hanks turned away, a lump in her throat. Griselda had spoken a truth, however, for before now she had been five—abortive—times to Golden Gate. But recently she had stopped going.

Matters continued even further to improve. She began to talk—about Knight. Nancy Hanks considered this a particularly good sign and was secretly elated. One evening at home Griselda suddenly unburdened herself of all she had been through since following Knight to Chicago. It was what Nancy Hanks had long been waiting for. Her strong weather-beaten face solemn, sometimes grim, always sympathetic, she sat listening with rapt attention as Griselda poured out her heart, her agony, until, after an hour, the sad chronicle had been totally externalized. Griselda then wept like a child. Finally Nancy Hanks led her off to bed, kissed her tenderly on the forehead, and put out the light. Griselda slept then as a child sleeps.

Thus things went for a month. Finally came the last week in May—with the long Memorial Day weekend ahead. On that Friday Griselda left home for the beauty salon and a shampoo but returned much earlier than her mother had expected. She let herself in the apartment and, hearing Nancy Hanks and her friend Lily Heller in another room in a strangely breathless, agitated, conversation, she went directly, unobtrusively, to her own room.

Seized by a strange premonition, however, she started to close her door. It was at this moment she heard her mother utter what sounded like a wildly distraught plea. "Oh, Lily, please, please!—don't say such a thing! You break my heart! . . ."

"I'm unhappy here," came the cold reply. "I feel I should move."

Griselda, now already fearful of hearing something she felt deep inside her she should not hear—did not want to hear—started to close her door again. She could not do it. She could not resist leaving it slightly ajar, as she stood against it listening with pounding heart.

"Lily, Lily, please don't leave me!" cried Nancy Hanks—"Please don't talk of such a thing! What would I do? I couldn't live without you!—you know that! But that's why you treat me as you do sometimes . . . you know I'm helpless, that I'm your victim, and *have* been since I first laid eyes on you! Have pity on me!—for God's sake have pity! Oh, Lily, you know you're the only human being on earth I love! . . ."

There was some kind of vague but audible struggle between them then—before Lily Heller, as if breaking free, said, "Nancy, control yourself! . . . let go of me, turn me loose. Don't create a scene . . . Nancy!"

"I love you," Nancy Hanks said, sobbing.

Griselda closed the door.

Memorial Day—Memorial Night. So now all that was left her was the moon and oblivion. A death grip on the bridge's iron railing, she took three more halting steps forward along the catwalk, feeling now in her fear the curse of the bright orange dust in the palms of her hands. She had never known such fright—was it the brightness of the moon making things so dire and ghostly? She began to tremble. Yet what was oblivion? It was merely, she imagined, the Pacific Ocean to which the tides receding from the Bay would take her before morning—an undulating gentle passage into blue-sea-green nothingness. So now she would stand perfectly still for just a minute or two—to summon the state of readiness. And as it had on countless humanity in travail, the moon shone on her, hallowing her in its lurid, impersonal light.

Memorial Day—the same.

Ornette had just hung up the telephone, and now stood in his kitchen door. "Something's happened," he said, for a moment reflectively, to Rosabelle in the kitchen. "That was Ferdie. He's coming by. When's he been here?—it's been a long time, I know that."

"What's he want?" Rosabelle said. It was noon, and she was making sandwiches for the children. Her mother, Mrs. Ransom, was visiting a son in Cleveland.

"He wants to come over and talk to us."

"About what?"

"He didn't say. He didn't sound good, though. He was so quiet, for Ferdie; today no laughing. Yeah, something's happened."

"Not necessarily. It's a holiday and Ferdie's got time on his hands. Before, he and John Calvin would probably be together, but now, ha, John Calvin's got other interests—no time for Ferdie."

Ornette gave Rosabelle a troubled, sour, look of affirmation—"You're telling me."

The baby, John Calvin, soon to be one year old—his name, however, still unchanged—was asleep. But the other four children —Sojourner, Nathaniel (Nat), Harriet, and Frederick—soon came trooping into the kitchen for lunch. Rosabelle, going around the table and pouring their milk, said, "You children try not to make so much noise this afternoon—Mr. Bailey's coming."

"What for, Mama?" Harriet said.

"Just to talk."

"And how," said Ornette, who then turned and left the kitchen.

Ferdinand came just before two o'clock. But he was smiling now, gracious, and even laughed when greeted by Ornette's comic bowing. "I hope I'm not interfering with something else you'd planned," he said to Ornette before taking a seat on the living room sofa.

"No, no, Ferdie," Rosabelle spoke up—"We're going to take the kids for a ride, but later on."

Ornette, who had been studying Ferdinand, said to him, "What's put that furrow in your brow, man?"

"Is is that obvious?" said Ferdinand, sighing. "It's nothing sudden, though. I've just been meaning to talk to you and Rosabelle for sometime . . . about—"

"Come on—out with it," Ornette said. "You've got around, I bet, to seeing what I told you is true—that day I came in your office. Nothing's happening, Ferdie; we're drifting—the organization's adrift. It's Knight. Am I right?"

Ferdinand hesitated, as if embarrassed. "Well, I do worry about John Calvin," he said, "and the organization. But he's been through so much since we left San Francisco and came here that sometimes I think maybe it's affected his mind."

"Haw!—that chick's what's affected his mind," Ornette said. "Honest to God, it's true—Mary Dee's turned out to be worse for him than Griselda ever was. And you and I engineered it all— own up to it, Ferdie—just to get rid of Griselda. So instead we get this—it was brilliant. I'll bet Griselda, safe and sound now back in San Francisco, would thank us from the bottom of her heart if she knew. Aw, Ferdie, we were out of our heads. Not about Griselda—she had to go—but about Mary Dee."

"It's not that bad, Ornette," Rosabelle spoke up again—"I think you're overstating it."

"But what worries me," said Ferdinand, "is that John Calvin's practically stopped traveling—he doesn't honor requests for speaking engagements around the country anymore. His periodic appearances helped the local organizations raise money. Recently they've been complaining. Even in the office now he can't concentrate on anything very long—his mind's apparently somewhere else. It's true, things are slipping some—a great deal, actually. It gives us cause for concern. I made up my mind to talk to you two about it—there's no one else except Mamie I'd dare talk to."

"Okay, just stop and analyze the situation for a minute," Ornette said. "What's eating John Calvin? It's this—he's so damned head over heels in love with Mary Dee, he don't know which end's up. He's forgot all about poor hungry nigger kids and things like that. He ain't got time to think about the organization these days; or about you or me or anybody else—except old slick Mary Dee."

"Ornette, now that's unfair," said Rosabelle. "Mary Dee's as honest as the average person, as conscientious and sincere—you don't know what she's thinking. Why would she have to be 'slick?'"

What's in it for her? What's John Calvin got that she wants or needs? Despite all your and Ferdie's plotting to bring them together, I've never been able to believe he's her type. Their relationship, for all we know, may be strictly a one-way affair."

"That proves my point, hon!" Ornette said. "Mary Dee *is* slick." He turned to Ferdinand as if for confirmation.

Ferdinand hesitated again. ". . . I don't know. I wouldn't say she's 'slick,' exactly. She's just hard to figure out. We all know how John Calvin feels about her. But it's not easy to tell the opposite. What are her motives? I don't know. But they're important, whatever they are—we can't ignore them. We must remember we don't really know much about her, her life, her past—only the bare outlines; so we can't tell what her real motives are about John Calvin. As for the organization, I've never been able to see why she took so strongly to it."

"She wasn't at first all that strong about it," Rosabelle said—"Ornette and I had to talk her into it. But why must we suspect her motives?—I don't see any basis for it and, again, I think it's unfair. In her way she's as honest as the next."

"But what's she think of John Calvin?" said Ornette. "That's the question."

"I think she admires him terrifically." Rosabelle was stubborn. "It's apparent—why else would she give him so much of her time? I hear they're together a lot nowadays. Why wouldn't she feel something for him?—look who he is, what he's accomplished; and what she is, what she's done, or hasn't done. There's no comparison. She'd be the first to admit it."

Ornette was shaking his head. "What you say, baby, would make sense in the ordinary situation, but this ain't the ordinary situation. I don't care what you say, I'd almost bet my youngest son, my own little John Calvin, that she thinks she's better than Knight. Don't ask me why she could think that—she just does."

"That doesn't mean she won't marry him, though," Rosabelle suddenly said.

Ornette stared at her incredulously. "What?—who said anything about marriage?" Ferdinand also seemed startled.

"Ah," said Rosabelle, "neither one of you had considered that, had you? Well, it could happen—it just might happen. I'm a woman and I know something about what Mary Dee might be thinking—and feeling."

"Jesus Christ," Ornette breathed.

"Oh, my," said Ferdinand, fearfully, almost under his breath. "What would that mean for us?—for the organization?"

"It just might be the greatest thing that could ever happen," Rosabelle said. "It might make a brand new man out of John Calvin. Think what he's been through in the last couple of years, and, before Mary Dee came along, how lonely he was all the time; upset and harried; distracted. That white girl, Griselda, try as she might, couldn't do anything for him; she only made things worse. So this might be just what was needed. It might bring him around."

"Well, it better happen fast," sighed Ornette, still shaken by the sudden turn of possibilities. "As of now, the organization's going down the drain. You know if Ferdie here all but admits it, it's sure in bad shape."

Ferdinand, who had been unhappily staring out the window, turned to Ornette and Rosabelle. "You've got to come back, both of you," he said—"you've got to give the organization more of your time. You haven't been very active lately, you know."

"And I told you why, Ferdie," Ornette said. "We don't stick our noses in where we're not wanted. Why should we?"

Ferdinand bristled. "For your children, that's why—and for their children."

Ornette and Rosabelle said nothing.

"Maybe," said Ferdinand, frowning in his distress and perplexity, "we expect too much of John Calvin. He's only human like the rest of us—he can make mistakes, can flounder, get lost occasionally, just like we do."

"No, no," said Ornette—"he's a *leader*, ain't he? Leaders don't act like that. They can't afford to."

"It doesn't always work out like that," Ferdinand said. "John Calvin's accomplished so much in his young life that we get the impression he's infallible. Well, he's not—and I know him better than most people. He needs help. We must help him—maybe save him."

Ornette and Rosabelle, silent again, gazed forlornly at each other.

713

"If he does have marriage in mind," Ferdinand said, "—and it had never occurred to me until Rosabelle brought it up—then we must support him, encourage him. We must stand with him. We *too* must regain our old dedication and fervor if we expect John Calvin to do the same. Ornette, I see signs, though, you're weakening some in your dedication to blacks, when before you were fanatical, a fire-eater. It makes me sad."

Ornette almost stood up. "Ferdie, you know that ain't true!—hell, how could you say such a thing? My kids never go to bed at night, never, without me telling them what it means to be black, what they can expect as blacks in a racist society; how they have come from a strong, a mighty, heritage they should always be proud of; how our black ancestors went through trial by ordeal and fire; and how they must fight the God-damned white man to the death to get their rights. And you come telling me I'm weakening!" He turned to Rosabelle. "Baby, go bring those kids up here," he said. "Go on!—I'll show him something." Rosabelle left the living room and went back to the rear of the apartment, as Ornette sat in smoldering silence, grinding his teeth and staring at the wall. Soon Rosabelle returned with all the children except the baby. They stood in an arc before their father, not cowed or afraid, but curious and serious. Frederick, however, the oldest, age eleven, seemed to have sensed something in the air and smiled faintly. Ornette turned to him first. "Son, tell Mr. Bailey here your full name and the man you were named after—and a little about him."

Frederick, clear-eyed, handsome-faced, athletic, already large for his age, turned to Ferdinand with an earnest mien. "My name is Frederick Douglas Hungerford," he said. "I was named by my parents after one of the greatest black men who ever lived—Frederick Douglas. He was a slave, but in 1838 he escaped from his white master in Maryland and fled north. There he educated himself and later, in Rochester, New York, founded and edited the abolitionist journal, *North Star*. He waged a long fight, by his writings and speeches, for less fortunate blacks still in slavery. When the Civil War came, he was even an adviser to Abraham Lincoln. All his life he was a fighter, a black fighter, as I and my brothers and sisters someday hope to be."

Ornette was moved and exultant. "Beautiful, son!" He turned then to Harriet, now age nine. "You're next, sweetheart."

714

Harriet, chubby, bright-eyed though wearing glasses, first glanced at her mother. "My name is Harriet Tubman Hungerford," she said in a clarion tone. "Harriet Tubman was also a slave who escaped and came north, but afterwards risked her life many times, nineteen times, to go back south and bring out other slaves. She brought out over three hundred, including her aged parents. Later, in the War, she was a Union spy. She said there was one of two things she felt she had a right to—freedom or death. She was a black heroine. I was named after her."

Ornette looked at Ferdinand in triumph. He turned now to his son Nathaniel—"Okay, Nat, what about you?"

Nat, now eight, looked his father in the eye, then smiled. "My name is Nathaniel (Nat) Turner Hungerford. I was named after Nat Turner." Then he hesitated, as if his memory had failed. He glanced at his mother, and recovered. "Nat Turner was a Virginia slave," he said. "In 1831 he led a big slave revolt. Many white slave owners were killed. But Nat was captured, and they hanged him for trying to win freedom for himself and other blacks. He died a black hero."

Ornette was beside himself. "You ain't kidding, Nat—a black hero if there ever was one!" He turned now to little Sojourner, age four. "Come here, babydoll, and give Daddy a kiss and a hug, then tell Mr. Bailey what your name is and how you got it." Sojourner, her eyes big, demure, her manner solemn, came to Ornette and stood between his knees. He lowered his cheek and she kissed him, then stepped back. "Hey, wait a minute," he said to her, grinning—"where's the hug?" Sojourner returned and dutifully hugged him. "That's more like it," he said—"now, what's your name?"

"Sojourner," came the diffident reply, as she looked across at her mother.

"Sojourner what?" Ornette said.

". . . Truth."

"Sojourner Truth, eh? What's the rest of it?"

Sojourner smiled for the first time. "Hungerford," she said.

"There you go. Now, why did we give our baby, that we love so much, that name—Sojourner Truth Hungerford?"

"She was a . . ." Sojourner, stumped, looked again at her mother.

"She was a what, honey?" said Ornette.

"... A good lady, I think,"

"There's more to it than that, honey," Ornette said, and turned to the other children. "Give her some help, you'all."

"She was a brave black abolitionist," Frederick spoke up. "She had been a slave but escaped. Then she went all over the north preaching against slavery—in very dangerous times. She was a black fighter for her people."

Ornette turned back to Sojourner. "Did you hear that, sweetie?" he said.

Sojourner, very solemn again, nodded her head. "She was . . . a black fighter, for her people."

"Beautiful—beautiful!" cried Ornette. He reached and pressed the child to him. Then he turned to the other children again. "What do I tell you'all every night after you've said your prayers and are ready for bed?" he said.

They answered almost in unison—"Be Black and be proud."

Ornette whirled around to Ferdinand. "*I* ain't weakened!" he said. "*John Calvin's* weakened!"

*   *   *   *   *

In her confusion, her distraught indecision, time was running out for Mary Dee. Yet she had at least reached a subconscious decision; though only feebly pulsating, it was soon, very soon, to take form, then rise to the surface of her expectant, indeed already-knowing, awareness. By now she felt it. The verdict would be positive, in the affirmative—or, depending on how one looked at it, in the negative? She would then tell her mother—as early as tomorrow. Telling her mother would somehow enable Irene Adkins to share the trauma, doubts, the tragedy. However, she had hit on an ancillary scheme to distract her mother, shock her, so that the decision, when communicated, might not have entire center stage—Irene Adkins' fragile sensibilities could stand only so much. Indeed would the double dose overload them? No matter; it must be undertaken. Tomorrow was a Saturday—and Ernestine's birthday. For the first time ever she would go bring Ernestine and Vernon home with her. It would be an early afternoon luncheon, a small celebration of the anniversary, now the child's thirteenth. Irene Adkins' shock might then cushion the other, more portentous, announcement she would also receive. Mary Dee's head spun with the difficulties of the situation. And as yet John Calvin Knight, for weeks now caught, held, in the cruel jaws of suspense, had no inkling of her thoughts in his favor, her finally maturing decision—his fate.

Next afternoon she arrived back home with the children at shortly after one o'clock. Ernestine and Vernon were awed by the apartment, causing Mary Dee to regret never having introduced them to the grandeur of the dear old house left behind that she could never erase from remembrance. What would they have thought of *it*? She had the children sit in the parlor while she went uneasily to the rear to somehow acquaint her mother with the larger decision, then to bring her up into the parlor to witness first-hand the other—to Irene Adkins both, doubtless, equally shocking.

Vernon's large eyes roved the room—the pictures, draperies, candelabra, the French and Italian chairs. "Where's the TV?" he asked Ernestine.

"How would I know," Ernestine said. "Maybe they got one in the back somewhere. Maybe they don't watch TV."

"I sure would like to watch it in *this* room," Vernon said, greatly admiring the general ambience. "Bet Momma would too."

"People such as Mary and her folks live different from the way most folks do," Ernestine said. "I'd like to live like her. Takes a lot of money, though." She stood up and observed what she could see of herself in the wall mirror. She was prim, immaculate, in her skirt, jacket, and blouse, and the bright tan shoes. "Money ain't easy to get," she said, finally sitting down again.

"That's what Momma says." Vernon, also jaunty in his well-pressed gray suit—he would be age ten before long—continued gaping around the room. "I'd put the TV there," he said, pointing at the wall space beneath the mirror.

"Oh, all you talk about is TV," said Ernestine.

"Mary never brought us to her house before. Just now on your birthday."

"She called Momma yesterday. Hell, Mary's nice."

"*I* sure like Mary," Vernon said.

717

"I like Momma too."

"Sure," said Vernon. "Everybody likes their mother. I like Mary too."

"Yeah, we always love to go places with her," Ernestine said. "Now she's brought us to her house. We were only at the garage behind her other house."

"Sometimes she don't say much," said Vernon. "She just sits—even if she's driving—and thinks."

"What's wrong with that?"

But Vernon himself was thinking—of something else. "Will she always be our friend?—and take us places?"

"Sure, because we're all friends—we sure are. If she was ever not our friend, we'd be sad probably."

"I bet," said Vernon, but again turning his head to look around him. "Whew, this room is pretty."

"Shut up," whispered Ernestine. "Here they come."

Soon Mary Dee, followed by Irene Adkins, a stricken expression on the latter's face, entered.

In the kitchen Mary Dee had told her mother two things. First, that the children, Ernestine and Vernon Carter, whom she had occasionally heard her, Mary Dee, speak of, were up in the parlor. "Oh, my God!"—Irene Adkins' hand had groped to her face— "Sitting on the furniture? . . . their clothes. . . ."

"Their clothes are clean, Mother."

"But where they have to live . . . where they must hang their clothing—there are sometimes insects. Some of the places even have rats."

"Mother. if you only knew what you're saying. That's what this is all about—my life now, these children and families like them, and John Calvin Knight. Your and other people's attitudes are so ironic. It *is* irony, isn't it?—Mother, you see, I'm going to marry him. I've decided."

Irene Adkins stepped back and an even more stricken, an appalled, look came on her face. "Oh, Suky!—this is incredible! . . . You could at least have consulted me!—you said you wanted me to think about it. Now look what you've done! . . ."

"It wouldn't have done any good—you were against it. I haven't told him yet, but I will today. It will mean a new life for me, Mother—maybe bring an end to all I've been through in the last two years. Already those children up in our parlor symbolize it."

"Oh, Suky! . . . you don't think about me at all—I'll be alone now."

"Ronald will soon be coming home. I've checked it—I've called him. Mrs. Grier will be here too. Come with me, now, Mother—I want Ernestine and Vernon to meet you, see you. They're wonderful children—very dear to me. It's Ernestine's birthday and I'm going to fix them lunch."

When Mary Dee and Irene Adkins entered the parlor, Vernon stood up at once, as if somehow divining, sensing in the air, he should not be seated in the downy white chair. Ernestine too then slowly, warily, stood, as both eyed Irene Adkins.

"Ernestine and Vernon," said Mary Dee, "this is my mother, Mrs. Adkins. Please sit down." The children eased into their chairs again.

Irene Adkins had tried her best to smile, but the expression had become a kind of hapless, feeble tremor of the mouth. "Hello, Ernestine," she said at last. "Hello, Vernon."

Vernon smiled. "It's Ernestine's birthday," he said proudly.

"My daughter has already told me. Congratulations, Ernestine."

Ernestine in a low, awed voice managed to thank her.

Irene Adkins, however, was already backing away. "Well, my daughter is going to prepare lunch for you," she said. "I hope you enjoy it. Have a happy birthday party." With that she left, went to her room, and closed the door.

"My mother's not feeling very well today," Mary Dee said. "But we shouldn't let that spoil our birthday party, should we?"

"Have you got a TV?" Vernon said, quickly relieved with the tension gone out of the air.

"Shut up, Vernon," Ernestine laughed.

"Yes, I have one in my room," Mary Dee said. "So does Mother. Vernon, do you want to watch television while Ernestine and I broil the hamburgers?"

"Yes, yes," Vernon said—"I want to see the ball game."

As they gaped at the apartment all the way, Mary Dee took them back to her room, where she turned on the baseball game for Vernon. Then she and Ernestine went into the kitchen. But when thirty minutes later the food was ready and the three of them were seated at the dining room table eating, Vernon suddenly, inexplicably, began crying. Ernestine was alarmed. "What's the matter with you, Vernon?" she said, and got up and went around to him. "Does something hurt you? What you crying for?—you don't hardly cry at all any more."

Vernon, who had put his fork down, now stopped chewing his food and lowered his head as tears rolled down his cheeks onto his jacket. He would say nothing.

"Do you feel badly, Vernon?" Mary Dee said. "Tell us. What's the trouble? Maybe we can help you."

Vernon only kept his chin on his chest and let the tears come.

"He gets moody sometimes," Ernestine, stilll standing over him, gave as her opinion to Mary Dee. "He used to cry all the time, but he ain't cried——"

"Hasn't cried," corrected Mary Dee.

"Hasn't cried all year—I don't know what's wrong with him today." Ernestine now bent down to Vernon and, laughing, began making all kinds of outlandish, grotesque, exaggerated faces at him. "Look at me, Vernon. You're nine, almost ten—you're a *big* boy now. You don't cry. Look at me." She put her thumbs in her ears and, still making faces, wildly wiggled her fingers at him, trying to coax him to laugh. "When he was smaller," she said to Mary Dee, "this used to make him stop crying and laugh. But now he won't look at me." Ernestine, sighing, finally returned to her chair. Soon, however, Vernon of his own volition stopped crying and silently resumed eating.

Although Vernon's unhappiness was mystifying to Mary Dee, his uncommunicative tears had somehow—she did not know why —made her too feel depressed and sad. But she laughed—"Say, what kind of birthday party is this? Pretty soon it will be like a funeral. Come on, let's snap out of it." She got up, went to the sideboard, and took out of the drawer a gift-wrapped package. "Here, Ernestine," she said, giving it to her— "Happy Birthday, from Vernon and me." Ernestine, her eyes already wide with pleasure and expectancy, at once began unwrapping the gift, as Vernon watched lugubriously. When she took out the red sweater and, with a great smile, held it up, Vernon began crying all over again. Then Mary Dee knew.

But so did Ernestine. "Aw," she said, still smiling, looking not at Vernon but at Mary Dee, "he's crying about *you,* Mary." Her eyes shone with pride. "He loves you. He's happy whenever we're with you. Only he doesn't laugh—he cries." But Ernestine herself laughed. "Vernon's nuts."

Mary Dee, embarrassed, flustered—and moved—finally looked at Vernon.

Ernestine said to her, "You came along, remember, and pulled us out of the cold and the snow. Vernon, he ain't never forgot."

Mary Dee ignored the lapsed grammar as her eyes began to sting.

Ernestine now went around to Vernon again. She wiped his face and nose with her paper napkin. "Vernon, you're a mess," she laughed—"Just look at you. And almost ten—Lordy, Lordy."

"Will Mary take us places again?" Vernon said.

"Sure. Won't you, Mary?"

"Yes," Mary Dee said. There was suddenly emotion, determination, commitment, in her voice. "We'll be seeing a lot more of each other now—you wait and see." Yet somehow thinking of her new life to come, she sighed.

After luncheon she took the children to a street carnival, and later to John Calvin Knight's apartment. It was in this setting then, his own living room, with the children only in the next room, that she gave him her fateful answer.

*   *   *   *   *

That night, far past midnight, Knight was still writing. His diary, over the years a sporadically-kept journal, containing great time gaps, had been mostly a record of his bad times, the crises, disappointments, failures—his agonies. Despite the famed accomplishments, his feats, all to the positive, such record as he kept of himself was negative. But now he wrote in this book of travail in a furious happiness, an exultation and rapture, such as he had never experienced, or imagined, before—certainly never involving himself. It had been, almost as much as the affirmative answer itself, her utter honesty and humility that had so moved, transported, him; now his extreme feelings for her, his yearning, welled up in him anew, flowing out toward her at last in a veritable torrent of love. He seemed not to know where he was, and wrote to himself—*of* himself.

His life now would change—his feverish words went down on paper. This heavenly girl would change his life by her vast integrity. Witness what candor she had used, he wrote. She had been miserable, numbed, since her father's death, she had told him today as the two children with her, themselves objects of her compassion, proof of her humanity, looked at television in another room. Her father had been part of her heart; and she his. Then he had suddenly gone away and left her, just at the time she needed him most. It had chilled her, her whole outlook, make-up, and character; she now found herself unresponsive to many things to which she would otherwise normally respond. It was imperative that he, her husband-to-be, try to understand her, be patient, generous; be noble as she knew from his career, life, he could be; more than once she entreated him to be kind to her; and that with his help she would grow, mend; she would somehow overcome the past and be his true and responsive partner. They as partners would then do much good for blacks.

It was this last that had really set him on fire. It confirmed what he had always held to: that with her he could fulfill his mission— the difficult mission he had set for himself on that first great occasion, the first time he had heard the itinerant Martin Luther King, Jr. speak, in a rural black church deep in the canebrakes of Louisiana. The leader even then had spoken of blacks' "long night of suffering" and prophesied the coming, after inevitable struggle, of a bright new dawn. It was then the young diarist had begun to see his own mission, though by comparison inchoate and puny, and pledged himself to the struggle. Yet then, after a famous series of successes, some while Dr. King still lived, the diarist had faltered, then floundered, lost his way, and finally—physically (gun fire) as well as psychically—almost expired. But now hope, assurance, thrilling and merciful, had come in the avowals of this brave, lovely girl who epitomized all the virtues of strength black women were known to possess. His heart grew fuller still as he wrote; he was moved, humbled, by the new chance he had been given, the opportunity to regain the sense of purpose, zeal, he had once had. Again now, he wrote, he might do great deeds. He did not go to bed, go to sleep, until after 2:30 A.M.

Then he dreamed. The woman's wet hair was long, disheveled, and almost black—a wild witch's dripping locks—and the evening gown she still wore, beaded, spangled, before the immersion showering sparks, fitted her svelte, yet decaying, body like a stocking. Her shoes were sapphire lamé. She had arrived ten minutes late for their appointment, yet at the crack of dawn. The appointed place was the huge, empty 43rd Street Amphitheater, where he sat waiting up on the great stage, watching eagerly as she entered through the main door and began the interminable trek up the center aisle of the half-dark auditorium toward the platform to join him. But as she came nearer, then yet nearer, his heart began to race, at first uneasily, then to pound with a hideous fear. It was her face, her ghastly face. Where before there had been the lovely hazel eyes, there were now only apertures, waterlogged sockets. And, strangest of all, her body with its bizarre apparel was soaking, dripping, wet. He somehow wanted to run; to flee through the rear exit; but now she had reached the front and was mounting the stage. Then he saw her arms, her hands, the watery flesh blue-white, soft, and tumid, ripe already to slip from their bones. The horror of it brought him groans in his sleep, then a loud outcry; yet, unmercifully, he did not, could not, awake. In his spasms he only spun over in the bed from his right side to his left, and vice versa, locked in the nightmare's grip.

Then he heard his own voice in the dream, grave and uncertain, filled with fear, echoing through the cavernous hall as once more he stood at the lectern and spoke to the great empty house. "I have betrayed you," he said to his spectral hearers, repeating what he once had said on that very platform. "I come before you a confessing sinner," he reiterated.

She had now sat down in a chair close behind him on the stage. She listened at first intently, then grew dour and sad. "I'm glad you didn't start your great speech until I got here," she said bitterly. "As you can see if you'll turn around, I've come, thousands of miles, from a dance, a ball—which went on so long it was like a marathon. At both the Mark Hopkins and the St. Francis I've danced for days, for nights—ah, John Calvin, the dance of death."

Furtively, guiltily, he tried to ignore her. "Brothers and Sisters," he said, addressing the vast house of apparitions, "my sin is that I've kept from you my doubts—my *doubts*, friends! As blacks, our suffering—the history, our *night*, of suffering, if you will—has been so terrible, so extreme, so outlandish, it has caused me to doubt the very existence of God. Were we abandoned?"

"Yes. I too was abandoned," she said—"by Frimbo. But that was not all."

"Really, did God early abandon us in our history?" he cried out into the great darkened grotto of a hall—"or did He himself *decree* our history?"

"Why, why, did you abandon me?" she said in almost a wail now, a keening, and rose, came to the lectern, and stood close behind him, her fetid breath like rancid wet ashes sickening him.

"I speak to your minds!" he said loudly to the house again, "not your emotions. I ask you, is *xenophobia* the answer? . . ."

"You knew then, in your heart, it was not," she said to him, as he quailed before her reeking breath on his neck—though he dared not turn around and look into the vacantly staring eye sockets. "You all but said it," she went on, pointing out at the sea of empty seats before them—"Seated down there only twelve rows in front of you, I heard you: 'Can we overcome by withdrawing into ourselves?' You knew the answer. Then a few days later you abandoned me—cast me out of your life as if I were a scruffy whore. Was it because you had once been in my bed? But I had no one but you. I had already been abandoned by the world—including my mother. Even, in the end, by Frimbo. There was only you. *Oh, John Calvin, John Calvin!*"

He yelled now, out at the echoing auditorium—"I speak to you of my doubts! . . ."

"And my death," she said.

Astonished, he turned around to her, only to meet her feverish embrace—as wet flesh parted from the radius bone of her forearm and remained on the shoulder of his jacket. Crying out again, lunging up from the bed, he awoke. He sat in the dark shaking, trembling.

724

Chapter 4

The grisly dream dogged his thoughts for days and nights. Soon he went into a period of deep depression and one whole weekend secluded himself in his apartment, even calling Mary Dee only to lie that he had caught a cold and was quarantining himself for a few days in deference to the health of his friends. The dream had filled him with a strange fear in which his guilt and remorse over Griselda would give him no rest. He knew he was hopelessly in love with Mary Dee, and that they would soon be married, yet Griselda's final, bitter reproaches still rang in his ears. It was torment. He could only hope she was well, that she had found new friends in San Francisco—she certainly hadn't pressing money worries now—and that soon her painful disappointment would ease; at last go away. Yet his gloom would not lift. "God, oh God, take care of, protect, Griselda!" he often breathed to himself. "Give her a long life and happiness. . . ."

He found now he wanted to hurry, rush, the wedding. It was as if it would validate, sanctify, what he had done, also bolster his spirits and moderate his contrition—restore some kind of normalcy to his life. Yet he knew he and Mary Dee had not discussed dates, and that only last week had he given her the ring. Moreover, he hadn't even told Ferdinand—his best friend. The following Sunday he called Ferdinand and asked to come see him.

"Congratulations!—I'm not at all surprised," Ferdinand, laughing, said when told in his living room. "It's a very natural thing, isn't it? Again congratulations! You're getting the best, the very best. Mary Dee's got everything—what a lovely girl, John Calvin."

"Thanks, Ferdie. I'm glad to get *your* blessing—you had a lot to do with bringing us together, you know. It was you, Ornette, and Rosabelle. I must tell them too."

Ferdinand grew serious, reflective. "Then when it's all over, John Calvin—the marriage—you can settle down to the real business of the organization again. You've been preoccupied, and it's understandable, but now you must get back in the harness, like in the old days, and give us the leadership we all know you're capable of. You can do it—you've *got* to do it. And look what a help Mary Dee will be—though it's you who must assume the leadership. The people in the organization expect it. I'll be frank with you, some feel Mary Dee has been calling the shots. You can't let this feeling get around too much."

"I know, I know." Knight showed impatience. "But you're talking mostly about Ornette. I know he's unhappy—that he resents Mary Dee's participation. But we must learn to *use* talent when it comes to us. It's an irony that it was you and Ornette who first pushed this relationship, wanted Mary Dee to really get active; now you seem to fear it. But you did the greatest service you'll ever do me. I can't describe my feelings about her—she's the most blessed thing that's ever happened to me. Ferdie, it's an awesome feeling—love. Love changes things."

Ferdinand, who had long since despaired of ever marrying, wistfully nodded assent. "I'm sure it does," he said, "and we all hope it will change your life, for the better; we believe it will. Ornette and Rosabelle, I'm sure, feel the same. Yes, you must tell them."

Knight hesitated. "Why don't you break the news to them, Ferdie?" he said uneasily. "It will go over better."

"Okay, then, I will. When's the wedding to be?"

"We agreed on the date just night before last. It will be two weeks from today—Sunday; a very simple, very private, ceremony in her mother's apartment. You'll stand up with me of course, I hope—won't you?"

"Absolutely," Ferdinand said. "You know I will. Are you going to keep your apartment?—will you still live there?"

"Yes, until we find the place we want. Mary Dee's brother, who's out of college now, is back and will live with her mother. It's all falling into place beautifully, Ferdie—only I've got a bad case of jitters. Somehow I can't imagine this is happening to me—that this girl, this good, very good, this sweet, lovely girl, is going to be mine. She's completely bowled me over. I've got it bad, Ferdie."

"It's returned, I'm sure. You're both lucky. Ah, I'm happy for you, John Calvin."

Knight somehow sighed though and would not look at Ferdinand. "I hope it's returned," he said—"one can only hope. I feel I can make her happy. She says she's never been in love—that might be to my advantage."

Ferdinand looked at him, quizzically. "It might be," he finally said.

"Ferdie, I want a family—I want another son. This one won't be named after me, though. His name will be Goforth."

"How nice. As time goes on, you're coming more to understand, appreciate, your father. That's marvelous. He'd be pleased."

Knight seemed oblivious. "Really, Ferdie, I'd like a house *full* of kids—like Ornette."

Ferdinand laughed. "Mary Dee, I imagine, will have something to say about that. Have you brought it up?"

Again Knight hesitated. "Yes, I did," he said, then tried to laugh. "But you know Mary Dee—she's not too communicative at times. Now and then you have to try to guess at what she's thinking. It's my belief, though, she'd really love having a big family."

Ferdinand laughed again. "She's already got two kids—Ernestine and Vernon."

"You see?—that's what I mean!" Knight said excitedly. "She loves those kids, Ferdie. They love her too. It tells a lot about her —about what a generous, compassionate, person she is. God, I'm lucky."

"Yes—yes, you are," Ferdinand said. "Only we must see to it that the organization is just as lucky. Okay—I'm going now and break the good news to Ornette and Rosabelle."

*   *   *   *   *

Knight returned to his apartment. As he showered and shaved, he thought of the evening ahead of him with uneasiness, almost trepidation. Mary Dee again had invited him to come to dinner, where he would meet her brother Ronald and encounter for the second time her formidable mother, and he was nervous. He had no way of knowing how the evening would go. He had already experienced Irene Adkins' cool, unhappy attitude toward him at their only other meeting, and he did not eagerly look forward to seeing her again. He was also uncertain about Ronald.

727

When he arrived shortly after six, he was admitted not by Mary Dee but by Ronald, who cordially, almost in awe, introduced himself and led him into the parlor where Irene Adkins sat. Mary Dee was nowhere in sight. Today, however, Irene Adkins had had no brandy and was smiling, though her face—octoroon, aquiline, delicate, fading—carried a harried look which to Knight, taking note, was disquieting if fascinating. But he was surprised and pleased by Ronald's deference and cordiality.

"Mr. Knight," said Irene Adkins, "my daughter is busy in the kitchen with Mrs. Grier. She'll be out in a moment. Please have a seat. Ronald, maybe Mr. Knight would like . . . something."

"May I fix you a drink, Mr. Knight?" Ronald said.

Knight, cooperative, asked for a bourbon over ice as he tried to size up the situation. He was inclined to believe Irene Adkins' surface graciousness was occasioned by her son's quite apparent approval of him. Could it be, he wondered, that her attitude had been influenced, softened somewhat, by Ronald's esteem? If so, he was grateful. He now began to feel better, slightly more relaxed, losing some of his natural suspicion, cold reserve. Moments of small talk followed.

"Mr. Knight," said Ronald, quitting some innocuous subject, "I've got friends in California, at Davis, who're members of the Black Peoples Congress. I knew about the organization before, though, long before. But these two guys, John Dudley and Tyrone Thompson, really made me aware of some of the terrific things you've done and are doing. It's pretty impressive."

Knight smiled. "They should have recruited you," he said. "We'd be glad to have you yet—you could help us."

Irene Adkins' face took shocked exception.

"I've got different ideas, though," Ronald smiled. "Different about how to help the black poor, as well as all the other poor—I don't think you can separate them."

"Interesting," said Knight, sipping the bourbon—"if true."

"The American people," young Ronald went on almost like a programmed robot, "—and certainly blacks—must vote themselves a constitution that will give them ownership and control of the means of production in this country, including the land and capital, and use them for everybody, for the general good; but all of course by free democratic methods and maintained only in the same way.

728

Then, if things didn't work out, though I'm pretty sure they would, the system could be voted out. Totalitarianism, repression, wouldn't be involved at all. Blacks should play a big part in this and they'll benefit accordingly. Their problems are economic, Mr. Knight. I don't think Black nationalism's the answer. Whites have the power —blacks have got to fight for a fair share of it, not take themselves off in a corner some place and starve to death. Don't you think—"

"I obviously *don't* think that," Knight interrupted—just as Mary Dee came in the parlor. At once he forgot everything. He had never seen her so beautiful—in a simple flowered summer dress adorned only by the Valentine brooch he had given her four months before. "Good evening," he said, rising.

"Hello, John Calvin. I hope you're not starved." Mary Dee then turned to Irene Adkins. "Dinner's ready, Mother, whenever you are." Soon they all went into the adjacent dining room.

Surprisingly, Irene Adkins participated more in the dinner conversation than Knight had thought likely. He regarded her behavior up to that time, though sometimes civil and polite, as mostly forbidding and taciturn. But now apparently she wanted to talk— about her daughter Mary Dee. Yet she seemed to address her remarks to Ronald, as Mary Dee watched her with what seemed apprehension. "Your sister here keeps extremely well-informed, Ronnie," she said, and gave a kind of manic, though blissful, smile. "She reads everything—books, magazines, newspapers—what have you. She even, whenever she's downtown, picks up out-of-town papers, like the Philadelphia *Inquirer*—I saw one in her room the other day."

Mary Dee looked appalled. What her mother had said was true. Yet none of the Philadelphia newspapers ever carried a single item relating even vaguely to what Mary Dee was looking for: something, anything, about the family that, with the exception of one member, she so despised. Whenever she could get them, she read the Philadelphia papers, the society pages, religiously, though in vain, for any reference whatever to the hated Wilcoxes, or to even a possible—almost certain?—wedding that, with pounding heart, she combed the pages to find. All was in vain. Hope then, though sadly flickering, was somehow kept alive. She had no idea, however, her mother had noticed she bought the newspapers and was angry with herself. She would stop it at once. Besides, she was able to buy the newspapers only irregularly, haphazardly; so they really meant nothing. Yet her heart ached for information, some word, although everything now and forever, she was convinced, was over, dead, academic. Dies had been cast and bridges burned, even if her heart, as opposed to her mind, would somehow, never, never, concede it. She was about to enter a new life now and prayed for better times, for an end to the confusion and anguish; for serenity and worthiness at last. Across the table then she saw Knight, with his piercing eyes, watching her. She quickly smiled. What had he seen in her face? she thought. What had made him stare? She wondered if he had seen the fleeting dark phantom of her dilemma—her vacillation of heart.

"Mother," said Ronald, "but how do we get Suky started painting again? I think she's stopped. Dad wouldn't like that, would he? —he always said her talent was so special; phenomenal, really."

"She has another talent also," Knight spoke up, though without raising his voice—"the talent for wanting to help people; the black poor, for instance."

Ronald smiled. "Why must it be the *black* poor, Mr. Knight?" he said. "Why can't it be just 'the poor?' "

Knight bridled, but Irene Adkins, who as she ate had taken only a few sips of her wine, insisted on discussing with her son her daughter Mary Dee. "Yes, I too fear Suky has lost the zeal to paint, Ronnie. Her talent was so beautiful; there was so much to be expected. Now she's become . . . she's become an administrator. It *is* good her father can't know—he thought she showed such promise. Now she's lost her . . ."

"I haven't lost my zeal at all, Mother," Mary Dee said. "In time I'll return to painting—it's just that lately I've been busy with other things."

Irene Adkins sighed. "How true, Suky."

"What she's been doing now is important, though," Knight said, quietly but defiantly. "In deferring her painting she's made a personal sacrifice for people who need her help. What she's chosen to do demonstrates her character."

Ironically, Knight's moralizing defense irked, irritated, Mary Dee. Besides, she felt in her secret heart her mother was right— she *should* be painting. For her, painting symbolized a very different

730

way of life from that she now led—a more creative, self-fulfilling, more exciting, way of life; a life redolent of an immediate blissful past. Yet out of vitriol and bitterness, her mission of revenge, she had chosen her present career and committed her future to it. It was something, however, she felt she was fated to do—that she was helpless, and though her heart was in her painting her spleen was in her work.

Irene Adkins talked on, until she had finished two glasses of burgundy and asked Mrs. Grier for "tea." Mary Dee was subdued and depressed. Yet she was also furious at the slighting manner in which Knight had been treated by her mother and brother. After dinner when they were alone, seated together on the sofa in the parlor, Mary Dee tried to make amends to Knight. "Oh, John Calvin, what a wacky family I've got," she laughed. "You can see."

But Knight was grave, almost self-righteous. "Your family's not unique," he said—"There are many such, unhappily. How can we reach them? This is where you can make a great contribution—helping us reach people like your family and friends."

"What friends?" she smiled sadly. "I have no friends—except you."

Instead of feeling complimented, Knight became prim. "I'm to be your husband, Dee," he said—"I hope you think of me as something more than a friend."

"Of course I do—I didn't mean it that way." But then her pique began to show. "I know, though," she said, "the kinds of people you're thinking about—blacks who've made it farther up the ladder than most, the people Dr. DuBois wisely called our 'talented tenth.' Well, these people have their ideas about things too, John Calvin. They think hard work, brains, culture, discipline, are all things highly desirable and that no group can advance without them. They don't like being put down. They think, and rightly so, they too are making a contribution—if for nothing else than the example they set for others; that is, as proof that achievement *is* possible. So you say that, unhappily, there are many such people, while I say there are, *happily,* many such people. That's what my father believed, that's what my mother believes now—and it's what I was taught. My mother gets upset when she sees, for instance, I've put aside my painting—which of course is only a metaphor for a whole range of things—in order to do what I'm doing with you and the organization. She thinks I'm squandering my time—in fact, my life."

"Do you think that too, Dee?"

Mary Dee paused, hesitated. "It's pretty clear I don't," she finally said—"or I wouldn't be doing it."

Yet Knight somehow sensed her inner turmoil, the perturbation of spirit, and grew fearful of further offending her. At once he became conciliatory, almost humble. "You're of course the most honest person I've ever known," he said. "That's why I treasure you for what you are—a rare gem. It's also why I need you. I need honest people in my life—people who'll help me by telling me the truth. But there's so much more in your case. I simply love you. That's an emotional state, I know—but it's far superior to any other. Besides, I've presumed to ask you to be my wife. I'm willing to spend the rest of my life trying to make you happy. Do you believe that?"

"Oh, of course I do!" Mary Dee too had become emotional. "How can I do other than admire you, respect you, for all the good you've done for so many people—for your accomplishments as a leader. Yes, yes, I do want to help you—I *will* help you. Only I must go through this transition period—it isn't easy—and you must help *me*. Please be tolerant with me, John Calvin—understanding, kind to me. This means, for instance, not expecting me to repudiate my family—what's left of it—and their views and way of life. There are so many things you must be forbearing with me about, until I've made this transition and am securely on the other, your, side. Do you understand what I'm saying?—are you willing?"

Knight was more emotional than ever. "You wouldn't doubt me for a minute," he said, "if you knew how I feel. It's *love* I feel—the purest, most exalted, selfless, love imaginable. All my life I've needed you, but that's not the point—the point is the passion and depth of my love. I know now, I'm absolutely certain, beyond any doubt, I couldn't live without you—my love's become an obsession. You can see the terrible state I'm in—I can't live without you, Dee!" He was pleading now. The veins stood out in his forehead and his eyes were wild.

The vehemence of his utterance momentarily startled, frightened, her. The old Paris fear and foreboding—of their two encounters—

returned. Her heart quailing, she stared at him in awe; for a moment she was unable to move or speak. It was fully a minute before her pulse began to slow and she became calmer again, at last pensive. "You honor me with such words," she said then. "I'll marry you and try to be the kind of wife justifying the love you feel. It's a tribute to any woman. I believe you're a great man who will become greater still, and I'm willing to be at your side. But be kind to me, please be tolerant, for I've been through a lot; then in time maybe I'll grow into the kind of wife you want me to be. I believe I'm capable, so I'm grateful to you then for changing my future. I am!"

Both were near tears. Knight took her in his arms and kissed her tenderly, saying, "I only know I could never live without you now. *I know that.* I also know that this is the greatest—absolutely the greatest—moment of my life."

*　　*　　*　　*　　*

Two days later the marriage banns, so to speak, were published —in that the word went out to the organization, nation-wide, that on the first Sunday in July the leader would marry. There was general gratification throughout, especially in Cincinnati, where Central Planning Committee member (and troublemaker) Jesse Lumpkins headed the local chapter. Ferdinand, himself elated, had wisely singled Lumpkins out for a phone call to brief him on who Mary Dee was, her record with the organization, and how it had all come about. Lumpkins, as well as other potential dissidents, had long since been told, reassured, that "that other person, Griselda Graves" was gone for good and that Knight was already courting an outstanding young lady in the organization who showed tremendous promise. There was therefore general relief over the turn of events. Even Ornette and Rosabelle, who from Ferdinand had learned of the impending wedding before most, had finally hearkened to Ferdinand's pleas to return actively, support Knight, and help rebuild the organization. Ornette, however, had given the decision long and careful thought before agreeing. Try as he might he could not rid himself of vast doubts and misgivings—as to both

Knight and Mary Dee. Yet Rosabelle had said that, on balance, it was the right thing for them to do and he at last acquiesced.

It was of course Mary Dee who was having difficulties—at home. The evening she informed her mother and brother of the wedding date she and Knight had agreed on, Irene Adkins sat down in the kitchen and emitted a long, heavy sigh. "Suky, you are my daughter," she said, tearfully biting her lip. "I love you—you know that—and if this is what you want to do, I wish you only the greatest happiness. But first you must tell me, look me in the eye and tell me, that it's something you really want to do—that deep down in your heart you want to do it. Can you tell me that, Suky?"

"Mother," protested Ronald—"that's hardly fair, is it? It's implied in her consent—*of course* it's what she wants to do, or she wouldn't have said yes." He turned to Mary Dee standing in the kitchen door. "Suky, I salute you. It's also because I admire Knight. I don't agree with him, and apparently you, on his black separatist stance, but the important thing is he's a guy with character, and also vision. He's trying to do some great things for blacks, and has succeeded in many ways. Mother, Knight's *doing things*—he's a mover and a shaker. You wouldn't want Suky to marry some vapid society doctor or lawyer who'd buy her a Mercedes-Benz and a long mink coat every year or two, would you?—you want her to do better than that, don't you?"

Irene Adkins' face was crimson. She stood up in a quivering fury. "How dare you say that! . . . Your father, a physician and surgeon, was one of the most respected men in this community! Yes—yes—I'd love to see her marry such a man! . . ."

"Oh, of course you would, Mother—I didn't mean it that way." Apologetic, Ronald went over, put his arm around Irene Adkins, and tried to soothe, placate, her. "*You* know Dad was my 'main man,' Mother. I didn't——"

"You shouldn'ta said it, then," Mrs. Grier, cooking dinner, spoke up in a rare huff. "How'd you get to know so much and just reached legal age?—talkin' when you should be listenin'. Is that what those professors taught you?"

Mary Dee was oblivious and cool, almost cold, to it all, and, ostensibly at least, obdurate, secure. Yet her heart was searching for answers—especially the answer to her mother's question. "I'm sorry to be the center of so much argument," she finally said. "But

I obviously have the greatest respect for John Calvin—and, more than that, I react to him emotionally. Mother, I'm sure you too, when you get to know him better, will appreciate and like him." Then she added a truth: "The first time I saw him, I disliked him heartily."

"It only shows we can change," said Ronald.

Irene Adkins, though still unappeased, at last remonstrated no further. Sniveling, she looked at Mary Dee for a long time. "What are you going to wear," she said at last.

"Mother, I haven't had time to think about it—something very simple, I guess; almost informal. Will you go with me downtown tomorrow to look?" Then impulsively she took a step toward Irene Adkins—"Mother, will you?"

Irene Adkins sighed again. "Yes, I'll go, Suky. But it should be something white—and with a small veil."

"Great," laughed Ronald—"I want to be able to give away a romantic, well-turned out bride."

Mary Dee, thoughtful, preoccupied, cheerless, withdrew to her room.

Next day she and her mother went downtown shopping for a modest wedding dress. When they had found what they wanted and, in Mary Dee's new Toyota, were driving home, Mary Dee suddenly said: "Oh, I just thought!—we musn't forget to invite Chauncey Stiles. Won't he be surprised to hear? He'd have a fit if he weren't there."

"Very well, I'll call him," Irene Adkins said. "And what about the minister?—I've never heard of this man you say you've got."

"*I* didn't get him, Mother—John Calvin did. He's a Reverend Bonbright, who's been active with John Calvin here in the Chicago organization."

Irene Adkins seemed apprehensive. "I hope, Suky, he's not one of the stomping and shouting kind."

"Mother, how could he find anything, at a wedding, to stomp and shout about?"

"Oh, it doesn't take much for that kind to get started—almost anything." The temperature was warm, the late afternoon beautiful. Mary Dee was headed south on Lake Shore Drive, where the lake on their left was calm and blue with a cloudless, almost infinite, horizon. Soon Irene Adkins glanced at Mary Dee out of the corner of her eye—tentatively, uncertainly, as if anything but sure of herself. Finally she said: "Suky, could we drive by the old house for a minute?—just to look at it again; not stop, just go by sort of as if to see if it's still there. Could we?"

"Oh, Mother, I'd rather not. . . . Do we have to? What good will it do?"

"We can live vicariously for a moment—in the past . . . when you skipped rope, climbed trees, and played the cello; and when Jocelyn and Ronnie ran after you wherever you went. That's the good it will do."

Mary Dee said no more. Heavy-hearted, she left the Drive at 51st Street, drove the two miles west to Woodlawn, and turned right. When the beautiful old house came in view, Irene Adkins— it was a paradox—rather than sad, was suddenly excited, elated. "Oh, look!—how well it's kept, Suky!" she said. "Ah, how wonder-ful—he's a white University of Chicago professor, you know. I'm so glad the broker was able to find people like that, aren't you? It looks every bit as good as when your father was alive!" Irene Adkins now seemed happy in her memories. Mary Dee, despite her own low spirits, was glad she had indulged her mother and, if only for a moment, brought her "home."

They arrived back at the apartment shortly after four o'clock. When they had gone up, Mary Dee, her packaged dress in hand, went directly to her room—where she removed the dress from the box, briefly viewed it again, then hung it in the closet. She was changing into slacks, when Irene Adkins reappeared and tossed down some mail. "Except for possibly one, it's all junk, Suky," she said and left. Mary Dee, though, her mind on other things, con-tinued changing clothes. It was fully five minutes before she thought to look at the mail.

* * * * *

Knight only the same evening remembered he had not even offered, suggested, to his wife-to-be that, if she liked, they could take a short honeymoon trip somewhere. Yet he debated calling her, feeling a strange reluctance doubtless born of his still gnawing,

736

intuitive, feelings of insecurity in the relationship; moreover, the more he yearned to be with her, to press his attention and devotion on her, to tell her a thousand times over how he worshipped her, again how he could never now live without her, the more he yearned to do these things, the more—strangely, weirdly—his guilt feelings about Griselda bore in on him and with a savagery calculated to tear out his insides. It was torture. He had dreamed of Griselda again last night, a swiftly-moving, tender, incomprehensible dream from which he seemed almost powerless to awake. But it was rather as if he had talked to her ghost, her disembodied presence, and had somehow been unable to come close enough to touch her, even see her; she was a mere insubstantiality, a wraith. He remembered asking her forgiveness, however; to which she had responded with sweet absolution and love. Yet, with her breath of ashes, she had warned him of something which was never quite clear, and now he was in a state of nerves like nothing he had ever experienced. He thought then again of Mary Dee. She was his refuge. How he wished he could somehow unburden himself of his immediate past to her, but knew he could not—she would never understand. Yet after dinner he phoned her—to suggest that after the wedding they briefly go away.

The phone rang many times. At last Irene Adkins answered, equivocally; she seemed nervous, upset. Then he asked for Mary Dee, and got the feeling now Irene Adkins somehow, surprisingly, welcomed his call. "Mr. Knight let me go call her," she said. "She hasn't felt well all evening—she didn't even have her dinner. But let me go tell her." When, however, she returned he could not help detecting the anxiety in her voice. "No, she's really not up to it," she said—"She's in her room with the door closed and won't say anything at all to anybody. It's plain she's feeling badly—but she's not the kind who makes a fuss."

"Should I call a doctor? . . ." Knight said.

"I asked her if I should talk to a doctor but she said no. I'm concerned, though. But I'm sure she'll feel better tomorrow and will call you."

Knight hung up in a quandary.

Later that evening the Adkins' apartment was quiet. Ronald, who had left during the morning, job-hunting, had asked that dinner not be delayed for him, that he would be late. Now it was after nine and Mrs. Grier had been gone since seven. When, at nine-thirty, Ronald finally came home, he was intercepted at once by Irene Adkins. "Something's the matter with Suky, Ronnie," she said. He could feel her worry. "She's been in her room since we got back from downtown and won't come out—and won't talk to anyone; neither me nor Mrs. Grier. She also refused any dinner. Why don't you go knock on her door, Ronnie, and see if she'll talk to you. Try to find out what's wrong with her. It's apparently not physical —I offered to call a doctor; she said no. I'm worried about her, though."

"What the heck's going on here?" said Ronald, almost to himself, as he headed back to Mary Dee's room. He knocked. No response. He knocked again. "Suky!—are you asleep, so early?" Irene Adkins stood behind him.

"No," Mary Dee said quietly through the door.

"May I come in?—are you feeling okay? . . ."

"I don't need anything." Her voice droned. "I'm going to bed soon. Don't bother—I'm okay."

"You don't sound okay!" Ronald turned the knob and opened the door. There was only one tiny lamp on; the room was almost in darkness. Irene Adkins, close behind him, peered in after him. Mary Dee, still in slacks and blouse, sat at the window where she'd apparently been gazing out at the star-studded night. Though her face was composed, her eyes were dulled, her manner inert.

Irene Adkins went and stood over her. "Tell us, Suky—what's the matter?"

"We want to help you," Ronald added. "Are you hurting anywhere?—is anything wrong?"

At last Mary Dee looked pleadingly at them. "If you want to help me," she said, "then please leave me and I'll go to bed. I think I need rest. . . ." Her voice now had taken on a low, hollow, sepulchral tone. "It's rest I think I need. I'll be okay in the morning." But her voice was in black mourning. "Please don't worry about me—just trust me. Goodnight, Mother—goodnight, Ronnie."

Ronald still stood staring at her. "Okay, then," he said finally —"we'll do as you say."

Irene Adkins, with fondness, tenderness, placed the palm of her hand against Mary Dee's cheek. "Would you like some hot chocolate?" she said—"and maybe a sandwich? You ate no dinner, you know. Aren't you hungry?"

"No, Mother—thanks. Now, goodnight."

Irene Adkins and Ronald left and closed the door.

Mary Dee still sat in the room's deep gloaming, yet no longer gazing out the window at the starry night. She only stared now at the opposite blank wall. Finally after fifteen minutes she got up and closed the draperies, then went to her dresser and rummaged in the top drawer until she found the pair of sunglasses. After putting them on, she went and turned on the bright reading lamp over her big chair near the bed. But even with the dark glasses on she shielded her eyes with her hand from the painful light—her eyes ached because she had so far been unable to cry. Now once more she took the stuffed, rumpled envelope—the letter her mother had brought her that afternoon—from her slacks pocket and sat down under the almost unbearable light. She held the brightly-tricolored air-mail missive, postmarked Paris, in her trembling hand for a moment as she whispered to herself something inaudible, like a prayer. Finally she took the four sheets of tissue-thin paper, close typewriting on both sides of each, from the envelope and once again (she had forgotten how many times) read his letter—Raoul's.

"My wonderful Dee: This is the most difficult letter I shall ever have to write—I am sure of it, *chérie*. It is a terrible, a horrible, task to have to perform. I really do not know how to do it. . . . It is even harder because I should have written to you before now. But I did not have the courage. When Philip completed his studies here—that was a year ago—he returned home, for good. He was glad to leave Paris—I have no doubt of it; he did everything but say it, and talked so often of 'the old days when things were better, when things were lovely.' So he disposed of all his effects—no small job—and went home. Yet within three months he was married."

For possibly the fifth time, even if now in a descending scale of force, the blow struck Mary Dee, yet almost sending her reeling.

"Many times," wrote Roaul, "I started to write to you about it, but I did not have the heart. I even tried to persuade myself that Philip, in his candor and honesty, would somehow have written to you himself and told you—I tried to tell myself that many, many times. Yet I feel rather certain he did not—he would have preferred that you not find out. He married of course to please his parents—most likely at the behest, indeed the command, of his father. So he married a girl chosen for him—a very rich girl, and from an old and established family. But he was miserable, I hear, inconsolable, and became more so every day. My information source —his younger and favorite brother, Kermit Randall Wilcox (remember his talk of Randy?) whom Philip had once even sent your picture—is unimpeachable. I'm sure, of course—and so is Kermit Randall—that Philip's torment, torture, was all because of you. He never got over you, *chérie.*

"But this now is the tragedy—it is a horrible thing to have to tell you: On the 15th of last month Philip was driving home late at night—alone. There is evidence that he had been drinking heavily. He took a rain-swept curve at a very high, an almost demonic, rate of speed—it was as if he were trying his best to commit suicide—and the car left the highway, hurtled down, rolling over and over, a steep rock embankment, and on impact caught fire. I can only say now how much I hate to have to tell you, *chérie,* that Philip is dead—that he was killed and his body burned almost beyond recognition.

"I repeat, *chérie,* this is a horrible thing to have to tell you, and I do so with the greatest reluctance and sorrow. You know, he and I were very good friends too—I lost a fine and noble friend. That is why his brother, Kermit Randall, who of course, as we both know, knew about you, cabled me; and why I later talked to him by oceanic telephone. He is well aware of what was wrong with Philip—that is, his desperation and agony over his love for you and the terrible mistake he had made in surrendering to his family. It is a sad, sad story, *chérie*—a heartwrenching, tragic, final chapter. It has troubled me—*you* have troubled me. I finally realized, after these weeks, that it would be perfidious of me not to write and tell you. What a final, final, chapter, *chérie,* when we think of the glorious times we had."

At last Mary Dee cried—sobbed.

Next day, explaining little or nothing to her family except where she was going, ignoring Knight altogether, she called her sister in Boston, where Jocelyn had a job for the summer to be near her fiancé, and told her she was coming at once to visit her. By noon she had left for O'Hare Airport.

740

* * * * *

In Boston Mary Dee did not answer Raoul's letter for a week. She was still so sickened and stunned she did not know what to say, or do. Though she had by now at last slightly recovered from the shock and grief of the news, she found herself in a perfect state of nascence; or as if she were newly reborn, or altogether in another, a brand new, world where she hardly new where she was. Yet as she pondered the tragedy in the blackest hours of her long, sleepless nights she could not help realizing Philip's death had brought change, a radical, if tragic, break with the past—her past. From this point forward her life would, had to be, different—not better, she thought, but different. She still felt the deepest sorrow, still loved him and his memory to distraction, still harbored dreams that were now so utterly baseless and void, yet all now was changed. Even her total feelings in the situation were not unmixed; there was a tincture of vanity, of self, in it all as well; a sense of fierce, just, retribution. How did the mighty Wilcoxes feel *now*? she thought. Justice had been dealt them with a swift and devastating hand— how now their mad cruelty and hauteur? But then there were moments of doubt—she even felt, in her own near-mad state, she might have been deceived by the letter, that Raoul's information could have been unwittingly false. It prompted her to go to the Boston Public Library, where she found the Philadelphia newspapers for that fateful week. Yet there it was, indisputable verification of the horrible fact, and front-paged: "Wilcox Scion Killed in Fiery Car Crash." Then suddenly it bore in on her addled brain that within three days—Sunday—she was to be married.

In Chicago John Calvin Knight's condition was beyond describing; he was in a hopeless, almost nauseous, state. Moreover, whatever the cause of Mary Dee's behavior, he felt its deep humiliation. He became angry then, less at her than at himself—for having been so unable to control himself, for having fallen so idiotically in love. He could sleep or eat but little, and erratically; and as for the organization, it was virtually without a head; his neglect of it was total. Another ordeal was his inability to get information. He had called the Adkins' apartment repeatedly, only to be told, by Irene Adkins, Mrs. Grier, or Ronald, that Mary Dee had left town briefly to visit her sister and was expeced back any day now. Yet the family was as much in the dark about Mary Dee's mysterious condition, malady, as Knight. Ronald and Irene Adkins talked on the telephone every day to Jocelyn, who had taken a very proprietary, protective, attitude toward her extravagantly-admired and unhappy older sister, but could learn only that Mary Dee was staying with her and was, at least physically, well and adjusting.

"Adjusting to what?" demanded Ronald.

"I have no idea," Jocelyn said. "I only know she needs love and understanding."

"As if she didn't get that here, eh?"

"Well, she's very upset about *something*."

"Do you think it's the upcoming wedding?" Ronald finally said.

"I don't know—it could be."

Irene Adkins, listening on an extension, said: "Or, as I told Ronnie, it could be something in a letter she received that day—a letter apparently from someone she knows in Paris. I brought it to her."

"Maybe in time I'll find out, Mother," Jocelyn said, "but at the present she's uncommunicative."

"Is she there now?" Ronald said. "If so, ask her to come to the phone, will you?"

"She's here, yes, but she's still not up to it, Ronnie. I want her to rest, to calm down. She wouldn't come to the phone anyway."

"I think it was something in that Paris letter," insisted Irene Adkins. "Maybe it's just as well—it may make her think twice about this marriage. Knight calls here every day, pleading for her address and telephone number. We refuse them, of course."

"Jocelyn," Ronald said, "go remind her that her wedding's *Sunday*. My God!—ask her what she plans to do, and what she wants us to do."

Jocelyn reluctantly left the phone, but soon came back with a message. "She says to postpone it for a month."

"Oh, thank Heavens!" Irene Adkins said before she thought.

"Postpone it!" said Ronald. "Good Lord!—this is a heck of a thing. You can imagine what it'll be like telling Knight that. Poor guy, I feel sorry for him—I know how I'd feel."

Later that day Ronald called Knight and asked to come see him. Though barely civil, Knight consented. That evening, the first thing

Ronald noticed on entering Knight's apartment was the leader's manic, glowing eyes and unshaven face. "Mr. Knight," he began even before he sat down, "I'm sorry, and embarrassed, as can be about what's happened, but we haven't had, until today, any more information than you've had. Mary Dee is in some kind of withdrawn state and doesn't communicate at all—in Boston with my other sister or with us. We don't know what ails her. The only thing she told us today was that she wanted the wedding postponed for a month."

Although Knight had brusquely motioned Ronald to a chair, he himself had dourly, nervously, remained standing. "Why, this is unbelievable," he said—"She can't mean that. I'd appreciate it if you'd just give me her address and telephone number in Boston."

"I can't do that, Mr. Knight—simply because she doesn't want it. She has your phone number, I'm sure, and can call you when she likes. It wouldn't be right for me to give her address either, against her will."

"Postpone the wedding. . . ." Knight mused aloud—"I can't understand it. It must be something I've done. Is it? Has she complained about me in any way?"

"No, not at all. I gather it's that she wants time to let this . . . whatever it is that's so upset her, let it die down some, not bother her so much, before she marries. In fact, maybe she's thinking primarily of you, Mr. Knight—doesn't want to begin the marriage on some sour note."

Knight brushed this theory off with an impatient wave of the hand. "You, representing her family, do me a great disservice—a dishonor, really—by refusing to tell me how I can get in touch with her. It shows you have no confidence in me. It's demeaning."

"It's only because she doesn't wish it."

"How do you know that?"

"Well, we sense it."

"You sense it!"

"Oh, I don't want to get in any argument with you, Mr. Knight," Ronald said, getting up. "I still think this will all come out all right —some way."

"But when you next get in touch with her," said Knight at last, in a subdued, disheartened, voice, "tell her that I send her my love, which she or no one else can destroy, and that I wish she would

743

call or write me; that I think of her constantly and hope she soon, very soon, feels better; that if it's anything I've done, I'd like to know about it and will try my best somehow to make amends. Will you tell her that?"

"Yes, Mr. Knight, she'll be told that yet tonight."

By the time Ronald was down on the street, his sympathy, pity, for Knight had all but overwhelmed him. He wanted to return immediately and give him the address and phone number, yet, having observed Knight's unsettled, obsessed, state, he was fearful of what he might do—Knight, he thought, would almost certainly fly to Boston at once; and probably make matters worse. It was too risky. He went home.

Later that evening Knight, his hand shaking, dialed the telephone to inform Ferdinand Bailey of this latest development. Alarmed Ferdinand, however, seemed as ineffectual as he was fervently solicitous. "Oh, John Calvin," he said, "don't take it so hard. Everything will turn out all right in the end—you watch. I've prayed over this thing and have faith right will prevail. The girl's inexperienced—she may be, temporarily, plain scared of marriage, for all we know. She hasn't been out in the hard, the real, world; knows nothing about it; she's lived such a sheltered life. You must be patient with her, understanding, knowing how naive she is. Plus the fact you're a national figure—she may be overawed at the prospect of being your wife. And, remember, you're ten years older than she is—think of that. Besides you're a very serious, no-nonsense, kind of person—she may be plain scared of you. I'll bet she'll come around, though, and real soon. So stop worrying—you're already losing weight. She'll write you. Or she'll call you, any evening now—so stay by your phone." Yet Ferdinand himself seemed as nervous, upset—fearful of what was happening—as Knight.

But Mary Dee did not write. Nor did she call. Night after night in his apartment Knight kept practically a vigil by the telephone, waiting, but no call came. He turned then to thinking about the mails, that she might still write him, but nothing came of that either. Thus two weeks passed.

Ferdinand, as he learned developments, had kept Ornette and Rosabelle informed. Ornette stopped by his office one morning to find if there was anything new. "Nothing, Ornette," Ferdinand

744

said—"absolutely nothing. John Calvin's taking it hard, too—he's about out of his mind. I'm worried about him."

Ornette sat down. He seemed cool, poised, almost inscrutable. But soon he said: "Let's own up to it. You and I, his so-called friends, got him into this. It's a fact. We did him no favor, though. You may argue with me all day, but we've got to face up to it—Mary Dee's thrown him over, Ferdie. She's jilted him practically in front of the altar. I feel sorry for him, but I feel still sorrier for the organization. It's the organization that's suffering. John Calvin's no leader any more, Ferdie, and you know it. Now it'll be even worse."

Ferdinand heaved a heavy sigh. "I don't like to think about it," he said.

That night, briefly, in the smallest hours, Knight dreamed again of Griselda. Her wraithlike insubstantiality unchanged, the loving kindness intact, she talked to him, it seemed, as if from a diving bell as she complained once, faintly, of the bends. "You too now, John Calvin," she then said, "are submerged—submerged by events of which I obscurely warned you, though I don't cry revenge. Rather, you were born to be a victim. You are wise and unwise at the same time, a wise and passionate man whose wisdom and passion have been squandered in tilting at windmills for a cause—the cause, the phenomenon, of color, which you let divide and destroy us both—that you have not fully investigated, whose profundities you have not sufficiently studied. Only a higher wisdom, predicated on long, ascetic studies into the night, will bring you the peace you seek before your untimely end. You are, then, forgiven—*all* is forgiven. *Oh, John Calvin, John Calvin!* But adieu . . . adieu . . . remember me—always."

What did it mean? he asked himself next morning. She had seemed so *unreal*.

*   *   *   *   *

At last from Boston Mary Dee wrote to Raoul in Paris. She tried in her letter for bravery, restraint. She thanked him for his steadfast friendship in a trying hour—for his courage, constancy,

745

in writing to her of tragedy. It had been a blow that staggered, she confessed, an unbelievable catastrophe, yet one few people were gifted, susceptible, enough to understand as could the two of them who, with Philip, had lived the beautiful, the glorious, Paris days. Anyhow lately, however, her life was destined to take a new, hopefully more constructive, course and she bespoke his understanding and good wishes. Again she thanked him, expressed hope his work went well, and signed the letter affectionately. Yet, only two days after she had mailed it, she received another letter from him, forwarded to her by her mother, bringing her to realize their letters— her first, his second—had crossed in the mails.

Raoul's letter was apologetic, almost remorseful. After mailing his first letter, he said, he had had tortured second thoughts, knowing how its contents must have affected her; that now he was not sure he had done the best thing, yet did not know either how he could any longer have refrained, considering the importance of the information to them both, from writing as he did. "These matters are always difficult, *chérie,* when the other person involved—here yourself—is a friend, a true friend. You think of your friend's great sensibility and moral fiber, one possibly in this case operating against the other, and you do not know what to do. One makes many false starts and is never sure. I only hope that what I did was, in the end, right—right for you. A partial parallel has been myself—my work. Last year, for example, I was persuaded, here at Beaux Arts, to become a member of the faculty administration, to give up, for a time, my pedagogy for the bureaucracy. It was a mistake, a false start, you see—I was miserable. I am only fitted for the teaching, the artistic, side of this business—I am not good at assuming responsibility for things and ordering people, some my colleagues, around. I like to think, *chérie,* of myself as an artist— not really, not the kind that you are, yet one, let us say, who holds art sacred. So I care nothing for business, for the prosaic—I am poor at it. In this connection I did not tell you that my mother died last April—a person dear to me. You recall she lived on the family property in Arles—a place which has been in our family nearly four generations, since before the Franco-Prussian War. She owned property here in Paris also and, with her investments, left quite a sizable estate. Well, as her only child, learning to administer it—it's all mine now—has been a virtual nightmare. I like no longer being poor, but the responsibilities I abhor. So I indulge myself, *chérie*, by telling myself this is because I am an artist. My only 'administrative' joy now consists in providing for my daughter's rearing and education. Nadine is nine years old now!—would you believe it? I would very much like to bring her up as your father brought you up—with indulgence and love, yet with a strong, suggestive, guiding hand. Ah, what a beautiful job your father did with you! Yes, you were spoiled, just as I'm spoiling Nadine—but to what good effect. So I've taken a rather nice place—sumptuous for me!—on the Ile St.-Louis, where Nadine, who thus far was reared by my mother—whom she misses terribly—has a governess and a grand piano on which she plays Clementi and Chopin. We have a regular household, including a cook. So you see my administrative duties are virtually awesome, *chérie*! I like them and I don't like them; for, you see, yes, I too am an artist."

The humorous, gossipy letter went on for three more closely-typewritten pages. But nothing that had happened since the arrival of his first, traumatic, letter had so sobered yet elevated Mary Dee's spirits. Her problems were legion and confused, but this second letter was sheer therapy. She read it quickly twice, then, before reading, savoring, it again, sat thinking of the old, the dear, Paris, which still to her could never be restored. But Raoul—how sweet he was. What a dear friend. Yet the letter ended with, for him, a rather stern reprimand: "I have a feeling—because you've not mentioned it—that you have abandoned your art, your painting, which, if true, I regard as both calamitous and sad." She had read the letter, however, with infinite pleasure—and answered it the same day. And again their answering letters crossed in the mails.

The Monday following the Sunday that was to have been the wedding day, Ronald Adkins took a plane to Boston to have it out with his sisters—both. When he had phoned the night before to say he was coming, Mary Dee went at once into what seemed an all-night brown study, hours of deepest meditation and hard thinking, under the heaviest pressure wondering what she would or could say to Ronald, what explanation, justification, she could give. The result was to compel her to confront the thorny considerations she had studiously avoided since Raoul's first letter had come in on her with the swiftness, force, and havoc of a meteor.

747

It concerned what she knew to have been the sole motivation for her professed ties with the Black Peoples Congress. Suddenly now —she felt almost sordid admitting it—the motivation was gone, vanished. With Philip's death, it had collapsed like the proverbial house of cards. She thought of his torn and grieving family and was somehow appeased—satisfied. Moreover, the tenderness of her feeling for him, their tempestuous, nostalgic, Paris love affair, and now his memory in death, had tempered infinitely her thirst for blood. Where then, she thought, with an already deadening remorse, did this leave her vis-à-vis the organization? And, alas, with Knight? She tried to steel herself, turn her mind away—she would think of it no more today. Maybe at least with Ronald the question would not yet have to be faced. She lived from day to day—hour to hour.

Ronald arrived from the airport shortly after lunchtime Monday. Jocelyn, who was now sharing with Mary Dee the room Jocelyn had taken for the summer in the home of family friends of her fiancé's parents, and who today had stayed home from her job to see Ronald, was the first to greet him in the living room. But Mary Dee, somehow looking none the worse for her recent experience, soon also appeared—she seemed perfectly composed and rational, as if she were home in the kitchen. They all sat down and Ronald wasted no time. "I have a four o'clock return flight," he said, looking at his watch, "so bear with me. Suky, Mother's worried almost sick about you." His young face was serious, his voice tinged with incipient anger. "Why would you do this to her? —I mean, go off like this and then even refuse to talk to her on the telephone. I'd like to know what happened—we, your family, are entitled to know."

"Now, wait a minute, Ronnie," spoke up Jocelyn—"Stop demanding."

"I'm not demanding. I'm pointing out her duty to her—her duty at least to her mother. Why're you so doggone protective, Jocelyn?—you must know a lot more, then, than we do."

"Oh, stop it," Mary Dee finally said. "Ronnie, I got word that day—in a letter—of the death of a dear friend I met in Paris. It was a shock, a blow, and I acted irresponsibly. I've come around to my senses now, I think. But I won't be home possibly for another week yet—though I'm imposing on Jocelyn in a cramped room. I need this time away, though."

748

"Have you forgotten Knight?" Ronald said, jutting out his jaw. "Do you realize you were to be married in our parlor yesterday afternoon? Have you contacted *him*?"

"No," Mary Dee said coldly, and looked away.

"Well, don't you think you owe it to him? I went to see him, and, although he's extremely upset, do you know what he told me?" There was a strained silence, yet no response. "He said if I contacted you to tell you that he sent his love, and that no one— you or no one else—could destroy that. I don't think there's any question he's a man of character, integrity—it's no accident he's such a hero to black people. True, this aura that seems to surround him, his personality, is a strange one. From what I can see it's partly a hot anger easily triggered combined with a kind of vain melancholy he carries around with him—neither of which he's aware of—that creates the impression he gives. But the man is anything but a phony. Yet, Suky, you treat him like someone beneath you. It's not like you at all."

Mary Dee seemed sad, troubled, reflective. "No one said he's a phony," she said—"I don't know why you bring that up. I've told you and mother how much I respect him."

"I know, but is respect enough?—that's another complication. But at any rate, Suky, shouldn't you call him and tell him the truth —whatever it is. Only *you* know the truth—and he's entitled to it. I feel sorry for him, I really do. He calls the house all the time for any news about you, but what can we tell him? He's in a terrible state—the poor guy's eating his heart out."

"Ronnie," Jocelyn said, now in a more conciliatory tone, "let me handle this. Let Suky stay here awhile longer, a week or so if she wants to, until she feels up to coming home. She'll feel better and things will be better."

Ronald shook his head. "I don't think so—she may feel better but things won't be better. I told Knight what Suky said about wanting the wedding put off for a month. He was shocked. Now even part of that time's gone. Suky, you've got to make up your mind pretty soon. Things are *not* going to get better, Jocelyn."

Mary Dee and Jocelyn, seeming not to know what to say to this, said nothing.

"Suky," Ronald said, "it seems to me—I could be wrong of course—that you're having second thoughts about this marriage; about Knight. Again, is respect enough?—I don't know. And I'm not asking you to comment—I just have my doubts. If I'm right, I certainly don't know what happened to change your mind so suddenly—the death of a dear friend? I don't get it. But whatever the situation is, I think you owe it to Knight to come home, sit down, and have it out with him. Don't go on avoiding him like this—really it makes you appear a little shifty. As I say, that's not you, Suky."

Mary Dee, staring off in space, gave another troubled sigh.

"Do you need any money?" Ronald asked her.

"No," she said.

"Will you call Mother tonight?"

"Yes."

"Will you also call Knight?"

Mary Dee flew into a rage. "Ronnie, you shut up! You're too big for your britches—Mrs. Grier was right. Where did you get so much wisdom that you can tell me what to do, order me around? You just shut up! You've said enough already—*too* much! What is this?—have you no breeding, no delicacy of feelings, to grill me as you have on such a private matter? I'll tell you nothing more—absolutely nothing!"

Jocelyn intervened. "Ronnie, let me handle this—Suky's had a bad time. Go home and tell Mother not to worry, that we'll work it out all right. Suky needs to be let alone for awhile so that she can solve some of these things herself. Only she can do it."

"With that I'll agree," said Ronald, now in a fierce pout. He was thinking of Knight—commiserating. "It's her decision," he said. Soon he bade them a very formal, frosty, good-bye and left to return to the airport.

* * * * *

Four days later Irene Adkins forwarded to Mary Dee Raoul's answer to her first letter. It also contained a snapshot of his daughter Nadine. The letter was again long, and humorously rambling and garrulous, with, however, a portion of it of uncommon—intriguing—interest to Mary Dee. She read this part with a grave and concentrated seriousness. "Ah, how great it was, *chérie*, to receive your nice, your very nice—though somewhat *triste*-in-tone—letter," Raoul said. "Much of it took me back to old times, more particularly to our last, our very last luncheon, just the two of us, remember?—at The Canary where the black man passed our table on his way out and so frightened you? We had a grand talk that day, did we not? I tried my best, I remember, to make the point to you that you have talent as a painter that you should never, never, neglect; that it should become, really, your *way of life*. Remember that? I meant it—I mean it now.

"Ah, *chérie*, but we talked of other things that day as well . . . am I right? And you cried a little, just a little—for you were so surprised—when I told you that while I used to think of Pauline, my deceased wife, all the time, that now I thought of you. Ha!—it flabbergasted you, bowled you over, didn't it? I shall never forget it. Though Philip was eternally on your mind, you didn't seem offended by my presumption, my brashness. But what I told you, was true, *chérie*. And, alas, it still is. Constantly I think of you. But I shall for the present eschew this, ha, difficult, shall we say, this slightly, delicately, embarrassing subject and go on to other things. Yet I fear it is rather like Banquo's ghost—it will not go away. Tell me, *chérie,* are you made uncomfortable by my bringing up these somewhat singular experiences out of the past?"

Eventually, however, the letter went on to other, though still not entirely unrelated, matters. "I am enclosing," said Raoul, "a new picture of Nadine to show you how she's grown since the last picture you saw of her. She is already, as you can see, a very proper young lady; and speaks English fairly well—reads it *quite* well. Her favorite novel at the moment—listen, I swear—is *Tristram Shandy*! Oh, she's *merveilleux,* and, I believe, gifted—ah, and has such a doting father!"

This letter bade Mary Dee pause. It was not one she answered at once. Rather, it sent her into hours, days, of deeply profound, if harried, confused, thought. She had always been a self-confident, self-reliant, person—a trait inculcated in her by her father. But now for the first time she wished she had someone to talk to, confide in, counsel with. Certainly Jocelyn, whom she regarded as totally inexperienced, would not do. Nor, of all people, Ronald. Not even her mother—alas, now somewhat erratic. There was no one. Even Ronald and Jocelyn had agreed there were decisions she,

751

Mary Dee, alone must make. For the first time now she was afraid. Then, less than a week later, she received from home Raoul's answer to her second letter. Matters were in no way helped; they had only become more serious.

What to her, midway into this chatty but crucial letter, that was by far its most significant section read: "Your second letter, yes, was so much better than your first—in tone somewhat less dismal. Yet it did not clear up for me a mystery I had found (or at least thought I had found) in your first—I have tried not mentioning this before, hoping it would clear up itself, but, *chérie*, it has not. You referred in the letter to the prospect that your life was destined to take a new, hopefully more constructive, course, and you asked for my understanding and good wishes. I have racked my brain trying to decide what you meant by that, but with no success. I can only hope, however, you meant you were going to devote your life now to the pursuit of your art—to painting. That was the only thing I could, and wanted to, conclude. But why would you ask for my understanding of *that*?—something I've always urged on you. Is this really what you meant, though, *chérie*? Please clear this up for me—it is important.

"For if you meant something else, that you were embarking on some other, very different, lifestyle or mission—not in any way connected with your art—then your statement at once takes on the gravest implications. *Chérie*, you were meant to be a painter— possibly, with the right tutelage and environment, a great painter. Who oversees this, who continues your instruction, also where it takes place, are all matters of the most vital importance to your future. When I tell people about your talent, your potential, people who never knew you, or, for that matter, never even heard of you, they are often very curious and ask all sorts of questions about you. Then when I tell them what a lovely, what a beautiful, girl you are—not only outwardly, but inwardly as well—they can hardly believe it; they can't understand how a young lady of such character and rare beauty could also have the exceptional talent that I am so confident your work shows. Ha!—if you were mean and ugly, *chérie*, wore thick glasses, say, and chewed your fingernails down to the quick, yes, they could believe then that you have *enormous* talent. But not someone of your personality and loveliness. It's really funny, isn't it?—funny in one way, yet a matter of

752

most serious consequence in another. It simply raises the question —poor Philip, alas, is out of your life now, *chérie*—of what you will make of your life from this point on. Will it slip away from you into an existence, no matter how 'constructive' you may think it is, of no real affinity or interest to you, or will it begin for you a bright new life, one of challenge and promise—*of fame*—in a field in which you have quite unique and natural gifts. Which will it be?—isn't that really the question, *chérie*?"

The letter had a profound effect on Mary Dee. She sat alone in her sister's room that morning pondering long the critical question Raoul had raised. Moreover, he had mentioned fame. She had never considered this. Was it conceivably possible for her? Although always confident in anything she undertook, she had never considered herself in this light. She had never thought of fame— of herself as potentially famous. Could it be? she asked herself, or was Raoul merely flattering her? She rejected this at once—right or wrong, Raoul sincerely believed what he had said; she was certain of that. Dear, dear Raoul, she thought—perennially her supporter and friend. But there was somehow something more in what he was saying here—it was anything but simple, elementary. She was not so oblivious, obtuse, however, as to miss what might be a deeper meaning, his possible true motivation, in what he had said in the letter; in effect, that the "tutelage and environment"—his words—that he felt it so necessary she have in her art should, of equal necessity, be provided by himself. It was almost too clear to be misunderstood.

He had mentioned their last luncheon. How could she ever forget that day! It was a week before Christmas and her last twenty-four hours in Paris—a time of lowest ebb for her. Philip, since her father's death two months before, had been acting so distant and strange, so furtive, and now, in his seeming hurry to get away, to go home for Christmas, had not even waited to see her off, though well knowing she was leaving Paris and would not be back. Though they had said an emotional good-bye, it rankled her even now; she had been terribly, dreadfully, hurt. Only Raoul, embarrassed by Philip's apprehensive, unchivalrous, behavior, had stood by her— dear, sweet Raoul. And what now, though only now, loomed so large in her memory of the luncheon were Raoul's words to her on that far-off, sad, but memorable day; words ironically prophetic today, though even then in the form and tone of a quasi-admonition: "This is your chance for a new beginning, *chérie*—you will see what I mean," he had said across their luncheon table. "In any event, you must come back to Paris. You must complete your studies and try to forget bygones. There are others, you know, who care for you." He had said it, then looked away—diffident, abashed, emotional. Yet tears had glistened in her own eyes even before he added: "It is true. I have thought of Pauline, my wife, who sadly now is gone—death is so final. Now I think of you." Suddenly then, impulsively, she had grasped both his hands in hers —as, unknown to them, the black man seated over in a remote corner of the restaurant watched them. But unmindful, she soon found herself crying, before she leant forward and kissed Raoul tearfully, clumsily, on the nose. He seemed her only friend. Then she had admonished *him*. "When I leave," she said, "be sure to think of me." And she fondly pressed his hand. "Always think of me, Raoul." Now, a year and a half later, in Boston, seated in her sister's cramped bedroom, his latest letter in her hands, she understood that her admonition had not gone unheeded. She was utterly lost now and had no idea what she should, or could, do. A psychological paralysis had taken hold of her and made her numb, inert.

Her state of inertia and bewilderment persisted. She did not know how to reply to Raoul's letter; so she deferred any answer. Finally she decided to call her mother—four days late on her promise to Ronald. It was a last resort. She had to talk to someone, be they erratic or not, who had lived longer than she had.

"Mother, how are you?" she said that evening on the telephone.

Irene Adkins gasped. "Oh, Suky! . . . I've been waiting for you to call! Why have you refused so long? Are you all right?"

"Yes, Mother—I hope you are. I've wanted to talk to you but there's too much—it's too involved—for the telephone. Sometime soon, though, we must talk."

"Oh, Suky!—why don't you come home? Come home at once! We can talk all you want! In times of trouble and perplexity one ought to be home—with loved ones. I'm your mother—you should be here with me. We should be talking all this out—it would be good for you and good for me. Also for Ronald and Jocelyn. Oh, promise me you'll come home—tomorrow!"

Mary Dee in her mind was already relenting, acquiescing. "No one must know, though, Mother," she said—"no one, of course, but Ronnie and Mrs. Grier. I don't want any visitors or any phone calls if I come. I'm coming just to talk to you, get your advice, or else I'd stay here. No one must know I've come home, Mother— do you understand?"

"Oh, yes, yes!" Irene Adkins had worked herself into a terribly nervous state. "Of course I understand, Suky! Don't you worry for a minute—no one will know except those right here in the apart-ment—Ronnie and Mrs. Grier—and you know they can be de-pended on. Oh, yes, you should be home!—I'll be so glad to see you! We can have long talks, just the two of us—as many as you like and as long as you like. Oh, don't disappoint us, Suky!"

Next day Mary Dee arrived home from Boston in time for din-ner. Despite everything—including Ronald's continuing, though temporary, pique—Mrs. Grier's sumptuous meal of roast loin of pork with glazed apple rings, served in the dining room, began as a festive occasion. Mary Dee was secretly glad, relieved, to be home and, in apparent good spirits, talked volubly to her mother and brother as though she had never been away and nothing had happened. Yet by dessert time a transformation had come over her. She had grown silent, introspective. It was the dread she felt now at having to talk to her mother—and of matters so private, per-sonal, so steeped in unhappiness and emotion. Though she had tried, struggled, she had never been able to accept the fact of Philip's death. How could she ever talk to her mother of this, or even related things—of Philip, Knight, or Raoul? Yet if she did not, was unwilling to unburden herself of her miseries, tell all, how could she gain her mother's understanding and counsel, or some measure of relief for herself? She did not know; her worries seemed compounded. But it was her grief over Philip, her final realization that he was no more, was to *be* no more, that weighed so heavily on her, afflicted, tortured, her, gave her no rest. She knew she could never love again. It was impossible—unthinkable; almost sacrilegious. Now her relationships with men—be it Knight, or Raoul, or eventually someone else—could only have other mo-tives, rewards . . . like vengeance, money, fame, yes, fame, or whatever. But not love. Love had died forever with Philip. Yet— although she realized that even had Philip lived it was beyond imagining they would ever have become restored to each other—her feeling of loss, of utter calamity, devastation, was undiminished; her grief would now be an eternal, aching flame. This was at least one reason she had not yet answered Raoul's last two letters— again she did not know what to say; her grieving passion over Philip, feelings both tender and undying, were nonetheless a frustrating mixture of confusion and searching. How could she ever tell her mother all this? At once she knew she could not. She would try then to confine the conversation to Knight—maybe mention Raoul—and hope for helpful reactions. But not tonight—she would defer this ordeal till tomorrow. This, however, was not to be. Dinner was hardly over, with Mary Dee, Irene Adkins, and Ronald now seated in the parlor, when the telephone sounded and Mrs. Grier, answering, came and called Ronald. "Some Mr. Bailey," she said. Mary Dee tensed. Ronald left his sister and mother and went to the telephone.

"Mr. Adkins," the unequal dialogue began, "this is Ferdinand Bailey, of the Black Peoples Congress—I'm an aide of Mr. Knight's. I was wondering if you could put me in touch with Miss Adkins, your sister—it's important that I talk with her. Mr. Knight is in the hospital—he collapsed in the office today, with another of his fainting spells or blackouts, and we don't know, really, what his condition is; he's now undergoing more tests. But I was hoping to get word to Miss Adkins—she might want to go see him. It's my personal opinion this is all connected with their relationship and the unfortunate turn it took recently. It's affected him severely and has now brought on what I think could even be a nervous breakdown. She could help him, I'm pretty sure, if she chose to go to him now. Is Miss Adkins in the city?"

"Yes," Ronald said, then, appalled, realized what he had done. ". . . But she's not here now. She's—"

"When do you expect her, Mr. Adkins?" Ferdinand suspected something.

"I don't know—I have no idea. Would you like to leave your phone number?"

"Yes—but I'll call her again early tomorrow." Ferdinand gave Ronald his number. "Or I might be able to get her later on tonight yet."

"I don't think so," Ronald said hurriedly. "I'll give her your number, though."

At once after hanging up Ronald was not only angry at himself but also at Mary Dee. He felt compromised—why should he have to lie, he thought, to cover up for her misdeeds? He returned to the parlor. "It was Ferdinand Bailey," he said to them. "I goofed and told him you were in town, Suky."

"Oh, heavens, Ronnie!" said Irene Adkins fearfully. "There's no telling what those people will do now."

"Knight's in the hospital," Ronald said. "He's had some kind of nervous breakdown, Bailey thinks—he blacked out in the office today. I put him off, but he's going to call again in the morning—if not later yet tonight. I took his number." Mary Dee only gaped at him. "But this is bad," Ronald said, shaking his head—"our being on the defensive like we've been. I don't feel comfortable at all—it's undignified for us to be behaving like this. We ought to be acting like responsible human beings instead of . . . instead of like—"

"You're right, Ronnie," Mary Dee said. "I'll call Ferdie tomorrow. No, we shouldn't be acting like this. We've—I've—finally got to face up to this whole thing, once and for all." She sighed. "Ronnie, leave Mother and me, will you? We want to talk—I came home to talk to her. Tomorrow I'll call Ferdie and tell him what I've decided!" Her face wore a sad, harried expression as she added, "Whatever it is." Ronald went to his room.

But Mary Dee now hadn't the slightest idea how to begin the crucial conversation with her mother. She sat quietly for a moment, vacantly staring at a far corner, as Irene Adkins watched her with strained expressions of both sympathy and anxiety on her pinched, pink face. "Oh, Suky, I somehow know how you must feel," she said, "even though I hardly know anything of what this is all about. I know about Knight, yes—we've talked about that—but I have this feeling there's more, much more, involved now than just Knight. What are all those letters you've been getting from Paris?"

"You've heard me speak of Raoul. Raoul Peyret was one of my professors—my favorite professor—at Beaux Arts. He's a wonderful man—a dear friend. But, Mother, I first want to talk to you about John Calvin Knight." But then Mary Dee could go no further. There was silence.

"Oh, Suky, must we?" Irene Adkins finally said.

"Yes, Mother, I'm afraid we must. I know your attitude toward John Calvin—I know you would prefer I forgot him. This issue is not so easily resolved, though. Remember he is a fine man."

"You've convinced me of that, Suky—yes, I believe you."

"What makes it so hard is that John Calvin needs me, Mother. It sounds egotistical of me, but it's true—he needs me. Not only in the work of the organization, but as a person, a man. He's become very personally, emotionally, involved. I take no pleasure in this fact—though I've shown little strength in discouraging him, either. I've been wishy-washy."

"You also said 'yes,' Suky, when he asked you to marry him— oh, I didn't feel right about it at all. You had said you were going to consult with me, but you didn't, Suky. Now, though, you want to—after the fact. It makes me a little disappointed, sad. You young people think you know so much, and that the rest of us are all old fogeys who are not abreast of life. Well, that's a mistake, Suky. We know much more about life simply because we've lived it—made mistakes, seen others do the same, and paid dearly for them. There's nothing, Suky, absolutely nothing, so important, so critical and decisive, in a woman's life—in her future happiness, or lack of it—as the man she marries. I'm proud to say I didn't make this mistake—I don't have to tell you, of all people, how fortunate I was in the man I married. But you may have made a mistake—though possibly not yet an irretrievable one—by acting so hastily; though I know Knight was pressing you. Now you have doubts—or worse." Ruefully, Mary Dee looked away again. "Suddenly something happened, Suky—you changed. What was it? You changed from the moment I brought you that first letter from your professor in Paris. Ronnie said it was because a dear friend of yours you'd met there had died—that you said that. Oh, I'm *so* in the dark, Suky! What's this friend's death got to do with your marriage to Knight? Ronnie thinks it's very bad that you postponed it. Now Knight's in the hospital. That's certainly bad. Why did you change, Suky?"

Mary Dee would not look at her mother. At last she shook her head forlornly, saying, "You must trust me, Mother. You must trust me without even asking me to tell you all the facts—they are powerful, though, I assure you. But, after days and nights of thinking about them, I know what the question is I face: From this point on, what should I do with my life? It's just that simple—or complex. Where, which way, do I go from here? That's why I wanted to talk to you, Mother—yes, maybe too late—and get your advice. Please don't be too harsh with me—I've been through a lot and have become confused. I've lost my way."

"No, Suky, I don't believe that—though you may really think so. No, it's not like you to completely lose your way. You already know, know well, at least on one level of your mind, what you want to do—what you're *going* to do. Yet you say you want my advice. How can I advise you when I know hardly any of the facts? Nor do I want to pry into your personal, private, affairs against your wishes—I only want to help you if I can."

"John Calvin Knight is carrying a heavy burden, Mother—he's engaged in a great work but is operating, I think, against unlucky odds. It's because lately he's had doubts, doctrinal doubts, about what all these years he's been preaching—his exclusionist, separatist, views. But they're views that up to now have been the keystone of the organization he founded and still, though feebly, leads. But his doubts now, along with other things—mainly his extremely complicated make-up, as well as his rare and sensitive intelligence—have at last caused him to falter. Immediately this got him in bad with the elders of the organization, and I was trying to help him, encourage him, bolster up his efforts and get things back on the track. But soon—he doesn't know it, of course—I myself began to despair of the organization's theories, even while I was trying to help him. My heart wasn't in it. I saw these theories as getting blacks nowhere and really lost my faith, my spark, in the organization's work. I couldn't have been very effective as his collaborator much longer—I saw it coming."

"Oh, Suky!" Irene Adkins threw up her hands distressfully. "You collaborated with him enough to promise to marry him!"

"You're right, Mother. Despite everything, I respected him, felt sorry for him, wanted him to achieve some sense of well-being. Besides, I was drifting myself—it was a very uncertain time for me. Perhaps I must have thought I also needed *him*. He's a very authentic and sincere person, an honest, dedicated champion of downtrodden blacks. They feel it—they can sense he's real. Yet he's unsure of himself, of what he's been teaching. This is a tragedy. It's because he wants *so* to believe blacks can make it on their own by trying in every way to separate themselves from the white mainstream. Yet deep down in his heart, as an extremely intelligent man, he doubts this, though his enormous pride—both as a black and a man—impels him to try to believe it anyway. I admire him and I pity him. Maybe that's why he became so dependent on me and why I hate so to let him down. How can I ever face him! He's already in the hospital. I shudder to think what will happen if I abandon him."

"Search your heart, Suky—what are your inmost feelings, inclinations? . . . what do you *want* to do?"

"I want to return to Paris, Mother, and resume my career—as a painter, an artist."

"Oh, heavens! *Do you really*? Oh, Suky, that sounds so beautiful! So right! Is it . . . can it really be true?"

"Yes, it's true—it's what I want to do. But should I?—that's what worries me!" Mary Dee's voice echoed her distress.

"Oh, goodness! . . . I don't know," Irene Adkins said, her hand groping to her face.

"There's also always the question of money in Paris—but I could get a job there."

"Oh, Suky, *I* would help you! You know that. If it's really what you want, if it will bring you happiness—and you haven't been happy lately—I'd gladly help you. Besides, I've thought so often what a pity it was that you had practically given up painting, neglected what your father had such high expectations for in you. Is it your professor who wants you to return, Suky?—is that what all those letters are about?"

Mary Dee was taken unawares. She hesitated. "Well, he's always advised me to return," she said—"even before I left Paris."

"Oh, how wonderful!" But then Irene Adkins had a second thought. "Suky, is he a gentleman?"

". . . What do you mean, Mother? Of course he's a gentleman— a man of unquestioned integrity and morality. He's also a distinguished art scholar and critic—an artist himself, really."

"Isn't that marvelous! Does he have a family?"

"He has a nine-year-old daughter—Nadine. He's a widower, Mother—his wife had recently died when I met him."

"He must still be rather young—to have a daughter that age."

"Yes," Mary Dee said, almost guiltily.

Irene Adkins now sat staring at her comely daughter. Glimmerings of understanding, almost full comprehension, were at last coming through to her. "I see," she said slowly, in dawning wonder. ". . . Suky, is this why you postponed the wedding?"

Finally at this Mary Dee cried out. "Oh, how do I know why I've done *anything* I've done?—I'm so mixed up!"

"No, Suky, again I can't believe that. It's perfectly clear in your mind what you want to do, and *will* do, for your own happiness. Only it's the effect it will have on others that troubles you. I can understand that, of course—you're a person of humanity and character. But you must think of yourself as well. Sometimes it's our duty, to ourselves and our family, to think of ourselves."

"But I'm needed here, Mother. The welfare of a lot of people is at stake in our work at the headquarters. Yet I think only of myself—of my own happiness, of what's going to happen to *me*. It isn't a picture of myself I like to see."

"What's the alternative, Suky? Are you really prepared to spend the rest of your life—as exceptional as you are, so attractive, well-educated, from an outstanding, cultured, family, you yourself a talented and promising artist—are you ready to leave all that for a life with Knight and his 'downtrodden blacks?' Certainly he needs you—hasn't he embarked on a mission to save the whole black world? He needs everyone he can get."

"No, no, Mother—you don't understand. One reason I think he needs me is that he links me somehow, though maybe only symbolically, with this black world. Before me, a white girl was trying to influence him. Oh, it's strange—I couldn't explain it in a year. He sees me probably as a kind of *idealized* black woman. Even I at times have spurred him on to think Black."

"Well, he's misguided—I don't think you're prepared to cast your lot with him, Suky, whatever his need. You can see the future as well as I, that when you reached your middle-thirties, were bored, disillusioned, your great opportunities gone forever, you'd be so sorry, so unhappy, that you'd be miserable for the rest of your life. In my experience I've seen not a few similar cases—potentially beautiful lives thrown away. You must not make this mistake, Suky—and you won't. Your father certainly wouldn't want you to, either. But what's more important, you owe it to yourself."

761

Mary Dee stared off in space again. "What about Ernestine and Vernon?" she said ruefully.

"What?—who are Ernestine and Vernon?"

"The two children—you remember I had them here recently for lunch."

"Oh, Suky, they're not *your* children. You said they had a mother."

"Yes," Mary Dee sighed—"me." Filled with a sense of utter futility now, she rose. "Thanks for talking to me, Mother," she said. "Come on, now, let's go to bed and get some rest." Soon Irene Adkins followed her out of the parlor. Mary Dee felt numb.

That night, however, despite the fatigue of the day's travel, she slept only fitfully—guilt-ridden. Her mother, she thought, knew her so well. Next morning she not only did not call Ferdinand Bailey, she refused, twice, to take his calls. Instead she spent the morning secluded in her bedroom answering, at great and fervent length, Raoul's letters—visions of the Champs Elysées and Jeu de Paume already swimming in her head. Suddenly then she thought of Philip. For a moment, wistful, pensive, sad, she stopped writing and gazed off in space. But only for a moment. That was the past, she realized; it could not be summoned back. It was her future visions she saw now, visions that filled her with sober delectation and wonder, visions of new beginnings, a new life. Yet, staring off in deepest concentration and solitude, she sighed.

Epilogue

Christmastime. In the dead of night he sought to collate—compare. Here were the excerpts which seemed to him during tonight's session to have special significance and relevance—from DuBois (two), then Douglas, and King. There was really in addition a fifth, a mere one-liner—from his late father, William Goforth Knight: "*We are what we were made.*"

It was 2:15 A.M., and in his motel room the books were spread out on the table before him, as the 75-watt yellow light came down on his clean-shaven head. His pate, frequently hot—not from the light but from his recent months of trials and afflictions—had somewhat cooled tonight. At times he went and put his head under the bathroom facebowl faucet, dousing, splashing, it for dear life with cold Georgia water—for surcease, which often came, at least temporarily. Now he opened the books, then untied a great sheaf of papers containing notes, and began anew his explorations. From so many continuous long nights of study his eyes pained him as he pored over the excerpts again to make sure he had read nothing amiss. Last night, for instance, he had sought, with only equivocal results, to collate just two minds—Garvey's and Malcolm X's. But even that, with his fatigued, raw eyes—he must finally get glasses, thought Knight—had taken him most of the sitting. The night before that, however, there had been three minds but easy collations—Tillman, Blease, and Bilbo.

But now DuBois: "The price of the disaster of slavery and civil war was the necessity of quickly assimilating into American democracy a mass of black laborers in whose hands alone for the moment lay the power of preserving the ideals of popular government; of overthrowing a slave economy and establishing upon it an industry primarily for the benefit of the workers. It was this price which in the end America refused to pay and today suffers for that refusal."

Again DuBois: "The true Negro folk song still lives in the hearts

763

of those who have heard them truly sung and in the hearts of the Negro people. What are these songs and what do they mean? I know little of music but I know something of men, and I know that these songs are the articulate message of the slave to the world. Not all the past South, though it rose from the dead, can gainsay the heart-touching witness of these songs. They are the music of an unhappy people, of the children of disappointment; they tell of death and suffering and unvoiced longing toward a truer world; of misty wanderings and hidden ways."

Next—in an 1847 speech—Douglas: "I cannot agree with my friend Mr. Garrison in relation to my love and attachment to this land. I have no love for America, as such. I have no patriotism. I have no country. What country have I? The institutions of this country do not know me, do not recognize me as a man. I am not thought of, or spoken of, except as a piece of property belonging to some *Christian* slaveholder, and all the religious and political institutions of this country alike pronounce me slave and chattel. In such a country as this I cannot have patriotism. How can I, I say, love such a country—a country, the church of which, and the government of which, and the constitution of which, are all in favor of supporting and perpetuating this monstrous system of injustice and blood? I have not, I cannot have, any love for this country, as such, or for its constitution. I desire to see its overthrow as speedily as possible, and its constitution shivered in a thousand fragments, rather than this foul curse of slavery continue to remain in the land." (Hisses and cheers.)

Finally King: "We have seen the old order in our nation in the form of segregation and discrimination. Living under these conditions, many Negroes came to the point of losing faith in themselves. They came to feel that perhaps they *were* less than human. The great tragedy of physical slavery was that it led to mental slavery. So long as the Negro maintained this subservient attitude and accepted this 'place' assigned to him, a sort of racial peace existed. But it was an uneasy peace in which the Negro was forced patiently to accept insult, injustice, and exploitation. It was a negative peace. Then something happened to the Negro. Factors conjoined to cause him to take a new look at himself. The Negro masses began to reevaluate themselves. The Negro came to feel that he was somebody. His religion revealed to him that God loves all of His children, and that every man, from a bass black to a

764

treble white, is significant on God's keyboard. So he could now cry
out with the eloquent old preacher-poet:

'Fleecy locks and black complexion
Cannot forfeit nature's claim.
Skin may differ, but affection
Dwells in black and white the same.
And were I so tall as to reach the pole
Or to grasp the ocean at a span,
I must be measured by my soul—
The *mind* is the standard of the man.' "

These great men, thought Knight, squinting under his yellow
light, were not addressing themselves to members of some learned
society, or the professorial savants of the academy, but to the
people. No matter the high tone, they were speaking directly to
the folk. The folk could, and did, change things; moved moun-
tains, wrought revolution. The revolution somehow now must not
be lost. Yet he himself had failed, collapsed, been through last
summer's maelstrom of total nervous breakdown following the
fateful girl's abandonment of him and her permanent flight to Paris.
As a consequence, he had returned, reverted, to first principles:
"We are what we were made." Finally his long, laborious investigations of his mass of primary materials, for this eventual purpose
gathered over the years, had begun in late July, after his last release from the Chicago hospital and his arrival, banishment, here.
But now, five months later, Ferdinand Bailey had said in a recent
letter that snow was on the ground up north. In contrast, though
it was only three days until Christmas, the weather here in Dixie
was temperate, most days filled with nearly tropical sunshine. But
in his deep preoccupation with nightly bookish tasks, weather was
taken by Knight for granted, hardly thought of. Thus, tediously,
life went on.

Today he had risen at noon and, on the motel's plain stationery
bearing only the legend "Sea Island, Georgia," had begun another
letter to his friend Ferdinand. He preferred to think of it as an ex-
planatory letter, seeking to elucidate—mollify, soften, really—some
of the language, language often harsh and bordering on the charge
of perfidy, he had used in a letter the week before to the little man
in Chicago he still hoped always to call his friend.

"But I'm becoming calmer now, Ferdie," the present letter said,

765

"less testy each day, I think—although as you sat in your office reading my last letter I doubt you would agree. I said you, as my best friend, seemed, however, almost as anxious as the others, including Jesse Lumpkins, to install new acting leadership—Ornette —until the extent of my recovery could be determined. It was done straightway. Yet I didn't mean to imply I felt you had breached our friendship. I know it was a hard decision—certainly for you. I guess I had only wished you personally might have humored me, ha, thrown me a sop, so to speak, by dragging your feet a little on the proposal that I, at least temporarily, step aside. But probably this thing had been festering in me until, now months later, I brought it up in an unfortunate letter to you. This past summer in Chicago, though—I don't have to tell you—was a difficult time for me. It was pretty bad—I never want to go through anything like that again. Yet I shouldn't have scolded you—and after letting all this time go by without mentioning it in any of my other letters. So I apologize for anything I said that wasn't just right, and ask your forgiveness. You are my only friend, of course. Besides, it was very decent of everybody—yes, including Jesse Lumpkins— to vote me money to live on while in 'exile' and with which to pay this motel's modest residential rate. I know you instigated it. I shouldn't complain.

"As I've said before, though only briefly, it's nice here. This is a truly lovely section of the state—the seacoast and its islands. You suggested it—a pearl of an idea—although I too then saw the merit, the fulfilled prophecy, in it at once. If I had to be exiled, this was the place for it to be to. No Elba this place. Yes, the state of Georgia is symbolic for me, isn't it?—an almost hopeless prophecy come to pass. It was a locality not far from here during Reconstruction that my forebears, Acts and Aaron Knight, were lucky to come away from with their lives and make it to Savannah (which is only sixty miles from where I am now). I'm restudying those events, those fateful times, trying to find answers from them —to learn what happened, what crossed our stars, as it were, made us such hapless, pitiable, victims, and what it augurs for the future. It was a terrible time for us, Ferdie. But now a century later, after much struggle, in some of which ten years ago your humble servant took part, it's all very different, by comparison almost paradise—whites coming and going here at the motel are ordinary,

766

matter-of-fact, not unkindly people, who don't much notice me. I've encountered no discourtesy. One day the woman who runs the magazine and notions stand in the lobby, seeing me from time to time lugging in books from the car, asked me whether I was a teacher or a preacher! We laughed.

"I do quite a bit of walking, in the afternoons, before coming back for a nap and dinner—after which in my room I work long hours into the night. I've cut off my hair too, you know, ha, my modest Afro—shaved my head. You should see me—I look like some kind of dark-skinned Krishna brother. But during the worst of my illness there in Chicago this summer, you'll recall (though it's still sometimes the case), my head was always hot, at times blistering hot, it seemed. It wasn't fever—my temperature was normal. It's weird—a phenomenon. It's the result apparently of all that's been going on, maybe seething, inside my head—my terrible defeat and all. But now that I keep it shaved, and often stand in an ice-cold shower, it somehow seems cooler; my mind doesn't seem so ready to blow, disintegrate, as it did this summer during my difficulties. Also my hands tremble considerably less— although, alas, I've taken up the dastardly cigarette habit again. But I avoid liquor—only occasionally a little sherry, though not much of that, for even then my hands begin to shake again. Yet, all in all, I think Sea Island is as therapeutic for me as anything those Chicago doctors did before I left—those well-meaning shrinks. The same is true there of the heart and blood pressure men, who this last time warned me so direly—though I do have to remind myself from time to time that I've had two blackouts down here too. But what's to be will be. Therefore in the afternoons I walk and think—plan my readings and researches for the night to come.

"So, yes, Ferdie, I've come home. Though I was born in Chicago, this is my metaphorical home. As Goforth would say, I've come 'back down home to the old country.' And, as I said, it's not at all bad here—now. It gets lonely sometimes—I know no one here, of course—but then I go for walks. On my walks, always with the ocean in clear view—where it's marshy on the mainland side of the road but sandy on the Atlantic side (beautiful on both) —I go through areas heavy, pregnant, with our history. I see the gaunt foundation stones that are the only remnants of once-proud

767

cotton and rice plantation mansions. There are the old cotton gin sites and also ruins of slave quarters. The dark, dense forests are awesome, the cypress trees dripping damp, mossy vines and foliage, where even the sun seldom penetrates. It's grand, magnificent, for walks—when you want to think, when you want to examine your screwed-up life, or what's left of it, to find out what happened, where your dazzling plans, all the dreams, went awry, and so forth, and so forth. . . .

"I speculate a lot on this these days. A thought that's plagued me as much, I guess, as any, especially on these long walks, is that it might have been better if I had died after the shooting incident, the attempt on my life. I think about it all the time. My death then, maybe as a martyr, or, ha, some kind of tinhorn saint, might have been a good thing for the organization, the movement, given it an impetus it decidedly didn't have during my latter days as leader—especially after Dee came into the picture. But, as it's turned out, I've lived to see failure and defeat—total. Wouldn't it be an irony, now, if already I've lived too long? Hey, how morbid I am today! Ah, Dee. . . .

"Okay, okay, finally, reluctantly, I'm forced to agree with you, Ferdie—she was a mistake. The relationship was foredoomed. But at one time, remember, you were all for it—so was Ornette, my illustrious successor. But we look *back* on it now—it's hindsight and a lot easier. Lovely, lovely, Dee—oh, hell, let's face it, I'll never get over her. It still seems, after five months, so incredible to me. She slaughtered me, wiped me out, didn't she? And to think —we expelled Griselda, sent her packing. We wanted Dee—*I* wanted Dee. Only, in the end, she didn't want us—me. But I also agree with you when you say you wish her no ill—only the best. Yet there can be no mistake now about why she fled to Paris— it wasn't just art, or her career as a painter, or even adventure; not at all. So when you wrote that she had married her professor, I wasn't all that much surprised. Considering everything, knowing what we know now, it was preordained—though of course we didn't realize it. But probably neither did she. She only knew what she wanted. Lucky girl!

"Oh, I know, from many things you've said in recent letters, that you don't agree she's lucky. You probably think just the opposite. Maybe she isn't. Maybe in the sense you speak of—her confrontation with herself, her self-recognition, the guilt—it *is* bad for her. You're right, yes—she left us, when we needed her most, and went over to the enemy. You even go so far as to say she turned out tragic—that her feelings are tragic because she senses her flaws. And that it was I, of all people, in the role I was fated to play, who brought it about—her self-awareness. If you only knew how I've pondered this—my role, as you put it. You claim that all along she unconsciously feared me, probably had this premonition about me, that I would someday bring her down, reveal her, to herself, for what she really is, for what she sadly harbors deep in her heart—the longing to be white. Well, of course, I've never been aware that she feared me, certainly not for the reasons you surmise, or any others. Maybe it's true I was an instrument in what eventually happened—to her and to me—but it was surely not my intention. I only loved her and wanted to marry her—if you'll allow a colossal understatement. What is your evidence of her tragic feelings of guilt? You even say, admit, yes, that you are speculating. Yet, as you also say, I can't, even if I tried, avoid the fact she's an extremely intelligent person and fully understands the implications of her act—the renunciation, repudiation, of all things Black. But the possibility that I was the instrument, knowingly or otherwise, of her self-revelation worries me a lot. I think about it constantly, for we're talking about a curse—on her. Was it I who, from the first—from Paris—put this plague on her? Had she felt this all along?—carried the burden about with her? I don't know, certainly. But it's strange, most unusual, that in all our talks she and I never really got around to talking at any great length about Paris, about what happened to us there. I was willing, but she always shied away from the subject—got very cold and forbidding whenever I'd bring it up. Something—though I don't know what—can be inferred from this, but it was something she didn't want to talk about. Yes, you could be right after all—maybe she's not lucky. The thought, though, is sort of astonishing, and saddening. Yet, Ferdie, let's not carry it too far—let's not be naive. Have you ever considered we might be wrong about her altogether?—about how she feels about herself. She may feel nothing.

"There's one thing, though, I haven't the slightest doubt about, something she proved to me that I'd never considered before: that love, pure, selfless, love—the kind I had for her—can be the most ennobling emotion we're capable of. This is true. Without knowing it, or meaning to, she really in a way ennobled me—at the same time, unable to help herself, prevent it, she cast me down, damned me, destroyed me. But by this, by being ennobled, for a time lifted up, I'm able, I think, still to love her. I'm relatively free of anger and bitterness—I understand her better now. The way she humiliated me, though, was a cup of gall—even if it wasn't at all her intention. I wasn't spared—I was disgraced, degraded, before the world. But, as I say, I see her more clearly—yes, in a kind of tragic light, maybe. Ornette can boast and brag all he wants to, though, about being the first to figure her out, see through her, as he puts it, but he could never understand Dee in a thousand years. She's far too complicated and he's far too insensitive. He can never explain her merely by saying she loathed being black and craved to be white. That's so naive, simplistic. There's much more to it than that. It's one of the things, night after night, I wrestle with here in my researches, my studies. It's a very involved, knotty, problem—a phenomenon. I certainly don't, at this point, understand it, but neither does Ornette. She knew we, all of us, needed her when she did what she did. She knew we needed her rare and special talents—needed her in the struggle—but in the end she couldn't oblige us, although she may have tried. So her talents went elsewhere, where they now contribute nothing—to us. This, Ferdie, may be where the tragedy is.

"But it was her ambivalence too, perhaps, that was ill-fated, tragic. Think, for instance, of those children, those two ghetto kids, she left behind—who still keep thinking, insisting, she's coming back. This is only one of many symptoms. Everything got too big, too difficult, for her—she couldn't solve, deal with, any of it. So she ran off—a kind of solution in itself, I guess. But it's still so incredible. No, I'll never get over her. I didn't know of course love could be so absolutely devastating—Ferdie, I loved her. Yet the fact that before she left she didn't try to contact me, or even write a letter explaining, or trying to explain, or that she wouldn't take your phone calls, doesn't prove anything—unless maybe that she didn't know what to say, or do. Besides, she may have been in a furious hurry to leave, may really have been desperate to go, driven by some inexplicable compulsion or need. I don't think, though, for the life of her, she could have said why she did what she did—she really didn't know. So now here I'm left merely singing the blues. It's laughable. It's clear I'm no hero. Just think of it, here I—ha, yes, the erstwhile hero—ending up a mere helpless, miserable whiner; when before there was so much to be proud of. My one chance now to salvage something out of it all, even if only temporarily, is in my studies here. You can see how crucial they are—my attempt to unravel what's among the greatest of all mysteries. Who can say if I'll succeed or fail? Pray for me, Ferdie. Pray, ha, for the fallen hero, the hand-wringing whiner, that the studies in the end will be fruitful. *Pray*, man! Is it possible now I've come to believe in prayer! . . .

"But no one can ever make me believe that Dee doesn't pity me, grieve about me, maybe—just as I've grieved about Griselda. With all my heart, with everything I'm capable of, I hope Griselda, wherever she is, whatever she's doing, whatever her life is now, has found happiness. Can anyone—anyone!—deny she deserves it? Hardly. Ah, Griselda. Ferdie, is what's happened to me retribution?—am I now reaping my just desserts? The very last time I talked to Griselda, do you know what—in her utter desperation—she told me, screamed at me, actually, over the long-distance telephone? She said (get this) that she was black!—that her father's maternal grandmother was an African slave in the Caribbean! I don't believe a word of it, of course; but it shows how desperate she had become there at the last. Ah, I wish her well. So, sure, I grieve. And yes, I'll bet Dee does too sometimes, secretly. It's all crazy, Ferdie. It's like the scattered pieces of a big jigsaw puzzle with no guide to it—who can put the pieces together right? I don't know—sometimes I despair. It raises that basic old question once more (a few nights ago I was reading again from the Karamazovs' *Pro and Contra*) of the very existence of God. There's a definite parallel here, that relates to us, to blacks, and to my present long and arduous—ah, and maybe futile—studies. Whether we realize it or not, we, we blacks, have always—historically—had this question to face. How do we account for 'our long night of suffering?' Think of it—of what we've been through. I even discussed it with Mary Dee, and another time with Griselda—two women with unusual minds and intuition. They saw the question, all right, clearly, and agreed, yet, like myself, neither could answer it—a question of course easier raised than answered. It's a great mystery, Ferdie.

771

Still every night I study it—I study it, man! I attack it!—from every angle. But will it ever yield, be solved? Who can tell?

"Ornette, though, will never be bothered by such questions as these—he could never see them; he's not capable, though you say he still fancies himself an artist with some sensibilities, a polemical painter of sorts, who dabbles. But he's not interested in the fine points of anything. Yet as a leader now he's probably better off for it. There's nothing doctrinaire about Ornette, and maybe, with Rosabelle's help, he'll do all right. He's a young man who sees, yes, only the fundamental things, a fellow of simple faith and direct action, with the passion and courage of a bull who will never give up until dead and who—ha, unlike one past leader—needs no long, inactive periods for contemplation and study of great questions. I must say I have a grudging respect for him. I do regret, though, he's finally insisted on changing the name of his son, the baby, once my namesake, to Malcolm instead. That was a low blow, I thought. It means he's written me off—as a moral factor.

"But I guess I, of all people, should know how one can feel about a son—when I think of how Goforth felt about me, and how I felt about my own late son, little Johnnie. Yes—as if you didn't know! —I once had a son. I lost him, of course. But I wanted—had hopes for—another. One night early last summer in Dee's parlor, before the debacle, getting carried away with myself, I told her this, about my hopes. She got very quiet—said nothing. At last, though, after some moments, she nodded sort of sympathetically, yet almost at once again became inaccessible. But my hopes were sky high in those days—I was in a state of euphoria, for by then she had finally said she would marry me. I was making fantastic plans—I had already determined our son would be named this time, as I've told you, not after me but after his paternal grandfather, one William Goforth Knight, ha! In the end, though, it wasn't to be. So now I, a direct descendant of Bymba Baptiste, who in the latter 1700s was born in Africa, will myself leave no offspring. The lineal line has ended. But it's strange—I still find myself wishing I could talk to Dee again, ask her many questions. Ah, wouldn't our son have had noble blood! How silly of me, though, to indulge in such fantasies, continue thinking about her. Yet maybe it would be therapy for me if just once more I could talk to her—say, for only twenty minutes. It might really, yes, be therapeutic. For you know I'm a crippled man—the shrinks say so. We are indeed what we were made. I repeat, Ferdie, I'm no hero—you can tell . . . all this self-pity. And one time I passed for a leader.

"In some humorous ways it all reminds me of Rodya. Remember Rodya?—or whatever his real name was—who had answers for everything? I think of him sometimes and laugh—Rodya the sleuth, the philosopher, the brain, Rodya the solver of all problems and mysteries; a graduate student, a mere gangling, brilliant kid. Yet somehow very few things he said were frivolous, or foolish. He could make you think—when he wasn't making you mad as hell. What would Rodya say about all this?—what would his sage comments be? How would he, were he here, presume to advise me on my present work, my studies?—in fact, I wouldn't be surprised if he showed up any day now. What too would he say about lovely Dee who broke my heart? He would probably absolve her. For that matter, so would Goforth—who always counseled tolerance to me. Yet I too, though, I trust, have forgiven. She chose the life she preferred—the life she really wanted. Is this tragedy, Ferdie? Despite what you say, I still sometimes try to make myself believe it may not be at all. Who knows?

"But the important thing is the organization. The movement, it will live. After a couple years' experience, Ornette will measure up —he's fanatical where blacks are concerned, and certainly has 'street sense'; this last is important. The organization, then, is indestructible; especially, Ferdie, as long as you're in it—which I hope will be for the rest of your life, a long life. But what happens to me now doesn't really much matter—my spirit and health are broken, gone, and occasionally I have feelings, a premonition, my time's not long. But life—death! What are they? Life itself is a terminal illness. Life is *fatal*, man! I only ask for time to finish my work—my studies. I live now for what, hopefully, they will reveal —the answer to that vast question, that vast mystery: the mystery of Blackness. There is a greatness there, a majesty, if it can only be found—Goforth said this. So wish me well."

*　　*　　*　　*　　*

Knight did not work on Christmas Eve night. Instead, though his hands shook, he treated himself to a glass of California sherry in his room and, smoking a half pack of cigarettes, tensely watched an ancient movie on television, his tensions yet springing from his craving to be at work. Time was of the essence, he thought. True or not, however, he told himself before going to bed he had become a fatalist—what was to be, yes, would be. Again the person now most in his thoughts was Goforth. He was almost sure Goforth would have wanted him to try to put the results, the findings, of his studies in book form. He was not, however, writing a book, or a treatise, Knight knew—he had never had any such intentions. His efforts, he was aware, were personal and subjective—he wanted, needed, answers for *himself*, while life yet lasted. Whose life, he asked himself, his or his father's, had really stood for more? There had been a time, in his vanity, he realized, when his answer would have been simple, ready, unhesitant. Now he was not sure. He had begun more to see himself as his father's son. He wished now, if only through the dreary, futile impasse of the grave, they could talk again. He was sure the opinions passed between them would be different from those uttered last time—especially by himself. What, though, would he say to his father? He would ask him to speak about life, of course—Goforth loved to hold forth on life. Yet his father might still have something of value, importance, to say— might even be able to make a start himself at fitting the great jigsaw puzzle pieces together. Knight knew that tomorrow, Christmas night, the studies would resume. Even now he could hear Goforth talking.

Author's Note

Any fictional verisimilitude achieved in the section of the novel (Book II, Chapter 1) dealing with the African slave abductions and the horrors of the Atlantic crossing was greatly aided by my reading *Black Cargoes—A History of the Atlantic Slave Trade,* by Daniel P. Mannix and Malcolm Cowley, Viking Press, 1962.

The section (Book III, Chapter 3) portraying events connected with the lynching of Parret Webb was prompted, and similarly aided, by my reading of a comparable episode in *The Black Book,* by Middleton Harris, etal, Random House, 1974.

Although, in writing the novel's "Paris section" (Book I, Chapter 2), I made two research trips to Paris, I am indebted to Professor Michel Fabre of the University of Paris (Sorbonne), noted French specialist in Black literature and biographer of Richard Wright, for his kindness in reading in manuscript and commenting on this chapter.

Chapter 1 of Book I first appeared, in slightly less extensive form and as work-in-progress, in Vol. 38, No. 4, of the literary quarterly *New Letters,* to whose editor, David Ray, I as a writer owe much generally.